# VAGABOND QUAKERS

# VAGABOND QUAKERS

*Northern Colonies*

**The Vagabond Trilogy**
**Book 1**

To Skye – Love, Olga R. Morrill

OLGA R. MORRILL

Morrill Fiction
Madison, NH

Morrill Fiction
Madison, NH

ISBN: 0998415103
ISBN 13: 9780998415109

**Publisher's Cataloging-in-Publication** ***(Provided by Quality Books, Inc.)***
Morrill, Olga, author.
Vagabond Quakers. Northern colonies / by Olga Morrill. -- First edition.
pages cm -- (The vagabond trilogy ; book 1)
Includes bibliographical references.
LCCN 2016920892
ISBN 978-0-9984151-0-9 (print)
ISBN 978-0-9984151-1-6 (Kindle)

1. Quakers--New England--History--17th century--Fiction. 2. Quakers--Persecutions--New England--17th century--Fiction. 3. Quaker women missionaries--New England--17th century--Fiction. 4. Puritans--New England--History--17th century--Fiction. 5. Freedom of religion--History--17th century--Fiction. 6. New England--History--Colonial period, ca. 1600-1775--Fiction. 7. Historical fiction. 8. Biographical fiction. I. Title. II. Series: Morrill, Olga. Vagabond trilogy ; bk. 1.

PS3613.O755455V34 2017 813'.6
QBI17-900007

# DEDICATION

*To Dearest MM*
*Who awakened me to the necessity of intellectual freedom*
*and to the librarians who preserve it*

# TABLE OF CONTENTS

# PREFACE

*Vagabond Quakers* is a work of fiction. It is based on historical references of actual events involving real people and places, but the details of those events and the characterizations of the people are fiction.

More than three hundred years have passed since the incidents depicted in this book and, predictably, the references contradict each other. Some maintain that the missionary Friends who came to the colonies in the mid-seventeenth century were heroes of equality, martyrs for freedom of worship, and victims of gross miscarriages of justice, while others downplay the abuse or pose the opinion that the Friends invited it. Most of the sources support the former premise, while the latter view attempts to preserve the myth that the founding fathers of the Massachusetts Bay Colony could do no wrong.

During the research my ignorance of the period became glaringly apparent. People were tortured and hanged in Boston? None of the events were included in my education despite their significance. History courses routinely jumped from Plymouth Rock and the Pilgrims to the American Revolution of 1776. With an occasional nod to King Philip's War one hundred and fifty years of colonial history were ignored. The benign image of our Puritan forefathers was originally conceived and propounded in the nineteenth century, but it is still widely accepted as fact.

The Puritans immigrated to the colonies to keep their religion pure from the taint of Anglicanism and "popery" they perceived as rampant in the mother country, but they did not accord religious freedom to any others—quite the contrary, as they zealously fined or banished dissenters. Governor John Winthrop's City on the Hill was to be a bastion of the pure religion, unpolluted by the coexistence of other faiths.

Furthermore, the Puritans transplanted the prejudices of the English class system into the social structure of the colonies. Their laws were based on the Bible, which clearly stated (in their interpretation) that some were born to serve and others to lead. The freeman system was established in every colonial English settlement, and it maintained the pervading rank and order.

To become a freeman in colonial New England was not a simple matter of owning land. One ran a gauntlet of interviews by the town's magistrates, ministers, and "peers"—landed gentry who were already freemen. Without this coveted status one could not vote, hold office, become a member of the church, or even receive baptism or communion. Fully two-thirds of the population—indentured servants, fishermen, sailors, laborers, and common folk—did not qualify. The worst punishment of the time, barring hanging, was to be banished, disarmed, and disenfranchised—stripped of property and the rights of freeman status. Church attendance was mandatory, and people were fined for absence from worship, membership or none. The hardships of distance and weather were no excuse, and as the services lasted all day, the journey to and from the church was a challenge for much of the year.

Enter the missionary Friends with a message of equality before God. All people were welcome to join their meetings for worship for everyone was capable of a personal connection to God Within. A minister's guidance was not needed, nor was a church, precluding the taxes required to support them. The Society of Friends worshipped in their homes or out of doors in small groups eliminating the hardship of travel to a distant meeting house. They were the first proponents of spiritually-based equality; they were guides to a divine connection for individuals; and they offered a tax-free religion with services close to home.

Most appalling to the Puritan theocracy was that the Society of Friends allowed women to preach. In the seventeenth century females were considered property belonging to their fathers or their husbands—vessels of procreation. Public speaking was considered "unnatural" for women, as was any intellectual activity. The Friends' concept of equality was spiritual and did not extend to social issues, but it was unprecedented. In addition Friends were considered rebels for refusing to honor social superiors by doffing their headgear or swearing oaths of allegiance, both commonly required at the time. To the Puritans it seemed a chaos of equality. Taken in context the Massachusetts Bay Colony's violent reaction to the Children of the Light was understandable, for they threatened the Puritans' social structure, their tax base, the power of their churches over the populace, and the livelihoods of their clergy.

Between 1656 and 1660 John Endicott and the Reverend John Norton devised the Quaker Laws that were subsequently approved by the Great and General Court of Boston to persecute Friends and drive them from the colony. The brutal laws had the opposite effect, attracting missionaries who came to the colonial capital to protest the injustice of the *ad hoc* laws. Hundreds of Friends and those in sympathy with them were disenfranchised, imprisoned for long periods without trial, flogged, tortured, branded, and forced to perform hard labor for their beliefs. Four were hanged. It is shocking to hear of the suffering perpetrated by the Endicott, his ministers, and the court that approved the brutality, for our history books have omitted these events and paint a very different picture of our Puritan founders. Although a bronze statue of Mary Dyer sits outside the State House in Boston, few know her story or the circumstances of her execution. The men who sentenced her and watched her swing from the Hanging Elm would be appalled that her memory is now honored by the city where she died. *Vagabond Quakers* reveals the surprising conflicts and complexities of a long-ignored period of American History.

*A note about the colonial calendar:* Prior to 1752, Great Britain and her colonies used the Julian calendar. The Gregorian calendar that we employ today was adopted after that date. The colonials of the seventeenth century observed the start of the New Year as March 24, Annunciation Day, rather than January 1st. Mary Tomkins and Alice Ambrose came to the colonies in June of 1662, but the year did not turn to 1663 until the following March 25th.

# ACKNOWLEDGMENTS

During the five years involved in writing this book, many people gave their time, expertise, and feedback. Marina Dutzman Kirsch redrew the maps, making them more specific to the book and helped with all the details of publishing, as well as editing. Key research information was provided by the Dover Public Library, the Woodman Institute Museum, the Friends in North Sandwich and Dover, NH, as well as the Salem Public Library of Salem, MA, and Lane Memorial Library of Hampton, NH. Carol Felice of the Remick Country Doctor Museum and Farm of Tamworth, NH consulted on botanicals and 17th Century medicine. Inspiration for the book originated from a prompt to write a piece of historical fiction for the White Mountain Writers Group, who patiently listened and gave feedback on early scenes and rewrites. Alice Davies reviewed procedure involving the Society of Friends. John Moody of Winter Center for Indigenous Traditions was an invaluable source for the Abenaki (accent on second syllable) language and accuracy in all aspects of the Indian characters. Nautical advice was given by Louise Taylor, Jay Rancourt, and my brother John Reigeluth. Ernest O. Brown created historically accurate and beautiful art for the cover. To my proven readers Cintra Warden, Jay Rancourt, Melissa Jordan, and Margaret Marschner, you have my undying gratitude for your patience and encouragement. Last but certainly not least, thanks to my husband Steve for his help with research, for listening to the early versions, for practical advice on logistics, and for believing in me.

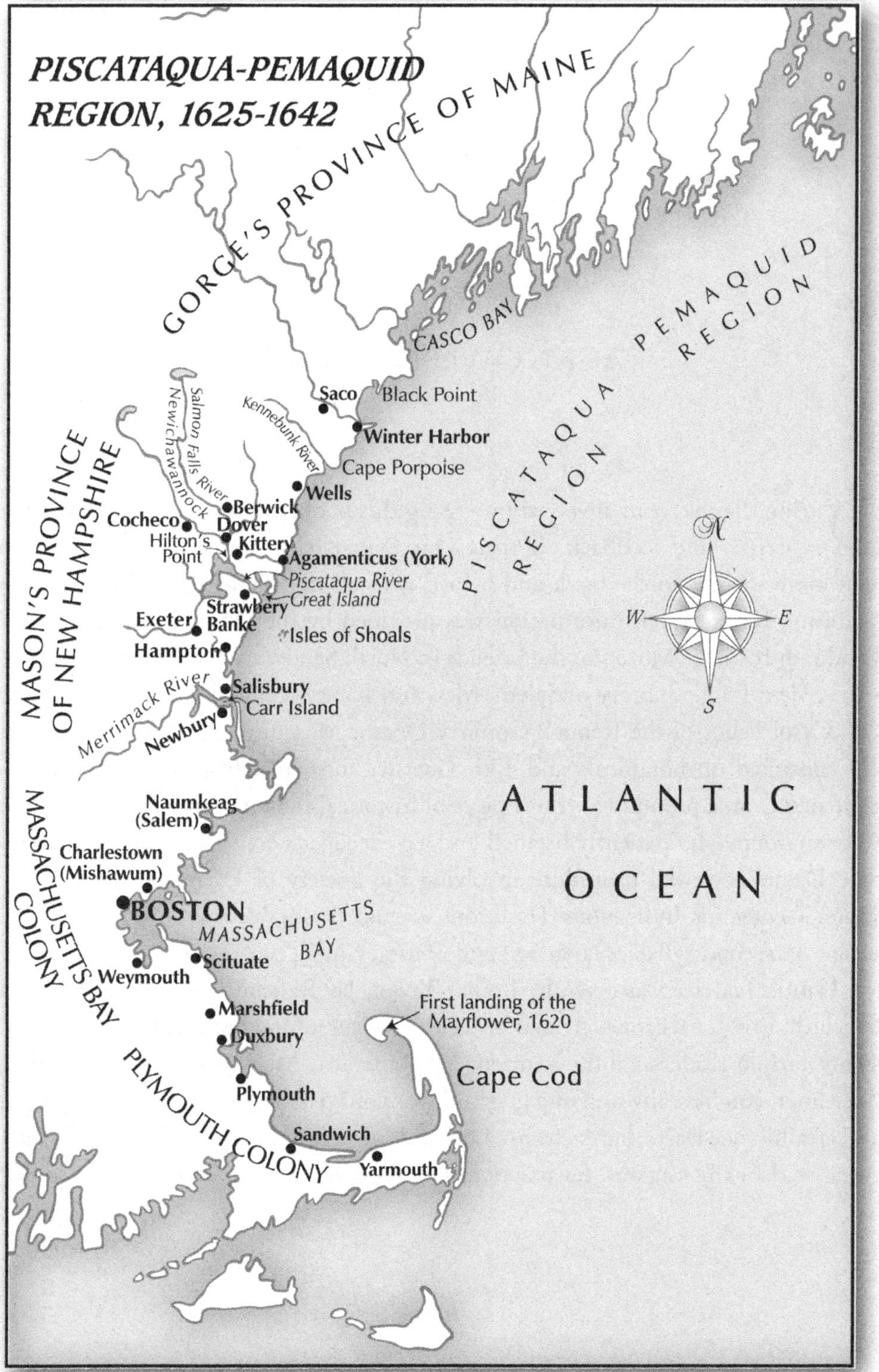

PISCATAQUA-PEMAQUID
REGION, 1625-1642
GORGE'S PROVINCE OF MAINE
CASCO BAY
PISCATAQUA PEMAQUID REGION
PISCATAQUA REGION
Saco
Black Point
Winter Harbor
Cape Porpoise
Wells
Kennebunk River
Salmon Falls River
Newichawannock
MASON'S PROVINCE OF NEW HAMPSHIRE
Berwick
Cocheco
Dover
Hilton's Point
Kittery
Agamenticus (York)
Piscataqua River
Great Island
Strawbery Banke
Exeter
Isles of Shoals
Hampton
Salisbury
Carr Island
Merrimack River
Newbury
Naumkeag (Salem)
Charlestown (Mishawum)
BOSTON
MASSACHUSETTS BAY
MASSACHUSETTS BAY COLONY
Scituate
Weymouth
Marshfield
Duxbury
First landing of the Mayflower, 1620
Cape Cod
Plymouth
PLYMOUTH COLONY
Sandwich
Yarmouth
ATLANTIC OCEAN
N
W
E
S

# *Part I*

# SUMMER

*Quakerism in its social and moral aspect was the synonym for brotherly love, purity, simplicity, integrity, and benevolence. The early Quakers not only advocated an enlightened revision of the criminal laws and a reform in the treatment of prisoners, which was then barbarous, but they visited the prisons, and sought out and aided the poor, the friendless, and the outcasts of society. They literally loved both friend and foe. Hated, reviled, and persecuted of men, they asked a divine blessing for their bitterest enemies.*

- *Richard P. Hallowell, The Quaker Invasion of Massachusetts*

# *Chapter 1*

## MARY AND ALICE *THE NEW WORLD*

June, 1662 Dover Neck, Massachusetts Bay Colony

Mary Tomkins stepped off the gangplank of the *Arabella* onto the crowded dock, breathing deeply. The odor of earth and plants warming in the June sun was a base note to the briny smell of the docks—damp wood and tarred rope, beasts of burden and their offal, cargo and people. It was a sweet contrast to the confined stench of the ship. A loaded hand cart rumbled by, narrowly missing her. She adjusted the satchel on her shoulder and made for a quieter spot away from the activity, but stopped, reeling. Seven and a half weeks aboard ship had altered her equilibrium, and the earth rolled beneath her feet disquietingly. She turned unsteadily and saw her friend and fellow missionary following. Allie's dark eyebrows rose, marking a similar effect. She staggered toward Mary, the leather bag over one shoulder causing her to list comically like a drunken sailor.

Laughter gathered in Mary's chest, like a cat readying to pounce. She tried to control an unseemly public display but failed. Once loosed, it fed on itself, and infected Allie, as well. The satchels slipped from their shaking shoulders, and the two friends grasped each other's arms, succumbing to raucous mirth. Sailors, laborers, fishermen, and colonists moved around them, mildly curious. The unexpected sensation of movement on dry land, the relief of having made the perilous crossing unscathed, and the prospect of the new life unfolding before them, all figured in the undeniable release of tension. The two women sank onto the bags they had dropped, wiping tears from their cheeks and gasping for breath. Thus did Edward Wharton first see Mary Tomkins.

The women rose, composing themselves hastily, as the two men approached. Their peaked hats, long hair, and unadorned broadcloth suits marked them as the Friends who had come to meet them. Mary was embarrassed to be caught in disarray, like children giggling in church. She was eager to make a good impression on these New World Friends. It was not the introduction she had imagined.

The two men were surprised. The perilous crossing and long confinement aboard ship had certes not disheartened the newcomers. Their laughter was infectious, and both men were smiling as the taller one stepped forward.

"Good morrow, Friends. We are Edward Wharton and George Preston come to greet you, if ye are Friends Tomkins and Ambrose?"

"We are. I am Mary Tomkins, and this is Alice Ambrose."

Mary was not tall, but she stood straight and lifted her chin. Her tone was more clipped than intended, as she struggled to regain her dignity. Her ribs hurt. Errant feathers of laughter tickled her throat and threatened to erupt, but she pressed her lips together and swallowed them. She avoided looking at Allie, as any eye contact would undo her. She concentrated on the two men, suppressing her mirth with effort, but when Allie coughed into her fist to cover a fresh burst of laughter, Mary's face broke into a wide smile.

"We do beg your pardon, Friends," she grinned, abandoning the illusion of dignity. The outburst had felt good, and she was not sorry for its sweet release. "'Tis our sea legs after the long journey. The ground rolls like the deck of a ship!" she explained.

The smile transformed Mary's plain face. Her teeth were even, and her eyes sparkled with merriment. Edward was fascinated by the change. He expected the women to be limp with exhaustion and dismayed by the colonial wilderness, unescorted as they were. Their spirit impressed him. He gazed at Mary and failed to respond to her explanation. His lack of polite reassurance was uncharacteristic, and George hastened to respond for them both.

"Oh, sea legs! Verily! Ye must become accustomed to solid land once more," he said heartily, glancing sideways at his preoccupied companion.

Mary met Friend Wharton's intent look. He must think her daft. Certes he was comely. She blushed, although the laughter still danced in her eyes.

George turned to Friend Ambrose and plunged on. "'Twill pass in time. Walking about helps, unless ye are fatigued?" He too had expected the missionaries to be debilitated by the crossing.

"No, not at all!" Mary responded, recalling herself. Edward Wharton's wordless scrutiny both pleased and flustered her. "We have rested aplenty these seven weeks past."

"If one considers convincing half the crew 'resting'!" Allie interjected, raising an eyebrow and smiling at their new acquaintances.

"We are eager to meet with the folk hereabout," Mary went on, ignoring this comment. "Margaret Fell informs us few Friends have journeyed to these northern settlements as yet."

"Ye are the first to come since Friend Hooten's brief visit last year," Edward said to George's relief, "and we transported two missionaries here in '59."

"Oh? Who were they?" Mary asked. "Mayhap we know them."

His face darkened, and he looked at George before answering.

"They were William Robinson and Marmaduke Stevenson," he answered gravely.

Recognition dawned on Mary's face, and she drew a sharp breath.

"The Friends who were hanged in Boston," she said. It was not a question.

"The same," Edward confirmed.

A heavy silence fell. Edward had known the men well and witnessed their execution.

"We were at Swarthmore Hall, when the news came," Mary told them. "'Twas a grave shock, for they were known and loved among us."

The women had trained for missionary work at Swarthmore Hall. Margaret Fell was the mistress of the manor and had devoted her life and home to the Religious Society of Friends. When the founder George Fox passed through Ulster in 1643, he had stopped at Swarthmore Hall. Margaret and her seven daughters became convinced the first time they heard him speak. Her husband Judge George Fell allowed their home to become a base for the fledgling faith—a training ground for missionaries, a refuge for recovery after abuse or imprisonment, and the hub of communication for the Society. Mary and Allie had lived there for three years, assisting in relief efforts during their training.

"At least the King's mandamus stopped the hangings," Allie murmured.

"Yes, thanks to Friend Burrough's audience with him," Edward responded. "But although the executions are stopped, the punishments grow in brutality at Boston. 'Tis why we met you here at Dover. Ye would be thrown in prison, and the ship's captain fined for transporting you as soon as the ship landed there."

"The Southwicks—our neighbors at Salem—lost everything," George told them. "An elderly couple who never did harm to anyone! They were whipped and imprisoned for nearly a year. All their property was confiscated, and Governor Endicott even attempted to sell their two children into slavery in Barbados, but no captain would take them and be party to such a heinous course."

"When they were finally released, their health was compromised due to their long confinement and the floggings they endured," Edward continued. "We took them to

Shelter Island in the *Sea Witch*—my shallop. The Sylvester Family has a large plantation there, and it is a refuge for Friends. The Southwicks died that winter within weeks of each other. Friend Mary Dyer nursed them, for she had gone there after her reprieve from execution at Boston in October. She held the Bay Colony responsible for their deaths and returned to Boston to protest Endicott's laws for the final time that spring."

Mary and Allie had known Mary Dyer personally for she was their spiritual mother and the instrument of their convincement. Her hanging in June of 1660 had galvanized the two young missionaries to complete their training and cross the Atlantic to take up her cause for the liberty of the truth in the Puritan-dominated colonies.

"After hanging was forbidden by King Charles, the General Court of Boston replaced it with the Whip and Cart Act," George said. "Many have suffered under the lash since."

Mary winced for this form of punishment was familiar in England. Offenders, male or female, were stripped to the waist, tied to the back of an oxcart, and flogged until out of the jurisdiction that had sentenced them.

"I cannot fathom why folk who left England for religious freedom deny the same to others," Allie commented.

"They are determined to keep that right for themselves exclusively, it would seem," Edward answered. "They tolerate no other faith. Even Anglicans are disparaged, although not persecuted as Friends and Baptists are."

The four Friends fell silent. The subject was a sharp reminder of the forces massed against them in the Bay Colony whose reach extended throughout the Piscataqua Region and into the Province of Maine.

"We should not keep you standing here," said Friend Wharton, breaking the heavy silence. "There is cargo on board for the Shapleighs, is there not?"

"Yes," Mary answered, returning with relief to the matters at hand. "Captain Walsh has the manifest. I believe he is with the harbormaster now."

"Then I shall see to it. The *Sea Witch* is docked nearby." Edward nodded at the missionaries' shoulder bags abandoned on the ground. "Ye have other baggage aboard?"

"Yes, a trunk," Mary replied.

"Just the one?" He seemed skeptical.

Mary smiled. "Yes, Friend Wharton, just the one trunk. We travel from place to place, and horses are dear. We carry only what is essential."

"Pardon my assumption, Friend Tomkins. I should not be surprised," he smiled wryly, recalling the women's robust laughter.

"Oh, Friend Wharton," Allie added mischievously, "we have only begun to surprise thee."

While Edward saw to the transfer of cargo and baggage, George suggested the new missionaries accompany him to the inn, where the men were staying. He attempted to carry their satchels, but they demurred.

"Quite capable, thank thee," Allie said, taking up the leather strap as George reached for it. Mary covered a smile, as she shouldered her own bag.

"'Tis many a mile we've carried our own, and many more to come, no doubt. Thou wouldn't wish us to become soft, would thee, Friend Bishop?" she asked, gently teasing.

"Yes! I mean, no!" George spluttered, as they started up the busy High Street, sea legs and all.

Of Edward Wharton's many skills, navigating the New England coast was by far the most valuable. Boats had ever been his passion, growing up around the docks of London, but he had been unable to afford a craft of his own. His widowed mother prevented him going to sea, so he apprenticed to a glazier and had made a livelihood installing and repairing glass windows before leaving England.

Upon his mother's passing in 1648, Edward immigrated to Salem. When missionaries for the Society of Friends arrived in the colonies eight years later, he became convinced along with a number of his neighbors for several had known the unorthodox Roger Williams before his banishment in 1636. The injustice against Friends, himself included, only strengthened his faith. He often transported missionary Friends along the New England coast for little or no remuneration, but, with the exception of the indomitable Elizabeth Hooten, women missionaries traveling alone were a rarity. Most traveled in groups and were accompanied by male Friends. With the exception of brides under contract, women did not travel alone, and the confidence of the new arrivals impressed him—not to mention their sense of humor.

The *Sea Witch* was twenty-eight feet long with a shallow draft. She had two sails, a tiller, a set of long oars, and a sculling oar, allowing her to maneuver the many coves and rivers where wind was not dependable. Most important, the craft had been affordable, although in need of some work. Edward had bargained with the former owner, William Hathorne, an influential citizen of Salem. By installing glass windows in the man's large manse, Edward's commission covered the lion's share of the purchase. The first improvement he made was a covered storage area to protect cargo and passengers when underway. The enclosure eliminated the use of the second set of oars, but was an overall gain, especially with Edward's navigational skills.

When it became apparent that most folk in the colonies could not afford glass windows like Hathorne, the Salem Friend had turned to trade, importing needfuls from England, such as sewing needles, scissors, tools, nails, pots, bolts of fabric, gloves, hats, and shoes—whatever might be found in London at a good price. Letters were often part of *Sea Witch's* cargo too.

George Preston was Edward's partner and a friend since boyhood. They peddled their wares in the coastal towns, where Edward also communicated the Friends' precepts to all who would listen. Since Salem was central to several busy harbors, their clientele had steadily increased, and Edward became familiar with the coastline and major rivers from Rhode Island to Casco Bay.

A ship's arrival was never sure, thus the Salem men had been in Dover for a week. They were staying at an inn on the Neck owned by the independent-minded Anthony Emery, who was sympathetic to Friends. Although June was usually a good month for the crossing, Edward was still relieved that the women had arrived safely. The shipping lanes were fraught with peril that was not confined to unfavorable winds and tempests. The dangers included privateers from Spain, Holland, or France who commandeered valuables and took English prisoners; corsairs from Africa's north coast who sold white captives into slavery or murdered them; and the on-board risks of spoiled food, rats, and ship-borne disease. It was no small wonder the women had landed safely.

At the inn Mary and Allie stowed their satchels in an upstairs room and washed quickly, using the basin and pitcher of water provided. In the excitement of arriving, they agreed to delay the time, work, and expense involved in arranging a hot bath. Besides, the tantalizing fragrances wafting up the stairs reminded them how hungry they were for fresh food after the weeks of ship's fare.

They found George sitting at a table in the common room, nursing a tankard of ale.

"There y'are then!" he said, jumping to his feet and nearly upsetting the bench.

"I am famished!" Allie commented, as she and Mary settled opposite him.

A fresh loaf of bread and a bowl of butter sat on the table. The three Friends closed their eyes and joined hands, sharing a moment of silent thanks then Allie cut three thick slices and smeared hers liberally with butter, using the bread knife. She took a large bite and sighed, chewing contentedly. The serving maid approached with a full tray and set steaming bowls of thick stew before them.

"Would you take some drink with that?" she asked.

"Small beer for us and it please thee," Mary replied, opting for the weaker version of ale.

"I took the liberty of ordering the meat stew instead of the fish, as I reckoned ye have had your fill of that these past weeks," George said.

"Thank thee, Friend Preston," Mary responded. "Thou must be familiar with the crossing to understand our appetites so well."

"Well, point of fact, yes. I usually make the crossing twice or even thrice in a year," George replied, taking up his spoon.

Allie looked at him, astonished. "Verily, twice or thrice each year?"

George nodded, his mouth full, then chewed and swallowed.

"Needs must. Our stock is bought up quickly. Edward knows what folk require, and they know him to be just. Also I have family back in London depending on me. I would live here, given the choice, but my wife does not wish to emigrate."

Mary and Allie exchanged a look at the mention of family. Who knew if they would ever be reunited with theirs? Although they had made their commitment to God's call over family ties, the women still missed their loved ones. George's comment brought this fact to mind.

They turned their attention to the food. Allie chewed slowly, savoring the full flavors of meat, green onions, turnips, and carrots. The taste of rich, sage-spiced broth lingered as she wiped her mouth on her handkerchief.

Edward rejoined them as they ate.

"Captain Walsh was singing your praises," he said, sitting on the bench next to George.

"Oh? Do tell," Mary responded, sipping from her tankard.

"He allowed your singing impressed everyone on board and was a lively diversion. He warranted the passage seemed less tedious than most. He is astonied that several of his most hardened crew attended your meetings and were changed by them. He reckons there is much to ponder from your discussions at table, as well."

He caught her eye and smiled warmly as he removed his hat to say grace. He closed his eyes briefly in prayer, and she found herself staring at the soft, brown curls that framed his handsome face. She reached for the loaf, hoping her blush was attributable to the sea captain's compliments rather than Friend Wharton's smile.

"Didst thou convince the entire crew, then?" George asked, once his friend began to eat.

"Oh no," Mary answered, intent on slicing bread, "not all of them."

"Not for want of trying," Allie put in lightly, scouring her bowl with a crust for every delicious bit.

"I warrant 'twas only about half attended meetings in the end," Mary added.

"Verily? Ye held meetings with the crew?" George asked his spoon arrested in mid-air. He was well acquainted with seasoned sailors and thought Edward had spoken in jest.

She smiled. "What else should a missionary do confined aboard ship?"

"Naught else! Naught else, I reckon," George said, impressed.

He set down his spoon, and rose with Edward, as a fellow approached their table.

"Greetings, Friend Furbush!" Edward said, shaking hands warmly. "Thou art acquainted with Friend Preston here, and these are the missionaries we spoke of, lately arrived from England. Mary Tomkins and Alice Ambrose, allow me to present William Furbush."

"Weel met and welcome to you, ladies!" Will said his Scot's burr evident. "Many folk here are eager to hear what ye would say of yer faith, as well as all the latest news of England."

Allie smiled and nodded but Mary rose and shook his hand.

"Friend Furbush," she said warmly, "we are also eager to meet with them. What location would serve, dost thou think?"

"If the Emerys are willing, this inn is a fine place," the young Scot replied. "'Tis central for many, and all know of it. I shall spread the word this verra afternoon," he added. "Shall we say after the sun has set, so none shall be thwarted by chores?"

"We look forward to it," Mary answered.

After they had eaten, the four Friends walked up Dover's High Street. The women still struggled to regain their land legs, but they walked slowly, relishing the earthy odors of wood smoke, livestock, and plants. People stopped work or turned as they passed, staring at the four Quakers. While newcomers were not unusual in the busy harbor town, these strangers stood out. Their peaked headgeat, the men's long hair, and the confident bearing of the women set them apart. Everyone knew of the punitive laws in

Boston, but Friends were a rarity in Dover. The missionaries spoke with any who met their eyes, inviting them to the meeting that evening.

The little group did not notice the minister, John Reyner, peering from a window as they strolled by the parsonage. He had come from the Plymouth Colony seven years ago. Dover had suffered both political and ecclesiastical turmoil over the years, enduring a succession of ambitious military men and ordained ministers since 1635. John Reyner was a strict Puritan and the fifth reverend for Dover Neck and the smaller settlement at Oyster River. The latter community was fractious in his view. They balked at his stipend of fifty pounds per year and attendance at Sabbath Day meetings was sporadic. They claimed that traveling from their homes upriver to the church on the Neck was a hardship. Why must they pay him for work he performed at Dover's First Church, whether they attended or no? At least the Puritans at Dover appreciated him.

But this now! This was a threat that could not be ignored. So far the northern settlements had largely been spared the invasion of the cursed sect called "Quakers." A few had passed through the region three years ago, and Reyner was aware of the turmoil they were causing in Boston. Everyone in the colonies knew of the hangings. The minister had expected that the harsh punishments devised to keep them away would discourage the heretics, but contrary to all common sense their numbers were increasing.

John Reyner paled at the sight of four of the interlopers strolling up his High Street. They embodied a severe threat to him and to his congregation—nay, to the very foundation of the tenuous social order and growing industry so painstakingly carved from the wilderness over the past thirty years. Clearly it was up to him to expose their seditious intent and protect his flock from their lies. He abandoned preparations for the Sunday sermon, donned his hat, and went to alert his most loyal parishioner and elder of the church, Hatevil Nutter. The man was true to his name, and the Quakers would soon regret coming to Dover.

# *Chapter 2*

## RICHARD WALDERNE *THE IMMIGRANT*

1635 Alcester, England

William Walderne ran a strict Puritan household. He was a successful advocate in the Town of Alcester, Warwickshire, and provided well for his large family; however, as was customary, he had little to do with his children unless discipline was called for. He believed that demonstrations of affection were effeminate and only corrupted right behavior. Human attachments were a sign of spiritual weakness, for one's love should be for God and God alone.

Now he listened with veiled interest as his seventh son Richard went on about a plan to immigrate to Virginia, or "New England" as the boy told him the northern coast of the New World was now called. As though that wilderness could ever resemble the Mother Country, William thought wryly. At nineteen Richard was mature beyond his years. He proposed buying a grant of land through a Captain Thomas Wiggin. The Captain was apparently in England on colony business and was also recruiting settlers for a place called "Piscataway" or some such ungodly name—a far-flung outpost north of the Bay Colony. The boy spoke of the resources, presumably parroting Wiggin, as he described timber aplenty and vigorously flowing rivers purported to be capable of powering mills. "Purported" was the word that stuck in the advocate's mind, though he made no comment and let the boy run down.

"'Tis all just beginning there, sir. If we invest now, the returns could make us both rich."

The clock in his father's study filled the silence, when Richard stopped speaking.

"I *am* rich, thank you." William turned from the window with no trace of the smile that had played on his lips as he listened. He assumed his patriarchal mask, though inwardly pleased by his son's initiative.

"Indeed, sir, and I would hope to follow your example," Richard answered deferentially, reining in his enthusiasm.

It amused the advocate to note this, as he settled behind his desk. His many years at the Bar had honed his perception of human behavior. He watched the lad straighten and draw breath deliberately slowing down. He had the energy of youth and the maturity to control his emotions—a fine combination. Mayhap his seventh son would go far, the advocate mused, sitting back in his chair and stroking his upper lip.

"My meaning, sir, is this:" Richard began again, adopting a reasonable tone. "I shall be able to pay back any monies you invest in relatively short order—with interest! This enterprise is bound to prosper. Captain Wiggin says everyone will be building. And not just dwellings and businesses but docks and ships in time as well. Lumber will be in great demand, and the forests are untouched! Captain Wiggin says but one sawmill has been constructed, and it is a distance upriver and has ceased production—miles from the Point and no competition in any case." Richard's composure was eroding as his eagerness reasserted itself. His words tumbled over each other.

William opened a drawer and bent over it, feigning to look for something. He was enjoying this earnest plea and wanted to play it out. He had never seen such ambition from the lad. It would not do to accept too readily. This was a good discipline for him.

Richard braced his hands on the desk and leaned forward desperate to engage his sire's attention.

"The Captain has recruited a group of some thirty accomplished gentlemen, Father—Puritans of good account and well established in their trades. There is even an ordained minister—a Mister William Leveredge. 'Tis not a gaggle of indentured servants, sir! These men are investing now because they know—"

"Yes, Richard, I understand," his father interrupted. Richard straightened, realizing the verdict was at hand. William stood and met his son's eye.

"Of course I shall support your endeavor. It sounds like a decent opportunity and a good livelihood for you in time. The authorities have established a civilized Puritan government there by now, I should think—at least in the Bay Colony. I am sure they can dispatch any salvages left in the northern regions."

"Oh they are quite tame, sir. Captain Wiggin says they trade land and fur pelts for the merest trinkets—especially with a little rum in them." Richard grinned, his relief evident. "He says the natives are unused to spirits and become like children—easily bested."

His father smiled briefly. "No doubt."

"I intend to set up a trading post and buy up their furs at the earliest opportunity. 'Twill be the first thing I build," his son confided, encouraged by his father's support.

William came around the desk and put a hand on Richard's shoulder.

"Fine, fine," he murmured then cleared his throat. "There's just one condition."

The young man froze. "Oh? What's that, sir?"

The hand on his shoulder tightened. "You must take William with you."

William was the Waldernes' firstborn son, their father's namesake, and Richard's elder by fourteen years. He had a fondness for drink and, as a result, managed to bungle every project their father devised for him. He was a drunken sot, as William senior tenderly put it, but even he admitted his eldest son had married well.

In Richard's memory Will had always been married. Barbara was his brother's saving grace. She was a strong-minded woman of good family and birthed children with commendable regularity. They had been married fourteen years, and Barbara had given him five sons and a daughter. Will had taken to fatherhood with surprising enthusiasm. He was affectionate and indulged his children to a fault, but they inspired him to maintain a level of sobriety previously considered impossible by his parent. The most recent was Isaac, not yet a year old, and Richard fervently hoped Will would refuse to immigrate. He would have to leave his family. The wilderness was no place for women and children. There was certainly no room for negotiation with his father on this point. It was too fine a solution for the advocate to be rid of his embarrassing namesake. Richard nodded reluctantly.

"Excellent!" his father exclaimed heartily. "Now, let us attend to the details, shall we?" He clapped his hands together and returned to his desk.

The young man sighed. His father was a stickler for documents.

As the seventh son in a brood of eleven, Richard had been schooled in competition from the day of his Breeching, the rite of passage when boys abandoned their nursery smocks for breeches and their complicated lacings. He learned early on that he must be one step ahead of the game to win. Losing was not an option. There was no love lost between Richard and his ten siblings. His elder brothers tested him at every opportunity, and he carried on their example by tormenting those younger and weaker than he.

His sister, Elizabeth, two years his senior, had doted on him in the nursery, but when Catherine was born, Lizzie had abandoned him for their baby sister. It was the first of many emotional blows, but the only one that was not dealt in the name of discipline. Ever since, he disliked babies. They were noisy, and they smelled bad, yet they commanded all attention. Once they were mobile, the little pests followed him everywhere and wanted whatever he held dear. He soon discouraged that.

Richard was a quick study and never transgressed in the presence of adults. When his younger siblings ran crying to the nanny, he asserted his innocence by quoting scripture. It invariably worked to his advantage. The Bible was his primer—indeed it was the only book he was permitted to read until boarding school. It was a constant source of tedious study, but in this capacity it served him well for there were passages for every eventuality. Before the age of eight while still living at home, it was a source of amusement to assert dominance over his younger brothers and get off scot-free. So eloquent were his defenses that none of the adults, including his father, ever credited the complaints against him. They believed him to be a pious and trustworthy lad. It worked every time.

Like his brothers before him, Richard was sent to the Shrewsbury Academy at the age of eight. Of course, new students were bullied, but Richard had dealt with that from his elder brothers since standing on two legs. The bullies soon learned that Walderne would not be cowed. In addition to the advantage of height and strength, his salient features were his confidence and piety.

Richard matured earlier than his peers, starting puberty at the age of twelve. His voice deepened, and by his thirteenth year, hair sprouted on his face and body. He looked two years older and was a head taller than most boys his age.

Life at the academy further sharpened his skills in manipulation. Richard never backed down from confrontations with his peers and wasn't afraid to risk punishment by intimidating them; however, he was also skillful at handling adults, and the masters at the school sang his praises. They marked him as a leader early on.

Boarding at the school taught him more than "might is right." Richard discovered that if he refrained from indulging in the base urges brought on by puberty, it afforded him superior strength in competitions and military exercises. He channeled his energy into being the best at any test of strength or endurance. In the dark dormitory, the furtive sounds of other boys relieving themselves disgusted him. They were weaklings with no backbone. They would never become leaders of men, if they could not control themselves. He felt superior. He was convinced that God favored him, as long as he did not succumb. If he spent himself frivolously, he would fall from Grace. He must retain his purity and his seed for marriage and procreation. At the age of thirteen, this became his credo.

# *Chapter 3*

## MARY AND ALICE *FIRST MEETINGS AT DOVER*

June, 1662 Dover Neck, Massachusetts Bay Colony

The Emerys' common room was filling up. Word had spread of the visitors from England and many were curious to hear what the Quakers would say. Once all were seated, Mary spoke to the gathering—some dozen folk, she reckoned.

"Welcome, friends," she began. "We thank you for leaving your homes after a long day's labor to meet with us. We are right glad to be on solid land once more!" There was a ripple of amused sympathy, as many of those present remembered their own crossing.

"Good people, we bring you a message of joy. The Revelation of God's Light is within your provenance this very day. But first, let us address your questions and concerns regarding the Religious Society of Friends and our practices. Whatever ye have heard from your minister is colored by his censure. When all inquiries are answered, those who wish may stay to join in a meeting for worship. Please, feel at liberty to speak."

There was a brief pause then a voice asked, "On what foundation do you rest your faith and hope of salvation?"

"Upon the Lord Jesus Christ, God's only Son, who died for us upon the cross. We do share the same tenets of Christianity as put forth in the New Testament," she answered.

There were murmurs of surprise, as John Reyner had, indeed, told them otherwise.

"However, the Children of the Light emphasize the original teachings of Christ. We hold with tolerance and love for our fellow man rather than the Old Testament's 'an eye for an eye.' But the greatest difference is in how and where Friends worship."

Mary went on to explain the core belief that the Seed of the Divine Spirit slept in all folk, and that a connection to God did not belong exclusively to the so-called ordained ministers.

"Mayhap some of ye have felt that Spirit as Conscience, an inner sense of right and wrong, or the uplifting sensation when helping another, or the warmth of love shared with family and friends," she suggested. "All of these flow from the Divine Spark, or what our founder, George Fox, calls That of God Within. For it is by conscience men should be led, rather than resorting to the outward sword. The Inner Light guides our actions, rather than words spoken by a minister. This Light cannot be found in a book. Every man, woman, and child is capable of experiencing it, for That of God sleeps in each heart, like a seed waiting for our notice to grow."

"But how does it waken?" a woman asked.

"Through silence and quiet contemplation," Mary answered. "Betimes, it does not awaken easily. But 'tis our greatest work as Friends to follow that Light and to recognize and encourage it in others. Does the Bible not bid thee to 'Love thy neighbor as thyself'? And does it not also say, 'Be still and know that I am God'?"

People shifted in their seats, exchanging glances, as they were all familiar with these passages. Outwardly, there was nothing particularly remarkable about this young woman fresh from England. She was plain of face and of medium height with a slight build. Her clothes were a simple skirt and jacket of different shades of brown. Wisps of light brown hair showed at the edge of her dust cap, her wide-brimmed hat set aside for the meeting. But she evinced self-assurance unusual for a woman, and she spoke well. Her eyes shone with intelligence and moved from face to face. She was poised, standing straight-backed, but not stiffly. Mary Tomkins had everyone's attention. She spoke for half an hour, until all questions were answered.

Then the first formal meeting of the Society of Friends in the Emerys' inn on Dover Neck commenced. The missionaries invited everyone to join in a hymn. As girls attending the Anglican Church in Kingsweare, Devonshire, Mary and Alice had loved the music most of all. Each was blessed with a clear voice and a good ear. They harmonized passing well with Mary's soprano and Allie's solid alto. The harmony lent grace to the rendering, and the volume swelled in response. Hymns were the only aspect of their Anglican upbringing that the missionaries could not bear to abandon. Even Margaret Fell had agreed that their singing was of use in their missionary work, for was it not to the Glory of God? It never failed to bring worshippers together. Yeomen, sawyers, fishermen, laborers, and wives were all affected by Thomas Ken's familiar hymn for evening worship.

*All praise to Thee, my God, this night,*
*For all the blessings of the light!*
*Keep me, O keep me, King of kings,*
*Beneath Thine own almighty wings.*

*Forgive me, Lord, for Thy dear Son,*
*The ill that I this day have done,*
*That with the world, myself, and Thee,*
*I, ere I sleep, at peace may be.*

*Teach me to live, that I may dread*
*The grave as little as my bed.*
*Teach me to die, that so I may*
*Rise glorious at the judgment day.*

*Praise God, from Whom all blessings flow;*
*Praise Him, all creatures here below;*
*Praise Him above, y'Angelick host;*
*Praise Father, Son, and Holy Ghost.*

Mary allowed a moment of silence following the "amen." Then she spoke.

"In silence and contemplation the Divine Light is revealed. Good people, set aside your daily tasks and worries. This is not a time to seek fulfillment of your needs. Banish these thoughts and be still. Our Father in Heaven will touch our hearts, if we but open to His Holy Light."

The worshippers were restive at first. People were not used to silence. It made them nervous, but those who stayed had chosen to do so. They wanted to experience a divine connection first hand. Gradually movement ceased, and the quiet deepened. Time passed. A door banged shut upstairs, but no one looked up.

With timing born of instinct Mary raised her head and looked around. Three of the worshippers were still in contemplation, and when they slowly raised their heads, their eyes were radiant. Two looked unmistakably bored, and the rest seemed bemused; however, most were convinced and eager for more. Encouraged by the response, the Friends determined to stay another day before going on to Kittery, where they would be entertained at the home of their friend Nicholas Shapleigh.

The next night the crowd was larger, and more women were present, some with children. Out of long habit couples separated, sitting on opposite sides of the room, facing each other. The Reverend John Reyner and Elder Hatevil Nutter stood against the wall near the door, glowering. They had come to hear what the heretics were saying for themselves.

"My neighbor was here yesterday and tells me ye take no stock in ministers or churches. Be this true?" asked one man, once the room had settled.

"Nor taxes neither, we hear!" another added.

"'Twould be a blessing all of itself!" commented the first, evoking an outbreak of amusement, which was speedily dampened by the reverend's blistering scowl.

The four Friends stood opposite the door before the fireplace, which was not lit on this mild June evening. Windows were open and mosquitoes foraged, their success evidenced by an occasional slap. The benches were full, and every face was turned to the missionaries. Mary took up the question.

"Yes, that is so. Why should your hard-earned coin go to pay a man whose experience of God is based on books? In the spirit, ye are his equal. In the spirit, we are all equals, for God's Light resides within us all. That is why members of the Society of Friends remove their hats only to worship God, for only He is above us. That is why Friends make no oath except to God, for no man is higher than another in spirit. That is why women may preach as well as men, because every person is capable of a direct experience of the Divine." She tapped her heart twice. "His Light dwells here."

"The ministers tell you there is no way to God but through them and their learned interpretation of the Bible, for it is by this yoke they harness you for their gain. Jesus tells us where two or more are gathered in His name, His spirit is with us. God needs no translator. He needs no house. He requires only a willing spirit and quiet contemplation to be revealed."

"But where then do ye worship?" a woman asked.

"In homes. In public places such as this. Out of doors, if 'tis not inclement. Wherever there is a quiet place with room to gather."

"And why are you called Quakers?" came a voice from the back wall.

"Our detractors call us so," Mary answered mildly. "Mayhap they call us Quakers because some are known to tremble when they experience the Divine Presence. Our proper title is the Children of the Light, and we call each other 'Friend.' By this title the founder, George Fox, reminds us of the Lord's words in the Gospel of Saint John, Chapter 15. 'Greater love hath no man than this, that a man lay down his life for his friends. Ye are my friends, if ye do whatsoever I command you. Henceforth I call you not servants; for the servant knoweth not what his lord doeth: but I have called you friends; for all things that I have heard of my Father I have made known unto you.' We use 'Friend' as ye would use 'Mister' or 'Mistress,' 'Goodman' or 'Goodwife.'"

The Reverend Reyner was becoming increasingly agitated and could stay quiet no longer. He pushed away from the back wall, declaring loudly, "This is an abomination!" Heads swiveled. "You would deny the magistrates, the ministers, the churches of Christ, and the three persons in the Trinity!"

He glared around and people ducked their heads and averted their eyes.

"Thy name, Fr—?" Mary began, but Reyner ignored her and advanced, addressing George Preston.

"Do you respect no authority? No churches? No ministers? You would throw us into anarchy! You preach the devil's chaos!"

George's quiet answer contrasted with the minister's raging tone.

"Thou dost mistake us, Friend, for we preach the Light of God and the Love of Christ, who bade us love our neighbors as ourselves. We own all the covenants of the Bible, including the Trinity. Thou dost wrongly accuse us on these counts."

Reyner's voice lowered, heavy with menace. He stood in the aisle between the men's and women's benches and raised his arm to point at the four Friends. "You do not own a house or property here. You are vagabonds poisoning the thoughts of these good people!" His arm swept the room, and his voice rose. "You upset and confound them! Leave off and quit this place or you will be arrested! You are not welcome here or anywhere in the Bay Colony!"

Edward stepped forward and raised his eyebrows, opening both arms. "I own a house and land in Salem and run a successful business, as many of these folk know who have purchased my goods. They have come, thirsty for knowledge of the Spirit. Should we deny them, because thou hast not filled their need?"

The minister's face flushed. The Quaker had struck a nerve.

"*I* am the ordained minister of this community! I have been educated to guide these people. *You* are deluded charlatans with no place here!" he fumed.

Edward paused, affording a moment of quiet. The clergyman's labored breathing was audible, and all present remarked his choler. The Salem man spoke calmly in contrast.

"Perhaps thy vehemence is fed by the fear of losing thy position, Friend. Thy very livelihood depends on the taxes paid by these good people."

There were audible gasps at this rebellious assertion and not a few in the room hid smiles.

Reyner shook with indignation and anger, temporarily speechless.

"You—!" He blinked rapidly, shook his head, drew breath, and at last responded in a strangled voice. "You have not heard the last of this! The wrath of God shall punish your heresy! Pray He does not smite us all because of it!" he spat, backing toward the door. "And do not think I have not remarked your faces!" he continued, sweeping an arm across the men's section. "The Bay Colony laws punish any who listen to these vagabond Quakers. You endanger yourselves and your families by being here. Mark my words!"

He reached the open doorway and, turning on his heel, left. A few of the men standing followed the minister. Elder Nutter kept his place, his eyes narrowed. He would not be so easily put off. Someone must stay to witness what these heretics were up to.

A collective sigh of relief passed through the room once the minister had gone. People turned to their neighbors to comment on the drama. Mary raised her voice, reclaiming their attention.

"Yes, take heed, people, for as ye have just seen, we are often wrongly accused. All the tenets of the Bible we own, as does the church here, but ye need no minister. The blossoming of thy Conscience is between thee and God. We worship in silence, deferring to none but the Highest Power. Freeman or servant, man or woman, we are all equal in His sight. Certes, the clergy tell you otherwise, for they depend on an order by which they profit. Friend Wharton is correct. They cleave to your taxes. Their authority is *not* God-given. It is man-made, and, as ye have witnessed this night, the ministers are undone by the truth."

The room buzzed, as people reacted to this revelation of freedom from the Puritan freeman system. Without that coveted status a man could not vote, be a member of the church, or hold public office, although he was still taxed to support the system. It was granted to the elite of every established community, and there was no alternative—until now. The Friends posed a visceral threat to the Puritan oligarchy.

"Many of ye labor over considerable distances to attend worship," Mary continued. "'Tis no small hardship to travel over rough roads or by water in all weather. Yet ye are fined, should ye fail to attend." There were vigorous nods and rueful smiles as all were familiar with the difficulties of travel, particularly the families with little ones. "But Friends require no meetinghouse. A neighbor's home or a quiet place out of doors serves just as well, for God's Light is with us anywhere."

The room was quiet now, all eyes on Mary, and she lowered her voice.

"But the greatest difference lies in how we treat our fellow man. Friends help the beleaguered and unfortunate. We stand by each other through sickness and lean times.

We call out injustice, wherever it may try to assert itself. All community decisions are agreed upon by the consensus of the head of every household. Good people, if we practice our Christian Faith as Our Lord Jesus instructed—with care and love for each other—how different might our world be! Let us join now in contemplation of that Kingdom on Earth. Let us find our strength in silence."

# *Chapter 4*

## RICHARD WALDERNE *WILDERNESS*

1635-1637 Bristol (Dover), Piscataqua Region, New Hampshire Colony

Civil war was imminent in England. The impending disruption caused a wave of immigration to the New World. Lords Say and Brooke bought up the grant for the Piscataqua Region from the Merchant Venturers of Bristol, England, who had broken up in the wake of political upheaval. Both Lords were military men sympathetic to the Puritan cause who remained in the Mother Country to aid in the effort to overthrow King Charles I. However, barring victory, they wished to establish a model Puritan foothold in New England to which they might escape. They employed Captain Thomas Wiggin as their agent, and in 1631 he made his first voyage to the region.

Edward and William Hilton welcomed Captain Wiggin with enthusiasm. They had built homes on a point of land they called Northam. Their partner David Thomson was an energetic Scotsman and the driving force behind the venture, but he had settled on the coast a few miles south of the Point with his wife and little boy. With just seven other young men to help them, they established a lucrative business catching, drying, and exporting fish. Thomson left in 1629 as soon as he met his obligation to the investors. He sold out to the Hiltons and took his family to live on an island in Boston Harbor. The Hilton brothers stayed at Northam, continuing the business, but they had done little to build a settlement fit for families. Wiggin brought back a favorable report of the site. Lords Say and Brooke granted him permission to recruit settlers, and within a year Wiggin garnered thirty men "of some account for religion," meaning Puritans like his employers. Among them were the Walderne brothers.

Richard's brother Will and his wife Barbara had decided that Will would go ahead to prepare their home in the New World and send for his family when all was in order.

Richard was vastly relieved. Women and children required a gaggle of servants for their maintenance—nursemaids, housemaids, kitchen staff, and menservants. Immigration would be difficult enough even without such a staggering contingent in tow. The brothers sailed in April of 1635.

During the crossing, the Waldernes forged friendships. Will was drawn to two brothers, John and Anthony Emery, who shared his love of spirits. Richard preferred to keep company with Captain Wiggin and the Reverend William Leveredge, serious men of good education whose friendship would serve him well in the new settlement. At twenty he was the youngest man in the group.

The Emerys were as alike as brothers might be. Their resemblance was such that, at first, Richard mistook one for the other if he saw them apart. Both were skilled carpenters, and each planned to establish an inn and ordinary in the New World. The younger Walderne frowned upon his elder brother's nightly excesses in the Emerys' company, but when they offered to assist with plans for Will's house and a trading post for Richard, he realized the value of befriending them and came to respect their professional knowledge.

Captain Wiggin called the company together every few days. He enumerated the priorities that must be accomplished in the settlement. The recruits had at least a year of hard labor ahead before they could purchase land. The colony's needs must be first—cutting trees and brush, improving existing paths, clearing others, and marking out house lots. Bachelors must defer to family men in the construction of dwellings, and all this was in addition to preparing for the long winter to come.

The *James* accomplished the crossing without mishap and landed at Boston in June. Richard was impressed with John Winthrop's "City on the Hill," now five years old, but the new arrivals did not stay long. Wiggin soon arranged for a smaller vessel to take them north to the Hiltons' settlement.

When they first arrived, there was insufficient housing for the immigrants. The bachelors slept on the ship anchored at Pomeroy's Cove. Those with wives and children—or influence, like the Reverend Leveredge whose family would soon join him—were entertained by the few local families. These included the Hilton brothers, Thomas Roberts, William Pomfrett, George Walton, Thomas Layton, and Captain Wiggin.

The new arrivals received a warm welcome, but they were not prepared for the rustic condition of the ten-year-old settlement, particularly compared to Boston. It consisted of seven homes plus a meeting house, all made of logs and linked by two rough tracks. Only William Hilton had built a proper house in Richard's opinion with clapboards, brick, and glass windows imported from England.

The original settlers of the Hiltons' group were Anglicans loyal to the King. Their number had been marginally increased by others of like mind, fleeing north to escape the rigid Puritan authorities of the Bay Colony and Plymouth Plantation. The Piscataqua Region consisted primarily of individuals whose priorities were aligned with the success of their livelihoods, rather than the practice of religion.

Richard was surprised by the general lack of enthusiasm to establish the model Puritan community of which Captain Wiggin had spoken. In addition there was more brute work to be done than the recruits had been led to believe. A log meeting house, completed just the year before, sat on a rise facing south. Trees and brush had been cleared around it to afford a fine view of both the east and west shores of the Point, but Richard was dismayed. It appeared so primitive it was sacrilegious in his view, although he kept this opinion to himself. It was a glaring reminder that the settlement was on the edge of a vast wilderness. Still, on the first Sabbath Day the Reverend Leveredge presided over his congregation with sincere gratitude and evident pride, and Richard soon became accustomed to it.

In addition to religious services on the Sabbath, weekly meetings were held on Tuesdays to address secular business. The thirty newcomers were a majority in the settlement, and at their first gathering, they voted that the town be named Bristol for the port from which they had journeyed. The vote demonstrated that the Point no longer belonged exclusively to the original settlers, but they still welcomed the increase in population.

Captain Wiggin organized the recruits into working teams. Although initially appalled by the rustic conditions, Richard was quick to involve himself in the planning and implementation of improvements. Even brother Will made himself useful as secretary, chronicling their earliest town meetings and eventually recording deeds.

Their first project extended the existing path in a northwesterly direction to the top of the next rise. Then lots were marked out and cleared for men with families whose homes were built first. That autumn was warmer than usual, and labor continued into November. Richard was tireless and able, and he was soon appointed supervisor of his team.

The first winter at Bristol was relatively mild by New England standards, the newcomers were told, but it was more severe than any English winter Richard had known. The snow held off until mid-December, but March and April brought heavy rains that delayed the resumption of outside labor. Progress was frustratingly sporadic on Will's house. The masons needed dry weather to set foundations and construct chimneys. Richard was frustrated by the delay. He longed to build his trading post and begin to generate profits, but a home for his elder brother's family trumped his plan.

Will missed Barbara and the children and became maudlin on the subject when intoxicated. His unbridled laments irritated Richard, and he ceased accompanying Will to George Walton's ordinary—one of the few existing buildings. After the day's labor, the younger Walderne walked the Point, familiarizing himself with the lay of the land. Several rivers flowed down from the north into Great Bay to the west and the Piscataqua River on the east side of Bristol. He realized he would need a boat to explore the rivers for an optimum location for a trading post.

Captain Wiggin took a liking to the earnest young Puritan, and during that first winter, Richard and Will were invited to his log manse on a regular basis. Richard noted that only the Puritan elite attended these dinners, and he counted it a victory to be included. William Pomfrett and John Damme were present, as well as Thomas Layton, Richard Pinkham, and Hatevil Nutter. The latter was one of the few immigrants in Wiggin's party who had brought his family. Conspicuous in their absence at these gatherings were the Anglicans loyal to the monarchy—William and Edward Hilton, and their friend and brother-in-law, Thomas Roberts.

In addition to the absence of civilized comforts, the settlement lacked marriageable women. Wiggin had recruited married men for the most part, although few had brought their families as yet. He encouraged the bachelors to follow suit, but there were few options—desperate widows or daughters of simple fishermen and yeomen, just coming of age. Richard had higher standards and wanted a wife of good family to bear his children. He realized he would not find her on this side of the Atlantic.

During their second winter on the Point, the Walderne brothers occupied William's house located on the newly improved High Street. While not finished, the house provided adequate shelter, and Anthony Emery arranged to winter with them, completing the interior work in return for his room and board. Anthony's lot was a short distance down the lane, but he had spent the summer helping his brother John build a house at Newbury Plantation thirty miles south and, like Richard, hoped to begin work on his own project the next spring. His wife, Frances, and three small children remained with his brother, John, until a house in Bristol was ready for them. Currently George Walton was the sole proprietor of an ordinary in the frontier village, but Anthony intended to change that—a plan that Will approved with enthusiasm.

The three men moved only essential furniture into the house, and Anthony set up his saws and cutting table wherever he happened to be working. Sawdust gilded every surface, and the smell of fresh-cut wood was pervasive, but the three men were not bothered by the chaos and got on well. Richard enjoyed helping the older man, for Anthony was good company. They talked as they measured, sawed, and fitted wainscoting and trim—Richard of his trading post and a sawmill and Anthony of an inn and ordinary. The only drawback was their new friend's company encouraged Will to drink. Anthony seemed unaffected the next day—the carpenter's work was always meticulous—but Will slept late into the morning, neglected his personal toilet, and revived only to lament the absence of his wife and children or to fulfill his duties as town secretary. Richard would retreat to a back room where he had set up a table of planks on two barrels. He kept candles there and worked on the plan for his trading post, though there was not enough coin left to build to his original standards. Anthony made some suggestions, familiar as he was with the workings of an ordinary, and the rough concept became workable. Despite his aversion to alcohol, Richard intended to serve spirits at his trading post, for liquor would give him the upper hand in bargaining with the Indians.

"Mark you, there is talk of prohibiting the sale of spirits to the salvages," Anthony warned him. "But then, away up here, who's to know?" he added with a grin.

The winter passed. Will's house was complete, and they celebrated the turning of the year at the Wiggins' on March 24$^{th}$. Shortly after, a letter came from England. Richard knew it must be dire news for it came by a rider a-horse, rather than by ship from Boston as usual. It was from their brother, George, second eldest in the family, and the news it contained was three months old. Following a visit to London for a friend's funeral, their parents had both contracted the plague and died within three weeks of each other—first Catharine in November of 1636, then William in December. There were family matters to address. The brothers must return to Alcester as soon as possible.

Captain Wiggin was sympathetic. Richard had indicated a preference for a particular lot of land bordering High Street, and the Captain promised to honor his choice. The brothers were just the sort of men Wiggin had hoped to find. Bristol could use more like them. After nearly three years in the colony, the Waldernes spent their last funds on passage to England. Richard determined to use the opportunity to find a wife.

# *Chapter 5*

## MARY AND ALICE *ON TO KITTERY*

June, 1662 Dover, Massachusetts Bay Colony/Kittery Point, Province of Maine

The day after the second meeting, the four Friends settled their bill and bade the Emerys farewell. They stowed their satchels on the shallop and climbed the bank above Pomeroy Cove to wait for the tide to turn. The June morning was overcast, but a fair wind from the southwest shepherded the clouds out to sea and no rain fell. They had a fine view of the activity around the docks, as they talked. To their right, the Point curved protectively around the cove. George pointed across the Piscataqua to the far bank.

"'Tis the Maine Province just over there," he told them. "Kittery Point is downriver on that side. Once the tide is with us, 'twill not take long to reach the Shapleighs' at Warehouse Point."

Mary's gaze turned upriver to the left, taking in the skeletal frames of the flakes where fish were dried. Below these was another landing. Several large piers extended well out into the river. Two large merchant vessels were docked there, and men were transferring milled lumber from flat river barges into their holds.

"What place is that with the piers?" she asked with a gesture.

"That is Richard Walderne's landing," Edward answered. His tone made her look at him.

"Who is Richard Walderne?"

"One of the richest men in Dover," George told her.

"Also a magistrate and a Puritan to the bone," Edward added grimly. "'Tis best we are leaving before the minister reports our presence to him."

"Why?" Mary asked. "We have broken no law."

"In Dover Richard Walderne *is* the law. He presides at the court," George said ruefully.

"No King's law, true," Friend Wharton went on, "but Dover is part of the Bay Colony, and they prosecute any who do not follow the Puritan creed, with the exception of the Anglicans. They are tolerated by the Puritans only because they are usually gentlemen of means—Royalists with connections and influence in England—like our friends the Shapleighs. Now the monarchy is reinstated, the King would never tolerate a colonial government harassing men of their ilk, and he has the power to revoke the Bay Colony's charter. But for ordinary folk—or Friends—there is no protection. Ye shall both be safer at Kittery with the Shapleighs."

"'Tis precisely such abuses of justice that called us here," Mary asserted. "Certes, we do not wish to avoid him. Our safety is in God's hands."

Edward gave her a hard look, which she met unflinchingly. George and Allie exchanged a glance.

"How are ye acquainted with the Shapleighs?" George asked her, changing the subject.

"From our childhood in Kingsweare," Allie answered promptly taking up the cue. "Our fathers were in the Shapleigh employ. Are ye aware of the family's shipping company based there?"

The two men nodded.

"Indeed," Edward answered, "they have oft obliged us by transporting cargo for our business. Nicholas' elder brother James runs the business, since their father's death."

"Oh, all of Kingsweare was saddened by Alexander Shapleigh's passing!" Mary responded. "We were fifteen, were we not, Allie?"

Alice nodded.

"He was loved and respected by many," Mary went on. "James carries on in his spirit and was most generous concerning the price of our passage. My father Ralph keeps the Shapleigh accounts, and Allie's father, Richard Ambrose, captained their ships for many years."

"In the '20s and '30s." Allie elaborated. "'Tis how he met my mother, Bernadette, who is French. Her father owned vineyards and engaged the Shapleigh ships to export his wine to England. He invited my father to dine at his home. It marked the end of Papa's days at sea, for my parents soon married, and voyaging lost its appeal for him."

Mary took up the tale. "Soon after Allie was born, word came that Captain Ambrose's uncle had passed. Having no issue, he left his inn at Kingsweare to his favored nephew, who had always stayed there, whenever he docked at Bayard's Cove."

The two women exchanged a smile, enjoying a new audience for an oft-told tale.

"The Hearthstone Inn and Tavern shares a back garden with the Tomkins household, and thus our parents became the best of friends," Allie added.

"We grew up with two homes," Mary went on. "My father gave us lessons once we were of an age to learn. Every morning except the Sabbath. He taught us everything we know."

"But to answer thy question, Friend Preston," Allie said, turning back to George, "we know Nicholas from the Yuletide gatherings that his father hosted each year for employees and their families. Nicholas is the youngest of the Shapleighs. He and his nephew John organized games for the children who attended. They are close in age, and the boys grew up as brothers."

"What riotous fun those parties were!" Mary exclaimed, her eyes sparkling. "Nicholas and John seemed so grown up to us as children, and we adored them. They led us in high hilarity with their games of 'Blind Man's Buff' or 'Button, Button!'"

"We sang carols, as well, I recall," Allie added. "'Twas the first instance we ever sang for folk outside of church."

"Oh yes! I had forgot that," Mary said. "And we all attended the Church of Saint Thomas of Canterbury, for Kingsweare is a small village. We saw the Shapleighs every Sabbath Day. Alexander always stopped to speak with our fathers after the service, and while they talked, Nicholas and John were ever kind and attentive to us."

"I do not believe our parents would have allowed us to journey here without Nicholas' patronage," Allie said softly, and Mary nodded.

The sun gained strength as it climbed, warming the travelers. Edward announced the tide had turned, though how he could tell, Mary had no idea. They made their way back to the dock and prepared to cast off.

Edward was relieved to note the women seemed familiar with boats. They boarded with cautious confidence and sat out of the way on the stern bench, as the two men loosed the lines. Edward and George pushed off and set to the long oars, skillfully maneuvering the shallop out of the cove and onto the river. Tide and current were with them, and the rowing was not difficult.

They soon cleared Hilton Point and caught some wind. The oars were shipped, the sails were raised, and the sturdy craft gradually picked up speed. Mary and Allie moved aside as Edward took the tiller, while George went aft to raise the jib. The *Sea Witch* headed for the landing at Warehouse Point, the closest landing to Kittery Manor.

Growing up in the little seaport of Kingsweare had prepared the women well for navigating the coast of the New World. Their village was located at the mouth of the

Dart River opposite the larger port of Dartmouth with its deep water harbor, Bayard's Cove. During Mary and Alice's girlhood, the traffic bound for the New World increased with each passing year. Ships docked to make repairs or provision their holds for the crossing, and it was just such a circumstance that had brought Mary Dyer to Kingsweare. The Quaker missionary was accompanied by two male companions, and she had spoken after the service at the church one Sabbath Day in October of 1657. Mary and Alice were twenty-two, and it was their first contact with the notorious Quakers. Friend Dyer had changed their lives. As she watched Dover Point recede, Mary realized it was five years ago now.

She tightened the shawl anchoring her headgear in the increasing wind and focused on the shoreline. It was wild here with few signs of human habitation, although the hills were not so steep. Everything seemed larger—trees, vistas, gulls—even the squirrels looked huge! Stumps dotted recently cleared land on the east bank, giving it a raw, denuded appearance, but on the whole, the confluence of river and ocean felt familiar.

The Friends' mood was ebullient. Their reception at Dover was encouraging; God had delivered His missionaries to the New World unscathed; and the four Friends were getting on well. A following wind was speeding them to their destination, and they would soon see Nicholas again and meet his wife, Alice, with whom Mary had been corresponding for over a year.

Wind and water made conversation difficult, and Mary was soon lost in thought. How far they had come, she and Allie! Not long ago her only option had been to live out her life in her father's house, since she refused to marry. It was the lesser of two evils, for at home she was subservient to her elder sister, Margaret, who treated her like a servant. From the age of twelve, Mary was enslaved to the demands of her brother-in-law and three nephews. Lessons with her father or working with the Ambrose family at the tavern next door were welcome respites from Margaret's sharp tongue and the drudgery of housework and childcare. During those ten years before Mary Dyer entered her life, Mary had never dreamed she would become a missionary, traveling the roads of northern England in the company of the dynamic Edward Burrough.

Friend Dyer had encouraged her protégés to become missionaries and gave them a letter of introduction to Margaret Fell at Swarthmore Hall. Mary had written Mistress Fell, asking to visit and work with the Society of Friends. The reply encouraged Mary and Alice to come to Ulster as soon as possible. Six months after Mary Dyer had left them, the two young women made the long journey north to Swarthmore Hall on a ship captained by a friend of Allie's father. It was their first adventure away from home.

Margaret Fell treated everyone under her roof like family. Traveling missionaries were constantly passing through. All received their training or found refuge at Swarthmore Hall. During the next three years, Mary and Allie wrote letters, helped with accounts, copied documents and treatises, organized relief packages of food, candles, blankets, and clothing, and made regular forays by wagon to visit Friends in prison. There were meetings for worship and stimulating discussions every day.

Free of her elder sister for the first time in her life, Mary blossomed. Thanks to her father's open-minded instruction, the Kingsweare women were unusually literate and well spoken. Margaret Fell encouraged them to contemplate missionary work. Although Allie was not inclined to speak publicly, she supported Mary emotionally, and, in any case, Friends were advised not to travel alone. Margaret realized the value of their relationship and recommended to the assessors that they work together. Once begun in earnest their training took a year, and the panel of experienced missionaries gave Mary and Allie unanimous approval. Edward Burrough was one of them, and he invited the new recruits to accompany him on their first assignment.

During their second year at Swarthmore Hall, Friend Burrough had come to recuperate from a severe case of catarrh contracted in the Lancaster Prison. Mary and Allie nursed him, tending not only his physical ailment but also reading aloud or, as he recovered, engaging in discussions of faith and the human condition. The two Devon women came to love Edward like a brother and were flattered and pleased to travel with him.

At twenty-five Friend Burrough was an experienced missionary who had convinced hundreds of the new faith. He was a prolific writer and rebutted many vituperative and fallacious pamphlets written by the Anglican clergy denouncing the "Quakers." His eloquence caused the Society's founder, George Fox, to dub him "Boarneges," meaning "Son of Thunder."

Although he was younger in age, he was their elder in spirit, and the two new missionaries willingly followed Edward's lead as they visited towns and villages across northern England, informing folk of the new faith. Friend Burrough radiated gentle good will, and people trusted him instinctively. No Anglican minister could best him in debate, and they invariably reacted with anger. Within a month the three missionaries were arrested and spent six months in the dungeons of Lancaster for "reproving a priest." Edward had humiliated the man before his congregation, and they suffered for the minister's wounded pride.

Edward Burrough's health was frail, but his unflagging spirit sustained them. The damp, the stench, the lack of light and fresh air still haunted Mary's dreams. The raw cold penetrated their bones. Sanitation was nonexistent. They became accustomed to vermin and rats, but worse were the guards. The meagre portions served once a day were often spoiled, and although Friends brought sustenance, blankets, and candles, little was left for the prisoners once the guards helped themselves. At first the warders took pleasure in taunting the starving Friends, as they consumed the fresh, savory-smelling food, but Edward returned their cruelty with calm compassion, eventually earning a grudging respect. Mary's heart warmed at the thought of Edward Burrough and Mary Dyer. She could do no better than to emulate them. Now God had led them here. Mary was not afraid of suffering, and she was eager to stand against injustice in the Puritan-dominated frontier.

Allie was contemplating her parents' resistance to her calling. It was the only time in her life that they had fallen out. Her three-year absence at Swarthmore Hall was difficult to bear, but they flatly refused to consider her crossing the Atlantic to a savage land. Did she not realize they might never see each other again? In the end it was the support of the Shapleigh Family that swayed them.

Shapleigh vessels sailed to New England regularly bringing supplies to a growing market and returning home with dried fish, timber, and furs. James Shapleigh generously offered the missionaries passage on a company ship at a fraction of the usual fare, but the deciding factor was that Nicholas and his wife Alice were eager to entertain the women at their plantation in the Province of Maine. The ship would land at Dover, not Boston where Quakers were immediately imprisoned. New World Friends would bring them on to Kittery Point, where they would be under Nicholas' protection. Without this assurance of their well-being Allie knew her parents would not have relented.

Even with James Shapleigh's generosity, lack of funds delayed them. The Friends provided some monies for traveling missionaries, but the women needed to purchase extra clothing, two pairs of sturdy walking boots, roadworthy luggage, and writing materials for reporting to Margaret Fell. It took another eighteen months working at the tavern and scribing for Mary's father to save enough coin to equip them, but the women savored the time with their families. Even censure from Mary's sister lost its sting, knowing departure was imminent. They had maintained a lively correspondence with Nicholas' wife Alice for more than a year. Now, at last, they would meet.

# *Chapter 6*

## NICHOLAS SHAPLEIGH *KINGSWEARE TO KITTERY*

1634-1662 Kingsweare, Devonshire, England and Kittery Point, Province of Maine

Nicholas did not remember his mother. She died soon after his birth, and his half-sister Katherine and her husband James Treworgy took on his care. Kat was seventeen years older and had married the year before Nicholas' birth. Her own first born, John, was delivered just three months after his Uncle Nick. Once she became a mother herself, Kat dismissed the wet nurse hired for Nicholas and suckled both babies. She loved her little brother as her own, and the boys were as inseparable as twins.

Nicholas' mother, Jane Egbeare, was his father's second wife. The widower married her soon after the death of Kat's mother for practical reasons. He had three small children: Kat, age three; Alexander Jr. (Zander), age 2; and Elizabeth, an infant. There was Kittery Manor to manage, as well as his international shipping business. His first wife, Marguerite Bloedel, was the love of Alexander Shapleigh's life. She had been fifteen, when they married, and died before the age of twenty, when complications arose after Elizabeth's birth.

Jane proved a competent partner and a gentle stepmother. Even as the eldest child, Katherine barely remembered Marguerite, who had died before Kat turned four. Jane wiped her tears and sang her to sleep. Jane taught her basic letters and numbers, needlework, comportment, and how to manage a household. Jane guided her through her first courses and the tumultuous years of puberty. Jane advised her throughout James Treworgy's courtship, assisted with the wedding preparations, and shared the joys and burdens of Kat's first pregnancy. Jane's three stepchildren were as devastated by her death as their father.

After losing a second beloved wife, Alexander was not inclined to marry again. Nicholas would be the last of his progeny. All his energy went into the family shipping concern he had inherited from his father, Nicholas, for whom his youngest son was named. The work was demanding, as Shapleigh vessels sailed the seven seas, exporting dried fish and importing oil, wine, and the fine French salt used in the drying process.

When Captain John Smith published his *Generall Historie of Virginia, New England and the Summer Isles* in 1624, Alexander's interest was piqued. He was not alone. King James had been encouraging expeditions to "Virginia," as he dubbed the entire coast of the New World, for two decades. England must not allow the French and Dutch to dominate the region. Smith's reports also caught the attention of an energetic group of businessmen based in Bristol called the Merchant Venturers. This consortium sought new sources of raw material the world over. Populations in Great Britain and Europe were swelling. The market demand was increasing as resources dwindled. Here was a potential solution. Alexander Shapleigh joined them, investing coin and ships.

Through the Merchant Venturers, Alexander met Sir Ferdinando Gorges, a decorated naval commander and Captain of the Plymouth Fort thirty-five miles west of Kingsweare on the Devon coast. Gorges owned a grant of land on the northern coast of New England and had financed several attempts to establish a permanent settlement on the mainland in the early 1600s. They all failed, until his ward David Thomson succeeded in 1622. Thomson partnered with two brothers, Edward and William Hilton, graduates of the Laconia Fishmongers Guild, and they hired only seven laborers. The outpost was a business concern producing dried fish, rather than a settlement of families, but it was a start.

The Shapleigh patriarch and Sir Ferdinando shared a love of ships and an enthusiasm for exploration. Consequently Alexander became his agent and made his first voyage to the region in 1634. Gorges called it the Province of Maine.

Lucrative fishing operations already existed on Monhegan Island and Smith's Isles, but Alexander wanted to settle on the mainland, using Shapleigh vessels to transport the valuable commodity of dried fish back to England. His children were grown. His two elder sons—Alexander, thirty-two, and James, twenty—were partners in the family enterprise. At last their father could leave affairs in their hands for a few months and make the crossing. Even Nicholas was seventeen now and three years into an apprenticeship in the family shipyard. Alexander planned to sail on his own vessel *Benediction* accompanied by his friend, Francis Champernowne from nearby Totnes, and Alexander's son-in-law, James Treworgy. Young Nicholas begged to go.

"'Tis of paramount importance that you finish your training here, Nico," Alexander responded to his son's earnest plea.

"But Father, I could learn on the crossing! 'Twould be a—"

"There shall come a day when we will all make the crossing, my boy. And when we go, 'twill be to settle there and build a plantation in the wilderness. I charge you to hone your skills and knowledge for that time, eh?"

Nicholas' eyes widened at this revelation of his father's ambitious plan to emigrate. Alexander chuckled at his expression and clapped his son affectionately on the shoulder.

"Continue your training and learn all you can," his father finished firmly.

Nicholas had faith in his father, for Alexander always made good on his claims. He swallowed his disappointment and concentrated on mastering his trade. It was no hardship, verily, for he loved ships and soaked up nautical information like a sponge. Nicholas' apprenticeship entailed working with the draftsmen, the carpenters, the sailmakers, and the riggers, but he also sought out captains, first mates, and navigators, listening eagerly as they held forth on the practicalities of sailing a large vessel on the high seas. They appreciated his inquiring mind, especially if he supplied the liquid refreshment as they talked.

Alexander returned home from his first voyage fired with enthusiasm. Such potential! The rumors proved true. The resources were prodigious and virtually untouched. The Hilton brothers welcomed him warmly and encouraged his plans, eager for neighbors like the Shapleighs with energy and means. William Hilton sold him a house and land on a point that Alexander named Kittery for the manor in Kingsweare. Once back in England he spoke of little else and was often at Plymouth, conferring with Gorges, or at Totnes speaking with the Champernownes, who also planned to emigrate. The Shapleigh patriarch was determined to establish a plantation in the New World.

His motivations were not entirely driven by profit. Like any shrewd businessman, he kept a weather eye on the political climate. There was a storm on the horizon in England. King James died in 1625, and his son succeeded him, but unlike his sire, Charles I had little interest in exploration. Royal hunts and sumptuous parties at court were more diverting. In addition, he married a French Catholic, alienating the Anglican Church, Parliament, and the Peers of the Realm—not to mention most of the populace, which harbored a deep suspicion of Catholics. He disdained Parliament's authority, insisting on his divine right as absolute monarch of the realm. Tension was growing between those loyal to the monarchy and those who wanted a return to a purer, simpler order. The former were mostly gentlemen of property, usually bearing an inherited title and Anglican in their religion; the latter were skilled professionals and Puritans, who disparaged drinking, gaming, the vanity of fashion, or religious ceremonies they considered "popish." The Shapleigh Clan was loyal to the King, but the growing opposition to Charles worried Alexander. The Puritans supported Parliament, and their resistance to royal decrees seemed ominous. If civil war broke out, Maine offered a refuge. Alexander's two eldest sons would stay in England to manage the business, but otherwise emigrating would be a family affair.

The next year Alexander was kept from returning to Maine by a new writ of tax on shipping imposed by the King, who was desperate for the funds denied him by Parliament. Alexander sent his grandson, John Treworgy, in his stead. Katherine and James' eldest child was unusually bright and at eighteen had just completed his studies as an advocate at Grey's Inn in London. Acting as his grandfather's factor, John bought five hundred acres on the east bank of the Piscataqua River and another eight hundred acres soon after on Spruce Creek. The "creek" was actually a river capable of powering sawmills—another of Alexander's plans, knowing lumber would be in demand.

John prepared the way for the family, overseeing extensive renovations to the house on Kittery Point purchased from William Hilton. Both Philip Swadden and Hilton were a boon to the young advocate, for they were familiar with the region and had bought the Point from the local Indians. They facilitated the negotiations for the Shapleigh purchases. By the spring of 1638, the year of Nicholas' majority, the extensive preparations for emigration were complete on both sides of the Atlantic. Alexander thought it not a moment too soon.

The family made the crossing in the *Benediction*. John had sent lists detailing what was needed, and the hold was packed with tools, provisions, bolts of wool and cotton cloth, and seed for crops. The transition to their new home would be smoother than most, thanks to their patriarch's foresight in sending John ahead. In addition to Alexander and Nicholas, the immigrants included Katherine and James Treworgy with their three younger children: Joanna, sixteen; Lucy, seven; and Elizabeth, a babe in arms. She was named for Kat's sister who was recently widowed and joined the group. In addition to various domestic servants, nine skilled employees with their wives and children accompanied the family, including joiners and a master carpenter, masons, blacksmiths, and husbandmen. Nicholas was eager to go and felt sorry for Zander and James, who must stay behind.

"If things become untenable, you must come to us post haste," Alexander told his elder sons at their parting. "Bring the *Golden Cat* and any who wish to accompany you."

Nicholas felt his life truly began when the family immigrated to the Province of Maine. His years of training had prepared him well, and he relished every aspect of the crossing. John was thrilled when *Benediction* dropped anchor off the Point, reuniting him with the family. He had been away for three years, and their reunion was joyous.

They arrived at the end of May with five months of hard labor ahead before the first winter. John had made a good start. The area around the renovated house and a new stable had been cleared, and construction was underway on a brew house and a warehouse, but progress increased markedly with the arrival of the skilled workers. William Hilton helped Alexander draw up plans for a publick house at the west end of the Point—a necessity in any English community where water was considered unhealthful to drink—but the patriarch's first priority was a proper landing on the ocean side of the point for docking large ships. It was essential for offloading livestock, and transporting cargo by longboat from ship to shore was tedious, risky, and time-consuming.

By the end of their first winter, it was clear that another trip to England was necessary to replenish supplies and transport animals, now there was a pier for docking. Nicholas accompanied Alexander, and their rapport deepened during the crossing.

Affairs were not running smoothly in England. James was struggling to manage the family business, as Zander was often away at foreign ports. Civil war seemed inevitable, and times were hard. The King's shipping writs were levied annually now and had cut into the Shapleigh profits. Debts had built up as a result of the investments in Maine, and Alexander realized the family business hung in the balance. He prudently transferred the Maine properties to Nicholas as protection from debtors, but his youngest son saw the acquisition as a loss, for it meant his father would not return with him to Maine.

"I have drawn up a document," Alexander said, as they discussed the practicalities in his study at the manor in Kingsweare. "Have John review it before you sign."

Seeing his son's downcast expression, he went on. "The Maine holdings would have gone to you in any case, Nico. Certes, you know that. There are few prospects for you here, especially with rebellion in the air. You and John shall make a good life in Maine, I have no doubt."

"But we shall miss you, Father. I would relinquish it all to have you there with us."

"I am afraid that is not possible at this time," Alexander said, turning away.

Three weeks later Nicholas returned to Maine on a loaded ship, reluctantly leaving his sire.

In retrospect Nicholas found it ironic that the ship bringing word of the birth of Zander's son also carried the news of his eldest brother's death. The letters were from their father. Upon returning from business in Barbados, Zander took to his bed. The physicians bled and purged him to no avail. They called it a tropical fever, and it took his life. His wife, Beth, had given birth to their long-awaited first child just weeks before his return, but Zander never held his son.

In addition to this dire news, their father asked that Nicholas return with the ship. The family business was at risk, and James needed his father's help more than ever with his brother gone; however, the Shapleigh patriarch required Nicholas' help "in another matter of great delicacy" though he offered no specifics. He waited until Nicholas arrived to confide in him.

"Beth is quite literally prostrate with grief and is unable to nurse the babe," Alexander began once they were alone in his study. "She has gone home to the comfort of her mother's arms, taking baby John with her, but I am concerned. Her mother tells me Beth is inconsolable and seeing the child upsets her, knowing he is fatherless and with few prospects. They have hired a wet nurse, but..." He trailed off, looking at his son expectantly.

Close as they were, Nicholas parsed his meaning. "You wish to adopt the boy, Father?"

Alexander nodded. "I wish *you* to adopt him, Nico, and take him back to Maine as your heir."

Nicholas was surprised. He wasn't even married as yet, but the more he considered it, the more the prospect appealed to him. Kat had not left him to be raised by hired help; it seemed mete that he adopt Zander's son in turn.

"I think it best you talk to them first, my boy," Alexander said once Nicholas agreed. "Beth trusts you. If anyone can convince her of this course, 'tis you."

A message was sent and Nicholas was received two days later. Beth's mother greeted him warmly, but warned him the young widow was yet in a delicate state. Beth made an appearance, but seeing Nicholas undid her for he resembled her husband. She burst into tears at the sight of him and ran from the room, embarrassing her mother, who apologized profusely.

"I understand," Nicholas assured her. "'Tis a tragic loss for all of us, but particularly for Beth. Still, I wonder if I might see little John, whilst I am here?"

"He is napping now," she answered, "but come up with me, and you shall have a look at him."

The baby was nearly six months old, and Nicholas gazed down at the sweet face, so cherubic in repose. Careful as they were, the baby woke, and seeing the faces bent over his cradle, smiled and kicked his legs. His uncle was smitten.

"Hullo there, little John-John," Nicholas breathed, bending closer. He turned to his hostess. "May I hold him?" he asked.

Beth's mother smiled. It was an unusual request for a grown man. "Certes, but I warn you, he's likely damp." She lifted Johnny and put the sturdy little body in Nicholas' arms.

"That's all right then," Nicholas answered, accepting him eagerly. "Come see your old uncle, Little Man."

The baby gurgled, grabbing at his uncle's nose, and Nicholas' heart swelled. Johnny was a healthy, happy child and favored the Shapleigh family. He responded to Nicholas immediately. His uncle realized he could not bear to leave his brother's child to be raised by hired help in another household. His father was right. Johnny was a Shapleigh and should be with them.

During the next several weeks, Nicholas visited often, patiently convincing Beth and her family to approve making John his heir. They realized the boy's prospects were better with the Shapleighs in Maine. In addition they were royalists and faced an unknown future in a country on the brink of civil war. A legal document was signed before witnesses, stating that the boy would inherit all of his uncle's assets.

More time was consumed in finding a wet nurse willing to emigrate, but at length Nicholas succeeded. Happy as he was to sail with his nephew, parting with Alexander was difficult. All hope of his father's return to Maine had died with his eldest son. Nicholas put on a brave face as they said farewell, but he was haunted by the premonition that they would not see each other again.

Within two years civil war broke out in England. Alexander's letter imparting this news also warned his family to stay away. Communication was sporadic in subsequent years, but Nicholas never forgot the missive they received from James. The Shapleigh patriarch passed in December of 1649. One month later, King Charles was beheaded, and Nicholas counted it a blessing that his father had not lived to see that dark day. Alexander was mourned by many, and the Shapleigh Clan was crippled by death yet again.

During the next two decades Nicholas was an active participant in the local government of Kittery. By weight of his character and popularity, he held a variety of public offices including selectman, special commissioner of the courts, and county treasurer. He was charged to survey the boundaries of the town, which was officially incorporated in

March of 1647. He helped to organize the York Militia and led the drills twice a month, achieving the rank of captain. His adopted nephew Johnny became an active partner as he matured, assisting his uncle in managing their extensive holdings—the sawmill, the brew house and ordinary, the livestock and crops, the exports and imports to and from England and Barbados, and the fishing fleet and flakes for processing. Nicholas and Johnny loved it all.

The family had built a church and procured Reverend Mitton to preach upon occasion. However, Nicholas was open-minded in his beliefs, a trait Alexander had encouraged in all of his children. His father liked to quote Sophocles, saying, "No good e'er comes of leisure purposeless; and heaven ne'er helps the men who will not act." It was the only comment touching on religion he ever made. As a result his children were energetic, free-thinking individuals who were not confined to following the well-worn paths of tradition.

When Edward Wharton brought two missionary Friends to Kittery, the Shapleighs welcomed them into their home. William Robinson was educated and well-spoken. Marmaduke Stevenson was a husbandman cut from simpler cloth with a warm and open spirit. Their conversation was thought-provoking, and the Friends' tenets appealed to Nicholas' own sense of fairness. His wife, Alice, became convinced, embracing the concept of That of God in every person.

Despite being among the wealthiest families in the province, the Shapleighs appreciated the skills of those in their employ. They did not let others labor while they reaped the fruits. Every day except the Sabbath, Nicholas and Johnny—now a capable lad of twenty—put on work clothes and got their hands dirty. John Treworgy lived in nearby York with his wife, Penelope and two sons, but he was often at Kittery Point helping with legal documents, accounts, and business concerns. It was a demanding life, but a good one for the family was free to follow the course they had worked out together.

Nicholas would have welcomed Mary and Allie's visit, even had he not known them from childhood. His wife, Alice, was eager for female companionship, and they were all hungry for the latest news from England. The monarchy had been reinstated for nearly two years. How different things must be after a decade of Cromwell and his Protectorate!

Mary's last letter to Alice Shapleigh said the missionaries would embark the second week in April. Their hosts expected them in early to mid-June. Nicholas arranged for the girls to be met at Dover by his friend and business associate Edward Wharton, who was also a missionary in the Society of Friends. He and his partner George Preston would bring Mary and Allie to Kittery Point along with the latest cargo the Shapleighs had ordered from England.

As June progressed, anticipation at Kittery Manor grew. The best guest room was ready, and Alice had the family on alert to welcome their guests any day. She could hardly wait.

Nicholas and Alice Mesant were married in the church on Kittery Point in 1647. They had met three years before at a gathering hosted by Nicholas' friend, Francis Champernowne, at his Greenland Plantation. It had been love at first sight for the eligible bachelor. Alice had a sweet nature and was beautiful, but she was also shy and difficult to engage in conversation. He felt sure that she loved him, yet she put him off. Nicholas was not deterred.

In the third year of their courtship, Nicholas' sister Elizabeth organized a party for him at Kittery House on the occasion of his thirtieth name day. Kat usually filled the role of hostess, but she and John were in Nova Scotia at the time, assisting John's father James Treworgy who was governor there. After dinner, as guests and family mingled in the drawing room or spilled out onto the veranda, Nicholas persuaded Alice to walk with him. He was determined to propose again. They strolled down the lawn to the landing at Warehouse Point to watch the sunset. It was a mild evening in May, and they stood on the pier overlooking the confluence of river and ocean. The timing was perfect, and Nicholas took Alice's small hand and knelt before her on one knee.

"Alice Mesant," he began, "will you not make me the happiest man in all of Maine and be my wife?"

"Oh Nicholas," she sighed, attempting to withdraw her hand. He held on.

"I beg you, Alice! There is no doubt in my mind. I cannot bear the prospect of a future without you. I would have your consent and the privilege of caring for you."

"I-I cannot, Nicholas! You do not understand!"

"How can I, if you will not explain?" He stood, still clasping her hand. "Is there another who has your heart?" he inquired gently, searching her face.

"No!" Her face softened, and she squeezed his hand. "No, Nico, there is no one else."

"What then? Please tell me! Nothing you say shall change how I feel about you."

Alice looked away and wordlessly shook her head.

He cupped her cheek and turned her face to his. Tears stood in her eyes, and one rolled down her cheek. Nicholas gently brushed it away with his thumb.

"Please trust me, my love," he implored softly.

She closed her eyes and more tears fell.

"I am damaged," she whispered.

"Damaged? What say you?" he responded, lifting her chin. Alice opened her eyes. "Never. Not to me!" he asserted without hesitation.

She was surprised that he did not recoil at her confession, but she feared even he would turn from her once he knew the truth. A sob escaped her, and Nicholas enfolded her in his arms, laying his cheek against her dark hair.

"Dear heart, you must trust me on this. Please believe that nothing you say will dissuade me," he murmured his lips close to her ear. "Confide in me, Alice, I beg you."

And there, cradled in his embrace, she voiced her shame.

"I can bear no children. I shall never bear children. I can give you no sons."

Her words came in a rush, and she bit back another sob, waiting for his reaction. It was not what she expected. There was a beat of silence then Nicholas held her at arm's length.

"How now?"

His surprise was genuine. She blinked. Must she say it again?

"You cannot bear children? *That* is why you will not marry me?" he asked, eyes wide.

Alice nodded, watching his face dubiously. "'Tis reason enough, I should think," she said in a small voice.

Nicholas smiled and pulled her close. Alice felt torn between relief and indignation.

"Oh my darling girl!" he exclaimed, holding her tight. "'Tis no reason in my view! Mine own mother died birthing me. 'Twas my sole concern that I might endanger you, as well. I warrant I am relieved!"

He held her at arm's length again and gazed fondly at her tear-streaked face.

"Dear, dear Alice, family I have aplenty. You and Johnny are all I could want. He is smitten with you already, and I need you by my side."

A tremulous smile appeared on her face. Was it possible this man she adored could abide such a glaring fault? He took her hand and again bent on one knee.

"So I ask you, Alice Mesant, will you marry me?"

Alice's smile broadened, and her ready tears fell again, this time in relieved happiness.

"Yes, Nicholas Shapleigh! Yes, I will."

# *Chapter 7*

## RICHARD WALDERNE *COURTSHIP*
### 1637 Alcester, Warwickshire, England

The Walderne brothers docked at Bristol, England in mid-May. Will's reunion with his wife and family showed no Puritan restraint. He greeted Barbara with tearful joy and embarrassingly deep kisses. He clasped each of his five children in his arms, ignoring little Isaac's wails as he plucked him from his mother's arms and held him aloft. Their emotion seemed overblown to Richard; however, Barbara and the children were in boisterous good health. They were living at the family manor, as Barbara had steadfastly nursed her plague-stricken in-laws. Will was both touched and horrified at the risk she had taken, but it seemed God approved Barbara's charity, for she and the children were spared the contagion.

Little Isaac, who was a babe in arms when the brothers had left, was now almost three. Initially he feared Will and hid behind his mother's skirts; however, after watching the warm affection his siblings and mother showered on this tall stranger, he was soon seated on Will's bony knees, giggling as his father bounced and tickled him.

Richard observed these demonstrations of affection with a stony countenance. He could not help but think of the caustic comments their father would have made. William Senior had raised his children with an iron fist, quashing such displays of emotion under his roof. He held with the Puritan belief that showing affection was effeminate. It did not surprise Richard that of the eleven children his parents had raised, only their daughter-in-law showed them any love or care in their travail.

Richard was not ashamed of his relief at the death of his parents. It was God's will. Death was the natural order, culling out the sick and weak—or the unlucky. His parents' time had passed, while his life was approaching its zenith. He was glad to be spared the indignity of begging for more funds at the mercy of his father's critical scrutiny. His sire no longer held the purse strings. Ever the pragmatist, Richard's major concern was the size of his inheritance, and the power it would afford him in the New World.

Soon after the brothers returned to England the ten surviving Walderne siblings gathered in the parlor of their childhood home. Their brother James had died in '33, kicked in the head by a fractious mare. Now they were eight brothers, three with wives, and two sisters with their husbands. Brother George was an advocate, like their father, and informed them they would not have to worry about finances once the will was approved and probated. True to form, their father had filed the document soon after he took to his bed with his second eldest son's help. Richard realized the estate must be considerable, or George would have sent an assistant.

"I shall, as a matter of course, subtract my fee from the estate before it is apportioned," George told his siblings smoothly. "The remainder shall be distributed as per Father's instructions. 'Tis a princely sum, I assure you, since it also includes the stipend he had designated for Mother. All is in order, and it should not take long."

"How long?" Richard asked from where he stood at the mantel.

George pursed his lips, looking alarmingly like their father. "A week, mayhap longer, if our clerks are overtaxed. Certes, not more than two, I should think."

The Walderne siblings were happy to let their George deal with the legalities and did not begrudge him his fee. Father would have approved. "Family brooks no favors," had been one of his hard and fast rules.

In the interim, Richard determined to find a wife, but he was not romantically motivated. A wife was another necessary component on the road to success. He needed sons and someone to manage his household and entertain guests, but how to find her? He almost wished his mother were still alive to help him. In her stead, Richard turned to his sister-in-law for advice. Barbara took action the very next Sunday.

Samuel Clarke was the minister at Alcester, assuming the post two years before Richard and Will emigrated. Reverend Clarke had earned some note as a biographer of prominent Puritans. He had been a good friend of their father's. The two men had much in common and had enjoyed many a discussion regarding literature and religion. Unlike Richard's father, however, Clarke had a mild temperament, unusual in ministers of his faith.

The Walderne residence was located on the edge of the village of Alcester, and in mild weather, the family walked the short distance to attend church. Most of Richard's siblings had returned to their respective homes. Only George remained as he had taken up residence in the family manse with his wife, Bridget, and their three small children. Richard and Will strolled along in his company while Barbara and Bridget followed, a plethora of children and nannies with babes-in-arms straggling across the lane in their wake.

The usual April showers held off, and new blossoms lifted their heads in the sun. The English spring felt impossibly mild, the air soft and fragrant. Richard had forgotten how much warmer it was at this time of year compared to New England and was regretting his wool frock coat and breeches. A trip to the tailor was definitely in order. How fine to realize anything one required was readily available in England. The neat village, the smooth, time-worn roads, the orderly landscape looked very different to him after three years on the rugged New England frontier. He savored the benefits of civilization as never before.

The twelfth-century church of St. Nicholas was more impressive than he remembered. Upon entering, the scents of aged wood and candle wax recalled his boyhood. He took in the stained glass windows lit by sunlight, the dark wood of the altar and pews, and the buttressed arches soaring overhead. He had taken these things for granted until now. Richard even enjoyed the service, impressed by Reverend Clarke's eloquence. He could not help but compare this Sabbath Day to Leveredge's ponderous sermons in the primitive log meeting house at Bristol.

After the service the minister stood outside at the foot of the stone steps, his wife and daughter beside him. Many lingered to have a word with him, for Clarke was receptive to each of his flock. Barbara had sent the children back with the nannies and insisted the adults wait to speak with their father's old friend.

When Richard last attended services with his parents four years before, he had not given the minister's twelve-year-old daughter a second thought. Now she was sixteen. He would not have recognized her were she not standing with her parents. The gangling girl had blossomed into a woman of arresting beauty. Richard had ample time to look at her, as they waited, although the crowd obstructed his view somewhat. He moved aside to get a better look. Her bonnet did not completely hide the auburn curls falling down her straight back. The sun awakened the chestnut highlights. He tried to see her face, but it was hidden by her bonnet. Her figure was slender, and she was taller than her mother.

At last Barbara and Will were greeting the Clarkes. Bridget and George were in front of him, and Richard craned his neck for a closer look at the girl. The curve of breasts and hips beneath the fine fabric of her simply cut dress distracted him from observing good manners. His gaze moved over her figure appreciatively, until she turned and saw him. Her green eyes brightened with amusement. She had caught him ogling her, but she did not appear offended or even embarrassed. In fact her smile deepened, and her right cheek dimpled. Then and there Richard determined to take her to wife. Here was the woman of good breeding he hoped to find. Their mutual interest did not go unremarked by either Barbara or Mistress Clarke.

For her part, Prudence was smitten from the moment she saw Richard. She remembered him and noticed his tall figure in the congregation immediately. Since the age of twelve, she had admired his handsome face and confident, military bearing. The intervening years had added maturity and strength. Comely appearance aside, as an immigrant to the colonies he was the embodiment of exotic adventure to the sheltered girl. Her life and her parents bored her. Her only escape would be through marriage, and here was a man who might rescue her from a life of predictable tedium.

As the rainy English spring warmed to summer, Richard devoted his energy to winning the trust of his prospective wife's family. He charmed Prudence; he prayed and discoursed with her father; he flattered her mother. His sister-in-law was his staunchest ally. Throughout April, May, and June, Barbara hosted dinners and teas designed to bring the two families together, and, of course, the Clarkes reciprocated. The young couple conversed in polite company at demure social gatherings under the watchful eyes of Prudence's parents.

Richard struggled with the contrast to his rugged life in Bristol, devoid as it was of the social niceties, barring the Wiggins' soirees. Courting was effortful, but the naïve girl drank in his descriptions—tailored somewhat—of the New World. Winning her affection was ridiculously easy. Richard realized the challenge was to gain her parents' trust. Prudence was their only child, fresh-faced, obedient, and pious. She was their darling, and therein laid the greatest obstacle to the match, for he would be taking her away from them to a savage land. It was likely they would never see her again. His powers of persuasion were taxed as never before, but with persistent charm he secured Reverend Clarke's blessing by the middle of June.

The engagement was announced to the unbridled approbation of all except the bride's mother. Mistress Clarke's initial enthusiasm waned, as she realized she would lose her daughter to this young emigrant. She would never guide Prudence through pregnancy and birth or know her grandchildren. She faced an advancing old age as though childless. She accepted the congratulations of family and friends with a stoicism that thinly veiled her dismay. She was an obedient wife and submitted to her husband's decision for their daughter's future, but she insisted on certain conditions.

Mistress Clarke would not be rushed into parting with her only child. Normally engagements lasted at least one year, and two was not untoward, but Richard was appalled when Prudence told him the wedding date was set for June two years hence. It was untenable. He wanted her now. A house could be completed in a year, now he had his inheritance. Money was no object, but time was. The summer was advancing and if he did not leave soon, he would have to wait until next spring to start the foundation of a home for his bride. Reverend Clarke must be persuaded to reconsider the circumstances, or Richard faced two more years as a bachelor. Soon after his bride-to-be communicated her mother's dictum, he appealed to the minister to expedite the marriage.

"Father Clarke," he began, using the appellation his future father-in-law favored, "Prudence tells me we must wait two years, but I fear time is of the essence. I must soon return to Bristol and had hoped to marry Prudence forthwith and bring her with me; however, I am willing to consider a compromise of, shall we say, one year?"

"Well, *you* need not linger in England all that time, my boy," the minister replied with a twinkle in his eye. "Now the banns are read, you may return whenever you wish."

"Yes sir, my thanks. That is true, but—" the young man groped for words, "Two years is a long time, and now that I know Prudence, being parted from her sweet company shall be a hardship. May we not consider an earlier date, Father Clarke?"

The reverend gazed at the young man as Richard pled his case. He had admirable drive, good resources, a strong bloodline, and plenty of ambition, though a touch impetuous. He would be a good provider for Prudence and her children, but the minister loved his wife and would honor her wish that their daughter not be taken from them so precipitously. Pru had just turned sixteen. It would be a good exercise in discipline for the young man to wait two years—a test of his abiding affection in fact.

"Yes," Reverend Clarke responded, suppressing a smile as relief flooded Richard's face. "*We* may consider it, Richard, but the ladies shall not, I wager. Their hearts are set on experiencing the full regalia of the matrimonial ceremony. 'Twill require some planning. I am sure *you* comprehend that to deny them that experience would engender a most inauspicious commencement to your marital bliss. The engagement is official, but Prudence shall stay here for the nonce, preparing for the wedding with her mother. I should think you would welcome the delay, Richard, for 'twill give you time to finish a proper house and insure that all is in readiness to receive her."

"But, sir, can you not—"

"My dear boy," Clarke interrupted, suppressing a twinge of irritation at the young man's refusal to accept the decision with grace. "I fear 'tis not a matter for debate; however," he paused, crossing to his desk, where he sat and took up a quill. "I propose to give you half the dowry now. Seventy-five pounds to expedite the construction and purchase appointments for Prudence's future home. You shall receive the balance upon your wedding day," Clarke fixed the young man with a stern look, "two years hence."

Richard was immediately mollified.

"That is very generous of you, Father Clarke," he said, already imagining how he would spend this second windfall.

The reverend smiled, as he wrote out the draft. If peace must be bought, so be it. At least they would have their sweet girl safe at home for two more years. "I am glad you understand, Richard," he said.

The young fiancé had no choice but to acquiesce.

# *Chapter 8*

## MARY AND ALICE *ARRIVAL AT KITTERY POINT*

June, 1662    Kittery Point, Province of Maine

As the shallop approached the landing at Warehouse Point, George brought out the small signal cannon and primed it with powder. He waited until they could clearly see Kittery Manor and its many outbuildings. There was even a church, as Edward pointed out.

"Ye may wish to cover your ears," George warned with a smile. They complied.

The report of the cannon echoed across the water, announcing their arrival far and wide. Soon after a figure appeared at the top of the pier and rang the bell there, waving at them with the other arm. They all waved back.

'Tis Johnny Shapleigh," Edward explained. "Nicholas' nephew, though they are like father and son."

Johnny recognized the approaching craft, for the Salem Friends were no strangers to Kittery Point. The youth had been taking inventory in the nearby warehouse, when he heard the signal cannon, and he was the first of the family to respond.

The arrival of the missionaries from England was the biggest event of the summer to the isolated colonists. Visitors with fresh news of the mother country were like water in the desert. The report of the cannon and the ringing bell signaled a rare respite from chores, as well. Folk were converging at the landing before the last notes faded. They came from the flakes where fish were salted and dried; they came from the warehouse and the brew house; they came from the trading post, the manor, and the kitchen house; they came from the barns and fields. The Point was a paragon of local industry, but visitors from England trumped all tasks.

Edward brought the shallop in smoothly. The wind cooperated, and he was able to dock without using the oars. Johnny was waiting on the pier along with several other workers by the time the craft landed. He was the first Shapleigh to know only the New World, having been a babe in arms when Nicholas adopted him. Alice had tutored him in letters and numbers from the age of six, but his real education was at Nicholas' side. His uncle involved him in all aspects of running Kittery Plantation, for he would inherit everything. At present, all of his considerable concentration was focused on welcoming their guests.

Had the southwesterly wind not carried the sound upriver, Nicholas might have missed the cannon's distant report. He was at the sawmill, scaling a load of pine logs hauled in by oxen the day before. The saw was quiet as the crew was stacking boards milled earlier that morning.

"Make haste, fellows!" he called. "Our guests are come, and we must make them welcome. Spread the word. Free ale at the ordinary! Clear up then no more work today!"

He finished measuring the last of the logs, marking the footage on the butts with his pocket knife then joined the others at the landing. For a wonder, the tide was in their favor. It would be a quick trip downriver to the Point.

Alice Shapleigh reached the dock just before the shallop landed. Most of the house staff accompanied her, except for Missus Beals, the cook, and two of her kitchen crew, who were scrambling to prepare for the feast in honor of the guests that night. How Alice had anticipated this day! Visitors to Kittery Point were always welcome, but these were the first women to come, and unescorted, as well! They must be brave and capable. Certainly Mary Tomkins was a lively correspondent. Alice fervently hoped the visitors would stay indefinitely.

As soon as the shallop was secure, Johnny helped the missionaries onto the dock. There was a flurry of activity as sails were rolled and bound, and eager hands assisted the Salem men in offloading baggage and cargo from the hold.

"I hope you brought those new saw blades, Edward!" Johnny called. "The old ones are near as thin as a razor!"

"Aye and we could use some of those, as weel!" a bearded young Scot called good-naturedly. Mary recognized William Furbush, whom they had met at Dover.

Everyone laughed. The air seemed to sparkle with energy and good will. Alice Shapleigh stepped forward to greet her guests.

"Mary and Alice at last! At last ye are arrived!" she exclaimed, kissing them on both cheeks in the French manner. She had no trouble discerning which was which after the letters they had shared. "Nicholas is upriver at the sawmill, but I am sure he will be along presently."

"Shall I fetch him, Friend Shapleigh?" William asked, pausing with a box in his arms.

"Do not make extra effort on our part, Friend Furbush," Mary interjected.

He gave her a smile at the use of his name. "'Tis an effort I would gladly make, Friend Tomkins, to be the bearer of such happy news!" he answered cheerfully.

"Why thank thee, William," Alice Shapleigh replied. "'Tis kind of thee to offer, but I wager he heard the canon and is on his way."

Mary and Allie exchanged an approving glance. Her warm words and respectful attitude marked Alice Shapleigh as a Friend already.

Two men took the missionaries' satchels up to the house despite their protestations. The arrival of guests was so exciting; everyone wanted to be involved in welcoming them. Edward and George urged the two women to go ahead with Alice, promising to rejoin them once the cargo had been stowed in the warehouse.

"We shall get you settled in," Alice said, as they walked the short distance up to the manor. "There shall be a feast tonight with the family, but we have you to ourselves this afternoon. Are ye hungry, or in need of a rest?"

"Oh, 'twas a quick sail from Dover, and I think we are far too excited to rest!" Mary answered.

"No lack of chimneys," Allie commented, as they approached the large manor.

"Why, this is as grand as any house in England, Alice!" Mary exclaimed, as they neared the columned veranda and the wide front door.

Kittery Manor was nearly as impressive as the original in Kingsweare. Inside the furnishings and appointments testified to frequent shipments from the mother country. The foyer gave onto a large front hall graced with a beautiful crystal chandelier. A carpeted staircase led to an open landing halfway up, where tall windows of imported glass gave a view of the fields behind the house. A large drawing room was located to the right of the hall; on the left a dining room boasted a table as large as the one Mary remembered from the manse in Kingsweare.

"We are so happy to have you here to help us fill it!" their hostess said warmly, leading them into the hall. She took each of them by the hand. "Come, I shall show you to your room."

They started up the stairs as the two men descended, having delivered the missionaries' hand luggage to their room. They were followed by the little chambermaid who had shown them up.

"My thanks, Ellen," their hostess said, as they passed.

"Y'are that welcome, Mistress," Ellen answered, her eyes fixed on the new arrivals, as she bobbed a curtsey on the landing. "All is in readiness for ye," she smiled shyly.

"We thank thee, Ellen," Mary said warmly, causing the girl to blush with pleasure.

"Ye know Nicholas' sisters Katherine and Elizabeth do ye not?" their hostess asked, as they continued up.

"Not well," Mary answered. "They seemed adults to us and did not join in our games with Nicholas and John."

"Katherine and her three girls lived with us for a year, after her husband, James, was killed in Nova Scotia," Alice told them. "Poor Kat was bereft. They were married near twenty-five years. Were ye acquainted with him?"

Allie shook her head, economic with speech as ever.

"From a distance only," Mary answered. "We were but nine when the Shapleighs emigrated." She took in the polished wood banisters, the black and white marble tiles of the hall, and the chandelier now at eye level from the open gallery at the top of the stairs.

Alice continued talking as they moved down the hall. "Katherine married Edward Hilton the next year, and she and the girls moved to his home in Exeter. The house has felt empty since, and your company is most welcome." She paused in front of a door. "Coincidentally 'twas Edward's brother, William Hilton, who first built on this site. Father Shapleigh bought the original house from him on his first voyage, though John Treworgy made extensive improvements before the rest of the family arrived." Alice opened the door with a flourish. "Here is your room."

Mary and Allie were stunned. It was a corner room, spacious and comfortable. Two canopied beds were to the right with a small table under the window between them. Two more windows opposite the door looked out over the river's wide mouth with a writing desk beneath them. A fireplace was on the left with two upholstered chairs flanking the hearth. A beautiful Turkish rug covered most of the floor. A large wardrobe sat left of the door and a chest of drawers was on the right with a basin and pitcher atop. The two Friends had not expected such comfort in the wilderness. Even their room at Swarthmore Hall had not been so well appointed.

"Oh, 'tis beautiful!" Mary exclaimed, going directly to the writing desk and touching the paper, quills, and ink waiting there. The windows were open, admitting the balmy, sea-drenched air.

"I hope ye find it comfortable," Alice smiled.

Allie sat on one of the beds and sighed contentedly, as the soft feather tick cradled her weight.

"Alice, 'tis perfect!" Mary exclaimed, turning back to her. "We shall be more than comfortable! Thank thee for entertaining us in such luxury!"

Their hostess blushed with pleasure. "We hope ye shall stay a long time," she said shyly. "I have enjoyed our correspondence, and the anticipation of your arrival has cheered us all. Now, would ye like to refresh yourselves? I can arrange a hot bath, if ye wish one."

Mary glanced at Allie then answered for them both.

"'Tis a tempting offer," she replied, "but while there is light to see, we would prefer to walk about and see more of the plantation. Might we bathe later, perhaps before dinner?"

"Certes! The bath house is in the kitchen, separate from the manor. Nicholas deemed it safer, after the original house was destroyed by a fire that started in the kitchen. I shall see the water is put on to heat for you." Their hostess made for the door, speaking as she went. "Nicholas will soon be here. He is as eager as I to show you all we have accomplished. Do settle in and come down when ye are ready." She turned at the door and smiled. "How wonderful to have you both here at last!"

As Alice was leaving, the same two hearty fellows arrived with the missionaries' trunk. They set it down and paused, eyeing the newcomers with frank curiosity. Unmarried females, barring widows, were virtually nonexistent in the colonies, where men far outnumbered women. In addition these two had made the crossing unescorted by any male companion. The only other single women to do so promptly went into arranged marriages. The men were further amazed when Mary asked their names, engaged them in conversation, and addressed them as "Friend." The missionaries could not have been more of an oddity had they sported two heads.

It did not take long for them to unpack. As Mary and Allie came down the broad staircase, the front door opened, and Nicholas entered. He wore work clothes and no wig. Tendrils of dark blonde hair escaped the black ribbon binding it. He was no longer the boyish youth the women remembered. At forty-five his lithe frame had evolved into a more substantial, middle-aged aspect, but he looked fit and radiated energy. His enthusiasm and high spirits were the same.

"Here you are at last!" he exclaimed, closing the distance between them with outstretched arms. He embraced them unabashedly, kissing them on both cheeks, as Alice had done.

"Mary! And little Allie!" he chuckled. It was an old joke they shared, as Allie was unusually tall. "Well met! Let me look at you. What fine young women you have become! You were little girls when last we met."

"'Tis true!" Mary laughed, pleased as ever by his warm regard. "'Tis twenty years, I reckon."

"Zounds! That long?" He was struck by this realization and turned to his wife, who had just returned from the kitchen house. "Imagine that, Alice! I have not seen these girls for twenty years!"

"Well, 'tis fifteen since we wed, dearest," she said, smiling at his high spirits. "But number not the years, for contemplating time can prove dangerous at our age!"

They all laughed at the verity of this statement.

"Besides, our friends are eager to see thy accomplishments before the afternoon wanes," his wife rejoined.

"Splendid!" Nicholas exclaimed. "Pray, allow me a few moments to make myself more presentable, and we shall have a grand tour. Has the family been alerted?" he asked Alice.

She assured him that they had.

While Nicholas freshened up, their hostess showed her guests the rest of the manor. Every room had a fireplace. In addition to the drawing room and the dining room off the Great Hall, there was a study with a large, untidy desk and an impressive collection of books, obviously selected and maintained with care.

"Nicholas loves to read," Alice told them, as the two missionaries avidly scanned the titles. "He and his father used to confer on the materials. 'Tis a memorial to Alexander. Indeed, the whole of Kittery Plantation is such. They were very close."

There was also a workroom for domestic projects. A spinning wheel and loom were currently operated by two women, who rose to greet the visitors. Alice introduced them as Elizabeth and her daughter, Meggie, skilled seamstresses and weavers in the Shapleigh employ. A large table was strewn with freshly cut rushes to be woven into baskets and mats, Alice explained.

Off the dining room was a cold kitchen—no fireplace—where food cooked in the adjacent kitchen house was prepared for service. Two enormous hutches held serving dishes, silver and pewter utensils, china plates, and crystal glassware. Two wheeled hand trolleys stood in a corner to facilitate the transportation of food and dishes between the buildings.

"Is it not cold in winter?" Allie wondered.

"We have this," Alice said, showing her guests a deep iron kettle three feet in diameter that sat on a platform of brick. "Our smithy, Mister Dudley, devised it to hold hot coals. The flat lid contains the fumes and provides a surface to keep food warm, as well. These holes provide air for the coals, and this lever closes them. We riddle the ash with the handle here, and it falls onto the tray beneath. 'Tis not so worrisome as an open kitchen fire and provides adequate heat in winter, as well," she finished proud of the ingenious device.

When they returned to the hall, the men were waiting for them. Nicholas had washed his hands and face, changed his work shirt, and neatened his queue. His tall form leaned casually in the open door frame, as he talked with Johnny, who sat on the steps.

It was still pleasantly warm. Puffy white clouds fled up the coast, but across the river to the southwest dark clouds were massing. The light breeze was redolent with the scent of lilacs and the fragrance of the ocean. It ruffled the women's skirts and dust caps and caressed their faces, as they came out onto the veranda.

"We shall have some rain tonight, I think," Nicholas said, straightening. "When we are done with our tour, we can take some refreshment at the ordinary. Folk are gathering there to bid you welcome." He proffered an arm to each of his guests. "Now, ladies, permit me to escort you."

Mary and Allie exchanged a brief smile. Nicholas was still the engaging gallant they recalled from girlhood. They fell in on either side of him, grateful their sea legs had been left in Dover.

It was a leisurely tour that began with the kitchen house, a single-story building with a large chimney some forty feet from the cold kitchen. The Shapleighs knew well the danger of fire. It was an ongoing fear in the colonies for good English brick was expensive to import. Before local brickworks were established, many chimneys were dubious constructions of mud and sticks. Even using brick, fires were frequent and devastating. Nicholas reasoned that a separate kitchen house at least averted the added danger of cooking in their living quarters.

The kitchen was steamy even with the doors and windows open. Preparations for the feast were going apace. The fragrances of roasting meat, boiling broth, and baking bread were thick enough to eat. A red-faced Missus Beals and her staff greeted the little group briefly with genuine warmth, but the visitors knew better than to linger and hinder their progress.

The hearth was impressive, made of sturdy English brick and high enough for Mary to stand in. Although the fireplace could accommodate four-foot logs, several small fires were maintained for food preparation. A variety of tripods and trivets positioned pots or skillets at different heights over flame or coals. Ovens lined with tin were cleverly built into the bricks. Nicholas proudly demonstrated a hand pump against an exterior wall, which drew water from a large barrel outside, filled daily from the well.

The pump was positioned over a slate trough, so the water did not splash onto the floor as it gushed out. The room on the other side of the chimney was cooler and quieter than the kitchen.

"This is our laundry room, bathing room, and dairy," Alice explained, closing the door on the chaos of the kitchen. Several cheesecloth bags hung from hooks, dripping whey into bowls set beneath them, and two young women were churning butter. Nicholas introduced them as Charity and Bridget, and Alice complimented their industry. This side of the chimney had a hearth as large as the other, but two large iron grates filled the space. One supported the largest iron pot Mary had ever seen over glowing coals.

"Oh, splendid!" Alice said upon spying it. "The water for your bath is heating."

In addition to the pots, kettles, and dairy equipment stored in racks along one wall, an enormous copper tub sat in the middle of the room. It had been scrubbed until it shone.

"Is that for bathing?" Allie asked eyes wide.

Alice blushed and Nicholas chuckled. "I had it made specially," he said, encircling his wife with one arm. "My bride insists on supervising my ablutions."

"Nicholas!" she protested, endearingly embarrassed. "'Verily, 'twas thy notion!"

He chuckled and kissed her temple, winking at Mary and Allie over her head.

The missionaries smiled, and Charity and Bridget stifled giggles at this demonstration of affection. The tub did indeed appear large enough for two. Mary anticipated immersing her travel-worn body in a rare hot bath later. Allie peered into the tub's depths; then looked at Nicholas.

"Has anyone ever got lost in there?" she asked in a mock-serious tone.

They all laughed.

"Take heart, little Allie," Nicholas joked. "Mayhap you shall be the first."

They moved on to the warehouse located near the dock. It was a full forty feet long and almost as wide. The double doors at either end were big enough to admit wagons and were currently open on the south side. Crates, kegs, barrels, and boxes of all sizes were stacked along the walls. They found Edward and George talking with young Johnny and his uncle, John Treworgy, who had just returned from Portsmouth on the ferry. The four men turned as the group approached.

"How now!" John exclaimed upon seeing Mary and Allie. "These are not the little girls I recall!"

"Well met, Friend Treworgy. Thou art kind to remember us at all!" Mary said, smiling.

"I am glad to see you survived the crossing unscathed, and please, call me John," he responded.

"We thought thou hadst gone to fetch Penelope and the boys," Alice said.

"I am on my way, sweet Alice. Your fellow Andrew is just fetching my horse. I shall bring the boys and Pen back in the wagon," he answered.

"The saw blades came, did they, Johnny?" Nicholas asked, looking around.

Johnny smiled, as it had been his first concern too. "Yes, Uncle, everything we ordered for the mill arrived, plus the writing paper and sealing wax, as well as the foodstuffs," he replied.

Alice drew breath to speak, but her nephew anticipated her question.

"Your tea and spices, also, Aunt Alice," he grinned. She returned his smile, the warmth between them evident.

"Excellent!" Nicholas exclaimed. "Duties accomplished! Shall we take some refreshment at the ordinary, then? I am starved!"

The ordinary cum trading post was located at the west end of the point near the ferry dock, affording liquid refreshment and food to travelers as well as basic staples for the locals. The brew house was hard by. William Hilton had built and managed the original, but it had gone through various renovations and proprietors since. Like most publick houses of its time, it had a long counter, where patrons stood. A room was added over the years with tables and benches for those who wished to sit. The hearth was unlit, and doors and windows were open to ventilate the crowded space. Smoke from several pipes swirled in the draft, and it was warm and crowded.

The welcome committee had not delayed in celebrating, and the guests were greeted with enthusiastic cheers. Tankards of local ale and cider were pressed into their hands, and all toasted the missionaries' safe arrival. The colonists were not hampered by shyness.

Nicholas introduced Mary and Allie to Walter Barefoote, a friend of the family who had recently sold his lot on Kittery Point. He was an apothecary and had established a practice after the death of Renald Fernald, the region's original physician. Dr. Barefoote told them he had immigrated to Kittery via Barbados with his sister Sarah in the mid-1650s. She was his only surviving relative and had run his household, until her marriage to young Thomas Wiggin, the Captain's son. The newlyweds took up residence in the manse on Captain's Hill, and the doctor had set up his practice on Dover Neck to be near his sister.

Unlike most of the men present, the apothecary wore a matching suit of fine Holland Lawn. Its muted green set off his eyes, which sparkled with interest, as they spoke. His light red hair was gathered in a neat queue with a matching silk ribbon. A cream-colored shirt looked clean and pressed, Mary noted, when he removed his frock coat in the crowded room. Walter was an Anglican and expressed relief that the monarchy was restored. Puritans made him uncomfortable. When he learned that Allie had an interest in healing plants, they became deeply involved in a conversation about the local flora.

Mary spoke with William Furbush, who introduced his wife, Rebecca. She was carrying their first child. Will related the story of his capture twelve years earlier after Cromwell defeated the Scots at Dunbar. He had survived the long forced march to London, during which many of his compatriots died. The traitors were banished to the colonies, but their departure was delayed. They languished in the hold of a ship in London Harbor for months in the heat of summer, during which more of the prisoners died in unsanitary conditions with inadequate food or drink. The prison ship finally sailed for New England over a year after their capture. In the colonies the young Scot counted himself fortunate to be assigned work at William Leader's sawmill on the Newichawannock River. The locals welcomed the prisoners warmly. Strong workers were needed, and Leader proved a fair employer. Furbush met his future bride in the river settlement, and they married as soon as his indenture was met in 1657. Their modest homestead was just north of Kittery.

Mary and Allie were closely questioned about conditions in England under Charles II, and the afternoon flew by. The shadows were lengthening, when the Shapleighs and their guests took leave of the jolly company and strolled back toward Kittery House. As a close friend of the family, Walter was invited to join them. Nicholas kept up a running commentary as they went, understandably proud of all they had accomplished in twenty years. Johnny added his comments freely, too. He was a gregarious young man who spoke with intelligence and confidence, every bit as excited as his uncle about their achievements and future plans.

Once back, Alice excused herself to check on progress in the kitchen house. Mary and Allie took a change of clothing and went for their long-awaited bath. The five men retired to the veranda on the south side of the house and, being in a celebratory frame of mind, breached a bottle of fine Scotch whiskey.

# *Chapter 9*

## RICHARD WALDERNE *A MAN OF MEANS*

1637-1638 Alcester, England and Bristol, Piscataqua Region, New Hampshire Colony

As soon as their inheritance came through, the Walderne brothers bought tools, clothing, staple foods, and good English brick. After living in the colonies, they knew better what was needed. They made their purchases efficiently and paid to store them in a warehouse at the Bristol docks until they took ship.

At a garden party celebrating their engagement Father Clarke blessed the match, and Richard kissed his fiancé's cheek. He thought it rather daring for a public gathering. There had been no opportunities for dalliance during their strictly chaperoned courtship, and the young Puritan had not sought them. His affection was reserved for their marriage bed, as his father had taught him.

With the engagement official and the wedding set for two years hence, the Walderne brothers booked passage, arranged for their cargo to be loaded, and set sail with Barbara and the children by the end of June. The parting on the dock at Bristol was chaotic. Will and Barbara's brood, the Clarkes, and brother George and family were tangled in embarrassing farewells with the exception of George and Richard. Prudence stepped close to her fiancée and put her gloved hands on his chest, turning her lovely, tear-stained face up to his. He looked down at her, surprised by the intimate gesture, and she closed her eyes. Richard hesitated, then quickly kissed her on the forehead and stepped away. She pouted prettily from under the brim of her bonnet, but he was already mounting the gangplank.

Once the ship was underway, and Barbara and the children had gone below, Will berated him.

"Why, in the Name of All That Is Holy," his brother said in a low but intense voice, "did you kiss your future wife on the forehead, you lummox. You will not see her for two years!"

"It was a public place, and her parents were present!" Richard declared indignantly, "All sorts of people were about! It was a proper kiss for the circumstances. We are not married as yet. Would you have me appear effeminate?"

"Fah!" Will responded with disdain. "Methinks we must have words before your wedding night, little brother."

Richard was affronted. "I know what is what!"

"I am not talking about *science* here, Dickie. I speak of *romance*. You have clearly demonstrated that you are ignorant in that vein," Will pronounced, peering at him from under thick eyebrows. He glanced around to be sure they were out of earshot of other passengers then leaned close. "A woman must experience *la petite mort*, as she is more likely to conceive as a result. Did you know that?" He pulled back, grinning. "Barbara is a living testimony, I assure you."

"But I do not need—" Richard began.

Will ignored his brother's protestations and slung an arm over his shoulders, turning him toward the common room below deck.

"Now is the perfect opportunity, I reckon. No labors, no demands, and no place to go. But we need a little something to make you more receptive. Come, little brother! I shall brook no dissent."

Richard rarely indulged in alcohol and never to excess, but his elder plied him with sweet rum toddies, insuring they were matched cup for cup. Although Richard begged him to get on with it, Will temporized until he deemed Dickie was ready; then he leaned forward, elbows on the table.

"Mark me now, for I shall impart the wisdom gleaned from years of wedded bliss," Will began, when their cups were filled for the third time. Richard felt pleasantly relaxed for the first time in months. He tilted his chair back on two legs, until it leaned against the wall. He recalled being caned for it as a boy in his father's presence. It made him smile to do so now with no repercussions. In fact, he felt inclined to smile at everything at present.

"Ah, the mysteries of the female form," Will began with relish. "There is a key to pleasuring a woman. 'Tis contained in the little bud just above the gateway to her womb, where you shall sheath your sword. But you must not wield your weapon precipitously. If you want issue—male issue in particular—you must prepare her with languid caresses and a light touch before you sow your seed. There are a number of ways to achieve the pinnacle of pleasure, so you must try them all. Mark me now..."

Richard brought his chair down, leaned in, and listened.

The *James* left Bristol with a full complement of passengers and a hold packed to the beams. After three months of courting Prudence and charming the Clarkes, of making compromises and smiling through gritted teeth, Richard discovered he relished the return to bachelorhood. As an independent man of means, it was no hardship to return to New England alone.

They made the crossing in seven weeks, arriving in mid-August without mishap. However, things had changed during their absence, and Bristol was in turmoil. The Reverend Leveredge had left "for want of adequate support." He was replaced by George Burdett, a charismatic clergyman newly arrived from England, who had seized the reins of power in the fledgling colony with his charismatic good looks and educated discourse. Men and women alike were charmed. He had preempted Captain Wiggin's authority and assumed leadership, styling himself governor as well as minister of the fledgling colony. He wrote a combination of governance that was subsequently signed by all the freemen. The inhabitants of the Neck had split into two factions—those following Burdett and those loyal to Thomas Wiggin. Richard was relieved to learn that the Captain still retained authority on allotments of land, representing his Puritan employers, but he was no longer the assumed leader of the settlement.

Despite the turmoil, the settlers had not been idle during the Waldernes' absence. The piers at Immigrant Landing had been extended to accommodate increased traffic. The original footpaths from Pomeroy's Cove were now wide enough for wagons to negotiate, and a new lane branched off the High Street providing access to the Fore River shore further up the Neck. It was called River Road. Will was quick to note that the brew house was nearly finished. New homes that had been skeletal frames when the brothers left were now occupied, and more were in various stages of construction. The rasp of saws, the clang of the blacksmith's hammer, and the cacophony of building was pervasive. Their friend John Damme had married William Pomfrett's daughter, Elizabeth, the year before, and she was great with child. In fact, it seemed nearly all the goodwives had babes in arms or were expecting one. Bristol was growing.

Will's family settled into their new home with customary confusion. In deference to Barbara, Richard helped. They hired laborers to unload their cargo. His brother's purchases were packed into wagons and transported to the house. It took ten trips and a staggering amount of manpower. Barbara was the eye of the hurricane, directing the placement of rugs and furniture, bedding and linens, trunk after trunk of clothing, and barrels, kegs, crates, and boxes of staple foods and kitchen equipment. Her seven-year-old daughter, Mary, tried her best to keep the two youngest boys out from underfoot, but Isaac usually escaped her to hang on Barbara's skirts, wailing. Richard's cargo of clothing, tools, and bricks was meager by comparison, and he stored most of it in a warehouse at the landing for the nonce.

Once his obligation to his brother's family was met, Richard focused on a house for Prudence. True to his word, Captain Wiggin had reserved his lot bordering High Street, and the young man paid in coin. Joiners and carpenters were in such demand that none could be hired until the next spring. However, Richard employed three masons and worked alongside them to expedite the project and insure the quality of their labor. They used the bricks he had brought from England, and the foundation and chimneys were done by November, when cold and snow brought construction to a halt.

Will and Barbara invited Richard to live with them, but after two weeks he could stand it no longer. He could not abide the children, or rather, he could not abide Will's lack of discipline. Both he and Barbara were far too indulgent, in Richard's opinion. Samuel, at five, and Isaac, at three, had no sense of propriety, and it seemed unlikely they would acquire it. No sooner had Richard sat his weary bones down of an evening, than the two little ones attempted to insinuate themselves onto his lap. Their sticky hands were always plucking at his pant legs or his sleeves to get his attention. Christopher, at fourteen, was the only one with whom Richard might have enjoyed a relationship, but the boy was easily distracted and seemed bored when Richard attempted to instruct him. Will had spoiled them all.

Their bachelor uncle deemed it worthwhile to spend his coin on a relatively quiet room at the Walton's establishment, still the only inn and ordinary on the Point. The couple had been gifted the house by Alice's father, William Hilton, when he removed to Kittery soon after Wiggin's recruits arrived. The Puritan influence at Bristol made him uncomfortable. Richard found a room in the Waltons' modest establishment a vast improvement over his brother's home. There were advantages to being a man of independent means.

The Waltons offered food and drink, as well as rooms, and Will was in the common room nearly every evening for a cup or two—or three. Richard was disgusted that even with Barbara and the children present his brother was indulging old habits. Will's joy at reuniting with his family was soon trumped by his love of spirits. Indeed a group of five or six regulars graced the Waltons' rustic ordinary of an evening. Richard himself drank the local ale, but Will and his friends practiced no such restraint. Although George Walton did not have a license for strong spirits yet, it did not prevent him from serving wine or rum on the sly to his friends or the various ships' captains, who supplied him with kegs from France or Barbados.

"One advantage to living in the wilderness is that one need not be concerned with tiresome laws issued from afar," the innkeeper asserted, toasting his guests and knocking back a dram of rum.

Although he did not care for alcohol, Richard agreed with putting lucrative business practices above the law. Living at the ordinary was an education of sorts. He nursed his tankard of ale and listened as the strong spirits loosened other men's tongues. In this way he learned the opinions of the colony's skilled workers and witnessed the developing social structure of Bristol.

The original settlers who had emigrated with the Hiltons and David Thomson were largely Royalists and Anglicans originally employed by John Mason or Ferdinando Gorges. They resisted the Bay Colony's attempts to wield control over their religion, tax their holdings, or regulate their businesses. The Anglicans feared the Bay was plotting to assimilate the incorporated towns to the north—and they were right. Governor Winthrop and his Deputy Richard Bellingham openly lamented the refuge dissenters were given, and the merchants of Boston resented the competition of the northern ports.

On the other hand, the Puritans who came with Captain Wiggin did not trust the Anglicans. They sought to establish Bristol as a stronghold for their religion in the north and spoke among themselves of the advantages of assimilation with the Bay Colony. Richard took it all in and aligned himself with the Puritan leaders of Bristol.

Captain Thomas Wiggin was his mentor. During the winter of 1637/38 with Barbara at Will's side and Richard engaged to be married, the Walderne's' inclusion in the captain's exclusive social circle was confirmed. Catharine Wiggin was a gracious hostess. She had emigrated with her husband shortly after they were married in 1632. Although Richard thought her plain in comparison to his Prudence, she was adept at making her guests feel comfortable and was a lively conversationalist, for a woman. She favored the younger Walderne, and Richard flattered her at every opportunity, knowing it pleased Thomas to see this deference to his wife.

The evenings were a welcome change from the more plebeian crowd at the ordinary. William Pomfrett, Hatevil Nutter, and John Damme were often there with their wives. Richard was the youngest—and the only unmarried man—among them.

"We shall forgive your bachelor status, Richard, since you are at least spoken for," Catharine Wiggin teased, sipping her watered wine.

"Your tolerance is commendable, madam," he responded, causing her to laugh merrily.

"You are no longer a threat to the female population," she smiled. "We anticipate meeting your Prudence. What did you say her age is?"

"I do not believe I mentioned it, madam, but I shall confide in you." He stepped closer and lowered his voice. "She is sixteen at present and shall be eighteen, when we marry," he imparted solemnly.

"Ah! How perfect!" Catharine crowed, titillated by the handsome young man's proximity and his inclusive confidence. "A blushing English rose, no doubt."

She leaned closer, placing her hand on his forearm. Richard was discomfitted. Was the woman tipsy?

"But how cruel, that you must delay for two long years!" she said *sotto voce* and winked. He stepped back embarrassed.

"We shall distract him by occupying all his energy, shan't we, Richard," her husband interposed smoothly, coming to his rescue. Richard turned to him relieved, and Catharine took her husband's arm, smiling at the comely young man conspiratorially.

"I doubt it not, sir, and am glad to hear it," Richard answered, grateful that Wiggin had deflected his wife's perceptive jest.

# *Chapter 10*

## MARY AND ALICE *THE DINNER PARTY*

June, 1662 Kittery Point, Province of Maine

Mary sighed with pleasure as she sank into the hot water. She had never experienced such a deep bath. The water rose to her shoulders when she settled. Allie was submerged with only her face and knees showing above the surface, but there was still room for Mary to recline, too. It was their first bath since leaving Kingsweare. The grime and tension of the crossing melted away. Mary closed her eyes and tipped her head back, wetting her hair to the scalp. The two friends luxuriated wordlessly in the bath's embrace. After a few drowsy moments, Allie spoke.

"The folk here are very friendly, are they not?"

"Mmm," Mary responded, eyes closed.

Sounds of frenzied activity came from the busy kitchen next door, but the noise only emphasized the peace and pleasure of their bath. At length, Allie sat up and began to lather a flannel cloth. The fragrance of the lavender soap was heavenly.

"I suppose their isolation from England is the cause, but I did not expect them to be so eager to keep company with us," Allie went on. "Dr. Barefoote has invited me to go foraging for plants on the morrow. I am eager to see more of the land and discover what grows here."

"I must write to Margaret and tell her we are arrived safely," Mary murmured not moving.

"I reckon Nicholas has a map of the area," Allie continued, following her own train of thought. "'Twould help us plan the best routes to reach folk and help those in need."

Mary sat up, water streaming from her hair, and held out her hand for the soap.

"Johnny mentioned there are but few roads that wagons can negotiate," she said, working lather into her scalp. "Most folk live near the water and travel by boat. Several people at the ordinary showed an interest in our message, and Nicholas has granted his permission to use the church on the Point for meetings. A map is hardly necessary."

"For Sabbath Day meetings, yes," Allie agreed, "but certes there are folk in the area who are in need of practical help, as well as spiritual guidance. It cannot be easy living in the wilderness. I reckon we can organize relief missions during the week. A map would show us distances and the time required to reach folk."

"Certes, Alice can help us plan a route for she told me she and Johnny take supplies to folk in need every Yuletide season and have for years. They shall be with us most like."

Allie took back the soap without comment. Her silences usually brought her friend around more readily than arguing. Although Mary spoke publicly, Allie organized their missionary work. Mary grinned, her lathered hair standing out in soapy spikes around her thin face. Allie could not help but laugh at the sight.

"We shall speak with Nicholas about a map," Mary owned and dunked to rinse her hair.

Allie smiled and submerged with a sigh.

Dinner that night was a family affair, as Alice put it, but the Shapleighs were more of a clan or, as Allie later put it, "a village in their own right." Happily, the various relations arrived before the rain began in earnest. John Treworgy and his wife, Penelope, came by wagon from nearby York. They had two boys, John Jr., nine, and little James, two. Nicholas' sisters—Elizabeth at Bloody Point and Katherine in Exeter—were alerted by messages delivered by swift riders. The former came with her husband Thomas on the last ferry at six of the clock, leaving their grown son, Zachary, to tend the inn and ordinary. The latter came by horse with her husband, Edward Hilton, taking the ferry from Portsmouth to Kittery Point. The party would number sixteen including the children, and all would stay the night.

"I feel several stone lighter," Mary said, as she and Allie descended the stairs, bathed and dressed in fresh clothing.

"Then I warrant we shall have to tether thee on windy days," her friend teased.

The parlor glowed with candlelight. The heavy green drapes were drawn, and a fire was lit against the damp. Gusts of wind pelted the windows with rain, making the room feel cozy.

Mary and Allie wore unadorned dresses of dark blue and brown serge, but the four colonial women wore silk or cotton dresses. The colors bloomed in the warm glow of candlelight, giving the scene a festive air. The Shapleigh men, Edward Hilton, and John Treworgy all wore white linen shirts with colorful waistcoats, their thigh-length jackets put aside for an informal evening with family. Edward and George came in soon after the missionaries, their hair still damp from their turn at the bathhouse. Once greetings were exchanged, Nicholas offered the missionaries cups of spiced cider, knowing they did not take strong spirits. All toasted their safe arrival.

Walter approached, smiling, a gleam of curiosity in his green eyes.

"I look forward to our outing on the morrow, when the weather clears," he said to Allie.

"As do I, Friend Barefoote," she agreed.

"Please, call me Walter."

"Only if thou wilt call me Allie," she smiled.

"With pleasure." He inclined his head politely then cleared his throat and addressed them both. "I am curious about your missionary work. What does it entail precisely?"

"I cannot speak for all missionaries," Mary responded, "but in general we travel afoot from town to town, explaining our beliefs. We also try to alleviate suffering and want among those in need."

"I am in accord with your message, although I am Church of England," Walter said, "but I am curious in a more practical vein. Inns are few and far between. How will you eat, and where will you sleep?"

"God provides through the kindness of those we meet, and we are able to give them some coin, when 'tis necessary," Mary explained. "Also we are better able to help people, if we stay in their homes. We provide succor, as well as awakening people to the Light Within. If a family is struggling due to some mishap, we alert their friends and neighbors to help them after we leave."

"Betimes they are ill or old with none to aid them," Allie added. "We try to bring comfort to the body as well as the spirit. Hence I would value thy knowledge concerning medicaments that can be found hereabouts. The supplies I brought will require replenishing before long."

Walter nodded sympathetically. "We shall certes address that," he assured her then added, "I believe you shall find fertile ground for your message here. As hard as folk labor in this rough place, the taxes exacted by the church are enough to turn survival into starvation. Add to that the burden of travel in all seasons to attend services on the Sabbath—"

Nicholas had approached to listen and now spoke up.

"And people are fined, if they do not attend!" he asserted. "I have ever chafed at the taxes exacted by the church, but worse is this freeman system implemented by the Puritans. 'Tis blatantly unjust! The ministers and magistrates determine who is worthy, but they are prejudiced. They exclude the majority of the population, according the status of freeman only to those who fit their measure, and to do that, a man must match or supersede their standards on religion, social background, or assets. How can our towns and industry be strong, when so many are excluded from participating? Those denied church membership have no vote and cannot hold public office! They have no voice, and there is no hope of improvement for them."

"Too true, too true," Walter agreed, as Nicholas drew breath. The Salem Friends had joined them and were listening keenly.

"Forgive my vehemence," Nicholas apologized, "but if there is one thing I cannot stand, 'tis an unfair system, and that is what prevails here."

"Thou hast the right of it," Friend Wharton rejoined. "I had hoped that in this New World we might make a fresh start with opportunities open to any man, be he honest and hardworking. Yet the established hierarchy is based on the Puritans' belief that some are ordained to lead and others to serve them. They fear abandoning the freeman system would lead to anarchy. Their authority is rooted in fear."

"And in coin," Walter added. "Their ministers depend on taxes for their livelihood. They have ever been suspicious of Anglicans, but they dare not persecute us openly—especially since the monarchy is reinstated. There is no such sanction for your faith, however," he said to the Friends.

"Our concept of equality and the disparagement of churches, ministers, and taxes threaten their system of governance as well as their livelihoods," Edward agreed. "They fight us tooth and nail, as evidenced by the laws enacted in Boston."

"I fear 'tis much the same in England, since Charles and his Parliament passed the Act of Conformity," Mary said. "It is aimed at Friends—specifically our refusal to swear oaths to any but God. Meetings of more than five persons are considered a threat against the government. 'Tis the reaction to Venner and his Fifth Monarchy Men. No doubt ye heard of that uprising?"

"Yes!" Nicholas answered. "Did they verily believe the Lord Jesus would return to sit on the throne of England?" He could not refrain from smiling at the image this thought engendered.

"'Tis hard to credit, I know," Mary allowed, "but ye must understand that even with the monarchy reinstated, the memory of Cromwell's rebellion prompts extreme reaction to any perceived threat. The Fifth Monarchy Men were deluded and poorly organized. They were easily put down, but they served to justify restrictive measures such as the Act of Conformity. As a result, hundreds of our faith are being abused and imprisoned."

"The clergy publicly accuse Friends of fomenting rebellion during our meetings for worship, despite all evidence to the contrary," Allie added, making a rare contribution to the conversation, "The ministers encourage the military and the common folk to violence against us, and King Charles does nothing to stop it, so the abuse has increased."

"Then your faith is disparaged on both sides of the Atlantic," Walter noted.

"Dinner is served!" a servant announced from the archway to the Great Hall. Mary noted that he wore simple, clean clothing rather than livery, as had the servants at the Shapleigh manor in Kingsweare, England.

Alice took Nicholas' arm, followed by the Hiltons and the Trickeys. The Treworgys shepherded their children along, and Walter escorted Allie. Edward caught Mary's eye.

"Friend Tomkins?" he smiled, proffering his arm. Mary felt a surge of pleasure at his notice, but she averted her eyes and took his arm smoothly, lest he perceive it.

"My thanks, Friend Wharton," she responded formally.

Behind them George and Johnny exchanged grins and followed them to the dining room.

The dinner was a sumptuous feast. Everywhere, the ready access to English imports provided by the Shapleigh fleet was in evidence. Silver service reflected the candlelight and was set off by a tablecloth of delicately wrought Irish lace. There were six courses, beginning with a light watercress soup flavored with green onions. A fish course of baked whole cod was followed by tiny stuffed game birds in cranberry sauce that Nicholas called "woodcock." Bowls of fresh garden peas and pureed squash from the root cellar graced the table along with platters of fresh bread, bowls of pickled vegetables, butter, and salt. By the time plates of tender sliced venison swimming in gravy were put before them, Mary could hardly manage a bite. A different wine was served with each course, although the Friends were content with cider. Dessert was a delicious cornmeal pudding sweetened with syrup made from the sap of maple trees, as their hostess explained. It was accompanied by a dark, steamy beverage that Alice called "coffee." It was bitter, but flavorful when tempered with mouthfuls of the sweet pudding. The final course consisted of artfully arranged platters of cheese and a bottle of Spanish Port.

Mary ate slowly, taking just enough to experience the flavors of each dish. Two years before, when she and Allie were imprisoned in Lancaster Gaol with Edward Burrough, her stomach had shrunk during the months of deprivation. Her appetite had been affected ever since. This meal was as far removed from that harsh experience as one might get. She brought her thoughts back to the present gladly.

All were eager for news from England, now that Charles II sat the throne. Did the missionaries think he dealt fairly with his father's executioners? His return must have affected the religious climate of the country, after eleven years of the Puritan Roundheads, but in what way?

"It seemed at first that the King would promote a more tolerant policy than his father to those outside the Anglican Church," Mary told them. "Friend Burrough had an audience with His Majesty, explaining that our beliefs forbid violent action against any man, and the King promised that our religion would be tolerated, but the Cavalier Parliament thwarted him on it, after the uprising of the Fifth Monarchy Men."

"Yes, we spoke of it earlier," Nicholas informed those who had not been part of that conversation. "The result is the Act of Conformity, forcing all to swear loyalty to the King."

"We heard that Charles has opened up the theatres again," Alice commented, attempting to divert the conversation to a lighter topic.

"Yes!" Mary rejoined. "And they say at London women play the female roles!"

The party was variously scandalized or highly amused at this stunning breach of convention.

"But there were reprisals for Cromwell and his government, were there not?" Nicholas asked, turning the talk back to politics.

"Not so harsh as one might expect," Mary answered. "Many were initially heartened by the Declaration of Brede, for by that agreement, Charles pardoned a great number of the Puritans. Nonetheless, nine were executed most cruelly—those who participated in the beheading of Charles I, one surmises."

"Extraordinary forbearance," Walter murmured with a wry smile.

"More a promotion of ignorance than forbearance, I fear," Mary continued. "The current government is determined to erase the fact that the monarchy was ever overthrown. Rumor has it that all the official documents of Cromwell's reign were modified to make it appear as though Charles had actually succeeded his father. People are forbidden to speak of it or be fined, not that anyone would be so rash in the presence of an official!"

"But tell us, if you might, what happened to the properties confiscated by the Roundheads?" Edward Hilton asked. "Have the Royalists got their original holdings back or at least been recompensed?"

"All the lands taken from the Church and the Crown were returned by the Act of Indemnity and Oblivion; however, my father thought it rather harsh that private holdings were not addressed," Mary answered. "Individual landholders must make their own arrangements to reclaim what once belonged to their families."

Hilton shook his greying head. "So much for rewarding loyalty to the Crown," he huffed.

"We heard they removed Cromwell's corpse from Westminster and beheaded it. That does not smack of tolerance, I reckon," Nicholas commented.

"But verily, Nicholas, he was guilty of treason and regicide," Alice pointed out.

"'Twas a decision made by his government, my love, not a personal one."

"It was unthinkable either way," his wife insisted.

"Tell them about Hyde," Allie put in, deflecting the debate.

"Good Lord! They didn't execute the Lord Chancellor, did they?!" Nicholas exclaimed upon hearing the name.

"Oh no!" Mary assured him quickly, "but it came out that his daughter Ann had secretly married the King's brother James and was carrying his child!"

Exclamations erupted around the table. This juicy tidbit had not been in the official news communicated to the colonies.

"It certainly worked in Hyde's favor," Mary continued, when the reactions quieted, "for the King has made him Earl of Clarendon, and many warrant he is now closer to Charles than anyone in the government. The Indemnity and Oblivion Act is attributed to him."

"A voice of reason in the darkness!" Nicholas quipped.

After a leisurely dinner, the company retired to the parlor. None of the men used tobacco, so they kept company with the women and children rather than retiring to Nicholas' study to smoke. Wind and rain were audible, but the well-appointed room was comfortable and warm.

"I realize I have been remiss in asking of your journey. Did Captain Walsh provide you a smooth crossing?" Nicholas asked the missionaries, as he poured out brandy for the gentlemen.

"Verily," Mary responded. "'Twas just the two tempests, was it not, Allie?"

Her friend nodded. "And Mister Lyons, the First Mate, opined they were not severe."

Edward chuckled, and they all looked at him.

"Forgive me," he apologized, "I am recalling the good captain's approbation, concerning his passengers." He nodded at Mary and Allie. "Our missionary Friends convinced half the crew during the crossing, and he allowed his seamen have never behaved so moderately. They were discomfited at the first, thinking two lone women might bring bad luck to the vessel, but within a week their grumbling had all but ceased. Ye won them over with your singing, apparently."

Mary colored at his approving look but managed to smile, inclining her head in modest acknowledgment.

"Ah, you continue to sing together, do you?" Nicholas exclaimed. "Even as girls they impressed us with their harmonies at the Yuletide celebrations in Kingsweare," he told the room without pausing for an answer.

"Oh please give us a tune!" Katherine enjoined. "I do recall how sweetly your voices blended!"

"I allow I have heard no songsters that compare to these young ladies since Kingsweare," John Treworgy declared.

"Mayhap a gentle tune would relax us all," Penelope said, as she cradled a drowsy Jamie on her lap.

The two missionaries were flattered and rose to stand before the company. When all were comfortably settled, Mary began.

*Alas, my love, you do me wrong*
*To cast me off so discourteously*

Her clear soprano captured the listeners immediately, and when Allie joined in with an alto harmony on the chorus, even the children were rapt. The servants stopped clearing the table and came to the archway to listen. By the sixth verse, little Jamie was asleep, so as the final chorus faded, the gathering did not applaud as heartily as they might. Several were misty-eyed.

"How fine it is to have you both here with us!" Alice said, embracing them each warmly.

"You have moved us deeply," Katherine declared, following suit to Mary's surprised delight. She thought it a fine ending to their first day on Kittery Point.

Edward Wharton was deeply moved as well but confined his praise to a smile and nod of his head. Still, as he drifted into sleep, Mary Tomkin's pure voice echoed in his dreams.

# *Chapter 11*

## RICHARD WALDERNE *CONSTRUCTION*

1637-1638 Bristol, New Hampshire Colony and Boston, Massachusetts Bay Colony

In November of 1637 a charismatic minister named John Wheelwright came to Bristol with his family and stayed through the winter. He had led a checkered career since his Anglican ordination in 1619. He had been dismissed for expressing Puritanical tenets and a year later immigrated to Boston with his family, including his second wife, Mary; her mother, Susannah; and five children. Mary was the sister of William Hutchinson, and the Wheelwrights followed her brother and his wife, Anne, to Boston in 1636.

For a year all was well. He was warmly received and served the Boston church as a teacher, sermonizing on Sabbath afternoons under the Reverend John Wilson. However, he became a vociferous proponent of Anne Hutchinson's radical ideas on religion, and an inflammatory sermon branded him a dangerous rebel. His loyal supporters circulated a petition in his defense, but everyone who signed it was subsequently disarmed, disenfranchised, and banished from the Massachusetts Bay Colony. Although many of the dissenters went south, eventually founding the colony of Rhode Island, Reverend Wheelwright ventured north with his loyal followers, hoping to find land to establish a town of their own. He sought advice from Thomas Wiggin, who welcomed the minister and his family, entertaining them in his home on Captain's Hill.

Wheelwright's strong personality enlivened the Puritan gatherings at Bristol that winter, and talk often turned to local issues. The Reverend George Burdett was considered a usurper in Wiggin's Puritan circle and was often the subject of criticism, but inevitably, the conversation turned to practical considerations such as building projects and future business plans.

Richard Walderne warmed to the latter topic, which was of paramount interest to him. He spoke eagerly of building a trading post, harvesting timber, and constructing water-powered lumber and gristmills. As the youngest of the group, Richard schooled himself to listen, but he could not stay mute on the subject of business. He concurred with the opinions of his elders on religion and politics and courted their favor, knowing it would serve him in future. Privately he determined to surpass them all in wealth and influence. The young Puritan fell onto his pallet every night with figures, plans, and the next day's agenda filling his head. His bride-to-be did not often enter his thoughts.

March came at last, bringing the new year of 1638 and a reluctant spring. Barbara was pregnant again. Predictably Will drank more than usual in celebration and had to be assisted home from Walton's ordinary. His companions thought it a lark, but Richard was disgusted. His brother's chronic weakness was encouraged by his friends at the ordinary. His association with Will became an embarrassing liability.

Work distracted him. The year proved to be the most demanding the younger Walderne had experienced. He turned twenty-four in April and did not even remark the day. As the weather warmed and the frost leached from the ground, he was up before the sun rose and first at the building site. The foundation, chimneys, and cesspit had been finished the previous November. The joiners and carpenters began the work of framing in mid-April. They found young Walderne to be a harsh taskmaster.

John Damme helped his young neighbor finalize the plan for a two-story edifice with a full basement. A kitchen ell on one side of the main house and a stable on the other were constructed around two chimneys of sturdy English brick. John came by regularly to oversee the progress. Anthony Emery had been useful with a preliminary plan for the trading post, but that project was again delayed. Pru's house was the priority. Damme was part of Wiggin's social circle, and the younger Walderne cemented their acquaintance by employing him. Carpenters were in demand, and Emery would not be idle. Besides, they had no formal contract, Richard reasoned. However, his former friend felt slighted when he heard Damme had been commissioned to build the house. Young Walderne was oblivious to the implied insult, but Anthony never forgot it.

The plans were finalized that winter, and Richard ordered glass for the windows and clapboards for the siding from England. The need for the latter was prodigious, and local production could not meet the demand. Glass was also a luxury few folk could afford, as it must be imported, but no stretched hides or linseed-soaked paper would do for Prudence. As the house took shape, it became a testimony to Richard's wealth and earned him the respect of his peers.

By June the skeleton of the house was complete, and word came that the shipment of glass and clapboards had arrived in Boston. Richard left John Damme in charge and made the trip on horseback, having purchased a fine steed that spring from Thomas Wiggin. His mentor also gave him a letter of introduction to his friend, Governor John Winthrop, who entertained the young Puritan for a week at his home in the capital of the colony. The Governor and his usually cheery wife, Margaret, were glad of the distraction. 1637 had been a contentious year for them with the controversy over Hutchinson and Wheelwright. The banished families had left in March, as soon as weather permitted—just ten weeks earlier. Over dinner on the first night of Richard's visit, the Governor expressed regret that his good friend and advisor, William Coddington, was among those who went south. Winthrop still hoped that Coddington might see the error of his ways and return. Richard kept quiet about Wheelwright's welcome at Bristol.

"They do not understand how tenuous our hold is here even now," Winthrop lamented to his guest, referring to the dissenters. "We must all hang together to survive in this wilderness. We can brook no heresy, for 'twould incite God's wrath against our enterprise. They stirred up rebellion, undoing all our efforts to maintain an orderly government in the Bay Colony!"

"We are not without our own troubles at Bristol," Richard said, commiserating with his host. "When we returned from England last year, my brother and I found a new minister in Mister Leveredge's place. The man had the gall to write up a Combination and many signed it, granting him the power of chief magistrate, as well as minister of the church. Captain Wiggin still controls the allotment of land, but Burdett styles himself as governor."

"What say you!" Wiggin looked shocked, eyes wide in a face gone pale. "George Burdett?"

The younger man was mildly alarmed at his host's reaction. His attempt at sympathy had got them out of the fry pan and into the fire, it seemed.

"Why, yes. Do you know the man?" he asked.

"Verily I do! He is a Papist!" his host exclaimed, squirming in his chair. "Some say he is a spy for Bishop Laud. He has no good word for the Bay Colony and would see us curbed by the Crown. Mark you, he was not welcome here, and we soon sent him packing." His host's face was flushed now. "I did not realize he had gone north to Wiggin's settlement. Oh, beware, Lieutenant Walderne. The man is up to no good! I must write to Thomas and warn him."

"'Twill do no good, I fear, as Captain Wiggin has no authority to dismiss him, sir." Richard replied. "A majority of the freemen support Burdett at present. I doubt they would approve his removal. Only Captain Wiggin and his supporters speak against him, but folk discount the Captain now. Burdett has a glib tongue and a quick mind. The goodwives especially hang on his every word and are swayed by his comely appearance."

Winthrop stroked his well-trimmed beard, but before he could comment further, his wife diplomatically changed the subject, prompting Richard to speak of his plans for the future. He responded with enthusiasm. When she heard he was building a proper house for his bride-to-be, Mistress Winthrop brought him up short by inquiring, "Were you able to find a suitable housekeeper in Bristol?"

His blank look was all the response she needed.

"You cannot possibly do without one! A good housekeeper will prepare everything in your new home to your wife's satisfaction, make no mistake," she asserted, visibly happy to be back in her element. "You would do well to seek one here in Boston."

"I fear I am quite ignorant on the qualifications required for the post," he temporized, unwittingly affording Mistress Winthrop the opening she sought.

"Permit me to assist you on that score," she smiled. "I shall make inquiries on the morrow. Our parlor shall serve for the interviews, I warrant."

There was no polite way to refuse, and being out of his depth, Richard humbly agreed.

Mistress Winthrop liked the handsome lieutenant, but she had no doubt a young bride straight from England would be dismayed by the frontier settlement of Bristol. Encouraged by his deference, she made a suggestion tactfully framed as an inquiry. "Mayhap you shall consider purchasing a dwelling here in Boston in future, should business call you here on a regular basis?"

"Capital idea!" her husband seconded. He had taken a liking to Wiggin's young protégé, too.

Richard was polite but noncommittal on this subject, though he did follow his hostess' advice concerning a housekeeper. During the next week between forays to the docks to make arrangements for his cargo to be shipped to Bristol, they interviewed three candidates. Mistress Winthrop was at his elbow throughout, coaching him on pertinent questions to pose.

The best candidate was a dour but capable widow from Scotland named Eleanor Cameron. The woman had no children and seemed older than her stated age of thirty-two. Her husband had been a ship's captain lost at sea. He left some small provision for her, but the funds were dwindling. She lived with her brother and had managed his household for two years, but he was engaged to be married, and his bride would soon displace her. She masked her desperation with calm dignity. Her austere dress and serious demeanor appealed to Richard. After a barrage of questions, which he would never have thought of asking, Mistress Winthrop judged the woman capable. They reached an agreement of twelve pounds per year plus the housekeeper's passage to Bristol by ship. She would come in October, when the house would most certainly be finished.

Two days later, Richard bade his host and hostess farewell and wound his way through the crowded streets to the harbor to witness the departure of the ship carrying his precious cargo. En route his eye was drawn to a cradle in a shop window. It was wrought of cherry wood and beautifully finished. On a rare impulse he purchased it and had it delivered to the ship. Perhaps one day his sons would be soothed by its rocking. He realized with a twinge of guilt that he had hardly thought of Prudence since leaving England. The purchase mollified him, and the cradle joined the shipment of glass and clapboards bound for the Point. He watched the ship leave Boston Harbor then turned his mount north with relief. The Winthrops were hospitable hosts, but they reminded him of his in-laws.

# *Chapter 12*

## MARY AND ALICE *FRIENDSHIP*

Summer 1662 Kittery Point, Province of Maine

It was still raining when Mary and Allie awoke on their first full day at Kittery Manor, but Mary was grateful. She needed to write Margaret Fell and her father of their safe arrival and initial success at Dover. She was eager to sit at the beautiful writing desk in her room and put quill to paper.

After breaking their fast, the men went to see the construction in progress at John Bray's lot further east on the Point. A little rain was not going to confine them to the house, but they would delay taking their families home until it cleared.

The women lingered over a breakfast of scones with jam and thick, fresh cream, leftover cornmeal pudding, and porridge, while little James played under the table with his wooden horse.

"How fare things in Kingsweare these days?" Katherine asked.

"Much as thou left them, I warrant," Mary answered. "Thankfully the Civil War did not affect us but for the shipping writs; however, all were saddened by thy father's passing. The town entire mourned his loss."

"As do we yet," Kat murmured then smiled at her. "But my thanks for 'tis a comfort to hear."

"The King was beheaded just weeks after," Allie added.

"I am glad Father did not have to see it," the older woman commented.

"Thy husband's death would have been a blow to him, as well," Alice put in.

"Yes, he and James were close. He accompanied my father on his first crossing. 'Twas difficult, losing them both within a year. Death has not been a stranger to our family," Katherine sighed.

Alice reached for her sister-in-law's hand. "Few families escape the Reaper's notice," she murmured. Kat squeezed it gratefully, mindful that Alice had lost her father at a young age. Rain pattered at the windows, and Jamie made clopping noises from under the table.

"We mourned when James was taken so unexpectedly," Alice went on, "yet I treasure the year that thou and thy girls lived with us."

"You and Nico were such a refuge," Katherine responded warmly. "I do not know what we should have done without you. Nicholas is more like a brother than an uncle to them."

"Small wonder, since thou wert the only mother he knew. He is ever grateful to thee," Alice said warmly.

Kat smiled. "I do love him like mine own, as did James. He concurred with me completely when I suggested caring for him. Poor motherless babe! Nico was ever sweet and loving. Even as I nursed him, his little hand would pat my chest."

"And in his turn he adopted Johnny as a babe, did he not?" Mary asked. She had been a child at the time, but her father had spoken of it approvingly.

Katherine nodded. "Another Shapleigh orphaned too soon."

"Certes Nicholas was ever kind to us," Mary said, and Allie nodded.

Kat laughed softly. "Nico tried not to have favorites among the children who came to our Yuletide celebrations, but one could see he was drawn to you both. I think he recognized that you and Allie are uncommonly close, as are he and my John."

"And I count myself most fortunate to be his wife," Alice added. "He has given me a family, when I had no hope of one."

Penelope spoke up. "Amen to that! When one marries a Shapleigh, one gains a clan!"

"I wager both my boys have married well," Katherine said, smiling at her daughters-in-law.

After breakfast, Penelope took Jamie to the kitchen house for a bath; Mary went upstairs to write her letters; and Alice, Allie, and Katherine spent the rest of the morning in the sewing room, carding the last basket of spring wool from the Shapleigh sheep. Although the family employed enough indentured servants and skilled laborers to populate a small village, Alice and Kat contributed to the endless chores necessary for survival. The Shapleighs and Hiltons enjoyed their comforts and lived in fine houses, but the two women entertained no airs and took up the task at hand cheerfully. Allie appreciated their warmth and energy. Alice might appear delicate, but their hostess was no fragile flower.

Elizabeth and Meggie soon joined them, shaking rain off their bonnets and cloaks and draping them over a bench by the fireside. The seamstress and her daughter set to plying the wool they had spun the day before. It would be washed and dried in the kitchen house later, then woven into warm cloth for winter garments, Elizabeth explained, when Allie showed an interest.

"Are the winters very cold here, then?" the missionary wondered.

The four local women rolled their eyes and nodded.

"I am afraid so," Alice told her, "much colder than England, I am told, though I have lived here so long I do not remember myself."

"Much colder," Kat emphasized, glancing up from her carding.

"The snow is that deep," Meggie told Allie with relish and held a hand at her ribs. "Ye cannot walk in't."

"The wind is the worst, tho'," her mother put in. "Blows right thru' ye, and squirrels its way thru' ev'ry crack o' the house, don't it just, Mistress?"

"Aye, 'tis so," Alice answered, slipping into their informal speech. "We labor spring, summer, and fall preparing for winter here."

"And if folk are in want, she takes 'em food and blankets and such," Elizabeth imparted.

"An' the master makes sure all have wood enow to keep 'em warm, he does," Meggie added.

The pair was obviously proud of their employers. Allie smiled at the girl warmly, which may have given her the courage to ask her next question.

"Why be'ent ye married?"

"Meggie!" her mother gasped, dismayed by her daughter's lack of tact.

The girl's cheeks colored. Alice and Kat exchanged a quick glance. They had wondered the same thing, but could find no circumspect way to broach the subject.

"I am not offended," Allie assured Elizabeth with a chuckle. "'Tis a fair question, and she is not alone in wondering, I reckon." Her strokes with the carding comb did not falter, but the others had paused in their activities, watching her. "Don't think on it much," she shrugged.

Alice found it hard to read her guest. She had noticed that Allie rarely initiated conversation or contributed to the talk unless posed a direct question, yet she did not appear to be shy. Alice would have recognized that sentiment herself. Her guest was simply quiet. Alice waited to see if she would say more. The missionary did not seem affronted, but she was so enigmatic, her hostess wasn't sure. Alice was casting about for a less volatile topic, when Allie continued.

"Had an offer once back in Kingsweare. I was sixteen. Dickie Miller was his name, though he wasn't a miller. Raised hogs. Smelly." Her nose wrinkled but her combing continued steadily. Her audience was rapt. "His Ma died the winter before. Left Dickie and his Pa and four little brothers with no woman on the place. I reckon they thought I'd be a good worker, strong and all. But I couldn't countenance taking care of all those pigs."

Her comb paused, and she met each woman's eye. "And most like they would have made me slop the hogs as well," she finished solemnly.

The four women stared at her. Had the missionary just made a joke? Then Allie winked at Meggie. Mary heard their laughter all the way upstairs.

By noon the rain had stopped. They all reconvened for a meal of chowder made from the leftover cod with "pop-robbins," tasty little balls of batter boiled in milk. Stomachs full, the Shapleigh relatives departed for their homes, promising to return for the missionaries' first meeting on the Sabbath. The Treworgy boys perched on a crate of tea in the back of their wagon. John held his little brother on his lap. They waved goodbye as the wagon jolted down the road to York. Katherine and Edward donned their spatterdashes, as the roads were muddy after the rain. They rode in the other direction to board the ferry to Portsmouth and take the road home to Exeter. Kat embraced the missionaries as well as her family at their leave taking.

Walter and Allie borrowed baskets from the kitchen house. Allie packed some scones and cider to sustain them, and they set off to explore the nearby fields and woods. In mid-June spring growth had matured, and everything seemed bursting with life after the rain. The warm air was fragrant with it. It was compensation for squelchy feet, as their shoes were soon damp.

"As in England, many plants here have tender, edible parts early on in the spring. Those are, unfortunately, past their prime at present," Walter explained, "However, 'tis easier to identify them at this stage of growth."

They walked east up the point toward York. The cleared area around Kittery House was soon behind them. The road rose and fell with the rocky topography, curving around the larger boulders and trees. In some places it rejoined the shoreline, and the same hardy bushes that Allie had remarked in Dover were in evidence. They were bursting with fragrant pink blossoms.

"Are these wild roses?" she asked.

"Yes, they call them '*Rosa rugosa*,'" Walter answered, pausing to afford her a closer look. "As you can see, they grow profusely here. The petals are quite tasty in a salad. They are also useful for ailments of the eye, steeped in hot water and applied topically, but their true value appears in late summer. Each flower becomes a small fruit, which makes an efficacious tea to prevent the onslaught of catarrh, or at least lessen its severity. They can be et or made into jelly, as well."

The trees opened up as they approached the construction site further along the Point. Nicholas' friend, John Bray, was building a modest post and beam dwelling. The frame was taking shape, and the rasp of saws and the thud of mallets reached them before they could see it. Walter had visited earlier with the men, so they did not stop but only waved as they walked by. Allie was gratified to see that one was not required to build a mansion to live on Kittery Point.

They abandoned the road where it angled left towards York. A wide meadow, currently pasturing livestock, gave onto a stretch of woodland before the land ended at the rocky coast. Walter and Allie spent a number of pleasant hours, poking about both field and forest, as Walter identified useful food and medicinal sources. Allie's favorite plant was the broad-leafed, long-stalked "King Solomon's Seal" or as Walter called it *Polygonatum biflorum.*

"Polly gone at him *who*?" she quipped, eliciting a chuckle from her new friend. It was evident that Walter enjoyed sharing his knowledge with her. Allie had judged him a fastidious person from his meticulous appearance, but in the field, Walter left his fine frock coat on the fence and rolled up the sleeves of his linen shirt for foraging, ruffles and all. He had no qualms about getting his hands dirty. His knowledge and clear explanations impressed her.

In the field he pointed out milkweed. "A prolific grower with many uses. The Latin name is *Asclepias syriaca*. The stalks may be eaten early on in spring, but not the leaves—never the mature leaves." He picked one and broke it open, revealing a thick, white sap. "You do not want to eat this, but applied topically, it rids the skin of warts and carbuncles. Later in summer, it forms large seedpods, which can be eaten in stews or boiled as a vegetable. When mature, the root may be crushed and applied to wounds and sores.

"And here," he said, moving on, "this is *Achillea millefolium*, commonly called Yarrow—a very hardy grower. One boils the flowers and leaves, and the result is used to wash wounds. It lessens the chance of noxious infection and can also be drunk as a tea to reduce fever."

They moved on toward the woods, but Walter soon stopped again.

"Ah, now this is Burdock—*Arctium lappa*—prolific and humble. Culpeper advises crushing the root and applying it topically to bites, but I think the seeds are the most potent part of the plant. I steep them in wine and use the result to treat sciatica, or it can be brewed as a tea for breaking down stones and gravels in the kidneys. Also good for treating bloody phlegm."

They clambered over a rough stone wall and were about to enter the woods, when the apothecary paused again.

"Ah, now here's a useful fellow," he said, stopping at the tree line. "*Eupatorium perfoliatum.* This serves for everything from fever to lung ailments. Rheumatics, bruises, sprains, aching bones, or fever aches, as well. Some call it Boneset, or betimes Feverwort, but because the Indians use it extensively, I like the term Indian Sage. The plant is most potent when picked after it begins to flower, however, so we shall leave it to flourish till mid-August."

Nearby Allie saw an old friend.

"Oh, I see Shepherd's Purse grows here, too," she said.

"Yes, *Capsilla bursa-pastoris.* Very useful in stopping bleeding of an open wound," Walter commented.

"I have used it as a tea for women's ailments, as well." Allie added.

Walter raised his eyebrows. "I must try that," he said. "You see, one can always learn more," he added with a smile.

"Indeed, one can," Allie answered, returning it.

He walked a few paces along the edge of the forest, "Now this is Sumac of the genus *Rhus.* The smooth variety here is *R. glabra.* Not very impressive at this time of year, but it grows quite tall. Then, as the autumn approaches, it develops conical tops of bright red berries. They make a very effective tea steeped in water and left in the sun for a day or so. It has a lemony flavor and quenches the thirst marvelously. The mature bark can be stripped and applied topically to wounds as a makeshift bandage. It slows the bleeding much as Yarrow does. I usually collect a supply before winter, dry it, grind it up, and keep it on hand as a powder. 'Tis useful in a salve."

The woods were cooler, but the blackflies were a plague. They tried to keep moving and ranged about, taking samples quickly. By the time they retraced their steps to fetch Walter's coat, the sun was lowering. They paused at the fence to share the snack Allie had brought. The bugs were not so bad here, and the bars were well placed for sitting. The sun warmed their feet and legs, which were damp to the knees. Their shoes and stockings would dry quickly on the walk back.

Allie removed her hat and turned her face up to the sun, chewing contentedly on a scone. The pale skin most ladies aspired to obviously did not concern her, the apothecary noted. She was unlike any woman he had ever known.

Walter broke a comfortable silence. "May I ask a question of a somewhat personal nature?"

She looked at him and smiled, having a notion of what was coming. He took her smile as leave to go on.

"Forgive me if I offend, but I have the impression that neither you nor Mary intends to marry, and this I understand," he added quickly. "I am not inclined to submit to the bonds of matrimony myself. But I wonder, is it forbidden to missionary Friends, or is it your own choice?" he asked.

As unusual as it had been for the two of them to remain single in England, it was even more of a rarity in the colonies. No doubt it was a question they would have to answer repeatedly.

"Marriage within our faith is encouraged, so 'tis our own choice."

He raised his eyebrows in a wordless question.

"The simple answer is that, until we have answered this call, we do not wish to be constrained by other responsibilities," she said, breaking the last scone in half and giving Walter the larger piece.

The apothecary's green eyes twinkled, as he took it. "And the complicated answer?" he prompted, taking a bite.

Allie sighed. She was reluctant to reveal things about Mary without her knowledge or consent, but Walter was becoming a good friend, and he was a doctor. Keeping confidences was part of his profession. Allie trusted him not to repeat the personal things she must impart to answer.

"The complicated answer is Mary, or mayhap I should say Mary's sister, Margaret." she said.

The apothecary chewed, waiting patiently. Allie took a sip of cider and passed him the jug.

"Margaret was nine when Mary was born. Sadly their mother died as a result of the birth, and Margaret never forgave her. She tormented Mary with it, but never in the presence of others. I think I am the only one in whom Mary ever confided, thus this is for thy ears only, Walter."

***"I understand," he responded solemnly. "You have my word on it."

"The summer of our twelfth year, Margaret married John Foster. Times were hard. 'Twas '42 and in October word came of the battle at Edgehill, although no one was sure who had won."

"I recall it well," Walter said. "I had just turned sixteen, in the third year of my training. It marked the start of the Civil War, and taxes rose precipitously. Many folk were ruined."

"John Foster among them," Allie agreed. "Thus Uncle Ralph, Mary's father, bade the newlyweds live at the Tomkins' home. Margaret was pregnant. She had three boys during the next five years and insisted on Mary's constant assistance, believing her own childhood had been devoted to caring for Mary. Mary was obligated to repay her in kind, she maintained, and out of guilt and to keep the peace, Mary acquiesced."

Allie sighed and looked at her new friend. "But Margaret sought a constant revenge in her expectations. She was never satisfied. Our morning lessons were Mary's only respite, but needless to say, Margaret did not see the sense in those either. She made mock of our education as a waste of time, for we would soon have husbands and children, and what use should all those books be then? Luckily for us, Uncle Ralph did not agree. He usually gave way to Margaret in everything—I warrant because she lost her mother at nine—but he enjoyed teaching us and would not stop. We repaid him with diligence."

Walter had not heard his new friend speak so long since he had met her. He was fascinated.

"When the boys were small," Allie continued, "Mary was enslaved to all the work they engendered. They were not docile babes or obedient children. They took their mother's cue and did not respect their aunt. It hurt my heart to see the Fosters treated her like a servant in her own home." She grimaced and shrugged her shoulders. "By the time Barty the youngest came, we were sixteen, of marriageable age. Mary wanted none of it. She vowed never to marry and suffer it all again. Her calling has merely confirmed what she decided long ago."

"And what of you, Allie? Shall you remain forever single, as well?" Walter asked gently.

Allie smiled and took back the jug. "Nothing is forever, Walter," she said, "except God."

# *Chapter 13*

## RICHARD WALDERNE *POWER AMONG PURITANS*

1638-1639 Bristol, New Hampshire Colony

By autumn of his last year as a bachelor, Richard had accomplished two major goals: the completion of a proper dwelling for Prudence, and a grant of land for a trading post on the Cocheco River. His friendship with Captain Wiggin served him well in the latter.

Upon returning from Boston, Richard moved to the stable at the house site. It was the first structure to be finished, as paying livery fees irked him. All that summer he slept on a military cot in the tack room. He was close to the work, and it saved coin, though he still took his meals at the Waltons' ordinary when he was not dining with his Puritan friends. Richard frowned on flagrant spending. His inheritance made him rich, but that did not mean he would squander his funds.

By the end of July only the interior work remained on the house for Prudence. To the laborers' collective relief Richard left John Damme in charge. He had more important concerns than finish work. At last he was free to search out a prime location for a trading post. He had purchased a twelve-foot shallop that spring from Hatevil Nutter. It was basically a rowboat with an excuse for a sail, but it was easily maneuvered alone. He wanted to explore the rivers to the north of Bristol.

Early one morning with the tide in his favor, Richard put out from Nutter's slip on Fore River and rowed up to its confluence with the Cocheco. The day was hot and still, but as he moved up the smaller river, trees shaded the banks, creating pockets of cooler air. The young Puritan reveled in his strength increased by the hard labor of recent years. The skiff shot forward with each pull on the oars, the forested banks slid by, and Richard smiled as he sweated. The forest was dominated by red and white pine, towering two hundred feet or more into the clear blue sky. He reached the first falls before noon.

Richard made for a spot protected from the current's pull by several large boulders. The bank was accessible, and he tied the bowline to a poplar growing close by. The falls were loud and their cool moisture was palpable. Richard threaded his way further upstream slashing through the growth along the bank with his sword, which he had brought for safety. Only a fool would leave the settlement without a weapon.

He rounded a bend in the river and saw another set of falls further upstream. He stopped, arming sweat from his brow, and watched the water rush past. All that power waiting to be harnessed. He would have to come back by horse, and he must talk to Wiggin, but Richard was sure he had found the prime site for his trading post. In his mind's eye he imagined the log building with a dock, a sawmill and stamping mill downstream, and eventually houses for the laborers he would employ. It didn't matter that the location was untouched wilderness at present. In fact it was better so. On the Point he would always be the younger man, deferring to his elders. Here he would be master. Richard Walderne had found his domain.

By the end of September Prudence's house was finished. Eleanor Cameron was due in ten days. Richard decided her first task would be to oversee the movement and placement of the furniture and appointments stored in the warehouse at Pomeroy Cove. Prudence and her mother had been sending shipments—everything from cutlery to curtains—for over a year. Storage was costly, but he fumed at having to pay the shipping expenses as well. The sooner the whole lot was moved to the house the better. He could test the new housekeeper and save himself the time and trouble of overseeing this tiresome task.

The young Puritan contracted John Damme to draw up a plan for his trading post, passing along Anthony Emerys' suggestions as his own. He walked the proposed site with Captain Wiggin, marking out the boundaries and building site. His mentor listened attentively and approved his ambitious young friend's ideas. They were closer than ever. Then two simultaneous events precipitated a change in the political situation at Bristol, distracting Richard from his project.

Late in October, Captain John Underhill came to the Neck with his wife and two young daughters. The man was famous. Everyone knew of his bold action against the Pequots in Connecticut in '36. He had led the attack that wiped out an entire Indian settlement near Mystic. The veteran soldier and his company were honored for this heroic deed by Harry Vane, Governor of the Bay Colony, but just months later, everything changed. Winthrop regained his position of power, winning the election in May of '37, and Underhill fell from grace. He had signed the petition supporting John Wheelwright and was disarmed and disenfranchised in spite of his rank and former glory. However, Underhill did not follow Wheelwright north or Hutchinson south, but took his family back to England in the company of his good friend, Harry Vane.

Unfortunately the employment Underhill had counted on in the mother country fell through. England's economy was unstable, and the political situation was deteriorating. King Charles dissolved every Parliament that refused to fund his excesses, and they all did. The monarch compensated with shipping writs and business tariffs, further crippling the economy. When there were objections, he cited the Divine Right of Kings and brooked no opposition. Underhill's Puritan friends were frantically plotting against the monarch and had no time to help him. Civil war seemed inevitable.

The Underhills returned to New England in less than a year, landing at Boston in the summer of '38. Governor Winthrop graciously allowed the former Captain of his militia to liquidate the assets he had left behind so precipitously. Underhill then took his little family north, but they were not alone. In their company was an ordained minister named Hanserd Knollys, whom Underhill had met on the crossing. The Wiggins and their friends welcomed the newcomers to Bristol and entertained them in their homes, until more permanent housing was available. This happened more quickly than any of them might have imagined.

Just weeks after the Underhills' arrival, George Burdett quit Bristol in disgrace. Wiggin's friends did a thorough job of spreading the rumor that the reverend was a spy for Bishop Laud, but in the end, Burdett hanged himself with his own rope. He was charged with "incontinency" and called to court. Dallying with a married woman was a serious offense punishable by death, if proven. Committed by a man of the cloth, it was unforgivable. The accusation itself ruined the minister's reputation—proven or not. Even his supporters turned against him, and Burdett beat a hasty retreat across the river to Agamenticus. Hanserd Knollys and his family moved into the parsonage, and the new reverend preached his first sermon on the next Sabbath.

A new earnestness marked the Puritan leaders' social gatherings that winter. Thomas Wiggin, William Pomfrett, John Damme, Hatevil Nutter, John Underhill, Hanserd

Knollys, and the Walderne brothers gathered once or twice a week at one another's homes. Of course, the men's wives were present, but Richard's regard was all for the business at hand. He paid the women little attention, barring his deference to Catharine Wiggin. The men often spoke privately among themselves in Captain Wiggin's library. They were planning a common goal—the election of Underhill as President of the Court in the May.

Wiggin was content to let the new arrival assume the reins of temporal power. Burdett's disgrace was balm to his wounded pride, but Richard's mentor also admired the newcomer as a decorated veteran of many military campaigns. Underhill was known for his success in the Netherlands and Ireland before his latest victory against the Pequots. In addition the Puritans were enthusiastic about the captain's plan to establish a First Church in Bristol with Hanserd Knollys as minister. It would be modeled on the First Congregational Church of Boston, which Underhill had been instrumental in organizing before he fell out with Winthrop.

Richard still believed that his sexual purity afforded him special dispensation with the Almighty, but public religion was different. It was a tool to gain influence and power. He was vociferous in support of Hanserd Knollys and the First Church, though in reality he was unconcerned who sermonized from the pulpit. The real issue was status among his peers. He was adept at discerning what people wished to hear for it secured their trust. As a result the Puritans of Bristol encouraged their young friend's business plans and helped with the legalities of procuring a grant for his trading post.

However, the Richard sincerely respected Captain John Underhill. One evening at Wiggin's home, the young lieutenant seized an opportunity to speak directly with the military hero for the first time. He began with flattery.

"Captain Underhill, we are most deeply indebted to your skill and bravery in quashing the salvages that threatened our neighbors to the south."

Underhill scrutinized the young man virtually standing at attention before him. After a slight pause he said, "You have obviously had some military training. Who was your sponsor, Mister...?"

"Walderne, sir, Lieutenant Richard Walderne," he supplied. "I regret I emigrated before that could be arranged; however, I trained daily for eight years at the Academy in Shrewsbury, sir."

"Hmm," the Captain said, keeping an eye on Richard, as he sipped his ale.

The younger man realized that compliments and academy training would not impress the hardened military veteran. He plunged on.

"Captain Underhill, it is my hope, sir, that you will instruct us in organizing regular drills. We have no formal militia at Bristol, as yet. You more than any of us know best how to proceed. We should be most grateful for your expert guidance, sir."

Underhill chuckled and lifted his chin, regarding Richard through half-closed eyes. "Certes Captain Wiggin is capable of training a troop here. Why, pray tell, should it be I rather than he?"

Richard realized his response might determine his relationship with this skeptical man. He glanced about to see who was near and noted no one listening. Wiggin was conversing with Reverend Knollys across the parlor. He turned back and took a discreet step closer.

"Begging your pardon, sir, but no man in this room can match your skill and experience. Your military acumen is known by all and emulated by many. Even children know of your success in routing the salvages from their nest at Mystic. I applaud your accomplishments."

Underhill's eyes opened fully and, for the first time, he smiled. "Mayhap you have read my pamphlet on it, *News from New England*? 'Twas printed last year in London, while I was there."

"Yes, sir, I have," Richard lied and pressed on before the Captain could ask for specifics. "Your action was a *coup de gras.* It sent a clear message of our superior military strength and training. In the long run it saved lives—English lives—and that is the heart of the matter, is it not? The salvages do not know God, and if they will not desist from practicing their heretical beliefs, we have no choice but to eliminate them."

Richard was relieved to see he had struck the right note. Underhill preened under his compliments and warmed to the subject.

"Harry Vane was Governor of the Bay Colony then," he began. "He sent us by ship—originally to secure Block Island. His concern was more with the Dutch than the Indians initially, but once the word came that an Englishman was murdered by salvages near Mystic, he directed us to look into that as well.

"We were a small company, just twenty men. We met up with John Mason, whose force was larger—local men plus a few Indians who counted the Pequots as enemies. They had a score to settle." His eyes glittered, and he leaned toward Richard. "One military man to another, Lieutenant Walderne, 'twas the easiest campaign of my experience," he confided, speaking quietly. The younger man nodded, thrilled by the inclusion. Underhill turned sideways, inclining toward Richard, and continued without looking at him.

"Our combined forces surrounded the native stronghold, expecting a pitched battle, but the Almighty rode with us that day. It came out later, that their warriors were absent. There were only women, children, and old men—no resistance to speak of. We torched their bark shelters from both ends of the camp, Mason and I. When the vermin ran out of their dwellings to escape the fires, we cut them down—hardly a pitched battle, y'see. Still, Harry insisted we be feasted as if we had risked life and limb!" he chuckled then quickly sobered. "There was a clergyman who had the gall to question our decision to attack. He happened to be present and was appalled by the aftermath. Mason knew him, though, and answered him smartly. 'We had sufficient light from the Word of God for our proceedings,' he said. That stilled the minister's churlish tongue." Richard was fascinated. He had never heard the story behind the glorious victory and counted himself privileged. Underhill set his tankard down, frowning. "Why he was concerned about the fate of heathens is beyond my powers of conjecture. We rid the Connecticut Colony of four hundred of the wicked imps that day, though, in retrospect, we should have stayed on. We learned later that their menfolk wreaked havoc when they found their stronghold destroyed and their families—" Underhill's mouth quirked. "Well, there were only seven left out of four hundred with any life in them, so I suppose there weren't many families to find, were there?"

"No, sir, verily not," Richard answered dutifully.

Without another word, the Captain turned abruptly on his heel and went to his wife's side. Richard was impressed by Underhill's ruthless efficiency, but his manners in polite company left something to be desired.

That winter Hatevil Nutter and Richard developed a mutual regard. It had begun with a shared distrust of George Burdett, but the two men soon discovered they shared similar views on business and a mutual disdain for liquor. Although Hatevil was dour and taciturn, Richard liked him. Nutter was a man of few words, but when he spoke, others listened. He was one of Wiggin's first recruits and was fifteen years older than Richard, as were most of the other men in their circle. Hatevil was one of the few who had brought a wife and family, and his house on Nutter's Hill was one of the first built. His lot had a commanding view of the Point to the south. He was an Elder of the church, and Knollys invited him to teach occasionally during afternoon sessions on the Sabbath. He was devout, but Hatevil came alive when talk turned to sawmills or shipping. He wanted a shipyard, and locally milled timber was an essential first step.

Richard hoped they might become partners in a sawmill in future. All of the men in Wiggin's circle agreed that water-powered mills would engender great benefits to the industry of the fledgling community.

Throughout the winter of 1638 /39 Hanserd Knollys spoke from the pulpit of the newly established First Church. Richard considered the long, cold Sabbath Day meetings an investment that would accrue to his best interests in time. He cloaked his ambition in piety and professed an unshakable devotion to the First Church of Bristol, but his prayers centered on a grant of land for a trading post and ordinary.

They were answered soon after the year turned in March. Just before Richard left for England to claim his bride, Wiggin made him a wedding gift of piece they had marked out for the trading post. His mentor presented the deed to him at a gathering a week before Richard was to sail. All present applauded. The young man determined to name his acquisition Cocheco, for the river that bore its name.

# *Chapter 14*

## MARY AND ALICE *FIRST MEETING AT KITTERY POINT*

June, 1662 Kittery Point, Province of Maine

The English missionaries held a meeting in the Shapleigh Church on the first Sabbath Day after their arrival. The June morning was idyllic, and people lingered outside, greeting each other and chatting, as wagons, horses, boats, and foot traffic arrived. George and Edward would soon return to Salem, but they stayed for this first meeting in Maine. Among those attending were several prominent families—neighbors or relations of the Shapleighs, including Pepperells, Brays, Treworgys, and Champernownes from nearby, and Hiltons, Chadbournes, Nasons, and Spencers from as far as Newichawannock and Exeter. A number of Shapleigh employees and Dover residents came as well.

Allie greeted Elizabeth and Meggie warmly and soon put them at ease. Mary noted them introducing her to the rest of their family and smiled. Allie had a warm presence despite her economy with words, and people took to her. Will Furbush and his wife, Rebecca, joined them. Rebecca's condition was visible, and Allie and Elizabeth were soon deep in conversation with her, suggesting food and teas to build her strength and calculating the date of birth.

Nicholas and Alice were welcoming Thomas and Rebecca Roberts with their youngest daughter, Sarah, from Dover Neck. The older couple was close to Katherine and Edward Hilton and greeted them warmly. Rebecca Roberts was Edward Hilton's sister. Thomas had met the Hilton brothers while apprenticing at the prestigious Laconia Fishmongers Guild in London. The three young men became fast friends and immigrated together, establishing the initial fishing venture on the mainland with their partner, David Thomson, in 1623. The term "fishmonger" was not derogatory.

Fish was plentiful, easily preserved, and efficient to transport, whereas meat spoiled quickly and was rare and costly. The first settlement in the region had depended upon the success of the venture, and thirty years later salt dried fish was still an important commodity worldwide.

Thomas met Rebecca through her brothers, and they fell in love while he was studying in London, but Thomas did not propose until he had gained freeman status and could provide a home for his bride. As friend and future brother-in-law to the Hiltons, he was among the first to choose a grant of land on the Point—a prime lot on the east bank at the top of the Neck overlooking Fore River. Rebecca gave him three sons and five daughters, and their farm prospered. Thomas was a respected member of the community and had served as President of the Court prior to the Bay Colony takeover in 1642. His even temper and ready smile were well known, in addition to the fact that he was a practicing Friend and former Anglican. Roberts had never embraced the Puritan faith.

Even in his sixties, Thomas retained his health. His white hair was thick, tied back in a neat queue, and his sturdy frame was unbent by age. Although her face was lined, Rebecca possessed the easy grace of a woman of good family, who has always been beautiful. Her hazel eyes sparkled with intelligence. The couple stood with arms loosely linked in casual affection.

"I have ever felt uncomfortable with the stance taken by the Puritan authorities," Thomas confided to Mary once Nicholas had introduced them. "That young man that passed through the area a few years ago..."

"Wenlock Christison," Rebecca supplied gently.

"Yes, Friend Christison. He quite convinced us, did he not, Mother? Such an intelligent young fellow! We have not attended services at Dover since."

"As a result the Reverend Reyner took one of our best cows," Rebecca added with quiet indignation. "He said 'twas to pay the fines for entertaining a Quaker and for our absences at church."

A small group approached, and Mary recognized the Dover innkeeper Anthony Emery and his wife Frances among them.

"Ah, 'tis our young friends the Wardells!" Thomas exclaimed with delight.

"Well met, Lydia," Rebecca said warmly, taking the young woman's hand.

Greetings and introductions were made. Eli and Lydia Wardell had come from Hampton with Anthony's brother, John, of Newbury. They were all staying with the Emerys at their inn in Dover. Lydia held a squirming toddler, and her young husband took him, setting the boy on his shoulders. Little Joseph crowed with pleasure from this higher vantage point and grasped his father's hair.

"The Wardells are also convinced," Thomas explained to Mary. "Eli and Lydia entertained Friend Christison at their home in Hampton before he came north to Dover."

"Indeed, my family entire was convinced by Friend Christison," Lydia asserted. Mary liked the young woman immediately. She spoke with confidence and met Mary's eyes with frank admiration. "But thou art the first woman missionary we have met," she added with a smile.

"The minister at Hampton is Seaborn Cotton," Roberts continued. "He is young and zealous. When Friend Christison was at the Wardells' home, Cotton came to their door wielding a truncheon with a number of his so-called loyal parishioners. In truth 'twas a gang of the lowest sort, for no true Christian would come upon his neighbors so."

"He said he was keeping the wolves from his sheep," Eli added wryly. "Mark ye, those 'sheep' dragged Friend Christison off to the gaol. We feared for him, they were so rough."

"When did this occur?" Mary asked.

The young couple glanced at each other, and Lydia answered. "'Twas almost three year ago now, was it not, Eli?"

He nodded. "'Twas '59," he confirmed.

Roberts spoke again. "And ever since, our young friends are constantly harassed! Cotton charged them an outrageous fine for harboring Christison and for absence from meetings at the Hampton Church. Tell her, Eli," he encouraged.

"He took our best saddle horse at the first—worth fourteen pounds, I warrant," the young man told Mary. "'Twas far beyond the value of the fines, but Cotton did not stop there. Over the past two years he has robbed us of our store of dried corn, so there is no seed for planting."

"The very fodder from our fields was taken, as well," Lydia added. "We had to borrow from my father and uncle to feed our stock last winter."

"And this spring he confiscated our only pregnant heifer for the fines he says we owe," her husband finished.

"'Tis outrageous thievery, and the magistrates do nothing!" Roberts fumed.

"The magistrates condone it!" John Emery asserted. "If there is no coin to pay the fines, the clergy may take whatever they wish in recompense."

"There is no accounting," Rebecca Roberts added. "The ministers have free rein, and their word is law. Reverend Reyner took one of our best milkers, but Cotton has reduced the Wardells to penury in the very town where Lydia has lived all her life—where her mother and father live still." Her eyes flashed with outrage.

"I would speak with these ministers," Mary said. "We have come to stand against such unjust practices. We bring a message of freedom from their tyranny." She glanced around. "I am glad so many folk have come today."

Thomas nodded then looked at his wife. "I wish our boys had come," he said quietly.

Rebecca hugged his arm in wordless agreement, and he patted her hand.

"They are the constables in Dover at present," he added, his face darkening. "They uphold the authority of the First Church, and I cannot say we approve."

"'Twas our own sons that came and took the cow from us," Rebecca said.

"I take it they do not share your beliefs?" Mary asked gently.

The couple shook their heads.

"Welcome, neighbors, friends, and family!" Nicholas announced from the steps of the church. Everyone turned to look at him. "Let us repair indoors, if our missionaries are ready to begin?"

He caught Mary's eye, and she smiled and nodded, but she was troubled by what she had heard. The greed of the ministers was bad enough, but she knew how difficult it was when loved ones did not countenance one's faith. Her own sister, Margaret, scoffed at the concept of That of God Within and mocked Mary's aspiration to become a missionary; however, for sons to bring the law to bear against their own parents was proof of the dire influence of the Puritan authorities.

The worshippers filed in, men to the left and women to the right side of the modest nave. It was cooler inside, and the interior was larger than it looked from without. The vaulted beams of the ceiling resembled a ship's hold turned upside down. Three windows on each side were embellished with colored glass transoms, no doubt from England. Penelope Treworgy sat at an organ on the left side of the nave poised to play the accompaniment for the opening and closing hymns. The four missionary Friends took chairs on the low platform of the altar. A modest wooden cross hung beneath a high window behind them. Nicholas stood next to the missionaries, as folk settled. When it was relatively quiet, he spoke.

"Most of you know this church has ever been open for worship, and many of you have attended services here. I had hoped that the Reverend Mitton, who has preached upon occasion, might have joined us today for a discussion on faith. Regrettably, 'urgent business' required him to be elsewhere today."

Glances were exchanged. Those who knew him would have been surprised if the reverend had agreed to debate the missionaries. He was not a man who relished confrontation.

"Therefore, without further ado, I introduce our missionary Friends, Mary Tomkins and Alice Ambrose, lately from England, and Edward Wharton and George Preston of Salem. They shall lead us in a meeting for silent worship as practiced by the Religious Society of Friends."

Nicholas stepped down, and Mary stood. It had been decided she would speak beforehand. Allie preferred her role as silent organizer, and the Salem Friends deferred to Mary. This was her calling, and they would soon depart.

"We gather this day to worship in silence," Mary began. "There is no sermon. We join in quiet contemplation of That of God Within. Betimes the Spirit may move one to speak; however, unless the call to share is very clear, we ask that ye respect the silence. If ye have questions, please speak with any of us"—she gestured to her companions—"after the meeting. Let us begin with a hymn," she finished and nodded at Penelope.

Johnny worked the bellows, and all joined in an enthusiastic rendition of "A Mighty Fortress Is Our God." Mary watched the group warm to the familiar hymn, as she sang. Once the voices stilled, she allowed the silence to linger a moment before speaking.

"In the words of our founder George Fox 'Out of everything and expectant silence, God's Light uses any worshipper as minister.' May ye find that Light this day and may it strengthen you in all circumstances."

# *Chapter 15*

## RICHARD WALDERNE *THE BRIDEGROOM*

1639 Alcester, Warwickshire, England

March brought the advent of 1639 unexpectedly soon for Richard. Prudence had sent letters faithfully every month since their parting. A surge of guilt smote him when he realized he would soon see her. His few posts delineated business plans and described their neighbors and the house, but he could think of little concerning the rough settlement that would interest his young, genteel fiancée. He did not deem it appropriate to write of the religious and political turmoil plaguing Bristol. Such things did not concern women.

It did not occur to the young man to express romantic blather, and he was surprised when Prudence did. Her missives became increasingly ardent. He was careful to read them in private. The first time that she wrote of kissing him in a dream *(and I mean not chastely upon the cheek, my love!)* he was shocked. During their brief time together, she had been demure, and he deemed her innocent of carnal thoughts; however, he did recall her dimpled smile at their first meeting, when she caught him ogling her. The memory evoked an embarrassing response, and Richard's will power was taxed. He was relieved to sail for England at the beginning of April.

On June 5th, 1639 the Reverend Samuel Clarke presided over the marriage of his only child to Richard Walderne in the church at Alcester. Although Puritan ministers did not normally perform this ceremony, leaving it to a civil official, her father had obtained permission by the weight of his influence. The wedding was attended by everyone in the parish, but only the family and closest friends were invited to the reception in the Clarkes' garden. The newlyweds would depart for Bristol that very afternoon and take ship the following day. Prudence's parents planned to accompany them and see them off. They would all stay in a fine hotel near the docks. The Clarkes wanted to be with their darling girl as long as possible.

It was a Puritan wedding. There was no music or dancing; rings were considered popish; and Prudence wore no adornment. Richard thought she needed none. Her auburn hair gleamed, and the fine material of her gown accentuated the curves of her graceful figure.

That night they enjoyed a sumptuous dinner with the Clarkes at the hotel in Bristol. Mother Clarke had arranged everything in advance, securing a private room for the little wedding party. Richard drank sparingly, remembering how lazy the toddies had made him on the crossing two years before with Will. He wanted his faculties clear for his wedding night. He gazed at Prudence, recalling Will's advice, and tried to envision how he would proceed once they were alone. Would it work? His bride turned to look at him, placing her hand on his thigh under the tablecloth. His response was immediate—an insistent throb that was both pleasure and pain. He covered her hand with his own, arresting it, and hoped his smile appeared confident.

The courtship of Prudence, the humiliating deference to her parents, and the years of waiting were all worth it, once Richard locked their bedroom door. At long last he was at liberty to indulge the passion he had so stringently controlled since youth.

Richard began by undressing his bride. He did not hurry, and his hands were steady as he unfastened the many buttons of her gown. He carefully removed the pins securing her luxuriant hair; then buried his hands in the thick, auburn locks, as he had longed to do, since he first saw her. They caressed his fingers like silk. He embraced her and kissed her lips for the first time. Her mouth opened under his, and his passion spiked, nearly overwhelming him. He broke off, breathing hard.

Prudence stepped back to remove her traveling outfit and carefully set it aside. She stood before him in her shift and unbuttoned his ruffled shirt, tracing the bared muscles of his chest and shoulders with her fingers. Richard grasped her hands, stopping their exploration. Her touch excited him too much, and he must retain control.

He placed her hands behind her back then pulled on the ribbon at the neck of her shift. The silk flopped open, revealing the hollow at the top of her collarbone. He tasted it with the tip of his tongue and nuzzled the soft skin under her jawbone. Prudence shivered. Richard pushed the soft material off her shoulders, and it fell to the floor, baring her breasts. She made no attempt to hide from him. Only her knee-length small clothes and stockings remained. She wore no corset or bindings. She did not need them. Her waist was delicate, and her breasts were exquisite, boasting the high firmness of youth, the nipples a rosy pink. He was enchanted.

Richard undid the laces of his breeches slowly, relishing the sight of her. Prudence blushed as he stared, his eyes rapacious and glittering. His desire was palpable. She sat on the chest at the foot of the bed and slipped off her stockings one by one. She removed her last undergarment and stood, naked and trembling before him. Her pubic hair was darker than the hair on her head. What mysteries did it conceal? This night he would discover them all.

The bridegroom pulled off his small clothes, releasing his phallus. Prudence gasped and took an involuntary step back. She had never seen a naked man, and the sight of him fully erect startled her. She looked up into his face, and he grasped her hips, pulling her against him and seeking her sweet mouth again. She wrapped her arms around his chest, raking his back lightly with her fingernails. The length of her naked body was pressed against him. His hands cupped her buttocks, and his member throbbed between them. The sensation was overwhelming. He broke off the kiss gasping for breath. His vision dimmed, and before he knew what was happening, Richard had spent himself. It was sweet agony. He stepped back mortified, but Prudence's reaction was a marvel in itself. She touched the sticky substance on her torso and chuckled. It was a low, seductive sound that made him look at her in wonder.

"Oh, husband," she murmured, closing the gap between them, "How potent and eager you are!"

She laid one hand on his chest and touched his quiescent member tentatively with the other. Her fingers were slippery, the sensation so intense it bordered on pain.

She smiled coyly, and her cheek dimpled. "We must practice until we learn the way of it," she purred, stroking him. Her touch caused waves of searing pleasure to pulse through his loins. How quickly his body responded to her! He must not be overcome. His brother had advised him to be masterful in the bedroom in order to maintain the upper hand in his marriage. He must assert control now.

"I shall show you the way of it," he growled and lifted her naked body in his arms.

Richard carried his bride with ease and laid her on the canopied bed. He took a moment to admire the sight. At eighteen Prudence was breathtaking. Her flawless white skin contrasted with the dark green counterpane. The candle by the bed caught the highlights of red in her hair as it fanned across the soft velvet. Richard closed the bed curtain, shucked off his unbuttoned shirt, and climbed in the other side, enclosing them. The newlyweds were alone and naked together for the first time. The curtained bed was their sanctuary, the only light a muted glow through the material. Richard stretched out beside his wife. She turned her head seeking his eyes. All that had been denied him was now his for the taking. It was time to test Will's advice.

Richard stroked his bride tenderly, exploring every curve and hollow of her perfect body with his work-callused hand, eventually resting it on the mound of her pubis. He suckled her nipples gently, one after the other, as he cupped her with gentle pressure. She moaned, and he reveled in the sound of it. He raked her nipples lightly with his teeth, and she gasped and clutched his hair, attempting to push his head away.

Richard leaned on his elbow and gathered her slender wrists in one hand, securing them over her head. It was a wordless command, an assertion of his power. He would do as he pleased. An obedient wife did not resist. With his free hand he firmly parted her thighs, clamping her leg between his knees so she could not close them. She whimpered. She was exposed. He had never seen a woman's private parts, and he leaned closer, scrutinizing them. He stroked the curly hair aside to get a better look and found it damp. Her female scent was intoxicating.

Prudence cried out as her husband touched her intimately, following Will's instructions to the letter. She squirmed against his restraint, whether in ecstasy or resistance he could not tell. In his own burgeoning excitement, he did not care. If his brother's methods did not work, he would take her in any case. She was his now. It was her duty. He silenced her mewling with a rough kiss that ended with a firm, damp finger against her lips in admonishment. Her eyes were wide, and she nodded wordlessly and went still. Satisfied with her submission, he returned to preparing her for his seed in earnest. Richard wanted sons.

He watched his bride's face, as his fingers explored. She was helpless, restrained by his superior strength. Her eyes closed, her cheeks and neck flamed, and she seemed incapable of silence, gasping and moaning. Her hips arched invitingly, but her groom would not be rushed, nor did he stop his caresses. He savored her wordless groans and his power over her, keeping her arms pinned above her head and her legs spread wide. He drank in the sight of her soft, white body so different from the hard planes of his own. His wife. *His* to do with as he pleased. Soon he would possess her completely, and she would bear him sons. Many sons. He was hard again.

As his member stiffened, Prudence's gasps reached a crescendo of wordless cries. She tried to curl in on herself, struggling to close her thighs and free her hands in earnest. Richard realized with a surge of triumph that he had done it. She was in the throes of the little death and ripe for his seed.

This was the moment he had anticipated. They were on the threshold of her deflowering and the consummation of all he had denied himself for a decade. Now at last with God's blessing he, and only he, would possess this perfect, virginal maiden. Never again would their coupling be so momentous. He released her hands and rolled atop her full length. Her legs clamped around his hips, and her arms encircled his neck. He kissed her, probing deeply with his tongue, as he soon would with his manhood. She was eager now. She sucked his tongue hard, sending a thrill of passion from his loins up his spine. He broke off to catch breath and shifted his weight to one forearm. Lifting his hips, he positioned himself with his free hand to enter her. She grasped his thick hair, and their eyes locked.

"Yes, Richard. Yes! Take me! Oh, my Love!"

He was careful at first, unsure if she could accommodate him. Her eyes widened and she gasped, as he slowly entered her. There was a subtle resistance. Will had explained there would be some pain for his bride the first time. The virginal hymen must be broken to gain access to her womb, the quicker the better. Richard withdrew almost entirely then thrust hard three times. Prudence cried out as she was deflowered. Girlhood and innocence were claimed by her lord and master. From this moment on she was a woman and a wife.

Pru's initial cries of pain became whimpers, which changed to soft exhalations in sync with his thrusts. This time the years of control stood him in good stead. The bridegroom settled into a slow rhythm, stopping whenever his urges threatened to overwhelm. Prudence shuddered beneath him, begging him to go on, but her husband was intent on savoring his own pleasure now. When he kept still, he reveled in her blatantly sexual movements, smiling down at the wild thing his bride had become. He had never imagined such intense sensation existed. He had thought the act of procreation was a duty necessary to get sons. He nearly laughed aloud. From now on this heretofore forbidden ecstasy was sanctioned—indeed, required of him as a husband. It was a duty he could relish.

During the pauses to extend his pleasure, he kissed his writhing bride deeply, nuzzled her neck, and suckled her soft earlobes, glorying in his mastery over her. After a lifetime of abstinence, Richard relished the build to his second release as long as possible; however, it was somewhat like running down a hill, and after a timeless interval of this novel pleasure, he was moving faster in spite of himself.

"This! And *this*, and *THIS* is the way of it!" he said through gritted teeth, as he climaxed deep inside her. Nothing in his life had ever felt so fine.

Richard filled his bride with his seed twice more that night, taking her again and yet again in their curtained sanctuary, whenever his energy returned. He claimed her, and she matched his passion with her own. The young Puritan vowed that he would never lose control in the marriage bed again.

# *Chapter 16*

## MARY AND ALICE *THE MISSION IN MAINE*

Summer 1662 Kittery Point, Province of Maine

The evening before the Salem men left, the four missionary Friends walked out to the ferry dock at the west end of Kittery Point. It was unusually calm with no wind to bedevil their headgear. The setting sun gilded the surface of the water and the landscape with coppery gold.

Mary felt unusually shy with Friend Wharton. There had been no opportunities for private conversation, since their arrival at Kittery, but when they were in the same room, she felt his eyes on her. No man had ever looked at her that way, and it was both disturbing and pleasurable—and dangerous. It was possible she misread him, and his interest was simply that of a friend, like Walter and Allie, but this was no time to form attachments of any sort. She was answering a call and must not deviate from her course. There was much work to be done, but Friend Wharton's regard distracted her. She was grateful for his help in transporting them to Kittery Point, but it was best he and Friend Preston were leaving on the morrow.

Mary and Edward walked faster than Allie and George and were soon some distance ahead. It provided a rare interlude to speak privily, but Mary was at a loss to begin. He seemed to be waiting for her to speak first, but she would not let her nerves govern her tongue. She was content to enjoy the view on this fine evening, and they walked some distance in silence.

"I love this time of day," Mary commented at length, breathing in the soft, sea-laden air. The day's heat had mellowed, but they had to keep moving to avoid the worst of the ravenous mosquitoes. Evidently they appreciated this cooler time of day as well.

"How long wilt thou stay with the Shapleighs?" Edward asked.

Mary looked up at him, mildly surprised by the abrupt question, but his eyes were fixed on some point in the distance. His hat was tipped back on his head, and brown curls brushed his collar. He looked so comely in the brassy light, that she turned back to the view quickly.

"I am unsure," she answered slowly. "Until the meetings here are well established, and we have organized practical help where 'tis needed, I warrant."

"And then where?" he pressed, kicking a stone aside.

"Two Friends from the settlement on the Newichawannock River have asked us to establish meetings there, when we have finished our work in Kittery and York—Friends Nason and Spencer. Allie reckons from there, we should continue up the river or cross to Somersworth or Unity and thence back to Dover, I think, as we had good response there. By that time the folk may welcome some further encouragement."

Edward sighed and removed his hat, pushing the hair off his forehead.

"Friend Wharton, is there somewhat thou wouldst say?" Mary asked gently.

He slapped his hat unnecessarily against his leg and replaced it on his head before answering.

"Certes, good progress was made in Dover..." he trailed off.

"But?" she prompted, attempting to catch his eye.

Edward stopped and glanced back at George and Allie. Seeing they were out of earshot, he turned and met Mary's gaze. The intensity of his expression caught her off guard.

"Thou hast also made an enemy there."

"The Reverend Reyner?"

Edward nodded.

"'Tis true, but not unexpected," Mary replied, realizing his message. He was warning her not to return to Dover. "We are accustomed to facing irate ministers and detractors of our faith. We have endured imprisonment and abuse in England. To have an enemy is nothing new, nor will it deter us from our goal," she said firmly. They had stopped, and now she turned and moved on.

"I do not mean to belittle thy courage or thy faith, Friend Tomkins," Edward said, matching her stride. "Thou hast both in good measure, but the Puritans hold sway across the river. I, too, was imprisoned, at Boston. I have felt their wrath upon my back. I endured months of hard labor in chains that chafed my wrists and ankles raw. I choked on the rancid air and spoilt food of their prison. I have witnessed Friends being hanged—good people blessed with more of God in their little finger than all the ministers and magistrates together. I thought they would hang me with William Leddra—" Edward's voice was rising, and he stopped, struggling for control. Mary stopped too, concerned and listening intently. He drew breath, glancing back at their comrades then continued with quiet vehemence. "I find the prospect of thee enduring such persecutions intolerable." He held her eyes.

Mary realized his expression of concern meant he cared about her, and she broke their gaze, confused by a wave of pleasure. She covered it by arguing the point.

"We cannot abandon our mission," she said, relieved her voice sounded normal, in spite of her turmoil.

"Verily not!" Edward rejoined. "But mayhap—"

"Mary Dyer was a spiritual mother to me. She encouraged us to become missionaries, and she died for the liberty of the truth. Allie and I are called to take up her cause. Should we shrink at the mere prospect of an enemy?" Mary spoke calmly, as her father had taught her for maximum effect in debate, but she did not pause for an answer. "We came to engage our enemies, the enemies of our faith. We came to join the struggle to end their bloody regime. If we refuse this bitter cup, the Puritan authorities shall prevail. We cannot allow Friend Dyer's death—yea, the deaths of all the missionaries who have suffered—to be in vain."

"I understand your calling, but there are many folk in need—other settlements that would welcome convincement. Reyner was publicly humiliated, and I fear he will seek revenge. I cannot—" he broke off, obviously frustrated.

Mary stopped, reining in her impatience. "Friend Wharton, speak plainly, I beg thee. What wouldst thou say?" she demanded.

Immediately she regretted the question, for she feared the answer. Surely the blood in her cheeks and the thundering of her heart gave her away. Would he declare affection for her? Did she even want him to? What would she do, if he did? In truth she realized she was drawn to him, as she suspected he was to her. He was comely and capable and shared her faith, but marriage would kill her mission more effectively than any Puritan minister. She might crave his regard in spite of herself, but she could not abandon her chosen course. She must be strong and resist her emotions. She forced herself to look at him and was nearly undone by his next words.

Edward met her eyes and his voice softened. "I fear for thee. The minister is powerful, and there is none can protect thee there. Please understand, Mary, I only—" He lifted a hand—to touch her?—then dropped it and stepped back. George and Allie had caught up.

Mary was stunned. He had used her Christian name.

As their friends joined them, Edward turned away. The opportunity to voice his feelings had passed. In fact, she did not need to hear them. He had called her Mary, not Friend Tomkins, and that told her everything that she was not ready to hear.

Early the next morning the household rose to see the Salem men off. They breakfasted quickly, and all walked down to the dock in the growing light. Mary was torn between relief and sorrow. She stood on the dock with Allie and the Shapleighs and shook the men's hands solemnly. Edward looked as if he would speak but in the end just held her hand for a long moment and nodded.

Johnny and Nicholas pushed the *Sea Witch* off, and they all waved, as Edward and George rowed out into the river. They watched the men ship the oars and release the mainsail. It flapped in the southwest wind, as it was raised. Then the jib went up, Edward took the tiller, they shortened the sails, and the craft made its first tack south.

"What fine fellows they are, eh?" said Nicholas, turning with Alice toward the house.

"Indeed," Alice said with a perceptive glance at Mary, "they shall be missed."

Allie knew something had happened between her friend and Edward Wharton on their walk. She had not pressed her about it but waited for Mary to confide in her. Now, watching the shallop sail away, sorrow was evident on Mary's face. Allie put a comforting arm around her shoulders.

"Oh, Allie!" Mary turned and embraced her tightly. "I fear he cares for me," she whispered over her friend's shoulder, her voice tight with unshed tears.

"Then the question is dost thou care for him?" Allie responded.

Mary stood back and looked at her. "Not enough to abandon our mission," she answered.

Without another word, Allie took her hand, and they followed their hosts. Each hoped Mary's words were true.

Later that day, Mary sat down with Allie and Alice to plan relief missions in the immediate area. Their hostess had made seasonal forays of this kind before, and knew of those most likely to need help. Of course, new difficulties constantly cropped up—the elderly, the sick, women with child, new mothers, or the luckless. The need was ongoing.

The settlements were always near a river or the coast, but as the land was rocky, homes were spread out to take advantage of arable soil and most were isolated from each other. Roads were not well maintained, as most people got around in boats or walked the shoreline at low tide. There were few actual villages on the coast. Looking at the map Nicholas provided, Allie suggested they expand Alice's route to include the settlements accessible by road in York as well as Kittery.

Donations were requested for this mission at the weekly meeting for worship, and the new congregation of Friends responded by bringing clothing, blankets, food, candles, tools, and a variety of useful household goods to the warehouse at Kittery Point.

By the following week they had enough to launch the first circuit of the Mercy Wagon. Johnny helped them load up and drove the team. He was as enthusiastic as the women about the project. They set out early with Alice on the seat next to Johnny, and the missionaries sitting in back, legs dangling.

An elderly couple was almost out of candles. A young mother needed clothes for her new baby and help cleaning her house. A pregnant mother of three could not keep up with the weeds in her garden or the prodigious laundry her family engendered. The Mercy Wagon eased their lack, but the comfort, company, and practical help the missionaries provided was of greater value. If they found illness that Allie's medicaments could not soothe, they sent a message to Dover asking Walter Barefoote to come in his sloop. And come he did, impressed by their industry. As they weeded, cleaned, fed, and laundered, the missionaries talked, and the grateful people listened.

It soon became apparent that one round a week was not enough to address the need. At the fourth meeting for worship in the Shapleigh Church, Mary asked for volunteers as well as donations and was rewarded with vigorous support. By the end of July, the rounds increased to two Mercy Wagons per week—one following the east bank of Spruce Creek and the other winding along the road to York. Attendance at the meetings was growing in response. As the summer progressed, the Friends gathered outdoors on the open ground bordering Back Cove.

Early in July, the first crop of hay was ready for harvest, creating more demands on the busy husbandmen and, indeed, any able-bodied person who could help. The missionaries and Alice Shapleigh organized the neighbors into cooperative groups that shared equipment and labor and accomplished the cutting, gathering, and storing more efficiently. Of course the haying also provided fine opportunities for social gatherings when the day's work was done. The Friends and their wagons became a welcome sight throughout the area. There was always music, dancing, and singing, for the people of Maine were seldom Puritans.

One afternoon on the York Road they came upon a group of Penacook women picking blueberries on a bank at the side of the lane. As soon as Johnny saw them, he stopped the team, passed Alice the reins, and raised both arms in greeting.

"*Kwai, nidôbak! Tôni kd'ôwllôzin?* (Hello, friends! How are you?)," he called.

The women straightened and stared at the *Iglismôniak* and their loaded wagon. Johnny sensed that if there had been other men with him instead of the three women, they would have fled. After a pause one spoke.

"*Newôwlôwzi.* (I am well)," she responded cautiously.

Mary and Allie jumped down as soon as the wagon halted. It was their first contact with Indians, and Mary was determined to communicate with the women. Language would not stop her.

"Allow them to approach us," Johnny cautioned, sensing her excitement as she came alongside.

Mary nodded without looking at him. She made eye contact with the Indian who had spoken, and imitated Johnny's gesture.

"*Kwai!*" she called, smiling.

The woman stared at her without expression. The others had moved closer to her, their eyes on the strangers. Mary lowered her arms, feeling foolish and desperate to allay their fear. She turned to Johnny.

"Canst thou tell them we mean no harm?" she asked him.

"I have greeted them with the word for friends, *nidôbak*," he answered quietly. "Now we must wait."

Instead of walking forward with Mary, Allie rummaged through one of the boxes in the wagon. She came to Mary's side with a pot of apple butter she had opened with her belt knife and slowly moved a few paces closer to the group on the bank. They watched her warily. She stopped at the edge of the road and held out the gift.

"For you," she said, and nodded twice.

The woman set down her basket and approached with caution. The others stayed back, watching. Her expression remained unreadable. Allie made an eating gesture and rubbed her tummy saying, "Mmmmm." The Indian took the proffered pot and sniffed it. The others gathered around her for a closer look, their eyes darting between the wagon and Allie.

Mary saw two had babies swaddled and strapped to boards on their backs, and their spokeswoman had hair streaked with gray. Their clothing was a hodgepodge of colonial cotton and tanned hides. Their dark hair was plaited in two braids, giving them a similar look, but up close their individualities were apparent. The elder native dipped a finger in the little crock and tasted the contents. The reaction was immediate. Her eyes widened and a slow smile transformed her stern features.

"*Oligen!* (That is good!)," she said to her friends, offering it to them. Each woman sampled the sweet condiment. She looked at Johnny. "*Gagwi yo?* (What is it?)"

"I do not know the word for apple butter," he said helplessly. "*Nda n'wawaldamowen* (I do not know)," he apologized.

The Indian women were all smiling, sampling the condiment and exclaiming, "*Oligen!*" The ice had been broken, and the Indians went from grave silence to chattering laughter, now they knew these *Iglismôniak* would not harm them or kidnap them for slave labor.

"*Awani gia?* (Who are you?)," the Indian woman asked Johnny. She appeared to have the weight of authority in the group.

"*Azo* Shapleigh *nia* (I am John Shapleigh)." he replied. "*W'pehanem* (wife) Nicholas Shapleigh—Alice," he gestured to his aunt on the seat beside him. "*Nidôba agema* (She is a friend)," he nodded at Mary and Allie.

"Ah, Shap-lee! *Oligo!* (He is good!)," she responded warmly. Nicholas had ever treated the Indians with respect. The woman's reaction proved their regard for him.

"*Awani gia?* (Who are you?)" Johnny asked.

"*Sozon nia* (I am Susan)," she answered. After two generations of interaction with the colonists, many of the Penacook assumed an anglicized name when dealing with them. The Indians guarded their personal names closely.

Johnny's command of the language was limited, but he knew enough words to roughly communicate their mission. Alice suggested the women each take a gift from the wagon bed. They accepted with enthusiasm, rummaging through the sacks and boxes, and exclaiming over the treasure trove of items. When one of them took two things, she was sternly reprimanded by *Sozon* and sheepishly put one back. The older woman said something to her in stern tones, and she fetched her basket of berries and shyly approached Allie, offering it to her.

"Do not attempt to refuse," Johnny warned her quickly, as Allie opened her mouth to protest. "'Tis a great honor and they would take offense."

Allie scooped a handful into her mouth and made a sincere show of enjoying the tiny, tart berries and sharing them with her companions.

"How does one express thanks?" she asked Johnny.

"*Oliwni*," he told her quietly, and Allie repeated the word to their new friends.

Johnny managed to learn the women were at their summer camp on a large pond to the north. Mary asked him to invite them to the First Day meetings at Back Cove, and the women seemed pleased. They parted with smiles, when the Friends continued on their mission. They left the Indian women happily comparing their gifts. The missionaries learned another word, *Adio*, for goodbye.

END PART 1

# *Part II*

# SUMMER AND AUTUMN

*Early Friends, as has been shown, had profound respect for authority leavened with justice, but when officials degraded it and themselves by acts of cruel tyranny, they were prompt to resist and to rebuke.*

RICHARD P. HALLOWELL, THE QUAKER INVASION OF MASSACHUSETTS

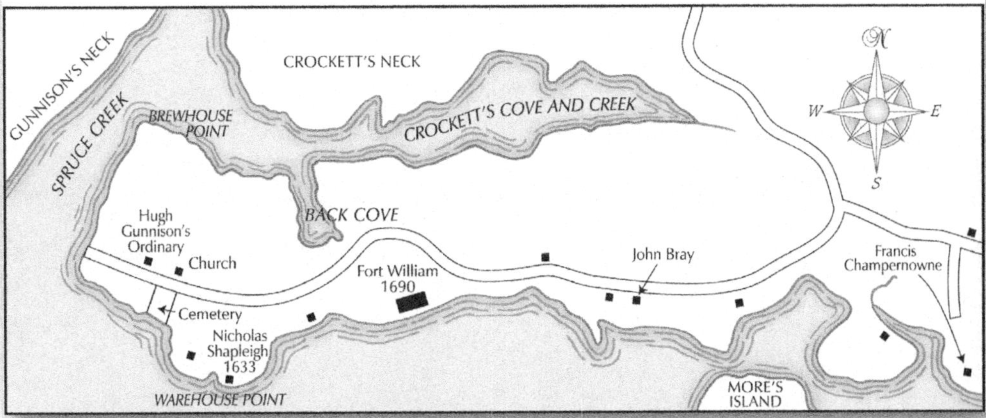


***KITTERY POINT, 1650-1700***

Taken from *Old Kittery and Her Families*

# *Chapter 17*

## REVEREND JOHN REYNER *THE COMPLAINT*

August, 1662 Dover Neck, Massachusetts Bay Colony

The summer was not going well for the Reverend Reyner. His congregation had dwindled since the humiliating encounter at the Emerys' ordinary in June. The increasing number of vacant spots on the benches alarmed him. The cursed Quakers were to blame. His humors roiled when he recalled the incident. He knew his rebuttal had been weak, and many nights since, he lay awake beside his sleeping wife, conjuring the responses that had eluded him.

Worst of all, Elder Nutter had witnessed his humiliation. Reyner longed for vindication, but what could he do? The next day the missionaries had fled across the river and were now protected by the influential Shapleigh family. At the minister's prompting, Richard Walderne sent a letter to Governor Endicott, complaining of the haven for dissenters on the eastern bank of the Piscataqua, but the response from Secretary Rawson laid all responsibility for dealing with the interlopers at the feet of the local authorities. The minister was powerless, unless the missionaries returned to Dover. But would they?

Reyner stood at the open door of the First Congregational Church of Dover, preoccupied by these concerns. His diminished congregation filed past with few comments to their shepherd. The weather was oppressively hot, and the humid air outside was stifling after the relatively cool interior. Heavy clouds hinted at a rainy reprieve with a growl of distant thunder.

The reverend was sweating in his fine black suit. Underneath the linen shirt stuck to his back, and a trickle of sweat tickled the ribs on his left side. A tight smile was plastered to his face, but he ground his teeth. He wanted to get home, change his clothes, and put up his swollen feet.

Reyner stiffened. Someone lurked behind him, craving words, no doubt, and delaying his release. He turned to find Elder Nutter towering over him. The reverend stepped back involuntarily. Even in his sixties the man gave an imposing impression of vigor, and few in the community could match his influence and wealth. They had not spoken since the disastrous encounter with the Quakers, and Reyner feared he had lost the elder's respect. Mayhap the man was recalling it at this very moment and wished to berate him.

"Reverend Reyner, I would have words with you," Nutter said, thrusting out his jaw and squinting down his nose at the smaller man.

"Yes, Elder Nutter, I always have time for you. How can I be of service?" the clergyman asked.

"Nay, not here," the other responded curtly, as the last worshipers cleared the steps.

The minister's heart sank. Goody Reyner had gone home to set out the meat pie baked the night before. She was a godly woman and knew better than to cook on the Sabbath. She would be fetching a pitcher of barley water from the root cellar, where it kept cool. It soothed his throat after preaching all day, but now relief must be delayed.

"As you wish, Elder Nutter," Reyner's smile resembled a grimace of pain.

"Come to mine house," Nutter mumbled, gesturing with his chin across the lane.

The big man looked around then leaned closer, although they were quite alone on the steps.

"We must discuss a course to correct these absences from worship, do you not think?"

Reyner's reluctance dissolved in a flood of relief. He was not to be censured—quite the contrary. Nutter wanted to help! Here was a powerful ally. Together they might find a way to correct this untenable situation.

"Verily, we must!" the minister agreed, speaking sincerely for the first time.

Nutter responded with a grunt and started down the steps without another word.

"I shall just close up here and join you forthwith," Reyner called to his retreating back.

The Elder's home was a stone's throw across the road from the eight-year-old meeting house on Nutter's Hill. Reyner hastily snuffed the candles and closed up. The air was deathly still, but thunder grumbled from behind him as he crossed High Street.

Hatevil had shucked his Sabbath Day coat, and the reverend followed his lead with relief, plucking discreetly at his damp shirt as he settled at the dining table opposite his host. Goody Nutter served them tea—no soothing barley water here—and left a plate of gingerbread on the table between them; then she took up her Bible and withdrew to a corner to read by a fine bronze lamp. Heavy clouds obscured the lowering sun, and the summer evening was prematurely dark.

The Nutters lived well. Hatevil was among Thomas Wiggin's first recruits and had lived on the Neck for thirty years. The big man felt a keen proprietorship for the town. His wealth came from land investments, timber harvesting, and shipping, and his tax rate was one of the highest on the Point. He was partners with Richard Walderne in the sawmill on Lamprey River, which provided materials for the Nutter shipyard, located east of the elder's house on the bank of Fore River. He preached on Sunday afternoons upon occasion, and although his delivery was ponderous, Reyner respected his piety. Now he spoke of the Quaker interlopers.

"The danger became apparent to me when we heard the heretics speak at the ordinary," he began. The reverend winced, but Nutter continued without further reference to the minister's humiliation. "Thus I sent my son, Anthony, to one of their 'meetings' at Kittery."

"Oh well done!" Reyner responded. "What said he?"

"They not only threaten our First Church but also our laws and the established social order," Nutter grumbled. "'Tis bad enough they support an unnatural equality and permit women to preach," he snorted derisively, "but they would deprive you of your livelihood as well, Reverend—no ministers or churches! No taxes! They flaunt the laws of the Bay Colony and fill the heads of the common folk with seditious notions. Their so-called missionary work encourages dissension at the very least, and outright rebellion at worst."

Reyner nodded, listening avidly. He lamented the empty seats and the resultant drop in church tithes, but he was more worried about his position. His entire means of earning a living was threatened by these heretics.

"God dwells within each person, they say. 'Tis blasphemy!" Nutter continued, fuming. "They would undo all our efforts to establish an orderly society here. They must be stopped."

The reverend had rarely heard the taciturn elder speak at such length, unless he was preaching. Nutter's vehemence gave him hope.

"I am in accord, Elder Nutter. 'Tis a grave threat indeed, but they are protected by Nicholas Shapleigh at present. How might we proceed, think you?" Reyner asked.

"We can do nothing unless they return to Dover. However, we must prepare for that possibility in advance," Hatevil answered. "We have two advantages—the law and our weight in the community. I propose we write up a formal complaint."

"A formal complaint?" Reyner repeated, straightening. This legal course had not occurred to him. The minister warmed to the idea even as he grasped it.

"Between us both, we are capable of procuring enough signatures, I warrant," Nutter replied, running a hand through his thick, cropped hair. There was an indent where the hatband habitually pressed, but very little grey, considering the man was over sixty.

The minister rubbed his palms together, a gesture that helped him focus his thoughts. "If sufficient folk sign it, we could present the document to a magistrate, who could then arrest them. That is precisely what we must do! Has Richard Walderne returned from Boston?"

The big man nodded. "I believe he is at Cocheco, overseeing the construction of a new house and tending to his interests there."

"You are well acquainted. Think you he would help in this endeavor?" Reyner asked.

"I have no doubt, Reverend. He is as staunch in his faith as am I."

Hatevil brought the reading lamp to the table, instructing his wife to fetch quill, ink, and paper.

"Some food, as well," he added, uncapping the inkpot, "And another pot of tea."

Fired by their plan, the two men labored over the wording of the complaint late into the August evening. Thunder rumbled increasingly closer, and gusts of wind thrashed the trees. The gathering gloom leeched the last meager light from the air; then the storm hit. Rain pounded the windows, lit by flashes of lightning. Peals of thunder sundered the air, but the storm did not distract the two men. Once satisfied with the wording of the complaint, they conferred on a list of folk that could be counted upon to sign it, along with a second list of those to be persuaded or coerced. There were more than sixty names.

By the time Hatevil Nutter showed his guest to the door, the storm had passed, the air was cooler, and clouds raced across the face of a half-moon riding high overhead.

"This complaint may serve a further purpose," Reyner said, donning his coat.

"That occurred to me as well," the Elder replied.

The big man ever surprised the minister with his subtlety of his mind. Their eyes met.

"'Twill be a divining rod, as it were, to point out the faithful who are with us," the minister said.

"And, of greater import, to point out who is not," Hatevil finished with a rare smile.

# *Chapter 18*

## MARY AND ALICE *CONTACT*

Summer, 1662 Kittery Point, Province of Maine

The summer was not all work. At the beginning of July, Alice Shapleigh took the ferry with Mary and Allie to Strawbery Banke, coming home at the end of the day with baskets full of tiny, wild strawberries. They made jam, which was exceedingly popular on the Mercy Wagon routes.

At the beginning of August, Nicholas and Johnny managed a rare break from their labors. The five of them, including Alice, sailed over to Great Island to visit George and Alice Walton at their inn. Nicholas and Johnny were skillful sailors, beating across the water against the prevailing wind. They all laughed, as the boat came about, ducking under the boom and moving from one side of the skiff to the other. The wind and salt spray were wonderfully refreshing in the summer heat, and the outing invigorated them all.

The Shapleighs entertained guests and received invitations often during the warm weather. The Champernownes, Brays, and Pearces were neighbors within a mile of Kittery Manor. There were dinners and picnics every week. The colonists created their own entertainment, and they took advantage of the fine weather, for the winters were long and confining. Nicholas liked to quote the old John Heywood poem, saying,

> *"Whan the sunne shinth, make hay. Whiche is to say.*
> *Take time whan time cometh, lest time steale away."*

Mary and Allie were pleased with the progress of their mission. Attendance at the meetings increased steadily, thanks to the Mercy Wagons. The hard-working colonists embraced the missionaries' message. The Society of Friends encouraged an open community based on consensus giving each man's opinion merit—freeman or not. Every person was valued, and all mature males participated in decisions of local import. The Friends did not go so far as to give women social or political equality, but all were deemed spiritually equal, and husbands were more likely to consider their wives' opinions than was customary. Most of those drawn to the meetings were outcasts, denied participation in the Puritan freeman system. However, a number were former Anglicans with property and influence, who believed in freedom of thought and worship. All welcomed an alternative to the existing system.

During July and August, as weather permitted, First Day meetings were held outdoors on the open ground overlooking Back Cove. It was a tranquil spot with a view north across the water to Crockett's Neck. Nicholas kept his skiff there for ready access to his mills on Spruce Creek, and the Friends who came by boat from the north also found it a convenient place to put in.

One fine Sabbath Day in August, Mary watched as people arrived and spread out—women to the right, men to the left in unconscious order. She rarely spoke now other than greeting the worshippers, and she realized the time to move on was approaching. Today's gathering numbered around forty. The sound of their singing filled the air and carried across the water in a most pleasing manner.

They were well into the opening hymn, when a large canoe appeared, coming from the direction of Spruce Creek and angling steadily toward the shore. Two others soon followed. Each canoe held six or seven Indians. The paddlers were swift and sure.

The Friends did not falter in their singing, but all eyes were on the approaching canoes. As they neared, it became apparent that several women were in the party, but most impressive was a veritable giant of a man with long white hair, who sat erect in the middle of the leading craft. Mary glanced at Nicholas and saw he was smiling broadly. He showed no distress—indeed quite the opposite. Mary looked for *Sozon* but could not be sure she was among them.

The Indians debarked gracefully, landing their canoes on the grassy bank with casual skill and scarcely wetting their moccasins. The hymn ended with a long "Ahhhhhhh—mennnnnnn," as twenty Penacook men and women joined the Friends led by the white-haired giant.

"This is a great honor!" Nicholas told the worshippers quietly then went to meet the tall native, raising both arms in greeting, as Johnny had with the band on the road.

"*Williani* (William)!" he exclaimed, using the name the Penacook chief had appropriated for interacting with the colonists.

The two men grasped each other's forearms. The Indian towered over Nicholas.

"*Nicola*! *Kwai!* (Hello!) *Tôni kd'ôwllôzin?* (How are you?)" His voice was deep and powerful.

"*Newôwlôwzi.* (I am well) *Ni tôni gia, oligo nidôba?* (And you, good friend?)" Nicholas answered.

They spoke briefly in the native tongue as Nicholas gestured to the group of Friends, explaining silent worship. He invited the visitors to join them. Everyone was smiling and nodding, but Mary noted mothers held their children close. The Indians did not appear to notice and grouped to men's left. When everyone was settled, Nicholas caught Mary's eye and nodded. She felt a formal welcome was in order and stepped forward, raising her arms.

"Greetings, Friends! *Kwai, nidobak*! I bid you welcome, one and all!"

The chief met her eyes. His face was impassive, but he nodded once, acknowledging the greeting. Mary had never seen such a big man.

"In the words of our founder, George Fox, 'God has a mission for every man, woman and child, and each person must work to discover his or her own assignment.' May the Light Within illuminate our way and guide us in recognizing and fulfilling that mission."

Mary willed her racing pulse to slow, closing her eyes and breathing deeply. God had brought these visitors to them. His Light resided in their hearts just as surely as it shone in hers, and this meeting would unfold according to His Will. As she relinquished her need to control the situation, her tension eased. She became aware of the warm sun on her back and the light breeze ruffling the edges of her dust cap. Her thoughts stilled, and the silence embraced her, broken only by birdsong and the lapping of water. Profound joy blossomed in her heart, and Mary surrendered to it willingly.

When the group began to stir, Mary opened her eyes. Her calm assurance persisted through the shaking of hands, and she met the eyes of the silver-haired woman who had been standing next to the tall Indian. Mary smiled, wanting to make a connection, but she was unsure how to surmount the language barrier. She looked around for Nicholas or Johnny.

Walter and Nicholas were speaking with the tall chief. Johnny and John Treworgy approached the Indian men with arms raised in greeting, and Alice was signing with the native women, but for the most part the colonists hung back with uncustomary shyness, stymied as Mary was, for most did not speak the Penacook tongue.

"Well, here's a first, then," Allie said quietly at her elbow. They shared a smile.

Nicholas looked around, and spotting them, gestured for the missionaries to join him. As she and Allie approached, Mary marveled at the contrast the three men made. Nicholas was tall, but the top of his head barely reached the giant's chin. His dark blond hair was pulled back and tied with a black velvet ribbon. He wore a black frock coat and breeches with knee-length military boots, his hat tucked under his arm. Walter, as always, was impeccably dressed in a dark green linen suit, white hose, and black shoes with silver buckles. His stylish hat sported an ostrich plume, which the chief was admiring. The Indian stood with innate dignity, his back straight, as he inspected the hat and its embellishment. He wore a red linen shirt, embroidered at the yoke and cuffs. His white hair was unbound, secured by a colorful headband that matched his shirt. White deerskin pants and summer moccasins completed his outfit. His dark, deeply lined face, long hair, and colorful attire contrasted with the colonists.

"Mary Tomkins and Alice Ambrose," Nicholas said formally in English, "allow me to introduce the *Sôgmô Williani* (Chief William) of the Penacook and *Ktsi Sôgmô* (great chief) of the *Wobanakiak*—the confederation of Abenaki Tribes. His true name is *Papisse Conewa* which means 'Child of the Bear' although the English have shortened it to Passaconaway. He prefers William, or as the Indians say, *Williani*."

Mary met the big man's appraising look. She had to tilt her head back to do so. Although he was not smiling, his expression was benign. His wisdom was palpable.

"I am honored to make thy acquaintance, *Williani*," she replied. Then matching the big man's serious expression, she put a hand to the side of her neck. "But I fear, if we are to converse for long, I shall have to stand upon a block!" she finished, eyes sparkling.

The big man's mouth twitched, then he laughed heartily. After a surprised pause, Nicholas and Walter joined in.

"Ah!" Mary exclaimed. "Thou dost speak English!"

"Oh yes!" Walter answered. "*Williani* has dealt with the colonists for many years; have you not, my friend?"

The old chief nodded. "*Ôhô* (yes). Many seasons. 'Tis simpler one *sôgmô* learn English than many *Iglismôniak* learn the language of the People." His eyes sparkled. "English tongues trip on our words. *Nicola* and Barefoote are..." he shrugged, "... different."

"I believe that's a compliment, don't you think, Nicholas?" Walter grinned.

"I warrant it is! And something of a rarity," their host declared, winking at the missionaries. The big *sôgmô's* mouth twitched again. Nicholas met his eye. "*Oliwni* (thank you), *Williani,*" he said, sincerely.

Alice approached with the silver-haired native woman, and the chief introduced her to the missionaries as his widowed sister, *Tolloti* (Dorothy). She wore an Indian dress of white deerskin decorated with patterns of porcupine quills. Tiny feathers were worked into the silver braids which fell to her waist. Once the formal greetings were exchanged, she spoke to her brother for some minutes in an assertive tone. Alice, Mary, and Allie shared a smile, watching the men nod and listen to her with respect. When she finished, her brother shrugged eloquently and looked at Nicholas, who responded, "*Cowi!*" (Sure!) Then he translated.

"This band consists of *Williani's* closest friends and relatives. They have spent the summer visiting villages and camps, encouraging peace between our peoples. They learned of our meetings from a group just north of here. The women spoke of meeting you on the road and praised you highly. *Williani* wanted to see you for himself. *Tolloti* proposes they set up camp in the meadow and stay a few days. They have a ceremonial drum and wish to celebrate our friendship with dancing and feasting." His eyes danced with excitement. "What do you think, Alice?"

"Oh yes!" Alice nodded enthusiastically and smiled at *Tolotti*. "I think 'tis a wonderful idea! We shall roast a pig and invite everyone!"

# *Chapter 19*

## RICHARD WALDERNE *THE NEWLYWEDS*

1639-1640 Bristol, England and Bristol, New Hampshire Colony

The day after their wedding night, Richard stood behind his bride at the rail on the crowded deck of the *Warwick* his arms encircling her protectively from the press of people. The Clarkes waved mournfully from the dock. They were understandably distraught, and Richard masked his triumph with grave sympathy at their leave taking.

"Keep her safe from the salvages," her mother had begged tearfully.

"I assure you, they are no threat, Mother Clarke," he said, forcing himself to kiss her doughy cheek.

"Be kind to our darling girl, Richard," Father Clarke instructed, gripping his hand so tightly it hurt. "Make sure she has all the comforts money can buy in that wilderness." Richard nodded, embarrassed by the tears standing in the older man's eyes.

"She shall be safe with me," he promised somberly. At long last Prudence was his.

Now as the distance between the dock and the ship widened, his bride raised her arm in a last farewell. He expected her to turn with tears on her cheeks at parting from home and family, but he was surprised. She was smiling radiantly. She placed her gloved hands on his chest and spoke quietly, surrounded as they were by other passengers, watching their loved ones dwindle as current and tide bore the ship downriver.

"My love, my all, you have set me free! I can scarce believe we are married and journeying to the New World!" she whispered her eyes shining with excitement.

Prudence wore her hair in a demure bun at the nape of her neck now that she was a goodwife. Her mother had cried upon seeing it that morning, for it was a sign of womanhood. Now she looked up at him coyly, her eyes sparkling beneath the brim of her bonnet, and his body stirred in response. He wanted to rip the damned hat off her head, bury his hands in her silky hair, and kiss her mouth right there in front of them all, the whole flock of sheep. Instead he stepped back, tucked her arm under his, and strode toward the hatch leading to their cabin. He had paid dearly for private quarters, but Richard was sure it would be worth every farthing during the next eight weeks.

Prudence had never felt so free and yet so possessed. She yielded to her husband's every whim, and their passion increased as they plumbed its depths. Richard was a different man behind closed doors. He confided thoughts and plans he had never expressed to anyone. Each day of the crossing, they spent hours in their cabin, extending the limits of their pleasure. He gave her all his attention, and Prudence was euphoric.

The *Warwick* docked at Pomeroy Cove in early August of 1639, having made the crossing in seven and a half weeks. Richard sent a boy to bring Will and the wagon and to alert Missus Cameron. Prudence watched her handsome husband supervise the offloading of their prodigious cargo, including her saddle horse, which seemed to have survived the crossing unscathed. Her mother had wanted her to take a lady's maid as well, but Prudence had refused. She did not want to be seen as the coddled daughter of well-to-do parents. She was determined to assert her independence as a married woman and prove a capable mistress of her own household.

"Missus Cameron shall be your right hand," Richard informed her, during one of their many discussions aboard ship. "Consider her advice; however, you have the final say on all decisions." He lifted her chin, giving weight to his next words. "Do not be cowed by her, Prudence. Remember that you are the mistress, subject only to me."

She gazed back solemnly. "Be assured, husband, I shall maintain authority with a firm hand." She gave him that dimpled smile and guided his hand to her bare breast. Their communication became wordless.

Prudence savored her newfound independence, as she waited on the busy dock among the trunks and hand luggage from their cabin. Weak sunlight filtered through an overcast sky, ameliorating the August heat. The young wife drank in everything around her. She watched the ponderous contra dance of ships' traffic to and from the docks. She observed the constant flow of cargo from ship to shore and vice versa. Brawny workers eyed her approvingly, as they hefted bales, kegs, trunks, and boxes on their broad shoulders or pulled loaded handcarts. Their sleeves were rolled up in the heat, and she could not help but admire their muscled arms. Perched on her trunk she was a small island in a stream of male traffic. These were not gentlemen, and she was unaccompanied in public for the first time in her life, while Richard saw to the cargo. She did not make eye contact with any of them, but she could feel their admiring stares. One was so bold as to emit a low whistle of appreciation, as he passed near her. A smile played upon her lips, as she demurely turned her eyes away, but Pru felt flattered. She was a woman now. She knew what men wanted, and their approval pleased her.

Her eye was drawn to a group of dark-skinned men with long, loose, black hair. She realized with a start that they were salvages. They were dressed like colonists, and only their skin and hair gave them away. No one seemed alarmed by their presence. Two white men were bargaining with them, using hand gestures. The Indians lifted a bale onto the pier and cut it open. Prudence saw the gleam of a pelt, as the traders held it up, inspecting the quality. There were six or eight of the Indians. She noticed the hair around their faces was plaited in two thin braids adorned with feathers and shells. Was it decoration? She was surprised they would care to embellish their appearance. It made them more human to her. Like the other laborers on the docks their sleeves were rolled up in the heat, showing coppery skin and the play of muscles, as they unloaded the canoe. She wondered how they smelled. Richard said they painted their faces, but these bore no paint. Still they looked wild, strong, and dangerous. The young bride was mesmerized and watched until their business was concluded. They shoved off and paddled efficiently through the traffic of fishing boats, ferry barges, small craft, and commercial ships. There were seven Indians she saw now—one in the bow and three paddling on each side. She was disappointed, when they disappeared from view.

Prudence turned her attention to the dusty road, leading from the landing up the Point. It was barely wide enough for two wagons to pass. Stumps were everywhere, although there were more trees than cleared land as yet. Columns of smoke rose from numerous chimneys further up the Point. Mayhap one marked her new home somewhere up that rutted lane, awaiting her supervision. She drew a deep breath and let it out slowly. This place was exotic, rugged, and thrilling. The young bride smiled.

By the end of August, Prudence was maintaining her household with Mrs. Cameron's subtle assistance. Together they hired a live-in cook and two sisters that came every day to clean, launder, draw water, make soap and candles, and tend fires. The first weeks were a flurry of activity, moving furniture and appointments up from the dock, and rearranging the interior of the house to her taste. Missus Cameron had established a fine kitchen garden, but Prudence wanted to improve the grounds as well. Once the house was arranged and the housekeeper had the staff running efficiently, the young bride hired a husbandman and walked the grounds, discussing the placement of flower and bush gardens. Of course, the plants must be ordered from England. She was attentive and kept a garden book, noting the local plants that might coexist with the imports and look pleasing together. Richard denied her nothing, concerning the house, and she reveled in her new-found authority.

With Richard gone each day to oversee the construction of his trading post at Cocheco, Prudence exercised her horse in the afternoon, familiarizing herself with the area and her neighbors. The newlyweds' social calendar filled quickly as a result. Their life together was progressing smoothly, and Prudence felt confident in her role as wife and mistress. Richard was proud of her ability to adapt. Although he discouraged affection outside their marriage bed, he was ardent once they were alone.

One morning near the end of August, the young bride woke feeling ill. Normally she was ravenous in the mornings, especially if she and Richard had satisfied their passion the night before. Not this morning. Missus Cameron was quick to notice her lack of appetite, when she joined Prudence at the dining table to go over the day's schedule. Nothing that occurred within her provenance escaped her eagle eye.

"Ye have'na touched your food, Mistress. Are ye not weel?" she said with her usual candor.

"I am feeling rather poorly this morning, Missus Cameron. I cannot countenance taking any nourishment, except, perhaps, a cup of tea," Prudence responded. "Is the Master about?"

"He left more than an hour ago, Mistress. Up to Cocheco he said."

Prudence sighed. She had no energy and wanted nothing more than to go back to bed. She wished they were back on the *Warwick* in their snug little cabin with nothing to do but—

"D'ye wish me to brew you a dose of chamomile, Mistress?" Missus Cameron was asking. She picked up the little bell on the table to ring for the kitchen maid but paused for the reply.

"No. Yes. Oh, I don't know!" for the first time since arriving in Bristol, Prudence felt overwhelmed. Uncharacteristically, she missed her mother, and tears stung her eyes, even as another wave of nausea assailed her. It made her mouth water, a sure sign of trouble to come. To her surprise, Missus Cameron smiled.

"Feelin' a bit weepy as well, Mistress? And tired, mayhap?" she asked more gently.

Prudence straightened, struggling for dignity. "What...whatever makes you say that, Missus Cameron?" She swallowed and lifted her chin, vexed to be caught in a moment of emotional and physical weakness in the company of a servant.

"Ah, weel," the rare smile surfaced again briefly, "Beggin' your pardon, Mistress, but I think ye may carryin'."

Prudence was not familiar with this particular euphemism, and her eyes widened in alarm. Did the woman mean she was harboring some disease?

"C-carrying what?" she asked fearfully.

Had it not been so alien to her nature, Missus Cameron might have laughed. As it was, she barely maintained her customary neutral expression. People thought her cold, but she was not. Prudence looked like a child, bewildered and fearful, and the older woman felt a wave of affection for her. The girl needed her mother and was most likely innocent, rather than dense. In that moment Eleanor Cameron's heart opened to her young mistress, and she answered with care and no hint of disdain.

"Why, carryin' a bairn, Mistress. I believe ye may be blessed with child."

Prudence lurched to her feet. There was no time to respond to this earthshaking diagnosis. In that moment all she wanted was to reach the commode in time.

Eleanor fetched a damp flannel and followed.

# *Chapter 20*

## MARY AND ALICE *CONNECTION*

Summer, 1662 Kittery Point, Province of Maine

The Penacook band set up camp in the open field east of Back Cove, erecting three lean-to shelters and digging a shallow fire pit. The Friends who had attended the meeting went home to prepare for the celebration. They would return with their most tasty recipes, comfortable clothing, and picnic rugs the next day. News of the Indians' visit and the impending celebration spread quickly.

Nicholas and Johnny supervised preparations for roasting the pig. During the summer an outdoor pit was maintained adjacent to the ordinary for this purpose. The hog would be slaughtered that afternoon, allowing the carcass to bleed out overnight. It would roast on a spit throughout the next day. Young lads were enlisted to load a wagon with wood and feed the fire all night to produce a glowing bed of coals by the morrow.

Alice arranged for trestles and boards to hold the food, and designated the kegs of ale and cider to be brought from the brew house. She alerted the kitchen staff and inventoried utensils and dishes from the house and the ordinary. There was much to be done. However, when Mary and Allie offered to assist her, their hostess firmly told them that their place was with *Williani* for he was there to see them.

"Our thanks, Alice!" Mary said, embracing her. "We should like nothing better."

"Take this for refreshment," Alice said, proffering a cloth-covered basket. "'Tis Johnny Cake—*skamanabôn*. We learned the recipe from the Indians, and they will be pleased to see we use it. There is also strawberry jam and cider. Our friends favor sweets."

"Oh, well done!" Allie exclaimed, taking the basket gratefully.

"Allie is not so particular. She favors anything edible," Mary teased.

"Verily," her friend agreed, lifting the cloth and sniffing the contents appreciatively.

They found the big man and his sister resting on blankets before one of the lean-tos in the shade of an old oak too twisted for the axe. *Williani* greeted the missionaries gravely and bade them sit. A small fire smoldered in a pit, smoking prodigiously. There was no sign of the rest of the band.

"*Pegwisak* do not like smoke," he commented, when the missionaries had settled.

"*Pegwisak*?" Mary repeated.

"Bugs, I warrant," Allie surmised. "And we do not like them."

The big man's lips twitched. "Just so," he responded. Mary realized this counted as a smile.

A pause ensued, and Mary found that she did not know how to begin a conversation with this extraordinary man. She recalled her father's axiom, "If you have nothing to say, say nothing." His advice stood her in good stead now. Silence was familiar, and she suppressed the urge to fill it. *Tolotti* picked up a branch with green leaves from a pile at hand and threw it on the smudge fire. They watched the smoke rise in the still air. It did seem to keep the worst of the mosquitos and biting flies at bay, although the former were worse after dark. Even in the shade, the sun's strength was evident this day.

Allie laid out the food on the cloth that covered the basket, gesturing for their guests to partake. Brother and sister set to with gusto, exclaiming over the strawberry jam and pleased by the inclusion of *skamanabôn*. *Tolotti* closed her eyes each time she ate some of the sweet condiment and directed her brother to inquire how it was made. Allie explained briefly.

"We shall bring you more," she assured them. "We have pots and pots of it!"

Her brother translated, and for the first time his sister smiled broadly, revealing strong, white teeth despite her age.

After they had consumed their fill, *Tolotti* lit a small pipe with a stick from the fire. She puffed until a cloud of smoke obscured her face. Once it was going, she offered it to the women. Allie took a tentative puff, and Mary followed suit, sensing the honor accorded them. Mary passed the pipe to *Williani*, and he smoked in silence for a time.

"So." His deep voice came between draws on the pipe. "Two *Iglismôniak* women leave their people (puff) to undertake a perilous journey alone (puff), crossing the Great Ocean to this wild place." He handed his sister the pipe and gave them his full attention. "Why?"

If an English person had asked her, Mary might have been offended by the bald question, but this man and his sister were unlike anyone she had ever known. The limitations of time as well as disparate languages and cultures necessitated candor. The normal rules of courtesy did not apply.

"We serve God, and He sent us to stand against the injustice suffered by people of our faith; therefore, we say 'tis a calling, and woe to us, if we do not listen," Mary answered.

"Your God speaks to you?" the *sôgmô* asked, more interested than incredulous.

"'Tis our belief He speaks to everyone who listens, for we believe His Light dwells in all hearts."

The big man considered this in silence.

"Has your God always spoken to you?" he asked at length.

"Oh no!" she answered. "I did not experience His Presence until Allie and I became convinced and joined the Society of Friends."

"Friends? *Nidôbak*? What is this Society of Friends?"

"That is the name given to our faith by our founder, George, Fox. We call each other 'Friend' rather than 'Mister' or 'Mistress.'"

"*Wôkwses*! Fox!" The big man chuckled. "Is it his *k'doodam* (totem)? Is he a good provider like a fox father?"

"Indeed, he has provided many people with a path to God's Light in their hearts," Mary agreed, smiling.

"But how do they find this 'Light'? At the meeting ye did not speak many words like John Eliot, the *Iglismôn* minister that came to us. How do ye teach them?" the big man asked.

"We do not use ministers or sermons. The Light is found in silent contemplation. When we meet, we speak very little. We quiet our thoughts and wait for God's Will to be revealed. If any be moved by the Spirit, they may express it, but on the whole we believe words are a distraction, used by the ministers. They wish folk to think that only the clergy can interpret the Bible and godly behavior. The Society of Friends believes that all people can connect with That of God. We do not need ministers or books or churches to find Him—only silence and an open heart."

*Williani* translated Mary's words for *Tolotti*. His sister responded, waving a hand towards the missionaries. He nodded and turned back to Mary.

"My sister says ye speak like an elder of the tribe. The People believe *Ktsi Niwaskw*, the Great Spirit, is in all things—people, animals, birds, fish—all that lives and grows. We honor what must die to sustain us, for we are all connected."

"'Tis a fine belief, but I fear our people do not share it," Allie murmured.

"This is true," he replied, fixing her with his keen gaze. "Where your people come, the land is changed. Trees fall to the axe; rivers are dammed for the mills and the salmon cannot spawn; land is plowed and planted season after season with the same crop, until the soil is weak; even the marsh grass is taken to feed your animals. The *Iglismoniak* claim ever more of our ancestors' land for themselves; then turn it to barrens. Tell me, why do ye not honor these gifts?"

Mary and Allie exchanged a look. There was no good response to this question. Mary answered with the truth.

"I fear we are a greedy people, *Williani*. Wisdom does not make a man rich, and the English seek riches above all else. The trees, the fish, the furs of animals are all in great demand across the ocean and can be exchanged for much coin."

The *sôgmô* shook his head sadly. "I do not understand this hunger for coin."

"In our country across the sea 'tis necessary, for it is used to purchase all we need to live—clothing, food, dwellings—all can be had with coin. Nothing of moment can be accomplished there without it," Mary explained.

"And yet there are people like your Fox leader. Does he crave coin also?"

"No." Mary answered, "He seeks only to do God's Will and help others to find the Light Within, but I fear he is rare among us."

The big man gazed at Mary impressed by her honesty. Spiritual awareness emanated from him, and a wordless communication passed between them.

"The Great Spirit has touched you, Mary Tomkins. It shines from your eyes," he said.

"And thee as well, *Williani*," Mary answered, galvanized by the connection.

"What is your story?" he asked softly.

Mary looked down at her lap. She wondered where to begin and closed her eyes briefly, willing the right words to come. He waited patiently, watching her.

"Before we became convinced," she began with a nod towards Allie, "I was dissatisfied with my lot. I was proud and vain. I thought I was smarter than everyone except my father, who taught me near everything I know—Allie as well, for we grew up together. She is like a sister to me." The two friends exchanged a smile. "Among the English, women are not considered capable of intellectual thought and are usually denied an education beyond basic reading and figuring. We are expected to marry, bear children, and keep a house. We own nothing and belong to our husbands. We are disparaged, if we try to do otherwise. The Society of Friends is the only exception, for it holds that women are spiritually equal to men, since That of God exists in all people. Serving God and awakening the Light in others is a matter of great import—greater to us than birthing children or keeping a house. We work to alleviate suffering, stand against injustice, and make a difference in the world by helping others. I found my calling and lost my vanity."

The *sôgmô* repeated this for his sister, who gazed at Mary as he spoke. Then *Tolotti* responded, and he translated.

"My sister says that among the People women are respected. Their words carry weight. Some become elders, as she is, and participate in tribal decisions. Although she understands your purpose and agrees it is of import, she does not understand why you cannot do both. She asks why you deny yourself the comfort of a husband and the joy of children. She wonders who will care for you in your old age."

"Mayhap 'tis possible for thy people to do both," Mary allowed, "but if we were to marry, we would not be free to continue our missionary work. A wife becomes the property of her husband and serves him in all things. We would be expected to obey our husbands and be confined to house and children. We would be forced to abandon our mission, but it is an imperative that we cannot ignore. There is joy and love in the Light and in helping others. As to who will care for us, we trust that God will provide."

"You make a great sacrifice," he commented gravely.

"We reap a great gain," Allie replied.

He grunted then spoke to his sister, relating Mary's explanation. *Tolotti* sniffed and threw another branch on the smoldering fire without comment. Her brother was silent for several long moments; then he spoke.

"I too have felt this 'calling,' as you say it. I felt the presence of the Great Spirit even as a boy, but I did not realize this was special until I reached nine or ten summers. As I grew, my power increased, and I believed I was superior. *Ktsi Niwaskw* touched my spirit, and the knowledge came through me. The People believed I made strong medicine, that I could call storms at will. I was both healer and destroyer—feared and respected. I was chosen *Ktsi Sôgmô*, Great Chief, of all *Wôbanakiak* tribes from *Malamak Sibo* (the Merrimack River) to *Kennebec Sibo*. I was proud and vain, like you."

He paused, watching his sister nudge unburnt sticks into the fire. The smoke rose in the hot, still air, and no one spoke for a time. Mary kept silent, hoping *Williani* would go on. He did.

"One day a runner came to our camp from the south. *Massassoit* was besieged by *Iglismoniak*. They were settling at Pawtuxet on tribal land. The People had fled inland during the Great Dying to escape the sickness. It was not so hungry away from the coast. Because the land had been cleared by the People, the strangers deemed it a good place to build. They were going back and forth from their ship many times, unloading supplies. *Massassoit* entreated me to bring a great storm upon them and sink their boats. He thought to drive them from his land forever."

The big man sighed and shook his head.

"'Twas long ago now. *Iglismôniak* had been fishing the northern waters for many seasons, but I had only seen them from a distance. My pride swelled, when I was asked to help our brothers to the south, and I went quickly, eager to demonstrate my power, certain of success. I took two of our strongest medicine men. We were young and strong. We made the trip overland, running, in two days. When *Massassoit* showed me the place, the *Iglismoniak* had begun to build their shelters of wood.

"We withdrew to a place of power to pray and fast. Then we returned and stood upon the shore out of sight. The sun rose from the sea. We joined our power and called to *Ktsi Niwaskw* and the spirits of wind and water to send a tempest to drive the strangers from our land."

He stopped and stared down at his hands then looked up.

"Nothing happened. We sang. We chanted. We prayed all that day and through the hours of darkness. By dawn the others gave up. I too was spent, but I refused to accept defeat. I had never known it, and I kept on. Another day and night passed, calm and clear. When the sun rose on the third day, and there was still no sign of a storm, I was forced to admit that I had failed."

The missionaries were transfixed. This was an unflattering truth that Mary was humbled to hear.

"I returned inland exhausted and alone to the village of *Massassoit* and asked that a sweat lodge be prepared. I feared *Ktsi Niwaskw* had abandoned me. I would sweat and pray and fast until a course was revealed.

"In the sweat lodge, it came at last. The message was clear. 'Ye cannot stop the *Iglismoniak*. They are as numerous as the leaves in the forest. If you make war on them, the People shall be destroyed.'

"Since that day, I counsel peace in all dealings with the English. As long as I live, no Penacook shall raise a hand against them. In return they have taken prime coastal land, occupying seasonal camps we have used for generations. Their fences and settlements change the habits of the game, affecting our source of food. I myself have been forced to plead with the English magistrates at Boston for the release of my son and his family, who were falsely arrested. Now I must petition the Governor to permit me to keep my island in the Merrimack, so that I have a place to die in peace. The English consume the land as sand drinks water. More come with each passing of the moon, and the promise of our hunting and fishing rights is forgotten. Still I counsel peace."

Mary could not speak. She understood the concept of loving thine enemy, but this wise, spiritually powerful man was suffering abuse and contempt at the hands of the English—the very people he had sworn to protect. Her countrymen's callous greed shamed her.

"The tribes to the south and west do not agree with me," the chief continued. "Some in mine own family protest, but better to bear their anger than leave the path so clearly shown to me by *Ktsi Niwaskw*. The People will die, if we resist. This I know. So, when you speak of this 'calling,' I understand," he said, meeting their eyes.

Mary was deeply moved. *Williani* was answering a call himself. How brave to stand for peace against the greed of the colonists and censure from his own people! Had he succeeded in his original purpose, would the English have survived here? He was truly God's instrument.

Once she could speak, Mary said, "*Williani*, I am grateful for thy understanding of our calling, but I am humbled by thy story and know not how to answer for my people."

She paused, gathering her thoughts.

"The Friends' mission is to fight injustice against any folk, for we are all God's children, but our weapons are words. We wish our enemies no harm. We only seek to worship as we please in peace. I fear we have made an enemy in Dover—the Puritan minister, John Reyner. We are warned not to return there, else we shall suffer."

*Williani* closed his eyes. Mary thought he might have drifted off to sleep, but when he opened them again, his gaze was disconcertingly intense.

"Tell me," he said. "Why do *Iglismoniak* treat their people so harshly? They fashion tools for the sole purpose of inflicting pain and humiliation. The prisons, the stocks, the whipping posts are in every village. You draw more blood from your own than any enemy, yet John Eliot told us the Christian God and His Son Jesus counsel love. Explain this to me, Mary Tomkins, for I do not understand."

He did not raise his voice, but his tone was urgent. For the first time Mary realized how the English system of punishment must look to one not brought up with it. He was not even aware of the dungeons of England, she thought with a shudder. Who were the "salvages" in truth?

"Their brutality is rooted in fear," Mary answered. "They believe one person's transgression will bring God's wrath down on everyone, unless it is publicly punished. The Friends are heretics in their view, inviting holy retribution, if unchecked. Also allowing women to preach is a sin in their sight. Indeed many of our beliefs threaten their theocracy—the ministers, the churches, the freeman system. They fear equality would bring chaos, and they would lose their power."

The big man considered these points, nodding gravely. He translated for *Tolotti* then went on.

"Among the People power passes from father to son and mother to daughter, but a wise leader listens to everyone. During my years as *sôgmô*, I found the counsel of women addressed the welfare of the families, while the counsel of men—especially the young ones—clamored for action to increase their glory as warriors. The women are wiser."

He summed up this observation for *Tolotti*, who snorted and replied with few words. Her brother laughed outright and passed along her retort.

"My sister says, 'and this surprises you?'"

# *Chapter 21*

## RICHARD WALDERNE *A HUSBAND'S RIGHTS*

1640-1641 Bristol/Northam, New Hampshire Colony

Paul was born at the end of May 1640. At first, Richard was pleased and proud to have fathered a son, but he soon became impatient with his wife's apparent obsession with the infant. Any sign of indulgence must be nipped in the bud, lest his family mirror Will's. When Paul was one week old, he asserted certain dictums concerning his son's care. Prudence was still confined to the bed in the birthing room. Her husband did not come to her bedside but stood stiffly in the doorway of the small, windowless room and informed her that he would tolerate no cradle in their bed chamber.

"That is why we have a nursery. I cannot have a squalling babe waking me at all hours of the night. The work I am doing is too important," he intoned. Prudence pressed her lips together stifling a protest. She knew better than to suggest that she sleep in the nursery with the baby.

Paul had been feeding and was asleep at her breast. He seemed healthy, but he was barely a week old. The new mother was loath to put him down, let alone have the baby out of her sight. A drop of milk hung from her nipple. She saw Richard staring at it, when she looked up. He averted his eyes, his face flushing.

"Cover yourself, wife," he grumbled.

Prudence pulled the nightdress over her breast.

"And *that* shall have to stop," he stated flatly. "You are not a cow. We shall procure a wet nurse. Certes, there is some—"

"What do you mean, Richard!?" she gasped then berated herself for the outburst—too late.

Her husband glared. "Do you question me, woman?" he asked coldly. "I have been discommoded these many months. 'Tis long enough. Your place is in our bed. I shall not permit an infant to dictate circumstances in mine own house! You are my wife, and you shall obey. Any wet nurse can feed him, but only you can fulfill your duty to me."

His face was stony, unmoved by her distress. He had never spoken to her like this. She was stricken by his ruthless tone. Where was the impassioned lover and confidant? Then realization dawned, and Prudence understood. For months her pregnancy had curbed their nights of pleasure, eventually preventing them entirely, and even after the birth, her confinement still kept her from their bed. Paul commanded all her attention, and in her husband's view, all her love. Richard was jealous.

Prudence suppressed her tears and groped for the words to change his mind. She must appear obedient and reassure him. That done, she might yet convince him on the point of nursing Paul. Certes she could not bear to watch another woman give her firstborn the breast.

"As you say, husband," she began meekly, placing the sleeping infant carefully to one side. "I am yours to command and shall obey with good cheer. Please do not be angry with me."

Richard stood stiffly by the door, and Prudence leaned toward him, holding out her hands. The top of her nightdress fell open again, revealing her bosom, if he looked down.

Richard looked down, and his eyes registered the effect. Prudence saw him swallow, as he gazed at her breasts, heavy with mother's milk. After a moment's hesitation he stepped forward and took her hands, his eyes moving to her face. She must tread a line between seduction and acquiescence.

"Dearest husband, you know I love you more than life! I live to please you, and that shall never change." Richard's eyes softened. Prudence kissed a callused palm and guided it to her breast. He squeezed reflexively, and his young wife caressed his cheek, still talking. "I am honored to bear your sons. I pray God will give us many more, but you, and only you, are my Lord and Master, my first concern and my true love. I wish our son to grow strong and hardy like his father, and there is nothing better for a weakling babe than the milk of his own mother. God has blessed me with this sustenance for our son. Would it not be wasteful to pay good coin for what I have in abundance, freely given by God?"

Prudence held her breath, while her husband looked into her eyes, his hand absently kneading her breast. She kept her face still, while he considered. Slowly he bent and brought his lips to hers, kissing her long and lingeringly, her breast still cupped in his palm. She could not suppress a shiver of pleasure. She did not try. He straightened and withdrew his hand, looking down. Breast milk was smeared across his palm. He looked at it wonderingly.

"Mayhap 'tis a gift from God," he mused. She handed him the flannel from her shoulder, and he wiped his hand. "You may feed him yourself then." She nodded soberly, masking her relief. "But henceforth he stays in the nursery, and you are to sleep in our bed tonight," he finished.

Her head snapped up, and Prudence put a hand to her throat. "Tonight! But, husband, I cannot—"

"Do you gainsay me, wife?" he asked, raising his eyebrows. His tone was dangerously light. Prudence shook her head submissively and looked down. "I thought not," he said satisfied. "I know what you can and cannot do, Prudence," he added, his voice husky.

Richard was recalling the conversation with Will the day before, while Barbara was visiting Pru and the baby. True to form, his brother coaxed him to confide how "things" were going, since the birth. On hearing of Richard's mounting frustration, he had imparted some practical advice about alternative methods of pleasure *postpartum*. Now standing over his young wife, Richard raised her chin, forcing her to look up at him. He smiled faintly.

"When I return home tonight, you shall be bathed, coiffed, and dressed in proper attire to dine with me at table. We shall enjoy a fine meal, after which we shall repair to our bedchamber." Prudence drew breath to speak, but her husband squeezed her chin, silencing her. "I shall not harm you, wife," he said, the steel returning to his tone. "In fact I shall hardly touch you." He loosened his grip and caressed her cheek, her neck, her breast. "'Tis you who shall pleasure me."

The year began peaceably in Bristol. Underhill assumed leadership, securing the appointment of President of the Court in the May election of 1639, and Hanserd Knollys presided over the log meeting house. By the time the newlyweds had arrived from England, the Puritans' inner circle held the reins of power in Bristol, as they had in Thomas Wiggin's day.

However, soon after Underhill's election, complaints surfaced. He was knocking on people's doors, using his position to solicit signatures for a document that called for the entire Piscataqua Region to come under the jurisdiction of the Bay Colony. Will reported the crowd at the ordinary was outraged. His friends claimed that some of the signees were not even landowners. Rumor had it that Underhill was corresponding with Governor Winthrop in secret, encouraging him to assimilate the northern settlements.

Richard was surprised. Upon his arrival at Bristol, Underhill spoke bitterly of the Bay Colony authorities that had disarmed and banished him. Why was he now coercing folk to submit to the very government he professed to oppose? The implied subterfuge disturbed the men of Wiggins' inner circle, but Richard suspected the former Captain of the Boston militia was tiring of life in the wilderness and missed his old post in the capital. He was likely aiming to regain Winthrop's good opinion by delivering the region into his hands. Whatever the case, after a year as the temporal leader of Bristol, it cost Underhill the election the next year.

In May of 1640 Thomas Roberts was elected President of the Court. Richard was barely acquainted with him. He knew Roberts was one of the original pioneers with the Hilton brothers and was married to their sister Rebecca. They had a fine farm, a growing family, and Roberts was a personable fellow. Everyone liked him, but he was an Anglican. Richard did not trust him. The Roberts Family's attendance at the First Church was sporadic. The balance of power in Bristol was shifting yet again.

Richard wished he could talk to his mentor about Underhill, but the Wiggins had left the log manse on Captain's Hill and moved to a farm with larger acreage on the east shore of Great Bay. The Wiggins had become close friends with the Wheelwrights, ever since the banished minister had stayed with them. Now the captain and his family attended services at Exeter, the fledgling settlement established by Wheelwright and his followers.

Bristol was not the same without the Wiggins. However, Richard was too busy to brood over the loss of his mentor. The trading post opened that summer, and he spent every waking moment overseeing its operation. The Indians had come around soon after the clearing commenced, and Richard had encouraged them. Before it was even finished, he was trading spirits, sugar, iron pots, and tools for valuable furs. He sold the cured hides for five times what he paid the ignorant salvages. His wealth was increasing, and with it the scope of his plans. His thoughts turned to the construction of a sawmill on the lower falls of the Cocheco. He needed a workable plan and an experienced builder to make the concept a reality, but they were hard to find.

The addition of a baby to the household was more disruptive than Richard had ever imagined. Although Prudence was back in their bed, his infant son still claimed most of her attention. She rose at all hours of the night in response to his bawling. She seemed incapable of ignoring the babe's demands. Richard would not countenance it.

When she rose, she woke him, disturbing his sleep. In a preemptive move he instructed Missus Cameron to hire a nanny, which she did with customary efficiency. Richard never suspected that Eleanor included her young mistress in the interviews, and the women soon agreed on a choice.

Bridget Cole was a widow whose only babe died at birth. One tragedy followed another, for soon after, word came that her fisherman husband was lost off the coast of Newfoundland— literally lost. The boat was found adrift, but there was no sign of the crew. The authorities determined pirates from Africa's north coast had taken them. Marauding bands of white slavers were feared above all other pirates for they wanted the men, not the cargo. Everyone knew of the tragedy at Baltimore, a village on the coast of County Cork in Ireland. The entire town—men, women and children—were taken to be sold as slaves in Morocco or Algiers. Bridget prayed that her Rob died fighting and was not now chained to an oar and plying the waters of the Mediterranean until he died of exhaustion and malnourishment. Bridget had no other family in New England, unlike Missus Cameron, whose brother had taken her in. Life was not kind to a young woman alone, and Bridget had no inclination to remarry. Employment in the Walderne household would save her from penury or a marriage of convenience.

Prudence brought Paul downstairs to test the young woman. He was nearly three weeks old and able to focus now. She watched her infant son's reaction to the prospective nanny carefully. He was fussy, being wakened from a nap, but Bridget soothed him in short order. She rocked him gently where she stood, humming softly. He quieted and gazed up at her. It was evident that Bridget doted on the babe, and more important to Prudence, Paul responded to her. The young mistress exchanged a glance with Missus Cameron, and they both nodded.

"When can ye start, Missus Cole?" the housekeeper asked briskly.

"Oh!" the woman's heart-shaped face flushed. "Am I hired then?"

The women nodded, and tears of relief welled in Bridget's eyes. She looked down at Paul and smiled radiantly. He gurgled in response.

"Oh! My thanks, Mistress! I thank you, ma'am!" She bobbed a quick curtsy to each of them, mindful of the babe in her arms. "Ye might call me Bridget, and it please you," she added shyly.

The new nanny slept in the nursery, so Prudence need not attend Paul when he cried at night. If he was hungry, Bridget soothed him with a flannel soaked in warm goat's milk, honey, and a dash of rum (Barbara's recipe). Richard was mollified.

Will's suggestions also proved sound. Richard instructed Prudence in pleasuring him with her hands and some scented oil. It aroused him to see her kneel before him, intent only on his pleasure. The new father found the alternative gratifying, if not fruitful. Abstinence was not an option he cared to contemplate now his considerable libido was satisfied on a regular basis. Pru was reluctant at first, but he insisted, and she complied. It was a good lesson for her to submit to his will, as any obedient wife must. Will's advice was put to frequent use, until his young wife's confinement ended, and even occasionally after, when her husband had had a trying day.

# *Chapter 22*

## MARY AND ALICE *CELEBRATION*

Summer 1662 Kittery Point, Province of Maine

The morning of the celebration was overcast, but the clouds burned off as the sun climbed. The air was humid, and the temperature increased steadily. Jackets were shed and sleeves rolled up, as preparations continued. Kittery Point bustled with activity, centering on the field by the ordinary. Trestle tables were set up, and kegs of ale and cider were brought from the brew house and tapped. Various small craft, wagons, and foot traffic began arriving before noon.

The fragrance of roasting pork taunted the workers for it had been cooking since sunrise. It had taken four men to skewer the carcass on the iron spit and position it over the pit of coals. Johnny chose a fresh team of boys to turn the spit and tend the fire, since the first group had been up all night. The pig would roast slowly throughout the day.

The missionaries joined their Indian friends as soon as they had broken their fast. They helped the women dig a shallow pit in a rare sandy patch among the rocks above the high tide line and were then enlisted to help collect wood. By custom the Penacook women owned the fire. Although she did not speak English, *Tolotti* was eloquent in sign language. She shook her head disparagingly at the missionaries' restrictive clothing and indicated they remove their shoes and stockings and tuck their skirts into their waistbands. At low tide the entire band took baskets and set off to forage for seafood—a family activity among the *Wobanakiak*. Mary and Allie learned how to find mussels under the seaweed, clinging to the rocks exposed at low tide. Clams gave themselves away by the air holes that bubbled up in the wet sand. Most impressive were the bizarre creatures called *sàga* (lobster) they found stranded in tidal pools on the rocky shore.

The missionaries thoroughly enjoyed clambering over the slippery rocks and wading through the pools with their new friends in the heat of the day. They returned with loaded baskets—sandy, wet, and laughing. The harvest was cooked over glowing coals between layers of seaweed in the pit they had dug.

It was a perfect day in mid-August, hot enough for folk to complain vociferously, while inwardly reveling in summer's warmth. Throughout the day people arrived, spread out quilts and blankets, helped with preparations, and conversed with each other. They sampled the kegs and the burgeoning feast, for everyone brought their best recipes or the fruits of their labors including wheels of cheese, pies both sweet and savory, puddings, cold pease porridge, baskets of cherries and blackberries, fresh breads, cold roast chickens, pickled vegetables, and a variety of stews and soups. The planks of the trestle tables bowed under the weight. By the time the sun was lowering, the crowd numbered close to a hundred.

The heat made everyone thirsty. Small beer, ale, and cider flowed freely. As the afternoon heat abated a little, the Penacook men and some young colonists engaged in a lively game involving a leather ball and two goals marked out with empty kegs. Johnny was among them. Mary and Allie sat in the shade with their new friends, cheering them on. As the spectators increased, the players responded with increasingly daring moves, until an especially hard kick sent the ball into Back Cove. The competitors chased after it en masse, shouting and laughing, as they splashed into the water. The game dissolved in good-natured tussling. Dunking each other proved more refreshing and just as much fun as chasing the ball around the field. The game brought the colonists and the Indians together as no amount of halting conversation could.

As the sun sank below the horizon, a breeze sprang up to everyone's relief. The sounds of fiddles and pipes being tuned lent a festive atmosphere to the gathering. There would be contra-dancing soon, when the twilight deepened and it cooled a bit more. Let the Dover Puritans frown, if they would. This was Kittery, where folk enjoyed music and dancing.

After roasting for fifteen hours, the pig was ready to be carved. The aroma had teased the revelers all afternoon, and everyone was eager to partake of the moist, flavorful meat. Appetites returned, as the heat abated.

Nonetheless Mary's favorite food of the day was the fare the native women prepared. The clams and mussels were delicious and easy to slurp from their shells, but *Tolotti* insisted they try the *sàga*. The missionaries were baffled by the bright red monsters with their impressive claws and hard shells. The Indians found their tentative attempts to breach them hilarious, until the elder took pity on them and demonstrated the process.

After eating their fill of the rich, white meat, the barefoot missionaries tucked up their skirts and waded into the water with their new friends to rinse their hands and cool off. They were soon splashing each other like children. The drops made arcs of silver in the gloaming. Mary and Allie enjoyed the informal ease and unexpected humor of the Indians. They were flattered to be included in their warm camaraderie.

It was full dark by the time the last of the food was consumed. Nicholas and Johnny enlisted help in lighting the torches set in a wide circle around the area marked out for dancing. The musicians sat on rough benches in the middle of the field—two fiddles, a concertina, and three fifes of varying sizes.

The Indians watched with bemused interest as the colonists formed up and followed the caller's singsong lead. Mary and Allie attempted to demonstrate some of the steps, but their new friends were overcome by such gales of mirth, watching each other's clumsy attempts, that the missionaries soon gave up, overcome by laughter as well. *Williani* and his sister witnessed the fiasco and were not immune to the infectious humor. *Tolotti* wiped tears from her cheeks, as her brother held his aching ribs and begged them to stop.

At length the musicians and dancers wound down and mugs were topped. The moon had risen out of the sea and cast a glittering path of silver on its surface. When the colonists' instruments were put away, *Williani* nodded to the men sitting near him. They responded efficiently. Two repositioned the benches, while two more carried the ceremonial drum to the center of the field. They were preceded by another who set up the custom-made frame in which it would rest. The drum was massive, measuring nearly three feet in diameter. The skin was secured with strips of rawhide and decorated sparingly with feathers woven into the thongs. The base was a tawny-colored wood with a distinctive grain. The men carried it carefully, positioning it with reverence. *Williani* and three of the elder Penacook men took their positions with synchronized dignity. Each held a drumstick padded with deerskin.

The curious colonists gathered around. Most had never seen the Indians dance. On a signal from their chief, the four beaters made the drum speak, claiming everyone's attention. The sound was powerful, deep, and rhythmic as a heartbeat. It resonated through the ground and carried across the water. Mary could feel its vibration in her feet and chest.

Eleven native men began to dance around the drummers. There was a definitive pattern to their movements, but it was unlike anything the English had ever seen. The dancers seemed to increase in number as their movements became more energetic. They leapt and whirled, now crouching then leaping high in complex and singular choreography. Some held gourds filled with dried beans, shaking them in time to the drumbeat. It was primal and compelling, and their audience watched fascinated.

The first dance ended, and the colonists demonstrated their approval, clapping their hands and stamping the ground. They wanted more. *Tolotti* stood up and took each of the missionaries by the hand, leading them out into the field with the other Penacook women. She demonstrated a simple step—one pace left, three in place, one pace left, three in place. THUMP, thump-thump-thump. THUMP, thump-thump-thump. Alice Shapleigh and Penelope Treworgy joined them, then Meggie and Elizabeth, and soon more of the colonial women were part of the circle. The men formed a second ring around theirs, repeating the step but moving in the opposite direction. Although simple to execute, the effect was thrilling.

When Mary felt able to look up from her feet, she saw that the men's circle now included many colonists too. After some initial hilarity, concentration deepened among the participants. Dancers and drummers were linked by sound and rhythm. The experience was compellingly inclusive. Mary realized that the Indians were not just dancing; they were creating a religious experience, connecting with each other and the Great Spirit through the beat of the sacred drum. Surely the Creator smiled upon this expression of communal joy and devotion!

The truth of it smote her like a revelation. What matter if different names were used? The Puritan God, the God of the Friends, and *Ktsi Niwaskw* were all One! The limitations of language or race did not affect His reach and power. They were all His children. Her eyes prickled with tears of joy, and she locked eyes with *Williani*. He nodded once, as though he shared her thought.

# Chapter 23

## RICHARD WALDERNE *CONFRONTATION*

1640-1641 Bristol/Northam, New Hampshire Colony

The relative calm following Thomas Roberts' election as President of the Court was threatened that summer of 1640 by the arrival of a dynamic and ambitious minister fresh from England. His name was Thomas Larkham, and he appeared to be a bachelor, although he was near forty. No one had invited him, but he was both eloquent and comely, and the isolated community accepted him readily. Boston did not suit him, he said, although he offered no specifics. He settled in quickly, leasing Thomas Wiggin's vacant manse on Captain's Hill and purchasing several shares in the patent for the Piscataqua Region. Richard surmised that the clergyman had some means at his disposal.

At first the Reverend Knollys welcomed the younger clergyman cordially and invited him to preach, upon occasion, during the afternoon service. In retrospect, Richard realized that Hanserd had initiated his own demise by this hospitable gesture, although at the time it had seemed mete to all but Hatevil Nutter, who grumbled at being displaced.

In autumn Thomas Roberts initiated his first definitive action as President of the Court by approving a Combination to be signed by the freemen of the colony. It was the second attempt to organize the frontier government, as Burdett's document had been eschewed, after his demise by dalliance. As a Royalist and Anglican, Roberts wished to reaffirm the colony's obedience to the King's law. Every landholder on the Point, as well as a few from its environs, signed it. However, the Combination also sparked the ambition of Bristol's newest cleric.

The first warning sign was Larkham's precipitous rise in popularity. The Puritans underestimated the new minister's influence, until he successfully instigated a vote at the weekly meeting to change the town's name from Bristol to Northam, from whence he came. Larkham did not stop there. Soon after the majority of the freemen asserted their preference for the newcomer in the pulpit of the First Church. With good grace Knollys gave way to popular opinion—initially.

The Puritans realized their mistake too late. Knollys was their man, upholding the tenets they held dear, including approved membership, baptism for adults, and avoidance of any rite based in the Anglican tradition, such as presiding over funerals or weddings.

In contrast Larkham received any who professed faith in God and a willingness to repent their sins, member or not. He performed funeral rites and baptized infants and children, even signing the cross over their heads—a blatant gesture of popery. An alarming number of the congregation embraced these throwbacks to the Anglican Church. All winter the Puritans suffered in silence, believing the popish excesses temporary, for was Knollys not their ordained minister?

In addition to preferring Larkham's preaching, his supporters resented Underhill's attempt to coerce them to join the Bay Colony. In fact a majority of Northam's citizens prized their independence and opposed assimilation. They considered Underhill a turncoat and did not trust him. Puritans that might have supported Knollys did not, because he was Underhill's man. There was a political divide among the townsfolk, as well as a religious one.

As President of the Court Thomas Roberts did nothing to curb Larkham. In fact the Roberts Family attended services more regularly than when Knollys was preaching. Like many families on the Neck they were in accord with the newcomer. No one seemed to remember George Burdett, but Richard thought Larkham was cut from the same cloth. The man's sudden rise in popularity was ominous. The young Puritan recognized unbridled ambition when he saw it.

The Puritans feared for their newly established First Church. In March they marked the advent of 1641 at a dinner hosted by the Underhills, but the mood of the gathering was far from celebratory. Larkham was flouting the tenets of the First Church, and the town could not support two churches and two ministers. A point of crisis was approaching.

"'Twill be a return to the Book of Common Prayer next, mark my words," Knollys intoned.

His friends shuddered at this prophetic statement. All devout Puritans knew of the Elder William Brewster's bold action, throwing the offending symbol of popery into the sea as the *Mayflower* sailed from England twenty years before. Was that sterling act of defiance to be undone by this upstart? Had they not left England to escape the Anglican yoke?

"Hanserd, you have been more than lenient with Larkham," Captain Underhill said, "but I fear he goes too far. You must assert your position as Bristol's ordained minister."

Will loosed a bray of laughter, startling them all. "Yes, we beg you quash this farce forthwith, Reverend, or you shall be the shepherd of 'Northam'!"

This provoked nervous chuckles from all but Knollys, who was not amused by this evidence of Larkham's popularity. The solution was obvious to Richard. Why even discuss it? He spoke for the first time.

"Excommunicate him," he said, when the laughter quieted.

Hanserd's chin dropped, and he stared at Richard with wide eyes. The young man was becoming impatient with his elders. Talk would gain nothing. It was time to act.

"As Captain Underhill says, you are the supreme authority in Bristol's First Church, Reverend Knollys," Richard went on, ignoring the shocked silence. "Larkham ignores our tenets and preaches like an Anglican. The benches are crowded with nonmembers. He should be excommunicated. Take up the reins, sir, and curb this runaway steed."

The minister looked to Underhill, and all eyes followed. The Captain and former leader of the colony slowly nodded his head, but his eyes were appraising Richard.

Hanserd Knollys bided his time and waited until Larkham overreached himself. The congregation's support went to his head and inspired the rogue reverend to fine George Walton for selling strong spirits without the required license. This was within a minister's right, but technically Larkham was not Bristol's—or rather Northam's—shepherd. Former ministers had heretofore turned a blind eye in deference to the local economy. Larkham was ignorant of this arrangement. It was his first unpopular decision, as well as a breach of Knolly's authority. Walton's was the only publick house on the Point, although Emery's ordinary would soon open its doors. People did not approve this high-handed action against their friend and neighbor—and only source of hard liquor. It was a chink in the armor of Larkham's popularity, and Hanserd was encouraged to make his move.

The confrontation took place on the last Sabbath Day of March 1641. Hanserd was emboldened by the company of his Puritan friends, as people gathered for the service. He was flanked by Underhill and Nutter, whose families watched from a few feet away. The Walderne's home was within easy walking distance of the log church, and Richard arrived with Prudence on his arm and Bridget carrying Paul, now ten months old.

"Mr. Larkham, 'tis I who first permitted you to speak as a guest here," Knollys was saying as the Waldernes arrived. "You have overstayed your welcome, sir. We insist that you be on your way." The reverend spoke loudly, but he was calm.

Larkham glanced around for support. James Nute and Edward Starbuck came to his side, and it bolstered his confidence.

"How now?" he asked mildly. "I have prepared a sermon, and these folk have come to hear it."

The onlookers murmured among themselves, and the volume rose, as those arriving put questions to those present. People unconsciously joined friends and family, and two distinct groups began to form in front of the meeting house.

"I am the ordained minister in this town." Hanserd replied, raising his voice above the hub bub. "You, Thomas Larkham, are henceforth banned from the pulpit, sir!" His face reddened.

"But the congregation prefers my sermons over yours, Mister Knollys. Would you ignore their good opinion?" Larkham asked, raising his eyebrows.

Richard felt Pru's gloved hand pressing his, and he looked down at her.

"Husband, I am frightened," she whispered leaning into his side. "No good can come of this."

He gently shushed her. She was right, of course, but he was eager to see how this would fall out. Bridget sidled closer to her employers, clutching Paul so tightly he squawked in protest.

Knollys ignored the slight to his popularity and spoke as though in the pulpit.

"Thomas Larkham, by the authority vested in me as ordained minister of the First Church of *Bristol*, you are banned from membership and are henceforth excommunicated."

There was a moment of stunned silence. Even the glib reverend was unable to find his tongue. It did not last.

Without another word Larkham bore down upon his would-be nemesis. Knollys flinched, expecting a blow. A few women cried out, and Prudence hid her face against her husband's arm. Underhill tensed, and Richard saw his hand go to his sword hilt, but Larkham only snatched the hat from Hanserd's head and walked away, holding it aloft.

"Has this been paid for?" The interloper shone with righteous indignation. He turned in a circle. All eyes were upon him. "I think not!" He turned back to Knollys, who was visibly trembling, whether from fear or anger, Richard could not tell. "You pay for nothing, Mister Knollys! All your needs are provided by the people of this parish.

Your house. Your sustenance. Your clothing!" He shook the hat clenched in his fist. "And what do you give them in return, *Reverend* Knollys, eh?"

He swept his arm over his rapt audience. Larkham was a fine speaker, and now he lowered his voice instinctively, turning his back on his opponent and addressing the crowd.

"He is not worthy of that august title," he pronounced scathingly. "Does he baptize your children? Does he say words of comfort over your dead? Does he allow those in need to attend *his* church?" Heads were shaking. "What say you, good people? The choice is yours." He paused dramatically and gestured at Knollys and the Puritan contingent. "The annihilation of traditional forms and submission to the Bay Colony?" He laid his hand on his chest. "Or an open church and self-government according to our Combination?"

There was a heavy pause, followed by conflicting responses.

"Larkham!" "Self-rule!" "No to the Bay!" cried several voices.

"Knollys!" "First Church!" "Get ye gone!" others called.

The town was split.

"*Lark*ham! *Lark*ham! *Lark*ham!" the chant was taken up loud enough to dominate the scene.

Ever cool under fire, Underhill pushed Knollys and his family into the meeting house and turned, guarding the door, his hand on the hilt of his sword.

"Those with the First Church, to me!" he roared over the tumult.

Richard shepherded his little family into the cool, dark interior. He left Prudence and Bridget with Barbara and the children. Little Paul was wailing, and he was not alone. Others were pressing through the door, blocking Richard's exit. He feared for Underhill, standing guard outside alone. Then Will was at his shoulder, and the brothers pushed through to stand with the Captain and Hatevil. He need not have feared. Larkham's supporters had gathered in the lane and were leaving en masse, following their leader south down Low Street.

"Come, men," Underhill said, watching them move off still chanting. "We had best prepare for trouble." The Puritans followed him into the church, but Will put a hand on his brother's arm, stopping him.

"I reckon this is better than listening to the ministers' droning—either of 'em!" he grinned.

Normally Richard would have frowned at this sacrilegious statement, but in this instance he could not help grinning back. This was exciting! Righteous indignation fired him, and the young Puritan longed to prove himself in a confrontation.

"Take the women and children home," Underhill was saying as the brothers entered. "Those of you with military training," his eyes found Richard, "arm yourselves and meet back here."

"What is your intent, Captain?" Hatevil Nutter did not often speak, but when he did, he got to the crux of the matter.

"Our minister's order of excommunication must be enforced," Underhill answered. "We cannot allow the man to walk away. He incites rebellion! His influence in our community is pernicious. Order must be enforced by lawful means. Larkham is excommunicated and banished. He shall be escorted to the boundary of Bristol's jurisdiction, there to make his way wherever he chooses."

"What action shall be taken against his followers?" Nutter asked.

"The mob must be dispersed. They shall be ordered to their homes."

"What if they resist?" Hatevil's tone was even, but Richard saw his eyes flash. As an elder of the church his friend had the authority to punish miscreants—a prospect he appeared to relish.

"Mister Nutter," Underhill answered with flagging forbearance, "one would hope 'twill not come to that pass. However, we must be prepared should it fall out thusly."

"Shall they retain their membership in the First Church?" Nutter persisted.

"That is up to Reverend Knollys," the Captain stated with finality and strode to the door. "They have departed," he said, after peering down the empty lane. "'Tis safe at present, but take the women and children straight home," he continued as the diminished congregation filed past. "We shall meet back here. As speedily as you may, gentlemen."

# *Chapter 24*

## MARY AND ALICE *HELPMEET*

October, 1662 Kittery Point, Province of Maine

The heat of August gave way all too soon to the first signs of autumn. The days were shorter and the nights turned cool. Allie and Mary were amazed by the vibrant foliage, for nothing in England compared to it. By the second week of October, frost gilded the landscape most mornings, and they could no longer leave the house without shawl or cloak.

The pace of work increased for snow might come any day. To be caught unprepared was life-threatening. Everyone labored from dawn to dusk, harvesting, preserving, and storing both fodder for the livestock and food for themselves. Prodigious amounts of hardwood, cut and left to dry the year before, must be transported, split, and stacked at every home to feed the fires during the long winter to come. The Mercy Wagons were busier than ever.

One unusually mild afternoon in mid-October, Mary and Allie were digging the last carrots from Alice's kitchen garden.

"'Tis time we moved on, I am thinking, Allie," Mary said.

Her friend straightened. "Upriver?" she asked with customary brevity.

"Yes, Friend Nason reminded me of his invitation to come to Newichawannock. I reckon 'twould be a good place to start. We have not journeyed inland as yet. His neighbor, Thomas Spencer, offered to entertain us, since Sarah Nason is not well. Katherine's daughter, Lucy lives there too. She is wife to Humphrey Chadbourne and expecting their first child, so we have not seen her this summer, but Kat says the Chadbournes are also eager for regular meetings. In another week or two folk will not be so occupied by their labors. They will have more time to contemplate the state of their souls in the winter months."

Allie nodded and bent again to the task at hand.

"We have prevailed upon the Shapleighs' hospitality more than three months now. We ought not to wear out our welcome," Mary went on.

"Aye," Allie grunted, working an especially large carrot free.

"We have accomplished much here, but the Kittery Friends can proceed on their own now. There are others in need." Mary paused. "I dreamt of Mary Dyer last night."

Allie straightened, brushing dirt from her prize, and waited for her friend to continue.

"I was desperate to find her," Mary continued, gazing into the distance. "I sensed she was near but ever out of my sight. Then of a sudden, as happens in dreams, I was on the slope above Warehouse Point. There was a boat." She stopped, meeting her friend's eye. "Friend Wharton's *Sea Witch*."

Allie had forgotten her carrot and watched Mary steadily.

"She was with him, moving away from me out to sea. Black clouds roiled above them, a tempest building visibly, but they seemed unaware. I tried to warn them, but the wind tore the words from my mouth. I could scarce breathe, so strong it was, yet the boat moved unnaturally on against it. They did not turn, nor take any notice of me." She blinked then looked at Allie. "I woke up feeling I had failed them somehow, that both were lost forever."

Mary looked desolate. Allie stepped over the furrow of earth between them and embraced her friend, forgetting the carrot still clasped in her hand. It bumped against Mary's shoulder, shedding dirt on her sleeve. It made them laugh and dispelled the dark mood of the dream.

"'Tis time we took up Friend Nason's invitation, then," Allie said, brushing dirt from her friend's dress.

The two missionaries left their full baskets in the kitchen house and returned to the manor. Alice Shapleigh had news. There was a letter from Edward Wharton. Mary and Allie exchanged a glance at the mention of his name. It seemed a portent they had just been speaking of him.

Friend Wharton planned to return to Kittery Point within a week. He was bringing a missionary Friend named Anne Coleman, recently arrived from England. They had met at the end of September while the Salem Friend was on a mission at Taunton in the Plymouth Colony. Friend Coleman was eager to join them, for she knew of the two missionaries from her own training at Swarthmore Hall. Friend Wharton was bringing her to Kittery, and they would arrive in a matter of days.

Mary and Allie took their leave as soon as courtesy allowed, excusing themselves to wash for dinner. They needed to discuss this new development privily.

"What dost thou make of this?" Mary asked, as soon as the door to their room closed.

Allie considered, as she poured water into the hand basin and picked up the lump of soap. She lathered her hands and began to clean the garden dirt from under her nails.

"I think we must wait for Friend Coleman before we leave," she said.

"'Twould be rude not to, since we have word of her coming," Mary agreed reluctantly, sinking onto the bed. "But Edward should not—" She broke off, took a breath, and continued more calmly. "Dost thou not think it presumptuous? Friend Wharton did not even consult with us!" She stood then sat again abruptly. "I feel such an urgency to be on our way!"

Allie was surprised by Mary's reaction. She thought it likely had more to do with Edward Wharton than the new missionary. She did not turn but asked gently, "To answer our calling or to avoid Friend Wharton?"

Mary opened her mouth to protest, then flopped back on the bed.

"Aaahhh!" she exclaimed, frustrated by her conflicting emotions. Allie was the only person to whom she could express them. She was angry with Edward for presuming to include this stranger in their plans, but the prospect of seeing him again quickened her pulse. She sought refuge in a familiar emotion—impatience. Mary sighed. "Thou knowest me too well, Allie," she said quietly to the ceiling.

"There is no gain in dodging thy feelings, Mimi," her friend reasoned, softening this statement by using Mary's nickname. She turned, drying her hands on a flannel. "'Twould be a blessing to know thy reaction at seeing him again, one way or t'other, and the delay is but a matter of days." She took the basin to the window, opened it, and poured the water out. "There is some good garden dirt for you," she told the bushes below, causing Mary to smile. "Mayhap 'tis God's plan for her to join us," she suggested, returning the basin to the bureau and pouring fresh water for Mary. "Friend Coleman may be a help to our mission."

Mary stood to wash her hands, silently hoping that Allie had the right of it.

The *Sea Witch* arrived early the next week. Mary, Alice, and Allie were at the warehouse sorting donations for the Mercy Wagon when the signal cannon sounded. They abandoned their work and headed for the dock immediately.

Mary strove for calm. The summer had been so eventful she had hardly thought of Friend Wharton. Now he was here, and her heart thudded alarmingly. She despised her lack of control. Allie glanced back and seeing Mary hesitate, waited for her. Mary grasped her hand, grateful for her friend's solid grip and perceptive understanding.

It was a blustery day. The wind tore colorful leaves from the trees in droves. They whirled through the air and tumbled along the ground, chased by the shadows of rapidly moving clouds. Alice reached the top of the dock first and rang the bell. Mary and Allie joined her, tying their shawls tightly to keep the wind from taking their dust caps. Johnny approached with three workmen from the brew house, where they had been storing cider in oak barrels. Nicholas was at the sawmill.

George and Edward had reefed the sails and were rowing toward the dock, as the wind was too unpredictable to put in by sail. Mary could not see their faces, but a small figure in the stern waved. The party onshore waved back.

Within minutes, the shallop was at the dock. George stowed his oar and tossed the lines to Johnny and one of his crew, while Edward helped the new missionary to disembark.

Anne Coleman stood on the dock, dwarfed by Edward beside her. Mary was shocked. Not only was the new arrival uncommonly short, but one shoulder was disproportionately higher than the other, misshapen by a hump. Her head appeared too large for her body with a broad forehead, long chin, and heavily lidded eyes, perpetually half-closed, giving her a sleepy look. Mary stammered a polite greeting. All worries concerning Friend Wharton were eclipsed. He greeted her with a warm smile, but it faded as he took in her strained expression. Mary struggled for composure, but she was appalled. Their new traveling companion was deformed.

Friend Coleman proved a hardy sort despite her handicaps. She was an enthusiastic conversationalist and evinced no embarrassment when it became apparent she could not eat at the table without a plump cushion. Her voice was surprisingly deep for her diminutive stature, and she spoke with an educated accent. Whatever she lacked in stature, Anne Coleman made up in spirit. Over dinner that evening, she warmly expressed her gratitude to her hosts and to the Salem Friends for bringing her to Kittery. Then she turned to Mary and Allie.

"And I am so very grateful for this opportunity to join you!" she declared. "All in the Society are inspired by the executions of the missionary Friends in Boston. More make the crossing every month. Friend Fell spoke highly of you both, and ever since, I have hoped to find you. When Friend Wharton said he had made your acquaintance and offered to bring me here, my hopes were realized at last!"

Mary looked sharply at Edward, but he was intent on his plate. He had arranged this awkward circumstance, yet he would not even look at her. So be it. She would take his lead.

"Didst thou make the crossing alone?" Allie asked, impressed by the little woman's pluck.

"Oh no," Anne replied. "I came with three other missionaries, Jane Millard and her husband John Liddal, and Joseph Nicholson. We landed at Newport in the Rhode Island Colony. Have ye been there?" She leaned forward to include Mary but did not pause for a response. "Our faith thrives in Rhode Island! Friend Easton entertained us most graciously—another Nicholas," she said to her host with a smile. "He holds regular meetings in his home and a goodly number attend. His son John is most solicitous of our cause. Indeed, the community of Friends there supports the protests in the Bay Colony. They stand ready to provide refuge. They are not plagued by the authorities, as one is allowed to worship as one pleases in Rhode Island, praise the Lord."

"Thou art very brave to leave that haven," Alice Shapleigh commented.

"One is not here to seek refuge. One is called to go where there is need. The four of us journeyed up the coast to Sandwich and met Friend Wharton, who had just come from Taunton. Both towns are in the Plymouth Colony, where the authorities do not hunt us down as in the Bay, so long as Friends do not disturb the peace or interrupt worship. Many at Taunton and Sandwich are now convinced."

Anne gave Edward a dazzling smile, which he acknowledged with a solemn nod. Mary saw everyone at the table was rapt and wondered if the woman ever paused for breath. Close on the heels of this uncharitable thought, remorse smote her, and she sipped her cider. Anne went on.

"I parted company with my companions then and sailed with Friend Wharton to Salem. Have ye visited there?" Mary and Allie shook their heads, and again Anne continued enthusiastically. "There is a strong community of more than fifty Friends at Salem despite censure from the Bay Colony. So many brave souls! A number of Friends at Salem have endured persecution in the Boston prison. They are fined or flogged for their beliefs, yet their faith remains steadfast. They have a high opinion of Friend Wharton, who has shared their suffering."

"Verily, Edward?" Nicholas was amazed.

"We were not aware of that!" Alice added, as they both looked at the Salem man.

"'Tis not a subject for polite company," Edward said quietly, avoiding their eyes.

"Forgive me," Anne said quickly. "I did not realize—"

"But what of thy companions?" Mary asked. She ignored the shocked faces that turned to her at this blatant interruption, but Friend Wharton's discomfort was evident. She did not like to discuss her suffering either. Despite her irritation, she felt moved to protect him by changing the subject. She softened her question with a smile and kept her eyes on Friend Coleman.

The little missionary blinked but rallied quickly. "They answered a call to Virginia. Much good work was accomplished there in the '50s by Friend Harris, but she stayed only two years. The Society suggested our group check on the Friends there and encourage their progress."

"How brave thou art to leave their company and journey here to join us. No doubt thy friends understood," Allie commented, further ameliorating Mary's bald question.

Anne focused on her. "I have wanted to meet since Friend Fell first spoke of you," she said warmly. "Also we were four missionaries, and ye are but two. I am more useful here."

"Is there some significance to the number three?" Alice asked, grateful for the change in subject, however awkwardly it came about.

"'Tis not a rule, but the Society recommends that missionaries travel in groups. They deem it safer," Anne answered.

"Well then! We must thank George and Edward for bringing you together," Alice commented, hoping to ease the unspoken tension plaguing her table this evening.

"We are happy to oblige," George replied when Edward did not immediately respond.

After an awkward silence Nicholas cleared his throat then asked, "What vessel did you cross on, Friend Coleman?"

For the remainder of the meal their hosts held the conversational reins, and Anne responded with unflagging enthusiasm.

Edward had brought letters from England for the missionaries—a thick packet with several pages from their families and a thinner missive from Margaret Fell in response to Mary's letter sent in June. They gave her an excuse to retire early. She did not see the disappointment that flashed across Edward's face when she excused herself, but Alice Shapleigh did.

Allie joined her within an hour to respond to her parents' letter. She did not bring up Anne Coleman or the strained conversation at dinner. She was blotting the ink, when there was a soft knock at their door. Mary rose from the bed, where she had stretched out, and Allie raised her dark eyebrows.

"Do come in," Mary called, smoothing her dress.

Anne Coleman opened the door but did not enter.

"Forgive me. I do not mean to intrude," she said from the threshold.

"Thou art most welcome," Allie responded, rising from the desk and going to her. "Do join us."

"We have finished our correspondence," Mary assured her politely.

Allie closed the door, and Anne focused on Mary.

"I wish to reassure thee," she began. Mary drew a breath, but Anne held up a hand. "I beg you, permit me to speak," she said gently. "The first meeting is ever a shock to people. Mind you, I have seen the same reaction many times, and I remarked it today."

Mary blushed, and Anne smiled with genuine sympathy.

"I do not berate thee, Friend Tomkins. 'Tis customary. No doubt thou fearest that I shall slow thy progress at the very least, and that my appearance may cause discomfort or censure among people at worst. I would assuage thy doubts. Although they are short, my legs work quite well. I am capable of walking all day if necessary. As to the rest," she shrugged her misshapen shoulder and gestured at her face, "I find that my oddities ultimately work to my advantage. Folk see that I can connect with the Divine Presence, even though I am small and crooked. They think, if That of God is attainable for me, it must certes be so for them. The women in particular warm to me, for I pose no threat where their husbands are concerned. And children, bless them, are frankly fascinated at the first then become the quickest to accept me. Instructing the children is my particular strength. Please be assured that I make no idle boast, when I say that I am capable of aiding thee in thy mission. I ask only for the opportunity to prove it."

Anne's candor both impressed and shamed Mary. For once she was at a loss for words. She met the little missionary's heavy-lidded gaze.

"'Tis I who must ask for thy allowance, Friend Coleman," she said.

"Please, call me Anne."

"I beg you forgive my faulty assumptions, Anne, for they are born of ignorance," Mary answered humbly.

Allie put a hand on the little missionary's shoulder without hesitation. "And thou must call us Allie and Mary as well. I am sure thou shalt prove a helpmeet to our mission, Anne," she said.

# *Chapter 25*

## RICHARD WALDERNE *CONFLICT*

1641 Bristol/Northam, Piscataqua Region, New Hampshire Territory

"They shall come after us, unless we go after them first," Thomas Larkham warned.

His supporters had gathered at the house on Captain's Hill once their families were safe at home, and they were discussing how to proceed.

"We must take legal action, gentlemen, and that swiftly," the minister said.

"You mean to take Knollys to court, Reverend Larkham?" Edward Starbuck asked.

"I mean to take Underhill to court, Mister Starbuck. I think we all agree his conduct in soliciting signatures to submit to the Bay Colony was an unlawful use of the power of his office," the minister said, looking around.

"'Twas tantamount to conspiracy!" Starbuck asserted.

"He duped us!" Thomas Layton agreed. "The man professed one thing and did the opposite!"

"And Knollys is his man," Larkham said. "They came to the colony together, did they not?"

Several nods confirmed this.

"If we bring down Underhill, Knollys shall fall with him," Larkham concluded.

"What of Thomas Roberts?" James Nute asked tentatively. "He is President of the Court. Should he not summon Underhill?"

"This is a moment of crisis, sir, and he is not here. However, Mister Roberts supports this cause, I am sure of it. As an ordained minister I have all the authority required,"

Larkham answered, staring the man down. Nute averted his eyes. "Who is with me to serve a summons to Underhill?"

They all were.

Richard left his distraught wife and nursemaid in Missus Cameron's capable hands, ignoring Pru's tearful pleas to stay. He would not shirk his duty, besides it was the most exciting thing to happen in years. He belted on his sword, donned his military hat and gloves, and went to the meeting house. Most of the others were there except Hatevil Nutter, who arrived soon after. He had affixed a bible to the top of a halberd for a standard but carried no weapon.

"God is our sword and shield," he asserted ponderously.

Although Will was an elected Deputy of the Court, he was behaving as if the incident was a lark. True to form, his armament was a flask of brandy "for courage." Only Richard, Hatevil, and Underhill refused to partake.

Knollys had fetched his wheel lock pistol from the parsonage. Richard was impressed.

"Do you deem that necessary, Reverend Knollys?" Underhill asked uneasily.

"Verily, sir." Knollys answered stiffly. "'Twill give them pause just at sight of it, and if they become fractious, I shall fire a shot over their heads. That will cow them. We hold authority in Bristol. We must demonstrate an unshakable steadiness of purpose, methinks."

The Captain sighed, but did not argue. Turning away, he caught Richard's eye. "This is why we need the established discipline of the Bay," he commented for Richard's ears only. "A popular government falls prey to base emotion."

The young man nodded. Although he had opposed the takeover initially, his opinion had changed. There would be advantages to joining the Puritan stronghold to the south. There were investors at Boston, and he already had a connection with Governor Winthrop. Who knew where it could lead? At the very least assimilation might stop the incursion of these rogue ministers with their papist tendencies—first Burdett and now Larkham.

Aside from the pistol, there were four swords among them. The remainder of their party disparaged armament; this was a church matter, and Knollys was clearly the ordained minister, they opined. Underhill arranged their marching order. He and Knollys led the party, with Nutter's formidable bulk behind them, carrying his bible standard. It rose majestically above their heads. Richard, Pomfrett, and Damme were next with their military swords. Will and eight others filled in behind, forming three rows of three men. A small group, but impressive in their show of military order, Richard thought. It was but ten of the clock, when they began to march down the lane in the direction Larkham's group had taken.

The parsonage sat at the junction of two lanes. The larger was Low Street, leading north to the meeting house and southeast to Pomeroy Cove. The smaller lane went directly south, ending at the manse on Captain's Hill, less than a quarter of a mile from the parsonage. The two houses between belonged to John Underhill and William Pomfrett. The road was straight, though rutted. The Puritans soon saw Larkham's group advancing toward them with some twenty men in an unformulated group. As the two factions drew closer, their progress slowed. They stopped twenty paces from meeting.

Larkham spoke first, his voice shrill. "You must give way, Captain Underhill! We have a summons calling you to Court! The majority of Northam stands with me!"

"The majority is not the rule here," the Captain answered evenly. "You are not the law, Larkham. Reverend Knollys is the ordained minister in Bristol, and I—" he faltered, remembering he was no longer in office, "—and we have William Walderne here, who is Deputy of the Court. You must give way to Mister Knollys' decree of excommunication."

"As you would have us submit to the Bay?" the other retorted. "We give way to nothing!"

Larkham's followers agreed vociferously.

Underhill drew breath to respond, but Hatevil Nutter chose that moment to make his move. He raised the halberd and pushed past the two men, causing Underhill and Knollys to stumble aside.

"We are the Scots, and you are the English!" Nutter's bass voice was so forceful as to startle those nearest him. It fairly boomed, and he advanced another step, shaking his bible-topped halberd. Richard marveled at his resemblance to an Old Testament patriarch. Larkham's group gave ground involuntarily.

"Mister Nutter, if you please—" Underhill began, but now Knollys' courage was bolstered by Nutter's reference to the recent Bishops' War. All were aware of the latest news from England that the Scots had trounced the English army and prevented them imposing the Anglican liturgy on their Presbyterian churches. The usually docile minister was eager to assert his authority. He stepped to Hatevil's side and raised the wheel lock pistol high, visibly cocking the firing mechanism.

"You shall not force the First Church to adopt your Anglican heresies, Larkham! You are excommunicated! Give over!" he yelled, brandishing the weapon.

"He has a pistol!" "Fall back!" "He's going to fire!" "Away, Larkham! Away!"

There was a scramble as Larkham's supporters pulled him into a hasty retreat. Those in front of the group tangled with those behind. Richard found their panicked haste amusing, as they turned tail and retreated back up the road. In truth there was no humor in the situation. Threatening with a loaded weapon was a serious offense.

It was all Underhill could do to keep Knollys and Nutter from pursuing. By sheer force of his considerable will, he turned the Puritans back toward the parsonage. The Reverend was triumphant. With emotions running high, Underhill gave up on maintaining their military formation. He let Knollys lead, while he brought up the rear, frequently glancing over his shoulder. Will passed the flask among them in celebration and scowled at Richard, when his brother refused again.

"Did you mark how they scattered?" the minister crowed. He was all but strutting. "You see, Captain? 'Twas the pistol undid them!"

Underhill did not deign to respond. The Revered seemed oblivious to the potential consequences of his action. Once they gained the parsonage, the Captain stood at the window, watching the street. A line had been crossed with the drawing of a loaded weapon, and he fretted about the repercussions. He had never intended to draw his sword against his fellow townsmen; he had just wanted Larkham's group to see it.

Knollys marked the encounter a triumph. Will's flask was empty, and the minister bade his wife bring them a bottle of his best brandy. The men stood around the dining table, toasting each other, caught up in the minister's excitement and too worked up to sit. Richard did not partake. He shared Underhill's sense of foreboding. Hanserd's pistol had forced the altercation into dangerous territory—from words to weapons. Richard recalled Pru saying, "No good can come of this."

Larkham's group was not cowed for long. Once their fear dissipated, they were outraged, and Larkham did little to allay their indignation. Inwardly, he was triumphant.

Knollys had gone too far, threatening them with a loaded pistol. Any objective party must side with him now. Once his supporters had calmed somewhat, he spoke.

"Where is the nearest authority to which we might appeal for protection?"

There was a pause, as the men considered.

"Governor Williams has a militia at Strawbery Banke," Edward Starbuck answered.

"How might we get word to him quickly?" Larkham asked.

"I shall go," Starbuck offered. "The ferry is large enough to transport them, I reckon."

"Without horses, certes," Anthony Emery added. "There are twenty of them."

"I shall accompany you," the minister said. "We are dealing with rebellion here, and these events must be related properly, if we are to induce them to come to our aid."

As the noon hour came and went, Richard's restlessness increased. If Larkham's group challenged them now, the Puritans would be bested. Most of their company was useless and continued to celebrate around the dining table. Knollys' cook and maidservant were kept busy, providing food and drink. The reverend's wife had discreetly absented herself soon after the men's raucous return.

By mid-afternoon, only Richard, Underhill, and Nutter were sober, when the militia from Strawbery Banke appeared, marching up the lane led by Captain Ambrose Gibbens. Thomas Larkham was at his side. The company halted before the parsonage.

"You in the house!" Gibbens called, "Come out and surrender your weapons. Do not force us to take arms against you!"

There was a pause. The door opened slowly, and Underhill led the Puritans out, his sword in its scabbard resting flat upon his two hands. Pomfrett, Damme, and Richard followed suit. Knollys held his unprimed pistol by the barrel. The rest followed with their empty hands held up to show they carried no armaments. The arrest cut through the haze of their celebratory mood. Richard was humiliated, surrendering his sword while Larkham and his group looked on in self-righteous triumph. The weapons were quickly confiscated, including Nutter's Bible standard.

"'Tis not a weapon!" he objected stoutly. "'Tis the Word of God!"

"He used it like a weapon," Larkham told the Captain. "He threatened us with it!"

"Any godly minister would not be thr—" Hatevil began hotly.

"If 'twas used to intimidate," Gibbens interrupted sternly, "then the court shall decide whether to consider it a weapon or no."

Nutter glowered at him but obeyed.

Captain Gibbens lined them up. Though they were now disarmed, the Puritans were placed under guard. From a distance the militia had looked impressive, marching in formation. At close quarters Richard realized there was not a full uniform among them. Five had military coats, but of these, three were naval. They were not soldiers; they were colonists with a modicum of training, which made submitting to them more of a slight.

Gibbens separated those who had not borne arms. He dispatched two of the militia to escort them to their homes, there to remain until called to the court. The Captain then turned to the six miscreants who had been armed. Richard had never been on the wrong side of the law. He stood at military attention, his face stony, inwardly seething with indignation. Larkham's version of the incident had been accepted without question. When Knollys and Underhill attempted to explain, Gibbens cut them off.

"I am not here to judge these events," he said, holding up a hand. "I only wish to distinguish the perpetrators from the followers. Governor Williams shall decide guilt or innocence in the court."

The Captain wasted no time but confined Underhill and Knollys to the parsonage under guard until their trial. Nutter, Damme, Pomfrett, and Richard were remanded to their homes under similar constraint. They were escorted by six of the militia. Folk peered from their windows and doors as the miscreants were marched up High Street. The young Puritan was mortified.

On approaching his house, the door flew open, and Prudence and Missus. Cameron came onto the porch, wide-eyed at the sight of the armed guard. His wife tried to embrace him, but her husband pushed past her without a word. Richard was twenty-seven, and it was the worst humiliation of his life.

The Roberts family did not attend church on that fateful Sabbath Day, as Rebecca had started labor in the wee hours of the morning. It was a long and arduous birth. Eleven-year-old John Roberts ran for the midwife at daybreak. None of the family was aware of the incident until later that afternoon, when Captain Gibbens sent one of the militia to the Roberts' farm with a message that he wished to speak with the President of Bristol/Northam's Court. Thomas was amazed. Having missed the encounter, there was little he could do to prevent the catastrophe of a public hearing. Captain Gibbens informed him that Governor Francis Williams of Strawbery Banke would preside.

Even more appalling was the Portsmouth Governor's harsh ruling. The hearing was held at the meeting house on the third day after the incident. Underhill and Knollys were found guilty of instigating a riot and fined the outrageous sum of one hundred pounds each. The rest of the men involved were publicly reprimanded. Larkham's supporters were jubilant. The Strawbery Banke contingent left the same day.

Mild-mannered though he was, Thomas Roberts would not accept Williams' *ad hoc* ruling. He felt slighted by the intervention of the Strawbery Banke Governor and his militia. He sent a rider to Boston with a letter to Governor Richard Bellingham, explaining events and requesting objective intervention. It came within a week in the form of three adjudicators—Simon Bradstreet of Boston, Hugh Peters of Salem, and Reverend Timothy Dalton of Hampton. Those illustrious gentlemen negotiated reparations between the two factions so well that ultimately the fines against Underhill and Knollys were waived, and Larkham's excommunication was revoked. All were cautioned to keep a tight rein on their choler in future.

However, there were long-term repercussions. The incident was proof that self-government was not proceeding in an orderly fashion in the northern settlements. At the next town meeting, the freemen did not balk when Thomas Roberts and the selectmen produced a petition to join with the Bay. Everyone signed. The following year the former New Hampshire Colony was assimilated by the Massachusetts Bay Colony. The first directive of the new government changed Thomas Larkham's "Northam" to "Dover."

# *Chapter 26*

## MARY AND ALICE *PEOPLE OF THE FALLS*

October/November, 1662 Newichawannock, Province of Maine

Edward and George did not linger at Kittery House. Their import business was especially busy as winter approached, and they were expecting a shipment of goods at Salem any day. They rose early the next morning to break their fast before leaving. Mary and Allie found them at the table with their hosts. Chastened by the conversation with Anne the night before, Mary avoided eye contact. She was ashamed of her behavior and realized during a restless night that her impatience was a defense to keep Friend Wharton at bay. She was subdued and spoke only when addressed directly. Allie rose to the occasion, relating their plan to go on to Newichawannock after the next meeting for worship. There was a chorus of approval round the table. Nicholas and Alice were pleased the missionaries would be near Katherine's daughter Lucy, and Friend Wharton smiled.

They all bundled into cloaks and mufflers and walked down to the dock together. The air was still, and frost coated every surface, crackling under their boots. A weak sun rose out of the sea, veiled by morning fog.

Friend Coleman shook the men's hands and thanked them warmly. Nicholas and Alice hoped for a longer visit next time. Allie shook hands, wishing them Godspeed. Mary felt Edward turn toward her and met his eyes. She wanted to apologize, but now he was leaving, the weight of all she wished to say tightened her throat.

"Friend Wharton," she began but was appalled to feel the threat of tears. She turned abruptly to include George, "and Friend Preston." For a wonder, her voice sounded normal. "Thank you for bringing Anne. She shall add both comfort and strength to our mission."

It was as close to an apology as Mary could manage. She shook George's hand firmly and turned back to Edward. He took her small, cold hand in both of his. His touch was warm and firm. He gave her a slow smile and nodded once. The shallop was well on its way out to sea before her hand stopped tingling.

The next Sabbath Day meeting in the Shapleigh Church was the missionaries' last. The people of the river were eager for them to establish meetings for worship and organize relief work, as they had in Kittery. Small settlements were strung along the eastern bank, but the most populous was called Newichawannock for the river it bordered. Some two hundred souls lived in the area between Pipestave Landing and Quamphegan Falls, including the Nasons, Spencers, and Chadbournes. There were several busy landings, and Friend Nason had spoken of the log drives, whereby the select King's Pine was floated downstream to Portsmouth and thence to England to serve as masts for the Royal Navy. The white pine of the colonies was the lightest and strongest wood in the world for this purpose. Although pipe staves were a byproduct, they were also in demand to make barrels, giving the lower landing its popular name. The river was literally a lifeline, providing a source of food, power to run the mills, and a navigable connection to the commerce of the coastal towns. Newichawannock boasted well-constructed homes, a burial ground, a school, and a meeting house and parsonage built two years before. However, no minister had yet come to preach so far upriver, and the folk were eager for spiritual guidance.

Richard Nason and Thomas Spencer would transport the three missionaries upriver after the meeting. Their wives did not accompany them, as Patience had given birth to the Spencers' eighth child, Joy, earlier that summer, and Sarah Nason was still recovering from Benjamin's delivery six months ago. Richard expressed the hope that the missionaries' presence would raise his wife's spirits and speed her recovery.

On the day of their departure, Mary was torn between excitement at moving on and regret at leaving the Shapleighs and the open-minded community she had come to know through them. Allie and Anne shared her eagerness, but it was hard to ignore Alice's downcast face, as they sat at the Shapleigh table for the last time.

Parting was difficult. Mary and Allie had changed their hosts' perspective, confirmed their spirituality, and enriched their lives. In turn, the missionaries were given safe haven and an invaluable introduction to the colony through the Shapleighs' extended family and friends, but their success did not make parting any easier. Anne said her goodbyes and joined Richard and Thomas in the skiff, perceptively allowing her new companions to take leave of their friends.

"I have got spoiled these months keeping your company. It shall be quite dismal without you," Alice said, holding Mary in a lingering embrace.

"We shall miss thee as well, sweet Alice," Mary said, returning it whole-heartedly.

"'Tis we who have been spoiled by thy hospitality," Allie rejoined, enfolding Alice in her long arms. "Thou hast made us feel part of thy wonderful family."

Nicholas kissed them warmly on both cheeks and took them each by a hand.

"You know you are ever welcome at Kittery Manor," he said, his voice husky.

As Friends Spencer and Nason rowed away from the dock, Mary looked back and saw that Alice was crying. Nicholas had a comforting arm around her shoulders, and they both waved. The three missionaries raised their hands in reply. Mary blinked back tears and fervently hoped Providence might reunite them.

The trip upriver against the current was demanding even with the tide in their favor. For much of the way, the southwest wind filled the sail, and they made good time at first. They passed between Great Isle and New Castle then headed north. They cleared Pearce Island at a good clip, and Mary recognized Strawbery Bank to port, reminding her of their outing with Alice. Dover Point and the bustle of Pomeroy Cove loomed then fell behind as they angled northeast. They moved up the Pisacatqua, and still the wind held. Less than two miles from their destination, however, they rounded an easterly bend in the river and were becalmed.

"'Tis like to happen here," Thomas told the missionaries, as he and Richard efficiently reefed the limp sail and set the oars.

"Not far to go now," Richard added cheerfully.

They reached Pipestave Landing tired and hungry at the last light of day.

"We cannot know how long this river has flowed past these banks before ever we were present," Thomas Spencer said through a cloud of tobacco smoke from his pipe, "And I reckon 'twill flow long after we are gone."

The three missionaries were sharing a quiet moment with their host after dinner. The evening was windless and mild for the end of October. They could hear the roar of the falls from across the dark field. Lamplight shone through the windows of the porch, where they sat rocking. The summer night chorus had quieted, since the recent killing frosts, but a few brave crickets sang from beneath the porch.

"I sit here often of an evening, and it causes me to ponder," their host continued, removing the pipe from his mouth and staring off toward the point where the Asbenbedick River split off from the Newichawannock.

"We have seen prodigious changes here in thirty years. How much more shall it be altered in another thirty? I shall not see the century turn, I reckon," he mused.

"When didst thou settle here, Friend Nason?" Allie asked.

"'Twas 1630," he answered, puffing. "I was just four and twenty. Came on the *Warwick* with Ambrose Gibbens and Roger Knight, hired by John Mason. There was nothing here then but the river, virgin pine, and the Old Fields." The fragrant pipe smoke curled above their heads and drifted out into the windless night. "Gibbens was here first and chose a fine location for a house on a rise just north of the Asbenbedick. 'The Great House' he called it, and it was large enough for all of us, at least at the first.

"The Indians proved curious about our activities and were more welcoming than we had hoped. Their *sôgmô,* Rowls, sold us this land, so long as his people could continue to grow corn and fish here. The Old Fields were their traditional planting grounds, y'see. For a time we employed near a hundred natives to plant corn each season, and we cleared more land for our own crop as well. Verily they helped us. In those years so many salmon came upstream in spring the river was thick with 'em. Betimes they overflowed the banks and spoiled, but the natives buried 'em to nourish the corn hills—an ingenious use of the waste.

"They don't run the river anymore, though—the salmon. Not since Richard Leader renovated the old sawmill back in '50. He brought a group of Scots with him, when he came up from Saugus Iron Works. Friend Furbush was one of 'em. Many of those men made a good start here, working Leader's saws—betimes twenty cutting all at once. An irksome noise, that was!" Thomas chuckled and knocked his pipe against the railing. "He showed us how 'twas done, did Leader, though he did not stay long. Eventually we built our own—Humphrey Chadbourne, my wife's brother, and I. Our son-in-law, Dan Goodwin, threw in with us too, in time. 'The sawmill is just across the field there." Thomas pointed with his pipe stem.

The women were fascinated by this glimpse of the early settlement.

"Did thy wife come with thee?" Anne asked.

"Not at the first. Patience and I were newly-wed and 'twas a hardship to part, but she joined me the next year along with the wives of Gibbens and Knight. We were a small company, just ten of us, and we all lived at the Great House, until Mason sent the joiners in '34.

"My father-in-law William Chadbourne was one of 'em. John Mason hired him and two others to build a water-powered sawmill. They brought a model and started early in July. It took 'em all summer to build, but it soon became evident that the practical application was trickier than anticipated." He smiled and shook his head. "We knew nothing then, and parts kept breaking from the force of the water. 'Twas a trial to mill boards of consistent thickness.

"Then the next year Mason died, and all his great plans of mills and mines and vineyards soon gave way to more practical concerns, like building homes. No wages were ever likely to come to us with Mason gone. On the other hand, here was a land where a man might carve out his own kingdom. We all opted to stay, pay or no. Father Chadbourne built this very house and gifted it to Patience and me. And none too soon, for we had three little ones by then!" Thomas chuckled then sobered adding, "He was a fine man, and we mourn his loss yet."

The door opened, and the sudden illumination broke the spell. Patience stood with Joy in her arms.

"I bid you goodnight," she said to the missionaries. "No, no—do not disturb yourselves," she added as they began to rise. "'Tis just the babe wants feeding and a good sleep. Ye share the bedchamber upstairs with Lizzie and Gwen," she went on, referring to the Spencer's daughter and a young niece who lived with them. They will settle you in, once ye are ready to retire. They are just clearing up."

"Oh, then we should help," said Allie, making to rise.

"No, I shall not countenance that," Patience smiled. "They are nearly done, and ye are newly arrived. Rest now. I promise we shall work you hard on the morrow."

"And I promise we shall hold thee to that," Allie answered, smiling back.

Joy began to fuss.

"Ah, my mistress bids me get on with it," Patience said, giving the baby's downy head a quick kiss. "Sweet rest then, and welcome to our home."

Patience Chadbourne Spencer was eight years younger than her husband. She had given him seven children with uncommon ease, but the eighth was a surprise, coming fourteen years later. At forty Patience had thought her childbearing days were over. Even their daughter, Margaret, married to Daniel Goodwin and living just across the road, had nine children older than their newborn aunt.

It had been a difficult birth. The infant breeched and had to be turned. Patience went in and out of consciousness during the long hours of labor, but God had seen fit to entrust another soul to their care, and far be it from the Spencers to gainsay His Will. Hence they named the baby Joy, but Patience determined she would be the last.

Sarah Nason's decline worried Patience and further confirmed this decision. The two women were neighbors, of an age, and good friends. They had shared pregnancies before, as well as during the past year and always attended each other's births, which had been smooth, Praise God—eight for Patience and nine for Sarah. Joy's delivery was the first difficult one for Patience, but Sarah almost died birthing Ben. The midwife could not stop the bleeding; nor could Walter Barefoote, who arrived ten hours later from Dover. Only the Grace of God stopped it, leaving Sarah within an inch of her life. Her milk never came in. The Spencers' daughter Margaret nursed the baby, as she had just weaned her youngest, and Ben thrived, but even after six months, Sarah was still abed, fevered, weak, and listless.

Patience visited her friend every day. It was a short walk, and Gwen or Lizzie usually accompanied her. Elizabeth was the only Spencer child still living at home, and her cousin was welcome company for her. They were both fourteen and adept at caring for Joy. They took turns staying with the baby or accompanying Patience, who was grateful for the help. It made her time at the Nasons' crowded household more productive. There were still four children between the ages of five and nine—plus Baby Ben—living in their home.

On their first full day at Newichawannock, the three missionaries accompanied Patience across the road to the Nasons' house. The mild night had given way to a raw, blustery day, punctuated by scattered showers of thick rain that was almost sleet. Lizzie and Gwen were glad to stay home with Baby Joy, and the four women donned their cloaks and mufflers and walked across the lane quickly.

They opened the door on chaos. A girl of about ten was holding a squalling baby, as she railed at three younger children, chasing each other around the kitchen table. A harried-looking woman stood in their midst with floury hands upraised over a lump of dough. At first the women's arrival went unnoticed.

"Good morrow, children!" Patience called pleasantly over the din.

Everything stopped with the exception of the baby's cries, and every face turned their way.

"I bid ye welcome our guests who have come from England this summer past. They intend to spend some time here and lead us in meetings for worship. This is Friend

Tomkins, Friend Ambrose, and Friend Coleman," she continued, as the children gathered around.

"Why is she so short?" asked the smaller of the two boys, pointing at Anne.

His elder sister blushed. "Mind thy manners!" she hissed, shifting the baby to her shoulder and patting his back. Mercifully the wailing stopped. "I beg pardon for my brother, Friend Coleman," the girl apologized.

"It is quite all right," Anne said in her deep voice. "I adore questions. Especially important ones like that. What is your name, young man?"

"D-Dickie," the child answered, confused. Everyone told him he asked too many questions, but now this unusual person, no taller than his sister Sarah, was giving him license to ask away!

"Whom shall I find to hear my stories?" Anne posed to the room at large. Patience smiled and began to unpack the basket she had brought. The woman at the table smiled back, shaking her head, and resumed her kneading.

"Me! Me!" the little girl shouted, jumping up and down.

"Me too!" the larger of the two boys insisted stoutly. Anne surmised the two were twins they looked so alike and appeared to be of an age.

"But why art thou so—" Dickie began.

"All questions shall be answered anon to the best of my ability," Anne stated firmly, taking his hand and making for the other end of the long, open room.

The three children followed her to a bench built into a large bay window, where the diminutive missionary settled with the twins on one side and Richard on the other. She did indeed have a way with children, Mary thought approvingly.

The baby found the fist he had been sucking unsatisfying and resumed fussing.

"He's hungry," the older girl explained. "Margaret should be here at any moment."

"Is thy mother asleep, Sarah?" Patience asked, setting her empty basket by the door.

"She was when last I saw her," the child answered, then turned to Mary and Alice. "I get Baby Ben up at first light for his morning feeding. Then my sister Margaret goes home to tend her family. She usually returns about now," she explained. Her smooth brow puckered, as she jiggled her brother. "This morning Mother slept so soundly she did not stir, when I took him from his cradle, though he was crying."

The three women exchanged a look.

"Well, I imagine she is awake by now," Patience said brightly. "I shall just see if she might like something to break her fast."

"I shall accompany thee," Allie added, hefting her satchel of herbal medications.

"And I shall visit with Sarah and Baby Ben," Mary said. "Thou must be a great help to thy mother, Sarah, as well as bearing her name. She must be very proud of thee," she was saying, as the two women made for the sleeping chamber behind the chimney.

The room was dim, lit only by a fireplace. The windows were shuttered against the cold and damp. The air was stale, and the small room felt stuffy compared to the open kitchen and living area. Sarah Nason lay curled on her side as if asleep, but when Patience put a hand on her shoulder, the body was cold and stiffening.

Patience was distraught but not surprised. After birthing Ben, Sarah had hovered at life's edge, barely summoning enough strength to take nourishment. A persistent fever weakened her, and the subsequent months of confinement engendered bedsores and a catarrh deep in her chest. The former made it hard for Sarah to sleep or even rest in comfort, and the latter wracked her thin frame with a deep, barking cough. Still, Patience had hoped that the missionaries' visit would somehow restore her dear friend to health.

"Poor, sweet soul," Patience wept, stroking Sarah's hair. "Thy trials are over now."

Allie put her hands on the older woman's shoulders, giving wordless comfort, and let her cry.

"We had best inform little Sarah," Patience said, rousing herself and blowing her nose on the handkerchief in her apron pocket, "And we must send someone to tell Richard. Oh, poor Richard!" Fresh tears fell.

Patience sank onto a stool by the bed overcome.

"Do not bestir thyself for a while," said Allie, rubbing her back soothingly. "We shall fetch Sarah first. She will want to prepare her mother for burial, and she will need thy help and comfort. I shall find Richard."

Patience wiped her eyes and took Allie's hand. "Thank thee, Friend Ambrose."

"Thy thanks can be expressed by calling me Allie," the missionary responded, "and thou art most welcome."

When the two women emerged, they found Margaret Goodwin had arrived and was nursing the baby in a rocking chair by the hearth. Mary was talking with her quietly, and Sarah perched on a stool near them, eating an apple. The younger children were rapt, listening to Anne's stories at the far end of the room. The cook had set the bread to rise and was scrubbing the table.

Allie took in the peaceful scene, her heart aching with the news that would tear it asunder. Mary looked up, and Allie shook her head slightly. It was all the communication necessary for her friend to understand. Allie donned her cloak and bonnet and went to find Richard Nason.

Patience helped Sarah to straighten her mother's limbs and gently wash her wasted body. Together they brushed her tangled hair, braiding it neatly, and dressed her in her finest clothes. Tears tracked their cheeks throughout the process, but Sarah did not falter. The child mourned her mother with a stoicism that was heartbreakingly admirable. She was a rock in the rapids for her three younger siblings, and in the following days Sarah alone seemed able to give her father some comfort in their shared grief.

Sarah Nason's long illness did not soften the blow of her death. Her family and friends had never given up faith in her recovery, and her loss was devastating despite living under its shadow for months. The community responded with both practical help and their loving presence. Friends and neighbors came and went bringing food and the bitter-sweet comfort of shared memories.

The Nasons' cook Molly Knight offered to live in for a week or two, until a housekeeper and nursemaid could be found. In the interim the missionaries moved their things to the Nason's loft to assist Molly and little Sarah with daily chores, childcare, and much-needed comfort.

Margaret took Baby Ben into the Goodwins' home, until he should be weaned. Sarah had an open invitation to visit him there and appeared relieved. Seeing the nine-year-old shoulder the burden of her baby brother's care altered Mary's perspective of her sister Margaret, who had done the same for her, and she was humbled. Anne was a wonder with the younger Nasons, both comforting and distracting them with stories and projects. Thomas Spencer sent word to the Nasons' four older sons, and they arrived with their families the next day, but there was no practical solution for grief.

Richard spent the afternoon building a simple coffin. The project distracted him, but now night had fallen, the neighbors had gone home, and the household was abed. His wife was laid out in their sleeping chamber, clean and at peace, cushioned by her favorite quilt in the sweet-smelling pine box. Candles burned at her head and feet. They would bury her on the morrow. Mary sat with him by the hearth on the first difficult night.

"She was the center of my life, and the best thing that ever happened to me," Richard said, staring into the flames. "How shall I continue without her?"

Mary knew he did not expect an answer. She considered carefully before speaking.

"My mother died birthing me," she said at length. Richard looked at her, momentarily distracted by this personal confidence. "My father might have resented me for causing her death, but he did not. He seemed to love me all the more. Thy manner with thy children today put me in mind of him. My education is due entirely to him, but his greatest gifts to me were his affection and understanding. When I was small, he comforted me. If I was out of sorts, he made me smile. He ever considered my childish assertions with tolerance. When I became convinced, he supported my determination to become a missionary, even though it meant losing me. I do not know if I shall ever see him again, but he is as much a part of me as my blood and bone. He infuses everything I say and do."

Richard turned back to the fire, nodding.

Mary waited for the tightness in her throat to ease, then went on. "No doubt ye were even closer as husband and wife. I cannot fathom thy grief, Friend Nason, nor can I parse why God saw fit to take her, but though she is no longer beside thee, yet I believe her spirit lives in the love ye bear for her and for each other."

Richard's eyes welled with tears. He buried his face in his sleeve and his shoulders shook. Mary laid her hand on his back and waited for the surge of grief to abate. At length he dragged his sleeve across his face and took up the poker, sniffing. He turned a log over and added another, then replaced the tool carefully and sat back.

"What happens when we die, dost thou think?" he asked, when he could speak.

Mary did not respond right away. It was not a question to be answered lightly.

"We cannot know," she said at length.

"But thou must have wondered, having lost thy mother. What dost thou reckon happens, when we die?" he pressed.

Mary closed her eyes, formulating a belief that was, until this moment, unexpressed.

"Hast thou felt God's Light in contemplation, Friend Nason?" she asked, turning to him.

He met her eyes and nodded slowly. "Aye, I believe I have."

"That joy that blossoms when we connect with That of God is profound but fleeting is it not?" she asked, carefully feeling her way.

"It is," he agreed, reading her face avidly.

"I believe that when we die, our souls enter a state of grace in which that feeling, that connection to the Divine, is sustained, and all sorrow and pain departs with our earthly form."

Richard gazed at her. "So, whenever I feel joy in contemplation, my Sarah is part of it?"

"Yes," Mary answered, "I believe her immortal soul has joined with God's Light."

He turned to the fire and gazed at the flames. "Dost thou reckon she is yet aware of us, her loved ones?" he asked, his voice breaking. Fresh tears caught the firelight.

"I believe she is aware of you all and of so much more, beyond our ken," she answered.

The widower sighed heavily. "'Tis a beautiful thought. My thanks, Friend Tomkins. Thou hast brought me great comfort."

They sat for some time in companionable silence.

"I think I shall make my vigil now," he said presently and rose to go sit by his wife for the remainder of the night.

At Richard Nason's request, the missionaries officiated over the service the next day. It was held at the meeting house next to the cemetery. Word spread quickly through the river settlement. Few were the families that had not lost a loved one. Even in England casualties of birth or illness were pervasive, let alone here in the wilderness. The meeting for worship originally scheduled was amended to a meeting to celebrate the life of Sarah Baker Nason. Although there would be an interval of silence, all were welcome to attend, whether convinced or not. Participants were invited to speak, sing, or read passages.

Mary was impressed when several Indians came from their camp above Quamphegan Falls. She could not imagine how they knew of Sarah Nason's death, but Richard was touched, and he and Thomas Spencer greeted them warmly in their own language. Both families had ever welcomed their Indian neighbors in their home, serving a favored treat—English tea loaded with sugar and cream. Once the area became more populated the Indians did not visit as often. Newer residents expressed outrage at their custom of entering homes without knocking, and sadly, in the original settlers' opinion, inter-racial visits had become rare.

The small meeting house was filling up. The three missionaries stood at the door, greeting people as they entered. Mary felt an affinity for the folk of Newichawannock. She saw curiosity but no suspicion or censure, as people shook her hand. Most were Anglicans and, like the folk at Kittery, they were open to the Friends' message. Lucy Treworgy Chadbourne was great with child, but she embraced them with awkward warmth for her mother had written letters all summer, singing their praises.

The service began with a hymn. There was no organ, but Anne Coleman had a fine alto voice and joined Mary and Allie in leading "Praise God, This Hour of Sorrow Shall Bring a Brighter Morrow." A few latecomers squeezed in during the singing, reaffirming Mary's decision to always begin meetings in this manner. Then she explained the Friends' procedure for the service.

"This is a time to mourn together the passing of Friend Sarah Nason," she began, "however, 'tis also a time to celebrate her life and recall what was most loved of her. We shall commence with silent worship. However, all are welcome to speak, if so moved."

After an interval of silence, several did. Among them, Patience Spencer was eloquent. The two women had shared immigration, communal living in the wilderness, adjustment to marriage, and the challenges of managing households, giving birth, and raising children. All were moved as she praised her dear friend.

Lucy Chadbourne spoke after her sister-in-law, recalling how kind Sarah and Patience had been to her as a young bride, newly married to Humphrey and establishing her first home. Several others rose to share memories. None of the Nason Family was able to speak, but Mary judged the sharing of praise and grief to be a comfort to them.

After the service, everyone trooped to the cemetery next door. The rain had stopped, but the day was bleak. The sun gave little warmth to comfort the mourners. Fortunately the frost had not penetrated deep enough to freeze the ground below a few inches. The Nasons' four elder sons had shared the task of digging that morning, and the family stood around the open grave. The coffin was redolent of freshly-cut pine. Each of the family threw a handful of earth into the grave and said goodbye. Five-year-old Richard was last, and his sister Sarah guided him to the edge. He opened his little hand, letting the dirt fall onto the coffin and inspired fresh tears when he expressed the unspoken fear of all who lose a loved one.

"Good-bye, Mamma," he said sadly, "Please don't forget me!"

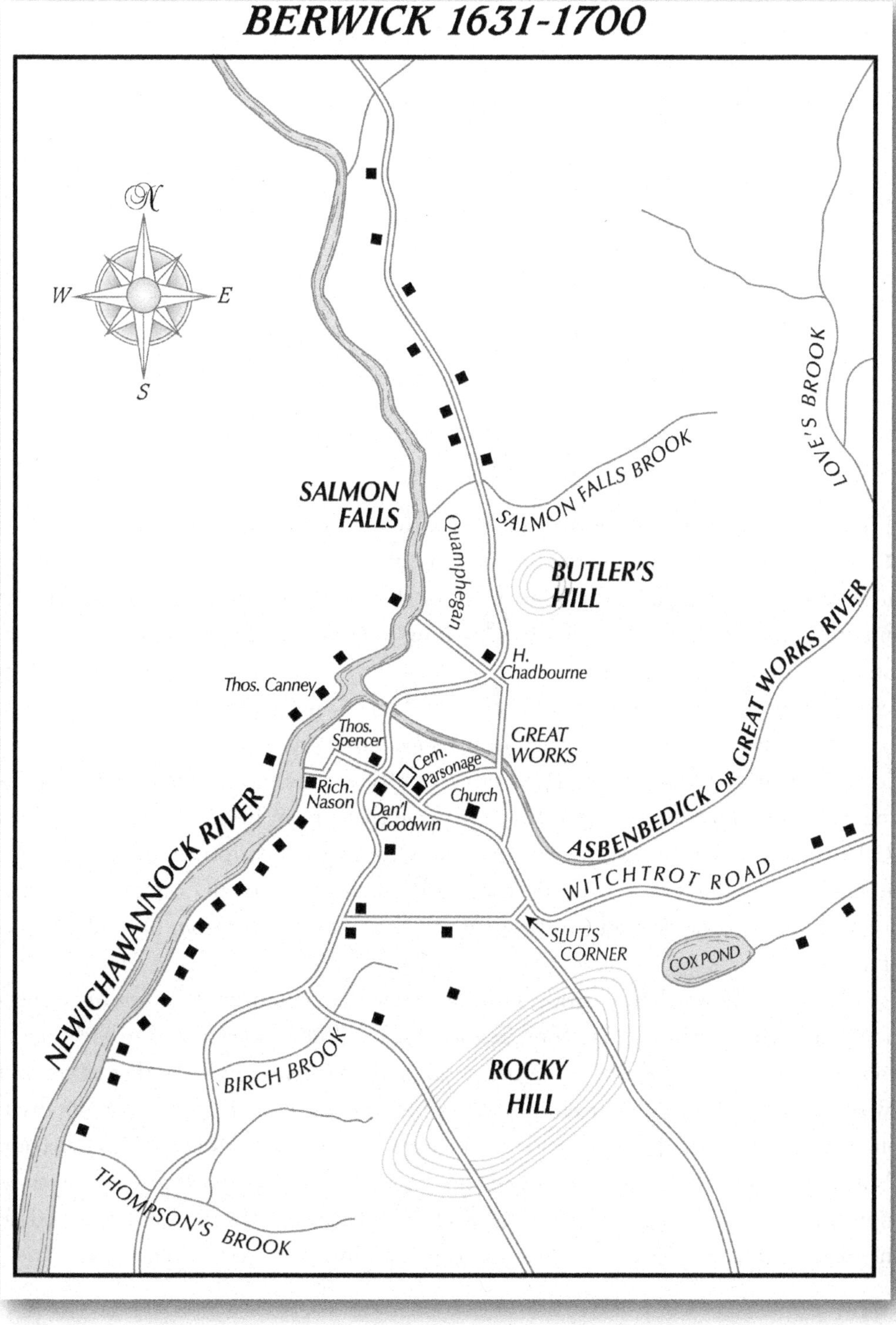
BERWICK 1631-1700
N
W
E
S
SALMON FALLS
Quamphegan
SALMON FALLS BROOK
LOVE'S BROOK
BUTLER'S HILL
H. Chadbourne
Thos. Canney
Thos. Spencer
Cem.
Parsonage
GREAT WORKS
Rich. Nason
Dan'l Goodwin
Church
ASBENBEDICK OR GREAT WORKS RIVER
NEWICHAWANNOCK RIVER
WITCHTROT ROAD
SLUT'S CORNER
COX POND
BIRCH BROOK
ROCKY HILL
THOMPSON'S BROOK

# *Chapter 27*

## RICHARD WALDERNE *COMMERCE*

1642-1644 Dover and Boston, Massachusetts Bay Colony

Prudence gave Richard another son. Timothy was born in the house at Dover Neck just as Paul was acquiring the knack of language. Bridget had her hands full in the nursery, but on the whole, the adjustment of the household to this second baby was smoother than the first. Prudence was learning to leave the children's care to Bridget, although she still spent most of her day with the boys and breastfed the newborn herself. Evenings were devoted to her husband and social engagements.

That summer Richard saw little of his sons, absorbed as he was in the construction of a sawmill. He often slept on a cot in his office at the busy Cocheco trading post and was training young Peter Coffin to manage the custom in his absence. It enabled Richard to make regular trips to Boston to keep his investors informed of the sawmill's progress. His ambition knew no limits, and Richard quite literally capitalized on the connections he made through Governor Winthrop. He was away from Dover for weeks at a time.

Whenever he was home, Bridget and Prudence presented the boys for his inspection each evening. After a quarter of an hour, the children were returned to the nursery and put to bed. Timothy was still a baby and held no interest for his father as yet, but two-year-old Paul required curbing. Their father did not touch the boys, barring discipline, but he monitored their development closely, ever on guard for fractious behavior. Paul's age was no disclaimer. Disobedience, inattention, and rebelliousness must be nipped in the bud lest the boy run wild. Richard's discipline was swift and brooked no interference. His sons learned to fear and worship him.

A few months after the incident with the pistol Hanserd Knollys departed for England. His enthusiasm for frontier living had waned. Richard regretted the clergyman did not witness Thomas Larkham's demise, which came soon after. Too comely for his own good the minister was accused of indulging in lewd conduct. There was insufficient proof for a conviction, but his guilt was evidenced by an abrupt departure, in Richard's opinion—another similarity to George Burdett. Will bought up Larkham's grant of land, crowing over the price the minister was forced to accept in his haste. Even after he was gone, gossip circulated that the man had abandoned a wife and children in England. The sun had set on Thomas Larkham's popularity.

Dover was without a minister, and it seemed an improvement in light of recent events. The elders and deacons of the First Church took charge of services until a replacement might be found, and contention in the congregation quieted. Hatevil Nutter and Edward Starbuck took turns preaching on alternate Sundays. There was still disagreement on points of religion, but governance was now monitored by the Bay Colony. Dover was permitted one representative to the General Court in Boston to voice the community's concerns, as were the other northern settlements. It became a coveted post to which Richard aspired.

The Underhills moved back to Boston that spring. After a formal apology to Governor Winthrop for supporting Wheelwright, the Captain was received back into the fold. Richard suspected the acquisition of the New Hampshire territories encouraged the governor's leniency. The young lieutenant was glad Underhill had opened the door for the assimilation; however, he was relieved to be out from under the feisty Captain's shadow. Granted, the man had organized a local militia most efficiently. Underhill's last military decree was to make Walderne's lieutenancy official and appoint him to run the monthly drills on the recently designated ox pasture. Dover had its own troops now, and the young Puritan aspired to the rank of Captain.

Since the incident with Knollys and Larkham, Richard kept his distance from the powder keg of religion. He still accompanied his family to Sabbath Day meetings, of course, but he would never forget the humiliation he had suffered in defense of the First Church. He left matters of religion to others and concentrated on his businesses and growing political influence in Dover and Boston.

The trading post and ordinary at Cocheco was turning a profit, and once he had investors for the prospective sawmill, Richard determined the site. In the process he discovered a large tract of freshwater wetland. It was unsuitable for building, but marsh grass was a valuable source of fodder for the increasing number of livestock on the

Point. Dover families were buying shares in six-acre lots, and once invested in the area, they began to purchase house lots along the river near the trading post as well. Richard was sure they would soon be clearing land and building homes, and his sawmill would supply the lumber. His ultimate goal was to build ships and conduct trade the world over, though he kept this to himself.

By June Richard had decided on a site. Construction was the next step, but he had no idea how to engineer or construct a sawmill. It had been three months since the disastrous incident involving Knollys and Larkham, and the young lieutenant swallowed his pride and sought out Ambrose Gibbens for advice.

Captain Gibbens had immigrated as an agent for John Mason, founding the settlement on the east bank of the Newichawannock River, where the first water-powered sawmill in the region was constructed in 1634. Although this first attempt had failed, Richard thought Gibbens might have some insight on the subject. The Captain had retired from his post at Portsmouth, and removed with his wife and daughter to Sanders Point on the southwest shore of Great Bay. Richard visited the fifty-year-old pioneer at his home. His ambition overrode any misgivings at seeing the Captain again. Gibbens remembered him, for he had been impressed by the younger man's stoic dignity even as he was arrested. He greeted Richard warmly.

"Lieutenant Walderne," he said, shaking the younger man's hand, "I trust circumstances at Northam are calmer now?"

Richard noted the twinkle in his host's eye and held his gaze steadily. "Indeed they are, sir," he answered, gripping the man's hand firmly. He did not bother to correct the Captain concerning the town's new appellation. Many still referred to the Point as Northam out of habit.

Gibbens quickly warmed to the subject of sawmills. He still had the original plan for the model the Mason men had used. Richard was fascinated, and the two men spent most of the afternoon poring over it, delineating the weak points and discussing how to correct them. When Mistress Gibbens interrupted them for tea, they were both surprised to realize how quickly the time had passed. Richard politely refused her offer, as he needed to cross the bay before dark. His host accompanied him to the landing, where Richard had docked his skiff.

"'Tis not a simple thing to construct a mill powered by water," Gibbens concluded at their parting. "You shall need a capable carpenter who is familiar with the factors of stress and maintenance. The building of the thing is just the beginning."

"Might you recommend someone, sir?" Richard asked.

Ambrose stroked his well-trimmed beard in thought, gazing across the water.

"James Wall might serve. He worked with us in '34. I believe he resides in Exeter now. Certes, he has more experience than most."

Gibbens' advice proved sound. By July construction began on Richard's first sawmill.

Within two years the trading post and ordinary on the Cocheco was central to the growing settlement that Richard had envisioned. The sawmill was producing lumber but could not keep up with the demand. He planned a second one and would need more investors. A trip to Boston was in order. Richard left a foreman in charge at the sawmill and Peter Coffin at the trading post and surprised Prudence with her first trip to the colonial capital.

It was June and the fifth anniversary of their marriage. The boys were four and two years old—healthy and rambunctious unless cowed by their father's presence. The young mother was excited. She had never been away from the boys, but her anticipation eclipsed any misgivings about leaving them. The Waldernes would be accompanied by the Wiggins. Thomas was an active participant in Bay Colony politics. He had prospects to serve as a Deputy to the Great and General Court for Exeter, and his connections in Boston had opened doors for his protégé. They would be entertained by the Winthrops.

Unencumbered by children, the young couple sent a trunk ahead to the Wiggins' farm on Great Bay and rode a-horse. The roads were dry, and they savored their rare freedom from home and business obligations. Thomas and Catharine greeted them warmly, and the Waldernes stayed overnight. The four of them would journey to Boston in the Wiggins' carriage the next day.

The break from routine revived her husband's ardor, and Prudence responded with enthusiasm. In the throes of their passion Richard was obliged to muffle her cries. Still, the next morning Catharine greeted them with a cheery "Ah, there are the love birds!" causing the young wife to blush prettily.

Prudence fell in love with Boston. The main streets were cobbled with stone. Shops and salons abounded, stocked with more wares than she had seen since leaving England. People, horses, and wheeled vehicles of all sorts crowded the thoroughfares. Thursday Market Days were especially festive with street vendors calling out their wares. There were mounds of local produce, fresh seafood, lamb, beef, and chicken—all dressed and ready to be cooked. There were imported spices, exotic oils, French wine, liquor from Barbados, and a plethora of dry goods from England to choose from. Brick townhouses fronted quiet streets, and church bells tolled the hour or called folk to worship. Prudence was charmed.

On their first full day in Boston, Richard surprised his wife with a gift to mark their anniversary. They strolled west from the Winthrops' manse bordering the High Street. Richard turned right onto a lane between two open fields that connected to a wider street called Tremont Row. There were fewer houses here, all newly built, overlooking the broad, green Common fenced for cattle and sheep. Richard stopped before a three-story brick edifice with steps leading up to a wide front door freshly painted a glossy black with matching shutters.

"Oh, what a lovely street, Richard!" Pru exclaimed. "Look you, such a fine view of the Common! Is it not beautiful?" She turned to him, her green eyes shining. "But why are we stopped here?"

She was glowing, and Richard smiled, savoring both her beauty and the moment of disclosure. He anticipated the full expression of her gratitude that night in their bed and had to restrain an impulse to take her in his arms on the public street.

"'Tis ours, my love. 'Tis my gift to you to mark our fifth anniversary," he answered.

Her jaw dropped, and she looked from her husband to the house and back again, overcome. Her eyes brimmed with tears, and Richard propelled her gently but hastily up the steps. He unlocked the front door and ushered her into the house before she might embarrass him on the street.

As Richard anticipated, Prudence spent their visit scouring Boston for furnishings and appointments for the house. He was generous in funding her purchases, for he was proud that he could afford whatever she wished. Catharine Wiggin was an enthusiastic cohort in the enterprise, and it kept the women happily occupied, while he and Thomas attended meetings and lunched with men of influence. Richard paid court to his investors and succeeded in finding others, gleaning funds for the second sawmill. Captain Wiggin seemed to know everyone of import, and the younger man was grateful for his help.

The days passed quickly and were productive for both of them, and the nights were blissful, rekindling the passion they had experienced during the crossing. But Prudence missed her children, and now that they owned a house here, she knew they would return in future. At twenty-three she was in her prime and anticipated a long and engaging life.

# *Chapter 28*

## MARY AND ALICE *SALMON FALLS*

November, 1662 Northeast of Dover Point

Will and Rebecca Furbush lived north of Kittery on the east bank of the Piscataqua. They kept a skiff tied up at the landing near the house, and they attended the meetings for worship led by the missionaries at Newichawannock regularly, as they had at Kittery Point. When the missionaries decided to move on at the end of November, Will offered to ferry them upriver to the settlement at Salmon Falls.

If Newichawannock seemed isolated, the tiny community at the Falls was even more so. The upper river dropped one hundred feet within a mile, creating a rushing torrent of power, and when William Wentworth came upon it in the early 1650's, he considered it a fine location for a sawmill. The little hamlet grew up around it. Wentworth was the law in Salmon Falls, as most of the residents were in his employ. He was an Elder in the Dover Church. Had he been at home, he would likely have frowned on the Friends' mission, but Wentworth was in Boston concluding business before the snow made travel difficult.

The people of Salmon Falls were not so open in welcoming the Friends. It was too far from Kittery Point for any of the residents to have attended the summer meetings. In addition the settlement was technically part of Dover and was taxed accordingly; however, most of the residents balked at the inconvenience of traveling to the Point every Sabbath, and a number were open to an alternative.

Will had friends there. William Styles and his wife Anna were among the original settlers of Salmon Falls, and they were happy to entertain the missionaries. Their children were grown, and they had no qualms about hosting meetings. Their home had a fine view to the east across the river. The Friends' practice of worshipping in people's homes without the burden of tithes and taxes appealed to them. William Styles was particularly taken with the concept of consensus.

"I removed here not just for the timber, ye understand," he said over dinner on their first evening together. "Sick and bloody tired of it, I was, if ye will excuse the expression. Those lords and landowners on the coast want to run things as if they were still in the Old Country. Each one ruler of his own little kingdom, mind ye, and it's all 'Do as I say or begone with you!' So we went," he chuckled, "and I'm sure they were that glad to see my back."

"And the women were just as bad," Anna added. "Always watching each other, they were, like cats on a mouse, if they caught the least scent of an indiscretion. Reverend Wilson called it the 'mutual watch' and said it would protect the community from God's wrath, but it was ever one person's word against another, and woe to you, if ye fell out of favor with anyone!"

"Was this at Dover?" Anne Coleman asked.

"Nay, we first settled at Boston in the Bay Colony, back when John Winthrop was governor," William answered.

"At least he was summat benign," his wife put in.

"Aye, summat," her husband allowed reluctantly. "But then he died in '49, and things went from bad to worse when John Endicott was elected. The man makes laws left and right with no sanction from the Crown. O' course, there *was* no Crown by then, thanks to the bloody Roundheads. We left Boston in '52, but Anna's sister says 'twas Endicott and the ministers set the laws against Quakers after. Even his neighbors from Salem were not spared—some twenty confined to gaol from his own town—and they had helped through a lean time! A right tyrant, he is now. He caused some of your lot to be hanged."

"Yes, we know of that," Mary murmured, laying down her spoon. Her appetite had fled.

"Oh, of course ye do!" Anna exclaimed mortified. "Forgive us for bringing it up and at table too!" She glanced at her husband reprovingly.

"No, it's all right," Mary said, straightening. "'Tis why we came to the colonies. Mary Dyer was our mentor, the instrument of our convincement." She nodded toward Allie.

"Oh, ye knew that godly woman, did ye!" their hostess exclaimed, impressed.

"Yes, she came to our village, Kingsweare, near Dartmouth on the Devon coast," she explained to their hosts, who were from Wessex. "She and two Friends interrupted the service at our church. She was en route to her family in Rhode Island after nearly six years in England, and their ship put in for supplies. She had come from Swarthmore Hall, where she trained as a missionary for the Society. She encouraged us to do so ourselves."

"Executing those men was terrible, but when we heard they hanged a woman..." William broke off disgusted.

"My sister lives in Charlestown and witnessed the executions," Anna Styles told them. "She wrote me of it, saying many were discomfitted for those being hanged seemed godly people and kept their faith to the end. The authorities insisted upon public attendance, but the crowd was gigantic, and when they made to cross the river all at once, the bridge to Charlestown collapsed under their weight!"

"How terrible!" Allie exclaimed. "Was thy sister harmed?"

"No, thank God!" Anna said. "She and her husband saw it from a distance. 'Twas a blessing it was June!"

"Folk will not countenance Endicott's brutal laws much longer, I think," William said. "The King's mandamus gave him some pause, I warrant, forbidding the executions, but the arrests and punishments continue, we hear."

"Ye should not go there for ye would certes be thrown in prison and flogged. Are ye not a-feared for your welfare?" Anna asked the missionaries.

Allie shook her head, as her mouth was full.

"We are in God's hands," Anne answered. "His Will be done."

Mary picked up her spoon. "I warrant 'twill not be long before we look this John Endicott in the face," she said quietly.

"It seems almost too easy, Allie." Mary whispered later, as they lay on pallets in the dark loft above the Styles living area. Anne had fallen asleep and was snoring softly.

"God approves, one supposes," Allie responded. "Is there no value without hardship?"

"'Tis only speaking of our dear Mary recalled our original purpose. By visiting these small outposts in the wilderness, we avoid challenging those responsible for her death."

"But these folk have a need too, because they are so isolated. The ordained ministers disdain these small communities that cannot afford their stipends. Wouldst thou go to Boston? We would soon see the inside of their gaol. Hard to accomplish much there."

"An unjust law should be challenged, but no, not Boston—at least, not yet."

"After your words at table I am summat relieved," Allie said, gently mimicking their hosts.

"We should return to Dover."

"Oh." All levity fled before this statement.

"A public protest there could be our first strike against the Bay Colony. There are many who would join us, I reckon. It might serve as a stronghold for Friends," Mary went on.

"Did Friend Wharton not advise against it?" Allie asked.

Mary seemed not to have heard. "We had good fellowship there in June with just two meetings. Dost thou not remember? Families like the Robertses and Nutes—"

"We made an enemy there as well," Allie cautioned.

"Certes," her friend replied undaunted, "But he is easily bested, as I recall."

"I warrant he is not entirely without support," Allie commented. "He is an ordained minister. An elder of his church lives here in Salmon Falls. We are fortunate he is away. Reyner's influence extends beyond Dover to the whole region. And what of that magistrate Friend Preston mentioned, the rich one with all the ships?"

Mary countered the question with another. "What of our call to stand against these unjust laws? Wouldst spend all winter in outposts such as this?"

Mary held her breath. She would not force Allie to take a risk against her will, even though she herself was ready for it, but Mary knew she could not proceed alone. She needed her friend's support.

"I reckon thou art already set on this," Allie sighed. "Whither thou goest, Mimi..." she said ruefully.

Mary groped for her friend's hand and squeezed it. Then she turned over and promptly fell asleep. Allie listened to her rhythmic breathing for a long time.

The trip down river to Dover Point went quickly with both current and tide in their favor. The Styles had business on the Neck before winter confined them to Salmon Falls, and they transported the three women in their open skiff. All were bundled in their warmest cloaks with mufflers wrapped around their heads and necks, for the weather was cold enough to snow. A month in Salmon Falls had served to establish regular meetings at the Styles' home. The group numbered around a dozen, but they were steadfast and assimilated the Friends' message readily. Mary was eager for a bigger challenge.

Although several families would welcome them on the Neck, the missionaries were aware they posed a risk to any associating with them. They planned to stay at the Emerys' publick house as they had the previous June. If meetings took place in different homes on different days each week, Mary hoped they might elude the authorities long enough to encourage the Dover Friends. If they were arrested, she was ready and willing to make a stand against the unjust law that forbade them to practice their faith. On the chilly trip downriver, Mary prayed for patience. She wanted to impart her message of freedom from Puritan tyranny to every person she met. She longed to speak out at Sabbath Day meetings, publicly challenging self-serving ministers like John Reyner, but she was not unmindful of the danger. She must follow her calling with care, exercise patience, and wait upon the Light Within to guide her course.

William Styles secured his skiff to the dock at Immigrant's Landing, which was busy as ever despite the cold. Everything felt familiar as the four of them walked up High Street to the Emerys' inn. It seemed ages since that June day they had staggered up the lane on sea legs with George Preston. Edward Wharton came to mind, his handsome face creased with concern, her name on his lips. She shied from the image and quickened her pace.

They walked briskly in the cold, clutching satchels and cloaks tightly. It was a relief to reach the ordinary, where a blazing fire warmed the common room. Anthony's wife, Frances, welcomed William and Anna Styles like the old friends they were, and she remembered the two missionaries. They introduced Anne Coleman, and Mistress Emery's smile remained genuine. Twenty years in service had exposed her to myriad configurations of humanity, and the innkeeper's wife evinced no shock or disdain. Mary was impressed. It was mid-afternoon and the common room was quiet, so Frances sat down with them. A kitchen maid brought steaming bowls of fish stew with a loaf baked that morning.

"Tasty stew, Frances," William commented between bites. "Where is Anthony then?"

"He is at Kittery for a few days," she told them. "He and James—our son," she clarified for the missionaries, "are taking up the ferry business there. We shall quit this place come spring."

"So 'tis true then," Anna Styles said. "We heard ye might be leaving." She glanced at her husband, who nodded, his mouth full.

"Not on our account, I hope," Mary said to Frances.

Their hostess gave her a wan smile. "There are many reasons. The custom is good here, but the authorities hamper us at every turn. If Anthony objects or tries to reason with them, they slap another fine on us for 'mutinous courage.' Each year they make some excuse to delay granting our license." She smiled without humor. "Though truth be told, we get on quite well with it or no." Her smile faded. "But now, well, you should all be told of this." She glanced around the room then looked at each of them. They stopped eating and stared back. "As soon as they learn y'are here, they mean to arrest you. They have circulated a formal complaint and bid folk sign it or be known as dissenters."

"Who has?" Styles asked alarmed.

"That Reverend Reyner and his crony, Elder Nutter."

"What does it say, precisely?" Mary asked.

"It calls for your arrest for offending the so-called god-fearing folk of this town with your heresy. Anthony refused to sign, but 'tis said there are more than sixty who did. They want you gone," Frances answered.

"Gone from Dover?" asked William.

Frances shook her head, "No. Their complaint is the key to open the door for the magistrates, the agents of the court at Boston. 'Tis backed by the Bay Colony entire."

# *Chapter 29*

## RICHARD WALDERNE *CATASTROPHE*

1644-1646 Dover and Boston, Massachusetts Bay Colony

A few weeks after their return from Boston, Prudence realized she was pregnant. She longed for a girl. Her husband had two strong sons. It was time she had a daughter. Barbara was but four months ahead of her, and Prudence was thrilled, oblivious to the fact that Barbara was not happy. This would be her ninth child, and she was near forty. On top of that, Will's penchant for spirits was affecting his judgment and his moods. His wife was worried.

One gloomy day in July Barbara was visiting Prudence. They sat in the window seat with their needlework, as summer rain peppered the glass, driven by an off-shore wind. Barbara's only daughter Mary was fifteen. She had taken ten-year-old Isaac upstairs to play with his younger cousins in the nursery. Barbara had left her younger boys at home with the nursemaid. The two women were alone.

"I dare not tell Richard, but I do so wish this babe shall be a girl," Pru said, speaking quietly though her husband was absent. She knew she could confide in Barbara.

There was no response, so Prudence went on, her eyes on her stitching.

"You must want that also, Barbara, with seven boys and just Mary to keep you company? Oh, would it not be lovely to have two little girls together?"

She glanced up to see silent tears coursing down her sister-in-law's cheeks.

"Dear sister!" Prudence exclaimed, laying her handiwork aside and moving closer. "Whatever is the matter?"

Barbara broke down completely at this sympathetic inquiry, and Pru embraced her, keeping an eye on the parlor door in case the children might appear.

"'Tis Will," her sister-in-law whispered, pulling back to remove the handkerchief from her sleeve and blotting her eyes. "Oh Prudence, I know not what to do!"

The younger woman was amazed. Will and Barbara seemed so solid, an older married couple to look up to. At times she had even wished Richard had more of his brother's playfulness and humor. Her husband was so strict and formal with the boys. He largely ignored them until after their breeching. Prudence thought his expectations were unrealistically high where the boys' behavior was concerned, though she kept quiet.

"Is he ill?" she asked, when her sister-in-law quieted.

Barbara expressed something between a laugh and a sob. "I suppose one might say he is ill. He is plagued by drink. He goes to the ordinary every night, and some days he does not rise until after noon." She paused and looked at Prudence searchingly, then confided in a low voice, "Last night, when I attempted to waylay him, he pushed me aside, and I fell against a table."

"Oh, Barbara! Are you quite—"

"It did no damage to the babe, I think," Barbara said quickly. "There has been no bleeding, though I am sore here," she touched her ribs, "but I fear for our future and for our children." Fresh tears fell, and she looked down. "I am afraid to have this babe."

"Oh, my sweet sister! This is untenable! I shall speak to Richard. Mayhap he can—"

"No!" Barbara gripped her sister-in-law's arm so hard it hurt. "No, Prudence, I beg you, do not!" She loosened her grip and added more quietly. "'Twould only make things worse, I fear. Will would be furious if he knew I spoke to you."

"But what shall you do? What if he harms you or the babe? Barbara, please let us help you!" Prudence pleaded.

Barbara shook her head and rose to her feet. "I should not have said anything," she muttered. "We must go home."

She hastily gathered her needlework and picked up the basket.

"Sister, do not leave like this—"

"I am his wife!" Barbara interrupted. "You know well what that means, Prudence. We have no recourse against our husbands. We *belong* to them. The law affords no justice for a woman who goes against her husband, no matter the cause. 'Tis our duty to obey and serve them without question or complaint." She started for the hall to summon her children. "You cannot possibly help me."

"At least let me ask Richard to give you some money!" Prudence said, following.

Barbara stopped, shaking her head. "So Will could spend it on drink? I think not," she said wearily. "But my thanks," she added laying her free hand on the younger woman's arm.

Prudence hugged her. "I shall keep your secret then," she promised. She held Barbara at arm's length. "But you must confide in me, if things become worse. Richard cares for you, and he will protect you. No one would countenance the abuse of a woman with child, especially if her husband is intemperate."

Barbara winced. "Thus shall all of Dover know of it, and I doubt not he would forfeit his post as Town Recorder. His reputation would be ruined," she said mournfully.

Prudence could not deny it. The women of their social circle would pounce on such a scandalous tidbit. Barbara donned her cloak and bonnet and called up the stairs to her children. Prudence watched them hurry off through the gusting wind and rain.

Barbara and Will's eighth son, William, was born at the end of October. Three months later, Prudence birthed the daughter she had prayed for and named her Elizabeth for her mother. Both births went smoothly, though Pru's delivery was several weeks early. The baby was small, but cried lustily and took the breast well. Prudence felt truly blessed; however, the women's delight was cut short that spring, when Will's decline became apparent to all. Things came to a head one Sabbath Day in early May.

The Reverend Daniel Maud had presided over the First Congregational Church of Dover for two years. He was the fifth minister in a decade of turmoil, and to the congregation's relief, he seemed a good fit. Maud had been a schoolmaster in Boston for six years. His demeanor was severe, but he was a quiet man who abhorred contention and had no designs to rule the colony. On the fateful morning the minister mounted the pulpit and was about to speak, when the door to the men's section opened abruptly. William Walderne staggered to his seat. He was not only late, but also inebriate beyond doubt. Heads turned. Barbara's face drained of color, and she gripped her sister-in-law's hand.

Still, the mild-mannered reverend might have simply frowned on the infraction had Will not gone on to commit the ultimate insult. During a pause in the sermon, a rude noise resounded through the meeting house. Will had fallen asleep in church.

The next Tuesday at town meeting, he was called to task and fined on three counts—tardiness, public inebriation, and sleeping in church. The minister and town officials banned William Walderne from membership, barring a public apology. He was sentenced to suffer penance before the congregation on the next Sabbath Day, bearing a sign labeled "Drunkard." William Pomfrett was chosen to replace him as town recorder.

Barbara's worst fears were realized, but she was not alone. Richard had avoided his brother's company for some time and had not realized the depths to which Will had sunk. He was mortified by the incident. It tainted the family name and Richard's own reputation by association. He had no sympathy for his elder. In fact he was furious.

Will was contrite. He bore Richard's considerable wrath without argument. He was stoic as his brother gave him a verbal dressing down and confiscated his alcohol. Will swore he would stay away from the ordinary. He made a humble public apology and another to Reverend Maud personally. The next Sunday he bore the long hours of his penance, standing before the congregation labeled as a drunkard without food or drink throughout the day, including the noon break.

Although this discipline allowed him to retain his membership in the church, Will had lost his livelihood. The years of excess had compromised his health and strength. At forty-five he was not fit for any job requiring physical labor, and there was little other work to be had locally. When he learned of a post as recorder of deeds at Saco in the Province of Maine, he applied for the job by post and was relieved to get it. After a month of sobriety and unemployment, William Walderne packed a trunk, bid his family a tearful farewell, and left Dover Point.

Soon after his departure Barbara was dismayed to note the well-known signs of pregnancy. She and Will had reconciled during his month of contrition and abstinence. This was the result.

Although Will sent funds sporadically throughout the summer, Barbara was forced to reduce the household staff. Her elder sons helped when they could, but they had families of their own and lived a long day's ride away. Barbara spoke of selling the house in Dover and moving to the family's townhouse in Charlestown to live with her eldest son, Christopher, and his family.

Prudence was horrified at this prospect and had words with Samuel, Barbara and Will's fourth boy. He was fifteen and had apprenticed to Edward Colcord as a cooper the year before. He lived with his employer in Dover, and in six years, he would be a paid journeyman. Until then, he had only his strength and company to share. Still Barbara was grateful when Colcord allowed the boy to live at home and help his mother. Sam was invaluable with the younger boys. They looked up to him and obeyed without argument and performed the heavier chores now most of the servants were gone.

Mary also rose to the occasion as her mother's tenth pregnancy advanced and her confinement began. She was nursemaid to her two youngest siblings, Alexander and William, four and two respectively. Mary also assisted the loyal and aging cook, Missus Higgins, who had been with the family for ten years. Prudence sent her hired girls over to help on laundry day. The family was struggling, but they would survive.

Barbara's labor started on the hottest day in August. Prudence attended the birth and helped Mary organize refreshment for the goodwives that came. She was at Barbara's side through the final hours of labor, laying cool cloths on her perspiring brow, and helping the midwife to support her on the birthing stool as she pushed. When she realized the babe was a girl, Barbara wept with joy and relief. She named her Prudence in honor of her loyal sister-in-law. She wrote to Will of the baby's birth but received no reply. In fact no word had come from him in weeks. Barbara confided to Prudence that she feared he was indulging in spirits again.

Pru secretly gave Barbara money from her household fund whenever she could manage. Richard forbid the mention of Will's name and silenced her if she tried to talk about his brother's family, but Prudence could not bear to see her sister-in-law and closest friend struggling to feed and clothe her children—the cousins of her own sweet ones.

Happily, Richard was often away that summer after Will left, citing his ever demanding business concerns. Prudence visited Barbara often, and the two women were closer than ever. They were together on a chilly day in September, when there was a knock on Barbara's door.

Mary answered it and came back with Reverend Maud and a stranger—a seaman by the look of him. Their faces were grave. The women stood up, and the minister introduced the man as Captain Fernald of Appledore Island in the Shoals. He captained a fishing craft and had come from Kennebunk with dire cargo. They refused Barbara's offer of tea. No one sat down. There was an awkward moment as Maud paused, turning his hat in his hands.

"Goodwife Walderne, God bless you," he began. "May He give you strength this day. There is sorry news, I fear."

Prudence felt dread uncoil like a serpent in her chest. Barbara groped for her hand.

"I take it you have word of my husband," the older woman said, searching the men's faces. Her voice was calm, but she gripped Pru's hand as if her life depended upon it.

The two men exchanged a look, and the minister continued.

"Yes, we do," Maud said, moving a step closer. "Mayhap you would care to sit?"

Barbara shook her head, and Prudence put an arm around her protectively. She could feel her trembling.

"He is injured?" Barbara asked.

To the reverend's credit Maud did not look away. "I fear 'tis worse." He drew breath. "He is gone to God," he finished.

Barbara swayed, and Prudence and Maud helped her to sit. She did not weep or rail. Her eyes were blank with shock.

"Dead then," she said dully. She straightened and fixed her eyes on the captain. "Were you there, sir? Tell me the circumstances, I beg you."

The man looked uncomfortable and glanced at Maud, who nodded encouragingly.

"He drowned, Mistress. He was alone, so we know not exactly what passed. His body—I mean to say, we found him after—well, he had been missing awhile, y'see."

He looked at the reverend in desperation. He could not bear to tell this woman, now a widow, of the condition of the body found some five weeks after folk realized the man had disappeared. It was an ordeal for the fishermen who recovered it and for the apothecary who examined the body for signs of injury. Even transporting the coffin was a trial. The smell even overpowered the stink of fish offal that clung to the boat. The captain looked forward to completing his Christian duty and getting shut of it. To his immense relief, the minister took up the narrative.

"There was no sign of foul play, according to the physician's report," he assured Barbara. "Mister Walderne's landlady said he went to his employment as usual that morn, but did not return. She thought perhaps he had moved on, although his things were still in his room. Captain Fernald brought them, as well, thinking you would want your husband's effects."

The captain nodded with a wary look at Barbara, who yet appeared stunned. When she did not respond, the minister continued.

"The last anyone recalled seeing him was mid-August. He left the ordinary in Saco sometime after the sun had set. The men who were—uh, who last saw him—said he was likely making for his lodgings across the river. It was his custom to stop there nightly on his way..." His voice trailed off, and they endured an awkward silence. William Walderne's wife knew well what her husband's "custom" entailed. "We can only assume some mishap occurred, as he crossed the Kennebunk," Maud finished.

Barbara nodded. The unspoken message was clear. Will had been drunk. The thought made her both angry and sad. More than twenty years had she lived and struggled with the man. Now the father of her ten children, her warm-hearted, weak-willed husband with his irreverent humor was truly gone. She would never see him more. Her face crumpled, and turning to Prudence, she succumbed to grief at last.

# Chapter 30

## MARY & ALICE *ARREST*

December, 1662 Dover, Massachusetts Bay Colony

Sarah Nute sprinkled dried parsley over the steaming fish on the platter. The aroma of baked cod filled the crowded room. There were many mouths to feed, but it was a fine big fish. She enjoyed cooking. It might be prideful, but she loved the compliments and attention even more than the food. Sarah was not a meek woman. She had come to the New World thirty years ago on the *Pied Cow* with twenty-one other women contracted to marry colonists. Thank Heaven her James proved to have a mild temperament, as few men would have tolerated her outspoken opinions.

There were oohs and aahs, as she placed the savory platter on the large table in the middle of the room. Sarah drank in the approbation of her guests and remarked the gleam of pride in her husband's eyes. The Nutes were happy to host meetings for the Dover Friends. Their farm had no neighbors in sight and was located on the west bank of Back River at a remove from the Point. The increasingly repressive influence of the Bay Colony had caused them to sell their original lots on Dover Neck two years before. It had been a good decision, affording the family more freedom to live and worship as they pleased away from the mutual watch.

Sarah and James Nute had been convinced three years before. They were living on the Point at the time and heard Wenlock Christison speak at the home of Thomas and Rebecca Roberts. Twice this past summer, they had attended meetings at Kittery Point, staying with their friends George and Alice Walton on Great Isle. They welcomed the missionary Friends, for even had they wished to, it was a hardship to cross the river for services on the Neck, especially once winter was upon them. The Nutes had no love for the Puritan Church and had supported Thomas Larkham in his day. The folk at this meeting were of like mind and would not gainsay their faith under threat of fines.

As folk grouped around the table for a portion of her delicious meal, Sarah surveyed the gathering with satisfaction. There were more attending than the first meeting at the Roberts's house last week. Some fifteen folk filled her home, Doctor Barefoot included, though he was an Anglican. Happily, George and Alice Walton had thought to bring extra trenchers and knives from their inn, where the next meeting would be held. Everyone in the close-knit group would take a turn at hosting, and their secret meetings were held on different days each week. The shared risk bonded the worshippers.

The door opened, admitting a raw gust of December air. Talk ceased and heads turned, as two men stepped over the threshold. Their hats and mufflers concealed their faces. Reverend Reyner and Elder Nutter followed and were more easily recognized. The men did not bother to close the door, and the candles on the table guttered and died in the chill draft. Nutter held a parchment, which he unrolled and began to read without preamble to the stunned folk.

> *Know all ye present this complaint by the righteous citizens of Dover that do herein humbly crave relief against the spreading and the wicked errors of the Quakers among them, and further that the General Court ordered by Captain Richard Walderne shall and hereby is empowered to act in the execution of the laws of this jurisdiction against all criminal offenders within the said town of Dover, as any one magistrate may do, until this Court shall take further order.*

"There they are!" Reyner declared, pointing. "Those three women there!"

The enforcers started toward the missionaries, but Walter Barefoote and George Walton blocked their way.

"Hold, I prithee." James Nute stepped between the men, his palms raised. "What law have they transgressed?" he asked in a reasonable tone.

"This is a formal complaint signed by more than sixty citizens and freemen," Nutter declared, thrusting out his chin. "'Tis all the authority required. Take them," he said to the constables.

Protests erupted, as the men moved to apprehend the missionaries. Allie put her hand on Walter's arm.

"Thou art more help to us free, Walter," she said quietly.

The doctor and the innkeeper stepped aside reluctantly. The missionaries did not resist, but they sank to the floor like rag dolls, as soon as the men laid hands on them. The constables were obliged to drag each of them bodily from the house. Reverend Reyner plucked the complaint from Nutter's hand and held it up, raising his voice over the objections.

"By this legal document the people of Dover seek protection from the pernicious lies spread by these heretics!" he declared, as the constables pulled Anne Coleman out between them. Her feet barely touched the floor. "They influence folk to absent themselves from proper worship for shams such as this." He flung out his arm, taking in the room then pointed at Mary and Allie. "These vagabond Quakers are unnatural women and a threat to our town! Any who defend them shall be fined!" He scowled at the company, then turned and followed the constables, shouting, "Secure her in the cart!"

The Friends were helpless to prevent the arrest without sharing the missionaries' plight. They watched in silence, except for their hostess, who continued to rail at the intruders. Her two youngest daughters clutched her skirt, eyes wide with fear, as the two men returned, seized Mary, and dragged her from the house, leaving snow on the floor and cold air in their wake.

"This is a travesty! Ye cannot do this! These are godly women!" Sarah admonished, following them outside. The little girls were loath to release their grip and were pulled along, as she berated the men. She seemed unaware of the girls in her righteous indignation.

The constables ignored her and returned for Allie, removing her as they had the others.

"Thy father shall be sorry to hear of this!" Sarah threatened, as they pushed past her again. The constables were John Roberts and his younger brother, Thomas.

The cart's progress was slow, and James Nute and Walter Barefoote followed on horseback, catching up at Hall's landing where the ferry crossed Back River to Dover Point. They brought the women's cloaks left behind in the rush. Sarah insisted they take a warm quilt and some hastily packed food as well. Their hostess would have gone herself but for her girls, whose wails rose in volume, as she made to leave. The Nutes would likely be fined for entertaining the Quakers, but their concern was all for the missionaries.

After the warning from Frances Emery, Mary and Allie had expected the arrest. The six months in the dungeons of Lancaster Prison had been much worse. The conditions at the Dover gaol were tolerable by comparison. The experience was new to Anne Coleman, however, and she shivered violently. Mary suspected it was not entirely from the cold. She and Allie put their small companion between them on the wooden plank that served as bed and bench, wrapping the Nutes' quilt closely around them. Walter Barefoote had taken the ferry with them and hastened home, returning in less than an hour with a pannikin of hot soup and two more blankets.

"I shall endeavor to do what I can for you," he promised earnestly. "Word is spreading already and many Friends shall attend your hearing on the morrow."

Young Thomas Roberts did not allow him to linger.

"You keep dangerous company, Doctor," the constable warned.

"Perverting the law is more dangerous than preaching the Love of God, I should think," Walter answered tartly. "These women have committed no crime!"

"That complaint says otherwise," Thomas asserted.

The soup and blankets warmed them, but the apothecary's loyalty bolstered the missionaries' morale. As the light waned and the cold sharpened, the constable locked the gaol and went home for the night, leaving the prisoners in the chill darkness. The women huddled together, exchanging stories of their training at Swarthmore Hall. Mary recalled their missionary work with Edward Burrough. They sang hymns, and finally, propped between her companions, Anne slept.

# *Chapter 31*

## RICHARD WALDERNE AND MARY TOMKINS
## *THE SENTENCE*

December 1662 Dover, Massachusetts Bay Colony

John Roberts informed Richard Walderne of the Quakers' arrest himself. He left for Cocheco as soon as the missionaries were locked up, leaving Thomas to guard them with strict instructions that no one but the apothecary was to see them. John wished to be the bearer of this good news, for it would accrue to his benefit in the powerful man's opinion.

Construction on the Waldernes' new mansion at Cocheco had started during the summer, and John found the captain in his office perusing the floor plans. He looked up scowling, when Paul Walderne rapped briefly and opened the door, but his expression changed when he saw that the constable accompanied his son.

"Constable Roberts," Walderne greeted him, standing and offering his hand. John was pleased by the gesture and reached across the desk to shake it firmly.

"Captain Walderne, sir," he responded warmly.

"Sit down, sit down. You are lately come from Dover?" John nodded. "To what do I owe the honor of this visit?" Richard could sense the younger man's excitement.

"My thanks, sir." John sat on the edge of the chair, eager to share the glad tidings. "I bring good news."

The captain's eyebrows rose in inquiry.

"We arrested the three Quaker women this afternoon," the constable said proudly.

"Well done! Where were they?" The magistrate leaned forward, resting his elbows on the desk.

"At the home of James Nute—the new one across Back River. We broke up one of their 'meetings.'" John answered the final word heavy with sarcasm.

"Hah! Never did trust that man. We shall see him fined for it." Walderne's eyes flashed, and John's smile widened under his approval. "So I presume you are come to fetch me for the hearing?"

John nodded, "Yes, sir."

"We shall not delay in making an example of these so-called missionaries." He glanced at the window. "The light is failing now. Allow me to entertain you this night. We shall go at first light on the morrow. Is all being prepared for the trial?"

"Yes, sir, Richard Pinkham is alerting the townsfolk to attend, and Reverend Reyner and Father Nutter were enlisting some men to set up the meeting house as I left."

"And the women are secured in the gaol?"

"They are, and Thomas is on guard until full dark."

"Excellent work, Constable!" the captain said with a rare smile.

Richard Walderne's approval was worth more than gold, especially since John's parents were known to have embraced the cursed sect. Their eldest son made it clear he was not in sympathy with them. He himself had confiscated one of his father's best cows to pay the fines owed for their many absences from the First Church. With Father Nutter and Captain Walderne as allies, John dared to hope he might become a magistrate himself one day. He was elated with this turn of events.

The next morning, the two men rose early and rode down to the Neck in high spirits. John went to the gaol to check on the prisoners, while the captain stabled his horse and joined Reyner and Nutter at the Emerys' ordinary.

The court would convene at ten of the clock, affording the magistrate time to take some refreshment and confer with Hatevil and the reverend. The outcome of the "trial" was assumed. The women were Quakers, and their guilt was evident. Richard had witnessed the havoc their fellows had wrought in Boston. He would not allow it here.

"The Quaker threat must be nipped in the bud," he said, as they discussed the sentence. "We must make an example of them to insure they do not return to Dover—ever. These clandestine meetings must stop."

"Would that the King's mandamus was not served last year," Reyner lamented. "We could hang them and be done with it."

"We must bend the law, not break it," the magistrate cautioned, lowering his voice.

"Even if 'twere still possible, Reverend, hanging is for a third offense and this is but their first," Hatevil reminded him. Reyner scowled, but the big man ignored him. "What do you suggest, Richard?"

"The Whip and Cart Act," the magistrate answered promptly.

The minister's face cleared. "Certes, 'twill humiliate them to be stripped to the waist and flogged in public," he said with satisfaction.

"The cold shall increase their suffering as well," the elder pointed out dispassionately. "Which towns shall we designate after Dover?" he asked.

Richard sipped his tea, thinking.

"Hampton and Boston?" Reyner supplied eagerly. "Or mayhap Ipswich and Boston?"

"No," the magistrate answered slowly, considering the towns along the King's Road. His lip curled, and he sat back. "According to the Act, they must be taken to the limits of the colony, must they not?" His companions nodded. "Then they must be taken to Dedham."

"Dedham is a far piece—over eighty mile, I reckon, but which town in beyween, think you?" Hatevil persisted.

"All of them," Richard responded.

The two men gaped at him.

"All of the major towns along the route," he repeated and ticked them off on his fingers. "Dover, Hampton, Salisbury, Newbury, Rowley, Ipswich, Wenham, Lynn, Boston, Roxbury, and Dedham." He had run out of fingers and held up a thumb for the last.

"Eleven towns?" Reyner asked faintly. Even the zealous minister was shocked.

"Is the Act not limited to three towns?" Nutter inquired.

"As the magistrate of Dover, my interpretation of the Whip and Cart Act is that they shall be flogged until they are out of the Bay Colony's jurisdiction," the Captain stated.

"But none could survive—" the reverend began then stopped. He sat back, looking at the magistrate with wide eyes.

"Who is to say?" Richard asked, raising his eyebrows. "Certes they shall not return."

Reyner and Nutter exchanged a look, and the elder shrugged eloquently. The minister smiled.

At ten of the clock the three men walked up High Street to the Fort Meeting House. Richard had donated the lumber from his mills, and his friends had followed suit with coin or other materials. The building had not been so full since its dedication in 1654.

The officials sat at a table on the north wall which served as a judge's bench. Richard looked over the crowd with satisfaction. No doubt there were dissenters among them, but they would learn a lesson this day. He would not stand by while the Quakers wreaked havoc in his town. Every bench was full, and spectators stood around the walls—even outside in the cold—awaiting the outcome. It did not matter whether people were for or against the missionaries. The event superseded the daily routine, and none would miss it.

The minister had quill, ink, and paper at the ready, for he was both accuser and recorder. Magistrate Walderne called for order in the crowded room, and the babble of conversation subsided to murmurs. The missionaries entered from the vestry, flanked by the constables. All talk ceased at their appearance. The clank of their chains seemed overloud in the quiet.

Richard assessed the prisoners through half-closed eyes, affecting boredom. One was small as a child and crooked. It was laughable the heretics allowed her to represent them, he thought with contempt. Another was tall as a man and met his eyes like one, though she was striking with black hair and green eyes. The third seemed unremarkable, until he realized she was searching his face with disconcerting candor. Certes, their confidence was bluff and would crumble under the lash. How had Reyner allowed himself to be bested by these motley women?

Mary looked at the magistrate. This was the man Edward and George had warned them about. He was comely in a severe way and exuded the assurance of power. She searched his laconic expression for any sign of That of God but saw only cold calculation, as he took stock of them. He glanced at the paper before him, cleared his throat, and spoke to the room at large.

"Mary Tomkins, Alice Ambrose, and Anne Coleman, this formal complaint," he brandished the document, "has been served against you for spreading your false doctrine in the Town of Dover, Massachusetts Bay Colony. It is signed by upwards of sixty members of the First Congregational Church and calls for your removal from this jurisdiction."

People stirred and glanced sideways at their neighbors, wondering who had signed the document and who had not. Walderne raised his voice, and the room stilled.

"The law of the Massachusetts Bay Colony forbids preaching by any unauthorized person, and further forbids the practice of any religion that deviates from the established church. You are charged with promulgating heresy. Do you deny it?"

The Tomkins woman responded with surprising eloquence.

"We do not deny that we have spoken, but we do deny 'tis heresy, for we speak God's truth."

The intelligence evidenced by this remark gave him pause and dispelled his lackadaisical attitude. He straightened, his senses sharpening as they did whenever he discerned a challenge. He retained his bland expression with difficulty as she went on.

"Our message is received with gladness. We do not constrain people to join us, unlike your minister who mandates that folk attend his church or be fined. Worship cannot be forced. Folk must be free to choose their own path to God, for He dwells within every person," she finished.

A collective gasp met this statement for it was heresy in itself. The three officials stared at her, astonied by the blatant infraction. Walderne recovered first and glanced at the reverend. Reyner raised his eyebrows as though to say, "You see?" The magistrate turned back to her, his expression grim. He was offended by the woman's temerity in stating such a bald lie in the court. She was unnatural and must be put in her place. He had never thought to hear such arrogance from a woman, and the prospect of besting her was strangely appealing. He began calmly.

"This document indicates otherwise," he said, gesturing to the complaint. "The good people of this town crave relief from your lies. They are not able to 'choose their own path.' They require guidance from the Reverend Reyner, an ordained minister who is educated to bring them to God. Salvation is found in the Bible. To claim any other source is a perversion and smacks of the Devil. It is blasphemy to compare yourself to an ordained minister!"

Richard's outrage gathered momentum as he spoke. His detachment was slipping, and his voice rose. The laconic attitude had fled. Mary watched him carefully.

"You have no education in religion. You are ignorant vagabonds! You own no property here and make no contribution to this town other than sowing chaos and dissension among its citizens. I have seen your ilk at Boston. You Quakers are like to a scabrous affliction—you are not welcome, yet you persist in staying."

Mary realized that as a magistrate and assistant to the General Court this man had been party to approving the laws and executions that had convicted and killed Mary Dyer and the other missionaries. Righteous fury coursed through her. Richard Walderne embodied everything she opposed.

The captain's eyes flashed. He forgot the avid audience. His focus was exclusively on Mary and bringing her to task. If she were his wife—God forbid—he would correct her outlandish behavior and relish it. His pulse was racing, but the Quaker woman seemed frustratingly unrepentant, looking up at him with dispassionate calm. He glared at her as he spoke.

"Furthermore, the offense is all the more heinous because you are *women* unbridled by a husband's discipline! You are abominations of your sex! If there be no law against women preaching, 'tis solely because no sane lawmaker would ever conceive of it!"

Mary longed to disparage the magistrate's prejudicial assumptions. She was no obedient goodwife to be cowed by male authority. The man was an affront to God, and she was His instrument. The magistrate was drawing breath to go on when she spoke, interrupting him.

"So there was a law that Daniel should not pray to his God," she said, citing precedent through scripture, as the clergy often did.

Richard froze. He could hardly credit his hearing. She was quoting the Bible in her defense with the presumption of an ordained minister. Besides that, it was a tactic he had used himself in his youth when pressed by authority. It created the last thing he wanted with this maddening woman—a connection. Her intelligence alarmed and fascinated him despite his fury. She was more dangerous than he had thought at first—both heretic and temptress.

Mary saw the biblical reference affected Walderne, but his abrupt change from choler to stillness filled her with foreboding. The hair on her scalp prickled. The heavy silence following her words was ominous. The entire room held its breath, awaiting his reaction.

The magistrate's eyes narrowed, and his voice was dangerously quiet. "Yes," he replied evenly, "and Daniel suffered, and so shall you."

Walderne sat back, fixing the woman with a predatory stare. No one moved. He would relish seeing her break under the lash on the morrow. His only regret was that he would not be present to witness the other ten floggings. His tone was now blandly official.

"In answer to the plea of the people of Dover for relief from this scourge, I hereby sentence you to banishment from the Massachusetts Bay Colony under the Whip and Cart Act enacted by the Great and General Court of Boston." He turned to the minister. "Reverend Reyner, make out the warrant as follows:" he glanced down at the complaint, "Mary Tomkins, Alice Ambrose, and Anne Coleman are to be secured to an ox cart and flogged ten stripes on their bare backs in each town from Dover to Dedham, until they are beyond the jurisdiction of this court. I shall sign it forthwith."

The meeting house erupted at the severity of the sentence.

"Any who protest shall join them!" Walderne roared, the banked coals of his rage flaring. "Constable Roberts, make the arrangements." He turned to the missionaries. "You are hereby confined to the cub from whence you came. The sentence shall be administered on the morrow at eight of the clock outside this meeting house." He addressed the crowd. "Attendance is mandatory. All citizens of Dover are called to witness the punishment and take heed. We are finished here."

Reverend Reyner penned the warrant, and Magistrate Walderne signed it. It read as follows:

*To the Constables of Dover, Hampton, Salisbury, Newbury, Rowley, Ipswich, Wenham, Lynn, Boston, Roxbury, Dedham, and until these vagabond Quakers are carried out of this jurisdiction. You and every one of you are required, in the king's name, to take these vagabond Quakers, Anne Coleman, Mary Tomkins, and Alice Ambrose, and make them fast to the cart's tail, and driving the cart through your several towns, to whip them on their bare backs, not exceeding ten stripes each on each of them, in each town, and so convey them from constable to constable, until they come out of this jurisdiction, as you will answer it at your peril; and this shall be your warrant.*
*At Dover, dated Dec. 22nd, 1662*
*Per me, RICHARD WALDERNE*

# *Chapter 32*

## RICHARD WALDERNE *BOSTON*

1649 Dover/Boston, Massachusetts Bay Colony

Richard was increasingly drawn to Boston. The second sawmill was as successful as the first. The Dover selectmen—of which he was one—granted him the right to harvest fifteen thousand trees of oak or pine at thruppence per tree, and he was appointed weirsman to oversee the harvest of fish from the Cocheco River as well. His influence in the colony was increasing.

During the summer of 1649 the family moved to Boston permanently. Prudence and Missus Cameron tackled this Herculean challenge together. Prudence undertook the myriad tasks involved gladly, for Dover had not been the same since Barbara had removed to Charlestown with Mary and the younger children a year after Will's death. Will had purchased the house during the peak of his prosperity, and Barbara's eldest son, Christopher, lived there with his wife, Ellen. He had steady employment as an advocate. The young couple had no children as yet, and they welcomed his widowed mother and younger siblings. Prudence was thrilled to be close to her sister-in-law again.

Well-appointed homes had sprung up and lined both sides of Tremont Row now. Paul, at nine and Timothy, at seven, were both of an age to attend school. Although Prudence taught them the rudiments of reading, writing, and sums, Richard wanted his sons to have the best education the colony could offer, and that was at Boston's Free Latin School. Reverend Maud had encouraged the family in this vein, for prior to coming to Dover the clergyman had been employed there, first assisting Philomen Pormort, the original headmaster, for several years then succeeding him.

Prudence organized social engagements for her husband, inviting the cream of Boston society. Following Mistress Winthrop's advice, she soon learned which invitations to accept or decline. At twenty-eight she was a credit to Richard's image—gracious, beautiful, and devout. All who made her acquaintance were charmed.

The colony was buzzing with the news of the capture of King Charles. The royal army was defeated by Cromwell's Roundheads with the help of the Scots, and the monarch was confined to the Tower. What would they do with him? None of the Waldernes' social circle mourned the fall of the monarchy. Cromwell was a Puritan, and the Bay Colony breathed a sigh of relief, knowing the new government would not threaten them with revocation of their charter, as the less sympathetic Charles had done. A number of the colony's Puritans were going back to England to participate in the glorious new regime.

Paul and Timothy walked to school each day. Little Elizabeth complained vociferously at being left behind. She wanted to go to school too. She was a precocious child nearing the age of five and was interested in everything. She talked incessantly. Any statement prompted her to ask "Why?" To placate her daughter, Prudence began teaching her basic letters and sums, though she deemed the child too young. Elizabeth's aptitude amazed her. She was quicker than either of the boys and soon knew her letters and could write her name. After morning lessons, mother and daughter would venture out to enjoy the diversions Boston afforded, especially on Thursday Market Days. Every week they lunched with Barbara and Mary at the house in Charlestown.

Richard was uncharacteristically lenient with his daughter. During the family's first winter season in Boston, he was home more often than ever before, and father and daughter formed a bond. She was the only one of the three children he permitted to touch him, even allowing her to sit on his lap. Her striking resemblance to Prudence and her enthusiastic welcomes when he came home of an evening overwhelmed her father's stalwart ban on affection. Elizabeth understood that his study was off limits, but if he sat in the parlor, he was fair game.

One evening when the boys had been attending school for several weeks, she accosted Richard with the full force of her personality. She pushed aside the book he was perusing and held up her arms. He lifted her onto his knees, and she placed her hands on his cheeks, gazing into his eyes.

"Papa," she intoned her small face grave.

"Elizabeth," he answered, nonplussed and amused in spite of himself.

"I must attend school with Paul and Timmy."

"Girls do not attend public school," he answered definitively, removing her hands from his face.

"Whyever not?" She drew back genuinely surprised.

"You do not require it. Boys go to school to prepare for employment when they are grown."

"What is empoyment?"

Richard's lips twitched. "EmpLoyment with an 'L,'" he corrected.

"Employment," she repeated carefully. Her smooth brow furrowed. "But I must prepare too."

"You must prepare to be a good wife and manage a household and family as does your mother." His amusement was waning. Young as she was, his daughter could not be allowed to entertain such radical thoughts as girls attending school. She must accept her role in society.

"But Mamma says I am quicker than the boys!" Elizabeth insisted.

Richard set his daughter firmly on her feet and stood up, giving Prudence a censorious look. She kept her eyes on her stitching, knowing she would hear of this later.

"Enough, Elizabeth," he said firmly, frowning down at her. "Education is not for women. 'Twould addle your brain to read and figure as men do. The only preparation you require is to learn to manage a household, obey your husband, and bear his children."

Her little head drooped, and Elizabeth was silent. He waited for the acquiescence he insisted upon, when instructing his children, but instead, his daughter took his large hand in her small one and looked up at him.

"Then I shall marry *you*," she said.

The marking of the New Year was subdued in 1649. Their friend John Winthrop was ailing and had taken to his bed in February. By the end of March, the founder of the Bay Colony, the chronicler of the Puritan faith, and the father of Boston—and sixteen children by three of his four wives—was dead at the age of sixty-one.

The occasion of his funeral was the largest Boston had ever seen. The week after the Governor's passing and before the burial was a busy one for the town's printers. Everyone, it seemed, was composing pamphlets and broadsides, lauding the man and his accomplishments. The presses ran round the clock, printing the black-bordered creations of some of the best minds in the colony. The Puritans did not hold with the "popish error" of speaking words over the dead, but they took up their quills with enthusiasm, honoring the deceased in verse, anagrams, puns, and other wordplay, often darkly humorous and embellished with grisly illustrations of skulls or the Grim Reaper. These were shared among friends, family, and acquaintances. Competition for humor and originality was stiff.

It seemed all of New England turned out for the feasting and drinking on the eve of the burial, despite the early April chill. Funerals were the only public event at which the Puritans condoned strong spirits, and the Winthrop Family was generous in providing both food and drink. The public was served outside in the gardens behind the mansion on Washington Street, while family, friends, and visiting dignitaries enjoyed a private party indoors.

In the high ceilinged drawing room Prudence stood elbow to elbow with a clutch of Boston goodwives. She glimpsed her husband across the room, hobnobbing with the powerful men of colonial society and sipped her own cup of funereal punch carefully, unaccustomed as she was to strong spirits. The committee selected to concoct the mixture had done their work well. The tenor of conversation was rising in response, along with the temperature in the room. Catharine Wiggin was a case in point. Prudence turned back to the group of wives, as her elder friend was tearfully praising Winthrop.

"We shall not see his like again," Mistress Wiggin lamented. "God could not possibly have blessed us with a finer man to lead this colony."

"He officiated at our wedding," Elizabeth Endicott put in mournfully. "He was as an elder brother to me."

"And mark you how he protected the colony from that witch, Goody Jones, just last year!" Rachel Rawson declared.

"Verily, the Governor's eye was keen as his intellect," Mistress Endicott asserted. "Margaret Jones could not conceal her Devil's imp from his sharp eye. At her Watching he saw it 'in the clear light of day,' he said. My husband witnessed it and told me so."

Anne Bradstreet gave Prudence a significant look and slipped unnoticed from the group.

Catharine grasped Elizabeth Endicott's arm, causing some punch to slosh on her own gown. Neither woman appeared to notice.

"And you shall soon be a Governor's wife, shall you not, my dear?" Catherine said in a conspiratorial tone. She attempted to wink but could not quite manage it. Prudence smiled into her cup but refrained from sipping the potent brew.

Endicott's wife blushed and evinced a modest denial, but the ladies chimed in like a veritable Greek Chorus with assurances that her husband, John Endicott, would doubtless be the colony's next governor.

Prudence took advantage of the moment to follow Anne, who, she noted, had exited by the French doors opening onto the veranda that fronted the back garden. There were rumors that Simon Bradstreet's wife wrote poetry, and Pru was intrigued. She wanted to speak privily with her and was relieved to slip away from the gaggle of increasingly tipsy wives. Their comportment was embarrassing, though she knew it was sanctioned on this occasion.

The cool breeze carried the potent odor of low tide and was a relief after the stuffy room. The revelers were becoming noisy out here as well, but at least it was in the open air. Anne was sitting on a bench against the wall of the house, and Prudence approached her. Anne looked up and patted the bench invitingly.

"I find it a trial to stand for long," she said smiling ruefully, as the younger woman settled beside her.

"I fear I find my friends a trial, when they indulge in spirits," Prudence responded frankly.

Anne chuckled but did not use the opening to gossip. Pru liked her better for it.

"Mistress Bradstreet," she began, but the woman held up a slender hand.

"Please tell me I am not so old you feel you must address me thusly," Anne said.

Prudence blushed. "No! Certes not! 'Tis only good ma—"

"Let us dispense with mannered talk, shall we?" Anne smiled. "Let us just be two women together." She patted Pru's forearm lightly. "You shall call me Anne and I shall call you..."

"Prudence and it please you," she responded, flattered.

"Prudence. A lovely name and a fine character trait. We shall see little of it today, I warrant."

As if in response, there was a chorus of whoops from the lawn, drawing their notice. An impromptu game was in progress. Young men sat on one another's shoulders and tried to knock each other down, but since few of them were capable of walking a straight line even unencumbered, the results were more comical than competitive.

"Is it true that you craft verse?" Prudence asked, emboldened by their shared mirth and use of Christian names.

Anne raised her eyebrows. "Why, yes." She paused. "Does that surprise you?"

Prudence's eyes widened.

"Of course it does." Anne sighed. "You have been told that women have no intellectual capacity, have you not?" She spoke without rancor, but Prudence sensed her disappointment.

"Verily I was taught that, but I do not believe it," she answered, realizing it was true even as she spoke.

"I am glad to hear it, Prudence," her new friend said sincerely. "Too many women define themselves by the opinions of men."

Prudence winced, recalling the censure her husband had heaped upon her for encouraging the inappropriate notion that Elizabeth was more apt than her brothers. She had not contradicted him, but sat mutely throughout the verbal reprimand, then humbly apologized. This dignified, intelligent woman was proof against his refusal to consider the possibility. It felt dangerous to be speaking with Anne Bradstreet. Richard would disapprove of these radical opinions, yet she longed to provide Elizabeth the opportunity to realize her full potential in addition to being a wife and mother. Anne Bradstreet was a living testimony that more was possible.

"Our daughter Elizabeth is but five years old, and yet I know she is quicker than her brothers. I have instructed them all in letters and numbers." Prudence glanced around and lowered her voice before adding, "She proved the most capable."

"And your husband is in accord?" Anne asked perceptively.

Prudence looked down at her gloved hands, clutching the cup of noxious spirits, and shook her head. "He will not countenance anything but traditional instruction for her," she murmured.

"Then you must nurture her intellect yourself," Anne said, touching Pru's arm and leaning closer. "In secret," she whispered.

Prudence looked up at this rebellious statement. The Bradstreets were known to be a pious family and had been among the original party emigrating with Winthrop in 1630. Anne's unconventional attitude surprised her until she recalled the woman had already broken society's mold by writing poetry.

"'Tis the course I took with my girls. I still have the lesson plans," her new friend confided quietly, her eyes dancing. She sat back and continued in a normal tone. "How fine to have the long winter behind us. I warrant the weather is improving. You must come visit us in Andover as soon as the roads are dry—and do bring Elizabeth."

The day of John Winthrop's burial was appropriately somber. Heavy clouds moved ponderously overhead, as a front approached from the sea. The wind gusted unpredictably, causing folk to grab at their headgear in a most undignified manner. Thankfully the King's Cross burial ground was a short distance up Beacon Street from the Winthrop mansion. It would not be a long walk. Once it began to drizzle, the wind quieted to the relief of all. Although no one liked being damp, they were all accustomed to it.

The funeral procession moved at a snail's pace led by the reverends Wilson, Norton, and Cotton with more than twenty ministers from outlying towns close behind. The coffin followed, carried on a bier bourn by six of Winthrop's eldest sons. A lavish purple pall embroidered with the Bay Colony Seal shrouded the coffin. The precious cloth belonged to the city and was used only for dignitaries. Four governors enjoyed the honor of holding a corner—William Coddington of Rhode Island, William Bradford of Plymouth, Edward Hopkins of Connecticut, and John Endicott, the prospective candidate for the Bay Colony. The Winthrop Family took up three coaches, each drawn by four black horses. The windows were draped in black crepe, shielding the bereaved widow and closest relatives from eyes of the public. Next were the officers of Boston's Honorable Artillery Company in full dress uniform on their mounts, leading a troop of sixty foot soldiers, smartly outfitted with rifles and pikes. The Bay's flag hung limp in the drizzle. It was a blank white canton on a red field, since fourteen years before Endicott had ordered the idolatrous cross of St. George to be cut out. The military bugles blared a slow dirge, counterpointed by the sharp report of the snare drums. Behind the troops eight canons rumbled over the cobbles drawn by horses caparisoned in black and flanked by the cannoneers. The mourners fell in behind, unconsciously pacing to the slow beat. As a matter of course, lesser dignitaries and prominent citizens took the lead. Commoners lined the street and joined the procession last. The bells of Boston tolled. The bells of Cambridge and Charlestown echoed in the distance. All the bells of the Bay Colony rang for John Winthrop on April 5$^{th}$ of 1649.

Richard and Prudence walked arm-in-arm behind the canons, each lost in thought. Richard contemplated business partnerships and political connections. It was the prime time to cultivate acquaintances as power shifted in the capital's government. He reviewed the names—John Endicott, Richard Bellingham, Thomas Dudley—all former governors of the Bay Colony. He was determined these men would soon know his name and face.

He also considered the friendships he was forming with two men closer to his age who shared his views on business and politics. William Hathorne was a successful merchant, and like Richard, headed his town's militia. He ran a successful shipping concern at Salem, as Richard aspired to do at Dover. As a protégé of Endicott, who was from Salem himself, Hathorne was a magistrate already—a position Richard coveted.

Edward Rawson was the youngest member of the General Court. He lived in Newbury on six hundred acres of prime land, but he also had a house in Boston. He had assisted Simon Bradstreet and Governor Winthrop in the formation of Hampton a decade before, establishing a Puritan outpost in the north prior to the assimilation of the New Hampshire Colony. Edward was well educated with a sarcastic sense of humor that appealed to Richard. Rumor had it he would be part of the committee to organize Winthrop's writings. Most impressive in Richard's opinion was Rawson's manufacture of gunpowder, a rare and essential commodity in the colonies. He had generously supplied the kegs required to honor Winthrop this very day. Richard anticipated cementing these friendships at the gathering after the burial and capitalizing on their connections.

Prudence's thoughts ran in an entirely different vein. She dreaded the post funeral gathering, with yet more sanctioned excesses of alcohol. She was weary of the vacuous conversations with the wives of the men her husband was courting. She wished to be home with her children by a warm fire on this dreary April day. The only benefit to the event was Richard's increased ardor. The combination of a little funereal punch and rubbing shoulders with powerful men ultimately accrued to her benefit. She savored images of the night before, as she paced demurely at her husband's side through the insistent drizzle, dodging the steaming piles on the cobbled street deposited by the horses in front of them. She was intensely aware of the strong arm beneath her gloved hand and the heat emanating from his body. She prayed for another baby.

The pain woke her. Prudence gasped, instinctively curling up to alleviate the agony, but it only worsened. It was a knife in her womb, and now it twisted. She clamped her teeth to contain a scream. She must not wake Richard—he would be furious. However, she could not contain the groan in her throat, and he stirred. She froze, holding her breath. He rolled toward her, encircling her with his arm and pulling her against him, as he had done hundreds of times. Her agony exploded in a scream that startled them both. He sat bolt upright.

"Prudence! What passes here?"

She was incapable of speech. She could hardly breathe for the pain.

"Is it the child? Prudence, tell me! What is it?"

She could only nod, curled around the fire in her womb. Something was terribly wrong.

Richard paced the hall at the foot of the stairs. He had never felt so helpless. He could not sit still, but crossed from the drawing room to the dining hall, frequently glancing up the stairs for a sign of Dr. Clark or Mistress Able. Surely between the physician and the midwife, something could be done. Prudence would be all right. He had to believe that. The alternative was an abyss, and he shied from its gaping maw. For the first time in a life defined by discipline, Richard's emotions threatened to engulf him. He loved her. He *needed* her. He could not recall ever telling her so.

He sank onto the stairs, leaning his elbows on his knees and clasping his hands. Richard attended church every Sabbath Day without fail, but religion was a tool for harvesting power and influence. Now he needed to believe that devotion to God would avert catastrophe and save his wife. Desperation opened his heart, and his supplication was sincere. Richard closed his eyes and prayed.

His breathing slowed. The muffled sounds of activity on the servants' stairs to the kitchen had ceased. The predawn quiet was broken only by the ticking of the grandfather clock. Calm flowed through him. It was a warm, physical sensation, like the hand of an angel, stroking from the crown of his head down his back. He had not felt the tension that clenched his muscles until it dissolved, and soundless tears tracked his face unchecked. One word repeated in his brain—*please.*

Dawn had brought a blush to the sky, when Mistress Able beckoned from the top of the staircase. He took the stairs three at a time and entered the bedchamber close behind her. Dr. Clark was packing his medical case. He looked up as Richard burst in, regret clear on his tired face. It caused Richard to fear the worst. Prudence lay in the bed, her face impossibly pale, eyelids and lips an unnatural blue. Richard looked at the midwife, eyes wide.

"Is she...?"

"She yet lives, Captain Walderne," Dr. Clark said, coming over to him, "but she has lost the fetus, and I fear the resulting loss of blood is prodigious. I cannot say how long she—"

"Is there nothing you can do? Either of you?" he asked appalled, looking from one to the other.

Their silence was eloquent. He could not, *would* not, believe it. The physician spoke again.

"We have tried all we know, but she has not responded to any—"

"Then leave us!" Richard shouted his shock turned to fury.

The doctor and the midwife exchanged a look.

"You shall get your damn fees," he growled. "Go!"

They left, closing the door quietly. Richard locked it then approached the bed.

"Prudence?" he ventured, his voice breaking. Dare he touch her? Cautiously he took up her slender hand. It was cold, so cold. He rubbed it gently between his own.

She did not stir or open her eyes. Her usually rosy complexion was deathly pale, and her beautiful hair had lost its luster. He smoothed a lock from her brow and gently kissed her forehead. Still nothing.

Richard lifted the bedcovers. He saw no blood, but he noted the bulk of bandages under her nightdress and knew they contained it. The odor was unmistakable, but it did not repel him. He must warm her. He stretched out beside her in his nightshirt and robe, carefully gathering her limp body close. Might not the force of his love revive her? He laid his rough cheek against hers and put his mouth close to her ear. He spoke of his love for her; how he had known she must be his wife from the moment he saw her; how he could not go on without her. He promised never to take her for granted again, if only she would come back to him. She stirred, and when he raised his head, he saw her lips were curved in the ghost of a smile, but Prudence Walderne never opened her eyes again.

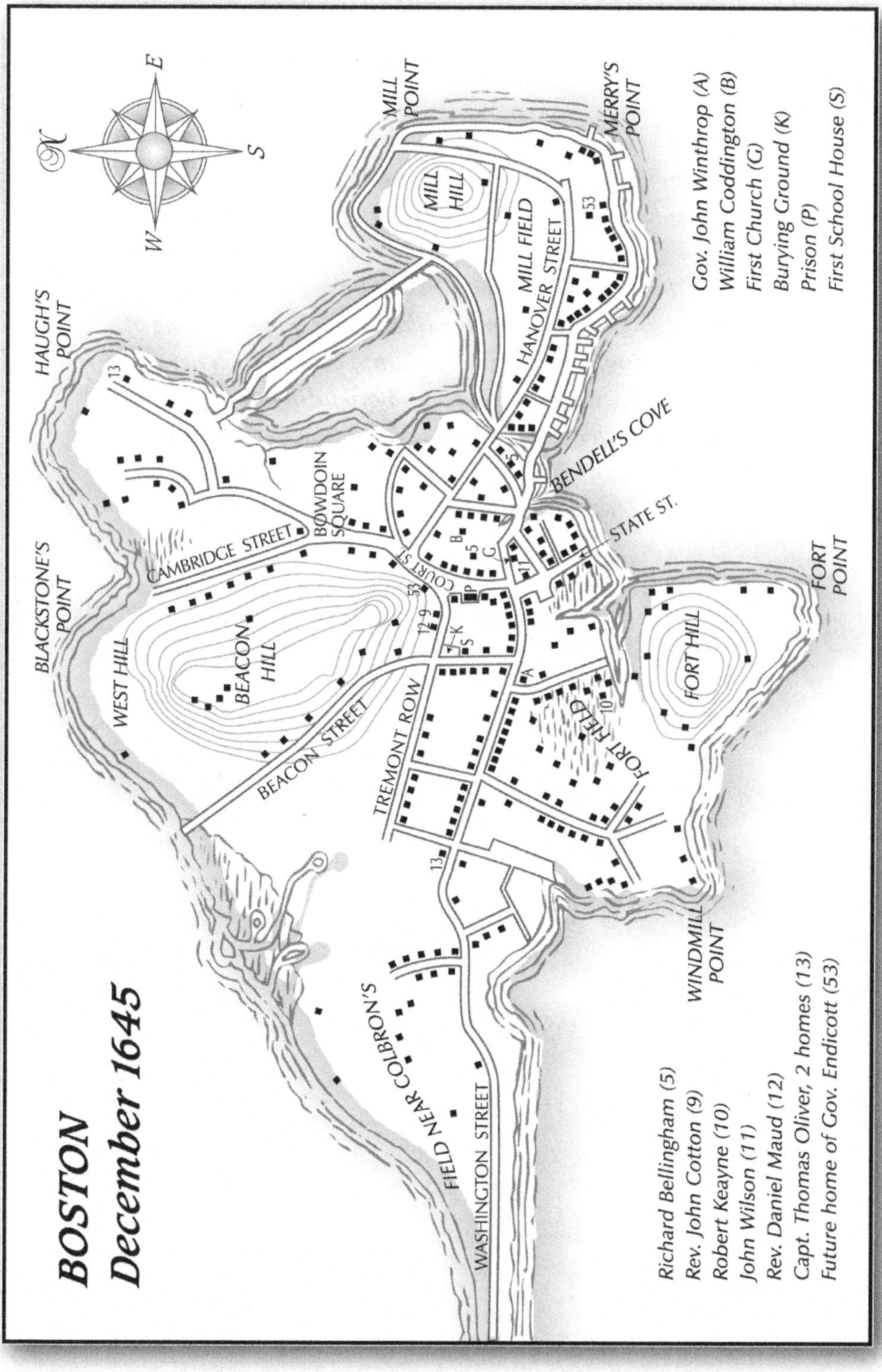
BOSTON
December 1645
Richard Bellingham (5)
Rev. John Cotton (9)
Robert Keayne (10)
John Wilson (11)
Rev. Daniel Maud (12)
Capt. Thomas Oliver, 2 homes (13)
Future home of Gov. Endicott (53)
Gov. John Winthrop (A)
William Coddington (B)
First Church (G)
Burying Ground (K)
Prison (P)
First School House (S)
MILL POINT
MERRY'S POINT
MILL HILL
MILL FIELD
HANOVER STREET
HAUGH'S POINT
BENDELL'S COVE
STATE ST.
BOWDOIN SQUARE
CAMBRIDGE STREET
COURT ST
BLACKSTONE'S POINT
WEST HILL
BEACON HILL
BEACON STREET
TREMONT ROW
FORT POINT
FORT HILL
FORT FIELD
WINDMILL POINT
FIELD NEAR COLBRON'S
WASHINGTON STREET

## HISTORICAL NOTE

In 1659 the General Court of Massachusetts Bay Colony passed the following law, viz.:

> *For preventing disorders arising in severall places within this jurisdiction, by reason of some still observing such ffestivalls as were superstitiously kept in other countrys, to the great dishonour of God and offence of others, it is therefore ordered by this Court and the authority thereof,* ***that whosoever shall be found observing any such day as Christmas or the like, either by forbearing of labour, feasting, or any other way, uppon any such accounts as aforesaid, every such person so offending shall pay for every such offence five shillings as a fine to the county.***
>
> —*Horatio Rogers, Mary Dyer of Rhode Island*

# *Chapter 33*

## MARY TOMKINS AND RICHARD WALDERNE
## *THE MISSIONARY AND THE MAGISTRATE*

December, 1662, Dover, Massachusetts Bay Colony

The constables escorted the Quakers from the Court and locked them in the gaol. Walter watched them go through the chaos of the meeting house, as folk milled about, talking of the sentence. No one wanted to leave. The town was divided once again into those who profited by the existing system and those who did not. Triumph or outrage characterized the knots of folk that lingered both inside and out. However, even those who had signed the complaint admitted they did not expect the sentence to be so severe. Over eighty miles! And in December with snow half the leg deep! In an ox cart? That would be slow going! Must they be stripped to the waist in this cold? Ten stripes in every town meant 110 stripes each! How would the missionaries survive? Whether in vindication, curiosity, or genuine support, none would miss the spectacle on the morrow.

Walter searched the crowd outside the meeting house for William Pitman. The Oyster River blacksmith was trustworthy for the little community upriver did not support John Reyner, and Will had participated in three of the meetings at Kittery during the summer. He also had one of the fastest horses in the colony. Indeed the man had been fined numerous times for organizing races and taking wagers. The blacksmith loved to ride fast. Walter found him talking with a group of young men and took him aside.

"How long would it take a horse and rider to reach Salem, do you think, Will?" he asked.

"Salem, eh?" The blacksmith considered. "With snow on the road ye would not want to go above a trot—too slippery for a good clip. Eight or ten hours at the least, I reckon. What is yer thought, Doctor?"

"Best not to say just yet, Will." Walter answered, glancing around. He moved closer and lowered his voice. "Can you get a message to Salem before nightfall, is the point."

The burly fellow sucked his teeth, calculating. "I might make Newbury by dark, but I doubt I could reach Salem before noon of the morrow—and that only if the weather holds. If 'twill help the missionaries, though, I'd ride to hell and back!"

"Good man! I believe it might save their lives. Take this coin for your expenses. No doubt you will wish to rest yourself and the animal at Salem. You must find Edward Wharton and inform him of what is afoot here. Tell him to meet us with his shallop at Salisbury, I reckon, for I doubt he can reach Hampton in time. Tell him 'tis a matter of life or death for the missionary Friends."

"Salisbury then. Were he the one bested the reverend last summer at Emerys' ordinary?" Pitman asked, having witnessed the scene.

"Aye, he and his friend George Preston. I have no doubt he will come apace."

"I'll take the grey. He's not my fastest, but he never tires."

"You ride for the Angels of the Lord, Will. God keep you."

The blacksmith hurried off, and Walter went to find Richard Walderne.

The magistrate was at the ordinary with John Reyner and Hatevil Nutter. They looked up from their food, when the apothecary approached the table. Walter did not remove his hat.

"I must speak with you on a matter of medical import, Captain Walderne," he stated formally.

"And a good day to you too, Doctor," Richard answered sarcastically. Inwardly he bristled at the man's lack of manners, standing there with his hat on like a damn Quaker. No doubt the Anglican was in sympathy with the prisoners.

Walter ignored the sarcasm. All his concentration was focused on containing his outrage. Venting his choler would not help his friends.

"The sentence is overly severe," Walter said evenly. "The Whip and Cart Act is usually limited to three towns."

"The Whip and Cart Act states that they shall be escorted to the limits of the colony, and so they shall," Walderne drawled, stabbing a bit of mutton with his knife and popping it into his mouth.

"They might have considered that, when they chose to harass the good people of Dover," Reyner remarked primly.

Walter gave him a withering look and drew breath before continuing. "It is over eighty miles and one hundred ten stripes for each of them. 'Tis like to kill them, particularly in this weather!"

The three men gazed at him wordlessly. He was appalled by their blatant cruelty but plunged on.

"As I understand it, the Whip and Cart Act is not meant to be a death sentence. The King's mandamus forbids executions pertaining to religion in His colonies."

Walderne chewed, delaying his response. The Anglicans were always hiding behind the monarchy. Still, the man had a point. The magistrate framed his answer carefully.

"I am aware of that document," he said slowly, pausing to take a pull from his tankard. "'Tis not a death sentence. It is, as I said, a legal escort out of the jurisdiction of this territory, the territory of the Massachusetts Bay Colony for—what is it now?" He pretended to calculate. "Twenty years, I believe." His eyes snapped back to Walter and his tone hardened. "It is an example—a lesson, if you will, for all who would corrupt the true church." His mouth parodied a smile, but his gray eyes were cold. "The warrant is writ, and I am not inclined to debate the legalities, particularly as I eat. What is your point, Dr. Barefoote?"

Walderne's hostile stare sent an involuntary shiver down Walter's back. These men did not care one whit if the missionaries perished. Indeed, he suspected it was their intent. There was not a shred of Christian charity among them. He covered the tremor by straightening his shoulders and clearing his throat.

"I propose to accompany the women on their march, tend to their wounds, and prevent them freezing or bleeding to death, as best I can. If—nay, *when*—I determine that their lives are in jeopardy, I shall exercise my authority as a physician to intervene."

The magistrate let the silence lengthen for an uncomfortable interlude, assessing the doctor through half-closed eyes. People usually reacted by babbling. Walter did not look away nor did he speak.

Walderne shrugged. "Why not?" he said lightly and returned to sawing at his mutton.

It was all the sanction the apothecary required, and he turned to leave, but the captain's final words chilled him.

"Be assured, Doctor, I shall personally oversee the administration of the sentence here."

After another restless night in the cold cell, the missionaries were awake at first light. Allie drew a blanket around her shoulders and paced, warming her muscles and working out the cramps. Her breath was visible in the meager light from the high window. Mary and Anne huddled together on the bench.

"Hast thou endured flogging before?" Anne asked tremulously.

"Nay," Mary replied. "They put us on public display at Lancaster with the Bridle, as punishment for reproving a priest, but they did not flog us. The dungeons were the worst of it. And thou?"

Anne shook her head, her heavy-lidded eyes wide. Mary feared the diminutive missionary would not be able to endure the flogging and the long journey exposed to the cold. She feared for all of them, but Anne would be more sharply challenged. She was so small! When Mary felt the call to take up Mary Dyer's work, a third missionary had not been a consideration. Mary felt responsible for Anne and ached to protect her. She took up her companion's small, cold hands, rubbing them gently.

"God will not abandon us, Anne," she said firmly. "We shall endure, and all who witness the cruelty of this law shall remember. We must stand against this abuse of justice, as Mary Dyer stood against the laws in Boston."

Anne's answer was barely audible. "Yes, but they hanged her."

"And now that law is no more. The King's mandamus stopped the executions. Many who witnessed the hangings became convinced by our martyred Friends, for they kept their faith in God unto death. Friend Wharton told us that one of the constables at Mary Dyer's hanging was so sickened, that he could not mount his horse. He had to be helped home, and Friend Wharton said he quit his post and is now one of us as a result."

"Her faith sustained her," Anne whispered, grasping at this meager straw.

"Yes, even as we shall be sustained," Mary said, squeezing her hands gently.

Then the glimmer of hope on the little missionary's face faded, replaced by fear. "But however shall we endure the cold over such a long distance?" Her lower lip trembled.

"We must find our strength in God," Mary answered.

She pulled Sarah Nute's quilt around them both and held Anne close, sharing her warmth in wordless comfort. Allie was standing beneath the high window. The sky was lighter now, and she could hear voices. Something was afoot outside. She managed to pull herself up by the cold iron bars to peer out. The oxcart had arrived.

The crowd before the meeting house was growing. People lined both sides of the High Street to the south, bundled and shivering in the cold. They made way for the three officials as they strode to the open space around the oxcart. Upon their arrival the constables fetched the prisoners from the gaol.

Walter Barefoote stood on the opposite side of the cart, his medical bag over one shoulder. Richard did not understand his intervention on the women's behalf. Why would an Anglican doctor insist on accompanying Quakers? It thwarted his plan to render the miscreants permanently incapable of spreading their heresy. The apothecary was one of the few people who could supersede his authority—at least in medical matters. What were the man's motives? It confounded and riled the magistrate.

The prisoners appeared, escorted by the constables. People made way to let them through. Mary was heartened to see the familiar faces of the Dover Friends, grouped around Walter at the side of the road. Even the Wardells had come from Hampton. Eli held two-year-old Joseph, and Lydia raised her hand. Thomas Roberts nodded to the missionaries soberly. Rebecca and their youngest daughter Sarah clutched his arms. James and Sarah Nute stood near with their four younger children. Will Furbush was there with Frances and Anthony Emery, but his wife Rebecca must have stayed home with her newborn. Then Mary saw the officials, standing by the cart. The magistrate cut an imposing figure in his military hat and greatcoat. He looked larger than he had in the court.

Richard was gratified to see the little Quaker was terrified, but the other two were disappointingly stoic. The Tomkins woman even met his eyes defiantly. She had a rebellious spirit, that one. He would enjoy seeing her break under the lash. He was careful to keep his expression neutral, but his eyes glittered with triumph and anticipation.

Reyner read the warrant, his pulpit voice carrying over the hushed crowd. Then he turned to the magistrate expectantly. Richard paused, savoring his power. He wanted the Quakers to realize they were at his mercy and would get none.

"Strip the prisoners," Walderne ordered, watching the Tomkins woman's face.

The crowd became restive at this prospect. It was a hard but necessary lesson for them, the magistrate reasoned, not unlike disciplining children. The prisoners had attempted to incite rebellion and chaos in his town, and they would suffer for it.

The constables used their belt knives to cut the women's bodices and small clothes open at the back. They pulled the ruined material down, baring the white skin of their torsos and arms. The missionaries did not resist, though the small one was weeping. John Roberts did not look at them, as he performed this awkward duty, but his younger brother got an eyeful. The women folded their arms over their breasts more for warmth than in shame. They shivered as the cold stung their bare skin, and the magistrate savored the warmth of his greatcoat and muffler all the more. The small one sobbed audibly now, and he hoped her fear would pass to the others like a contagion.

"Secure their hands," he ordered.

The constables set to this task, and Anne wailed, when her arms were wrenched from her chest, robbing her of their scant warmth and cover. An angry shout interrupted the proceedings. Eli Wardell was pointing at the Reverend Reyner.

"Look ye! The minister laughs! Remark how he revels in their suffering!" he exclaimed.

"This is no man of God, delighting in the pain of tender women!" Will Furbush added.

All eyes turned to the minister.

Richard saw Reyner dampen his smile, but smile he had—the idiot. Did he not realize it would incite sympathy for the prisoners?

"Set those men in the stocks!" the magistrate ordered. Dissenters in the crowd hissed. "They are obstructing justice!" he declared, as the constables led the protestors to the pillory on the north side of the meeting house. "They shall remain there until sundown, as shall any others who object!" he barked, glaring at the Quaker sympathizers.

The hissing stopped, but the crowd was restive, during the awkward interval before the constables returned. It was necessary to punish sinners to protect the community from God's wrath. It was difficult for some to witness—especially women and children—and for this reason it must be done dispassionately. Though he shared the reverend's triumph, expressing delight was untenable and inappropriate. It called the minister's motives into question and discomfited the spectators. Worse, such behavior might alienate the good Puritans in the crowd.

"Contain yourself, Mister Reyner," he admonished the red-faced minister quietly.

At length the Roberts brothers came back and resumed tying the prisoner's wrists to the pole at the back of the oxcart. Once their hands were secured, the women were fully exposed to public view. Richard moved his contemptuous gaze over the Tomkins woman's torso. Her skin was stippled with goosebumps, her nipples puckered by the cold. He hoped to make her squirm. He addressed the townsfolk while staring at her.

"Do not fear good people. We brook no heretics at Dover. You shall soon be free of this unnatural contamination," he announced and was gratified to see the Tomkins woman's pale face redden under his gaze.

Mary had feared being publicly stripped more than the whip. Humiliation was worse than pain for her, but the intensity of the cold was so shocking that loss of dignity became a minor note in a symphony of physical abuse. The ropes abraded her wrists, her hands and feet were numb, she could not stop shivering, and her teeth chattered spasmodically. Only when the magistrate raked her with his predatory stare, was her shame resurrected.

Captain Walderne turned to the constables. "Administer the punishment," he ordered.

Thomas climbed onto the seat of the cart, and John positioned himself behind the Quakers, shaking out the whip. He had oiled it the night before, and the supple leather strips were braided and knotted at the ends; however, as he prepared to strike, the women launched into a hymn.

*A mighty fortress is our God,*
*A bulwark never failing;*

The singing amazed everyone, but it confounded John Roberts. He lowered his arm and looked to the magistrate. Richard's surprise was brief, and he gestured impatiently for the constable to get on with it. The show of godliness irritated him, for it was an obvious ploy to gain sympathy among the witnesses. He wanted to silence the women, but realized he could hardly censure the singing of a hymn. He scowled as voices in the crowd joined—Quaker sympathizers no doubt, but would it spread to others? It compromised his control of the situation. Annoyance became anger, and he curbed it by remembering the bravado would soon be beaten out of these unnatural women.

John Roberts nodded to his brother, and the cart lurched into motion, forcing the women to keep up or be dragged. Their singing did not falter.

*Our helper He amid the flood*
*Of mortal ills prevailing.*

Anne was at the left side of the cart tail, and the constable began with her, delivering the first strike as the cart crept through the dirty snow. High Street was lined with spectators. Mary had not known there were so many people in Dover. Anne's cries of pain caused some to cover their ears or turn aside, while others craned their necks to see. She bled by the third stroke and was hard put to keep pace with the moving cart. The hymn gained volume. Richard ground his teeth in frustration.

*For still our ancient foe*
*Doth seek to work us woe --*

Again, and again, the whip bit into the thin flesh on Anne's misshapen back, drawing more blood with each stroke. She staggered and slipped, clinging to the pole to keep from falling, as the cart moved on relentlessly. Her cries became ragged gasps, but the singing grew louder, as more along the road took it up. Lydia Wardell's strong voice led the Friends. She and Walter walked as close to Mary as they could, and people gave way for the apothecary and the brave young woman with a child on her back. The Friends followed, keeping pace with John Roberts and singing loudly.

*His craft and power are great,*
*and armed with cruel hate,*
*on earth is not his equal.*

The constable was nearly finished with the small one when she lost her footing. Anne Coleman hung by her bound wrists, her feet furrowing the slush. The cart did not stop nor did the whip; however the hymn was now pervasive. The officials glared at the people, but their disapproval had no effect.

The first ten stripes were done, and John Roberts turned his attention to the tall woman in the middle. At least with this one, it did not seem like beating a child. He was rarely called upon to perform this duty, and it was a far cry from collecting taxes, dealing with inebriated laborers, or corralling errant livestock. The hymn unnerved him. His own family walked beside him, singing for all they were worth. Their censure was palpable. Father Nutter and Captain Walderne had convinced him these women were unnatural and dangerous. It was his duty to protect the people of Dover—even if they did not appreciate it. He must persevere.

*Did we in our own strength confide*
*Our striving would be losing,*

Allie sang through the first blow, but the second robbed her of breath. When her own voice ceased, however, she realized how many others had taken it up.

*Were not the right Man on our side,*
*The Man of God's own choosing.*

The grim cavalcade continued down the Neck, and the hymn swelled, echoing off the clapboard buildings. Those singing were no longer passive spectators forced to watch an act of brutality sanctioned by law. They were infused with the power of this protest without violence. Mary was encouraged and lifted her head, willing the Light to use her voice and her spirit.

Richard was infuriated. The hymn was an act of dissent that could not be punished. The Tomkins woman sang clearly, her head held high. He had thought her plain at first sight, but even shivering and stripped to the waist, she was impressive—her face lit from within by her faith. He felt a twinge of admiration and sharply recalled himself. Her appeal made her more dangerous.

*Dost ask who that may be?*
*Christ Jesus, it is He --*
*Lord Sabaoth His name,*
*From age to age the same --*
*And He must win the battle.*

John Roberts' found strength in anger. He felt betrayed by his own family and the town he served, and he struck with more force. He was protecting these people. They should be supporting the law he represented, not singing with these heretics.

Allie grasped the wooden pole and clenched her teeth to keep from screaming. The slush soaked her boots, and her feet were blocks of wood. Staying upright was a challenge. She clung to the support evidenced by the singing and turned her head to the right to take strength from Mary.

*And tho this world, with devils filled,*
*Should threaten to undo us,*

Mary locked eyes with her friend, willing her to endure, as she sang for them both.

*We will not fear, for God hath willed*
*His truth to triumph thru us.*

Allie was bolstered by the connection then John Roberts slipped, and his final stroke went high. One of the knotted thongs caught her face, and she staggered, her cheek blossoming with blood.

Richard saw the Tomkins woman stifle a cry. He wondered if the constable had struck the blow deliberately. Roberts looked irate, his face set in a grimace. No doubt the singing rattled him. The woman's head hung between her arms. Blood dripped from her face and flowed down her neck and breast, but she kept her feet. The damned hymn grew louder.

Mary nearly cried out when Allie's face was struck but realized it would only please the officials, watching avidly for weakness. Outrage for her dear friend obliterated her own duress. She sang the next words directly to the magistrate.

*The prince of darkness grim*
*We tremble not for him;*
*His rage we can endure,*
*For lo! his doom is sure*
*One little word shall fell him.*

Richard bristled at the implication. *She* was the agent of darkness. He was an official of the law, protecting his town, but even as he glared back, her expression changed.

As she sang to the magistrate, Mary realized that outrage and defiance would not best him. They would only feed his pride and self-righteousness. She reached for the Light more intently than ever before, surrendering her will and opening her Self to That of God Within. Mary Dyer's beloved face came vividly to mind, followed by a surge of spiritual strength that warmed her. Her shivering stopped. The Light heightened her perception, and she looked at Richard Walderne and *saw* him.

Even this brutal man had the potential to connect with That of God. He was only misguided, believing he was doing the right thing. In that moment Mary Tomkins forgave him. The mask he habitually wore was stripped away, revealing his naked soul. She saw his pride and his desperation. She recognized his addiction to power and his craving for approval. She felt the devastation of his losses. She mourned for the child whose vulnerable emotions had been bludgeoned from birth. Commanding and comely as he might appear, the man's heart was literally broken for it held no love. His spirit was crippled by cynicism.

It took a moment for Richard to register the expression on the heretic's face. Compassion replaced defiance. Her expression was tender, but it penetrated his soul. He felt exposed. Her pity was a blow. It was inconceivable, and it shook him. He looked away quickly lest she see that too.

The whip struck in counterpoint to Mary's strong voice.

*That word above* (one) *all earthly pow'rs* (two)
*No thanks to them* (three) *abideth;*
*The Spirit* (four) *and the gifts are ours* (five)
*Thru Him who with us* (six) *sideth.*
*Let goods and* (seven) *kindred go.*
*This mortal life* (eight) *also;*
*The body they* (nine) *may kill:*
*God's truth abideth still* (ten)
*His kingdom is forever.*

A ragged chorus of "ah-men's" echoed up and down the lane. In the abrupt silence the cart rumbled on, its wheels churning the slush. The fresh blood of the missionaries' wounds was vivid in the colorless scene.

Richard Walderne kept his expression blank, but he was dismayed. She had not broken, in fact *she* pitied *him*! How had she sung throughout her whipping? Common folk might misconstrue her strength as God-given, undoing all his efforts to expose the Quakers as charlatans. His only satisfaction was that she could not possibly sustain her stoicism through ten more floggings and the long trek to Dedham. He hoped she would die. He could not bear the sight of her, bleeding but unbroken, saintly in her damn compassion, despite humiliation and pain. He must get away.

The cart approached Emerys' ordinary, and the magistrate signaled Thomas to stop there. Walter did not question the abrupt halt. His attention was all on his friends, and he rushed to their aid. Lydia Wardell handed little Joseph to Sarah Roberts and joined the Friends assisting him.

Masking his turmoil Richard instructed Hatevil and Reyner to see the prisoners onto the ferry. He avoided eye contact and left quickly. Snatches of conversation surfaced as he crossed High Street, heading for the stable.

"Did ye hear that? 'Tis a wonder, I warrant!" "She sang thro' it all!" "A miracle, do ye not think?"

Richard ignored the talk and strode through the press of people with all the dignity of his considerable status. They made way for him and watched his retreating back; however, the footing was treacherous, and his pace was overlong. He slipped in the slush, narrowly avoiding a graceless exit. He bit back a curse, his face flushed, and he glanced around, but none met his eye. He had cleared the crowd and was nearly at the stable, when the Roberts brothers caught him up.

"Begging your pardon, Your Honor!" John called, hampered by the slush. He came alongside, panting. "Are we to take the oxcart all the way to Hampton, sir?"

Thomas came up on Walderne's other side. "Certes, 'twill be slow going in the snow for twenty mile. Don't reckon we can reach Hampton by dark," he added.

The magistrate stopped and looked at them, exasperated.

"What do you want of me?" he barked. "I can neither shorten the distance nor melt the snow!"

"And it please you, Captain," John said, giving his younger brother a keep-your-mouth-shut look, "Might it not be more practical in these conditions to transport the prisoners on horseback, sir?" A gust of cold wind caused him to shiver, as his sweat dried. Flogging was hard work.

Ignoring his elder brother's look, Thomas added, "'Twould be four or five hours to Hampton a-horse instead of twice that with the cart. We were only able to get the one ox, y'see, and if we were to get stuck on the road to Hampton, which is like to h—"

"Fine! Do whatever you deem necessary," Walderne snapped, resuming his awkward progress. The brothers gaped, bewildered by his anger. Had they not carried out his sentence to the letter? The magistrate paused at the barn door.

"Just get those vagabond Quakers out of my town!" he ordered over his shoulder and disappeared inside.

Richard wanted nothing more than to put Dover behind him. He pushed his mount hard on the ride back to Cocheco, but the ghost of Mary's compassion dogged his heels and nipped at him long after.

# *Chapter 34*

## MARY AND ALICE *DELAYED*

December, 1662 Dover, Massachusetts Bay Colony

Reverend Reyner and Hatevil Nutter were surprised by the magistrate's precipitous exit. He seemed pressed to leave, and they agreed to see the prisoners onto the ferry. The minister protested as the Friends started to help the women indoors but gave way reluctantly to Walter's assertion that it was a medical necessity. The townsfolk dispersed to their homes, seeking warmth and shelter from a quickening wind.

Anne was the apothecary's first concern. Her wrists were bloody and her skirt was wet to the thighs from dragging behind the cart. Because her hump protruded, the skin on her right shoulder was flayed almost entirely away. She cried out every time Walter touched her mangled back, but once the wounds were blotted with a mixture of yarrow and sumac powder, the bleeding lessened. He applied salve and bandaged her back. Mary and Allie had fared little better.

Allie's cheek worried Walter. It required stitching, which she endured stoically with eyes closed and jaw clenched. He was afraid the scar would permanently disfigure her face, but she seemed unconcerned. His admiration for her—for all three of them—swelled. He concentrated on the work at hand, and professionalism overcame emotion, but as their friend, he was outraged.

The missionaries were in too much pain to eat, and Walter dosed them with willow bark tea. Once they were bandaged and warm, Lydia Wardell and the Nutes took hot soup to Eli and Will in the stocks. Frances Emery also supplied mittens, mufflers, and blankets to warm them. The Roberts family offered to scavenge fresh clothing for the missionaries to replace their torn and bloodied garments, and the small group of Friends walked back up High Street together.

After fetching their mounts for the mile-long ride to the ferry landing, Reyner and Nutter took their noon meal in the common room of the Emerys' ordinary. Frances refused to serve them, but Anthony had no such scruples.

"Their coin is as good as any," he told his wife. "Let us relieve them of as much of it as we can. 'Twill not aid our friends to refuse it."

Still, Frances sent the kitchen maid to serve them and took food and tea upstairs for the apothecary and the missionaries. Walter was hungry and thanked her profusely. He ate quickly then left to replenish his medical bag, pack his saddlebags, and fetch his horse for the long journey ahead. Frances stayed with the women, encouraging them to take a little broth. Thomas and Rebecca brought fresh clothing, and the two women helped the invalids to dress. Walter was back in less than an hour, for his home and practice were nearby.

It took the Roberts brothers longer to return the ox and cart to William Pomfrett then procure three extra horses and three saddles with pillories for the trip to Hampton. There was no time for the constables to take refreshment, though they had not eaten since sunrise. They returned to the ordinary more than two hours later.

"I reckon we shall have this done and be home on the morrow," Thomas said to his brother, as they secured the horses to the rail outside.

John did not answer. In his experience things rarely went as planned.

The constables were eager to begin the twenty-mile trek to Hampton. It was already well past noon, and darkness came early in December. They insisted on leaving immediately and escorted the missionaries from the inn with Reyner and Nutter's help.

"Certes, thou hast the warrant with thee," Mary said to Thomas, when they reached the horses. Her voice was weak but clear.

"The warrant?" Thomas repeated blankly.

"Yes, the warrant dictated by the magistrate that defines our punishment. Reverend Reyner wrote it up." She turned stiffly to the minister, as pain flared in her back at any movement. "No doubt thou knowest that a legal document must be shown to the constables of the other towns," she told the minister, "else there are no lawful grounds for the sentence to be executed."

All eyes looked to the clergyman for confirmation.

"Nonsense! List not to this heretic!" Reyner blustered. "She only seeks to delay—"

Walter was quick to seize upon this point.

"Nay, 'tis true! It is the law!" he asserted. "The constables of the other towns will not prosecute so brutal a sentence without proof of its legality. You must have the document upon your person ere we can leave," he said gravely. Inwardly he exulted at Mary's quick mind.

The brothers moved off a few paces to confer with the minister and the elder in hushed voices. Walter met Mary's eye and gave her a slow nod. His experienced eye noted her pallor and the intermittent tremors that still wracked her body, but otherwise, she appeared calm and alert. Allie watched her friend through a haze of pain, but she was prepared to take her cue from Mary's behavior. She sensed a strategy unfolding.

Reyner broke away from the whispered consultation.

"I shall fetch the warrant," he announced with a murderous glance at Mary. "Secure them on the horses and prepare to leave," he directed the brothers.

"I shall stay and assist the constables," declared Elder Nutter, "but make all haste, Reverend."

The minister mounted his horse and disappeared up the High Street toward the meeting house at a brisk trot, slush flying from the animal's hooves.

The elder and the constables turned to the women. The Nutes and Lydia had returned from their mission of mercy at the stocks and joined the Roberts family, bearing witness in the cold. Other folk watched from the windows of the ordinary. Three of the horses had saddles with leather pillories affixed by heavy thongs. The prisoner's wrists would be secured on either side of the saddle horn, exposing their hands to the cold. Until the warrant was in evidence, Mary would not suffer it. As soon as John Roberts touched her arm, she went limp and sank to the ground. Allie cautiously followed suit.

"None of that now!" John ordered, remembering the missionaries' arrest. "Get up from there!"

The women remained limp, neither hindering nor helping their captors. Even laboring together, the three men had little success. At last they got Mary hoisted into the saddle, but she slipped off as soon as the men let go, falling onto Thomas and tumbling them both into the snow. Her face went white with pain, and Walter winced in sympathy, but it undid the men, and they left her there in frustration. Anne did not have to pretend to collapse, as Walter and Mister Roberts were holding her up. The constables lifted her small, inert body easily, and Nutter held her in the saddle, while the constables secured her wrists in the leather cuffs. She slumped over the horse's neck and Walter went to steady her, as she was too weak to endure a fall. The enforcers turned to Mary once more.

The Friends watched the struggle in silence, and more faces peered from the windows of the ordinary. The three men became increasingly short-tempered and overwarm despite the cold wind. Although the scene had a comic aspect, the spectators looked on gravely for the missionaries' protest was effective, albeit painful for them. The Friends began a hymn to hearten the prisoners. Wrestling with limp missionaries while an audience of Quakers sang, further infuriated the keepers of the law, yet they had no recourse but to bear it, as before.

By the time Reyner returned, Mary and Anne were pilloried a-horse, but the constables and Elder Nutter were sweating and irritable.

"I have the warrant, Constable," the minister said, producing it from an inside pocket.

The Friends were quiet now, grouped around Walter and watching intently.

Thomas turned on the clergyman, poised to vent his frustration. "About bloo-"

"Thank you, Reverend," John interposed, sharply elbowing his brother aside before his loose tongue could get him arrested for public slander against an ordained minister. He put the warrant inside his greatcoat. "We have had some difficulty here," he continued, glaring at the prisoners. "I fear we shall need your assistance lifting the tall one into the saddle."

At a nod from Mary, Allie struggled to her feet and went to her mount. The wound on her face made speech difficult. Wordlessly she put her hands on the saddle, wincing at the gesture, and lifted a damp boot for a leg up.

The men gaped at her.

"Now the warrant is in hand, we are willing to proceed," Mary explained.

Thomas boosted Allie into the saddle, and the brothers secured her hands in the leather cuffs. John scowled at Thomas over the saddle horn. "Mount up!" he growled as they finished. "And mind your tongue!"

The apothecary shook hands with the Friends, thanking them for their help. He hid a smile as he mounted his own horse. The missionaries had successfully delayed their progress by more than an hour.

The horses picked their way through the slush on High Street, and the loyal Friends followed in the Robertses' sleigh. The wind hit them full force, as they reached the open ground at Hilton's Point and approached the ferry landing.

John feared to make Hampton before dark. At least the ferry was at the dock, preparing for the crossing to Bloody Point. He was relieved they would not have to wait for it to arrive in the chill wind.

Thomas Trickey ran the ferry with his son and a hired man. They looked up as the group approached the dock.

"Where might ye be going with this lot then?" Trickey asked, as the bizarre procession drew up.

"To Hampton," John answered shortly.

"For us, any road," Thomas smirked. Each brother held a rope attached to the women's horses with Nutter leading Allie's mount. "These prisoners here are going to Dedham at the cart tail." He indicated the missionaries.

Trickey turned to John for confirmation. He knew the Roberts brothers well, and Thomas was known to exaggerate. "Verily? All the way to Dedham?"

John nodded and shot an angry look at his brother. Thomas and his unbridled tongue!

"That's a far piece! More than eighty mile, I reckon." Trickey paused, taking in the pilloried women, wrapped in quilts and shawls—one slumped over the horse's neck, the other two pale and shivering. He recognized those two. They had been guests at Kittery Manor. "Are these not the English missionaries?" he asked, incredulous.

"A formal complaint was served against them by the citizens of Dover. Certes, ye know about this," John answered, peeved and chilled by the cold wind after his exertions. He despaired of reaching Hampton this hellish day. "Just get on with it, Thomas Trickey!" he finished, his temper flaring.

Trickey went still. Whenever someone berated him, he deliberately slowed down, "Like molasses in January," his wife Elizabeth said, and she knew from experience.

"Ye think to make Hampton, leading this lot?" the ferryman asked skeptically after a marked pause.

John had the grace to blush. He did not mean to be rude. He had known Trickey all his life, but his nerves were raw. The whippings, the singing, and the missionaries' passive resistance left him emotionally exhausted and physically chilled. On top of that, his father-in-law was watching his every move. John feared his disapproval, and it made him gruff.

"If you get this ferry moving, I hope to!" he retorted, then sighed. "Please, Thomas," he added more softly.

The ferryman gazed at John for a long moment then looked at the grave-faced folk in the sleigh. He recognized all of them and supposed they were showing support for the prisoners, whatever they had done—or were accused of doing, more like. He noted the presence of Elder Nutter and Reverend Reyner. He had refused to sign their complaint, excusing himself as a resident of Bloody Point. Apparently they had got enough signatures without it. He turned away, shaking his head, and bade his crew prepare to cast off. He would leave it for his wife to berate them. Elizabeth was better at it than he.

Reverend Reyner gave John coin for the journey, while Thomas began the boarding process. For a wonder, none of the horses balked at the gangplank, and they stayed steady once tethered on board. The prisoners were not allowed to dismount. As the barge pulled away, John watched the figures of his father-in-law and the minister diminish on the dock. Beside them the loyal Friends waved, though only the doctor could respond.

John glanced up seeking the sun's position through the murky clouds. He did not want to be on the road after dark. Attacks by wolves had diminished due to the bounties awarded for their hides, but those that remained were desperate in winter. He had, of course, brought his flintlock, but he did not favor risking travel after sunset.

He glanced at his brother, smiling and nattering on to Thomas Trickey, as if they didn't have three prisoners in custody and a long, cold journey ahead. He was more of a liability than a help. Even when their duty was done, there was the long trek back, leading three rider-less mounts. Reyner and Nutter turned their horses up High Street and rode off. He envied them going home to their wives and warm hearths.

END PART II

# *Part III*

# WINTER

*The early Quakers...were abreast, if not in advance, of the foremost advocates of religious and civil freedom. They were more than advocates; they were the pioneers who by their heroic fortitude, patient suffering, and persistent devotion rescued the old Bay colony from the jaws of the certain death to which the narrow and mistaken policy of the bigoted and sometimes insincere founders had doomed it. They forced them to abandon pretentious claims, to admit strangers without insulting them, to tolerate religious differences, and to incorporate into their legislation the spirit of liberty which is now the life-blood of our institutions.*

*-Richard P. Hallowell, The Quaker Invasion of Massachusetts*

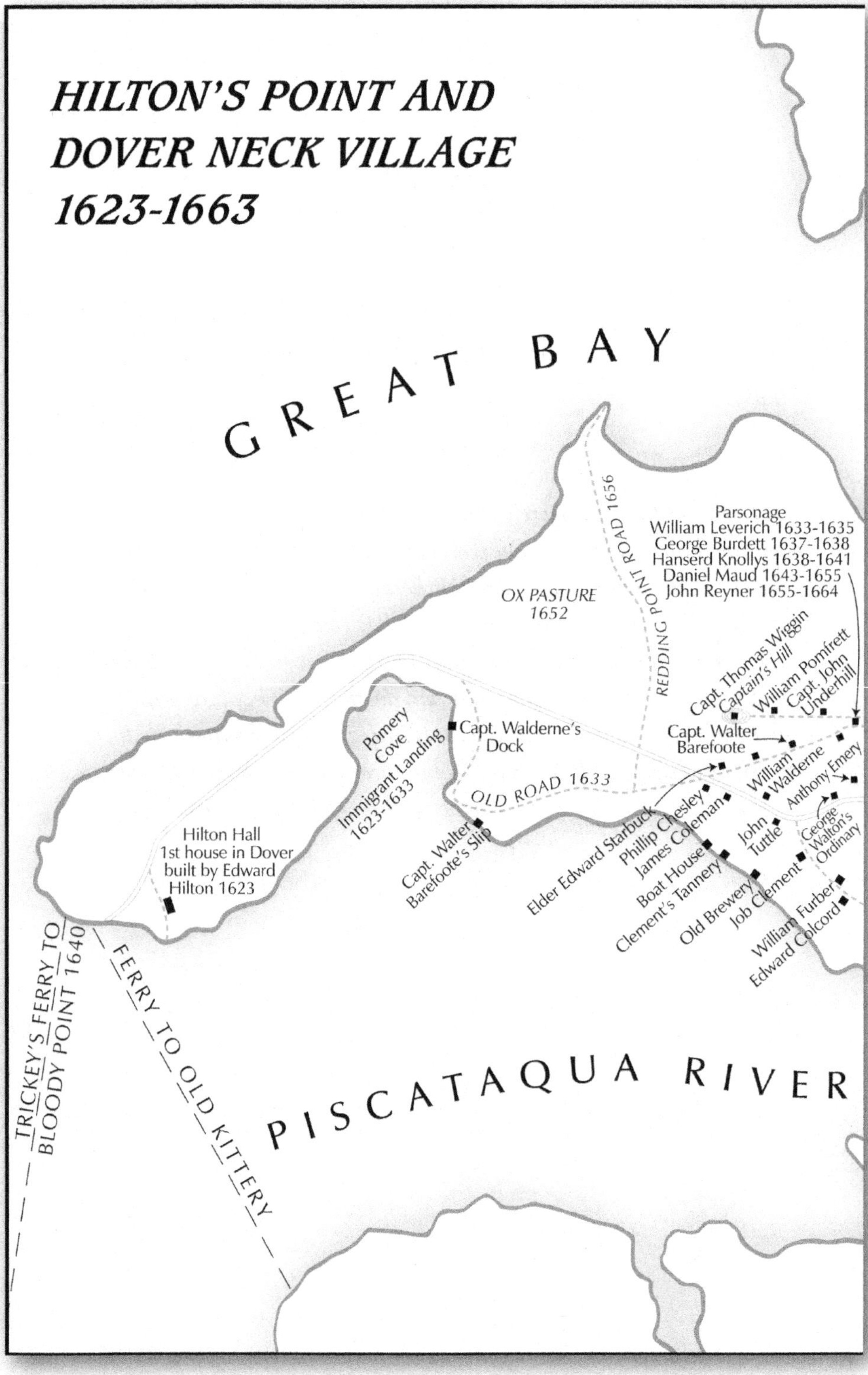
HILTON'S POINT AND DOVER NECK VILLAGE 1623-1663
GREAT BAY
PISCATAQUA RIVER
OX PASTURE 1652
REDDING POINT ROAD 1656
Parsonage
William Leverich 1633-1635
George Burdett 1637-1638
Hanserd Knollys 1638-1641
Daniel Maud 1643-1655
John Reyner 1655-1664
Capt. Thomas Wiggin
Captain's Hill
William Pomfrett
Capt. John Underhill
Capt. Walter Barefoote
William Walderne
Anthony Emery
George Walton's Ordinary
John Tuttle
Elder Edward Starbuck
Phillip Chesley
James Coleman
Boat House
Clement's Tannery
Old Brewery
Job Clement
William Furber
Edward Colcord
Capt. Walderne's Dock
OLD ROAD 1633
Pomery Cove
Immigrant Landing 1623-1633
Capt. Walter Barefoote's Slip
Hilton Hall
1st house in Dover
built by Edward
Hilton 1623
TRICKEY'S FERRY TO BLOODY POINT 1640
FERRY TO OLD KITTERY

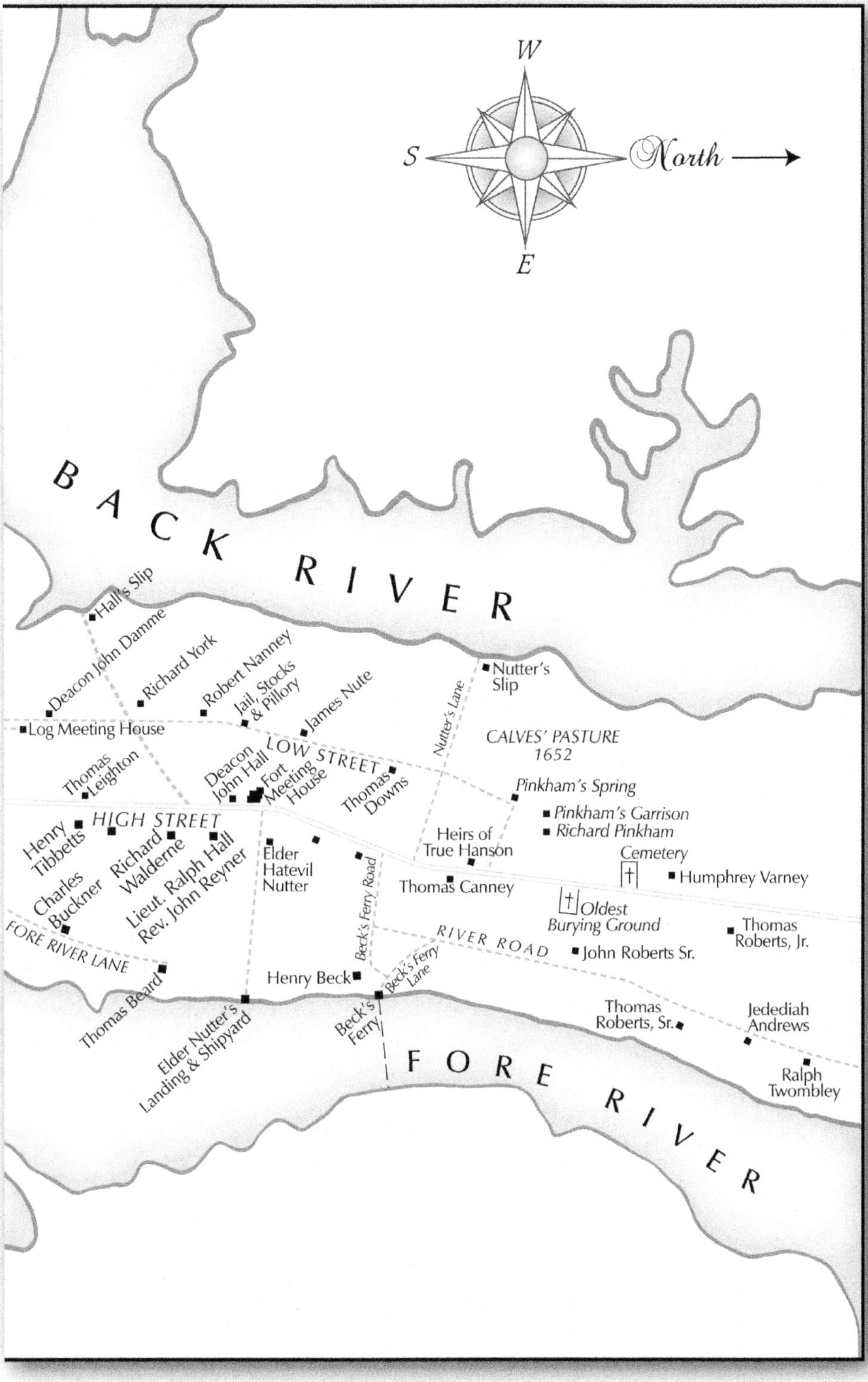
W
S
North
E
BACK RIVER
Hall's Slip
Deacon John Damme
Richard York
Robert Nanney
Jail, Stocks & Pillory
James Nute
Log Meeting House
Nutter's Lane
Nutter's Slip
CALVES' PASTURE 1652
LOW STREET
Deacon John Hall
Fort Meeting House
Thomas Leighton
Thomas Downs
Pinkham's Spring
Pinkham's Garrison
Richard Pinkham
HIGH STREET
Henry Tibbetts
Richard Walderne
Lieut. Ralph Hall
Rev. John Reyner
Charles Buckner
Elder Hatevil Nutter
Heirs of True Hanson
Cemetery
Humphrey Varney
Thomas Canney
Beck's Ferry Road
Oldest Burying Ground
FORE RIVER LANE
RIVER ROAD
John Roberts Sr.
Thomas Roberts, Jr.
Henry Beck
Beck's Ferry Lane
Thomas Beard
Elder Nutter's Landing & Shipyard
Beck's Ferry
Thomas Roberts, Sr.
Jedediah Andrews
Ralph Twombley
FORE RIVER

# *Chapter 35*

## MARY AND ALICE *HAMPTON*

December, 1662 Bloody Point and Hampton, Massachusetts Bay Colony

The passage to Bloody Point was quick, but further travel that day proved impossible. Some two hours of daylight remained once they docked. There was no choice but to stay at the Trickeys' ordinary. John Roberts came to this conclusion reluctantly. The next day was the Sabbath, and travel was forbidden, engendering a further delay. The constable's mood was foul.

The missionaries were confined to an upstairs room as speedily as possible. John did not want the sight of them to incite sympathy among the clientele. The independent-minded families of Bloody Point mistrusted Reyner as it was. Thomas Trickey's black looks were bad enough, particularly when he learned that Allie's facial injury was John's work too.

Mistress Trickey led them upstairs herself and gave Constable Roberts the key to the room with a look that matched her husband's. She was Nicholas Shapleigh's sister, and John had no doubt the captain would hear of this. He hoped the Sabbath would delay the news, and that they would be on their way to Hampton before Shapleigh might intervene.

Walter counted the delay a blessing for his patients. Elizabeth Shapleigh Trickey knew Mary and Allie from Kingsweare and had seen them more recently at her brother's home on Kittery Point. She was a sympathetic and able assistant and helped Walter to remove the women's bloody bandages and treat the wounds. There were no signs of infection as yet, and the apothecary was grateful for an extra day to afford his friends warmth, rest, and sustenance before the long ride to Hampton and a second flogging. The women were still in too much pain to eat a full meal, but they took some bread soaked in broth. Walter dosed them with his tea, built up the fire, and left the exhausted missionaries dozing on their stomachs.

The Sabbath was a veritable day of rest for the invalids. After helping Walter change their dressings in the morning, The Trickeys went out in their sleigh, leaving their son Zack to tend the ordinary. They returned hours later with clothing for the missionaries.

"We are blessed with friendly neighbors," Mistress Trickey said with a significant look. She placed the bundles in Walter's arms. "Ye shall have need of them at Hampton," she added gravely.

Young Thomas Roberts was unconcerned by the delay, happy to be spared the long Sabbath Day sermons in the unheated Fort Meeting House. A day by the Trickeys' warm hearth with a flagon in his fist and food for the asking was no hardship for the younger constable. Besides, his brother was fretting enough for both of them.

The day of reprieve passed all too quickly. John Roberts had them in the saddle at first light on Monday, although Thomas was the only one to complain. It was December $25^{th}$, but all Yuletide celebrations were banned in the Bay Colony. Feasting or neglecting normal labor would incur a fine. John was glad to go, for he was discomfited by the Trickeys' disapproval.

Progress was excruciatingly slow. An unrelenting wind made the cold day frigid. The horses managed a jogging trot at best, but mostly they walked in the icy conditions, picking their way and jerking on the lead ropes, as one or another slipped repeatedly. The jolting was painful for the missionaries. Their wounds bled, and the bandages became stiff, chaffing at every movement. Riding behind them, Walter watched grimly as blood began to show through their cloaks. Elizabeth's fresh clothing was needed already, and they had not even got to Hampton, he thought despairingly. He prayed Pitman had found Edward at Salem. Elizabeth Trickey would inform the Shapleighs, but the apothecary doubted their friends could help. These days Nicholas' influence on the west side of the river was marginalized by his association with the Friends. The Bay Colony was aggressive against any who supported them. Walter's musings were gloomy on the dismal ride.

Several times in open territory John tried to go faster, but the vista was misleading. The wind created drifts in some places and exposed treacherous patches of ice in others. It stung exposed flesh and insinuated itself ingeniously through the tiniest gaps in clothing. The increased pace made the horses slip and stumble more often. The unrelenting pain exhausted the missionaries.

Mary ached from the constant shivering. Her back burned but did not warm her. It felt wet, sharpening the cold. Every jolt sent a fresh stab of pain up her back. She could not feel her hands, pinioned in the thick leather cuffs, even though Walter had wrapped them in flannel. Her wounds throbbed with the beat of her heart. They traveled in single file, and she was but dimly aware of her companions on their separate mounts. She longed to bury her fingers in the thick coat of her horse's neck, but the cuffs denied even that small comfort. It was a relief when the road took them into the woods. The trees afforded a modicum of protection from the wind, and John was obliged to keep the horses to a walking pace in the deeper snow.

It took over four hours to reach Hampton. It was approaching noon, but the light was muted by heavy clouds. The smoke from many hearths was visible before they reached the town, bringing the welcome odor of habitation and warmth. Mary roused from her stupor at the fragrance with its promise of journey's end. The road was packed as they got closer, and they came into town at an agonizing trot. Candle and lantern light shone from windows, dispelling the gloom of the day within doors. They saw no one abroad and finally stopped in front of a house.

"Hark you, William Fifield!" John Roberts bellowed from the saddle.

Figures moved behind the windows, and the front door cracked open.

"Who goes there?" Fifield called, loath to brave the cold.

"We have prisoners to deliver into your custody," John Roberts told him. "We have been on the road from Bloody Point since daybreak. Come forth and do your duty!"

The door closed and presently Fifield stepped outside pulling on his cloak. "You have prisoners? By whose order?" he asked, regarding the group with suspicion.

"By order of Captain Richard Walderne, Magistrate of Dover and Assistant to the General Court of Boston. I am John Roberts, constable of Dover, and the warrant is here. Now delay no more! We have need of warmth and refreshment, man!"

"I must fetch the keys," the Hampton constable replied and disappeared back inside.

Faces peered from the windows. Fifield was evidently a family man. Roberts huffed with impatience. The man reemerged wrapped in a muffler and holding a storm lantern.

"But these are women!" he protested, as he peered at the figures behind the men more closely. "What is afoot here?"

"They are Quakers. Now take us to the gaol for we are cold and weary and would be done with this!" Roberts insisted.

"I would see the warrant first," Fifield answered stiffly.

"Think you we made this journey for *sport*?" John roared. His horse shied, almost jerking the lead rope out of his mittened hand. All patience was spent. Relief was so near. "Take us there forthwith!" he ordered, struggling with his mount. "You can look at the warrant when we are out of this wind!"

As though cued by the Almighty, a gust nearly took their hats. Fifield relented reluctantly and led them the short distance to the meeting house. The gaol was located in the back, facing the town common. Fifield unlocked the door, but insisted upon reading the warrant before securing the missionaries in the single cell. John fidgeted, impatient to be away and at least return to Bloody Point this day. Leading three horses would slow the constables, and the air was heavy with oncoming snow, but there would be sufficient daylight, if they were not delayed here.

Walter and Thomas Roberts supported Anne, and she revived on moving indoors. Mary and Allie limped on numb feet but managed to walk unaided. The three prisoners sat stiffly on a bench. Thomas plunked down on a stool and dozed off in the relative warmth. Fifield perused the warrant carefully, reading it over several times, as John paced impatiently.

"But this cannot be correct!" the Hampton Constable exclaimed at length.

Thomas jerked awake. John's face was a picture of dismay. Walter suppressed a smile.

"Ten stripes at the cart tail in each town?" the Hampton constable went on. "They could hardly survive the trek to Dedham in this weather, let alone being flogged in every town along the way! 'Tis more than an hundred lashes apiece!" He was sincerely amazed.

"There is no mistake," John Roberts replied, holding his temper by a thread. "'Tis signed by Captain Walderne, Magistrate of Dover, look you!" He pointed with a grimy finger. "The citizens of Dover made a formal complaint to be shut of them. 'Tis signed by many. They are heretics and vagabonds. Now do your duty!" John finished, pulling on his mittens. "Mine is done."

He turned on his heel and left. Thomas hurried after him.

"Begging your pardon, Constable," Walter said when the door closed.

"And who might you be?" Fifield asked peevishly. He felt out of his depth and did not like it.

"Doctor Walter Barefoote, at your service, sir. I am an apothecary and charged with the care of these women. At this moment they are in need of sustenance. We passed the publick house as we rode in. Will you allow me to fetch some refreshment for them?"

"Well." The constable cleared his throat and swallowed visibly. "Warrant or no, this...business must wait until the morrow. I must arrange for an ox and cart and alert Reverend Cotton and the townsfolk..." He trailed off, brow furrowed in consideration of all the necessary preparations. "I reckon they must eat, though certes, these women have caused trouble enough for one day," he opined, unlocking the cell door and gesturing them in. "I profess, you must not think to make fools of men," he admonished, as they filed past.

Mary met his eye. "We are able to deal with thee, as well as the others," she answered and smiled, recalling the constables laboring to get them a-horse—a small victory but satisfying.

Fifield was amazed the woman could smile after being flogged and exposed to a twenty-mile trek in the cold. He urged the apothecary to make haste as Walter left to fetch food for the prisoners. The Quaker women unnerved him, and his own noon meal was waiting at his warm hearth. He must guard them, until he could lock up the gaol.

It was snowing lightly as Walter rode the short distance to the publick house. A spry lad took his tired horse, and he gave the boy a coin for grain. His mare had earned it, and the gaol was an easy walk. He did not envy the constables' mounts their journey homeward, though he rather hoped the men would suffer.

He found the ordinary nearly deserted and attributed it to the blistering cold. A blazing fire filled the hearth, broadcasting blessed warmth. An elderly gentleman sat at a table in the corner, the ledgers before him marking him as the innkeeper. He rose as Walter approached.

"I bid you good morrow, sir," the doctor said. "Walter Barefoote, Apothecary of Dover, at your service." He held out his hand.

"Robert Tuck, proprietor. Well met and welcome," the man responded, eying Walter keenly, as he shook his hand. "I also have some small skill in that area." He sank back into his chair, pushed his accounts aside, and gestured for the apothecary to join him. "What business brings a man of physic from Dover to Hampton on such a day, may I inquire?"

Hearing voices, a woman appeared in a doorway near the table, wiping her hands on her apron. She listened attentively, as Walter related the events at Dover. By her confident bearing and interest in his story, he assumed she was Tuck's wife, and this was confirmed, when the proprietor introduced her. Joanna Tuck looked a deal younger than her white-haired husband.

"I hope to procure some sustenance for my friends. They have endured a long and painful ride in this cold, and they are in a weakened state. Constable Fifield intends to administer their flogging on the morrow," Walter finished.

The Tucks exchanged a look. Without another word Joanna went back to the kitchen and returned carrying a covered kettle. The fragrance of chicken soup made Walter's stomach churn in anticipation. She carried a wrapped loaf in the other hand, along with four wooden spoons.

"Oh bless you, madam!" he said, removing his purse from the pocket of his waistcoat. Tuck put a hand on his arm, stopping him.

"Your room and the fee for your horse is payment enough, Dr. Barefoote," he said. "I deem it a privilege to help a fellow physician, especially one that is aiding those who suffer for their beliefs." His wife nodded gravely. "Mayhap we shall find time to converse anon, when your duty to your friends is done," he added.

"I should enjoy that," Walter smiled wearily.

A maidservant passed through the room and up the stairs with an armful of clean linen to make up his bed.

"Might I borrow some blankets, as well?" he asked. "It shall be a long, cold night in the gaol."

"Certes," Mistress Tuck answered and fetched three woolen blankets for him.

"I scarce know how to thank you for your kindness," he added, resettling the strap of his medical bag on his shoulder. He put the bread and spoons in a pocket of his greatcoat, donned his hat and gloves, and took up the blankets and kettle of soup.

Robert Tuck nodded, "No thanks are necessary. You shall find little sympathy for the Bay Colony in this house," he said quietly, "And there are good families in this town who do concur."

Walter walked back to the jail as quickly as possible. He was relieved to find these kind people after the cruel prejudice of recent events.

Mary Fifield watched from the window when her husband was called out. The figures on horseback were distorted through the glass, but did she not see skirts? What had these women done? Might they be witches? But if that were so, why bring them here from Dover? She hid her concern and fed the children, setting her husband's meal to keep warm on the shelf in the fireplace. At least the gaol was not far. Still she was uneasy. Sensing her tension, the two elder girls took the three little ones up to the loft to play, but eleven-year-old William stayed by the hearth, whittling and glancing at the door periodically. Mary took up her mending and sat by the window. The weak afternoon light dimmed, and large flakes of snow whirled with the wind.

They both jumped up when the door opened.

"What is the matter, father? What did they do?" young Will asked without preamble.

William's hat and cloak were coated with snow, and he removed them carefully, avoiding eye contact. They had been wed for twenty years, and Mary could see her husband was upset.

"Father is tired now, Will," she said, laying her hand on the boy's shoulder, "Let him eat in peace."

She felt her son draw breath to protest and tightened her grip, "Mind now, son," she repeated in the tone her children knew well. She patted his shoulder. "The wood box wants filling," she added more gently.

Will looked to his father, but the constable was intent on removing his boots. No reprieve there. The boy sighed, donned his coat, muffler, and mittens, and reluctantly obeyed.

Mary set her husband's food on the table and ladled some warm cider into cups for each of them. William stood warming his hands at the fire, and she could not see his face.

"Come eat while 'tis still warm, husband," she invited.

"I have no appetite," he answered without turning.

Mary went to his side. "What is it, dear heart?" she asked, laying a hand on his back.

He turned and put his arms around her. She held him close and waited for him to speak.

"Ah, my sweet Mary." His voice was muffled against her dust cap. "What am I to do?"

The whole sorry situation came out then—the Quaker missionaries, the brutal warrant issued by Walderne, and the public stripping and flogging he must perform on the morrow.

"I do not think I can bear it, Mary! But if I shirk my duty, I shall be marked as a weakling or a Quaker sympathizer. Yet how shall I smite tender women on their naked backs?" he finished, turning from her in anguish.

"Sit now, husband. Sit down and list to me. Mayhap there is a way."

Mary drew him down on the bench before the hearth, her agile mind racing. Will was a gentle soul. He had never raised a hand against her or the girls, and she could count on the fingers of one hand the instances he had taken a switch to his sons. Why had God put this duty in his path? Her husband's sweet nature was among the things she loved most about him, but it would not serve him in this stead. Only his family knew that he abhorred blood. He was like to sicken and swoon at the sight of it. How *would* he bear it? William had served Hampton well as selectman, advocate, and now constable, but if he failed to carry out this task, he might well lose all the status and respect established over two decades. His fear was not groundless, but she had an idea.

"Consider this, husband. If you go early on the morrow, before first light, before folk are up and about, then mayhap the punishment could be administered within doors, privily. You need not bare their backs at all! No one would know you had not, and you could strike with a light hand on their clothing, and none would be the wiser."

William rubbed his lower lip, a habit when considering. Slowly he nodded then grasped her hands. "Ah, Mary," he exclaimed with relief, "You are a wonder!"

Fifield surprised the prisoners by appearing before sunrise. He rattled the latch and banged the door as he entered then stamped his feet, ostentatiously knocking the snow off his boots to insure the women were alerted to his presence. He held up the lantern and approached the dark cell.

The missionaries moved slowly. They were stiff from sleeping on their knees in the cold, heads pillowed by their arms on the wooden shelf that served as a bed. Their rest had been fitful, as lying down or leaning against a wall was impossible with their torn backs. Once on their feet, they regarded him silently. Only the smallest of them evinced any pain, and the others supported her between them. The constable suppressed the urge to exchange pleasantries. Inquiries as to their health or how they had slept were, certes, not appropriate. William suppressed a bubble of hysterical amusement at the thought. He had no doubt they would be gratefully relieved upon hearing his wife's plan. He cleared his throat.

"As Constable of Hampton I have the authority to amend the implementation of this sentence somewhat," he began formally. "'Twill be best for all concerned."

He paused, expecting a reaction, but the women regarded him as before. Fifield plunged on.

"The sentence can take place within doors, privily, without removing your—"

"Nay," said Mary firmly.

The constable thought he might have misheard and persisted. "You need not be publicly stripped and flogged in the cold with all the town—"

Mary cut him off again. "We are not ashamed of our suffering."

Fifield gaped at her.

"Do according to thy order or set us free," she said, holding his eye.

"Best fetch a cart," Allie put in, moving her lips as little as possible.

Will flushed. It had not occurred to him that the women would not comply.

"Mark you, I would spare you pain and humiliation. You cannot wish to suffer!"

"How else shall people know of this unjust law that forbids us speak God's truth?" Mary asked.

Fifield hid his dismay with anger. "So be it then," he snapped, "but 'tis on your heads."

He turned on his heel, a man unjustly used, but Mary's words cut him to the quick.

"Nay, Constable," she said softly, "'Tis on the heads of men who abuse justice, and those who stand by and allow it."

Two hours after sunrise the town crier beat his drum, calling the people of Hampton to witness the punishment. The clouds had cleared overnight, leaving a few inches of snow. It sparkled prettily on every surface, belying the ugliness of the impending event. The area around the meeting house filled with townsfolk, bewildered by the summons and bundled against the cold.

Mary Fifield pushed her way to the front of the crowd, her son beside her and the girls following with the little ones. A cart with two oxen stood before the meeting house, their breath pluming white in the early morning sun. The sight of them filled her with dread for it meant her plan had failed. Mary did not see her husband and surmised he was fetching the prisoners.

Walter helped Anne as Fifield led the missionaries out to the cart tail. The constable's face was set, and he looked neither left nor right. The women did not relate their earlier exchange with Fifield for they doubted their Anglican friend would understand. There was no point in their suffering, unless it engendered outrage against the law that dictated it.

They reached the cart tail, and Fifield hesitated, reluctant to begin. Then the crowd parted for Captain Thomas Wiggin and the Reverend Seaborn Cotton, and he was trapped.

"Shall I read the warrant, Constable?" Cotton asked. He seemed in high spirits, his fair cheeks rosy with cold.

Will handed him the document, and the two officials turned to the crowd, flanking him. As the minister read the sentence, there were shocked reactions to its unprecedented severity.

"You may proceed, Constable," Wiggin urged, when Fifield did not move immediately.

Will approached the prisoners, pale and shivering at the cart tail. He looked at Walter in desperation, but the apothecary looked back with raised eyebrows. The physician would not help him strip the women, but might another be persuaded? The constable scanned the crowd—a woman preferably. His eye fell on Elizabeth Hussey, his neighbor's wife.

"Goodwife Hussey," he said, beckoning her, "I require assistance in removing their clothing."

She shook her head and backed away. "Not for all the world," she answered.

She had never looked at him so coldly, and his heart sank. Did she not see that he had no choice?

"Why, I profess I will do it myself, then!" he exclaimed with forced bravado.

He turned back to the prisoners. Rust-colored spots marked their cloaks, and the constable removed them gingerly. He winced at the sight of their bodices. Walter had been unable to treat the wounds in the unheated gaol, and the dressings had been applied before the long ride from Bloody Point. Folk reacted audibly. Fifield slit the stained material with shaking hands and pulled it down to their waists with his fingertips. The bandages were stiff with blood, and the reactions rose in volume.

The apothecary stepped forward to remove the soiled dressings, but Fifield's relief at his help was short-lived. The freshly mangled skin of the prisoners' backs engendered outcries of distress and horror from the onlookers. Peeling off the bandages made the wounds bleed afresh, and the constable turned away, gagging at the sight and smell of it. He had ever been an active supporter of the law, but this felt like a sin. For the first time in his life, he feared his actions might damn him to Hell—*if* he was even capable of carrying out the order without succumbing to a faint.

The three missionaries stood half naked, bloody, and shivering. Tears tracked Anne's cheeks, but she was too weakened to voice her pain and fear. Fifield busied himself with binding their hands to the pole across the back of the cart, but this action brought him uncomfortably close to their exposed breasts. He could not focus. Spots danced before his eyes, and his hands trembled, fumbling with the ropes.

Thomas Bradbury was charged with driving the oxcart, and he moved to help Fifield, lest they be there all day. He was Clerk of the Court for both Hampton and Salisbury and had willingly served both towns in a number of official capacities. He knew William was a gentle soul and sympathized with him, but there was little he could do with the officials standing by. The crowd was ominously quiet. At last the prisoners were secured with Bradbury's help, and Fifield stepped away quickly. Thomas went to the front of the cart to await the signal to move ahead.

Captain Wiggin put the whip in the constable's hand. Will looked at it blankly for a moment then gripped it with both hands to still their shaking. He must face those bloody backs again, and his stomach roiled. His conscience screamed at him to cast away the whip and refuse this brutal duty. He looked at the magistrate and minister in hope of a reprieve, but they both nodded encouragingly, unperturbed. Only the resultant humiliation and loss of respect from men of their ilk prevented him from walking away.

At a nod from Mary the three women began to sing, and the Hampton Friends joined in immediately—Eli and Lydia Wardell; her father, Isaac Perkins, and her uncle, Abraham with their large families; five of the Husseys including Lydia's sister Rebecca and her husband John; and William Marston's family—more than thirty voices. Others roused to sympathy at the women's condition also took it up. Things were going from bad to worse. Fifield realized he had best get this over. He nodded to Bradbury, and the ox cart lurched into motion. The constable ignored his wailing conscience and applied the whip.

In spite of his reluctance the stripes were agonizing, scouring wounds that had had no time to heal and creating fresh ones. Walter forced himself to watch, his kind face stony, as he paced beside the cart. The Wardells walked with him, and Lydia took his hand. He was glad of it. Wiggin and the minister flanked the constable, encouraging him to strike with force and admonishing him if he flagged—which was often. The Friends followed, bearing witness, and the crowd along the lane fell in as the cart labored by, circling the town common counterclockwise.

They halted in front of Robert Tuck's ordinary. The circuit had taken less than half an hour, although it felt like an eternity to William Fifield. He breathed raggedly. After the final blow he flung the bloody whip aside as if it were a snake and staggered around the corner of the building. Cotton retrieved the discarded item, wiping off the blood in the fresh snow.

"Well done, Constable!" Captain Wiggin called after him.

There was no response. Mistress Fifield told her son to take his siblings home and build up the fire, then she hurried after her husband.

Thomas Wiggin permitted the apothecary to treat the prisoners' wounds indoors. The Hampton Friends were quick to assist him. Robert and Joanna Tuck had hot water and bandages ready, and the two doctors worked efficiently together. Joanna and Lydia helped them. Anne had been dragged again and was semiconscious as they carried her in; however, she roused screaming, when they tended her. Mary and Allie had not sung for long this time and were incapable of speech. Tears wet their cheeks, and they gasped at every touch or movement. Even warmed their bodies convulsed with intermittent spasms. Walter attributed it to the dual shock of cold and pain. Lydia was gentle and kept up a steady stream of comforting talk, but her eyes flashed with anger.

Eli sat in the common room with little Joseph asleep on his lap. He had survived his ordeal in the stocks at Dover without losing any fingers or toes, thanks to the Friends. The Wardells knew the importance of bearing witness to injustice for they had suffered abuse at Cotton's hands for years. The only hope for change was public censure.

Fifield returned to the ordinary in less than an hour, outfitted for the six-mile trek to Salisbury and eager to be done with it. It was not yet noon, but he insisted the prisoners be loaded in the cart as soon as they were bandaged. He did not chain them for it was evident the women would not leap from the cart and escape.

The constable did not wait for Walter to saddle his mount but set off immediately. The missionaries were barely settled in the back with blankets borrowed from the Tucks before he moved out. The Hampton Friends stood in the road, watching until the cart was out of sight.

Walter bid the Tucks and Wardells farewell, thanking them profusely. As he mounted his mare, Thomas Bradbury rode up. He lived in Salisbury and suggested they ride together. Walter did not object. The man had driven the ox cart and bound the women to the pole, but he had also untied those bonds and helped them into the ordinary.

They soon caught up to the cart. Captain Wiggin's two oxen labored slowly but steadily through the snow, covering the six miles to Salisbury in three hours. Walter wished it were farther. Raw and bleeding as their wounds were, the missionaries would soon be subjected to a third beating.

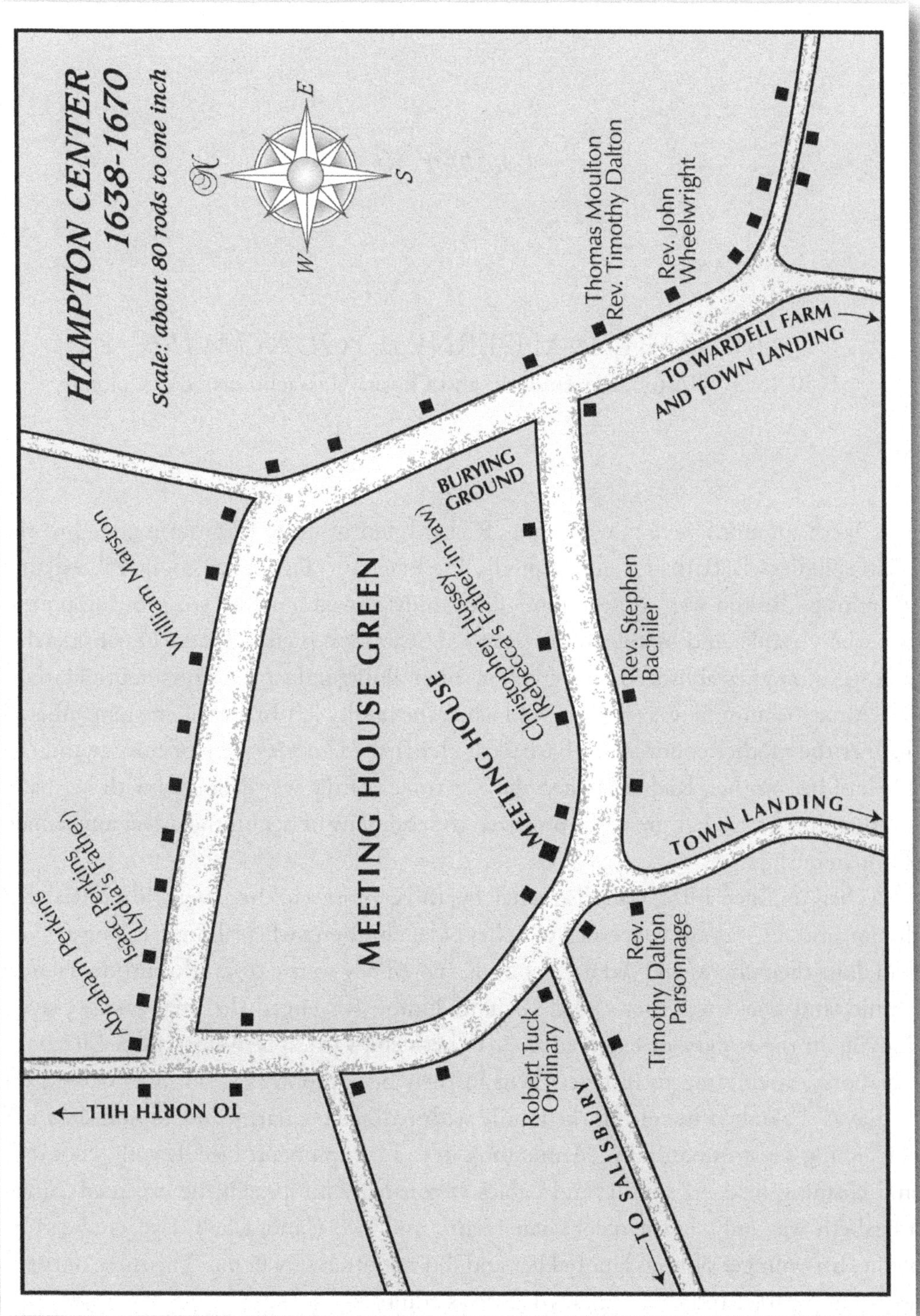
HAMPTON CENTER
1638-1670
Scale: about 80 rods to one inch
N
E
S
W
Thomas Moulton
Rev. Timothy Dalton
Rev. John
Wheelwright
TO WARDELL FARM
AND TOWN LANDING
BURYING
GROUND
Christopher Hussey
(Rebecca's Father-in-law)
William Marston
MEETING HOUSE GREEN
MEETING HOUSE
Rev. Stephen
Bachiler
TOWN LANDING
Isaac Perkins
(Lydia's Father)
Abraham Perkins
Rev.
Timothy Dalton
Parsonnage
Robert Tuck
Ordinary
TO NORTH HILL
TO SALISBURY

## *Chapter 36*

### RICHARD WALDERNE *A YOUNG WIFE*

1650-1652 Boston, Portsmouth, and Dover, Massachusetts Bay Colony

The Scammons were not Puritans. Richard and his wife Eliza immigrated to the colonies via Barbados and kept the Presbyterian faith. They soon realized that Winthrop's Boston was not for them. The family moved north to the growing port at Strawbery Banke and by the 1640's, Richard Scammon owned a farm of considerable acreage and was established in the growing shipbuilding industry at Portsmouth Harbor.

Annie Scammon was two years old when the family left England. She remembered neither the mother country nor Barbados. Her first memories were of Boston and the birth of her brother, Richard, when she was three. Annie was delighted with her baby brother. In fact, as they grew, she preferred the company of her brothers over any female companionship.

Their mother Eliza was distracted by three more children born after Richard Junior, and she was not concerned with her older children's whereabouts, as long as they had done their chores and did not get underfoot. They were constantly outside. Henry, Annie, and Dickie, as they called Richard Junior, scavenged the tidal pools, played Indians in the woods, or explored their father's shipyard. Their elder sister Elizabeth was bossy, attempting to instruct them in their busy mother's stead. She focused on Annie as the only other girl in the family with tedious regularity and admonished her for "acting most unnaturally." Annie took it as a compliment. Needlework, cooking, and cleaning held no appeal, and babies were smelly lumps, Dickie excepted. Since Elizabeth was only a year older than Henry and two ("and a half") years ahead of Anne, her younger siblings ignored her and did not often stay home. The three of them were inseparable, and they remained close as adults.

Annie was not sorry when Elizabeth married in her twenty-first year and moved to the Atkins' farm on the Kennebec River with her husband Thomas. At eighteen, the younger Scammon daughter was in no hurry to wed. The boys who attempted to woo her could not hold a candle to her father or brothers, and she spurned them. Helping her mother keep house was much more enjoyable without Elizabeth's constant censure. They all got on well. Henry was on the brink of his majority and worked with their father at the shipyard, but Dickie evidenced an interest in weapons and at fourteen he apprenticed to the gunsmith Thomas Matson of Braintree. Annie missed him.

Whenever her younger brother came home for a visit, Dickie brought a variety of rifles to test and evaluate. As a result Annie was familiar with the latest firearms. She was a passing good shot "for a girl," he teased. In truth she had a keener eye than most men.

Dickie was home on a rare mild day in April, when Annie Scammon's life changed irrevocably. He was up from Braintree for Eastertide on a week's leave and had brought one of the new flintlock rifles. Their father was expecting a guest—a business associate due to arrive at the Portsmouth dock that afternoon on a gundalow loaded with lumber from upriver. The man owned one of the sawmills that supplied the Scammon shipyard, and he wanted a tour.

Richard Senior was uncharacteristically tense, as they broke their fast that morning. He usually cared little for the opinions of others.

"Captain Walderne is an important man and a Puritan, so I must ask you to be on your best behavior this eve," her father told them.

"He is also a widower and one of the richest men in Dover," Dickie put in, winking at Annie.

"Do not be japing at me, Dickie," she responded tartly, smacking him lightly on the side of the head, as she set the cider jug on the table. "I have no desire to marry an old Puritan gaffer, no matter how rich."

"Look you! That is the very behavior I do not wish our guest to witness this night, Anne!" their father exclaimed. His customary good humor was not in evidence this morn.

"Zounds, he is serious, *Anne*," Dickie intoned. The family always called her Annie.

Richard senior put his head in his hands and let out an exasperated sigh.

"Oh, fret not, Pa," Annie assured him with a touch of impatience. "I promise to play the role of dutiful daughter to Mother's gracious hostess. I shall not smack my brother in company—unless 'tis called for," she added. Brother and sister laughed. Their father did not join in.

"But verily, Pa, the question is why must *we* be on our best behavior?" Dickie was not so ready to acquiesce. "You are buying *his* lumber, so he should be courting *your* favor."

Their father took a long pull from his tankard before answering. The two siblings exchanged a look. It was a familiar tactic, and they both knew he was hiding something. They waited while he set down his cup and stood up.

"There are matters of business pending , which I cannot discuss at present," he said avoiding their eyes. "Just attempt a semblance of courtesy at dinner this night, I beg you."

By late afternoon all was nearly ready in the house. Eliza had enlisted their part-time cook, Missus Fernald, for the occasion. It was lavish by Scammon standards. Annie had helped prepare the food and clean the little-used parlor and dining room. The big dining table was set with their finest cloth and service, the candelabra gleamed, but their father and his guest had not appeared. Dickie was target shooting in the field behind the house with their younger brother, John. Annie joined them as soon as her mother let her go. She was eager to try the new flintlock Dickie had brought. She admired the relative lightness, as her brother explained the principles behind the new firing mechanism. It was superior to the matchlock with its dangling rope fuse, unpredictable at the best of times, let alone in wet conditions. However, Annie soon lost patience with her brother's detailed explanation and cut him off.

"Just show me how to load the bloody thing, so I can get off a few shots before 'tis too dark to see," she demanded.

All three were intent on this task, and they did not remark their father rounding the corner of the house with Richard Walderne at his side. Once loaded, Annie positioned the rifle in its frame, braced her feet in a wide stance, sighted the target, and released the hammer. The puff of smoke from the barrel was echoed by a small explosion of straw and dust from the scarecrow target's midriff.

"Oh well done, sister!" "Rum shot!" the boys crowed, laughing.

"Nonsense," Annie sniffed, straightening. "I was aiming for the head."

"You put him out of commission in any case," a deep voice said, startling them all.

Annie turned and met Richard Walderne's amused look. She assumed her father's guest would be an older man, pious and stodgy. He was mature, well into his thirties, she reckoned, but he radiated virility. She was unprepared for his comely face, his tall,, fit figure, and the glint of approval in his gray eyes, as he took her in.

Her father made introductions, and his guest shook hands with the boys. Then he turned to Annie and grasped her ungloved hand. He held her eyes and brushed her knuckles with his lips. Her hand tingled, and she blushed, causing his smile to deepen, as he straightened.

Richard noted the girl's heightened color with amused satisfaction. He released her hand slowly and assessed her with frank interest. It had never occurred to him that a woman could shoot a gun, let alone enjoy it. Wind-whipped tendrils of blonde hair framed her pleasant face, the thick braid falling to the middle of her back. Her breasts were small, but her hips widened into a pleasingly voluptuous pear shape. Richard imagined wrapping that golden braid around his hand and pulling her head back to nuzzle her smooth neck.

The captain turned his attention to the flintlock. Little crumbs would soon have her feeding from his hand—best not to give too much too soon. In the months since Pru's death the previous June, several Boston widows had demonstrated an interest, but desperation clung to them like heavy perfume. They were used goods, and none appealed to him. This one did. Even as he feigned indifference, conversing with her brothers and hefting the gun, he could feel her eyes on him. He would woo this intriguing girl that fired a rifle like a man and take her to wife.

In minutes Dickie was near as smitten as Annie, responding to Walderne's informed questions about the rifle and inviting their guest to take a shot. The Captain was more than personally interested, for he headed the militia at Dover. He handled the firearm with easy confidence and, ignoring the frame, set the stock against his shoulder, sighted, and fired. The shot nearly took off the target's head. Puritan or no, Annie was impressed.

During dinner with the Scammon family that evening, Richard laughed for the first time since losing Prudence. For months her loss was unsupportable, a constant drag on his energy. Her presence lingered in the house on Tremont Row. After the funeral he had fled to Cocheco, where there was nothing to remind him of her. Still, his sorrow howled for attention like a ravening wolf. It attacked at unguarded moments, devastating him with the teeth and claws of grief and loneliness. Keeping busy was his only defense. The trading post and two sawmills thrived under his desperate attention, but it was not enough. He determined to make a study of shipyards in the region, preparatory to building a fleet of his own for an international shipping business.

Marriage was the last thing on his mind when he had arranged to view Richard Scammon's shipyard among others at Portsmouth. After he left their home that evening, he could think of little else. The wolf was silenced. Her father had mentioned Annie was twenty-two—old for an unmarried woman. Richard supposed her bold spirit and lack of ladylike comportment had deterred suitors. However, she was a virgin, not a widow. This mattered. He would be her first and only lover.

Once he communicated his intention to Annie's father, the courtship progressed quickly with the wholehearted approval of her parents. Scammon agreed to the match with such alacrity that Richard suspected the man had planned it from the first. The Scammons' religion did not concern him for Annie would become a member of the First Church once they were wed. Annie's parents were close to his own age and openly admired him. He respected Scammon's expertise in turn and commissioned the construction of his first ship with his future father-in-law. Annie's dowry was a goodly portion of the cost. Their courtship was as straightforward as the girl herself. There was none of the strain he had endured with the Clarkes.

However, the widower could not refrain from comparing Annie to Prudence. His first wife had been physically perfect, a gracious woman of good Puritan blood, who obeyed him without question. Annie was passing fair, of more common stock, but she was spirited enough to contradict him, and he discovered her defiance aroused him.

She challenged his wit, and Richard liked a challenge. Her brothers had schooled her in holding her own. She conversed like a man—not in manner but in content—and preferred male company, as their interests appealed to her intelligence and independent nature. Female frivolities irritated her. In short Richard was more himself with Annie than with his perfect, ladylike first wife.

The greatest difference between the two women, however, was Annie's sense of humor. She understood and approved his sarcasm, as no one ever had, with the exception of his friend Edward Rawson. In addition the girl was smitten with him, although she tried to hide it, which amused him. Their attraction increased with every visit.

Mastering Annie would be a lively diversion from business demands. He anticipated seducing her, claiming her virginity, and instructing her in the pleasures of their marriage bed. He anticipated burying his hands in her hair, which was her best feature—thick, straight, and honey-colored. She was neither slender nor graceful, but Richard found her small stature and wide hips appealing. He could overpower her easily, yet she was sturdy. She was fifteen years younger than he and would give him sons for many years. Their offspring would be strong in temperament and physically hardy. For the first time since Pru's death, his ardor awoke in anticipation of their wedding night.

They were married in September at Portsmouth, and Richard brought his bride to the house on Tremont Row. Construction had begun on his ship, and by the time it launched fourteen months later, his young wife had given him a son. It was an easy labor, as births went, her mother Eliza said. They named the boy Richard and laughed about it.

# *Chapter 37*

## MARY AND ALICE *SALISBURY*

December, 1662 Salisbury, Massachusetts Bay Colony

It was past noon when Fifield drew rein before the meeting house at Salisbury. Though piercingly bright, the winter sun gave little warmth. When the cart halted, Mary and Allie struggled to sit up, shivering and trying not to imagine what lay ahead. Anne did not move. At least the painful jolting had stopped.

Mary could not feel her toes, even when she thought she was moving them. Her fingers were numb as well, and she could not stop shaking, but these were minor discomforts compared to her wounds. Her back was afire, chafed by bandages already stiff with blood. Pain flared with each breath and the slightest movement of head or arms, but how much worse it must be for their small companion! Mary turned her head carefully to look at Anne who lay on her stomach. The little missionary's face was obscured, but her breathing was audible, and she too shivered with duress and cold. Allie looked frightful. The wound on her cheek had bled through the bandage, but she sat erect, surveying the curious folk, who gathered to gawk at the prisoners.

The apothecary pleaded with Fifield to move his charges indoors, but the constable insisted they stay in the cart until custody was transferred to the Salisbury authorities.

"My duty ends with transporting them hence," he told Walter stiffly. "Constable Challis shall make all decisions concerning their treatment from here on. You must ask him when we return."

"At least allow me fetch them some food," the doctor insisted. "Look at them, man!"

Fifield did with reluctance then averted his eyes quickly.

"Some food, then," he allowed, "but they must stay in the cart."

The man was adamant on this point of law and left without another word. Thomas Bradbury kindly pointed out John Severance's tavern across the road then followed Fifield.

Walter watched them go, too weary to pursue and argue. Besides, he did not want to leave his friends. The past three days were taking their toll on the apothecary, as well as the women, and a wave of despair overcame him. The cold exacerbated their condition, and he longed to get them warm and change the soiled dressings. It was hard to judge how they were faring during the trip from Hampton, as the women lay on their stomachs, covered in blankets, while he followed on his long-suffering mare. Walter climbed into the cart to assess their condition. He was alarmed at the amount of blood. The bandages were stiff with it, and the apothecary struggled to retain his composure.

"I shall fetch some refreshment post haste," Walter told them, when he could speak.

The doctor was relieved to find an ordinary that was efficiently run and spotlessly clean. The common room went quiet when he entered, but Rebecca Severance greeted him at the door. She had noted the arrival of the cart, as had all her custom. She introduced herself and bid him welcome then led him back to the kitchen, where they might talk without an audience. Walter followed, dazed by the blessed warmth of the place.

"They must have done something dreadful to be given such a hard sentence, Dr. Barefoote," she commented, after his brief explanation. She put a bowl of hot soup in his hands and indicated he sit at the kitchen table with a nod of her head. She ladled more of the steaming liquid into three pannikins while Walter tucked in and spoke between mouthfuls.

"'Tis enough they are missionaries for the Society of Friends, Mistress Severance," he said. His energy was returning with every delicious bite. "In addition they publicly embarrassed the minister John Reyner. He wrote up a formal complaint and procured enough signatures to justify an arrest. I suspect many were coerced. The magistrate, Richard Walderne, set the sentence."

"But eleven towns and over eighty miles! Is it not excessive?" She knew it was and did not wait for an answer. "Hi there, Kit!" she called across the large, warm kitchen to a rosy-cheeked maid, stirring a pot at the hearth. "Wrap one of those loaves, will you, and bring it here? Richard Walderne?" she asked, turning back to Walter.

"Yes, he set the punishment," he confirmed.

Rebecca was surprised. "I thought he had a cooler head on his shoulders. Were they offensive to his face? In the court?"

"Their very existence is an offense to the man. He did not want me to accompany them. It incenses him that women preach religion. He deems it unnatural. Add to that the Friends' concept of spiritual equality..." Walter trailed off with a shrug.

"Ah, yes, that would topple his empire, would it not?" Rebecca shot him a rueful smile, and Walter decided he liked this outspoken woman.

He returned her smile, as she put two pannikins on the table.

"I think I should like to meet these criminals who hold with equality before God," she continued, fetching her cloak and muffler.

Walter drained his bowl and shrugged into his greatcoat, as Rebecca took up the third container of soup and the loaf.

"Just cover that pot and swing it off the flame now, Kit. I shall return shortly," she called as she accompanied the apothecary out the back door.

More townsfolk had gathered to stare at the women in the oxcart. When they saw Mistress Severance with the apothecary, they peppered her with questions, but she waved them off, her attention on the missionaries.

"Where is the constable?" she inquired indignantly. "These women are wounded and freezing! They must be brought indoors."

"I quite agree—" Walter began, when a familiar figure broke through the knot of onlookers.

"Edward Wharton!" Walter exclaimed. "Well met! You are a welcome sight!"

The apothecary seemed on the point of embracing the man, despite the soup he carried. Then he registered the look on his friend's face and contained himself.

"What abomination is this?" the Salem Friend asked without preamble, going directly to the women. Mary and Allie looked up at his voice.

"'Tis the work of Reyner and Walderne," Walter said barely able to speak through the rush of relief. "They were flogged in Dover Saturday and again in Hampton this morning at first light."

Edward's angry expression became concerned, as he took in the missionaries' pain and exhaustion. They were shivering pitifully, and he shucked his mittens and reached under the blankets to rub their cold hands. He searched their faces, and noting Allie's facial wound, turned to Walter, inclining his head toward her in wordless outrage.

"It happened at Dover. The constable's whip went high," the doctor told him. "Help us feed these poor souls now, my friend, for they are spent and must take nourishment."

Walter quickly introduced Rebecca to Edward, and the three of them set to the task.

Edward's voice evoked a surge of hope so strong, it smote Mary physically. For the first time since their arrest, she felt the threat of tears. Edward was here! Was it possible he could help them? Her throat constricted, making speech impossible, but she managed a tremulous smile. The warmth of his touch was an anchor in a maelstrom of pain and cold. All too soon he stopped rubbing her hands to feed her, but the soup warmed her belly and tasted divine. Edward's face broadcast loving concern, as he gently pushed the wooden spoon past her chattering teeth. She realized with undeniable certainty that she loved him.

"Where is the *Sea Witch*?" Walter asked quietly. He had climbed into the cart and was supporting Anne as he fed her. She was semi-conscious but took the soup greedily.

"At the dock on Town Creek. I arrived yesterday," Edward answered. "Thy messenger did well. Also, we have an ally here in Salisbury."

The crowd parted as a man rode up to the cart. People made way, indicating he was known and respected. He nodded at Edward as though acquainted, and Rebecca greeted him warmly, when he dismounted.

"Lieutenant Pike!" she exclaimed. "I was on the point of sending for you! Doctor Walter Barefoote, this is Lieutenant Robert Pike. He is an officer of the local militia and a man of influence in Salisbury. Verily, he is a voice of reason in our town."

"My thanks, Mistress Severance," Pike said, giving her a dazzling smile. "Well met, Doctor," he continued, offering a firm handshake. Walter liked him instantly.

"When I put in yesterday, Friend Pike was the first person I sought," Edward told Walter. He turned to the man. "We have arrived none too soon, Lieutenant, as thou canst see."

Pike began a polite bow, but he froze and his expression hardened, as he took in the missionaries' sorry state.

"Doctor Barefoote," Pike said, "Where is the Hampton constable? I assume he has the warrant, and I would read it for myself."

"He went to find your Constable Challis, last I knew," Walter answered.

"They are likely at the goal. Let us go there forthwith. At the very least, these women should be taken within doors. Will you accompany me, sir?"

Walter hesitated. He was loath to leave his charges, but Edward and Rebecca reassured him.

"Go with the Lieutenant, Doctor. We shall stay with the missionaries," she told the apothecary.

Walter gave them a grateful look, and Edward climbed into the cart to take up feeding Anne. The doctor climbed down and started off with Pike, but no sooner had they cleared the crowd, than his new acquaintance stopped abruptly with a mild oath. Walter looked at him, confused.

"Your pardon, doctor," the Lieutenant apologized, his eyes fixed over Walter's shoulder. The apothecary turned to see a figure approaching rapidly. His cloak billowed, revealing the black suit of a Puritan minister. "I fear the circumstances are about to become more challenging than I anticipated," Pike finished.

"Who is it?" the doctor asked, as the man bore down on them, fury flashing in his eyes.

"That is John Wheelwright," Pike answered, "the minister here at Salisbury."

"Pike! Hold up!" the reverend called petulantly, as if the two men had not paused, awaiting him. "What is afoot here?" he asked gesturing to the crowd. "Are those prisoners not women?" he continued, huffing up to them and squinting at the oxcart.

"Reverend John Wheelwright, allow me to introduce Dr. Walter Barefoote of Dover," the lieutenant interposed with unshakable good manners.

"Your serv—" Walter began but was cut off.

"Yes, yes." Wheelwright brushed the pleasantries aside impatiently. "Where is Constable Challis? What passes here?" He spoke loudly, his tone suggesting he had purposely been kept in the dark.

Pike chose to address the first question. "I believe Challis is at the gaol. We are on the point of going to speak with him. Would you care to—"

"Then I shall accompany you," Wheelwright stated and set off without waiting for a reply.

Pike glanced at Walter, his look expressing volumes. The apothecary raised his eyebrows, and they followed in the minister's wake.

When Reverend Wheelwright burst through the door, the two constables and Thomas Bradbury looked up, startled. Bradbury had read the warrant three times and still could not believe the severity of the sentence. He thought the flogging would end at Salisbury, the third town, but the warrant called for eight more. It was unthinkable! He frowned at the minister's rude entry. Wheelwright had been at Salisbury for only a few months, yet he acted as though all authority in the town was his and his alone. The man *had* established several settlements that were now incorporated towns, but Salisbury was not one of them. Bradbury's friend, Robert Pike, had already clashed with the assertive reverend several times.

Wheelwright stopped in the doorway and glared at the three men.

"Constable Challis!" he admonished. "Why was I not summoned? What passes here?"

Philip Challis froze, staring at the reverend open-mouthed.

Pike and Walter appeared behind the reverend, blocking the open doorway. The Lieutenant caught Bradbury's attention and rolled his eyes. Thomas was relieved to see him. Robert was one of the few in Salisbury who might supersede the influence of the feisty minister.

"Begging your pardon, Reverend, but might we enter?" Pike inquired politely.

Wheelwright glanced over his shoulder frowning but moved into the room. Walter closed the door behind them.

"Allow me to explain, Reverend," Thomas Bradbury interposed, since Challis seemed unlikely to respond. He handed over the warrant and recounted the situation as the reverend perused it.

"Constable Fifield transported the prisoners by oxcart from Hampton, after administering the sentence there this very morning. I witnessed it and rode down with them after. They have only just arrived," Bradbury explained.

"I would see that document, and it please you, Reverend," Pike said.

Wheelwright hesitated then relinquished the paper reluctantly.

"Well done, Constable," the minister said to Fifield. "Now let us perform our duty forthwith," he added turning to Challis.

Philip Challis looked at Robert Pike with wide eyes.

"Sir! Look not to Pike for direction on this. I am in authority." The minister pointed at the warrant in the Lieutenant's hands. "The order is here."

Robert Pike could tolerate no more of the cleric's high-handed assumptions.

"Verily, Reverend, Mister Bradbury and I are the authorities concerning matters of the civil court in this town," he stated firmly. "Constable Challis serves the civil law. He is not a deacon of your church."

"But this is a religious matter! They are heretics!" Wheelwright protested. "As an ordained minister I am the higher power in this matter. The law comes from the Almighty, and I am His instrument!"

"I beg to differ, sir," Pike responded calmly. Walter marveled at his composure. He himself wanted to throttle the cleric. "As this warrant reads, the arrest of these missionaries is based on a formal complaint by a number of citizens in the Town of Dover. Technically they have broken no civil law, and, certes, they have not disturbed any citizens of Salisbury."

"But the warrant states—" the minister began.

"That warrant is a travesty!" Thomas Bradbury asserted, venting his indignation. "No person could survive one-hundred-ten stripes, as well as travel such a distance in winter. And these are women!" His voice rose in outrage.

Wheelwright evidenced no concern for the prisoners but rounded on Bradbury, pressing his point. "'Tis signed by Richard W—"

"It matters not who signed it! 'Tis tantamount to murther most f—"

"Gentlemen, please," Pike interrupted firmly. "The subject is an heated one, but we do not need to become overheated ourselves."

The two men fell silent, glaring at each other. The Lieutenant went on with calm logic.

"The legality of the warrant is questionable, as the Whip and Cart Act is usually limited to three towns."

"Just so," Bradbury put in emphatically. Pike shot his friend a warning glance.

Wheelwright opened his mouth to protest, but the Lieutenant held up his hand. Walter had never known a man to wield authority so temperately—an iron fist in a velvet glove.

"Permit me to finish, gentlemen," Pike said mildly. "Dr. Barefoote has determined that further flogging shall endanger the prisoners' health—even imperil their lives. He is not only a physician; he is also a Deputy of the Great and General Court, representing Dover. At his professional recommendation the women shall *not* be flogged a third time—"

"You cannot mean to release them!" Wheelwright interrupted aghast.

"Sir." The lieutenant's patience was cracking, for though he did not raise his voice, his eyes flashed at this latest interruption. The minister made a moue of disgust, but held his tongue, and Pike continued. "I propose to deputize Doctor Barefoote and remand the prisoners into his custody. As a Deputy of the Court he is charged to remove them from the jurisdiction of the Bay Colony as soon as possible."

Walter barely contained a shout of triumph. Wheelwright did not erupt in protest as the doctor expected, but his face flushed, and he spoke through clenched teeth.

"You overreach your authority, sir, and I shall not forget it," he seethed.

"He overreaches nothing, Reverend," Bradbury responded tersely. "An officer of the military has the authority to deputize any freeman he chooses, particularly a representative to the Court." He looked around the room. "As Clerk of the Court in the towns of Hampton and Salisbury, I submit that I am in accord with this decision."

All present agreed except the minister, who left without another word, slamming the door behind him. Only then did Constable Philip Challis find his voice.

"We do not whip women in Salisbury," he said indignantly. William Fifield winced.

In his capacity as Clerk of the Court, Thomas Bradbury wrote up the document deputizing the apothecary and Robert Pike signed it. Walter secured the precious paper in an inside pocket of his coat, and the five men went back outside. Fifield went straight to the ordinary, ignoring the cart and its contents. Challis, Bradbury, and Pike broke up the crowd, telling them to go about their business, as there would be no flogging that day. They were assaulted with questions, but firmly declined to answer, explaining the missionaries must be tended forthwith. As the crowd dispersed, Walter informed Edward and Rebecca of Robert Pike's ruling. At last they could move the women inside.

Rebecca went back to the inn to prepare a room and to alert her husband. Pike and Bradbury went ahead, carrying Anne. John Severance came to meet them, holding the door open. Then he assisted the apothecary with Allie, who winced as she limped on numb feet. Between them, they supported most of her weight. Edward followed slowly with Mary leaning on his arm. As they crossed the lane, Walter asked the innkeeper about getting a message to Kittery Point.

"You write it, and I shall find a rider to deliver it," John replied, grasping Allie's arm with two hands, as she stumbled. "Easy there, my girl! 'Twill require some coin, I fear, for I reckon there will be no volunteers for such a journey." Walter nodded. "My leg tells me we shall be getting more snow," John continued, as they slowly mounted the steps to the wide porch.

"An old injury?" Walter asked.

"An altercation with a log in Plymouth in '35," the innkeeper told him, opening the door. "The log came out on top—verily—but it brought me to this business, so no complaint. It has kept us coming up short in our supplies many a time," John grinned.

Once Edward had got Mary inside, the warmth of the tavern made her lightheaded. She had not been in a heated room since Bloody Point. She swayed, and sounds faded in and out. Edward gripped her upper arms to steady her.

"Mary is flagging," he said to Walter. "I shall have to carry her up the stairs, I reckon."

It was the last thing she heard before the world went black.

Rebecca supplied clean flannels and hot water, to which the apothecary added powdered sumac, cayenne, and yarrow. As the tincture steeped, he removed the bandages, sniffing for signs of infection. Anne roused from her swoon, unable to contain her cries of pain. Edward held her hands and spoke soothingly, as the apothecary and their hostess gently blotted the oozing wounds with the tincture then coated them liberally with salve. The Salem Friend comforted Mary and Allie in their turn. Mary gripped his hands and fixed her eyes on his, welcoming the distraction during the sharp agony of the ministrations. Edward's eyes were a warm brown flecked with amber. She had not remarked them before. Walter put off applying bandages, until the women must be moved again. He was grateful for the clothing the Hampton Friends had supplied but did not dress them yet.

The apothecary examined the women's feet and hands for signs of frostbite. The pain as their extremities warmed rivaled the agony of their wounds. As circulation returned, toes and fingers first tingled then burned. Walter was relieved to find no blistering.

The missionaries had had soup in the cart, so the doctor dosed them with a tea of willow bark, powdered sumac, and honey. Rebecca ground some precious nutmeg and added it as well, saying it would help the invalids sleep—their only escape from pain. Edward built up the fire, and they left the women resting on their stomachs in the warm room.

Walter was hungry, but first he penned a message to Nicholas Shapleigh, giving it to John Severance with coin for the delivery. He wanted their friends to know the missionaries were safe and would soon return to Kittery Manor to recuperate. At present they were in no condition to undertake a day-long journey tossed about in an unheated shallop. His friends were reprieved, but he worried where to take them until they were strong enough to travel.

He found Edward and Lieutenant Pike at a table in the common room with Bradbury and the two constables. The men were assuring William Fifield he was not at fault in obeying the warrant at Hampton, but the man was inconsolable. The missionaries' release only heightened his remorse. When the doctor joined them, Fifield rose and bundled up for the journey home.

"I only wish we might have had a Lieutenant Pike at Hampton," he said mournfully.

Thomas Bradbury and Philip Challis took their leave and followed him out. When they had gone, Edward related Pitman's arrival at Salem the Saturday before.

"Thy message said to meet at Salisbury, and I thought of Lieutenant Pike," Edward said.

"We became acquainted some years ago, when Friend Wharton glazed the windows in my house," Pike explained to Walter.

"I knew Robert for a man of integrity and thought he might assist us," the Salem man continued, "So I gave Friend Pitman a message to deliver to him on the way back, explaining the situation."

"Thank God you did," Walter said with a grateful look at Pike. "And I am relieved Pitman found you," he told Edward. "I said nothing to our friends, as I was unsure of success. But now where can we keep them until they are strong enough for the journey to Kittery Point?"

"Can they not stay here?" Edward asked the lieutenant.

"I fear Reverend Wheelwright will attempt to prosecute the original warrant," Pike warned. "The man never gives up without a fight. No doubt he will inform Reverend Reyner of this turn of events, and he will alert Richard Walderne."

"In any case the tide is against us and, even were it not, 'tis too late to set out for Kittery Point this day," Edward worried.

"I would entertain them myself," Robert said, "but 'tis the first place Wheelwright would look after here." He sat back a moment, thinking. "There is another possibility," he resumed, leaning forward. "Is either of you gentlemen acquainted with George Carr?"

Edward shook his head, and Walter said, "I have not had the pleasure."

"I thought you might know him or at least have heard of him," Pike continued. "He lives hard by on an island in the Merrimack. He has a shipyard and runs the ferry between Salisbury and Newbury. Have you not heard of the float bridge he built in the '50s?"

"Oh, I know of that enterprise," Walter responded. "Quite a feat of engineering, I understand. I should like to see that!"

"Well, mayhap you shall," Pike said. "More to the point, Carr is an independent thinker, as well as an ingenious man of business. 'Tis the reason he chose an island for his home. He has no love for the Puritan authorities. His brother William joined the Friends years ago and lives in Rhode Island Colony. William Carr was among those who left the Bay with Roger Williams in '36, when he was banished." Pike glanced around then leaned forward, lowering his voice. "I propose to tell George of our situation. We are well acquainted, and he may agree to shelter the missionaries. Wheelwright would not dare to look there even if he thought of it. They would be safe under his protection."

"I hesitate to ask more of you, after all you have done for us, Lieutenant Pike; however, I see no alternative." Walter rubbed his chin. The stubble itched. He was normally fastidious in his toilet, but it had not been a priority since leaving Bloody Point. "Once again, we are in your debt, sir."

"You owe me nothing, Doctor," Pike answered. "Allow me to speak with George," he said, rising. "I am happy to thwart a miscarriage of justice, in any case."

"Shall we go in the *Sea Witch*?" Edward asked, standing with him.

"My thanks, but no," Robert assured him. "'Tis a scant mile's ride, and there is a well-kept track to the float bridge. If I find George at home—which is likely at this season—'tis best I speak with him privily. 'Twill afford him the opportunity to refuse with grace, although I am willing to wager he will welcome the missionaries. I shall return as speedily as possible."

Once they had eaten, Walter went to shave, and Edward checked on his friends. He knocked softly and looked in. Anne and Allie dozed, but Mary's eyes were open. She lay on her stomach, her mangled back shiny with salve, but she reached out a hand wordlessly, wincing at the movement. He set a stool close to the bed and took it gently. Her eyes were heavy with pain and exhaustion, and her fingers were bright red. He suppressed the urge to kiss them.

"However did thee find us, Friend Wharton?" she asked her voice barely audible.

"Walter sent a messenger to Salem on the day ye were sentenced."

"He said nothing of it," she murmured.

"He did not wish to raise false hope," Edward explained. "Friend Pitman arrived at Salem the next morning. I barely made Rockport before dark. I slept onboard and set out before first light, so none would chastise me for sailing on the Sabbath."

Mary's eyes widened. He might have been fined for it. A mischievous grin lit Edward's face, and he leaned close. The pain did not prevent her heart skipping a beat in response.

"Aye, I risked my soul for thee," he confided, eyes dancing then he sobered. "But despite my wickedness, God's breath filled my sail, for I have never made that stretch to Salisbury so speedily. I went to Robert Pike forthwith, and he did not disappoint. 'Twas he deputized Walter and granted him custody of you. There shall be no more flogging." Mary's eyes closed and tears of relief wet her lashes. "I shall take you all back to Kittery Point as soon as ye are strong enough to sail," he said softly. Their faces had never been so close.

Mary opened her eyes. "Then we have triumphed," she whispered.

Edward saw this news made her exultant in spite of her agony. He looked down, stroking her palm with his thumb. He had hoped the ordeal would fulfill her call and was dismayed to realize it would not. He had known the agony of the lash himself, but he was a man of rugged build with the courage of his convictions. He could endure pain, but Mary's suffering was harder to bear than his own. Why had she returned to Dover after his warning? It was a question born of frustration, and this was not the time or place for remonstrance. Besides, he knew what she would answer. He sighed and looked up. Mary was asleep.

He studied her face in repose, committing every aspect to memory against that barren time when, inevitably, they would part again. Walter found him there when he came to check on his patients. The apothecary informed Edward that Pike had returned with good news. George Carr was intrigued and would welcome the Friends to his island sanctuary.

# *Chapter 38*

## RICHARD WALDERNE *THE STEPMOTHER*

1652-1654, Boston and Dover, Massachusetts Bay Colony

Annie assumed her place in the house on Tremont Row with unstudied grace. She was a child of the New World, unfettered by the social constraints of an England she did not remember. She had grown up largely doing as she pleased, and she was not content to be a figurehead mistress. Annie was hands on. Missus Cameron and Bridget were more like her mother than the matrons of Richard's social circle. Left to their own devices, the housekeeper and the nursemaid had run the house efficiently and cared for the children since the death of their former mistress. Annie respected that. She deferred to their wisdom and experience, although she asked to be included in major decisions. She gave no orders at first but watched and listened. Then she sat down with the two women to define her part in the household. She was confident without being overbearing, and they liked her for it.

"There is no guesswork with this one, mind ye," Missus Cameron opined to the nursemaid after the meeting.

"And no airs, neither," Bridget answered, smiling.

Although Richard's public demeanor was all business, Annie encouraged his sense of humor when they were alone. His caustic comments made her laugh even when she was the target, for her brothers' teasing had prepared her well. She was not cowed by her husband's choler or daunted by criticism and went head to head with him in private.

In polite company, she was appropriately demure and acted with decorum, until boredom made her desperate. Then she discreetly teased him with eloquent facial expressions only he could see. She crossed her eyes or ran her tongue slowly over her lips or pouted alluringly. Her skill at nonverbal, clandestine communication sharpened over time. It amused her to see him struggle to maintain a straight face. He never cracked and continued to converse as though he did not see her, but Richard was deeply affected. His young wife's flair for discreetly mocking convention tickled him. They shared a delicious wickedness. When they got home, he made a show of disciplining her for these infractions, and she eluded him, laughing.

"Do you mock me, woman?" Richard growled, finally catching her up in a rough embrace. He carried her to their bedchamber, kicked open the door, and dropped her on the bed. One passion led to another. Her irreverent humor aroused him, and his young wife enjoyed the "discipline."

Annie embraced role as stepmother. She brooked no nonsense from the boys, but she understood Paul and Tim instinctively, thanks to her brothers. She recalled her own childhood fondly and wanted her stepchildren to experience the same freedom. She set them daily chores, but once these were accomplished, she encouraged the boys to roam outdoors and did not make a fuss when they came home filthy. They tried to shock her with gifts of snakes, frogs, and various insects, but Annie surprised them with sincere delight and stories of her own wild pets. Unlike their father, she listened to the boys without criticism, encouraging discussion on everything from scrapes at school to the latest technology in ships or weapons. Paul—now ten—and Tim at eight were soon won over. They adored their new Uncle Dickie who taught them to shoot—with their father's permission, of course. Annie's brother was a frequent visitor at the house on Tremont Row, and he usually brought weaponry from Braintree, where he now worked as a gunsmith, following his apprenticeship. The boys adored him.

Elizabeth was harder, but Annie had a second sense where her stepdaughter was concerned. She did not press the six-year-old to accept her, but was sympathetic when Beth missed her mother, which was often. The child tried to spurn her stepmother, for would it not be disloyal to love her? Still, Beth was young and bereft and in desperate need of comfort.

Annie counted it a triumph the first time the girl allowed herself to be held, as she mourned Prudence. Richard forbade the children to speak of his late wife and censured any show of grief, but one day, Annie came upon Beth in the sewing room, clutching a project her late mother had never finished, and crying. It was a heart-wrenching sight, and ignoring her husband's rule, Annie held out her arms, saying, "Aw, Bethy, are you missing your mamma? Come here, poor sweetling. Come, let me hold you whilst you have a good cry." This time Beth gave in, and Annie considered it a breakthrough.

Thereafter their relationship improved steadily, despite occasional setbacks. Annie and Elizabeth shared regular outings together until Annie's first pregnancy and the winter months confined activity to the house. They took up the girl's lessons, when the boys returned to school that fall, although Richard would have frowned upon it.

"We girls must hang together in this men's world, Bethy," she told the girl conspiratorially.

Beth's eyes widened. "Mamma used to say that too," she said, wonderingly.

Annie held out her arms. "Then 'tis verily so twice over," she said as they embraced.

The child had a keen mind. The more she learned, the more she hungered for information, posing questions that amazed her stepmother.

"Why did they cut off the King's head?" Beth asked one day, as they were discussing the English Monarchy.

"He was a very wicked king. He declared he was God's instrument and would not honor the Parliament, as kings must. He also married a French Catholic," Annie answered. "We are better off without him."

They visited the Boston book stores and millinery shops. They watched street puppet shows in season. They wrote poetry and attempted painting landscapes *en plein air*, laughing at the results. They strolled the Common, climbed Corn Hill for the view, and watched the traffic on the Charles River.

"Mayhap they shall rename it the Wicked River now King Charles is dead," Beth said, and Annie laughed until her sides hurt.

"Only a weak man wants an ignorant wife, Bethy. An accomplished woman is a credit to her sex," Annie told her repeatedly, but she cautioned the girl to keep such ideas to herself. "Your father might not agree, and we do not want to upset him. Besides," she smiled, "secrets are so delicious."

The last of Beth's resistance to her stepmother dissolved when baby Richard was born the next summer. Beth adored him from the start, and Annie wisely allowed her to be involved in his care whenever possible. Beth sat with her even as she nursed the infant, and Annie answered her many questions as openly as she could. The girl would be a mother someday herself, God willing, and she must know what was what. The baby released the floodgates of Beth's heart, just as Annie's little brother Dickie had for her. Annie loved being a mother.

Richard and Annie's second baby was born in April of 1652 and was as spirited as her mother from the start. This labor was shorter, though more intense than the first, and the birthing was quicker. Eliza Scammon attended her daughter again and declared

Annie was a natural with her wide Scammon hips. They named the baby girl Anne and joked about producing replicas of themselves—a little Richard and a little Anne—thus the two children became "the Littles." Richard thanked God for his young wife's sturdy build and appreciated her all the more.

When Annie's confinement began a month before the birth Richard went to Cocheco, tending to business. Annie did not mourn his presence, for she encouraged a boisterous household, and her husband did not. The three women ran things efficiently, Eliza came to help with the birth, and the children were fine company. Annie also discovered that her husband's extended absences kept their relationship novel.

When he was at Tremont Row, Richard's presence always generated a flurry of social activity, but the months following little Anne's birth were unusually busy. Once her confinement was past, Annie resumed the role of gracious hostess. Richard was providing the materials for a new church at Dover, and construction started that May. He wanted his generous donation to be common knowledge for it would increase his influence in the northern community, cultivating the approbation and respect of his Puritan friends, who followed suit with their own contributions.

In addition to the church project, Richard was lobbying for two representatives from Dover to the General Court in Boston. Currently the town was permitted one, but the population had increased substantially over the past decade. He wanted the Bay Colony to approve two—one from the village on the Point and a second from the growing town of Cocheco. Richard was employing all his political clout to that end, and the prospects were good. An appointment as Assistant to the Great and General Court was in his sights.

Annie admired her husband and was proud to be his wife. He was not yet forty, yet he rubbed shoulders with the rich and influential men of the colony. The often tedious social gatherings were a necessary penance for the fine life and children Richard gave her.

However, not all the gatherings were a chore. In the autumn of 1653 Richard made a new acquaintance at a dinner given by the Rawsons. Thomas Lake and his young wife, Mary, had just immigrated to Boston. The two men were of an age and had military training in common. Mary and Annie were contemporaries as well. Lake took Boston by storm, for he was energetic and well spoken. Although a relative newcomer, Lake was appointed Captain of Boston's prestigious Honorable Artillery Company the next spring.

The Waldernes invited the Lakes to Tremont Row for a quiet dinner to deepen their acquaintance. Thomas was excited when he learned Richard had sawmills and access to timber in the Piscataqua Region.

"I am on the point of investing in a vessel," Lake confided, when Annie and Mary had gone upstairs to see the children. "A three-hundred-ton barque with three masts. She is not known for speed, but she is dependable. The future of the colonies is in shipping, Captain Walderne. The Royal Navy is hungry for mast trees and lumber. Your timber and my ships are a winning combination, I warrant."

Richard responded with a rare genuine smile. "Call me Richard, and it please you," he replied.

1654 was a demanding year. Everything seemed to happen at once. The new meeting house at Dover was finished, and of course, the Walderne Family must attend the dedication ceremony. Richard hired local workers to prepare the house and grounds on the Neck, but Annie, Missus Cameron, and Bridget still had their hands full, moving the household for the summer. In mid-April they took the boys out of school early and went by ship. The dedication was planned for the second Sabbath in May.

That year Richard was also appointed by the Bay Colony to survey the Town of Dover's boundaries. Nicholas Shapleigh was given the same responsibility for Kittery. The two men arranged a meeting at the Emerys' ordinary on Dover Point to coordinate procedure. Each man was actively involved in the formation and governing of their communities, serving in various public offices. They drilled their local militias, owned sawmills and considerable land holdings, and both came from moneyed English families. The similarities ended there.

"Captain Shapleigh, I presume," Richard said, proffering his hand.

"Captain Walderne." Nicholas shook it.

A serving girl brought two tankards of ale to their table.

"My thanks," the Kittery man said, smiling at her.

Walderne ignored her. The two men toasted their project and drank.

"I have employed a crew to accomplish the surveying," Richard began, setting down his mug. "Have you capable men on your side?"

Nicholas smiled. "I believe I am up to the task. My son and my nephew will assist me."

Walderne raised his eyebrows. "As you wish," he commented, after a pause.

They discussed origins and ending points, approximated the time required to complete the job, coordinated mapping methods and symbols, and determined a date for their next meeting to compare the results. Business concluded, there were several beats of silence. Both men drank.

"You have a son, did you say?" Richard asked.

"Yes. His name is John," Nicholas answered. "He is almost thirteen."

Richard nodded then furrowed his brow. "Just the one?"

Nicholas kept his expression pleasant. "Yes. And you?" he asked politely.

Walderne's smile widened and involved his eyes for the first time. "I have three and hope for more. The two eldest are of an age with your John. Paul is fourteen, and Timothy is twelve. The youngest, my namesake, is but four. One cannot have too many sons, I warrant."

Whether the man meant to mock him or was simply unaware of his childless marriage, Nicholas was unsure. He changed the subject.

"Have you not just built a new church here in Dover?" he asked.

Walderne took the bait. "Why, yes! Quite a project—two years of near constant labor."

"Yes, so I heard," Nicholas responded. "You provided the materials and raised funds for it, did you not?"

Richard adopted his humble affect. "I am fortunate that my business interests are thriving. One must repay the community that enables one's success, especially when 'tis to the Glory of God."

Nicholas contemplated a number of responses to this assertion and rejected them all.

"Have you a church at Kittery?" the Puritan asked.

"Two, actually," Nicholas answered. "One in the town and one on the Point, where we live."

"Have you clergy enough for both, may I inquire?" Walderne probed. "Ordained ministers are somewhat rare in the region."

Nicholas sipped his ale before answering. He realized the man was attempting to pinpoint his religious beliefs. Aloud he said, "Certes, you may inquire, but the answer is not simple. The Kittery church leans toward the Baptist Faith. Our church on the Point is more difficult to define. The Reverend Mitton preaches there upon occasion, but he is called to other parishes betimes. We observe the Anglican traditions at Kittery Point."

Walderne's face went blank, a sure sign of disapproval masked, and Nicholas suppressed a smile. He had anticipated the reaction, knowing Walderne was a staunch Puritan. The man's superior attitude was irksome, but now he felt contrite.

"You have sawmills, do you not?" the Kittery man asked, steering the conversation into safer waters.

Richard's face lit up, and the two men spent the next half hour discussing their mills, timber, and the growing shipbuilding industry, ending their meeting on a more positive note. Still, parting was a relief for them both.

# *Chapter 39*

## MARY AND ALICE *CARR ISLAND*

December and January, 1662 Carr Island, Merrimack River

Pike changed his mount for a sleigh pulled by two matched bays to transport the missionaries to Carr Island. By the time he returned, the sun was swallowed by a bank of clouds, but there was no wind. The air was laden with the tang of impending snow.

The missionaries had not slept deeply, and they bravely endured the application of bandages. Worse was getting dressed, though Walter, Edward, and Rebecca did not hurry and were as gentle as possible. Then the innkeeper and Pike helped transport them to the sleigh. Although their exposure to the cold would be short, the invalids had had only two hours of warmth, and their feet and hands yet burned and tingled. Even aided, walking was difficult and the men all but carried them.

Once in the sleigh, Walter covered the invalids in all the blankets the inn could spare. Robert promised to return them on his way home. When the apothecary started to pay the Severances to keep his horse, Pike stepped in and offered to board her until the doctor could return. Walter thanked him profusely for his new friend would take no coin for the mare then the doctor turned to the Severances.

"I know not how to express our gratitude—" he began.

Rebecca cut him short. "'Tis no more than any Christian folk would do, Doctor," she said and patted his arm. They shared a smile.

John Severance shook each of the men's hands. "It heartens us to know there are some brave enough to stand against the abuse of justice," he said solemnly.

Edward was loath to leave his friends, but his shallop was at the town landing. Current and tide favored him, and it would be an easy scull downriver to Carr island.

Walter rode on the seat beside Pike. The road to the river was packed, and the sleigh seemed to fly after the hours spent plodding behind the oxcart. The float bridge was less than a mile from the inn, and they could see it well in advance. The snow pack on its planks contrasted with the black water.

"'Tis two-hundred-seventy feet in length," Robert explained, slowing the horses to a walk as they approached.

They moved up the wide access ramp and onto the bridge itself.

"The base is made of sturdy planks affixed to a series of barges. You can see their ends are tapered, the better to deflect currents and tides." Pike explained, as they began to cross. "The sides are reinforced with iron bars, as a precaution against nervous animals precipitating any watery mishaps," he added.

After Pike's comment Walter was relieved the team seemed accustomed to the bridge and did not balk. From his high seat he could see over the top rail to the river on either side. He was thrilled, as they passed smoothly over the dark current. The horses' hooves were muffled by the snow, and the sleigh moved silently but for the susurrus of the runners. The island was small. They could see Carr's dock off to the right and were on the lane to his mansion sooner than Walter expected. The crossing seemed over before it began. The entire sleigh ride took twenty minutes. They had spent more time preparing the missionaries to go out and settling them in the sleigh.

George and Elizabeth Carr were waiting for them. Physically, the man did not cut an imposing figure, but it took only moments in his company to be impressed by Carr's energy and intellect. His wife was twenty-five years younger than her husband. Mistress Carr was not tall, but she gave an impression of strength and authority. She was as calm as her husband was vigorous. She had birthed eleven children, nine of whom survived. They ranged in age from two to twenty, and she was both parent and teacher. The Carrs did not hold with relegating the care and education of their children to others. The two eldest had left the nest, but seven younger children yet lived with their parents. There was little that could shake Elizabeth Carr's composure.

Fourteen-year-old William was keeping watch and alerted his parents of the sleigh's approach. When Pike drew up, the entire family was gathered under the portcullis. Mistress Carr assumed command.

Although the ride had been short, the weakened missionaries were visibly shivering again in spite of the blankets. Elizabeth took one look at their pale faces and shuddering limbs and waved aside Lieutenant Pike's attempt at polite introductions.

"I commend your manners, Robert," she interposed, laying a gentle hand on his arm, "but I think, in this circumstance, form may be abandoned." She turned to the doctor.

"Walter Barefoote at your service, madam," he said briefly, touching his hat brim, "Apothecary of Dover and acting physician for the missionaries."

"Are they able to walk, Dr. Barefoot?" Mistress Carr asked, ignoring the formalities.

"Anne—the smallest—requires carrying," he answered, indicating her. "The other two are capable of walking with support, but we must avoid touching their backs."

"I understand. James," she continued without turning or raising her voice. A tall figure materialized at her side. He was dressed like an English servant, but Walter realized he was not. Indeed, he was the largest Indian the apothecary had seen, barring *Williani.*

"Would you be so good as to carry the small one to the sick room?" their hostess said to the man. "Avoid touching her back, if you might."

Anne moaned but did not cry out, as James lifted her from the sleigh bed with surprising gentleness, settling her against his shoulder with an arm around her hips in her cocoon of blankets. Elizabeth followed, her children trailing behind, as they glanced over their shoulders at the strangers and whispered excitedly to each other. Walter and George Carr helped Allie from the sleigh.

Mary gripped Robert Pike's arm and limped into the house on aching feet behind them. Her first impression of the Carr's home flooded her with relief, as warmth and the aroma of roasting chicken enveloped her. The no-nonsense attitude of their hostess made her feel both safe and welcome.

Elizabeth reappeared to lead them to the windowless sickroom situated between two chimneys on the ground floor. It was tiny with barely enough room for the three cots and six people now crowding it, but it was the warmest room in the house. Aside from that, it was near the stairs to the kitchen, located in the basement, and so was handier for hot water, food, and fresh medicaments than the formal guest rooms on the second floor. Elizabeth had birthed all her children there. Although the cots were nursery size, they were comfortably made up with pillows and quilts. Mary sank onto the feather tick stunned by warmth. Her back throbbed and burned, but they were safe now and would not have to move again, until they were stronger. At last she could believe their ordeal was verily behind them.

Edward arrived at Carr Island and docked in the early winter dusk. He was guided by a lantern that James held aloft for he and Will Carr had come to meet him. They helped batten down the shallop for the coming snowstorm. Edward was grateful, and the task was accomplished more speedily than usual.

"How didst thou come to be with the Carrs, Friend James?" Edward asked as they walked up the track from the river.

Will and Edward followed the big man who led with the lantern, and the light swayed as James shrugged his broad shoulders. "In trade. Carr build ship for old master. I am part payment."

They approached the house.

"And we have got the better part of the deal, I reckon!" Will commented heartily, as they mounted the steps.

James seemed not hear the compliment. He opened the wide front door and stood to one side, allowing the others to precede him, but in the light Edward saw his eyes twinkling.

George Carr and Robert Pike were in the parlor, and Will introduced Edward to his father.

"Would you care for some liquid refreshment, Friend Wharton?" his host offered.

"My thanks, sir, but not at present—though I should welcome it anon," Edward responded. "I would like to see my friends, if I may."

George showed his guest to the sickroom without delay and then rejoined Robert, leaving the care of the invalids to his capable wife and their friends.

By the time Edward appeared the missionaries were settled face down on the cots. Walter and Elizabeth had removed their outer clothing—thankfully unsoiled—and were peeling off the bandages. Edward made himself useful by folding the blankets from the inn and piling them outside the door. The Carr children had been banished upstairs, ostensibly to prepare for dinner, which would be served at six of the clock, no matter that three fugitives from the law had landed upon their doorstep. As Edward looked up from his task, he saw small faces peering through the banisters. They scattered at his notice, and it made him smile.

Walter was encouraged. There was less blood despite the move, but the wounds would heal more quickly with an application of fresh salve and no bandages. Edward helped apply it, and Elizabeth asked the ingredients, as she doctored her family herself.

"The base is fat, of course," Walter told her. "Coconut oil is best, but hard to come by. Any rendered fat will serve. I add powdered cayenne and sumac—both berries and bark—and willow bark to inhibit the bleeding. I use a tincture to blot the wounds in the early stages that has all those plus yarrow. I add honey, when I can get it."

"What is your opinion on the Culpeper publications, Dr. Barefoote?" Elizabeth asked, as she salved Anne's glaring wounds. Her eyes had widened at first sight of the missionaries' backs, but she recovered quickly and remained unshaken.

"In my opinion he has been much maligned by the established medical profession. His *English Physitian* is my bible along with *The Complete Herbal*," he answered.

"Oh, I quite agree!" their hostess exclaimed. "'Twas a tragedy we lost him at an early age. How much more might we have benefited had he lived beyond his thirty-seven years!"

Walter was grateful to the Carrs, but now he warmed to his hostess. They shared a respect for the ground-breaking "physitian."

The apothecary removed the bandage from Allie's face with great care for it stuck to her cheek. He soaked it with tincture before removing it completely. The welt was livid and the stitches made it look worse. It marred her lovely face, but Walter hid his dismay, as he blotted the wound, applied fresh salve, and left it exposed to the air. At last he dosed the three Friends with strong willow bark tea sweetened with honey and fortified with a dash of brandy.

"Not too much," he cautioned. "Alcohol thins the blood, and we do not want the bleeding to resume."

Little more could be done to alleviate the missionaries' pain. They were exhausted by the duress of the past days and literally overwhelmed with relief. As Elizabeth closed the door of the cozy little room, all three were drifting toward the blessed oblivion of sleep.

Robert Pike waited to bid his new friends good-bye, and he stood up when Walter, Edward, and Elizabeth joined them. He had done all he could for the missionaries and wished to return home for dinner with his family. The Carrs brushed off his fervent thanks.

"'Tis quite the most exciting thing since our daughter's marriage last May," Elizabeth said.

"With none of the cost and bother!" George added, earning a good-natured thump from his wife.

Edward and Walter collected the Severances' blankets and followed Pike outside to see him off. Will had brought the sleigh from the barn, where he and James had watered and rubbed down the horses. Darkness had fallen, but Robert delayed, fiddling with the storm lanterns on the sleigh and checking the horses' feet and tack. They debated the approaching weather, but once this familiar topic was exhausted, conversation ceased. The three men had faced a crisis together, averting disaster, and the experience had created a bond too profound for a casual good-bye.

Edward broke the silence. "Robert, we owe thee a debt of gratitude. God bless thee," he said, holding out his hand.

"Edward," Pike replied, shaking it warmly, "may we meet again under happier circumstances."

Walter grasped his hand. "I do not know how we would have managed without your help. I shudder to think on the alternative." The doctor blinked. "You saved their lives. There are no words to adequately thank you, Lieutenant," he finished, his voice husky.

"We shall meet again, when you come for your mare, Doctor," Pike smiled. He climbed onto the sleigh and took up the reins. "I do not hold with laws contrived at the whim of arrogance," he said. "Faith cannot be mandated. Although I count myself a Puritan, no religion need bring such brutality to bear. As Mistress Severance said, I have done no more than my Christian duty. God keep you all safe on your journey to Kittery."

He snapped the reins and his team took off with a will, sensing they were going home.

"Mistress Severance spoke true," Walter said, watching the sleigh's lanterns diminish in the dark.

Edward looked at him quizzically, and the apothecary went on.

"Robert Pike is indeed a voice of reason—in any town."

Mary and Allie regretted missing Lieutenant Pike's departure, but they were able to join Edward, Walter, and their hosts for dinner the next evening. Anne was still abed, but she took some bread soaked in broth. Her agony had eased to a bearable pain. The two missionaries hobbled slowly on feet recovering from frostbite and moved stiffly in their fresh bandages. The bleeding had stopped, but Walter had bound the wounds to prevent the salve rubbing off on their clothing. Although they still tired easily, their appetites had returned, and dinner with the family was a welcome distraction.

The Carrs were lively conversationalists. All but the two youngest children sat at the table. Mary could not help but imagine how Anne would have delighted in their company. Allie's facial wound had stopped bleeding, and Walter advised no bandage. Chewing or talking was a chore, but everyone did an excellent job of ignoring the stitches and the livid welt, shiny with salve; however, six-year-old John sat on her right, and from the corner of her eye Allie saw his head turn repeatedly toward her. At last during a lull in the conversation, as the soup was cleared, he could contain his curiosity no longer and leaned toward her.

"Does it hurt?" he asked in a loud whisper, staring at her cheek.

"John..." his mother warned, causing him to straighten and blush.

"S'alright," Allie said, barely moving her lips. "Less each day," she told him.

"It *looks* like it hurts," the boy went on, encouraged by her response and too fascinated to stop. "This morning at lessons Mother told us what happened to you, so we would not ask embarrassing questions."

Elizabeth closed her eyes and put two fingers to the bridge of her nose at this revelation, and the three men stifled smiles, but John continued, oblivious in his innocence.

"But she never said anything about your face. She said flogging meant they hurt you with a whip on your back."

Allie put her hand on her lips to still them. Smiling hurt more than talking or eating and she tried to contain it.

"When people have suffered, they rarely wish to speak of it, John," his father admonished gently, mistaking her gesture.

Allie shook her head and looked at Mary who explained for her.

"Friend Ambrose is not upset, John. She is trying not to smile, for it pains her," Mary told him, smiling herself, "Your father is correct, though. In most cases, folk do not wish to speak of their tribulations, but we are not so constrained," she added. "We believe the law by which we suffered is unjust. The Children of the Light are being punished for worshipping God in their hearts and homes instead of in a church with a minister. We believe this is wrong, that one should be allowed to follow one's conscience in matters of faith. When people see our suffering, we hope they shall realize that this law is a perversion—um—a misuse of justice and change it."

"Then the law is unjust?" Will asked, quickly parsing the heart of the matter.

George raised his eyebrows, but his son oft surprised him as he matured. "Not always," he prevaricated. "We need laws and magistrates to sustain order in a civilized society."

"The law dictating a person's faith is unjust. 'Tis complicated, Will," Elizabeth put in.

"But is it not the responsibility of the magistrates to insure the law is just?" the boy persisted.

Carr sighed. "They are human like everyone else, my boy. There are occasions when they make mistakes," he allowed.

"But who corrects them on those occasions?" Will asked.

The adults at the table exchanged looks, at a loss for a ready reply. Then his father answered.

"Brave people like our guests here," he answered.

The snow had started that afternoon with deceptively tiny flakes. By the time Mary and Allie excused themselves from the table and returned to their beds, it was a full-blown tempest. Edward read to them awhile, and Mary dozed off, but then the wind woke her. The room was dark and Edward had gone. She lay on her stomach, listening to it keening in the chimney tops like a demented banshee. Anne's soft snores and Allie's even breathing told her the others were asleep. Mary had refused the willow bark tea proffered at bedtime—she abhorred being an invalid—but now she regretted it.

Her back throbbed and burned, but it was her mind that kept her awake. It refused all strategies to quiet her misgivings, which were legion. They might well have been sleeping on their knees in some unheated cell en route to Dedham—muscles clenched against the cold, fresh wounds congealing, unable to eat for the pain—had their three saviors not succeeded. Most like they would have suffered a lingering, painful death, if Edward had not come; if Robert Pike had not been a man of conscience; if Walter had not accompanied them. She was grateful, but restless and confused. Was this deliverance God's way of encouraging their calling, or was it a warning to stop now? Should they return home to England or should they continue to follow His call? Should she abandon all of it and consider marrying Edward?

She could not sleep for wrestling with these questions. She rose from the cot slowly, pulled the quilt carefully over her borrowed nightdress, and crept from the sickroom in her stockinged feet.

The parlor was dim, lit only by the soft glow of the fireplace. Mary did not see her host in the wingback chair until she came up beside it, and he uncrossed his legs to stand.

"Oh, Friend Carr! Forgive me, I thought—"

"Not at all, not at all," he said rising. "I welcome the company. Please, join me." He indicated the chair on the opposite side of the hearth and reached for another log.

"Only if thou canst forgive my attire. I did not expect to find myself in mixed company," Mary said, holding the quilt at neck and waist. She smiled wryly and bobbed a tiny curtsey.

"We shall not stand on ceremony," George responded, bowing slightly in response before settling the log on the hearth. He straightened. "Would you care for a brandy?"

Mary started to refuse out of habit but changed her mind. Perhaps some brandy would calm her thoughts and help her sleep.

"I believe I would. My thanks. A very little bit," she said, remembering Walter's advice. She lowered herself carefully to the edge of the chair.

The dry wood caught, warming her legs and feet. The flames brightened, creating a cozy circle of light on the hearthrug and the chairs. It shone through the dark amber liquid in the glass, as he put it in her hand.

"To freedom of thought," he toasted.

The crystal snifters chimed as his glass gently touched hers. Mary took a cautious sip. The heat spread from her throat to her belly, and she sighed.

"Elizabeth and I admire your courage," her host said, as he resettled.

Mary moved her glass in slow circles, inhaling the aroma of the spirits. Compliments made her uncomfortable, and she felt far from brave at the moment.

"I imagine it is not easy to sleep," Carr continued, when his guest did not respond. "You have experienced a harrowing ordeal, and however justly motivated one may feel to take up a challenge, the actual experience quite annihilates the carefully constructed equilibrium of one's accustomed way of being."

Mary looked at her host more closely. He had expressed exactly what she was feeling.

He smiled and met her gaze. "I imagine I must seem a rather stodgy old man to you, settled comfortably in a fine house on my own island with my large and happy family about me. What could I possibly know of hardship? But, 'twas not always thus, I assure you. A long and difficult path led me here."

"I do not think thou art old or—" Mary began, but he stopped her, raising a finger.

"'Methinks the lady doth protest too much,'" he said with mock solemnity.

"Ah, Shakespeare's *Hamlet*. Art thou a scholar, sir?" she responded.

"No, no," George chuckled. "I am a merely a shipwright who enjoys good literature. I have read all of the Bard's plays and poetry. But I am impressed, Friend Tomkins, for you are obviously an educated woman. Who taught you?"

"My father—" Mary intended to say more but was swamped by a wave of longing that robbed her of speech. She was appalled to be overcome so unexpectedly. She sipped her brandy, and its warmth eased the tightness in her chest.

"I see you love him very much," Carr said softly. "You must miss him, especially at this time of crisis in your life."

Again her host surprised her. She wanted nothing more than her father's comforting presence and wisdom. She feared it would undo her if she looked at George Carr's sympathetic face. She stared into the flames and nodded. Her host surmised a distraction was in order.

"Would you care to hear how I came to these shores?" he asked.

"Yes, I would. Very much," she answered gratefully and shifted a little to face him.

"I was one-and-twenty, newly-wed to my first wife, Lucinda. I was young and foolhardy. I believed 'twould be a great adventure to emigrate from England and carve a new civilization in the wilderness. I should have had my bride join me when things were more settled, but I did not. I am not certain I could have prevented her even had I tried. We were in love, you see, quite smitten with each other and could not bear to be parted."

He paused and sipped his drink before continuing.

"We sailed on the *Mayflower*." Mary's eyes widened. "Yes, that *Mayflower*. I have no doubt you have heard the stories. We arrived late in the season and further north than originally planned. Leakage on the *Speedwell*, our sister ship, had delayed us. She never did complete that crossing, but our ship did. How often after did I berate myself, wishing we had gone with our sister ship."

Carr sighed and rose to replenish his glass. He raised his eyebrows and gestured at her drink. Mary slowly shook her head. Her host continued speaking from the sideboard.

"That first winter was horrendous—a complete catastrophe. Our shelters were inadequate, hastily constructed. They barely kept the snow off our heads, let alone held any heat." George returned to his chair. "On top of that, our food supply was soon depleted. Hunger weakened us. People became ill, and sickness spread. Many died. Lucinda was among them." He drank.

Mary's first impulse was to say some sympathetic cliché, but she thought better of it. George Carr was not telling her this for sympathy. He would only brush it off and perhaps even be disappointed that she hadn't waited for his deeper meaning. She kept quiet.

Carr set down his glass and leaned forward, elbows on his knees. Firelight emphasized the lines of sorrow on his intelligent face.

"I thought to tame the wilderness, but it broke me. Took the only thing I held dear. My sweet Lucinda." He was silent a moment then said, "God may love us, but Life finds us wanting."

Mary nodded, and they both stared at the flames. George went on.

"For a long period after, perhaps 'twas even years, nothing held meaning. There was no sense in what I was doing without her. Everything that had been so important became superfluous. I almost returned to England, but then I thought, why? Lucinda died for our dream. I had buried her with the others, when the ground thawed. I could not abandon her, and the colony needed strong young men. I could at least be of some use at Plymouth Plantation."

George rose to put another log on the fire.

"You see, Mary—may I call you Mary?" he asked, turning toward her.

"Yes, certes, George," she replied, knowing he would ask her to do the same.

He acknowledged the appellation with a brief smile and positioned the log as he spoke.

"In time I regained my equilibrium, but the ordeal of that winter is ever with me. Watching the one I loved most in the world waste away from cold and sickness and starvation, powerless to avert it—" He broke off and leaned on the mantelpiece, watching the fire embrace the wood. When he turned back to her, his face was composed.

"I would be so presumptuous as to say, I understand what you are going through right now," he said. "You question beliefs that have been the linchpins of your existence. When the body is weakened, the emotional humors rear their ugly heads and all conviction becomes doubt."

"Just so," Mary said softly, watching the flames brighten. She was honored that George had confided in her and gratified that he understood how she felt. She knew she could trust him.

"What can I do?" she asked, her voice breaking.

He resumed his seat and leaned toward her. "My dear girl, I cannot tell you what to do, but I can advise you what *not* to do."

Mary looked at him and nodded once, unable to trust her voice.

"Do not credit your doubts, Mary. Acknowledge them but let them pass. They are born of your suffering and a weakened physik and have no true merit. You are young and strong—"

Mary looked down at her glass, pursing her lips ruefully.

"Mayhap you do not feel that now, but in time you shall recover, my dear," he said gently. "Make no decisions until you are fully healed, until you are your true and balanced self again."

He regarded her in silence for a moment then drained his glass and stood. Mary looked up at him.

"I shall bid you goodnight now," he said kindly. "Pray, sit here as long as you wish. Feed the fire, but do not feed your doubts." He waggled a finger at her and smiled. "May sleep refresh you."

He started for the archway but turned back. The child-like figure wrapped in the quilt looked small and vulnerable perched on the edge of the chair.

"Have you had a good cry yet?" he asked.

Mary slowly shook her head. He returned to her side and held out his handkerchief.

"I would recommend it."

Mary looked up into his face expecting pity, but saw only warm commiseration.

"There is no shame in it, Mary, and you have most certainly earned one." He held her gaze as she took the proffered hanky, then he started for the stairs again, saying, "Clears the humors. Most therapeutic."

As with everything her host said, this also proved true. The fire was a bed of glowing coals when Mary used George's handkerchief to wipe her eyes and clear her nose. Carefully she added more wood to keep it going on this stormy night then crept back to bed, where the soft wings of sleep enfolded her at last.

The tempest raged throughout the next morning. The hall was chilly, and Mary and Allie discovered they could move faster when necessary. A fine fire warmed the dining room, and they closed the door quickly on the cold draft.

The Carr children were regaling Friend Wharton with the grisly details of winter storms past, talking over each other and jumping up from their chairs to demonstrate the height of the snowbanks. They froze when the missionaries entered, staring at them with awe. "Table," Elizabeth intoned, and they quickly sat. Whatever their mother had said about the missionaries, the children were fascinated and watched their every move.

Edward smiled to see his friends up and about, and they settled on either side of him to break their fast. Pleasantries were exchanged, and breakfast proceeded without further theatrics. Mary welcomed the return of her appetite and enjoyed crispy fish cakes with cream sauce. Allie applied herself to a large bowl of porridge with butter and maple syrup, which did not require chewing. Elizabeth was interested in their missionary work, and Mary told her of their summer at Kittery and the Mercy Wagons. The room was cozy and smelled of good food.

Outside the wind buffeted the house with alarming gusts. Wood creaked and windows rattled. The few without shutters revealed dizzying views of swirling white. The missionaries had known only the mild winters of England's south coast, growing up in Devonshire. Even at Swarthmore Hall, more than three hundred miles north of Kingsweare, there had been nothing to compare with the intensity and length of this storm. The wind wailed around corners and over the chimney tops, seeking entry and finding it. Every fireplace blazed, and all were vigilant for sparks blown onto the wood floors by errant gusts. Interior doors were closed to the cold drafts of the hallways.

When James came into the dining room with a loaded canvas sling from the woodshed, he reported clearing a deal of snow from the floor, driven through the crack at the bottom of the exterior door. Edward had finished eating and rose to help him replenish the woodbins at each of the eight hearths in the three-story manse. The native's response was impassive as ever, but he nodded his thanks. Tending the fires on a day such as this was a prodigious chore.

There was no sign of Walter, as yet, and they let him sleep on. Once the family had broken their fast, Elizabeth herded her protesting brood upstairs for morning lessons, storm or no storm, and guests notwithstanding. George Carr and Edward took another cup of tea to the parlor and sat by the hearth, discussing the float bridge, boats, and the perils of the New England coast. Mary and Allie perched in a south facing window seat that was not shuttered and watched the snow dance to the wind's whim. They could barely make out the ghostly shapes of trees in the yard. The rise and fall of the men's conversation was soothing, and the missionaries shared a wordless gratitude, wrapped in warm shawls on the interior side of the thick, wavy glass.

Anne was still too weak to leave the sickroom. She sat up for short periods of time, but as she could not lean her back against any support, soon returned to lying on her stomach, dozing. They took turns reading to distract her from the pain, when she was awake. George Carr had a fine collection of bound books and generously shared it without reservation. Mary was impressed to see some of the volumes were published in Boston, but she chose a London printing of Chaucer's *Canterbury Tales* to cheer their companion. She and Allie still tired quickly. By midmorning they returned to their cots in the cozy sickroom. Edward rose and came with them, offering to read to them as they rested. The missionaries fell asleep to the reassuring sound of his voice relating "The Wife of Bath's Tale."

Edward was restless. He left off reading when he realized his friends were asleep. He marked the place, and gazed at Mary's face, so childlike in sleep, but he needed to move and soon left. Although a man of deep conviction, he was not a contemplative sort and was happiest when active. Most like they would not have left for Kittery this day, even without the turn in the weather. The missionaries were still too weak to endure the December cold in an unheated boat all the way to Kittery Point. It would take a full day, he reckoned, mayhap longer, unless the wind shifted to the south by some miracle.

Edward believed in miracles. The missionaries' reprieve was one. That none of the women had lost any fingers or toes from their prolonged exposure to the cold was another, though most probably Walter could be credited as God's instrument in that. He had thought the apothecary was a dandy, but he had revised that opinion. Difficult circumstances engendered miracles, but this stasis, this waiting, was unbearable. He had to find something to do beyond filling the wood boxes, reading to the women, or assisting Walter with their treatment.

By the time he returned to the parlor, his host had gone. Edward put more wood on the fire and decided to explore the house. He had seen the upstairs and ground level rooms while helping James fill the wood boxes, but he had not been to the kitchen located in the cellar.

He paused on his way down the stairs, taking in the room. The large space ran the length of the house and was half its depth. The south and east walls were comprised of the granite foundation blocks that supported the house. The floor was slate to reduce the danger of fire, Edward reckoned. A walk-through hearth of brick was to his left. Small and medium-size pots and kettles hung from iron rods set at various heights; larger ones sat on trivets over hot coals or small fires. Their steamy fragrances filled the air.

The kitchen was warm, well lit, and bustling—not just with food preparation but also with projects and repairs. Workbenches lined the side of the room opposite the hearth with wall sconces above each one for light. Edward was interested to note the windows positioned six feet above the benches. Currently they were blocked with snow, affording only a feeble, bluish glow. He imagined they would otherwise provide additional natural light. His glazier's eye estimated the glass to be eighteen by twenty-four inches. He was wondering how often they needed replacement when young Will came to the bottom of the stairs.

"Good afternoon, Friend Wharton," the boy greeted him.

"And to thee, Friend Carr," Edward said, returning the boy's formality, as he descended the remaining the stairs.

The lad smiled and flushed. "You can call me Will, and it please you," he said shyly.

"Then thou must call me Edward," the Salem Friend replied.

"Would you care to join us?" Will gestured to a workbench, and Edward saw James was there. "We are just repairing some snowshoes, and James is helping me make a pair of mine own as well. Would you care to see?"

Will's voice had only recently deepened, and on the last word, it regressed to its childhood timbre with a comical squeak. Edward could not contain his laughter, and, blushing anew, Will joined him.

"Why yes, Will," he answered, clapping the boy's shoulder. "I would care to see very much."

There turned out to be quite a trick to making sturdy snowshoes. The ash wood frames were already steamed, bent, and secured in an oval shape. Holes had been drilled for the laces, and Will was applying a mariner's varnish to the frames. James demonstrated how to weave and knot the rawhide strips tightly on a finished frame, but after several botched attempts, Edward limited himself to oiling the rawhide straps and leather foot pieces and listening.

James was a fount of information once drawn out. His English was abbreviated, using only major nouns and verbs, but his pronunciation was clear, and he had no difficulty understanding. It seemed more a case of economy than ignorance. His practical knowledge and dexterity were impressive. Edward learned that the Indian had set fishing weirs in the river between Carr Island and Ram's Isle a short distance to the south. James and Will planned to go check them the next morning.

"But what of the storm?" Edward asked.

"Snow stop. Clear by morn," James answered.

"Shall you accompany us?" Will asked Edward hopefully.

"I would enjoy that, though it may be necessary to prepare the *Sea Witch* for the trip to Kittery," Edward told him, standing up. "And speaking of that, I must check on her before dark."

"Oh splendid!" Will exclaimed. "I shall go with you and test my new snowshoes."

James shook his head. "New ones not ready. Use those," he said, gesturing with his chin to the ones they had repaired.

"Shall we brave the storm then?" Edward asked.

His new friends nodded.

It was still snowing, when they ventured out, but the wind had dropped. The flakes fell straight down, and the world seemed unnaturally still, muffled in white. Edward fell twice before he got the knack of using snowshoes, but his new friends cheerfully came to his aid, hauling him to his feet once they had stopped laughing. The Salem man laughed with them, but the cold snow down his back inspired him to learn quickly.

The *Sea Witch* and the dock were buried under a more than a foot of snow. Edward was glad of the help in clearing it. By the time the three adventurers returned to the house, it was getting dark and tea was being served in the parlor. Anne Coleman was up, sitting on a stool close to the hearth with the younger Carrs clustered around her. She looked pale and fragile, but her spirits were reviving. The children appeared to adore her already.

Mary caught her breath, when Edward entered. He grew more comely every time she saw him. He greeted his hosts, accepted a cup of tea and a slice of lemon cake from Elizabeth, and looked around. His face lit up when he spotted Mary, and she felt a rush of pleasure in response. He came to her side. He smelled of fresh air and oiled leather. His hair was damp, and he was smiling, causing his usually grave face to look boyish.

"Friend Wharton, wherever hast thou been?" she asked, attempting a light tone. She clasped her hands, restraining the urge to push a damp curl off his forehead.

"Will and James helped me clear the snow from the shallop, and we went on snowshoes. They take a bit of getting used to," he grinned, pushing back the curl that had tempted her, "but we would have been floundering without them. There is a deal of snow out there! James says the storm is passing and will clear by the morrow." He sobered and glanced at the small figure by the fire. "How fares Anne?" he asked, lowering his voice.

"She took good nourishment at the noon meal, and as thou canst see, she has joined us for tea," Mary answered. "No doubt she shall soon tire, but Walter reckons she is on the mend now." She turned as the apothecary joined them.

"I believe she may be strong enough to travel in another two days, if there is no relapse," the doctor said. "but I wish I knew if the Shapleighs received my message. I hope they are not worrying about us in this storm."

# *Chapter 40*

## RICHARD WALDERNE *URGENT OCCASION*

1654-1657, Boston and Dover, Massachusetts Bay Colony

The summer of 1654 was the last the Waldernes spent at the house on Dover Neck. In autumn Paul would start his final year at Boston Latin, and Richard expected his eldest son to distinguish himself among his academic peers and continue his education at Harvard. In truth he realized Timothy was more apt to fulfill that role for Paul was a reluctant student. Throughout the summer following the dedication of the new First Church at Dover, Paul disdained all boyhood pursuits and accompanied Richard to Cocheco, watching and listening to all his father did and said. Richard was pleased, but he hid it by badgering Paul to apply himself to his studies more stringently. It would never do to reveal his pleasure in the lad's interest. Paul and Tim returned to Boston with their father at the end of August to continue their education.

The women stayed to close up the Dover house. By October it was denuded—emptied of all furniture and appointments Annie deemed useful at Tremont Row. Missus Cameron went ahead by ship with the bulk of the cargo and their personal effects, while Bridget stayed with Annie, Beth, and the Littles. They carried minimal baggage and took the ferry to Portsmouth to visit the Scammons for a week, until the Boston house should be organized under Eleanor Cameron's efficient directives.

Although she had been a wife and mother for over four years, Annie felt like a girl again upon entering her childhood home. Her parents had visited the Dover house several times that summer. They doted on their grandchildren, who returned their affection with enthusiasm. Beth was particularly smitten, as she had never known grandparents, and Eliza was equally thrilled with her. The ten-year-old shadowed her grandmother and was soon kneading bread, peeling potatoes, and concocting chowders at her side. Eliza rarely hired a cook, as she enjoyed preparing meals for her family and friends. There were no restrictions of age or class. All were welcome at the Scammon table, including the Littles and Bridget, who, after fifteen years of tending Walderne children, was a member of the family as far as Eliza was concerned.

"So Richard is selling the house on the Neck, eh?" her father asked the first night at supper.

Annie nodded her mouth full of her mother's good cooking. She swallowed. "Dickie. Elbows," she said to the four-year-old.

"There's a good lad, then," his grandmother added, when he obeyed. She was holding little Anne on her lap, feeding her tender morsels from her own plate and gently distracting the two-year-old's attempts to grab the food herself. "She is a fine eater, this one," Eliza commented, chuckling.

"Oh, aye! She is that!" Bridget responded brightly.

"D'you know what he might be asking for it?" her father pressed. One had to be persistent to maintain the thread of conversation at the Scammon table.

"No idea, Pa," Annie replied, her focus on her plate. "He only just decided. Best ask him yourself, if you have an interest."

"'Tis your brother who might have," he said.

"What, Dickie?" She looked up surprised.

"Yes, Momma?" her son piped.

They all laughed.

"A deal too many Richards in this family," her mother smiled.

The visit went all too quickly. Annie's parents saw them onto the ship for Boston. There were tears and hugs and kisses, but as Bridget shepherded the children on board, Annie's father said quietly, "Tell Richard to talk with me first before he sells to anyone else, would you, sweetling?"

Annie embraced him and promised she would.

Richard had determined to sell the house he had built for Prudence, as Dover was now a backwater for him. Henceforth he would be in Boston or at Cocheco, and it was impractical to keep it. He did not acknowledge the vague nostalgia the house evoked.

In November he rode down from Cocheco and walked through the cold, empty rooms, insuring nothing of import remained. Only the most unwieldy furniture was left. He remembered Pru sending that damn sideboard from England. It had cost him dearly to move it up to the house, not to mention the shipping. Now it was an abandoned bulk under a sheet and would most like sit there till it became dust.

His study was empty except for the massive desk. The fireplace was denuded of ash. The bare bookshelves looked skeletal. He had a finer desk in Boston, but early in his magistracy, he had deliberated minor cases from behind this behemoth. He lifted a corner of the dust cloth and touched the dark wood in a last salute.

Satisfied that nothing of value had been overlooked, Richard walked briskly to the front door, his steps reverberating through the empty rooms. He turned to look around one last time. An image of Prudence moving gracefully down the stairway struck him with searing clarity. The house echoed with more than his footfalls. He exited quickly and locked the door.

As he rode back to Cocheco, floorplans occupied his thoughts. Richard was planning a new house there for his growing family. It would rival the finest homes in Boston. The proceeds from the Dover house would cover most of the cost, and he had access to all the lumber he might need from his mills. Once he cleared the Neck, he spurred his mount into a canter and left Dover without looking back.

In the winter of 1655 Reverend Maud delivered his final service then died in his bed at the age of seventy. Once again, Dover was without a minister. Richard mourned the ecclesiastical calm the clergyman had sustained for ten years, more than the man himself, but an admirable replacement turned up from a surprising source.

The Waldernes attended a social gathering hosted by Boston's Governor John Endicott on the eve of the new year of 1656. Richard considered it a privilege. Men of influence were invited for the Endicotts were entertaining William Bradford, Governor of the Plymouth Colony, for a week. The old Pilgrim had made a rare trip to Boston, but it would be his last. Upon hearing Richard speak of Dover's need for an ordained minister, Bradford had a suggestion.

"Mayhap you have heard of the Reverend John Reyner? He is our teacher at the Congregational Church in Plymouth for, oh," he cast his rheumy eyes to the ceiling, "upwards of ten years now, I warrant. He assists our minister Charles Chauncy. Mister Reyner is a man of stalwart faith and a fine fellow," Bradford asserted.

"Then I confess, Governor, I am surprised you wish to part with him," Richard observed.

The elderly Puritan cleared his throat, realizing excessive praise was suspicious. He did not want word of the rift between Plymouth's ministers to circulate here. Charles Chauncy and John Reyner were divided over the issue of infant-versus-adult baptism, and the congregation was split between them. If Reyner found a post of his own, it would diffuse the tension and none the wiser, but he must guard his tongue with this sharp young man.

"Well, uh, Mister..."

"Captain, sir, and it please you," Richard supplied pleasantly. "Captain Richard Walderne of Dover."

"Yes, yes, of course! Captain Walderne."

Bradford peered at him. The Plymouth governor was showing his age, as well he should. He was approaching seventy and had endured more hardship than most as founder of the original plantation. His palsied hands shook, as he pulled out his handkerchief. Endicott's drawing room was crowded and over warm, despite the raw March weather outside. Bradford took time to word his response while blotting his wrinkled brow.

"You see, Captain Walderne, we have a superior minister in the Reverend Charles Chauncy, who has seniority in his favor. Reyner assists him as teacher, but, since Dover is in need, mayhap he would accept a post as minister in his own right—a step up for him, if you catch my drift. You shall find him more than capable, I assure you."

This proved true. By the end of April the new minister and his family moved to the parsonage at Dover, and John Reyner became the new minister at the First Church.

Paul Walderne was a comely lad. He had his father's build and his mother's coloring, but he was a reluctant scholar. He balked at attending Harvard for more years of tedium and had determined to convince his father that an education in his employ would be more practical.

"I would emulate *you*, sir," Paul said, earnestly pleading his case. "I am eager to learn business and trade at your side."

They were in Richard's study at Tremont Row. Paul was fifteen, and his last term at Boston Latin would soon end. Richard assessed his eldest son as objectively as possible. He appeared older than his age and cut a fine figure. His father felt proud to have sired him, and his son's words were flattering. What father did not want his heir to succeed him in business? The boy matched him in height and energy, but could he plan ahead and handle negotiations? Could he command respect from employees? There was only one way to find out.

"Since you appear bound and determined to abandon your studies," Richard began drily, "we shall give it a trial," he finished, surprising his son with this about face. "What do you imagine you might do?" Best to know if the boy entertained unrealistic aspirations.

Paul had been ten, when his mother died, and they had shared a strong bond. He had witnessed her combination of humility and manipulation in handling her assertive husband. Paul learned early on that outright resistance was futile, where his father was concerned. The young man knew exactly how his training should start but deferred, knowing it would please his parent. Paul's response to this loaded question proved he had learned well.

"I shall apply myself to whatever task you set me, Father, if you will but let me try. I have much to learn, sir, but what interests me cannot be found in a book or a classroom. I entreat you to permit me to make a start and accomplish something of practical merit under your tutelage."

Richard could not contain his smile. He remembered voicing a similar sentiment at the age of sixteen, when procuring permission from his father to pursue a military career.

Encouraged by this rare evidence of approval, Paul dared to hazard, "Mayhap I could start at the trading post in Cocheco, sir?" He made it a question and was awarded an affirmative response.

At the end of May Paul rode north with his father to Cocheco. He was elated. His days of tedious book learning were behind him, and he had his father's exclusive attention for the first time in his life. Richard was a harsh teacher, but Paul was accustomed to his father's scathing criticism and bore it stoically, remembering he the alternative was languishing at Harvard. Ultimately he dreamed of traveling to foreign ports and exotic places as his father's representative in trade. In the interim he strove to impress him, Herculean as the task might be.

Timothy was sorry to see his elder brother go, but he did not share Paul's antipathy for academics. He was a quiet lad with a quick mind, though he lacked the physical prowess of his brother. Tim wanted to attend Harvard and become an advocate like his cousin Christopher in Charlestown. Richard encouraged this, for knowledge of the law would be a boon to his business concerns. Certes, the boy did not have the makings of a military man.

Upon graduating from Boston Latin, Tim prepared to attend Harvard and live across the river at one of the boarding houses for students. He loved his siblings but was particularly close to Beth. Paul had been a rambunctious playmate, when the brothers were small, always stronger, faster, and louder. Keeping up with him was a struggle, but Beth had a sweet temperament and was easily bested in their games. Losing did not upset her. In fact she became irritated, if she sensed he was letting her win. He worshipped Paul but preferred the less challenging company of his sister.

As they matured, Beth's thirst for knowledge did not abate, and Tim secretly shared his lessons with her. Her aptitude was impressive, belying the belief that women could not be scholars. She soaked up Latin like a sponge and was decent at mathematics. Her reading comprehension exceeded Paul's, although the two siblings wisely kept this fact to themselves.

Beth was inconsolable at the prospect of Tim leaving and sat on a stool in his room, watching him pack.

"Can you not live here and attend classes during the day?" she asked, not for the first time.

"You know I cannot, Bee," he replied, using his pet name for her. "University life is more than classes. There are clubs and lectures and activities that I would miss, if I stay home."

She did not respond, and he went on.

"I shall see you every week on the Sabbath for the service at First Church and dinner after."

Glimpsing him on the other side of the nave or across the table with their father present was not what Beth had in mind, and she stayed silent. Tim turned to look at her. She was picking at her skirt and did not meet his eye.

"I shall bring notes from my lessons for you. I swear," he tried.

She nodded but did not raise her head.

"You shall be the most educated woman in the colony," he said, smiling and tilting his head to catch her eye.

She looked up, and he was alarmed to note the glitter of unshed tears.

"Why must everything always change?" she asked tremulously. "I shall lose you to new friends and interests. I shall be left to molder here, until Papa arranges some lucrative union for me, and then I must fulfill my duty as a good wife and populate the colony."

He could not deny the truth of her words. However generous he might be in sharing knowledge with his sister, it would not change her fate as a woman.

"Your husband shall be the luckiest man in the Bay," he said softly.

She stood and they embraced. They had always comforted each other since losing their mother. Tim did not hold with the popular belief that demonstrations of affection were effeminate in a man. When Bee was sad, he held her, as she did him.

"You shall never lose me," he said stoutly, moved by her sorrow.

"Thank you, brother," she whispered. "I could not bear it."

As representative for Dover, Richard Walderne had never missed a session of the General Court until May of 1657. He requested leave to absent himself upon urgent occasion and was excused.

Boston was struck that spring by its first epidemic of measles. The disease ravaged the city. The physicians had no recourse but to bleed and purge their patients of the noxious humors, then let the sickness run its course. There were but few casualties—a few elderly folk, two babies, and one young student at Harvard University, Timothy Walderne.

## *Chapter 41*

### THE SHAPLEIGHS AND MARY AND ALICE
### *NEWS AT KITTERY AND FAREWELL TO CARR ISLAND*

December/January, 1662, Kittery Point, Province of Maine &
Carr Island, Merrimack River

The storm held off until after Boxing Day. Alice, Nicholas, and Johnny celebrated the holidays with the Treworgys at York. Christmas was infinitely more enjoyable with children present. Few in the Province of Maine obeyed the Bay Colony law prohibiting such "superstitious ffestivals." Kat and Edward had come too; however, the Trickeys were unable to join them, since the ferries must run according to law, as they did every Monday.

When they returned to Kittery Manor, there was a message from Elizabeth. It was not a holiday greeting. It bore the dire news of the missionaries' arrest at Dover and the sentence imposed by Richard Walderne.

"However shall they survive!" Alice fretted, as she read the letter again.

Nicholas and Johnny exchanged a look over her head. How indeed?

"At least Walter is with them, dear heart," her husband said, putting an arm around her. "Certes, he shall intervene, if 'tis called for." His voice was soothing, but his face was bleak.

The snow began that afternoon. The three of them were restless, confined by the weather. The storm raged through the night and continued most of the next day. Alice was tense, and Johnny escaped by reading in the study. Nicholas chafed at his helplessness. How would he explain to the girls' families? They trusted him to protect them. If only he had known they were at Bloody Point, he might have got them away before they were taken to Hampton. He considered writing to their parents, but put it off, hoping for better news from Walter soon.

The day after the storm ended the Shapleighs rose early. Kittery Point was buried under a foot and a half of snow. Nicholas went to check the outbuildings. Roofs would need clearing. Johnny coordinated two teams of oxen to pack the major roads so that folk could go about their business.

Alice was in the sewing room with Meggie and Elizabeth—the only employees to have braved the deep snow that morning—when they were surprised by the distinctive rap of the knocker at the front door. Alice rose to answer it herself. It was her nephew Zack Trickey.

"Well met, Zack," she greeted him warmly. "I hope your family was able to keep Christmas despite running the ferries."

"Mother roasted a goose, Aunt Alice," he answered, "but 'twas otherwise unremarked. We missed your company. But I did not come to give greetings of the season," the young man continued, pulling a letter from an inside pocket. "This message reached Portsmouth two days ago."

Alice's eyes widened and the color drained from her face. Zack was looking at the missive and went on oblivious to her reaction.

"'Twas delayed there by the storm. The messenger was told to deliver it into Nicholas Shapleigh's hands only, but he let father have it when he learned he was married to Uncle Nico's sister. I reckon the fellow was glad to end his journey there and avoid the ferry ride to Kittery Point," he smiled and held it out.

When Alice made no move to take it from him, he placed the folded paper in her hands.

"I thank thee," she said faintly, regarding the sealed letter on her palm with dread. What tragic news might it contain? She was loath to open it.

"Wouldst thou take a cup before going out again?" she asked, delaying. She wished Nicholas was here.

"I would, but I cannot," Zack answered ruefully. "I am running the ferry today and must keep to the schedule else Father will have my hide." He grinned but she did not respond. He peered at her nervously. "Are you quite alright, Aunt?" he asked noting her pallor.

Alice nodded. Zack gave her a wary peck on the cheek and left. Once the door closed behind him, Alice summoned her courage and broke the seal.

*Dear Nicholas,*

*Excuse brevity. Our 3 Friends flogged at Dover and Hampton, but reprieved at Salisbury! I am deputized by Lt. R. Pike and they are now in my Custody. E. W. here with boat. We sail for Kittery Manor, depending upon their condition—as*

*yet too weak for travel. Prepare 3 sick beds. Their wounds are grave, but not life-threatening.*
*Fervent Thanks from Your Friend,*
*Walter Barefoote*

Alice sank onto the bench by the front door. *Their wounds are grave.* Thank God Walter was with them and bringing them here! She read the message again, but the day of their arrival was frustratingly vague. *Their wounds are grave.* Alice rose. Succumbing to emotion would not help her friends. She returned to the sewing room in a daze. Elizabeth took one look at her face and rose, concerned.

"What news, Mistress?" she asked, noting the letter still clutched in Alice's hand.

"Put aside thy work," Alice answered with studied calm. "Meggie, find James and Joseph. We must prepare this room for the English missionaries. Elizabeth, please help me clear away and make room for three cots. Along this wall, mayhap."

"Be they comin' back then?" Meggie asked eagerly, donning her cloak and muffler.

"Yes, but they are not well," Alice said. "They were arrested and—and flogged twice."

Nicholas and Johnny did not return for the mid-day meal until nearly two of the clock. They found the household in a mild uproar, as the sewing room was transformed into an infirmary. They were removing their snowy outer garments and boots in the foyer, when James and Joseph came down the stairs and crossed the hall carrying a cot. One of the housemaids trailed after without seeing the two men by the door, so laden was she with quilts and pillows.

"Ellen?" Nicholas said, stopping her. "What passes here?"

She gave a small squeak of surprise and attempted an awkward curtsey. "Yer pardon, Captain Shapleigh! I didna see ye there," she said her voice muffled by her burden. Johnny relieved her of two pillows, revealing a flushed face.

"Just tell us what is afoot, and it please you, Ellen," he said kindly.

"'Tis the English missionaries are comin' back," she explained, embarrassed and pleased by the two gentlemen's intent focus. "The mistress had a message from Dr. Barefoote." Her voice lowered as if she were imparting a secret. "They bin flogged, it said, at Dover and Hampton both! They are in a bad way, and we are preparin' the sewin' room for their arrival."

Nicholas and Johnny exchanged a look.

"Do you know when they will arrive?" Johnny asked.

"Nossir," she answered, deflated by her ignorance.

"That is fine, Ellen. Where is Mistress Shapleigh now?" Nicholas asked with admirable calm.

"She is in the kitchen house at present," the maid told him, glad of a question for which she knew the answer. "She was for makin' a batch of salve to treat their wounds."

"My thanks," her employer said, shrugging into his damp greatcoat once more. He made for the kitchen house without another word.

"I shall just help you with these," Johnny said to the girl, assuming more of her load.

"Oh thank 'ee, sir," Ellen sighed with relief. "I thought me arms was about to break!"

As the winter dusk deepened, it became apparent the refugees would not arrive that day. Johnny went out at dusk to light the two signal lanterns above the landing in the event of a late arrival. The lane was packed, and the walk was not taxing. It was clear and starkly beautiful in the wake of the storm. Just short of full, the moon's luminous edge rose from a pewter sea. There was no wind, and Johnny gazed south into the gathering gloom, his keen eyes searching for the *Sea Witch*. There was no sign of her. He knew none of them would rest well that night for worrying about their friends.

Indoors Alice sat before the hearth, occupying her hands with mending, but the rote work did not ease her mind. Her distress was palpable. Nicholas stood at the mantelpiece, his back to the flames, waiting patiently for her to give vent to her fears and worries, as he knew she eventually would. She kept nothing from him, and he was glad of it.

"I had a premonition when they left, that they were going into peril," Alice began, stabbing her needle into the material with uncharacteristic force. She yanked it out so quickly the thread tangled and broke. "God's Bones!" she swore, tossing the piece into the basket and covering her face. Nicholas sat down beside her and took her hands in his.

"Dear heart," he said gently, catching her eye, "we knew they came to broadcast their faith and stand against the Quaker laws. 'Tis their mission. How else are they to demonstrate their dissent but by breaking them?"

"But Nico, verily, didst thou expect the sentence to be so severe? Elizabeth's letter said they were to be flogged from Dover to Dedham—eleven towns! 'Tis tantamount to murther!" Alice protested, indignant tears shining in her eyes.

"And Robert Pike realized this and stopped it at Salisbury, God bless the man!" he responded. "They are safe in Walter's custody now. Edward shall bring them, mayhap on the morrow or the day after." He smoothed a tendril of dark hair off her forehead and cupped her cheek.

Alice covered his hand with hers and kissed his palm.

"How is it thou art so accomplished at comforting me?" she asked with a weak smile.

Nicholas gathered her into his arms, holding her closely.

"Because I love thee more than life," he whispered.

Edward did not accompany young Will and James to check the weirs for fish. He spent the morning clearing the storm's last inches of snow off the shallop and preparing to sail. Will assisted him once he and James returned to the dock empty handed.

"Big storm. Fish sleep," the native commented and went to tend to his chores.

Will was fascinated and impressed by the modifications to *Sea Witch*. The cabin measured eight by sixteen and had four berths in the bow. There was space for cargo in the widest area amidships. Edward had even installed small portholes of thick glass to let in light. Will spoke of apprenticing in his father's shipyard come spring. They enjoyed their shared interest in boats and each other's company.

When they returned to the house, Walter told Edward that Anne would be ready to travel the next day. They planned to depart with the outgoing tide at first light. The Carrs insisted they take sufficient bedding to keep the missionaries warm and comfortable. James helped Edward, Walter, and Will transport feather ticks, blankets, and pillows to the landing, tying it all to a sledge that the big man pulled easily over the packed snow of the lane. They made up all four berths, as Walter and Edward would take turns on deck, during the long trip. There was no heat on the shallop, but the women would be out of the wind—dry and cushioned in the event of rough seas.

Edward prayed for a southerly wind. His main concern was gaining Kittery Point by dark. If the blow was against them, he planned to a make a reach for White Island, the closest of the Isles of Shoals. They would have to overnight there and go on to the Point the next day, which meant additional hours in the cold. At least the island folk were an independent lot who had no love of the Bay Colony. They would not be harassed, but his hopes were set on a wind from the southwest or the southeast, rare though it might be at that season.

Walter emerged from the hold and stood beside Edward on deck.

"All is in readiness," he said and sighed, his breath pluming in the still air. "Do you reckon we can make it in one day, Edward?"

Walter owned a sloop. He understood the improbability of a favoring wind, but Edward realized it would only worry the doctor to voice his own misgivings. He looked up at the clouds. Their slow movement was the only indication of a light wind. It was from the north as usual.

"God willing," he said.

That evening the adults at the table were glad of the Carr children's company. Oblivious to the underlying tension on the eve of departure, they kept the conversation going. Anne had been up most of the day, telling stories and answering their many questions about England, once morning lessons were over. Mary marveled at her skill with them, weak though she was. Anne's melodious voice had regained its strength, and Mary realized how much she had missed hearing it the past days. However, the little missionary still tired easily. After supper she went to bed. The rest of the adults soon followed.

"Please do not feel constrained to rise with us on the morrow," Mary said to the Carrs, as they bade each other goodnight at the foot of the stairs. "Ye have done so much for us already."

Elizabeth hid her concern for her new friends with a brusque manner. "Nonsense," she asserted. "The children would be desolate to miss seeing you off. You are heroines in their opinion." She turned abruptly and went upstairs.

"And you have our undying admiration as well," George added gently and followed his wife.

Young Will appeared holding a pair of snowshoes. He went to Edward, his face coloring even before he spoke.

"Friend Whar—I mean, Edward." He took a breath and cleared his throat. "These are for you."

Edward began a polite protest, but Will overrode him. "James and I are in accord," the boy stated. "You need the practice." His face broke into a grin.

Edward chuckled and accepted the gift. "That I do, Will. That I verily do."

The boy sobered. "Mayhap, when you use them, you may remember us a little?" he added shyly.

Edward put his free arm around the boy's shoulders. "I shall never forget thee, Will," he said quietly. "Not ever."

The boy ducked his head and beat a hasty retreat before Edward should remark his tears.

The next morning the household was up and about before the sun. They shared a hearty breakfast of oatmeal, bread, and ham with steaming pots of strong English tea sweetened with milk and sugar. Elizabeth saw that a hamper of food was packed for the Friends' journey as well.

Although the landing was not far from the house, George insisted the women ride in the sleigh, including his wife and the three youngest children.

"Skirts drag in the snow," he said. "You do not want to start the journey with wet clothing."

None could argue with his logic. Seeing his son's long face, George put Will in charge of driving the sleigh to the dock. The boy's spirits rallied and he rose to the task admirably. It was no small job transferring the women and small children to the sleigh. Once they were packed in, Will climbed onto the driver's bench. Edward held up the snowshoes.

"I promise I shall use these at the earliest opportunity," he told Will seriously, then smiled, "but not today. I do not wish to start the journey with wet clothing either!" They both laughed. "Oh! I had hoped to bid farewell to James. Is he about?"

"I know not," Will glanced around then shrugged. "He abhors sentiment."

The impending sunrise brightened the sky over the Salisbury bank, but the temperature was frigid. The men walked behind the sleigh with the older children. The track to the dock was packed, and the fresh snow squeaked under their boots. At the landing the tide had turned, and a breeze sprang up, cutting through their wraps with knife-like severity. Edward was encouraged by its westerly direction.

The Carrs came aboard to help settle the women below deck. Elizabeth deemed the arrangement adequate, while the children swarmed over the small space. Allie and Anne settled in their berths gratefully, but Mary returned to the deck with the Carrs, who herded the children ashore then turned to say goodbye. The conversation by the fire with George had forged a bond. Mary was reluctant to part from this perceptive man who understood her like a father. Their eyes locked. George took her mittened hands in his and kissed her forehead then he passed her into Elizabeth's hands and stepped back unable to speak. Elizabeth kissed her cheek.

"Our deepest thanks—" Mary began.

"Hush," Elizabeth said, kissing Mary's other cheek. She smiled, gave Mary's hands a gentle squeeze then George handed her onto the landing.

Mary stood on deck while Walter and Will released the bow and stern lines then the doctor hopped aboard and took up an oar on the bench beside Edward. Will and his father pushed them off, and the boat began to drift downriver. Elizabeth and George linked arms and slowly waved. Will stood apart, looking forlorn. The younger children bounced around the dock, shouting farewells and waving exuberantly. Mary gazed at

George Carr. Tears stung her eyes, and she raised her hand, ignoring the flair of pain. She waved until the dock was lost to view then made her careful way below.

As they passed the southernmost tip of the island, Walter nudged Edward and pointed with his chin. James the Indian stood, facing east. He wore snowshoes and a Navy great coat with brass buttons that caught the first rays of the rising sun. He cut such an impressive figure that the two men stopped rowing and gaped at him, until current and tide bore the shallop past Ram's Isle. Just before they lost sight of him, James raised both arms in farewell.

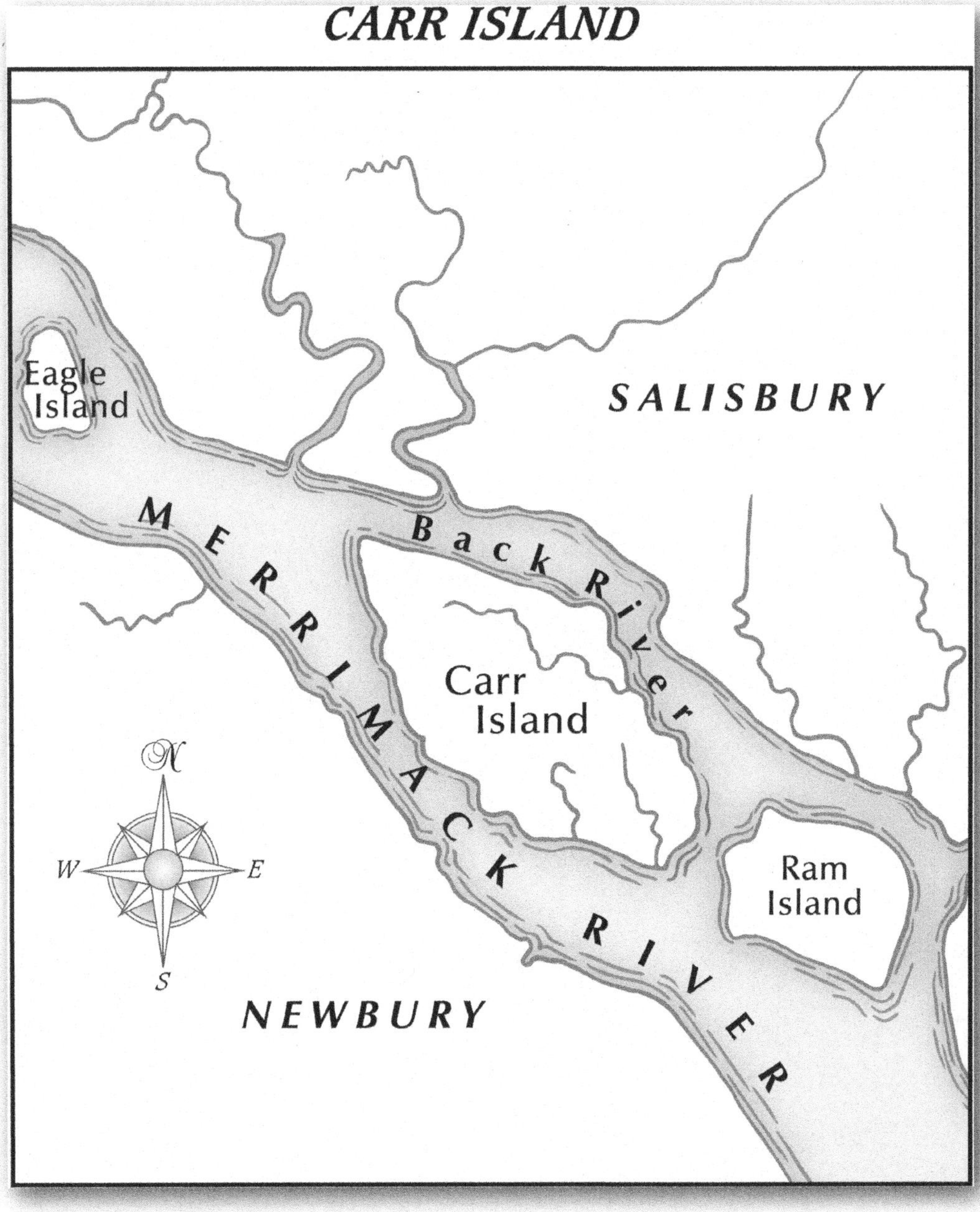
CARR ISLAND
Eagle Island
SALISBURY
Back River
MERRIMACK RIVER
Carr Island
N
W
E
S
Ram Island
NEWBURY

# *Chapter 42*

## RICHARD WALDERNE *THWARTED*

January, 1662 Dover and Cocheco Falls, Massachusetts Bay Colony

The Roberts brothers reached Bloody Point at dusk, exhausted by the ride to Hampton and back, leading three mounts, on the coldest day of the year yet. They were too tired to care about the Trickeys' stiff disapproval and were on the first ferry to Dover the next morning. After stabling the extra horses, the constables rode wearily to the parsonage on Low Street. John reported to John Reyner that he had left the prisoners in the custody of the Hampton constable, William Fifield, on December 25th.

"You did not stay to see the punishment properly administered?" the reverend queried.

John was affronted by the implied criticism, as well as the fact that Reyner kept them standing in the entry hall and did not invite them to sit or take any refreshment.

"There was insufficient coin to board us and five horses overnight at Hampton, Reverend," he said stiffly. "We were delayed by the Sabbath on the way down and had to stay at Trickey's Tavern two nights as a result. We spent most of the coin you gave us there. The remainder paid for the ferry back to Dover. We have been four days dealing with this business. Are you suggesting we shirked our duty?" John's eyes narrowed.

"You did not say we must witness the sentence," Thomas added defensively. "We saw the prisoners into Fifield's hands and gave him the warrant." For once John did not shush him.

The minister sniffed. "Well, 'twould have been best had you stayed to oversee the punish—"

"'Twould have been best, if you had overseen it yourself," John shot back. He was road-weary and in no mood to be called out on this point from the man who had instigated the whole mess, yet stayed warm at home while they labored. "Look to your own duty, Reverend. There are empty seats in your church of late."

He did not wait for a response, but turned on his heel and left, seething. The man had no appreciation of the hardship they had endured.

Despite the constable's rude comments, John Reyner savored his victory for three more days. The news of the aborted sentence was delayed by the blizzard, but inevitably it came. Reverend Wheelwright of Salisbury ensured that his counterpart in Dover was informed by post, and Reyner wasted no time sharing the information with Elder Nutter.

"Richard Walderne shall know of this," Hatevil growled upon hearing the news.

"Mayhap he is at Cocheco presently," the minister said hopefully.

The elder nodded. "I shall inform him of this travesty of justice," he asserted.

The response was swift. Two days later, Reyner and the Roberts brothers met with the magistrate at Nutter's home. They sat at the big dining table except for Reyner, who paced the room visibly upset. Mistress Nutter poured their tea and left them.

"They have evaded the sentence and made fools of us all!" the minister fumed, as soon as she had gone.

"Wheelwright's missive," Nutter said, handing it to the magistrate.

There was silence, as Walderne read the letter. He kept his expression blank, but he was furious. The damn Quakers had persuaded some of the most powerful men in the region to protect them—first Shapleigh, then the doctor, and now Robert Pike. How were three women capable of creating so much bother? It was that she-devil, who yet disturbed his sleep. He was unable to forget her discerning look, that inexplicable compassion. No one must ever know how the Tomkins woman affected him. She must be silenced.

"Please modulate your tone and sit down, Reverend," he said with studied calm. "Where are the Quakers presently?" he asked, once the minister was seated.

"I do not attend them! How would I know?" Reyner answered peevishly, ignoring the magistrate's scowl at his tone. Few people spoke to him that way without repercussions.

"It matters not," Nutter said, bringing attention to the matter at hand. "We can do nothing unless they return to Dover, which is not like to happen now, I warrant."

Walderne snorted. "If they are anything like their fellows at Boston, it is *very* like to happen. Even hanging did not stop them returning. We must be prepared, in any case."

"Certes, we must go after them. They must be apprehended. They are fugitives from justice!" Reyner asserted. "As Reverend Wheelwright says, Robert Pike overstepped himself, deputizing Barefoote and releasing the prisoners to him. 'Twould not have fallen out thus had the constables followed through by wit— "

"Would you have us arrest them on sight, if they return, sir?" John Roberts interrupted. He would not countenance being blamed for this unforeseen turn of events, particularly in the company of the magistrate and his father-in-law. Reyner huffed but was generally ignored.

"I charge you to apprehend them at one of their 'meetings,' Constable," Walderne answered. "A firm message to all who participate in this heresy is in order. We must make an example of them. 'Tis obvious Pike does not perceive the danger these unnatural women pose to God-fearing folk. The man must be a libertine! I doubt the constables could have foreseen this tangle, Reverend. Certes, you did not. Barring the Lieutenant's interference, the Quakers would now be...," he groped for a less volatile word than *dead*, "...incapable of creating more mischief. Pointing fingers will not serve. We must work together to protect our town from this threat."

The minister flushed at the mild reprimand but did not argue. John sat straighter, heartened by it, and gave the reverend a hard look. There was silence, as the men waited for the magistrate's directions.

"Nothing we discuss this day shall be repeated," Walderne stated after a thoughtful silence. "To anyone." He fixed each of them with a keen eye. They nodded. He leaned in, and the others followed suit. "Evidently the usual means are not sufficient to deal with these miscreants. They are more devilishly subtle than we anticipated. Their pernicious influence must be stopped—permanently." He looked at Nutter. "Whom can we trust with a private landing and a small boat?"

"I have a number of small craft at my shipyard," the elder answered.

"This must be done privily," Walderne said his voice quiet. "Your shipyard is too public, I fear."

Looks were exchanged.

Thomas spoke up. "Our father has—"

"That we can *trust*, numbskull," John cut in.

"Thomas Canney, mayhap," Nutter said slowly. "'Tis small, but he has a landing on Fore River upstream from my shipyard. He secures his skiff to a small pier."

"Canney," Walderne repeated. He sat back, considering. "Yes, he may serve."

"But the man is an adulterer!" the minister protested. "He is not fit for an Indian to live by!"

"As I recall there was a lack of evidence," the magistrate answered.

Reyner snorted. The Captain's expression sharpened. "The court released him, Mister Reyner, although his reputation has suffered since." He thought for a moment. "A circumstance that may be in our favor," he mused. "Send him to me," he said to John. "I shall speak with him at Cocheco." He looked around the table. "I am here another week or so, attending business," he said and pushed back his chair. "We shall meet again, once I have spoken with Canney. Keep me informed, if there are any developments. And remember, not a word of this to anyone."

There was a chorus of assent. The men drained their cups, and the meeting broke up.

# Chapter 43

## MARY AND ALICE *SAFE*

January, 1662 Kittery Point, Territory of Maine

Once she settled in her berth, Mary remembered little of the journey to Kittery Point. The motion was soothing, the sound of the hull plying the water a lullaby. Walter checked on the missionaries periodically and roused them at midday to sit up and eat, but even this small activity proved exhausting and painful, especially for Anne. Walter took his turn at the tiller, affording Edward some rest and refreshment. When he came below, his face and ears were red with cold but the Salem Friend was in high spirits.

"We have a following wind!" he told his friends, but sobered when he noted their strained faces.

"Good news indeed," Mary said warmly. "Our thanks, Friend Wharton, for all thy effort."

"You might call me Edward from here on." He spoke to the three of them, but he was looking at Mary. "That would be ample thanks."

"Agreed," said Anne promptly, as Allie nodded.

"From here on then, Edward," Mary agreed. They shared a smile.

He closed his eyes for a brief blessing then turned to his food. "And let us all give thanks for this wind. If it holds, we shall make Kittery Point before dark," he added with cautious optimism.

Soon after partaking of Elizabeth's nourishing food and a cold dose of the apothecary's willow bark tea, the women crawled back into their berths. Edward covered them with the Carrs' warm quilts. By the time he returned topside, the missionaries were dozing again. They roused hours later when Walter came below for the signal cannon. The shallop was approaching Kittery Point.

Alice Shapleigh had checked everything a dozen times. The sewing room was ready. The little housemaid, Ellen, kept the fire blazing all day, and the room was warm in spite of a brisk southwesterly wind that rattled the shutters. Stacks of rolled bandages and pots of salve were at the ready. A nourishing batch of fish chowder simmered in the cold kitchen, thick with potatoes and cream. There was plenty of hot water in reserve. Three canvas stretchers were borrowed from the militia at Kittery to transport the wounded women from the dock to the house. Alice felt sure their friends would arrive that day. She was too distracted to eat, but Nicholas insisted she take nourishment at midday.

"You shall need all your strength once they arrive, my love," he reasoned.

"Oh dear," Johnny said, attempting levity, "Uncle Nico and I shall just have to eat this lovely kidney pie ourselves. However shall we manage?"

Alice smiled weakly in response but sat at the table and picked up her fork.

As soon as they had eaten, however, she asked Johnny to round up four steady fellows to help carry the stretchers.

"Thou and Nico can carry Anne," she reasoned, "but we shall need four more for Mary and Allie. They must be ready. Ask them to wait at the ordinary for the signal cannon," Alice instructed before hurrying off to check on the preparations yet again.

Nicholas accompanied his nephew to the door. It was just past noon, and he knew it would take their friends a full day to reach Warehouse Landing from Salisbury, if, indeed, they made it at all that day. As to his wife's idea that the men wait at the ordinary...

"Perhaps you had best keep them company, Johnny," he said, giving his nephew some coin for the men's food and drink. "We don't want our stretcher bearers to be in their cups, staggering about with their precious loads."

They shared a smile.

"Not to worry, Uncle Nico," the young man answered. "James and Joseph are level headed fellows, and they shall help me choose two others to assist us. You have drawn the sterner duty by far, staying with Aunt Alice."

His uncle agreed.

The afternoon passed at a snail's pace, and Alice's patience eroded with every tick of the clock. Nicholas tried to distract her with a game of backgammon, but she routinely forgot to play her turn.

"Is it dark yet?" she asked, peering at the unshuttered bay window that glowed with the orange light of a lowering sun.

"No, my love," he answered patiently, throwing the dice. "Oh look, I have doubles."

"Dost think we should light the lanterns?" she fretted, still staring out the window.

"Let us wait a little, dear heart. Mayhap when our game is done. 'Tis your turn."

"I think I should check the fire in the sewing room," Alice said, making to rise.

"Alice, sit down," Nicholas said gently. "You know Ellen is taking care of that."

"Yes, but—"

A dull boom interrupted her.

"They are here!" she cried.

Alice leapt up so quickly, the board fell to the floor, scattering backgammon tiles. She ran for her pattens, cloak, and muffler without registering the mishap.

Nicholas sighed. As he knelt to retrieve the pieces, he said a silent prayer of thanks that the *Sea Witch* had arrived, for none of them would have slept that night had it not. Then he followed his wife to the dock.

The tide was approaching its height, and the light had faded to gloaming by the time Edward and Walter rowed in with sails reefed, affording a gentle landing. The lanterns were not necessary, but Alice insisted they be lit, and no one wished to gainsay her. Much as she wished to embrace her friends, she restrained herself to kissing their cheeks—one cheek in Allie's case. The sight of the livid welt and stitches elicited an involuntary gasp, but Alice recovered quickly, kissing Allie twice on one cheek. She was firm, however, when Mary and Allie made to walk up to the house, insisting they be carried like Anne, and Walter agreed.

The missionaries were tenderly borne up the snowy track. Alice led the procession, turning around every few seconds to see all was well and repeatedly admonishing the bearers to take care.

The warmth of the house was balm to the travelers, chilled from the long day at sea. The concern and love of their friends was palpable, as they settled the three women in the familiar sewing room. Kittery Manor felt like home after all they had endured. Now they were safely arrived, Alice focused on the tasks at hand with steadfast calm. She assisted Walter in blotting and dressing the wounds without comment, though her eyes widened at first sight then filled with tears. She controlled them with ruthless efficiency.

After the necessities were brought from the shallop, Nicholas and Johnny persuaded Edward to sit and drink a hot toddy by the blazing hearth. Walter had Alice's help, and the long sail had tired the Salem Friend. He recounted the events since receiving Walter's message at Salem. They marveled at Pike's role in rescuing the women from a painful death and securing them refuge with George Carr.

"Thank God you had Lieutenant Pike and the Carrs to help you!" Nicholas exclaimed.

"Yes," the Salem Friend replied, "we have much to thank Him for." He glanced at the archway then leaned forward and added, "I did not tell the others, but I doubted we would make Kittery Point in one day. I am grateful to the Almighty for the providential wind as well."

The Friends healed quickly in the safety and comfort of Kittery Manor with the exception of Anne. She contracted a catarrh deep in her chest and was once again too weak to rise from her cot. Her wracking cough did not respond to the usual medicaments. Walter stayed on at Kittery Manor until her condition improved.

Walter and Alice applied salve to the missionaries' backs morning and night. As their wounds formed scabs, the three women spent most of their time in the warm sewing room, bared to the waist and exposing their backs to the air. At this stage bandages and clothing only retarded healing by rubbing the scabs. Mary and Allie spent hours with Anne, talking, singing, and reading aloud. They were both up and about, but regular activity still taxed their strength. Alice encouraged them to rest, but this proved difficult for the wounds itched maddeningly as they healed.

Mary's antipathy returned as she mended. She craved Edward's company, but feared his effect upon her resolve. The imperative of her call revived, but it faltered in his presence, giving way to doubt and yearning. She was embarrassed by the potency of her attraction, and the lack of control over her emotions shamed her. She could feel his gaze, but when their eyes met, she was overwhelmed and turned away, blushing.

After two days Edward felt impelled to leave. Another storm might come any time, and the wind had resumed its usual northerly direction. If it held, he might make Salem in a day and a half. The *Sea Witch* was comfortable and beamy but not swift. Although he was reluctant to part with Mary, he had responsibilities to his business. In any case, he saw her only at meals.

The incident had defined his feelings for her, and Edward longed to declare his love, but there would be no opportunity for them to speak alone while she healed. He could not bear another formal farewell and opted to go early the next day, before the household awoke, ostensibly to catch the tide. He informed Nicholas that night, once everyone else had retired.

"I think it best I leave with the morning tide, Nicholas," he began.

His host frowned. "I wish you could stay longer, my friend, but I understand. 'Time and tide wait for no man.' Shall we drink a dram to your safe voyage?"

"My thanks, I should enjoy that," Edward answered, following him to the sideboard. He did not often indulge in strong spirits, but he was glad of an opportunity to talk. He needed to confide his feelings to someone, and he trusted Nicholas.

"'Tis a fine thing you did for our girls, Edward," the older man said, pouring two neat measures of scotch. He handed one to Edward. "May your journey home be swift and safe," he toasted, clinking glasses.

He put a hand on Edward's shoulder. "Come let us sit by the fire. We have had little time for conversation, you and I."

Now he had his friend's attention, Edward was unsure how to begin. Nicholas was not blind, however, and had noted the younger man tracking Mary whenever she was present. Nor had he missed her heightened color in response.

"'Tis difficult to see those we care for abused," he now said carefully, as they settled.

Edward sighed. "Thou hast read my heart. Are my feelings so transparent, then?" he asked.

Nicholas smiled. "I think mayhap 'tis more obvious to someone like myself, who has experienced the all-consuming certainty of true love. It took years to convince Alice to wed."

"I thought women were weak, frivolous beings, but Mary is unique. She is like no other!" Edward stopped himself with a wry shake of his head. "I do not know mine own self." He sipped his drink. "Was it so for thee? I can scarce think of anything else," he finished.

"Oh my friend, you do have a severe case! And yes, it was so for me from the moment I met Alice," Nicholas chuckled, then sobered. "But I fear it is the things you love about Mary that shall work against you. You know she is dedicated to her calling and is not inclined to marry."

"But I would not expect her to abandon her call!" Edward said rising and pacing to the hearthside. He placed his glass on the mantel and turned back. "I understand her commitment to missionary work. I am not minded, if we have no children. I do comprehend that much about her, Nicholas, but I fear for her. She does not credit the danger and has no regard for her own safety. I feel compelled to protect her. She is so rare, so precious! I want her beside me in my home and in my life." He leaned on the mantle, staring down into the flames.

"I understand, Edward, but 'tis Mary you must convince, is it not?" Nicholas responded gently. He drank then straightened. "In truth I think she may be frightened."

"Frightened? Of me?" Edward turned to him, alarmed.

"No, not of you, exactly. More the feelings you engender, when she is with you," his host answered slowly.

Edward considered this. "Dost think...art thou saying she has some regard for me as well?"

"We are drifting into dangerous waters, my friend," Nicholas said, holding up a hand. "I should not venture to guess what our Mary feels. But I have remarked her cheeks bloom at your notice."

"Verily?" Edward's expression was so vulnerable, Nicholas winced. "I have remarked her blushes and dared to hope she might return my affection," Edward admitted. He retrieved his glass and sat on the settee next to Nicholas, encouraged.

Nicholas leaned back and propped his feet on a stool. "'Tis hard to say for sure, but allow me to venture this—for years I labored under the assumption that Alice did not accept my proposals because she did not love me. When she finally opened her heart to me, I learned she feared herself lacking. Whatever Mary feels, you must declare yourself; else you shall never know."

"I am in accord. 'Tis good advice, Nicholas, but I do not know when that opportunity may come," Edward said, peering into his glass morosely.

"Then you shall have time to prepare, for I have no doubt it will come upon you one day," Nicholas smiled and held up his glass, "Most like when you least expect it."

The crystal tumblers chimed, and the two friends drained their glasses and went to bed.

The next morning Nicholas watched Mary's face, as he informed the table at large of Edward's early departure. Her expression remained neutral amid the exclamations of surprise and regret. He noted Allie's quick glance at her friend and Mary's subsequent lack of involvement in the conversation. She excused herself and left the table soon after. Her behavior indicated that she cared for the Salem man—or at least cared that he had left—and Nicholas was glad for Edward, but he did not envy his young friends. Circumstances did not favor their relationship. The missionaries were in danger—indeed, all Friends were. Only the river and his influence protected them in Kittery, and Nicholas was uncertain how long the latter would hold against the growing aggression of the Bay.

As their strength increased, Mary and Allie tried to keep busy. They were desperate for distractions from the constant itching. They caught up on correspondence, relating the incident to Margaret Fell. Their families received an edited version. That accomplished, they begged Alice to put them to work. She set them dipping candles, sewing warm woolen cloaks to replace their ruined ones, mending donated clothing, and knitting shawls, scarves, mittens, and hats for the Mercy Wagon—or rather, the Mercy Sledge at that time of year. Winter passage on the outer roads was challenging, if not impossible, so there was but one sturdy sledge each week. Alice forbade the recovering invalids to lift anything heavy or go on rounds as yet. Instead they stayed warm and dry, dipping wicks, reading aloud, singing, and playing word games, as their knitting and sewing needles clicked and flashed in the flames from the hearth. Although their discomfort was unrelenting, the sounds of song and laughter were often heard from the sewing room. Anne was recovering at last, and Alice delighted in their company, when she was not managing her household or making winter rounds on the sledge with Johnny.

Two weeks after the missionaries' return, they planned a meeting for worship at Kittery Manor. The scabs had fallen away revealing tender, pink skin that felt tight when they moved, but the itching subsided to a minor irritation. Her energy and assurance had returned, and Mary looked forward to the meeting. Word circulated that the English Friends wished to celebrate the Yuletide they had missed and would lead the next First Day meeting on January 15th. There would be caroling, silent worship, and, of course, tea and refreshments after the service. The holiday was openly celebrated on the east bank of the Piscataqua.

Near thirty folk responded in addition to the household. Among the familiar faces of the Friends some new ones appeared, curious to see the women who had eluded the wrath of Richard Walderne. Contrary to the intent of the Puritan authorities, the incidents at Dover and Hampton engendered new interest in the Friends' message.

Walter came to ensure the women were physically ready for the event and planned to stay overnight for the celebration. He was received with joy, for the ordeal had sealed their friendship. Anne was up, and Walter approved her attendance but cautioned her to stay indoors, as exposure to the cold air might exacerbate her cough.

The meeting was held in the Shapleighs' large drawing room and began with a lively rendition of "The Holly and the Ivy." Mary and Allie led the carol and their harmonies and syncopated singing thrilled the worshippers. The story of their suffering had circulated, making their presence all the more precious. After a blissful silent worship Mary rose to speak.

"Dear Friends," she began then paused, savoring the warmth and safety of this fellowship. "We stand before you today only by God's Grace and the good work of Dr. Walter Barefoote, Lieutenant Robert Pike, and Friend Edward Wharton." A wave of emotion constricted her throat, but she breathed deeply and continued. "I have no doubt that without them we would number among those who have sacrificed their lives for our cause.

"Mark ye, the brutal sentence brought against us is a measure of the Puritans' fear. The Children of the Light threaten them, for we represent a new order. Once folk discover a connection to That of God Within, there is no going back to ignorance. There is no returning to the empty words of the ministers and the constriction of an authority that recognizes a select few.

"This day, as we celebrate the birth of God's greatest gift to us, His only Begotten Son, let us recall His words. '... resist not evil: but whoever shall smite thee on thy right cheek, turn to him the other also.' Jesus bids us turn the other cheek. 'Tis the embodiment of meekness, is it not?" Her eyes moved from face to face, as heads nodded. "'Tis a difficult lesson to suffer a blow and not return it in kind. Our first response is to retaliate."

People stared at her, unsure of the direction she was taking.

"Yes!" she asserted. "We all know the Old Testament councils 'an eye for an eye.' Turning the other cheek seems a coward's response and is contrary to our base nature." She paused, allowing this thought to register. The room was still.

"But it is right behavior. Our Lord asks us to be meek in the true sense of the word, which is to abandon pride, to negate the self. Otherwise pride, anger, and fear shall rule us, as they rule the Puritan authorities. The Son of God does not council us to bring outward strength to bear against our enemies but rather a potent and loving spirit. He clearly instructs us to 'resist not evil' but to turn the other cheek."

Mary paused and reached for Allie's hand. Her friend stood beside her, grasping it.

"That is why, before long, Alice Ambrose and I shall return to Dover."

The gathering erupted. Nicholas stood up. Walter's mouth was agape. Mary clearly heard Alice Shapleigh's "No! Oh, no!" but she raised her voice and spoke calmly over the reaction.

"We shall turn the other cheek to the Puritan authorities in the Massachusetts Bay Colony, and by our meekness shall they be undone."

# *Chapter 44*

## RICHARD WALDERNE *CANNEY ENLISTED*

January, 1662 Dover and Cocheco, Massachusetts Bay Colony

Thomas Canney was not a happy man. At first he had prospered in the New World, building on one of Captain Wiggin's lots, raising a family, eventually gaining freeman status and membership in the church. He was selected for the Grand Jury one year, served the town as constable, and at the peak of his good fortune was voted a selectman, though he could neither read nor write. However, his luck seemed to depart with the death of Mary, his first wife and mother of his four grown children.

Her successor did not prove as biddable as Thomas anticipated. They had not been wed a year when Jane went after him with a rolling pin just for coming home at a late hour from the ordinary, where he had, justifiably, been celebrating his partnership in a sawmill. He put her in her place by taking her to court for the assault—he had the bruises to prove it— but as a result his home became a battlefield. She drove off his daughter, Mary, and her husband in similar fashion a few months later. God's Blood, the woman had a sharp tongue! She was apt to grab up whatever was handy and lay on with it, when her choler was up—which was often.

Jane's opinion of him went from bad to worse, when he was called to court himself, accused by Ronald Jenkins of tempting his wife Anne to "unchastity." The charge against him was dismissed for lack of evidence—no witnesses—but he was fined nevertheless, and his reputation suffered. Bad as things were after Mary's death, at least his friends and neighbors had supported him. Now he was shunned. The past two years had been abysmal. He sought solace in spirits.

He thought he had kept his attraction for Goody Jenkins well hidden. She had flirted with him for months, smiling sweetly whenever he passed her on a village way or saw her at church. Jane never smiled at him that way. He prided himself on his ability to mask his desire, so someone must have seen them that day—or more disturbing, had she told her husband herself?

Even now, two years later, Thomas winced at the memory of the summons and the resultant public degradation. Of course, it had been William Walderne's brother presiding. Stammering, red-faced, Canney had denied the charge hotly. Sweet Christ, he had only stolen a kiss and a feel! He had not bedded her! Of course, he did not admit that, oath or no.

*She* was the one leading him on all spring and summer with her smiles and the breasts of an angel—so temptingly plump. He fell asleep of nights dreaming about hefting them in his palm, while that sweet smile warmed and welcomed him.

An opportunity presented itself one day on the River Road behind the brewery—a spot less frequented by the usual foot traffic. It was a hot day in August. Thomas was resting in the shade at the back of the brew house, refreshing himself with pulls from his hip flask. He had been there awhile when Goody Jenkins came round the corner of the building. She wore no shawl or jacket, and her apron tied at the waist and had no bib. His eyes went to her breasts. They were not bound, and she wore a light cotton blouse over her shift. She carried an empty basket on one hip, and that promising smile lit her face as she approached. She waved merrily, causing her bosom to sway enticingly under her blouse. Thomas licked his lips and smiled back.

There was no one else in sight, and he acted on impulse. He pocketed his flask and stepped away from the building, intercepting her. Her smile did not falter until he grasped her upper arms and pushed her against the wall of the brew house. This was their chance! Her basket tumbled to the ground. He ignored her feeble protestations—certes, all for show—and stopped her mouth with his. She wriggled against him, but he held her arms firmly, and her hands beat feebly at his sides. He pinned her against the building with his wiry body. Her bosom was crushed against him, more wonderful in reality than his dreams. He let go of her left arm, and her breast seemed to leap of its own accord into his hand, the nipple a tantalizing little nub against his palm through her thin summer clothes. He squeezed the soft flesh and forced his tongue past her clenched teeth, drinking in the sweet taste of her. His erection throbbed between them, insistent on a little rime in ree.

She twisted from the kiss with a strangled exclamation and stamped her heel on his toes. He howled and let go of her, jumping on one leg. Then she butted him with her shoulder, the cow! He nearly fell over! When he looked up, she was gone, leaving him with an embarrassing bulge in his britches and a sore foot. The next time he saw her was in court, where her husband accused him of encouraging her to lewd behavior. She had encouraged him with her come hither smile! Women! They teased you or abused you. What was a healthy man to do?

Now John Roberts and his little sheep of a brother said Richard Walderne wanted words with him. Thomas could not imagine why. Walderne had avoided him for years. Roberts said it would be worth his while, but naught else. Still, it was enough to revive a hope of salvaging his reputation. It might even impress Jane, if he could regain the magistrate's good graces.

In '52 Canney was partners in a sawmill with Walderne, Nutter, Emery, and some others he didn't know. It had been his last good year. He was a selectman and had just married Jane. His run of bad luck was not apparent as yet, but it all began with Richard Walderne's censure.

Thomas had been a good friend of Richard's brother Will, who had died in '46. Now there was a man who had known how to balance labor and leisure! He and Will had enjoyed many a cup at the ordinary together before Will's untimely death in Maine. The Waldernes were as dissimilar as brothers might be. Thomas' decline started the day Richard Walderne called him a drunkard. He maintained that Canney had been a bad influence on his brother, and it was "friends" of his ilk who had killed William. Will *had* loved his cups—more than Thomas himself—but it stung that the younger Walderne blamed *him* for Will's death! Furthermore Mister High and Mighty Walderne insisted on buying out Thomas' share in the sawmill, although the sum he offered was considerably less than Canney's original investment. When Thomas objected to the amount, Walderne sneered, "You have drunk all your profit, Canney. You are fortunate to get this."

Thomas still smarted from that accusation, more than the loss of coin, though it was years past. What could the Captain want with him now? More to the point, how might he turn Walderne's need to his own gain?

The morning after the Roberts brothers came, Thomas chipped the frozen bilge from the bottom of his skiff and rowed up to Cocheco in the cold. He found Walderne at the trading post, finishing his midday meal. The smell of meat pasties made his stomach rumble. The magistrate pretended not to remark him, until hat in hand, Thomas cleared his throat.

"Why, Thomas Canney!" Walderne drawled, feigning surprise. He sat back, wiping his mouth with a handkerchief. Thomas could not tell if the magistrate's tight smile was a greeting or a smirk of disdain. His face colored, as the latter seemed more likely.

Walderne stood. "Let us repair to my office," he said and quit the room without looking back.

Thomas followed, his hopes fading. Obviously the man's attitude had not changed. After coming a long, cold way, it was humiliating. Walderne closed the door and sat behind his desk. Thomas stood.

"'Tis best we discuss this matter privily," the captain began, gesturing to a chair. Thomas sat as the man went on. "I must ask that you keep this discussion to yourself. What we speak of here must not leave this room." He speared Thomas with a hard look, as though doubting his ability to govern his tongue.

Thomas stared back then realized a response was expected. He swallowed and nodded once.

"You must swear it," Walderne insisted.

Thomas sat up straighter. "I—" He cleared his throat. "I do so swear," he managed.

"Good," Richard said. "If you prove useful in this endeavor, I may grant you a favor in return."

This crumb fed the desperate man's hope, and he leaned forward, encouraged.

"'Tis a matter of justice thwarted," the magistrate began, watching Thomas carefully. "I propose to deputize you. The constables require assistance in apprehending some fugitives of the law—three heretics that threaten the First Church and the good folk of Dover. By scurrilous means they have evaded their sentence. You would be acting in the best interests of the town."

"Speak you of the Quakers that were flogged at the cart tail?" Canney asked his eyes wide. He had witnessed that show along with the rest of the town. He had not sung, but he had appreciated seeing all those bare titties.

Walderne nodded once. "The same. They were released at Salisbury—a miscarriage of justice. I have reason to believe they may return, as many of their ilk do. Your job as deputy is to assist the constables in apprehending them, when and if they appear in Dover."

"You want me to help arrest three women and take them to the gaol?" Thomas asked. It seemed suspiciously easy.

"No," the magistrate answered cryptically. "Not the gaol."

Canney's brow wrinkled in confusion. "Then wh—"

"List to me now, Thomas Canney," Walderne interrupted. He leaned forward and lowered his voice but his tone was intense. "You must assist the constables in dealing with them so that we shall be troubled by them no more."

There was a heavy silence, as Canney parsed the Captain's meaning. It took a moment.

"What?" he exclaimed, frankly shocked. Walderne put a finger to his lips and stared at him with narrowed eyes. "But 'tis a sin," he hissed. The man was talking of murther! Thomas might be damned to Hell!

"Not in this case," the magistrate said firmly. "As I said, they are fugitives from the law. They have evaded the sentence proscribed by the court. In addition they are unnatural, an affront to God. Think you the Almighty approves of women spouting heresy against His First Church? The Reverend Reyner himself supports this course, as does Elder Nutter. You are God's instrument and are absolved of guilt, but discretion is called for. None may remark where you take the prisoners. This mission must be secret."

Thomas was silent. Another man might refuse. Another man might walk away.

Seeing Canney waver, Walderne continued. "On top of that, *if* all goes well, I shall put in a good word for you, should you wish to assume public office. You were a selectman before and might serve the town again in that capacity—or mayhap the position of constable appeals?"

Canney imagined the respect he would command as a figure of authority in Dover once more. Constables carried truncheons and wielded whips. Folk would fear and obey him. Even Jane would have to obey him and cease her harrying. Goody Jenkins would regret spurning him, but he would be gracious and forgive her. It would turn his life around. If Elder Nutter and Reverend Reyner approved, verily, it could not be counted a sin.

"When is the arrest to be?" Thomas asked.

Walderne's smile was genuine this time. Canney's lingering doubts dissipated with this evidence of the influential man's approval. When Richard Walderne smiled at you, good things happened.

"The constables shall alert you of our next meeting to finalize the details," the captain answered, "*If* we know you are with us."

Thomas took a deep breath and nodded. "By God, I shall do it, then."

The magistrate rose and shook his hand on it but did not offer to seal the bargain with a toast. No surprise there. Canney corrected the lack in the common room before the cold trip downriver. His luck was changing. The more he thought about it, the more the plan appealed to him. He would be doing the town a service and would be welcomed back into the fold as a respected official. He ordered a refill. It would feel good to teach some fractious women a lesson, as well as restoring his good name. Two birds with one stone. He downed his second dram quickly and called for a third.

# *Chapter 45*

## MARY AND ALICE *SECOND INCIDENT AT DOVER*

January, 1662 Dover Point, Massachusetts Bay Colony

Barring her initial reaction to Mary's announcement, Alice Shapleigh governed her tongue until all the worshippers had left but Walter. Johnny excused himself as soon as the front door closed on the last of them, sensing the oncoming storm. Nicholas opened his mouth to speak then shook his head and closed it again. The apothecary regarded them balefully but without surprise. However, Alice could not contain herself.

"Ye cannot mean to go back to Dover!" she exclaimed and did not pause for a response. "Ye have only just recovered and Anne is too weak to endure the cold—besides 'tis dangerous! They are like to k— "

Nicholas stopped her with a hand on her shoulder.

"I agree, 'tis upsetting, but it is not our decision to make, my love," he interrupted gently. She allowed him to take her hand and lead her to her usual chair, though her expression said she was not finished. "Let us hear out our friends and support them in any way we are able," he said, standing at her side. He looked at Mary and raised his eyebrows.

"Anne cannot accompany us, as ye well perceive. We hope she might remain here until she recovers," Mary said.

"Certes," Nicholas replied promptly, but Alice was not to be distracted.

"My dears, ye cannot mean to willfully endanger yourselves! Your wounds are barely healed! Anne, dost thou agree with this course?" Her anger was becoming sorrow.

Anne smiled sadly and nodded. She supported the decision for she understood the imperative of a call. Mary spoke for all of them.

"Dear Alice, I beg thee understand. These unjust laws cannot be allowed to prevail. Our return shall prove that God's Truth is unstoppable. We spread the knowledge of God's Light to folk, but we are called to stand against the abuse of justice as well. Our return is the strongest response possible. This is not the time to stand down for safety's sake. 'Tis the time to press our advantage."

Alice shook her head. "How is getting flogged to within an inch of your lives an advantage? Ye cannot depend upon God's Grace to save you again."

Nicholas drew a sharp breath at this bald statement of doom.

"'Tis all right, Nicholas," Mary assured him. "She speaks out of love and concern for us. This we understand." She smiled at Alice, who held her gaze but did not smile back. "Thou art like a sister to us, Alice, and because we love thee, we would have thee understand this decision, as we understand thy objections."

Alice crossed her arms and held her tongue, though her husband knew it must be an effort for her. Mary sat on a footstool near Alice's chair and continued.

"We have prepared for this challenge for years. God approved our effort by enabling our friends to save us, but we must not falter or lose faith. We were spared so that we might continue the struggle, not abandon it out of fear."

"But why can ye not continue your work here, on this side of the river, where ye are safe?" Alice demanded unconvinced. "Ye have already accomplished much, and the people here love you!"

Mary reached for her friend's hand, which Alice relinquished reluctantly, and went on.

"In Salisbury the authorities set to punish us recognized the injustice of the sentence and refused to honor the warrant signed by Richard Walderne. That was a great victory, but the evil laws against Friends yet hold sway throughout the Bay Colony and flourish in Dover. If we convince folk, the practice of their faith endangers them. We cannot rest until those laws are abolished. More than convincement this is our true calling, our Life's Work. We can make no stronger statement than to return and protest publicly. Our presence shall alert everyone at Dover of the authorities' failure to stop us."

At these words, Alice's eyes filled with tears, and she stood up, breaking Mary's grasp. She realized she could not win. Mary rose with her.

"Thou speakest well, Mary, but whatever thy fine reasons, I fear for your *lives*." Her tears spilled over. "Walter, is there nothing thou wouldst say to dissuade them?" she asked, desperately.

The doctor gazed back at her. "They are grown women, Alice," he said ruefully. "I can suggest they wait, but, in truth, they are recovered physically. I cannot tell them what to do, particularly in matters of faith." He sighed, as though he wished he could. "However," he went on addressing Mary and Allie, "I intend to accompany you, and I shall do everything in my power to protect you."

Alice turned to her husband, but he shook his head, agreeing with Walter. Allie stepped forward and embraced her, but Alice was distraught. Her friends would risk their lives again, and she was helpless to prevent it.

Two days later, Nicholas himself drove the missionaries and Walter to the ferry landing in the sleigh. Alice did not see them off, and the missionaries understood she could not bear it. They were taking Emery's ferry to Beck's Landing on Dover Point where the missionaries planned to stay at Anthony's ordinary. They would be welcomed by the feisty innkeeper and his wife.

Anne was gratifyingly supportive, but she was in no condition to accompany them. The cold air alone would compromise her lungs, and the women would likely be flogged again. Mary still felt responsible for Anne's suffering and was relieved. It was enough to return to the lion's den without that burden too. She expected it would be a matter of days before she and Allie were arrested and punished, but the reprieve at Salisbury would be public knowledge, striking another blow against the unjust laws.

They were quiet on the short sleigh ride to the landing. The women could see Nicholas was upset, but he did not try to dissuade them. Walter was stoic. The four of them stood on the landing as the ferry approached.

"We shall never be able to repay thy kindness, Nicholas," Mary said, looking at his glum face.

"Thy understanding most of all," Allie added at his other side.

The corner of his mouth rose, but his eyes were sad.

"Your families trusted me to protect you. I am afraid I have failed them," he said.

"That is the Lord's provenance, not thine," Mary answered, laying her mittened hand on his arm.

Nicholas covered it with his. "Then I pray He is better at it than I, for I warrant your parents would not agree. Shall we see you again, Mary?" he asked, as the ferry docked.

Mary met his eyes and squeezed his arm wordlessly. He embraced her gently, holding back tears. "Be careful, you wonderful, foolish girl," he managed.

He turned to Allie and enfolded her in his arms. "I know you cannot keep her safe, but don't allow her to be too daft, Allie," he whispered. "God keep you both."

Beck's ferry retained its original name out of long habit, though it was now Emery's ferry. The Trickeys ran the routes from Hilton's Point to Portsmouth and Bloody Point. The Emerys went from Beck's Landing on Fore River to the Town of Kittery and Kittery Point. Anthony's son James was working the passage that day. The young man was surprised to see the missionaries.

"How now!" he exclaimed, as they boarded, toting borrowed saddlebags stuffed with fresh clothing the Kittery Friends had supplied. Their satchels had been lost during the first arrest. "We did not think to see *you* return to Dover!' he said, amazed.

Mary gazed back at Nicholas on the landing and did not respond.

"The Lord works in mysterious ways," Allie told him solemnly.

Walter left them at Emerys' ordinary and went home, arranging to see them for a meal at noon the next day. The warmth was a relief after the ferry ride and the walk from the landing. The missionaries were more sensitive to the cold now. At mid-afternoon there was little custom in the common room, where their first meetings were held.

"Why, 'tis the English missionaries!" Frances Emery exclaimed upon seeing them. "We did not expect to see *you* back here!" she added, unconsciously echoing her son.

"Is thy husband about?" Mary inquired, once greetings were exchanged, and they sat at a table by the blazing fire.

"He goes below stairs to fiddle in his carpentry shop, when 'tis slow," his wife explained.

"We do not wish to endanger thee by our presence," Mary said.

Frances snorted. "We entertained those two missionaries that came through a few years back. Anthony helped them get about on the ferry as well. They called him to the Court in Ipswich on it and slapped a fine of ten pound on him." She seemed unperturbed, as she poured steaming bowls of tea to warm the women. "They may fine us all they wish. We shall not lick their Puritan boots. Who are we to refuse custom? It pays the fines," she smiled, then sobered. "We do not hold with the Bay Colony poking into our business. Few folk here appreciate their interference, the ones with any backbone, that is."

"Friend Emery, is there talk about us?" Mary asked.

"There was plenty of talk after the flogging last month! Many were astonied by the sentence. People judge you incapacitated or even dead by now," she answered. "Do ye mean to keep your return a secret?"

"No, not at all," Mary said.

"Quite the contrary," Allie put in, savoring the strong, sweet tea.

"Ha!" Their hostess exclaimed. "Now ye sound like my husband!"

While the missionaries took their tea, Frances sent a girl to light a fire in their room and make up the bed. They went up as soon as she was done. Parting from the Shapleighs had been emotionally taxing, and the ferry ride and walk to the ordinary was the longest they had been outside since Salisbury. The two Friends removed their boots and put up their feet gratefully, lying back on the freshly made bed. The linens smelled of rosemary.

"Shall we hold the meeting here then?" Allie asked.

"I hope to," Mary answered, "but I would speak with Friend Emery first. We must have his consent."

"His wife has no objection, it would seem, but how shall we get word to the Dover Friends?"

"Perhaps our host or Walter can help with that," Mary said and yawned.

It was good to lie on her back without pain, although the scarred skin felt tight when she moved. Mary closed her eyes.

Allie lay on her side and watched Mary succumb to sleep. She was tired but restless. Excitement and foreboding warred within. She anticipated the shock their return would engender, but she feared the repercussions. She expected no mercy. Her imagination supplied various scenarios of their arrest and punishment, none of them pleasant. No doubt confinement in the unheated gaol and flogging or the stocks would be involved. Once it was known they were back, Allie knew it would not be long in coming.

It was dark by the time they went down for the evening meal. The common room was crowded. The workday was done, and the last ferry had landed. A cold wind thumped at the shutters, but the fire blazed, and the ordinary was warm and redolent with the aromas of cooking, spiced cider, spilled ale, and pipe smoke.

Their host had his hands full at the bar, drawing ale, pouring rum and wine, and ladling steaming spiced cider into flagons. Busy as he was, he saw them and gave a cheerful nod in their direction. The missionaries looked around, but every table was occupied. Anthony noted their dilemma and held up a finger, bidding them wait. He soon came around the bar, wiping his hands on his apron, to seat them himself. He led them to a table fronting the hearth.

"Come, gentlemen," he said to the three men seated there, "give way to the ladies, will you?"

"Oh, 'tis not necessary for them to move, Friend Emery," Mary interposed. "There is room for all of us at this table, if ye do not mind sharing, Friends?"

The men rose at the women's approach. They glanced at each other and shrugged.

"We welcome the company of ladies," one said, politely indicating the two chairs closest to the fire. The other two nodded, resuming their seats once Mary and Allie had sat.

"What refreshment would you have?" their host asked.

"Two ciders and two suppers, thank thee, Friend Emery," Mary answered.

The use of "Friend" and the familiar pronoun between adults marked the women as Quakers. The men exchanged wary glances. They were carpenters at the shipyard owned by Hatevil Nutter. They were discomfitted to learn they were sharing a table with the missionaries who had been flogged just weeks before. The women's reprieve struck them as miraculous.

"Mister Nutter bid us sign that complaint," the first man told them quietly, "even though most of us did not know ye existed."

"My wife was that upset by the flogging," the second fellow added. "Yer singing brought the tears to her eyes, it did. She feared the sentence would kill you, if not the cold. She will be that glad to hear they did not whip you all the way to Dedham."

"They took you from the Nutes' place, did they not?" asked the third shipwright.

"He was fined for it too, I heard," the first added.

"We are sorry to hear the Nutes suffered on our account," Mary said.

"I warrant 'twas nothing compared to yer suffering," the second allowed.

The third carpenter spoke again, his face intent. "Ye ought to quit this place. 'Tis not safe for you here." He glanced about then lowered his voice. "Why have ye returned?" He seemed uneasy.

"Dost thou think the law against worshipping freely is just?" Mary asked him.

The men ducked their heads and squirmed.

"Well, I reckon not," the first responded. "Certes, there are few in Dover that think the sentence was so."

"But we do not question the law here," the third man said darkly.

"Then mayhap 'tis time to start," Allie rejoined, giving him a scar-graced smile.

When the missionaries' food came, the men took their leave. Mary and Allie joined hands, closing their eyes to say grace, and did not see the third man's parting glance of surreptitious guilt. His employer would pay good coin for any news of the Quakers' return to Dover, and his family had need of it.

As the tavern quieted, and custom dwindled to those staying at the inn, Frances and Anthony ate their supper with the missionaries.

"'Tis a publick house," he said in response to Mary's question about a meeting, "and you are paying guests. Have all the meetings you like."

"We do not wish to cause thee trouble, Friend Emery," she said.

Their host emitted a short laugh. "Life is trouble," he replied, wiping his mouth with the apron he wore to tend bar. "We have had little else, since the Bay Colony took over. Frances and I have survived their interference before, and we shall again." He broke off a piece of bread and mopped his bowl with it. "'Tis your own safety you should be thinking of."

"Our safety is not at issue here," Mary responded. "There has been a misuse of justice."

"You sound like those two fellows who came through here in '59. Robertson? Stevens? I misremember their names."

"William Robinson and Marmaduke Stephenson," Allie prompted.

"That's them," Emery said. "They stayed here two days before I took them to Kittery. Did ye know them?"

"No, but our friend Edward Wharton did," Mary answered. "He brought them north originally, and he witnessed their hanging at Boston. They are martyrs known by all Friends in the Society."

"Godly men they were, I warrant. I'd sooner listen to them than John Reyner. He puts me to sleep and lines his pockets with our coin. Frances and I welcome the Friends. But mark my words, the minister shall stop your meetings and have you arrested soon enough," Emery warned.

"We are counting on it," Mary answered.

# *Chapter 46*

## RICHARD WALDERNE *A NEW LAW*

1658 Boston, Massachusetts Bay Colony and the Penacook Region

After Tomothy's funeral Beth took to her bed. Neither Richard's threats nor Annie's cajoling moved her, but Eliza was present and succeeded where all others failed. In half an hour the girl was up, and her grandmother helped her pack. Beth left with the Scammons to spend the summer in Portsmouth.

"'Tis best if she is not minded of her brother for a while, poor dear," Eliza said at parting.

Richard Walderne dealt with the loss of his son stoically in public. In private his ardor was fueled by desperation. His own sire had fathered nine boys out of eleven children, and Richard measured his virility against this high standard. He had but two sons now and was fixated on producing more. He applied the same vigor he brought to bear in his business concerns. He was zealous in preparing Annie to conceive more readily, but it felt like a military exercise rather than lovemaking to the young wife. She was not religious, but Annie prayed daily for a boy.

The women of the household were her allies. Missus Cameron and Bridget conferred with the cook, Missus Murphy, pooling their knowledge of tried and true methods to produce a male child. Annie had never consumed so much red meat and schooled herself to eat it rare. The butcher's wife also told the cook that the mother-to-be should keep a coin in her mouth while her husband "did his business," but after nearly swallowing it, Annie abandoned that method. It was not without benefit, however, for when the copper slipped to the back of her mouth, she sat bolt upright. With a mighty cough it flew out, hitting her husband on his bare chest. Richard was overcome with laughter—the first time since Tim's death. Thereafter his sarcastic humor resurfaced again.

Annie welcomed the familiar signs of pregnancy. It had been six years since little Anne was born; however, her relief was not entirely personal—the family needed a positive event. Tim's death had shocked and saddened them all, and they yet labored under its shadow. She hoped a new baby would serve as an antidote for the gloom that pervaded the house on Tremont Row.

Soon after Annie's good news, Richard received a summons from Edward Rawson, who was now Secretary to the Great and General Court. His friend had the Governor's ear, and his message communicated urgency, if not the reason for it. Edward's townhouse was on Rawson's Lane, which also bordered the Common. The October morning was cool, and Richard welcomed the autumn tang after the heat of summer. He crossed the greensward, unconsciously vigilant for the byproducts of the livestock pastured there, and considered the issues his friend might wish to discuss.

Boston was experiencing unparalleled controversy, barring the crisis over the Hutchinson woman in '37. Endicott was plagued by Quakers intentionally breaking the laws he had created to stop the spread of their heresies—particularly banishment. The Governor's punishments failed to staunch the flow of vagabonds and so-called missionaries converging on Boston to protest the brutalities. An increasing number of people supported them, and alarmingly, public opinion was turning in the Quakers' favor. Perhaps the governor had come up with a new strategy to combat them.

A servant girl answered the door and showed Captain Walderne to the study. Edward rose from his desk to greet him.

"Well met, and welcome, Richard," he said, shaking hands warmly. "Rachel tells me that Annie is with child. Congratulations. She is well, I trust?"

"My thanks, Edward," Walderne responded. "'Tis a blessing, and she fares well, indeed."

"Will you take some refreshment?"

"My thanks, but no. I have recently broken my fast," Richard replied, masking his impatience with the niceties.

The two men sat in armchairs before the hearth, and Edward got down to business.

"I would speak with you concerning this Quaker business. All efforts to expel them from the colony come to naught. 'Tis a conundrum. They return to protest the laws, but there would be no need for the laws, if they did not return. They are too thick to care for their own well-being and force us to increase the severity of the punishments. What choice have we?"

He rose and paced to the window, gazing out on the sunlit Common. Richard knew all this, but he stayed silent, waiting for his friend to come to the point.

"'Twas the Brend man that turned folk against us," Rawson fumed. "He nearly sparked a riot!"

"I do recall it," Richard said. "That physician Clarke set it off, publicly announcing the man was like to die. The mob wanted the warder's blood, but the prisoner refused to work! Michaelson was merely doing his job."

Edward turned. "Verily! And Endicott only made to bring charges against the man to placate public opinion temporarily. He never intended to prosecute Michaelson," he responded then smiled. "Reverend Norton was not so constrained in the warder's defense, though, was he? 'William Brend has beaten the gospel black and blue,' says he, 'so 'tis only just that he be beaten black and blue himself.'"

Both men chuckled, recalling the clergyman's gall when facing the angry crowd outside the prison.

Rawson returned to his chair and became grave. "Richard, I must tell you what is afoot. Norton and Wilson have rallied the clergy since the Brend affair. They are pressing for the death penalty for a third offense."

Richard was surprised but covered it with a sage nod. Here was the crux of the matter—a law of execution against Quakers who ignored their sentence of banishment a third time.

"The ministers clamor for blood on one side, while public opinion rails against it on the other," Edward went on. "The Governor disdains public opinion, Praise God, but others are cowed by it." He looked at Richard keenly. "Have you heard about the letters?"

"To what letters do you refer?" his friend asked. Normally Richard would not admit ignorance, preferring to appear knowledgeable, but he was curious, and Edward was privy to information from Endicott, being Secretary of the Court.

"The governors of several other colonies wrote to John, pleading for clemency. They would dissuade him from this course. Two even offered to take the miscreants into custody, rather than see them hang."

Richard's mind reeled at this news. It was a blow that other colonial governors, as well as the common public, disapproved. "What was Endicott's response?" he asked.

Edward snorted derisively. "He spurned them out of hand—called them cowards. He fears only the loss of the Bay Colony's charter, should the monarchy be reinstalled. My sources in England say that may be sooner than we think. Cromwell is ill."

"Then we must act speedily," Richard said, "before we have a papist monarch to deal with."

Rawson nodded. "Endicott is pressing for a vote forthwith."

Richard straightened. He understood his friend's urgency now. "A special session?" he asked.

"The notice to convene shall go out this day," Edward answered. "We meet next week."

"Certes the Assistants shall approve it on the advice of the clergy. I shall vote for it gladly," Richard asserted.

Rawson smiled and clapped his shoulder. "I knew you would, my friend. 'Tis the Deputies that worry me, as well as a few of the assistants. They argue 'tis contrary to the laws of England. We shall need to employ all our wiles to persuade them otherwise."

Before 1658 the Great and General Court of Boston did not have a particular meeting place, although the need of one was widely discussed. The cost of constructing a suitable edifice was staggering. No individual Bostonian could manage it, and none was inclined to coordinate funding for such a mammoth project. Then Captain Robert Keayne stipulated a bequest of £300 sterling toward the construction of a town-house in his will. Keayne was a prosperous merchant and respected citizen, who was instrumental in forming the Ancient and Honorable Artillery Company and acted as its first commander. His prosperity made him benevolent toward the city that had engendered his wealth. He dreamed of a building that would grace the colonial capital and serve all of its citizens.

Keayne's bequest encouraged the business community to rise to the challenge. Merchants, artisans, and professionals donated goods and services. The total value was a princely £500 in addition to Keayne's provision. At a town meeting in March of 1657, the freemen voted to begin construction. Edward Hutchinson and John Hull were appointed to hire workers and oversee the construction.

It was an ambitious plan. The building was 66 feet long by 36 feet wide, supported by twenty-one columns, allowing for a covered but open market space on the ground level. Above were several meeting rooms, storage for the Honorable Artillery Company's weapons, and a library—the city's first for the public. The largest meeting room was designated for the General Court.

On October 20, 1658 the Great and General Court of Boston convened in the new Town-House to vote on the proposed death sentence for Quakers returning a third time after banishment. Richard Walderne, Edward Rawson, Deputy Governor Bellingham, and other stout Puritans had lobbied relentlessly in favor of the law, but in the end, only two of the forty-eight Deputies consented to change their vote in favor of it. The deciding factor was Fate. A magistrate who disapproved of the law was ill and could not attend. It passed by a majority of one.

Following this political victory and the confirmation of Annie's pregnancy, Richard rode up to Cocheco. He felt released. It was early November and brisk. Wood smoke rose from multiple chimneys, perfuming the air around the towns he passed. Warm in his greatcoat and muffler, Richard relished the day's ride. He alternately slowed his mount to a walk and gave the mare her head, enjoying her eagerness to run in the bracing weather. It was good to be out of the city. The trees were stripped of their autumnal finery, but it was best to judge the lay of the land, when foliage did not impede the view.

Richard was contemplating the purchase of a piece of land in the Penacook region. The Merrimack was a major route for the transport of pelts from the North Country where game was still plentiful. He planned another trading post on the east bank. The one at Cocheco was turning a fine profit; why not have another? The tribes from the northern interior used the Merrimack more than the Piscataqua now, as there were no mills to impede their progress—yet. He offered his factor, Peter Coffin, a partnership in the new venture. Paul could manage things at Cocheco for the lad was eighteen now, a full adult. He learned quickly and had proved himself capable, which gratified his sire.

In addition Richard had laid ground for a future shipping concern involving his timber and Thomas Lake's ships. As he loped along the King's Road, his old confidence swelled. The prospect of another son, the narrow victory at the General Court, the challenge of the new business with Lake, and the purchase of land for another trading post—all energized him. He was forty-four but felt younger. Richard rode north, leaving his melancholia behind.

Two days later he left Cocheco with Paul and Peter Coffin to determine the site for a trading post on the Merrimack. He wanted his son to witness the negotiations. They left early and reached the east bank of the river by noon.

They would meet with the aging *sôgmô Williani* at his winter camp on an island in the river. A delegation of four solemn-faced Indians ferried them across, leaving a boy to watch their mounts. Both Richard and Peter spoke enough Penacook for trade, but they did not need to struggle with the language. The old chief greeted them in their own tongue, and they settled in his warm, smoky lodge around the fire pit.

Formalities observed, Coffin produced a map, and they spent some time negotiating the boundaries.

"What will you do with this land?" the chief asked.

"I shall build a trading post around here," Richard answered, indicating an area on the map.

"No town? No mills? No fences?" The old man raised his eyebrows.

"A simple business establishment to trade with your people for pelts. 'Twill benefit all."

*Williani* grunted. The changes the English wrought rarely benefited his tribe.

"What will you trade?" the *sôgmô* pressed. He was well aware of the threat liquor posed. It made men foolish and easy prey to greedy colonists. Paired with weapons, it could mean disaster.

"Iron tools, pots, clothing—the usual," the captain said casually.

He knew why the old man was probing. Selling spirits to the natives was now against the law, but the new trucking post would be far from any town or constable. Even if it was discovered, Richard knew all the officials. A share of the prodigious profits would encourage them to look the other way. It was an advantage he did not intend to lose. Trading with inebriated Indians had accrued to his benefit at Cocheco for years. The thought made him smile.

*Williani* was regarding him intently. Richard's smile faded, and his scalp prickled. It felt as if the old man read his thoughts, but that was impossible.

The old chief knew the *Iglismônak* captain was dissembling. The man's mouth curved in a smile, but his eyes spoke of avarice. The *sôgmô* did not trust him, but the People depended on trade with the English now, and the coin for the land would provide security in his old age. Once he had held sway over the entire region; now he feared dying a beggar, at the mercy of the colonial magistrates, such as this one.

Paul looked from face to face. He felt something pass between his father and the chief, but he was unsure what. He looked at Coffin, but Peter's attention was riveted on his employer. Their escort sat with them but did not deign to look at him, gazing impassively over his head.

"The Penacook shall continue to fish and hunt on this land you wish to purchase," the old chief stated at length, holding the captain's gaze.

"Certes," Richard agreed, silently adding, "Until time and the English drive you heathens away." The old man's keen look was disturbing, and it made him irritable.

"What is your price?" he asked finally, when he could stand the silent scrutiny no longer.

"What do you offer?" the *sôgmô* returned.

Richard realized the old man was no fool and was grudgingly impressed. *Williani* was apparently subtle enough not to limit his options by naming an amount.

"There is no urgency," Richard said with studied insouciance. "We need not determine that at present. I shall have the deed drawn up based on the boundaries we agreed upon. Shall we meet again, say, in two weeks?"

*Williani* nodded once then closed his eyes. Their escort stood. It was a dismissal, and they left.

*Tolotti* had been listening and now materialized from the shadows at the back of the lodge. She carried a half-finished basket of sweet fern and sat beside her brother.

"You did not offer the pipe," she observed, after a moment at her work.

"I do not smoke with men whose eyes are greedy," *Williani* said.

# *Chapter 47*

## RICHARD WALDERNE AND MARY AND ALICE *MEETINGS*

January, 1662 Dover Neck, Massachusetts Bay Colony

In the days leading up to the meeting at Emery's inn, Mary and Allie frequented the common room, talking with the people who came in. Walter visited daily, but they declined to go to his home not wishing him to be fined. The Dover Friends were jubilant. Word soon spread that the missionaries were back and would hold a meeting in Emery's common room on Sunday after services at the First Church; however, the Friends were not alone in responding to the news.

Elder Nutter sent word summoning the others to his home again. Richard arrived last, as he came from Cocheco. The January afternoon was gloomy and bitterly cold. Clouds hid the sun and spat snow intermittently, heavy with the threat of more to come.

Richard gave his damp cloak, gloves, and hat to the servant girl at the door. He was put out at leaving his warm trading post upriver, but the threat the women posed must be eliminated. They were back, just as he had anticipated. It was time to finalize the plan.

The captain sipped his tea, wrapping chilled fingers around the warm cup, and addressed Elder Nutter at the head of the table.

What news?" he asked without preamble. He wanted this done so he could return to Cocheco before the weather worsened.

"As I informed you in the message," the big man said heavily, "two of the three Quakers were seen at Emery's ordinary. One of my shipwrights talked with them. Word has it they plan a meeting Sabbath next, following the afternoon service at First Church."

"Which two?" the magistrate asked, keeping his tone bland.

"The little, crooked one is not with them," Nutter answered.

She was back. Walderne turned to John and Thomas Roberts, his face a mask of calm. "You shall arrest them at this 'meeting' then," he directed.

Thomas nodded, but John looked confused. "Do we not wish to avoid notice?" he asked.

"Their arrest must be public, so all present shall know the law cannot be flaunted in Dover," the magistrate explained, as to a child. "No one will know where you take them. If any press you, say you are removing them from the colony, which, verily, you are."

Thomas Canney had been making mental calculations and now spoke hesitantly.

"The tide is against us that time of day, Captain Walderne," he ventured.

Richard sighed. "Then you must wait until it turns," he said with exaggerated patience.

"We cannot put out in the dark so t'would be mid-morning the next day," Canney said.

"But all shall know we take them to the gaol, and their cronies will follow us there. How do we deal with that?" John asked nervously.

"Do not take them to the gaol," Walderne said blandly.

"But where else can we confine them overnight?" John's voice rose. He had not realized they would not use the jail. Complications made him anxious.

There was a weighty silence as they pondered.

"I have a root cellar," Canney said, tentatively. "The door bars from the outside, and Jane keeps it locked against filchers. Would that serve?"

"Admirably," the magistrate answered with a nod.

"What of your wife, Canney? Can we trust her not to speak of this?" Nutter asked.

The question startled Thomas, as Jane worried him. He doubted she would approve, and if she voiced her objections, these men would know he lacked control over his own wife.

"'Twill be dark. If we take them directly to the root cellar, she will not see—" he began.

"Unless she has need of some potatoes," Thomas Roberts interrupted, chuckling. They all glared at him, and he ducked his head.

Canney was not amused. "I will keep her quiet," he growled and prayed he could.

"But how do we feed them without alerting her to the situation?" John asked.

"Do not feed them," Walderne replied. "They shall not be hungry long."

"What if they freeze during the night?" John persisted. He was intensely uncomfortable with this plan. Too many things could go wrong, and who would be called on it? He and Thomas. The magistrate, the reverend—even his father-in-law—would deny any knowledge of the plan, he was sure.

"Then your work shall be done for you," the magistrate said, narrowing his eyes. The constable was prevaricating. They could afford no loose links in this chain.

John squirmed under the captain's cold stare. "I am only trying to anticipate any difficulties, so as not to be taken by surprise," he said defensively.

"Root cellars do not freeze," his brother grinned. "That is why folk store their food there. Everyone knows that, Johnny!"

"Do not call me that!" John hissed, infuriated by this reference to his childhood name.

"Gentlemen." Walderne's tone was sarcastic, as he reclaimed their attention. "Let us concentrate on the matter at hand. You arrest them at the ordinary and take them to Canney's root cellar. How shall you transport them?"

"By sledge or sleigh, I warrant," Reyner assumed.

"No," said the magistrate. They all looked at him surprised. "They are too easy to follow and would confine you to the lane. Remember, no one must know where you take them."

"How then?" Nutter asked, perplexed.

"By horse?" John asked alarmed, remembering their former struggle.

"Afoot," Walderne stated, "but not by High Street. You must avoid the road and go through the fields. Approach Canney's from the back."

"But 'tis near a mile!" John protested, "The ground is uneven and deep in snow!"

The magistrate frowned and spoke severely. "Secrecy is of the essence, Constable. You cannot march them up High Street to Canney's for all to see. Mark you, there can be no witnesses. If you require more assistance, you shall have it."

"They go limp as rags, once hands are put upon them," the elder warned.

"They must be dragged then, but they are women," Walderne said dismissively. "Two men for each Quaker should suffice—unless you are not strong enough?" He raised an eyebrow.

John colored. "I only say 'tis a hard way in the dark with snow to the knee and stumps and such." He was on the defensive again.

The magistrate snorted. "Then 'twill be a rough passage for them, will it not? If they refuse to walk, they bring it upon themselves. 'Twill serve to subdue their rebellious spirits." The thought, made him smile. He turned to Canney. "Your son Joseph is a strapping lad. Can you trust him to assist in this, Canney?"

"What Joe? Uh, certes," Thomas answered, hoping this was true, "but—" he broke off.

"Go on, man," Walderne prompted impatiently.

"His, um, his discretion would be assured, if there were some, uh, recompense involved," he said and braced for a rebuke.

Walderne stared at him then sighed. "I reckon that could be arranged," he agreed reluctantly.

"I would accompany the constables at the arrest," Nutter said, straightening his broad shoulders. The others stared at him. "We cannot have another mishap," Hatevil stated. "I would see this over and properly done this time."

"That is an excellent idea," Reverend Reyner said, gazing dolefully at John Roberts, who ignored the implied rebuke.

Walderne nodded. "So be it, Hatevil."

John was both relieved and uneasy that his father-in-law would accompany them.

The captain went on. "Then in the morn, when the tide is favorable," a nod to Canney, "you shall remove them from the root cellar and take them out on the river. There are no houses between the shore and Canney's place. You have only to get across River Road unremarked," the magistrate emphasized, looking from face to face.

"What if they make noise or cry for help?" John asked, still uneasy. Now it was coming down to it, he was unsure he could throw women—even unnatural ones—overboard and watch them drown. Most like the frigid water would do for them first, he realized, suppressing a shudder. The magistrate was regarding him keenly, and John wished he could take back his question. He sipped his tea. It had gone cold.

"Gag them," Walderne answered coldly.

Now Father Nutter was regarding John skeptically too. "We do God's work here, John," he stated. "These women are aberrations of their sex—criminals and deluded heretics. They are nothing like our goodwives, whom we protect by this course."

John met his eyes and nodded. There was no option but to believe him.

On the afternoon of the meeting, Anthony, Frances, and Walter helped the missionaries set up the common room. People began to arrive at dusk. Many of the Dover Friends were present, including the Robertses and Nutes. Several families, the Pitmans among them, came from Oyster River, where Reyner was not popular. Their beloved Reverend Fletcher had returned to England two years prior. John Reyner was a poor substitute, in their opinion, and they balked at paying fifty pounds a year for his stipend. Reyner retaliated by refusing to make the trip upriver for their spiritual edification, forcing them to attend church at Dover or be fined. The Friends were a welcome alternative.

Walter had attempted to dissuade the missionaries several times. They would be at the mercy of men who had no regard for their lives, and it could only end badly for them, but Mary was set on a public arrest. The apothecary attended out of concern for his friends. He would witness the arrest, bring food and blankets to the gaol, and provide medical attention after they were flogged, as he was sure they would be.

Some forty folk gathered in the common room. Benches and chairs faced each other in two groups, one side for men, the other for women and children. There were few empty seats. Mary and Allie sat together in the front row of the women's section. After the opening hymn, Mary remained standing and spoke.

"Welcome, dear Friends. We gather this day to join in silent worship. Verily, we have no need of a minister, for our Lord Jesus Christ tells us, 'If ye continue in my word, then are ye my disciples indeed; And ye shall know the truth, and the truth shall make you free.' Let us open our hearts to that truth. If any be moved by the Holy Spirit to speak, please do."

Lamps and candles reflected from the windows as the winter darkness deepened outside. The gathering settled into silence as a weary traveler settles into a soft bed. Peace was the counterpane, and it covered them all. The moments slid past soundlessly, but for the crackling fire.

The door burst open, shattering the silence. Heads rose at the abrupt noise and rush of cold air. Folk were wrenched from contemplation. Mary and Allie kept their heads bowed, eyes closed. The intrusion was no surprise to them.

Four cloaked men strode down the center aisle, faces concealed by mufflers and hats pulled low. A fifth closed the door and stood in front of it. The men moved purposefully. Their boots shook the floorboards, and people flinched as they strode by. A child began to cry. The invasion so contrasted with the warmth and peace of the meeting that the worshippers were stunned.

As the men seized the missionaries by their arms, the cloaked figure at the door pulled his muffler aside and spoke.

"Alice Ambrose and Mary Tomkins, you are under arrest by authority of the Massachusetts Bay Colony. You are banished, yet here you be, harassing the good citizens of Dover yet again in violation of the sentence put upon you. In the name of the law, you shall be removed from this colony once and for all."

It was Hatevil Nutter, elder of Dover's First Church. Everyone knew him. Several of the worshippers were in his employ and hid their faces, afraid to be recognized. Walter Barefoote was the first to react for he had not been in contemplation nor was he surprised by the intrusion. He stood.

"Mister Nutter!" all heads turned to the apothecary. "When will their sentencing take place?"

There were murmurs of assent, but Nutter's response silenced them.

"They have been sentenced and eluded the just punishment put upon them. That mishap must be corrected," he growled.

He held the door wide, as the men approached, dragging the women by their arms. The missionaries were limp and did not resist. Like lambs to the slaughter, Walter thought despairing.

Stop, man!" he called, striding after them "For the love of God, allow us to cover them! They shall freeze without cloaks!"

The missionaries' things were upstairs in their room, but several Friends offered their own cloaks. Thomas Roberts and Anthony Emery helped Walter drape them around the women, while the enforcers paused impatiently.

"I weep to think mine own sons are party to this!" the elder Roberts lamented with a baleful look at John and Thomas. He secured a cloak around Allie's shoulders then straightened. "John, Tommy, these are godly women! Ye do great wrong here!"

"They flaunt the law, Father!" young Tom exclaimed.

"So do you by supporting them!" John added hotly, stung by his parent's public rebuke.

Nutter still held the door open and gestured for the constables to make haste, but Anthony stalled their departure, blocking the way as he addressed the elder.

"This is a publick house, Mister Nutter. All are free to meet here!" he insisted stoutly.

The big man glowered down at the innkeeper, but Anthony did not quale.

"Do you stand against the law of the First Church?" Nutter said ominously.

"'Tis not a law worth honoring, if it forces folk to deny their beliefs," Emery shot back.

"My boys, I beg you! Will you not desist from this brutal course?" their father pleaded.

"Enough, Thomas Roberts!" Nutter bellowed, rounding on him. Children whimpered into their mothers' skirts. "Your sons are righteous and uphold the law! They are not at fault here! Carry on, Constables!"

The men dragged the inert missionaries out into the cold. It was full dark now. Elder Nutter took the lead with a storm lantern he had left on the porch. The five men moved at speed across the road and disappeared behind Job Clement's barn. Walter, Anthony, and Thomas Roberts watched them go, confused. It was open field back there, some of it recently cleared. There was no conveyance or horses waiting in the road. Others crowded behind them on the porch.

"Where are they taking them?" the apothecary wondered aloud.

"And why are they afoot?" Anthony added.

"I like it not. We must follow," Walter said, ducking back inside for his own gear.

"I shall accompany you," the innkeeper said, following. "Frances! Fetch two lanterns! We shall see nothing without them," he added, shrugging into his greatcoat.

Others offered assistance, but Walter deferred, explaining briefly that it was best they be undetected, and to that end, two were better than a crowd.

"Go to your homes. We shall learn what we can!" he said to the concerned Friends, as Frances put a lighted lantern in his hand.

Thomas Roberts was distraught. He stood on the porch, watching as Nutter's lantern appeared briefly then disappeared again behind the Tibbetts place. They were headed north. His wife and daughter clung to his arms, shivering. Silent tears slid down the older woman's cheeks.

"Oh woe that I was ever a father to such children!" the old pioneer lamented.

Walter had no time to comfort them. He pushed through the crowd on the porch with Anthony close behind. They crossed High Street and found the distinctive tracks left by the missionaries' feet. Lanterns aloft, the two men plunged into the deep snow and hastened after the figures swallowed by the dark contours of the land. The apothecary had expected the arrest, but this was bizarre. He feared for his friends. Walter prayed that he and Anthony could prevent this night playing out to a bitter end.

# *Chapter 48*

## MARY AND ALICE *A GREAT STORM*

January, 1662 Dover Neck, Massachusetts Bay Colony

Pain. Cold. A strong odor, familiar somehow. Darkness so complete she was not sure her eyes were open. She was lying on her back. She blinked then raised a hand to touch her lids. Pain flared at the movement. The floor was damp, packed dirt. Where was she? Where was Allie?

"Allie?"

Her voice was an unfamiliar croak. Her tongue felt thick and her mouth was dry. Such thirst. She rolled over carefully onto her elbows, wincing. Everything hurt. The men had pulled them swiftly and carelessly, forging through unpacked snow, heedless of the rocks and brush underneath. Her skirt and cloak were ripped and her dress was damp to the armpits, chilling her. She must have fainted, as she did not remember arriving here, wherever "here" was. Something solid bumped her left side, when she turned over. Gritting her teeth against the pain, Mary got to her hands and knees.

"Allie? Art thou here, dearest?" Her voice was stronger, but it still sounded flat. Not a large space then. She reached out cautiously, exploring with her hands. Cold and aching as she was, her concern was all for Allie. Separation was worse than any physical pain.

"Allie, I beg thee!" Her voice choked on a sob. "Please answer, if thou art able!"

Silence. Mary fought rising panic. Was she alone? Was Allie—no! She would not think it. She forced herself to breathe deeply and be calm. It was a barrel on her left. She recognized the shape and feel now. It did not rock, when she bumped it, so it must be full. She realized she was in a root cellar—that familiar smell. She used the barrel as a reference point and positioned her feet against it. The darkness was absolute.

Mary swept her arms before her and inched forward on her knees. A groan came from behind, to the right. She turned blindly toward the sound, her relief so profound it provoked a sob.

"Allie! I am here. Do not move!" Mary's fingers scrabbled through empty air then connected with a wet boot.

"Oh, Allie dearest, Praise God! How farest thou?"

Mary felt her friend's damp clothing and moved her hands carefully upward. She gently explored her friend's face and hair for bleeding and was relieved to find no sticky wetness. Allie's cap was gone. Mary pulled Allie's head and shoulders onto her lap, ignoring the pain it caused them both. She kissed her cheek and stroked the hair from her face. Allie stirred and moaned then coughed and grasped Mary's arm.

"Where am I?" she asked weakly. "Oh! Ow!" she continued, as she made to sit.

"Stay still! Lie still a moment, dearest, whilst we find thy wounds," Mary cautioned. "Where does it pain thee most?"

"What is this place? It stinks, and I can't see a bloody thing!" Allie proclaimed, her voice gaining strength with each word. She moved her head as if trying to look about.

Mary was relieved at this sign of spirit. "I think 'tis a root cellar," she answered, gently pressing her friend's ribs. "Does it pain thee here?"

"Ouch! Yes! Uh, just bruised, I reckon. I can breathe, at least. My shoulders and legs hurt most. They about pulled my arms off! But what of thee, Mimi?" Allie asked, groping for Mary's face and laying her hand on her friend's cheek.

"I hurt all over, and 'tis cold," Mary answered her teeth chattering, "But everything seems to work. Dost thou recall coming here?"

"No," her friend said after a pause. "They meant to punish us with that rough treatment, I reckon. They seemed to seek out the rocks and stumps. I think I fainted before we reached this place."

"Why are we not in the gaol?" Mary asked. Allie had no answer for that, or at least, no answer she wished to contemplate.

They huddled close, spooning back to front and laboriously switching when their exposed sides got too chilled. There was comfort in each other's warmth and presence. Mary began to hum, and soon they were singing softly in the chill dark. Hours later the men found them thus, when they unlocked the door at mid-morning.

Clouds had massed overnight and hid the sun, but even this dull light was blinding after hours in total darkness. The women recoiled, squinting. The sight of them bedraggled and shivering in their torn, damp clothes, gave John pause. Their singing was sweet; the men had heard it through the door. With mussed hair and eyes blinking in the sudden light, they looked like two children, clinging to each other on the dirt floor. Then the constable recalled his father-in-law behind him, and his shame became anger.

"On your feet!" he snarled. "We shall soon be rid of you once and for all."

His words filled Mary with foreboding. She squinted up at him, tightening her hold on Allie, and tried twice before she could speak. "Wh-what is your intent?" she asked, trying to keep her voice steady through the shivering. She feared the answer.

"You should not have returned to Dover," Nutter admonished portentously.

"Wh-why are w-we not in the g-gaol?" Mary croaked. Her heart was pounding.

The elder sniffed. "So you might seduce another man of influence with your female wiles and escape justice again? We shall not be swayed, and you will trouble us no more."

Mary gripped Allie harder, as she parsed his meaning. "Ye cannot act outside the law—"

"We *are* the law," he interrupted. "We are charged by the authorities of this town to deal with you. Our actions are sanctioned by the magistrate and the Almighty."

"Enough talk, Father Nutter," John urged, motioning for his brother to help him with the tall one. Best get this over and done. "If you refuse to come of your own accord, we shall treat with you as before," he warned, standing over them.

"Are we to g-go to our deaths willingly?" Mary asked appalled.

Thomas Canney stepped forward, grinning. "Walk or we drag you." He slapped his rag-bound hands together and rubbed them as if relishing the thought.

Panic seized her. These men verily meant to kill them. The women clung to each other. "No!" she cried. "This is not—"

Her protests were abruptly cut off, as Canney and Joseph grabbed her arms, separating the women easily. The Roberts brothers seized Allie. The women were dragged outside into the snow. The flare of pain at the rough treatment robbed them of breath and their parched throats were mute. They had had neither food nor drink for twenty hours. Crying out was beyond them. Mary was face up. This time her recently healed back would receive the abuse. Elder Nutter shut and locked the root cellar door.

Jane Canney knew her husband was up to something. His boy, Joseph, was in on it as well. They had gone out yesterday afternoon and did not return until after dark. Their boots and britches were wet to the knee, as though they had waded through snow. Contrary to custom, her husband did not smell of drink, though he soon corrected that. Joe went to his bed in the loft immediately after supper, another irregularity. When Jane asked what they had been doing, Thomas said they had cleared snow off the landing and the skiff.

"What? Y'are going fishing tomorrow in this cold?" she asked amazed.

"What of it?" he said, rounding on her with uncharacteristic vehemence. "Fetch my supper, woman! And more rum."

Something in his face stopped her customary retort. There was a nasty gleam in his eye, as though daring her to cross him. Thomas was weak; Thomas was lazy; Thomas loved his cups, but he had never scared her. It was unsettling. Something or someone was giving him a dangerous confidence.

The next morning as they broke their fast, there was a knock at the door. Jane rose to see who it was, but Thomas pushed her aside and answered it himself. Constable John Roberts was there with his brother and father-in-law. She thought they had come to arrest him. Elder Nutter never visited their house, and it was clearly not a social occasion, as the men made no move to come in. They had come to fetch him, for what reason she could not imagine. Her husband did not explain. He brushed off her questions, as he donned his gear, and hurried outside with Joseph at his heels.

"Tend to your chores, woman," he said gruffly and slammed the door.

She watched them from the window and was perplexed when they did not make for High Street. They went around to the back of the house. What could they want there? She hurried to the window in the spare room and peered through the crack between the shutters. The five men talked for a bit, looked around then went to the root cellar, unlocking the door. Four of them disappeared inside, while the elder stood in the doorway. The goodwife waited, mystified.

Jane clapped a hand to her racing heart. Through the wavy glass she saw the men drag two women out into the snow by their arms. What mischief was this? Women secreted in her root cellar! Had they been there all night? The men moved at a fast clip away from the house across the field, dragging their burdens toward River Road with Elder Nutter striding behind. Jane was appalled and afraid.

Moments later there was a knock at the door.

It was a scant quarter mile from Canney's house to his landing on Fore River. Once they crossed River Road, the bank sloped steeply. The incline was fraught with boulders, stumps, and other debris. Canney was enjoying himself. It felt good to teach these willful women a lesson—defying the law then refusing to walk! They invited it. Pulling this smaller one downhill was no chore with Joseph helping. Thomas and John were just ahead. The four men moved swiftly on the downhill cant, dragging the Quakers like two sacks of seed corn. The woman made no sound, but Thomas figured she could not. The impact of her body against stumps and rocks was satisfying. Furthermore it was sanctioned, and he was in control. Thomas almost laughed aloud. This was fine sport.

Mary was terrified. This was no ordinary arrest—no gaol, no stocks, no public flogging. These men meant to kill them in secret. It seemed planned in advance. They were hurtling downhill through unbroken snow. Each blow to shoulders, back, hips, and legs was excruciating, and she could not see what was coming. She tried to summon strength from the inner light but could not focus. She struggled to pray for deliverance, for some intercession from the Almighty, but pain and fear commandeered all thought. Then the back of her head struck a rock, and Mary lost consciousness.

The skiff was at Canney's makeshift landing. A rickety ramp extended from the bank to a small pier. The craft was secured bow and stern to iron rings with enough rope to allow the craft to rise or sink with the tide. The skiff was twelve feet long with three rough planks for seats and a single set of oarlocks. Nutter would push them off and wait ashore. The tide was going out and would speed their passage downriver. Coming back would take more effort, but then, the skiff would be carrying a lighter load, John reckoned.

The Roberts brothers reached the ramp first. A sharp wind gusted from the northeast, biting at their faces, and the men ducked their heads against it. The river was a pitted, gunmetal gray broken by whitecaps. A half-hearted attempt had been made to clear the snow from ramp and pier, John noted. He did not realize that the ever-present moisture of the seacoast had frozen overnight, coating the residue with a thin layer of ice.

The Roberts brothers started down the ramp, intent on their task. They did not remark the ominous clouds building on the east bank of the river. The thin ice on the ramp broke under their boots, but the constables barely slowed, as they jostled down with Allie between them. Then they reached the pier, where the ice was thicker and treacherous.

Thomas was first to go down. His feet flew out from under him. John followed. Both landed hard, losing their grip on Allie's arms. She slid across the slippery surface face down, carried by the momentum. Her upper body fell into the skiff, pushing it out as far as the lines allowed. Her legs fell into the water between the skiff and the dock.

The shock was so great that at first she could not breathe. She clung to the icy gunwale with her arms, and the boat nearly capsized. The far side lifted out of the water and near side dipped, wetting her to the waist. Only the tension of the bow and stern lines kept the small craft from flipping over on top of her. Freezing water saturated her boots and skirts. Battered, weakened, and handicapped by the weight of her soaked clothing, she was barely able to hang on, let alone pull herself into the rocking skiff.

The brothers swore eloquently, more upset by their fall than by their prisoner's plight. They got to their knees and crawled to the edge of the pier.

"Do you fancy a bath, then?" Thomas jeered.

"Mayhap she shall do for herself, and we need not go out in the skiff at all," John said, hoping it might be true. He looked around to see if anyone was about, watching them. There was no one, but it caused him to notice the approaching front. The east bank of the river was obscured by a massive wall of gray. He clutched his brother's arm and pointed wordlessly. Thomas gaped. John turned to alert the others. The Canneys had just gained the top of the ramp with the elder behind them. With hats pulled low and heads down, they were oblivious.

"Father Nutter!" John called. "Look you!"

The wind gusted mightily, prickling their exposed skin with the first icy needles of the tempest. Nutter looked up, clutching his hat. At first he seemed unable to comprehend what he was seeing. The storm filled the sky and approached visibly. A sibilant hiss, increasing in volume, filled the air. John realized it was sleet smiting the river. It would soon be upon them in full force.

"Sweet Christ! A tempest!" Canney's voice was shrill, his words garbled by wind. "Get back! Get back to the house before we cannot see!"

He and Joseph turned awkwardly with their burden, but Nutter blocked their path, mesmerized. John had never seen his father-in-law look so shocked. His habitual composure was shattered, his expression so surprised it looked comical on his grave face.

"Nutter! Mo-ove!" Canney screamed.

His raw panic broke the elder's stupor. Nutter stepped aside, and the Canneys lurched up the bank, hampered by Mary's unconscious body.

John was stunned himself. How had they missed it? The storm had come so quickly! Out of nowhere like the wrath of—. Dread smote him. Might this be the hand of God?

Allie cried out. Her arms were sore, and she shook with exhaustion and cold. When she tried to kick her legs, the water felt thick as jelly. The weight of her wet clothing fought her and was winning. A sob escaped her laboring lungs.

"Help me, Tom! She cannot be found here!" John shouted over the keening wind.

Kneeling on the icy landing, the brothers hauled the skiff closer. They grabbed the woman under the arms and heaved her out with difficulty. Water sloshed across the dock, soaking their pant legs instantly. The brothers jumped to their feet, swearing, grabbed her arms, and dragged the unconscious Quaker up the ramp, slipping on broken ice. Water streamed from the clothes on her limp body.

The others were lost to sight for the wind-whipped snow reduced visibility to mere feet. The men's wet pants soon stiffened, hampering their progress. The missionary was in a faint, yet her body was shaking. He could feel it in the arm he clutched. Had he not feared Father Nutter's censure, he would have dropped her and run for shelter. Dragging her uphill was so much harder than the precipitous way down!

The two men scrambled in panic, as though pursued by wolves. John's labored breathing caused icy snowflakes to tickle his throat, making him cough. He could not feel his legs or feet and had lost all sense of direction. He tried to keep to the tracks they had made on the way down, but they were rapidly filling with snow. The others had abandoned them, and it seemed the brothers struggled up the bank for hours, burdened by the woman's dead weight.

At last the ground levelled off. They crossed the River Road at an awkward lope without bothering to check for witnesses. They would not have been seen in any case, so thick was the driven snow. John's chest hurt and he could hardly breathe by the time Canney's house appeared, an amorphous dark shape in a world gone white. The brothers staggered through the door, dropped the Quaker on the floor, and joined the other men at the hearth, leaving soaked hats, cloaks, mittens, and mufflers in their wake.

Outside the wind howled like a beast denied its prey.

END PART III

# *Part IV*

## SPRING

*The tale is one of an evil time,*
*When souls were fettered and thought was crime,*
*And heresy's whisper above its breath*
*Meant shameful scourging and bonds and death!*

*What marvel, that hunted and sorely tried,*
*Even woman rebuked and prophesied,*
*And soft words rarely answered back*
*The grim persuasion of whip and rack!*

*If her cry from the whipping-post and jail*
*Pierced sharp as the Kenite's driven nail,*
*O woman, at ease in these happier days,*
*Forbear to judge of thy sister's ways!*

*How much thy beautiful life may owe*
*To her faith and courage thou canst not know,*
*Nor how from the paths of thy calm retreat*
*She smoothed the thorns with her bleeding feet.*

—*John Greenleaf Whittier, How the Women Went from Dover*

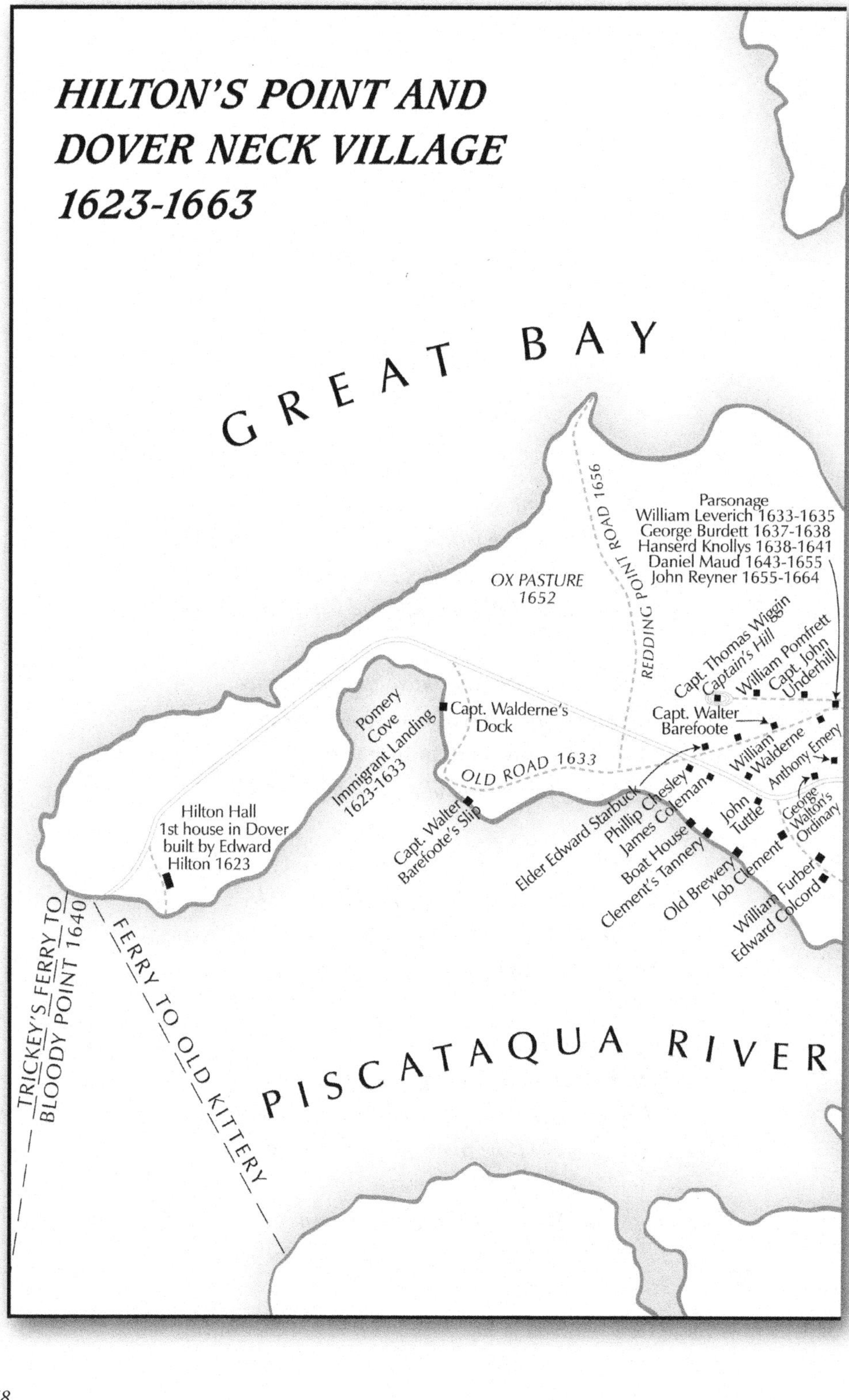
HILTON'S POINT AND
DOVER NECK VILLAGE
1623-1663
GREAT BAY
REDDING POINT ROAD 1656
Parsonage
William Leverich 1633-1635
George Burdett 1637-1638
Hanserd Knollys 1638-1641
Daniel Maud 1643-1655
John Reyner 1655-1664
OX PASTURE
1652
Capt. Thomas Wiggin
Captain's Hill
William Pomfrett
Capt. John
Underhill
Pomery
Cove
Immigrant Landing
1623-1633
Capt. Walderne's
Dock
Capt. Walter
Barefoote
OLD ROAD 1633
William
Walderne
Anthony Emery
Hilton Hall
1st house in Dover
built by Edward
Hilton 1623
Capt. Walter
Barefoote's Slip
Elder Edward Starbuck
Phillip Chesley
James Coleman
Boat House
Clement's Tannery
John
Tuttle
George
Walton's
Ordinary
Old Brewery
Job Clement
William Furber
Edward Colcord
TRICKEY'S FERRY TO
BLOODY POINT 1640
FERRY TO OLD KITTERY
PISCATAQUA RIVER

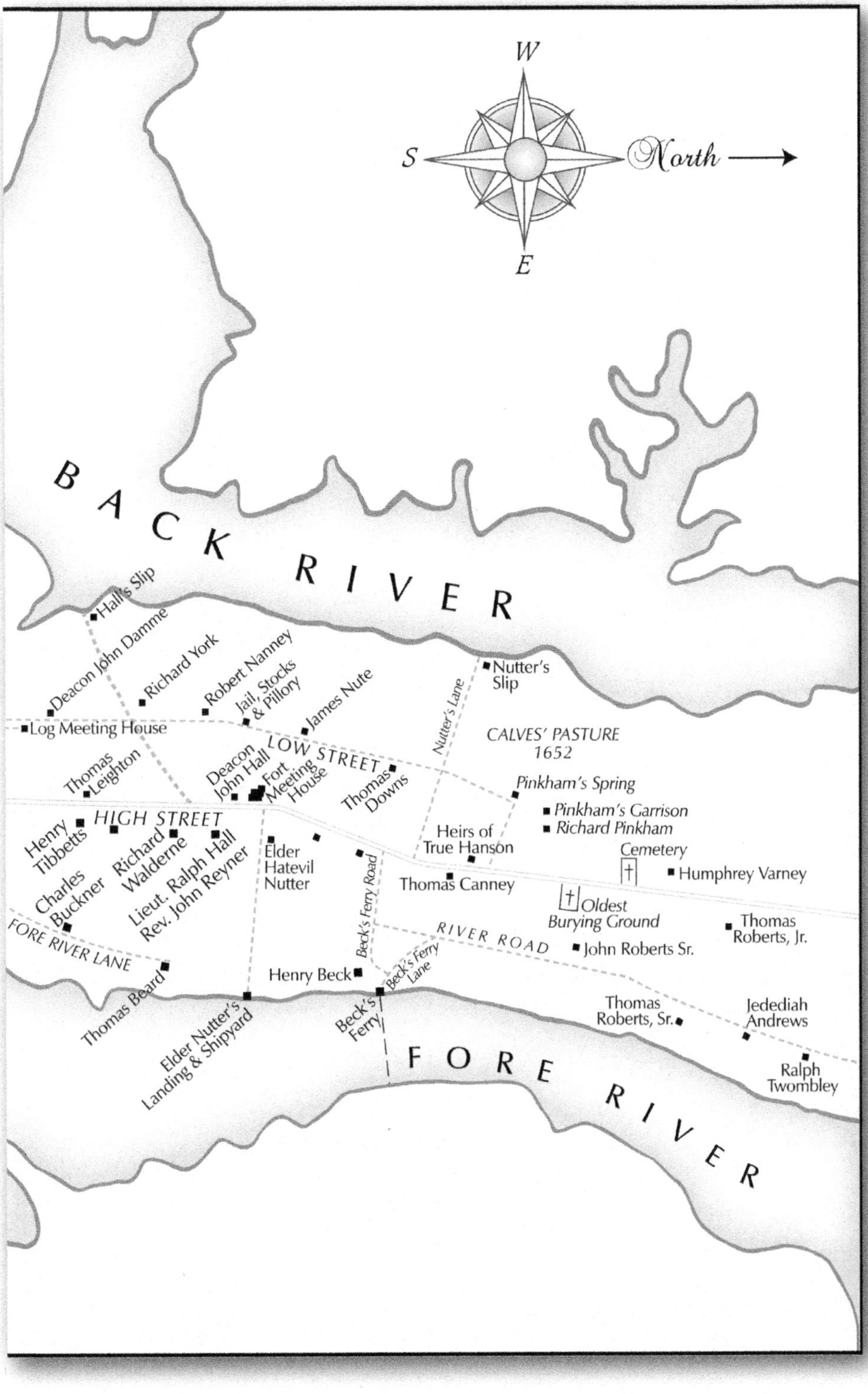
W
S
North
E
BACK RIVER
Hall's Slip
Deacon John Damme
Richard York
Robert Nanney
Jail, Stocks & Pillory
James Nute
Log Meeting House
Nutter's Lane
Nutter's Slip
CALVES' PASTURE 1652
LOW STREET
Thomas Leighton
Deacon John Hall
Fort Meeting House
Thomas Downs
Pinkham's Spring
Pinkham's Garrison
Richard Pinkham
HIGH STREET
Henry Tibbetts
Richard Walderne
Lieut. Ralph Hall
Rev. John Reyner
Charles Buckner
Elder Hatevil Nutter
Beck's Ferry Road
Heirs of True Hanson
Thomas Canney
Cemetery
Humphrey Varney
Oldest Burying Ground
Thomas Roberts, Jr.
FORE RIVER LANE
RIVER ROAD
John Roberts Sr.
Henry Beck
Beck's Ferry Lane
Thomas Beard
Elder Nutter's Landing & Shipyard
Beck's Ferry
Thomas Roberts, Sr.
Jedediah Andrews
Ralph Twombley
FORE RIVER

# *Chapter 49*

## MARY AND ALICE *THE GOODWIFE*

January, 1662 Dover Neck, Massachusetts Bay Colony

Jane Canney was startled by the knock on her door, coming moments after the men left, dragging the women towards the river. Who were they? Why had they been shut up in her root cellar, presumably all night? She suspected whoever was at the door was associated in some way, and she peered cautiously from the window. Dr. Barefoote and Thomas Roberts stood on the stoop. She was confused, unsure if she should fear or welcome their presence, but curiosity won out. Mayhap they knew what was afoot.

"Come in, come in, gentlemen," she urged, opening the door wide.

"Forgive the intrusion, Mistress Canney," the apothecary said, removing his hat.

Mister Roberts nodded, but said nothing, his kind face grim. She knew the constables were his sons and they had fallen out. The whole town knew of it.

"I reckon I can guess why you are come," Jane began, quickly shutting the door on the frigid air. The wind was rising. "D'you know aught of this, Doctor?" she asked, turning to them. "Who were those women in my root cellar?"

"We must be brief," Walter answered. "Your husband may return at any moment."

"A front is moving in," Thomas Roberts explained. "They seem bound for the river, but likely they shall turn back, if their intent is to put out in a boat."

Walter quickly related the events of the day before from the arrest at the Emerys' ordinary to following the tracks and seeing the constables and Elder Nutter leave the Canney's place. Once the men were gone, Walter and Anthony had tried to rescue their friends then and there, but the door of the root cellar was secured with a large screw key padlock, and the key was not in evidence. They had called to the women as loudly as they dared and thumped the thick door, but got no response.

Fearing to attract Canney's notice, there was no choice but to leave the missionaries overnight.

"We prevailed upon your neighbors, the Hansons, this morn. They are sympathetic to our purpose, as Mistress Hanson is a Friend, and she allowed us to watch from their window. We saw the constables and Elder Nutter come to your door. We were hoping you might know their plan. Did your husband say nothing of this?" Walter finished.

"I know less than you," Jane said. "Thomas told me nothing and became feisty when I pressed him last night about where he had been. I feared they were up to no good."

Mister Roberts sighed. "I am glad thou art not complicit in this scheme, Friend Canney," he said, "and we hope the storm shall thwart their plan—whatever it may be. But assuming the men do bring our friends back, how are we to get them from this house?"

There was silence, as they considered the problem.

"I reckon I might help," Jane said slowly. "I have no love of Quakers, mind ye, but these are women. I like it not that my husband is mixed up in this—and dragged young Joe into it as well."

"I am in accord, Friend Canney," Roberts said glumly, "I am sick to think my boys are involved in this nefarious business. We must help the missionaries."

Walter held her eye. "We would be most grateful for your assistance, Mistress Canney. You might well save their lives," he said gravely.

Jane returned his look and nodded. "Then here is my thought. When they come back, the men shall be cold. I know my Thomas will want his toddy—sweet tea and rum with a dash of cider vinegar. I imagine they shall all want some. I shall not spare the rum."

Walter caught her drift and nodded encouragingly. Jane went on.

"After two or three potent ones and the warmth of the fire after the cold, I reckon they shall soon be stuporous. I can tend to your friends then and get them ready to move. When I deem it safe, I shall set a candle at the window, there." She pointed to a window at the left of the front door, facing High Street. "You should see it from Hanson's across the lane. Then you can get them away while the men sleep."

Roberts furrowed his brow. "What shall ye tell them, Friend Canney, when the men discover the prisoners are gone?" he asked concerned.

"They shall find me abed," she answered. "I shall tell them the women left whilst I was asleep, and I did not remark it. I am no warder to guard them."

Walter looked at the older man, and Thomas shrugged.

"I can think of no better plan, Doctor," he admitted reluctantly. "We hesitate to endanger thee, my good woman. 'Tis not foolproof and we are, certes, dealing with fools here, but I can think of no other way."

"We shall await your signal at the Hanson's then," Walter said. "Our deepest thanks, Mistress Canney. God bless your endeavor." Feisty the woman might be, but betimes that was a Godsend, he thought.

As the two gentlemen left, Jane heard the first icy pellets ticking against the shuttered windows at the back of the house, driven by a howling wind. Mister Roberts proved correct, and the tempest was raging by the time her husband and Joseph returned. They staggered in dragging an inert woman between them with the elder on their heels, all of them covered with snow. They dropped her on the floor and made for the hearth, shedding wet gear. The Roberts brothers returned minutes later with the other woman. These last had all got wet somehow, their clothing stiff as boards.

"Well." Jane Canney said, regarding the unconscious captives on her floor, "Look what the cat dragged in."

She hid her concern with sarcasm, but she feared for the women. The smaller one lay on her back unnaturally still. The other lay face down, and water pooled around her unconscious form, as it melted from her clothes. She shivered spasmodically in her faint. It was upsetting to leave them lying there so obviously in need of care, but it fortified her determination to help the poor things, dropped on her kitchen floor like offscourings, as the men scrambled for comfort.

Like most of the modest homes in the colony, the kitchen and parlor was one long room. The central chimney had two hearths, one on each side, and there was a loft above. Thomas had added a room ostensibly as a bed chamber, when they were first married, but it was too cold in winter and became a storage area. The Canneys' bed was in the kitchen to the left of the hearth.

The five men huddled close to the fire on the parlor side out of sight of the kitchen. John and Thomas stripped off their soaked boots, socks, and trousers immediately and stood close to the flames, drying their woolen small clothes. Wisps of steam rose from their legs and the clothing they had draped over stools to dry. Thomas complained vociferously, oblivious to the comical figure he cut, ranting in his state of undress. Jane looked away, stifling a nervous giggle, and busied herself gathering up the sodden outerwear the men had dropped.

"Never mind that," her husband ordered. "We near died out there! Fetch us some toddies, woman!"

Jane straightened and smiled. "Certes, husband, straight away."

Thomas was too distracted to notice her unusual compliance to this curt demand. She had started the mixture heating as soon as Dr. Barefoote and Mister Roberts had left. Now Jane added the entire jug of rum and ladled out five flagons. For once she was grateful that her husband kept the house well stocked with rum. Even Elder Nutter drained his first cup quickly. The men had pulled chairs close to the hearth and were talking urgently, taking no notice of her as she served them.

Young Joe left the group as soon as his cup was drained. He wanted nothing more to do with the scheme, even for coin. The sudden storm seemed divine intervention to his mind. He would risk the wrath of Richard Walderne over the wrath of God any day. He ducked past his stepmother, avoiding eye contact, and escaped to his bed in the loft, though it was just past noon.

The others argued with increasing vehemence about what had happened, what should have happened, and what to do next. Jane was solicitous in refilling their cups. It became apparent that, indeed, they had intended to take the Quakers out in Thomas' skiff and throw them into the river! Only the weather had stopped them. The men assumed that abusing the missionaries was justified, and Jane was appalled to hear them speak so callously, though she kept her face impassive. It dispelled any lingering doubts about helping the women. It seemed the men's greatest concern was Richard Walderne. From their talk she learned it was *his* plan, and they feared the repercussions if they failed—again—to rid Dover of the Quaker scourge as directed.

"What shall we tell him, Father Nutter?" John Roberts asked morosely, as the tenor of their dialogue began to be affected by the rum. An hour had passed, and Jane was refilling their tankards a third time.

"The truth," the Elder responded slowly. "No one could venture out in this and survive."

"That's it then!" Canney sat up. His cheeks and nose were red from windburn and the toddies.

The others looked at him blearily.

"D'you not catch it?" he continued. "If no one can venture out in this storm and survive, then all we need do is take 'em out and leave 'em someplace—somewhere they cannot be found."

John Roberts responded first. "He has the right of it. They are in rough shape as 'tis. Folk would think they wandered out in the storm and got lost. No one would connect us with it, if we take 'em out a ways."

"But what of all those folk at the inn? We were seen with them last," Nutter said gloomily, staring at the steaming liquid Jane poured into his tankard.

John was undaunted. "But they could not prove our part in it," he said, warming to the idea. "We could say they escaped us—that we knew nothing of it."

Young Thomas Roberts was sitting on the floor with his feet nearly in the flames. He was having trouble following the conversation and had seized on "take 'em out."

"How now? Go out of doors in *this*?" he interposed with dismay then belched. The rum seemed to affect him more than the others. His speech was slurred. "Not me! Me brishes (britches) are not yet dry…yet."

He shook his head against the idea, causing him to sway where he sat. When he steadied, Jane topped off his flagon unnoticed and moved on. Thomas looked down, and his eyes widened in surprise upon finding his cup full. He smiled and took another pull.

Nutter turned ponderously in his chair to peer at the window. The blizzard had brought on an early twilight. The wind shrilled, and snow fell so thickly that the Elder saw only a featureless white, but he could discern that it was not dark outside.

"We shall wait for the cover of darkness," he said, sighing and leaning back in his chair.

As Jane added more wood to the fire, a bizarre noise made her turn. Young Roberts lay on the floor, his head pillowed on his arm, snoring. Within another half an hour, all the men dozed.

Jane went to the Quakers. The women had not moved. The taller one first, for she still shook as though in a fit. She must have fallen in the river—or been thrown in. Her clothes were no longer frozen, but she was soaked through. She lay on her stomach, and Jane rolled her about with difficulty, removing her sopping boots and clothing.

As she peeled off the wet smallclothes, the woman's scarred back gave her pause, for she had never seen the effects of flogging, but what was all this? The front of the Quaker's body was rife with bruises—ugly purple marks from the shoulders down. Had the men beaten them? She was outraged that her husband was party to this evidence of abuse.

Goodwife Canney dried the battered body gently. Allie began to revive as Jane wrapped her shuddering body in a quilt. Her lips looked painfully chapped and dry. A cup of tea was in order. She propped the semiconscious missionary against the side of the bed with her feet toward the fire and turned to the smaller one.

She was drier, though not by much. When Jane tried to remove her dust cap, it stuck to the back of the woman's head. The goodwife had to use a wet flannel to soak the area before she could peel it away. Blood was matted in her hair, and an ugly gash on her scalp oozed more. Small wonder she was unconscious. This one had bruises front and back as well. What did they do to you? Jane wondered, dashing tears away impatiently. No time to go soft now! She would amend this sorry situation no matter the risk. She pressed the flannel against the wound with one hand and patted missionary's cheeks with the other, whispering with low urgency.

"Come on, my girl, wake up! What is your name? Tell me your name now."

She was relieved to hear a moan. The woman's eyelids fluttered then stayed open.

"What is your name, girl?" Jane whispered, smoothing Mary's hair from her face.

"M-Mary," the missionary croaked. Her lips were dry and chapped too. "Wh-who art thou? Where am I? Where is Allie!" She startled and tried to sit up but eased back, wincing.

"Hush now!" the goodwife cautioned. "She is right here, but you must be quiet. The men are close by!" In truth Jane was relieved. "I reckon they didn't knock out all yer brains," she muttered.

She helped Mary sit up slowly and knelt on the floor behind her to tend her head wound. She used warm water to blot the oozing gash, covered it with a piece of clean flannel, and bound it tightly. It seemed to contain the bleeding.

Once both of the women were dry and sitting up against the bed, Jane gave them strong tea with plenty of milk and sugar. She had to hold the cup for Allie, whose hands were shaking too much to manage without spilling. As the tea warmed them and soothed their parched throats, Jane quietly explained about the apothecary and Mister Roberts waiting to take them away as soon as they were able to move.

"You cannot stay here long," Jane warned. "They mean to leave you out in the storm to die. You must be gone before they rouse. We must get you dressed. Then I shall signal the doctor to come and get you. Stay quiet now whilst I fetch some clothes."

Allie's spasms were easing but so was the numbness in her legs and feet. Feeling was returning with a vengeance. The pain was far more intense than at Salisbury. She massaged the offending limbs methodically, containing her agony by force of will. Her bruises were mild discomfort by comparison. She doubted her ability to stand, let alone walk.

The goodwife returned with an armload of clothing and saw Allie rubbing her legs.

"The doctor and Mister Roberts have got a sleigh," she whispered. "You shan't need to walk far, and we can help you. I fear if you tarry, they shall waken and do you more harm. Put these on now."

Jane left the clothing and crept around the chimney to check on the men. They all appeared to sleep except Elder Nutter, who stared into the fire; however, he did not look up or react to her presence. Mayhap he slept with his eyes open. The thought sent a shiver down her spine.

The goodwife decided the doctor must be summoned, whether the tall one could walk or no. She lit a taper and set it in the kitchen window. Frost coated the pane, and she rubbed it away and peered through the thick glass into a swirling wall of white. Would the doctor see it? When she returned to the women, they appeared to be sleeping. She had hoped they would be dressed or at least in the process. She knelt and pinched Mary's cheek gently but firmly. She knew enough about head wounds to know sleep was not good. Besides, the women were in danger and must prepare to leave!

"No, no! You cannot sleep here! They mean to kill you sure!" she whispered urgently.

Allie's shivering was easing, but she was spent. She knew she should rub feeling back into her legs and feet, but the warmth of the fire and the hot tea in her belly persuaded her to rest. At Jane's admonishment she roused herself, but her customary perceptiveness was still intact.

"Thou w-wouldst go ag-gainst thy h-husband to help us?" she asked, concerned.

Jane snorted, then covered her mouth and glanced toward the parlor. "I am ever going against *him*!" Her voice was harsh but subdued. "Besides," she added, working a dry shirt carefully over Mary's tender head, "Y'are women. We must hang together in this rough world."

She turned to Allie with an old shirt of Joseph's and helped her dress with a gentleness that belied her gruff manner. The dry clothes felt wonderfully warm and soft after the abrasion of frozen material against their bruises. "I know who is behind this scheme," Jane went on, keeping her voice low. "Betimes I am hard, but I am not stupid. I do not countenance my husband taking part in any plot devised by Captain Walderne. He lords it over folk as though he were the King Himself!"

Mary was too exhausted and muddled to respond, but the statement surprised her. Few folk were so discerning. Mistress Canney was verily no meek goodwife.

"D'you reckon you can stand?" Jane asked when the women were half dressed. She did not wait for an answer. "Let us try, shall we? I will help you. Up on the bed first."

She put an arm around Allie's waist and grasped her elbow, hauling her to her feet. The missionary winced at the pressure on her bruises and the weight on her legs, but Jane was strong and got her onto the bed. Mary was smaller and easier to lift, but her drowsiness was worrisome. Her lids were heavy and her head lolled. Jane wished the doctor would come. Surely he and Mister Roberts could carry the larger woman between them, and she could manage this one, but would come before the men woke?

As Mary and Allie pulled on Joseph's old britches and wrestled socks over their numb feet, Jane ladled out thick bean soup she had made for supper. She was ever conscious of the sleeping men. She tried to contain her anxiety, but reviving the women was taking longer than she had anticipated. She had not expected their condition to be so severe. As she spooned soup into Allie's mouth, she prayed the rescuers would come soon and save these poor souls. Tremors still wracked the tall one's body and getting food into her mouth without spilling was a challenge. At least the other one was able to feed herself, if she did not fall asleep. The women ate ravenously, and the soup seemed to revive them.

Jane barely heard the scratching at the door over the wind. She realized she had been straining to hear it for some time. Her relief was so profound her own limbs trembled. After a glance at the dozing men, she went to the door, which opened onto the kitchen end of the house. Still, the doctor and Mister Roberts entered quickly, lest the cold air rouse the sleepers. Jane had never been so glad to see anyone in her life.

The early winter darkness was gathering in earnest, and it was still snowing hard when the Quakers limped from the house, dry, fed, and bundled in Joseph's old clothes. Allie could not get her legs and feet to work, and the two men virtually carried her, while Jane assisted Mary. They made their exit as swiftly and quietly as possible.

While the doctor and Mister Roberts tucked blankets around the missionaries in the bed of the sleigh, Goodwife Canney went back inside to fetch the women's wet clothing. It would not do to have that evidence about, when the men awoke, else they would never believe Jane's story of waking up to find the missionaries gone. As she left the house for the second time, the hair stood up on the back of her neck, and she braced for a shout. It did not come, and the men slept on.

The wind gusted, and the snow still fell heavily. There was no time for proper thanks or farewells, but as Jane straightened from putting the wet clothes on the floor of the sleigh, Mary leaned forward and embraced her. The goodwife returned it briefly then pushed away.

"Go on now, off with you!" she said impatiently, masking her pleasure.

The hot food and dry clothes had revived them, but Jane Canney's gruff kindness warmed the missionaries most of all.

# *Chapter 50*

## RICHARD WALDERNE *DISSENT*

1659 Boston, Massachusetts Bay Colony

On August 2, 1659 Elnathan Walderne was born at the house on Tremont Row. Annie was vastly relieved. The delivery was smooth, the baby was healthy, and Richard had another son.

Eliza Scammon had come in mid-July to help with the children and to attend her daughter's third birth. After the infant was wiped down and swaddled, she sent for his father.

"What do you think of your fine baby boy, Richard?" his mother-in-law asked, holding the newborn out to him.

Richard did not take the mewling bundle. He peeled back the swaddling blanket, looked at his squirming, red-faced son, and replaced it.

"I think 'tis a start," he said and went to Annie's bedside.

It was not long before Governor Endicott's death penalty was put to the test. Out of hundreds of Friends residing in the colony, only six responded to the order of banishment on pain of death by removing permanently. Rather than driving them away, the new law brought the Children of the Light to Boston in droves, where they entreated the authorities to rescind it. Unmoved by the protests, the General Court punished the dissenters with increasing vehemence—imprisonment, flogging, amputation of ears, branding, forced labor, and banishment.

The abuse had culminated in the near-death of seventy-year-old William Brend. When he refused to perform the labor required of him in prison, he was shackled wrists to ankles, beaten over one hundred stripes with a tarred rope, and left for sixteen hours on the floor of his cell—still shackled—without food or drink, let alone medical treatment. The next morning the prisoner was cold and barely breathing, and the authorities hastily called for a doctor. A dead Quaker would turn the tide of public opinion against them permanently. The physician announced that Brend could not possibly survive, and public outrage exploded. Governor Endicott placated the angry mob outside the prison by promising the gaoler would answer for his cruelty in court. It was a piecrust promise—easily made, easily broken—for it never happened. Miraculously the old Quaker had recovered, but the brutalities continued.

In the summer of 1659, eleven-year-old Patience Scott walked from Providence, Rhode Island to Boston in company with Mary Dyer, William Robinson, Marmaduke Stephenson, and Nicholas Davis to protest the death sentence. Patience was deemed too young for the prison and was confined to the governor's house for three weeks before she was brought before the Court in September. Her astounding eloquence did not move the officials, although her tender age gave them pause. When she ceased her plea to rescind the law, the court was unusually quiet. Then Secretary Rawson broke the spell.

"What! Shall we be baffled by such a one as this?" he exclaimed, recalling the Court to its callous attitude. "Come, let us drink a dram!"

Nervous laughter rippled among the assistants, but the deputies' benches stayed silent.

"There is a spirit in her above a woman," John Endicott commented, when the members of the Court had finished interrogating the child. "It must be the devil," he concluded.

It was determined that Patience was an instrument of Satan sent to confound them. They reasoned that a girl of her years could not possibly understand the principles of religion she parroted, and therefore could not be convicted as a Quaker. She was excused without punishment, but her four adult companions were banished upon pain of death.

On his day before the Great and General Court William Robinson spoke so eloquently, they deemed him to be a minister of note among the heretics and in need of additional reprimand. He was stripped to the waist and lashed to a gun carriage, which the Honorable Artillery Company stored on the ground level of the new Town-House. He was publicly flogged twenty stripes before being banished with his three companions.

Upon leaving Boston, Mary Dyer returned to Rhode Island, but Robinson and Stephenson did not depart the Bay Colony as ordered. They went to Salem, where the community of Friends received them warmly and treated Robinson's wounds. They stayed with their friend, Edward Wharton, holding meetings in the woods outside the town. Within a month they were discovered. More than twenty Friends were apprehended and imprisoned at Boston, including Edward.

In early October of 1659 Mary Dyer heard of their arrest and, ignoring her banishment, came to Boston with Friend Christopher Holder to entreat the authorities to rescind the brutal laws. Holder had been imprisoned and maimed at Boston the spring before, losing his right ear at Endicott's decree. He was returning to England, where he hoped to alert the newly reinstated King Charles II of the rogue laws being implemented in the Bay Colony. The authorities were unaware of his intent and glad to be rid of him, but Friend Dyer was arrested for this third violation of her banishment.

Richard Walderne sat among the assistants, when, one by one Robinson, Stephenson, and Dyer were brought before the Great and General Court. Endicott ordered the hats pulled from the men's heads and did not allow them to read the statements each had prepared. Genuinely perplexed, he asked why they had returned, knowing they would be put to death. All three maintained that God had called them to do so.

"All your laws and punishments shall not avail you," the Dyer woman warned the officials, "for the Almighty shall send tenfold more in our place."

Richard Walderne listened with scorn as each of the Quakers exhorted the General Court to rescind the new law. Surprisingly, none of them asked for leniency or evidenced fear for themselves. They were concerned for the officials sentencing them, whose hands, they said, would be stained by "innocent blood." Richard found this laughable, coming from criminals sentenced to death. He hoped to see every one of them swing by the halter, including the Dyer woman. Public opinion be damned and good riddance of bad rubbish.

Governor John Endicott made a fine show of reluctance, but stuck by his new law, condemning the three heretics to be hanged the following week on October 27 at nine of the clock. The General Court approved the sentence, and Richard was satisfied. If the Quakers thought to call the Governor's bluff, they would suffer for it.

The procession to the gallows reminded Richard of Winthrop's funeral. One hundred militiamen came out to guard the prisoners on the mile-long walk to the Neck, where a great elm tree served as the gallows. The drums beat before and behind the Quakers to drown out any seditious lies or inflammatory exhortations, which might incite the crowd to violence. The mass of humanity overflowed the street for as far as the eye could see in either direction. A frisson of dread prickled Richard's scalp at the sight. He had not realized how many would turn out. He revised his opinion that a hundred militia were unnecessary. Reverends John Wilson and John Norton headed a large group of clergy from the outlying towns. Richard fell in with the other assistants behind Governor Endicott, Deputy Governor Bellingham, and Secretary Rawson. The deputies of the Court, constables, marshals, selectmen, and lesser officials followed.

Richard could not see the prisoners during the procession, surrounded as they were by their military escort. However, space was reserved for the officials near the elm. They would have an excellent view of the execution. The militia cordoned off an area around the tree, separating the officials, the clergy, and the prisoners from the crowd.

William Robinson was first, and John Wilson could not refrain from a last triumphant jibe.

"You see, we shall not permit such jacks as you to come before authority with their hats on!" he smirked, standing near the ladder for the condemned set against the elm.

Robinson gazed at him as the marshal tied his hands behind his back.

"Thinkest thou it is for not putting off the hat we are put to death?" he asked incredulously. Wilson's face flushed. The question made him appear ignorant. It spread through the crowd, passed along by those near enough to have heard. A low, ominous hissing rose in response. The clergyman's flush deepened.

Two soldiers guided the bound prisoner up the ladder to the third rung. The crowd hushed as he appeared over the heads of the militia. The marshal bound his legs and feet to contain his death spasms, as the Quaker addressed the crowd.

"I commend my life to the Light of Christ. Be minded of it, for it dwells in all of you. Follow that Light and be guided by it. I do testify of it and shall seal that testimony this day with my blood."

Already publicly embarrassed by the man, Wilson was infuriated by this pious statement and shouted, "Hold thy tongue! Be silent! Thou art going to die with a lie in thy mouth!"

A kerchief was tied around Robinson's head to hide his face, sparing the witnesses his facial contortions in death. The noose was secured at his neck.

Robinson raised his chin. "I suffer for Christ, in whom I live, and for whom I die," he said clearly. At the Governor's signal the ladder was turned, dislodging him. The crack as his neck broke was audible in the heavy silence. He thrashed but little and was still.

Richard perused the faces of those nearest him. The Governor, the assistants, and the clergy looked satisfied, but the deputies of the court looked grim, and lamentations came from the crowd. Beside him Edward Rawson shook his head impatiently, scowling at this evidence of disapproval from the rabble. Endicott gestured for the marshal to get on with it. There were two yet to go.

Marmaduke Stephenson was led forward and prepared in similar fashion. He was as calm as Robinson, and although he was not as eloquent, God's Light shone in the face of the yeoman from Yorkshire. His last words were simple and clear.

"Be it known to all this day that we suffer not as evil-doers, but for conscience's sake."

Two bodies hung from the elm.

It was the Dyer woman's turn, and Richard felt uneasy. The men's courage in the face of death was impressive, though no doubt it was of the devil. Lamentations ceased, and the crowd was ominously quiet. Mary Dyer was no strumpet or witch. Would they revolt at her hanging? The soldiers stood between the authorities and the people, but were they capable of drawing weapons against their own townsmen if a riot broke out?

The marshal tied the woman's hands, and she did not resist as she was guided up the ladder. Her legs and feet were bound, yet she seemed joyful at the prospect of meeting her Maker. The Reverend Wilson himself supplied the handkerchief to cover her face, but at the point of putting her off the ladder, a shout was heard.

"Stop! She is reprieved!"

All turned to see a horseman approaching apace. Dyer's son, Christopher, had spoken with Endicott just days before and secured a pardon for his mother upon the promise that she would never return to Boston. The arrangement was secret. Richard learned later that Edward Rawson had been in on it but had kept his council. The three men had agreed it would be a good lesson to her, and the authorities need not engender more public outrage by hanging a woman. In fact they would appear merciful. They all assumed Mistress Dyer would be relieved, grateful, and repentant, but they misjudged the depth of her spiritual strength.

The prisoner's legs and feet were untied, but the woman did not move from the ladder. The marshal bade her come down, but she refused.

"I am willing to suffer as my brethren did," she stated, "unless ye would annul this wicked law."

They ignored her brave words and pulled her down bodily, quickly escorting her back to prison. Christopher Dyer was a ship's captain, and his vessel sailed that afternoon. He had a scant hour with his mother, but her fury at the reprieve and her willingness to die disturbed him. Her own family did not understand her faith and thought her fanatical.

The next day, Mary Dyer was released and escorted a-horse by four men to the border of the Bay Colony, where they left her to make her way home to Rhode Island. Governor Endicott counted it a victory. A strong message had been imparted by following through on the death sentence, but the court had also shown clemency for the Dyer woman. He doubted the Quakers would test his resolve again.

November brought cold weather, but Annie still went for romps with the younger children before the winter snows confined them all to the house on Tremont Row. Nine-year-old Richard was an apt pupil at the Boston Latin School, but he also excelled at fencing, archery, and wrestling. The boy did not inherit his father's height, though he was strong and quick. His Uncle Dickie taught him to shoot a pistol, as the boy could not yet handle the weight of a rifle. He had the Scammon coloring of blonde hair and blue eyes and favored his uncle physically. Little Anne was seven and showed no interest in baby Elnathan, but fifteen-year-old Beth doted on him. Little Anne was like her mother in this respect and preferred her brother Dickie's company.

Richard returned to Boston after purchasing the land on the Merrimack. He had paid the native *sôgmô* a fair price, for the Captain knew he would soon make it up in lucrative trade. At any rate the old chief discomfited him. Better to pay the old man's price than spend time negotiating with him. He left Paul to manage things at Cocheco, as Peter Coffin was now occupied overseeing the construction of the new trading post.

Whenever he was home at Tremont Row, Richard dined alone with his wife. Annie would have preferred to have the Littles at table with them, but it was not worth raising an argument. Betimes she could see his point, as their conversations would have been quite different.

"That town is growing apace," Richard said at dinner on his first night home from Cocheco. "I am considering building a new house there myself."

Annie raised her eyebrows, as her mouth was full. She swallowed and sipped her watered wine. "I am surprised you would consider leaving Boston, husband. Do you not wish to participate at the General Court any longer?" she asked. It *had* been a contentious year, she knew, but she thought her husband was satisfied with the executions implemented the month before. Sedition and heresy must not be allowed to run rampant.

"Not hardly!" he exclaimed. "I am needed more than ever with these damnable Quakers invading the city!" He cut his meat, as he talked. "The prisons are overcrowded.

The Governor has his hands full maintaining the Court's authority in the face of public whining." He stabbed a morsel with his fork. "No, I cannot possibly step down at this juncture. We shall keep this house as well," he finished.

"What of Dickie's education?" Annie asked, absorbing the ramifications of the move.

"'Twill be some years before the house is finished. He shall be done with his studies by then," her husband said, chewing. "I have been working on the layout and shall solicit an architect for the final plan." He sat back and looked at her. "'Twill be as fine as any house in Boston, Annie."

"Do tell." She patted her mouth with the linen napkin and placed it beside her plate. "Will you not show me your layout, husband?" she asked, looking at him coyly.

"Indeed." Richard gave her a lopsided smile that engendered a shiver of anticipation in his young wife. "We have all winter to improve upon it," he drawled.

Annie rose from the table. She knew what that smile meant.

Bridget had been with the Walderne family for nigh onto twenty years. She had come to them at the age of eighteen, and next month she would be thirty-eight. Elnathan was her sixth charge. She had witnessed each child's growth and seen them leave the nursery, one after the other. Privily she considered them hers and was not tempted to marry and leave them. She rejoiced with her mistress at the birth of this latest baby, for now she was of use again. Even the Littles had disdained her attentions of late.

Elnathan was a sweet babe, content and easily soothed. Still, it was a trial in the cold weather to rise from her warm cot to tend him when he woke in the night, as inevitably he still did at five months. Thus, when she roused at his usual waking time and did not hear him fuss, she stayed in her warm cocoon and went back to sleep gratefully.

The morning sun woke her with a start. The babe was sleeping later than usual by its light. She rose quickly and went to his cradle. He appeared still asleep on his stomach, and she gathered him up. His head lolled, and his soft little body was limp in her arms. Elnathan was dead.

# *Chapter 51*

## MARY AND ALICE *REFUGE*

January - February, 1662 Dover Neck and Kittery Point

Thomas Roberts could barely make out the turn off High Street onto Beck's Ferry Road through the snow. It was dark, more than a foot had accumulated, and it still came down. Fortunately the team knew the way home, and he let them find it. There were no houses along the stretch of River Road that led to the Roberts Farm, and no one was abroad in the storm to see the sleigh.

They pulled into the yard and stopped at the front door. Rebecca and Sarah were watching and hastened to help. Rebecca held a lantern as the two men carried Allie into the house, and Sarah assisted Mary. The family's hired help had been dismissed that morning to avoid being trapped by the storm, and Walter was relieved. The fewer people to know of this, the better.

The Roberts women had made two pallets on the floor of the parlor near the hearth. While Thomas stabled the horses, they helped Walter with the missionaries. It was his first opportunity to examine them, and it was a shock. Rebecca and Sarah were horrified at their battered condition and the state of Allie's legs and feet, which were swollen and red. Sarah would have wept had she not been so angry at her brothers, and Rebecca was grimly stoic. Walter shaved the hair around the gash on Mary's head and stitched it up, while Rebecca wrapped Allie's feet and legs with warm, wet flannels—a trick she had learned from their Indian neighbors when the settlement at Dover Point was new. Sarah supplied hot water, then brought soup, bread, and tea.

Once the women were settled as comfortably as possible, the four of them talked as they took some refreshment. Their friends must be removed from Dover as soon as the weather allowed, and they discussed how and where to take them.

"They would be safest across the river with the Shapleighs, I warrant," Walter suggested. "I only wish there were time to get a message to them and alert them of our coming."

"If I know Nicholas, 'twill matter not," Thomas said. "We can use my skiff, but it offers no cover. Can they endure the cold?"

"They must, for I see no alternative," Walter answered. "We dare not keep them here. The storm is our best protection and will fill in our tracks this night, but once it stops, I fear the constables will be out looking for them."

"We shall pray they do not come before the tide turns then," Thomas sighed.

"'Tis a sad day when we fear our own sons," Rebecca said quietly, reaching for her husband's hand. "Thinkest thou they verily meant to—" her voice trembled, "—to kill them, Tom?"

Her husband met her eyes and nodded wordlessly.

"I hesitate to ascribe such a dire judgment upon them without substantial proof," Walter put in gently. "However, 'tis evident from their wounds, they meant them harm."

Thomas Roberts gave him a grateful look. It was bad enough to learn his sons were capable of hurting such godly women, but it was unbearable to think they would be complicit in murder. The apothecary's words were a straw for the distraught parents to grasp in the flood of their misery and guilt.

For some years now, the gap had been growing between those benefitting from the Puritan system and those suffering under it. The Friends offered a viable alternative, and that made them dangerous to the established order. Friends respected each other, no matter their age, sex, or social status. How could any true Christian find fault with that? The old pioneer took a deep breath, determined to see that the changes erupting in the colonies would have a positive result.

Exhausted as she was, Mary did not sleep well. Her head hurt even when she kept still, and any movement, however slight, woke a chorus of pain from her battered body to accompany it. Every part of her was afflicted. She remembered the next day in disjointed flashes—the agony as Walter changed the bandage on her head wound; the blinding glare of sun on fresh snow; the pain as her bruised ribs expanded in the sharp air; the awkward transfer from house to sleigh and sleigh to skiff; the ache of constant shivering as the cold penetrated her abused limbs despite the quilts. Her first clear image of that day, as she roused in the warmth of Kittery Manor, was Alice's dear face, looking down at her.

"How did this happen?" her friend asked with dangerous calm.

Mary moved her eyes—not her head—and saw Walter stood beside Alice. He answered, but his voice was a low rumble, and Mary could not parse the words. She was drifting away again, and she surrendered with gratitude, secure in the knowledge that if Alice was present, they were safe.

During the following week, it was Anne Coleman's turn to help Alice nurse her companions. Their bruises slowly faded from black and blue to green and yellow. Allie lost one of her small toes to frostbite, but Walter saved the rest, and although she limped, she was otherwise mending quickly. The agony of Mary's head wound subsided to a dull ache.

To Alice's credit, no remonstrance was expressed concerning the disastrous outcome of the missionaries' return to Dover. It had not been the public protest they envisioned but rather a clandestine attempt to kill them. As she recovered, Mary contemplated the providence of the storm often. She felt no triumph this time, only grateful humility to be alive, for somehow her panicked attempts at prayer had been answered.

Walter left to collect his mare from Lieutenant Pike and tend to his neglected practice, but he returned by ferry a week later to check on the missionaries. Anthony Emery accompanied him as he was concerned for the women as well.

"The talk is all of your disappearance," the innkeeper informed Mary and Allie. "The constables are saying they took you to the border of the colony and turned you out in the storm. The conclusion is that you are banished and gone for good—or dead."

"Neither Thomas nor I have been questioned," Walter added, "and there has been no search, for 'twould contradict their lie. I reckon those responsible realize that further attention might raise awkward questions, risking exposure of their nefarious scheme."

In mid-February Nicholas arranged a meeting. The only evidence of the missionaries' injuries two weeks prior was Allie's limp. Ten people sat around the table at Kittery Manor—Penelope and John Treworgy, Nicholas, Alice, and Johnny, Walter, Anthony, and the three missionaries. Nicholas wanted to discuss a course of action in light of the unlawful violence the two women had suffered. Fines and the seizing of property were one thing; officials plotting to kill was quite another. The danger for Friends was escalating. Nicholas had no power to stop it, but might they devise a course of action before others were unjustly abused?

Once they were settled, Nicholas looked to Mary to open the discussion. She no longer wore a bandage, and her dust cap covered the shaved area and the scar on her scalp. Walter marveled at her confidence and energy so soon after the near fatal abuse.

"Our thanks to ye all for your concern and for coming this day," she began. "We are joined in a struggle against justice gone awry. It is clear that God's intervention in the form of a tempest and Jane Canney's kindness saved our lives, but we still might have perished in the storm had Dr. Barefoote and Friend Roberts not risked their own safekeeping to remove us from harm's way.

"As the forces set against us are entrenched in every community of the Bay Colony, an organized plan of action is required. What can we do to protect our faith and the Children of the Light?" she asked, looking around at each face. There was a short silence then Walter spoke.

"Our missionary Friends have opened a path for us in this thicket of Puritan brambles, but they cannot continue this struggle alone. The laws against Friends increase in brutality."

"And missionaries come in increasing numbers because of them," Mary put in quietly.

"Just so," Walter acknowledged. "They protest bravely by breaking the laws, but would it not be more effective if we coordinated these protests? We might send messages to key people in the Society of Friends, communicating where and when to act."

"Yes!" Mary responded quickly. "Such as Catharine Scott in Rhode Island!"

"And Margaret Fell, for she communicates with all the missionaries." Allie added.

"We should make a list," Anne suggested.

There was hopeful energy around the table now, as Johnny fetched ink pot, quill, and paper. The list included six people to whom they could appeal for help, including Margaret Fell in England; Catharine Scott, William Coddington, and Nicholas Easton in the colony of Rhode Island; Robert Pike in Salisbury; and Edward Wharton and George Preston in Salem.

Ever the advocate, John Treworgy said, "Now let us discuss the language of this missive."

"A succession of challenges aimed at the Puritan clergy would be most effective, I wager," Walter opined. "They are the most vociferous against Friends. When I removed from Kittery to Dover, Reverend Reyner pressed me to join the First Church, but as an Anglican, I refused. The town needed an apothecary, so he did not persist, but they are rarely so tolerant. The Puritans' power depends on the allotment—or withholding—of church membership. If folk do not seek membership, the ministers lose power."

Nicholas spoke up. "Some of the wind has been taken from their Puritan sails now the monarchy is restored. The King would not approve what they do, I am sure of it. The mandamus he sent last year stopped the executions, but the Whip and Cart Act is near as lethal, if they allow flogging in more than three towns. Men like Walderne and Endicott flaunt royal authority by perverting the King's law. They must be challenged on this point—repeatedly."

"As we did in Dover," Mary said, taken with the idea, "but one protest following upon another, so that the courts and the ministers are besieged." She smiled at the thought.

"Yes," Walter agreed then expanded on Nicholas' proposal. "To that end we must define the key locations, concentrating on the towns that have reacted most stringently against Friends. Which are the strongest bastions of Puritanism, think you?" he asked them all.

Anthony Emery spoke up. "Salem with that magistrate Hathorne. Friend Wharton said he and Endicott were ruthless, imprisoning more than twenty folk who attended meetings in the woods. Endicott and his minister Norton created a bloodbath at Boston with their death penalty until the King's mandamus stopped the hangings."

"Friend Christison barely escaped execution. The King's rule saved him," Mary added.

"Would that I had been there to see Samuel Shattuck serve the document to Endicott," Nicholas chuckled. "The Governor was forced to comply, but how it must have galled him to receive the order from the hand of a Friend he had banished!"

"Boston is too dangerous and should be avoided, I warrant," Walter cautioned. "The authorities there encourage brutality, as in the case of William Brend. But certes Hampton and Dover must be on the list, for they carried out Walderne's sentence against our friends here."

"Those same towns abused the earlier missionaries, as well," Anthony put in.

"That is why any confrontation with the authorities must be undertaken by trained missionaries," Mary said, looking carefully at each of them. "Ye may offer refuge to Friends. Shelter us, feed us, help us heal, if necessary, but do not join in the fight other than refusing to attend Puritan services. Ye should not risk lives, children, and property. The cost is too dear. Leave it to us who have prepared for this fight and have nothing to lose," she finished.

"Except your lives," Alice said softly.

All were in consensus. The letters were penned and copies made for each person on the list, informing them of the plan and asking them to encourage missionaries to come to northern New England, specifically targeting Salem, Hampton, and Dover. As an Anglican and a doctor, it was deemed safest for the responses to be delivered to Walter. The apothecary promised to inform them when he received replies.

This accomplished, Walter and Anthony had a quick cup of tea and made to leave. Mary accompanied the two men to the door and took the opportunity to speak with Anthony.

"Friend Emery," she began, after glancing back toward the drawing room, "dost thou think thy brother might entertain us at Newbury for a time?"

Anthony grinned. "John never turns away custom!" His broad brow furrowed. "But why would you lodge there?"

Mary looked over her shoulder again, but Alice was not in sight. It was safe.

"I am unsure as yet," she answered. "I wanted to talk with thee first."

"You wish to go to Newbury?" Walter asked, concerned. "Why?"

"'Tis closer to Hampton than Kittery Point by some miles, is it not?" she asked, arching her brows.

Walter ignored the question, answering with his own. "When would you leave and by what means? The roads are nigh impassable," he persisted. He loved his friends, but they were exasperatingly cavalier about their own well-being. Twice he had snatched them from the jaws of death. Did Mary seek to tempt fate—or God—again?

"Most like, we shall take the ferry to Portsmouth and walk, but not until March, when the weather breaks," she assured the apothecary.

Anthony chuckled. "Mayhap in Devon the winter ends in March. Here 'tis April—*if* we are in luck!"

"You cannot walk that distance!" Walter protested with increasing vehemence. "'Tis near forty mile to Newbury from here, and you pass through Hampton and Salisbury to get there. Robert told me Wheelwright has not forgotten the incident. You would be arrested!"

"Walter, please," Mary begged, "I do not wish to upset Alice. We must speak of this privily for the nonce."

The doctor sighed and shook his head, looking at Anthony. The innkeeper shrugged.

"You cannot prevent them, doctor," he said ruefully amused. "Did you think they would agree to this plan and then allow others to take the risk?" He turned back to Mary. "John will be glad to have you, and I shall alert him."

"Thank thee, Friend Emery," she said gravely and offered her hand.

The innkeeper looked surprised, then chuckled and shook it. Women did not usually do so.

"I beg you not to leave precipitously," Walter said stiffly. "Give this more thought, will you?"

His concern made her want to smile, but Mary refrained, sensing it would offend him. She stood on tiptoe, kissed him on both cheeks, and said, "Dear Walter, I promise."

As ever, Mary's restlessness increased with her strength. Comfortable and safe as they were with the Shapleighs, there was much work to be done to curb the injustice running rampant through the colony. The three missionaries discussed their next step often.

"We cannot return to Dover," Mary said, "but Hampton might serve. There is a strong community of Friends there, and their minister, Seaborn Cotton, has grossly abused his power."

"I do recall Lydia Wardell telling us of his greed," Allie responded.

"Oh, little Joseph's mother?" Anne asked typically recalling the child before the parents. In the next breath she answered her own question, as her companions knew she would. Although this trait irritated Mary initially, now she found it endearing. She and Allie exchanged a smile as Anne continued. "They came to a meeting here in October, I recall. They were the ones that harbored Friend Christison at Hampton, were they not? And the Reverend Cotton has harassed them ever since."

Mary nodded. "They witnessed our floggings, as well. They are stalwart Friends, but they have suffered for it. People in Hampton know Cotton fined them, but I doubt the extent of his greed is known. No one has called him out on it publicly."

"Then 'tis time someone did," Allie responded. "When do we leave?"

By the end of February, Walter had received several responses to their letter and came to share them with his friends. He stayed overnight at Kittery Manor.

George Preston informed them that Edward Wharton was on a mission in the Connecticut Colony, visiting settlements along the coast. George would forward their message, but it might be some time before it caught up to Edward. George added that the meetings in Salem had not ceased despite the laws and concurred with the towns they had chosen.

The Rhode Island Friends deemed their plan "timely and just." The missionaries' ordeals at the hands of the Puritan authorities were the talk of the colony. They promised to spread word of the plan and offered to entertain the three women whenever they came to Newport. Catharine and Richard Scott also extended an open invitation to stay at their home in Providence. It had been Catharine who wrote Margaret Fell of Mary Dyer's execution, and Mary Tomkins had responded. As a result they had corresponded for the past two years, and Catharine was eager to meet Mary and Allie.

The responses were encouraging, and after a merry dinner, Mary deemed it a good time to communicate their plan to go to Newbury.

"The roads are near impassable this time of year," Nicholas warned at the news.

"We shall not leave immediately. The weather must turn first," Mary responded.

"But how shall ye get there and where will ye stay?" Alice asked, biting back the blatant protests that sprang to her lips.

"Friend Emery's brother, John lives in Newbury and will entertain us. Our friends the Wardells are being ruined by the Reverend Cotton. His greed must be exposed publicly."

"Will they not arrest you?" Alice's voice rose. Her composure was eroding.

Walter cleared his throat, and they all looked at him.

"I shall transport you to Newbury in my sloop," he stated. There was a stunned silence. "I like it not that you persist in putting yourselves at risk again, but I support this endeavor."

Mary gave him a radiant smile, but Walter's face remained grave.

"How shall you quit the colony?" Nicholas asked. "If you have no transport, the authorities will leave you in the wilderness after you are flogged." Alice winced.

"I shall attend them," the apothecary said. "The least I can do is treat your wounds and insure that you are transported to safety. But this is the last time, Mary."

She met his eyes and nodded once.

"After Hampton you must quit this region. As a physician and your friend, I insist you subject yourselves to life-threatening abuse no more." His eyes flashed. "Following this protest, I shall take you to the safety of Rhode Island."

For once Mary humbly agreed.

# *Chapter 52*

## RICHARD WALDERNE *MARY DYER*

1660 Boston, Massachusetts Bay Colony

"The Dyer woman has returned," Edward Rawson said without preamble.

"How now?" Richard closed the door of his study and turned to his friend. Rawson's unannounced visit alerted him that something was afoot, but he had not expected this! The Dover magistrate was not easily surprised, but this statement shocked him.

"Who says this? Did her son not swear to keep her away?"

Edward shook his head. "Evidently he could not. She appeared this morning at the market, spouting her poison and protesting the Governor's law, brazen as ever. Quite a crowd gathered before the marshal removed her to the gaol."

"I cannot fathom it. Does she *wish* to die?"

"So it would appear," Rawson said, sitting heavily.

"Shall there be a special session?" Richard asked, too put out to sit.

"No," his friend answered curtly. "John deems it best to let her stew in her cub until the regular session. 'Tis but ten days. He is furious that she reneged on their agreement. She forces his hand, for he knows people shall censure the hanging of a 'tender woman.'" His last words dripped with sarcasm. "He would prefer to leave her to rot in prison, but too many saw her. The whole city knows of her arrest by now."

"Then the whole city shall see her swing," Richard said grimly.

"Are you the same Mary Dyer that was here before?" Endicott asked, peering down at the prisoner. Richard was unsure if the Governor would credit a denial, although it appeared he would welcome it. The point was moot, given the Quaker's response.

"I am the same Mary Dyer that was here the last General Court," she answered, leaving no room for doubt.

Endicott grimaced with irritation. "You will own yourself a Quaker, will you not?"

"I own myself to be reproachfully called so," she responded.

"We passed the sentence of execution upon you the last session. You were reprieved by the mercy of this Court, yet it would seem you spurn our good intentions, for here you are again." Endicott shook his head and sighed with reluctance. Richard admired his show of sincerity. "Mistress Mary quite contrary..." came to mind, and he suppressed a smile.

Then the Governor straightened and delivered the sentence. "Mary Dyer, you must return to the prison and there remain till tomorrow at nine of the clock. Thence you must go to the gallows and there be hanged till you are dead."

"This is no more than what thou saidst before," she replied, disdaining her former pardon.

"But now it is to be executed," Endicott spat, venting his irritation at last. "Prepare yourself for tomorrow at nine o'clock."

Mistress Dyer was not cowed and proclaimed her calling yet again. She was God's instrument to stop the flow of innocent blood. The new law must be repealed. Richard rolled his eyes, and happily the governor cut her off, all patience gone.

"Away with her! Away with her!" he shouted.

"Yea, joyfully I go," she said, as the marshal hastened to remove her.

Richard maintained a stoic facade, but Elnathan's death ignited a spiritual crisis. All the promise, all the hope he had felt at the birth of his fourth son was shattered. Had he lost God's favor? Certes, the Almighty would not afflict his chosen so. How had he transgressed? Sincere in his anguish, the bereaved father sought solace in the Bible and found an answer. The succession of losses—Prudence, Timothy, and Elnathan—were lessons. It was his punishment for holding his family too dear. His father had always maintained that human attachments were the work of the devil, distracting one from devotion to God. Now Richard believed it. He must forsake all human frailty and love only His Maker.

Lost in her own grief, Annie did not notice the change in her husband at first. Initially they fell out over Bridget's dismissal. Richard deemed the nursemaid responsible for the tragedy, and nothing Annie or even Dr. Clark said could dissuade him.

"I have unfortunately seen similar cases prior to this," the physician had said to the distraught parents. "'Tis perplexing, but not without precedent. A perfectly healthy babe expires in the night. We cannot parse the source of the ailment, but 'tis doubtful anything your nursemaid did or did not do could have been prevented it. God has called His little angel home. We cannot fathom His Will. There is no blame."

Richard did not agree. The baby died on the nursemaid's watch, and after twenty years of service, he turned her out that very day. Missus Cameron prevailed upon her brother and his wife to take Bridget in temporarily. Annie missed her gentle companionship and worried about the loyal nursemaid. Under the circumstances, Bridget would find no work in the colonial capital. She had no family and nowhere to go.

Eliza Scammon provided a solution. Of course the Scammons came to comfort their daughter and grandchildren and attend the burial—the coffin had looked so pitifully small! Unbeknownst to Richard, Eliza took the devastated nursemaid back to Portsmouth. Annie's family had a large circle of friends and acquaintances, and her mother would help her make a fresh start there.

Gradually Annie realized the change in her husband was not temporary. He had no interest in social engagements, and when he was home, he stayed in his study, working, she supposed. He always closed the door—an indication of his manner with her in general. When they did interact, he demanded nothing short of unquestioning obedience. He called her Anne now, like a disapproving parent. Once her pregnancy was confirmed, he went north to tend to his many business interests. The very house on Tremont Row seemed to breathe a sigh of relief.

After a four-month absence Richard returned to Boston to attend the May session of the Great and General Court. The officials approved another hanging, and it was the talk of the town. This time it would be a woman, Mary Dyer.

On the eve of the execution husband and wife were preparing to retire. Annie sat at her vanity, brushing her hair, before plaiting it into a night braid.

"I wish to accompany you to the hanging tomorrow," she said.

Richard froze in the act of unbuttoning his shirt. "I forbid it," he stated, meeting her eyes in the cheval glass.

Her brush did not falter. "May I ask why?" she said lightly.

The magistrate did not voice the response that came to mind—because the Dyer woman is dangerous, brave, and well spoken—instead he addressed her mild challenge.

"Because I forbid it," he repeated blandly.

She watched him turn away dismissively in the smoky glass and barely stifled a retort to his implacable decree. Richard was distancing himself by asserting his authority again—an increasingly common occurrence. The argument over Bridget drove a wedge between them, when she had hoped they might comfort each other, but now months later he still shut her out. At first she had been too sad to care, but she had conceived within a month of Elnathan's mysterious death—passion not withstanding—and the new life in her womb was reviving Annie's spirits. Although she hardly showed in her fourth month, she felt the first flutters of movement. It energized her enough to contemplate rebellion. This would be the biggest event of the year, the hanging of a woman.

"The city entire is called to attend," she began reasonably. "Certes, the wife of an—"

"The *pregnant* wife of *this* assistant to the General Court shall obey her husband and stay home on the morrow." Richard pulled off his shirt, overriding her without turning around.

It was unlike him to use so bald a term, and she realized he would not be swayed. Pressing him would only make him angry. She began to braid her hair. Annie knew when to keep silent, but it did not mean she would comply.

The drums ceased their racket abruptly once the militia reached the gallows elm with the prisoner. The contrasting silence was ominous. This time the Right Honorable Artillery Company formed a double guard between the crowd and the prisoner with her entourage of officials and clergy. It seemed the entire Bay Colony had come to witness the hanging of the Quaker woman.

Over the sea of headgear between Annie and the elm she saw only the top half of the ladder and the empty noose dangling beside it. People pressed forward for a closer view, jostling her, and she clutched the hat containing her long braid. Missus Cameron had insisted on accompanying her, and now she linked arms, keeping her young mistress close. The tall housekeeper had gained them a position a third of the way back from the elm on a slight rise, but they struggled to hold their ground. Annie was glad of Eleanor's familiar, solid presence. Even disguised as a boy in Tim's old clothes, she felt vulnerable in the press of humanity. She need not have worried. All attention was on the elm. A hodge-podge of humanity was present from professionals and business owners to servants and vagrants, although as a matter of course, the latter were farthest back.

The Quaker became visible as she mounted the ladder. Exclamations erupted at the sight.

"There she is!" "'Tis the heretic!" "That is the Dyer woman!"

Someone was speaking to the prisoner, but Annie could not see who nor make out the words from her vantage point. The reply was clear.

"Nay, I cannot, for in obedience to the Lord I came, and in His Will I abide faithful to the death," Mary Dyer proclaimed. It was likely the clergy wanted her to recant her faith.

Captain John Webb of the Boston militia was vociferous as ever and spoke reprovingly. "You were here before and had the sentence of banishment upon pain of death. Now you have broken the law by coming again. Therefore you are guilty of your own blood!"

All hushed to hear the Quaker's response.

"Nay, I came to keep blood-guiltiness from you, desiring you to repeal the unrighteous and unjust law of banishment upon pain of death, made against the innocent servants of the Lord. Therefore my blood is required at your hands, who willfully do it."

The woman looked down at the ministers and Court officials. Even standing on the gallows ladder with her hands bound at her back, she evinced impressive calm and a steadfast spirit. Every eye was on her. Mistress Dyer raised her voice.

"But for those who do this in the simplicity of their hearts, I desire the Lord to forgive them. I came to do the Will of the Father, and in obedience to His Will, I stand even to death."

There were audible reactions to this statement. Had the Lord Jesus Christ not said similar words at his death? "Father, forgive them for they know not what they do." She forgave those that acted in ignorance, although it was doubtful any such were present.

Annie put her mouth close to Mrs. Cameron's ear. "How can she have such courage?" she whispered.

"Faith," the housekeeper responded briefly. She put her hand over Annie's, her attention on the Quaker. "List now."

The Reverend Wilson was berating her, his strident voice carrying in the morning air.

"...Dyer, oh repent and be not so deluded, and carried away by the deceit of the devil!"

"Nay, man, I am not now to repent," she responded. Her voice was gentle in comparison to the minister's shrill railing, but all could hear.

Her assertion prompted the ministers to a cacophony of admonishment. They beseeched the prisoner to deny her heretical notions and save herself, but she gazed out over the throng unmoved—even as the marshal bound her legs.

Every eye was upon her and Mary Dyer addressed the people of Boston. "I commend my soul to God. My life availeth me nothing without the Liberty of the Truth," she declared.

Marshal Michaelson covered the prisoner's face with a handkerchief and tightened the noose around her neck. Endicott nodded curtly, and two soldiers turned the ladder. Hundreds of people gasped then fell silent, watching the body twitch. The rope creaked, the spasms subsided, and Captain Webb broke the heavy silence.

"She hangs as a flag for others to take example by," he announced contemptuously.

There was no chatter as the crowd dispersed. Some were weeping quietly. Annie clung to Missus Cameron's arm, as they made their way back among the press of people. Like everyone around them the two women were stunned and did not speak. Annie was unsure the example of which Webb had spoken would accrue to Boston's credit.

## *Chapter 53*

### MARY AND ALICE *PROTEST*

March, 1662-1663 Newbury and Hampton, Massachusetts Bay Colony

A small group of Newbury Friends celebrated the New Year on March 25th with a meeting for worship and a fine meal at the Emerys' ordinary. Three days earlier, the missionaries had arrived by sloop with Walter, who stayed overnight. John Emery and the doctor made plans to get the women to Hampton. The innkeeper would take them to the Wardells' farm by wagon, when the roads were drier. It would insure their safe arrival, and John promised to alert the apothecary in advance. In the meantime, Walter would prepare for an extended absence from his Dover practice. It would take a week to reach Rhode Island, and he would need to rest a day or two before returning north.

"Pray, do not act without me," he cautioned Mary at parting. "They will take you into custody if you do not have means to leave the colony, and we know how dangerous that can be. We shall meet at the Wardells'."

"We understand," Allie said firmly. "Thank thee, Walter. We shall not proceed without thee." Mary agreed without argument.

Instead of progressing predictably into spring, however, the beginning of April brought renewed cold and more snow. The English Friends were dismayed, though the Emerys maintained it was normal. Back in Devon, trees were budding, fields greening, and bulbs blooming, but in northern New England, April was as cold as March, and March was a winter month.

The Newbury Emerys welcomed their guests warmly. Like his brother, Anthony, the innkeeper was fearless in challenging the authorities if he thought them unjust. He had served his town on both the Ipswich Petit Jury and the Boston Grand Jury, had been voted a selectman in '55, and became Clerk of the Market the following year. He was respected by his fellow townsfolk and was not a man to be trifled with, in spite of his cavalier attitude toward Puritan authority. He spoke of sheltering Wenlock Christison, the first missionary to come north from Boston. He had been fined for it, but the Newbury minister, Thomas Parker, was a rare, mild-mannered clergyman and not inclined to persecute contributing citizens like John Emery once their fines had been paid. Although sympathetic to the Quakers, the Emerys had no quarrel with their reverend and still attended Newbury's First Church.

John was the elder of the two brothers by a year, and their resemblance was striking. They had emigrated together in 1635 with Captain Wiggin, but John had settled his family at Newbury Plantation, gaining freeman status by 1641. The Emerys had two children—a small family by Puritan standards. Their daughter Ebenezer was thirteen, and her brother Jonathan was ten.

The missionaries spent many a chill evening with the Emerys, huddled close to the hearth in the family's private living quarters—nights that would have been tedious without a rapt audience for Anne's stories and Mary's accounts of her fractious nephews back in Kingsweare. The children had endless questions about England and became openly affectionate with their guests.

Mary was plagued by impatience, as Walter had known she would be, but she honored her promise to him. The roads were still impassable, in any case. The three missionaries went over their plan often. John would take them to the Wardells', where they would stay until the next Sabbath. On that day they would expose Cotton in the church before his congregation, citing his many injustices against the Wardells. Mary would speak, while Allie and Anne delayed anyone trying to stop her. If touched, they would go limp. After the inevitable punishment, they would depart for Rhode Island with Walter.

During their time with the Emerys, the missionaries pitched in, helping Mary Emery, Ebenezer, and two hired women with the many tasks of running an ordinary. Their work at the Hearthstone Inn in Kingsweare had prepared them well. One dismal afternoon in mid-April, they were peeling and seeding winter squash in the kitchen.

"Shall this rain ever stop?" Allie wondered. "'Twill be June before we can travel!"

"I am in no hurry to see you go," John's wife said, rolling pie crust at the wooden table in the center of the large room.

"I hope it rains forever, and you shall never go!" Ebenezer added with a grin.

"Aargghhh!" Allie responded pulling a face that made the girl laugh.

"Thou hast been so kind to entertain us," Mary said, "but I wish thou wouldst take some coin for thy trouble—for our food at the least."

Mary Emery shrugged and smiled. "Your company and your help is payment enough."

"You are like family to us now," Ebenezer declared, as she separated seeds for spring planting from the sticky, orange pulp.

Mary appreciated the girl's affection and smiled at her, but she took the opportunity to gently remind the family that the missionaries must soon depart.

"Thy husband deems the roads shall be passable in a week or two," she said to Mary Emery. "Mayhap we should send word to Dr. Barefoote, affording him time to prepare."

"'Tis hard to credit," Allie sighed, watching from the window as a miserable-looking horse and rider picked their way along the edge of the morass in front of the inn. The rain fell relentlessly. She thought it would be at least another two weeks before John's wagon could negotiate *that*.

"At least 'tis not snow," Mary Emery said brightly.

"Oh, bite thy tongue!" Allie rejoined, and they all laughed.

Their hostess shook her head, her merriment fading. "I cannot fathom why you wish to return to Hampton," she said, sliding the pies into the oven built into the hearth. It was not the first time she had made the comment, and Anne repeated the response in her deep voice.

"Reverend Cotton must be publicly called out for his actions against the Wardells."

"Besides," Mary Tomkins added, "He will not expect it. We shall have the element of surprise."

Mistress Emery snorted. "Shock is more like. Those folk have not seen you since you were flogged at the cart tail. They shall probably faint at sight of you!"

In the final week of April the missionaries bid farewell to the Emery Family. Anne sat on the wagon seat with John, while Mary and Allie sat in back, on their saddlebags. Ebenezer and Jonathan stood with their mother in the dooryard to see them off. They would sorely miss the women's company. John snapped the reins, and the horses lurched into a trot, heading up Country Road for the ferry to Salisbury and thence to Hampton.

The lanes nearest the town center had been passable for a week, but there were rough spots further out. Materials for spring repairs were in evidence at intervals along the way. Landowners were responsible for the section of road abutting their property;

therefore, conditions varied drastically. Some stretches showed signs of recent improvement, while others were sorely in need of attention. John knew the road well and was a good driver, however, and they managed a steady pace for the most part and did not get stuck. They reached the Wardell Farm on the outskirts of Hampton by early afternoon. John did not linger. He shook the missionaries' proffered hands with a reaction comically similar to his brother's and took his leave, planning to visit his friend and fellow innkeeper Robert Tuck on the way back.

The farm looked shabbier than Mary remembered. The detritus left behind by the snowmelt had not been tidied. Indoors an attempt to pack was evidenced by sundry items piled against one wall, crowding the kitchen and living space. The Wardells' home, though small, had always been neat as a pin. Now it was in chaos.

Mary was more alarmed by the absence of Lydia's brisk confidence. Eli was not at home, and his young wife seemed harried and unkempt. Little Joseph, now three, sensed her tension and clung to her skirt, fussing for attention, until Anne engaged him. Initially Lydia was overjoyed to see them but became distracted, as they chatted over tea without sugar or milk.

The younger woman was embarrassed by the state of her house. She did not sit for long but jumped up to straighten things, apologizing constantly. The three Friends helped her, and Mary tried to draw her out as they worked, but Lydia avoided eye contact and responded in monosyllables. Anne took Joseph outside for a walk, and Allie swept the floor while heating water to wash trenchers encrusted with food. The Wardells' one bed was in a corner by the hearth, and the linens and quilts lay in a tangle. Mary was helping Lydia straighten them, when she looked up to see silent tears on her face. Mary went around the bed to embrace her, and the younger woman dissolved in sobs.

"Forgive me," she gasped, wiping her eyes with her apron—a rather soiled one, Mary noted. "I do not wish to—"

"Thou hast no need to apologize to me, Lydia," Mary said firmly. "We are more than friends. We are sisters in spirit." She smoothed strands of hair from Lydia's wet cheeks and pulled her close again. "We are here to help thee, not to criticize. Come, sit a moment." Mary kept an arm around her, and they sat on the rumpled bed.

"'Tis upsetting to leave thy home and family," she began, "particularly under such uncommonly difficult circumstances. Thou hast struggled with Cotton for two years now—"

"Two and a half," the young woman put in morosely, employing the hanky tucked in her sleeve.

"Just so," Mary agreed. "In another light, removing from Hampton shall lead to worshipping freely with neighbors of like mind. You shall not find that here."

"Not while hypocrites like Seaborn Cotton stand in the pulpit; and his bulldog, Captain Wiggin, supports him," Lydia said bitterly.

Mary winced at her tone, but who could blame her? The young woman was an outcast in her own town, ruined by the minister's insatiable greed. Aloud Mary said, "Those men are false. They believe themselves righteous, but the truth shall out, Lydia. Do not allow their greed to poison thy heart. Be guided by the Light Within. Let faith soothe thy spirit, for thy suffering shall give way to a finer time, when thy family shall prosper again and worship openly with joy."

"Mary," Lydia's tears had dried, and her face was intent. "How can one be certain of a calling?"

Mary was surprised by the sudden change of subject and considered carefully before answering.

"'Tis based on faith, Lydia," she answered slowly. "I warrant 'tis different for every person. My call to take up Friend Dyer's mission came from the stillness of God Within and humble contemplation. It is a great burden and should not to be taken lightly, for once accepted, it cannot be denied."

"I want nothing more than to be led by the Light Within, as thou art," Lydia said fervently. Her eyes glittered, and Mary felt a twinge of alarm, but her young friend went on in a rush. "When we watched the flogging in Dover and again here in Hampton, I had never witnessed such clear evidence of God's presence. He was *there* among us, working through thee. Ye were all so brave, but when thou sangest through thy suffering," her breath caught between a laugh and a sob, "the Light shone from thy face! My faith is strong because of thee, Mary Tomkins." She smiled radiantly and squeezed Mary's hands. "'Tis *thy* torch burns in my heart."

Before Mary could react to this unsettling statement, Eli's voice sounded outside, and they went to greet him.

Walter hired young Job Clement as crew for the voyage to Rhode Island. At fourteen the lad was eager for an excursion and happy to be paid in coin. He stayed onboard at the town landing, and the apothecary walked into Hampton. The Tucks greeted him warmly, and Walter left his bag in a room at the ordinary, since the Wardells could not entertain him with the missionaries occupying the loft.

He arrived at the farm in time for the last meeting for worship and an evening meal with the missionaries. It was a veritable last supper. The thought saddened him. Once they were in Rhode Island, he doubted he would see his friends again. He would miss them, but they were in danger here, and their safety was paramount.

Walter's practice was suffering from inattention, but since witnessing the blatant malevolence of the Dover authorities, the women's mission had become his priority. Friendship was a major motivator, but as an Anglican and a stout Royalist, Walter wanted to see the Puritan stranglehold on the Bay Colony broken. The Friends were striking at the very roots of their power—the unjust laws, the clergy, and the exclusive freeman system—and he could help.

The meal was simple. Lydia's parents, her sister Rebecca with her husband John Hussey, Walter, the Wardells, and the three missionaries crowded around the table to partake of the meat pies Susannah had brought. The little house was tidy, and Lydia's spirits were buoyed by her friends and family. The apothecary was concerned, however, for her demeanor struck him as excessively bright. He wondered if she might have a touch of fever, but found no opportunity to speak with her about it that evening.

The Sabbath dawned cool and windy. Cloud shadows raced before them on the road, as the three missionaries walked to the Hampton Church with the Wardells. Buds were swelling, and a few brave bulbs were green exclamations in the drab landscape. Little Joseph ran ahead or rode on his father's back, as he was becoming too heavy for Lydia to carry any distance. Their mood was subdued despite the promise of spring. The missionaries had rallied the young couple's spirits, but parting would be all the harder. Each moment together was precious, for they all knew the Wardells would walk home alone.

Walter spent a restless night and rose early to take food to Job, who had slept on the sloop. They made sure all was ready for departure then the apothecary returned to Tuck's, conversing quietly with Robert and watching from a window for his friends. When he saw the little group approaching, Walter took his leave reluctantly, dreading to see his friends suffer again. The Tucks declined to witness the protest and its aftermath but assured him they would help in treating any wounds.

The Reverend Seaborn Cotton stood on the steps of the Hampton church, greeting his parishioners as they filed past. Son of the well-known Boston minister, John Cotton, Seaborn had earned his name by entering the world on the crossing from

England. He was a Harvard graduate, following in his father's footsteps as an ordained minister. The young reverend had come to Hampton five years earlier, acting as teacher in tandem with Timothy Dalton, the town's long-time minister. When Dalton passed away three years later, Cotton became Hampton's shepherd. He was an earnest young man, fiercely dedicated to his flock. He pursued his calling with a fervor bordering on fanaticism, as though to make up for his youth and boyish features.

As the last worshippers mounted the steps, the bell—pride and joy of the community—ceased tolling, and Reverend Cotton turned to go in. He did not see the little group turn onto High Street, heading for the church.

Lydia's family had alerted the Hampton Friends, and they gathered outside to bear witness and give moral support. Her parents and Uncle Abraham arrived first. Soon after, her sister, Rebecca, came with John and several of the Hussey family. William Marston crossed the village green with his wife, joining them last.

The Friends communed in silence outside the church. It was the last Sabbath Day in April. The clouds had burned off, and the sun's warmth was a blessing on heads and shoulders. The windows were shut though not shuttered, and the Friends could hear the cadence of Cotton's preaching but not the words.

Mary closed her eyes, breathing deeply, and prayed for the Light Within to guide her. It was her final mission in the northern settlements. Just four months before they had been flogged here. She hoped the townsfolk would spread the word that the Quakers had returned and were alive and well against all odds.

The sun was at its zenith when the Cotton launched into the closing prayer. There would be a short break for the noon meal before the afternoon session. It was the cue to act. Walter stood behind them, and when Mary turned, he nodded, indicating that all was in readiness. The two missionaries thanked each of the Friends who had come, shaking hands and bidding them farewell. Lydia embraced Mary fiercely but could not speak. The three missionaries mounted the steps, Eli and his father-in-law opened the double doors, and they entered the Hampton Church.

Heads turned. Cotton was in the pulpit and looked up when the door opened. It took him a moment to realize three Quaker women were in his church. Then he recognized them, and his face went pale then flooded with color.

"You!" he exclaimed, as the congregation gaped.

The missionaries ignored him, and Mary spoke, her voice ringing off the rafters.

"Good people, take heed! Your minister is corrupt!" She gestured at Cotton.

"You cannot speak here! Begone!" he shouted.

"He perverts the law for his own gain and calls himself a man of God," she proclaimed.

Cotton's mouth worked, but nothing emerged. Mary did not pause.

"Your neighbors, the Wardells, have lost a fine saddle horse, a heifer soon to calve—"

"Lies! She speaks lies!" Cotton interrupted in a strangled voice.

"—the fodder from their fields, and their store of dried corn to this man's greed."

"They harbored a heretic and absented themselves from worship more than twenty times!" Desperation made the minister's voice strident. "My actions are within the law!"

"Verily?" Mary responded. "The horse is valued at fourteen pounds. That alone is a deal more than their fines, I warrant."

"They flaunted the law!" Cotton insisted over the audible reactions to this information. Most of the townspeople were not aware of the extent of the retribution the minister had exacted from the Wardells. He was flustered by frowns and shaking heads among his flock. "This is not your concern!" he hissed at her, leaning over the pulpit.

"A miscarriage of justice concerns all," Mary asserted.

"Do not credit this slander!" the minister admonished, as the buzzing among his flock increased.

"What is the value of all thou hast taken?" Mary posed reasonably. "The Wardells are ruined."

Cotton hesitated, torn between defending himself from the pulpit and descending to deal with the interlopers. He chose the latter, his shoes clattering on the steps in haste.

Mary continued. "There is no accounting. Your minister bends the law for his own gain and can do the same to any of you." She swept her arm over the entire congregation.

"Arrest them!" Cotton shouted from the altar. He looked over the men's section. "Fogg! Where is the constable? Fogg, arrest them now!"

Samuel Fogg had been appointed constable in January, when William Fifield resigned the post. He rose from his bench then paused, unsure how to proceed in arresting the women. All three at once? One by one? Must he lay hands on them? He balked at the thought. Mayhap some of the men could help him. He glanced around.

The congregation was transfixed. Were these not the same women flogged here in December? They were alive and well! How had they survived that brutal sentence? God must have protected them, for here they were again! Everyone stared at the missionaries, astonied.

"The fines are set at your minister's whim," Mary went on. "If there is no coin, he takes whatever he chooses. There is no record and no end to his greed. Is this just?" Her calm assertions contrasted with the reverend's frantic shouting.

Cotton started down the aisle, gesturing impatiently for Fogg to follow. Allie blocked their progress with outstretched arms, and Mary was undaunted by his glowering approach. He slowed as he reached Allie, who planted her feet and raised her chin. They were the same height.

"Life is not easy in these colonies," Mary was saying. The people quieted to hear her. "Ye are all brave folk who labor from dawn to dusk to survive. Yet this man lives by your coin, and for what? He does not plow or fish or harvest or saw. He talks."

"Seize them!" Cotton barked, pushing Fogg toward Allie. He was under attack. This must stop. Fogg bore down on her, but Allie stood firm, and he stopped short of grabbing her, stymied. Mary used the delay.

"Your honest labor supports him, and he keeps you in ignorance, believing he is the only path to God."

"Now, Constable!" Cotton roared. People were listening! Desperate to stop the heretic's poison, the minister pushed Allie aside himself. She promptly fell to the floor. Fogg acted then, stepping over her and reaching for Mary. She twisted away, still talking.

"God's Light is found in your hearts, not in the words of a thief!" Mary declared.

People reacted to this accusation audibly, and the room became chaotic. Folk stood up talking among themselves or making for the aisle. Samuel Fogg realized the Quaker would not go peaceably, but trying to wrestle her out the door would be an ignominious struggle. He approached her from behind, bent his knees, and pinioned Mary in his arms, lifting her and carrying her toward the doors. She did not resist, but now the little one blocked his exit, arms outstretched. Mary continued to speak while the constable went back and forth with Anne, trying to get around her. Folk began to crowd the aisle. Then, to the constable's relief, a deacon advanced on Anne from behind and picked her up in similar fashion. Both men headed for the door.

"No true man of God would ruin..." Mary's voice faded as the women were carried out.

Allie remained on the floor. Her part was accomplished, and she did not resist as Thomas Wiggin helped the reverend drag her awkwardly down the aisle by her arms. She pushed down the memory it evoked.

The meeting house was in an uproar. Some were angry at the intrusion; others were confused; some wished to hear more; but all were determined to miss nothing.

"Are ye not the ones who got the lash here in December?" Fogg asked, as he set Mary down outside.

"That we are," she answered, turning to look up at him. Her gentle expression surprised him. He expected anger.

"Why are ye back here and breaking the law yet again?" he asked, sincerely bewildered.

"We protest an unjust law, Constable. Your minister has stolen valuable property from the Wardells and other good folk in this town. What harm did they do?"

Samuel Fogg shook his head. "Ye have riled the parson without a doubt."

The minister and Elder Wiggin pulled Allie down the steps and dropped her roughly on the ground. Lydia and Eli helped her up, and the group of Friends gathered around the three missionaries in silent support.

"This is all *your* doing, Wardell!" Cotton accused, when he saw Eli.

"Nay, Cotton," Eli answered gravely. "'Tis thy own greed undoes thee."

"We shall decide who gets undone," Thomas Wiggin growled. The aging captain was an elder of the church at Hampton and had been a magistrate for over fifteen years. He was a staunch Puritan, for the system had always afforded him power, land, and influence.

"As you can see, Constable, these are the very miscreants punished here in December!" Cotton pointed out self-righteously.

"Aye, I do recollect," Fogg admitted.

"Come, man! You heard their blasphemy," Wiggin admonished. "They are unnatural women and a threat to god-fearing folk. That one has the devil's own tongue!" he pointed at Mary.

"Are words now against the law?" Eli asked at Mary's side.

"Certes, heresy is. You know the law, Wardell." The magistrate raised his voice to address the crowd. "We brook no heresy in Hampton Town! They shall be flogged for interrupting worship!"

"They spoke at the end of the service, Thomas. None were at prayer," Isaac Perkins put in reasonably.

"I was not finished!" Cotton stated hotly. "I was saying the closing prayer!" He sounded like a petulant child.

Fogg winced and glanced around. The entire congregation was observing the exchange avidly. Arguing with heretics was undignified and unworthy of a man of God.

"The point is moot," Wiggin interposed, apparently reaching a similar conclusion. "Calm yourself, Reverend," he added *sotto voce*, indicating the rapt onlookers with a nod of his head. He spoke up. "In any case, 'twould appear they are slow to learn, since they are returned."

Cotton agreed with relish. "Certes, the lesson shall be repeated!"

The two officials looked at Fogg expectantly. He had hoped that the situation would not come to this, but they gave the orders, and he must do the dirty deed. He understood now why Fifield had resigned his post.

"Ye cannot sentence them in the road like this! Ye have no authority to punish these women without a trial!" Eli protested.

Fogg was quick to agree. "'Tis true! They must go before the court, Reverend."

"They have already *been* tried in Dover and were sentenced to the Whip and Cart Act," the minister retorted. "They were banished from this colony last December, yet here they stand! There is no need for a second trial. They must be flogged forthwith!"

"I concur," Wiggin agreed. "They were tried and found guilty previously then evaded their just sentence. I charge you to do your duty and enforce the law, man!"

Mary spoke up. "I do not shrink from the lash, for what I say is true, and I am willing to suffer for the truth," she interposed calmly, "but Friends Coleman and Ambrose said nothing and should not share the same fate as I."

Allie opened her mouth to protest, but Mary silenced her with a look.

"Clap those two in the stocks, then. They may watch their companion suffer," Wiggin ordered. "They took part and are not entirely blameless."

The stocks and whipping post were adjacent to the meeting house, facing the town common. The crowd parted as the Quakers and the officials walked to the back of the building. Everyone followed, murmuring in hushed tones.

As Fogg secured Anne and Allie head, hands, and feet in the stocks, Mary spoke to the onlookers. Others who were not members of the church saw the crowd and joined out of curiosity.

"Remark how the minister is confounded by the revelation of his greed, good people," she said. "A godly man would not be so undone!"

"The lash shall temper thy speech," Cotton snarled, but his face colored.

Constable Fogg returned from the gaol whip in hand.

"Strip the prisoner, Constable," the reverend ordered coldly. "Fifteen stripes."

Abraham Perkins spoke. "Ten lashes is customary sentence for a woman, Reverend."

"That one is unnatural," Wiggin pronounced. "If she will not behave as a woman should, she shall not be punished as one."

"*And* she evaded the original sentence," Cotton added. He looked at Fogg. "Fifteen."

Captain Wiggin stood with Cotton near the whipping post, the better to observe the punishment. His friend, Richard Walderne, would be glad to hear of this. These very women had caused trouble at Dover and were now attempting to do so here. Mary's calm dignity riled him, and he scowled at her.

Mary met his censorious glare with composure. "My body may be scourged this day, but 'tis your souls that will suffer from this course, Thomas Wiggin and Seaborn Cotton. There shall come a day of reckoning for your sins."

Samuel Fogg's face was stony, as he slit the back of her dress open and bared the prisoner to the waist. There were audible reactions, when Mary's scars were revealed. The constable stepped back, dismayed by the sight. Cotton waved his hand as if shooing a fly. Wiggin frowned at his show of sympathy.

"Shirk not your duty, Constable Fogg! Those are the marks of a sinner!" Wiggin said.

"'Tis evidence of her guilt!" Cotton added hoping to squelch the sympathetic reactions.

"'Tis evidence of your brutal law!" Eli countered, outraged.

Fogg bound Mary's thin wrists to the iron ring on the post, studiously averting his eyes from her naked torso. The crowd muttered, and someone was crying. Mary feared it was Lydia. She turned her head to see and caught the reverend's eye.

"I fear for thee and pray God will forgive thy ignorance, Seaborn Cotton," she said, as Fogg moved behind her and shook out the whip. In the stocks Allie and Anne began to sing. They could see only the boards of the platform, but they knew what was coming and willed strength to their friend through the hymn. The Friends took up the familiar words of "A Mighty Fortress Is Our God." Cotton fumed. They had done this before, and he could not stop it. The dissenters in the crowd took it up.

Samuel Fogg prevaricated, shifting from foot to foot, wiping his hand on his britches, and shaking out his arm. Clearly many in the crowd did not condone this punishment.

"Carry on, Fogg!" Cotton urged stridently.

The constable pulled back his arm and struck.

Mary Tomkins suffered fifteen stripes that Sabbath Day in Hampton with the same whip that had torn her back in December. The hymn heartened her, but she was not able to sing through the flogging. The spiritual power that had fueled her at Dover had been unique. Each time she was whipped, the pain was worse, and the five extra stripes undid her. She lost count of the blows and soon after, lost consciousness as well. When it was done, the minister and the magistrate went to take their noon refreshment, well satisfied.

As soon as the constable untied her hands, Walter and Eli caught Mary's limp body by the arms. Lydia and her sister wrapped her in linens that Rebecca had fetched from her father-in-law's house nearby. The four of them carried Mary as gently as possible across the road to Tuck's Tavern. The Tucks had a room ready in their private quarters, and Robert Tuck and Lydia helped the apothecary treat Mary's wounds, while his wife handled the sudden increase in custom that crowded the common room in their wake.

The Friends stayed by the stocks with Allie and Anne. The missionaries endured the long afternoon stoically. A group of young swains came to taunt them for sport, but the Friends deflected their censure, both verbal and vegetable. Their loyal companionship made the ordeal bearable, providing food and drink, and singing or talking quietly. A few brave folk came to speak with Anne and Allie. Some were concerned about the Wardells; others had questions about the Children of the Light. Keeping company with Quakers was forbidden, but neither Cotton nor Wiggin was there. Samuel Fogg was among the seekers.

When they returned for the afternoon service, the minister and the elder went directly inside, ignoring the women pilloried in the stocks at the back of the building. However, as the congregation took their seats, Cotton was dismayed by the number of vacant places.

Despite the renewed order of banishment, Thomas Wiggin allowed the apothecary to remove the missionaries from the colony the next morning with the tide. The old captain was strict and self-righteous, but he was not murderous. The heretics had been duly punished, and he honored the medical grounds upon which Walter based his plea.

At sunset, when Constable Fogg released Anne and Allie from the stocks, Eli and Walter helped them to the ordinary. After five hours of confinement their muscles cramped and walking was painful.

Mary dozed on her stomach, her wounds covered with poultices. Lydia sat by the bed, loath to leave her friend. Walter convinced her to join them in the common room for a bite, but the young woman soon returned to her vigil. Mary's suffering had stolen her appetite, but she took a bowl of broth in case Mary roused and needed nourishment.

Eli, Allie, Anne, and Walter discussed the incident as they ate. Little Joseph had gone home with his grandparents.

"D'ye reckon it was worth it?" Eli asked the two missionaries.

Allie nodded and wiped her mouth with her apron. "Several folk asked about the Society of Friends," she told him. Her wrists and neck were red and raw from the rough wood of the stocks, and the abrasions were shiny with salve, but she seemed unperturbed. "They kept us diverted with their questions, did they not, Anne?"

The little missionary nodded. "Indeed they did," she answered with satisfaction. Being smaller had worked in her favor for once, and she was not so affected by the stocks as her larger companion. The doctor was relieved to note she had survived the ordeal well. "Several are outraged by Cotton's actions against thee, Eli," Anne went on. "I think they may try to get thy horse returned to thee. At least, some were talking of it. It does not bode well for Cotton now his avarice is public knowledge."

"I reckon the seeds we sowed this day found fertile ground," Allie said, glad the protest was behind them. "Mayhap they shall bear fruit in time."

## *Chapter 54*

### RICHARD WALDERNE *BOSTON TRIALS*

1660-1661 Boston, Massachusetts Bay Colony

News of the restoration of Charles II reached the colonies in August of 1660. Although the coronation would not take place until the following spring, there was no delay for reprisals. Puritan heads were rolling in England, and the glory of their great experiment was past. Under the Protectorate the Bay Colony enjoyed the advantage of a sympathetic Puritan government. Now that had changed. With the monarchy reinstalled the Bay Colony's charter was again prone to His Majesty's whim. The news was a major topic of conversation in the drawing rooms of Boston throughout the autumn. Richard lamented the King's return along with his peers.

However Captain Walderne did not indulge in fruitless speculation for long. Monarchy or no, as head of a Puritan household, he had a responsibility to expand his wealth. Convinced that God disdained human attachments, Richard pursued his business enterprises and public service with all his considerable energy. He engaged with Clarke & Lake Shipping through his friend, Thomas Lake, supplying lumber and masts that were transported to England on the thriving company's vessels. The enterprise proved successful, and Richard invested the profits in a shipyard and dock of his own at Pomeroy Cove. His first ship launched just a year later.

When not called to the Court at Boston, Richard stayed at the trading post in Cocheco monitoring the construction of piers on the Point and production at his two sawmills. He was surprised when his brother-in-law arrived unannounced one day in August. Dickie Scammon informed him that he was engaged to be married and wished to purchase the Walderne house on Dover Neck.

"Who is the fortunate bride-to-be?" Richard asked, after congratulating him.

Young Scammon looked surprised. "Did Annie not tell you?" he asked.

Richard did not wish to reveal the rift in their relationship. He had not seen his wife since the beginning of June. "I do not recall it. No doubt my thoughts were elsewhere," he temporized.

"Certes, you would not have forgotten, had you heard!" the younger man exclaimed with a grin. "Granted, she is young, but we shall wait another year to marry when she is sixteen. We both thought it fitting to live in the house you built for her namesake. 'Tis your niece, Prudence."

Annie did not miss her husband, although she worried that their marriage had changed irrevocably. It was not just his withdrawal since Elnathan's death. She was profoundly affected by Mary Dyer's execution and was disturbed by her husband's participation in bringing it about. She was glad to be spared his company, for she feared she would ultimately voice her misgivings. Annie knew how Richard would react.

She blamed her conflicting emotions on her advancing pregnancy. At one moment, she agreed that the Quakers were seditious and would bring chaos to the colony; at the next, she was haunted by images of the brave and godly woman on the ladder reduced to a twitching corpse. Mary Dyer did not urge rebellion. She spoke of God and professed forgiveness for her enemies, but it was unthinkable that the governor and his court were hanging innocent people. Twisted nightmares plagued her sleep, in which she stood on the ladder with the noose abrading her neck, while Richard looked on impassively. The ill dreams depleted her energy and filled her with dread. She mourned her former ignorance and wished she had not disobeyed her husband.

The fetters were the worst of it, barring the beatings twice a week. William Leddra had endured imprisonment three times during the past two years—twice at Boston, plus a ten-month stint at Plymouth. However, he had never been shackled like this. The iron cuff had abraded the skin of his ankle. Even moving a few paces to the bucket in the corner provoked agony, as the wound was chafed afresh. The chain was attached to a log, and he marked the days of his confinement on the wood with a link. They numbered seventy-eight—most of the winter. He could escape the cold, the stench, the hunger, and the darkness in the solace of God Within or betimes in dreams of the

Barbadian sun, but the pain of his ankle pierced his consciousness and was never completely gone. He missed the solace of his cellmate, Edward Wharton.

Edward had been in the dark, airless cell in the basement of the Boston Prison for nine months, when Leddra was arrested. They had met in 1658, when Friend Leddra first visited Salem, and they had been close ever since. Edward returned from a session before the Great and General Court to find William in the cub. They took comfort in each other's company.

"What happened in the court, Edward?" Leddra asked after they had embraced.

"I asked to know the charge laid against me, for keeping me locked up these many months," his friend answered, "and Endicott said 'twas for not putting off my hat."

William shook his head in disbelief.

"'Wearing my hat is no legal grounds for persecuting me,' I told him. 'I would know what law I have broken.'"

"Thou didst press him then. What said he?"

"The man had no answer. 'You shall know that afterwards,' he said, and sent me back here. I am sorry thou must endure this, William, but I am heartened by thy presence," Edward finished.

The next day the Court called for Wharton again, and the Salem man repeated his question.

"For what am I treated as an evil-doer?" he asked Governor Endicott.

"Your hair is too long," his former neighbor asserted. As Edward began to frame a response, he added hastily, "And you have disobeyed the commandment saying, 'Honor thy father and mother.'"

"Wherein?" the prisoner inquired, bewildered by this *non sequitur.*

"In that you will not put off your hat to magistrates," Endicott answered.

"I own and love all magistrates and rulers who are for the punishment of evildoers and for the praise of those that do well," Wharton maintained.

Secretary Rawson smirked. "Hold up your right hand," he said, knowing Quakers did not swear public oaths, especially at the whim of temporal authority.

"I will not," the accused replied calmly. "Thou hast no evil to charge me with."

"Hear your sentence of banishment then," Rawson snarled, losing patience.

The new law applied the death penalty for ignoring banishment, and Edward had no intention of leaving his home and thriving business. He addressed the governor. "Have a care what you do, for if you murder me, my blood will be heavy upon thee."

"Edward Wharton, attend to your sentence of banishment," Rawson's voice rose. "You are, upon pain of death, to depart this jurisdiction; it presently being the eleventh of March, by the one-and-twentieth of the same. On pain of death," the Secretary stressed.

The words seemed to echo in the chamber of the Great and General Court. In the silence following, Edward Wharton spoke.

"For nine months I have suffered imprisonment with no charge against me. I was taken from my home, where I was following my lawful business, led through the country like a culprit without being able to discover of what I was accused, and now I bid you take notice. There is nothing alleged against me but the length of my hair and the wearing of my hat. I think I shall be here tomorrow," he finished.

"You are dismissed!" Endicott declared. Damn the man's eloquence!

In truth the governor feared the repercussions, should a man of Wharton's stature be hanged. The other miscreants were vagabonds or in the Dyer woman's case from Rhode Island—a known refuge for dissenters and heretics. Wharton was a citizen of the Bay Colony—a successful merchant, well known and respected by the people of Salem. His death would create more trouble than it was worth. Endicott was eager to be rid of him as speedily as possible. There were other prisoners in Boston's jail to use as an example.

Once released, Edward did not desert his friend. From October to March, Leddra suffered whippings twice a week, bitter cold, and deprivation, while continuously chained to the log. Edward and George helped the Boston Friends bring food, candles, writing materials, blankets, salve, and flannels for his ankle and his torn back. They kept him alive and sat with him for as long as the warder allowed it—several hours if they brought rum. Edward posted letters for William and wrote some himself, informing the Society of Leddra's imprisonment and suffering in Boston.

On March 9th of 1660 five months after his arrest, William Leddra was brought before the court, still shackled. Two soldiers carried the log with the prisoner limping behind.

"When then shall these chains be removed?" Leddra asked the warder dismayed to learn the cuff would not come off for his hearing.

"Upon the day of yer hanging," the man replied with a sneer.

The officials were mildly surprised when the bizarre little parade appeared, log and all. The prisoner could barely walk. He was unkempt and squinted in the light after months in the dark cell, but he held his head high and spoke clearly when questioned.

Endicott was on the point of pronouncing the death sentence, when there was a disturbance at the doors. Wenlock Christison strode into the chamber, interrupting the procedure. He was of an influential family in England, educated in the law, and no stranger to legal procedure. He had also been the first missionary Friend to visit the Piscataqua Region in 1659.

The Governor's mouth was open to pronounce Leddra's doom, and it remained so in shock. Christison had been banished on pain of death, yet he entered the court of his own free will.

Edward Rawson recovered first. "Here is another," he said. "Fetch him to the bar."

He glanced at the Governor, still amazed and speechless, and took up the questioning.

"Is not your name Wenlock Christison?" Rawson began.

The interloper confirmed this statement, and Endicott rallied.

"Were you not banished on pain of death?" the governor asked.

"Yes, I was," Christison replied calmly.

"What do you here?" Endicott was nonplussed.

"I am come to warn you that ye shed no more innocent blood, for the blood that ye have already shed, cries to the Lord for vengeance."

Richard Walderne spoke from his seat among the assistants. The Quaker's high handed bravado incensed him, and he could not keep still.

"Unless you renounce your false religion you shall both surely die," he stated harshly.

Wenlock looked at Leddra, chained, weakened, and filthy from his confinement. William slowly shook his head, indicating he would not recant his faith.

"Nay, we will not change our religion to save our lives. Neither do we intend to deny our Master. But if I lose my life for Christ's sake, I shall save my life," Wenlock asserted.

Endicott addressed them both. "What have you to say, why you should not die?"

"I have done nothing worthy of death," Leddra answered. "If I had, I would refuse not to die."

Richard threw up his hands in exasperation. Several groans echoed his reaction. Why did these damned Quakers ever deny their guilt? They were blatantly breaking the law!

"You are come amongst us in rebellion, which is the sin of witchcraft and ought to be punished," Endicott said with customary logic.

"We came not among you in rebellion, but in obedience to God; not in contempt of any of you, but in love of your souls and bodies," Christison answered. "*That* ye shall know one day when ye must give an account of the deeds ye have done." He looked around the chamber, but saw only contempt on the faces of the officials. "Take heed for ye cannot escape the righteous judgments of God," he finished with sincere concern.

Major-General Adderton sat among the assistants. Like Richard he was not cowed and responded to this statement laconically. "You pronounce woes and judgments, and those that came before you pronounced woes and judgments," he made a circling motion with one hand, "But the judgements of the Lord are not come upon us yet." He spread his arms.

Nervous laughter rippled through the room.

"Be not proud, nor let your spirits be lifted up," Christison warned. "God doth but wait until the measure of iniquity is filled up. Then shall His wrath come upon you." He fixed on Adderton and lowered his voice. "And as for thy part, it hangs over thy head and shall come as a thief in the night, suddenly, when thou thinkest not of it."

Two months later this statement would prove chillingly prophetic, when the haughty major-general was thrown from his horse and broke his neck, dying instantly.

Adderton snorted and flapped a hand dismissively. Christison turned back to Endicott. "By what law wilt thou put us to death?"

"We have a law, and by our law you are to die," the Governor snarled.

"Who empowered you to make that law?" the Quaker pressed.

"We have a patent and are patentees. Do you judge whether we have not power to make laws?"

"What! Have ye power to make laws repugnant to the laws of England?" Christison asked.

Endicott scowled and was forced to answer, "Nay." Inwardly he cursed the man and his education—and the monarchy too for good measure.

Wenlock pressed his point. "Then you have gone beyond your bounds and have forfeited your patent. Are ye subjects to the King, yea or nay?"

The interloper struck at the root of their fears, and the officials stirred restlessly in response.

"What will you infer from that? What good will that do you?" Rawson challenged. He was shaken by the direction this was taking, and he masked his anxiety with anger.

"If ye are, say so, for in your petition to the King, ye desire that He will protect you and that ye may be worthy to kneel among his loyal subjects."

"Yes, we are so," Secretary Rawson declared, but his voice sounded strained, even to himself. He was confused. Somehow the Quaker had gained control, first turning the session into a debate and then making threats. Members of the Court exchanged troubled glances.

"Well, so are we," Wenlock continued, including Leddra with a gesture. "And for anything I know, we are as good subjects as ye, if not better, for if the King did but know your hearts as God knows them, he would see they are as rotten towards him as they are toward God. Since we are all loyal subjects of the King here, I demand to be tried by the laws of my own nation."

"You shall be tried by a bench and jury," Endicott prevaricated, although in their dealings with the Quakers, the officials had exercised the powers of accuser, judge, and jury.

"That is not the law but the manner of it, for if ye are as good as your word, ye must set us at liberty. I never heard or read of any law in England to hang Quakers." Christison pointed out.

"There is a law to hang Jesuits," the Governor asserted.

Richard groaned inwardly. Endicott was grasping at straws. Christison had him on the defensive and was clearly besting him. All present could see it.

"If ye put us to death, it is not because we go under the name of a Jesuit, but a Quaker;" the accused said reasonably, "therefore I appeal to the laws of my own nation."

Rawson leapt to the Governor's defense. "You are in our hands and have broken our laws, and we will try you," he declared. Richard felt a flood of relief. The old, confidant Edward was back.

Christison paused, glancing at the Secretary as at a yapping dog. He addressed the governor.

"Your *will* is your law, and what thou hast power to do *that* wilt thou do. Thy jury will deliberate upon our lives, and this I say to them: Jury, take heed what ye do, for ye have sworn before God that ye will true trial make and just verdict give, according to the evidence." His eyes scanned the benches. "What have we done to deserve death? Keep your hands out of innocent blood."

Rawson rose from his seat and whispered to the Governor. Endicott nodded and promptly dismissed the assistants to deliberate on a verdict. Rawson went with them and charged the officials to disregard Christison's testimony, as it had no bearing on Leddra's case. His intervention was deemed an irregular interruption and therefore moot. Richard's mind was made up, anyway, and his peers concurred. They soon returned and ruled both men guilty. Christison was remanded to prison, and William Leddra was sentenced to hang one week hence.

The day before the execution, Edward Wharton, George Preston, and a Salem Friend named John Chamberlain sailed to Boston in the *Sea Witch*. Edward was determined to witness William Leddra's death and give his body a proper burial. He could not endure another mishap like the one following the first hangings. When the two martyrs were cut down, the drop from the gallows elm caused William Robinson's skull to burst, disfiguring the corpse. The memory haunted Edward's dreams, and he would not allow it to happen to William. He also wanted a last chance to speak to his friend and was waiting outside the prison, when Leddra appeared under guard. His chains had, at long last, been removed for his execution. His pale face shone with relief in spite of his imminent death. Edward moved to embrace him, but Captain Oliver of the militia barred his way.

"'Twill be your turn next, Wharton," the military man sneered.

"What! Wilt thou not allow me to comfort my friend on the day of his death?"

"If you speak one more word, I shall stop your mouth!" Oliver threatened, going toe to toe.

The Salem man bristled and drew breath to retort, but William distracted him.

"Edward!" he called over the heads of the guard. They locked gazes. "God be with thee! Thou art the finest frien—"

Oliver signaled the drums to start up, cutting off his last words. William smiled ruefully and shook his head, as the escort herded him away. Even a brief farewell was denied them. His eyes stung with tears, but Edward set his jaw, determined to be strong for his friend's sake.

The morning of March 14, 1661 was overcast and raw for Boston's fourth execution. A morning fog was dispersing, and Richard hoped the rain would hold off. Anne was still asleep. The baby was due any day now. He donned his military greatcoat and hat over his full dress uniform and ceremonial sword. The officials of the Court were gathering at the prison for the procession to the Neck, and he did not want to be late. He left the house and strode purposefully up Tremont Row toward the prison.

The crowd was the largest yet. It pooled around the prison and flowed down both sides of the street, but the soldiers cleared the way, flanking the limping prisoner and beating the drums. The procession reached the elm, the militia took up their positions, and the condemned man was assisted up the ladder. The procedure was familiar now. It did not occur to Richard to be bothered by this.

"William, do you have anything to say to the people?" Rawson asked, once the ministers had finished haranguing the prisoner to recant his faith.

"For the testimony of Jesus and for testifying against deceivers and the deceived, I am brought here to suffer," Leddra said, gazing out over the sea of upturned faces.

The crowd reacted sympathetically to this statement, and one of the clergymen tried to diffuse its effect by admonishing them.

"People, be not so moved to see a man willing to die. You may read that the apostle said that some may be given up to strong delusions and even dare to die for it."

Richard tensed. There was no such passage to his knowledge, and he knew the Bible well.

The Governor waved the minister off impatiently and gestured for the marshal to get on with it. The sympathy for the miscreant made him nervous. Words of courage from the condemned only inflamed public censure and worked against the officials.

"I commit my righteous cause unto Thee, oh God," Leddra said, as Michaelson tied a kerchief over his face.

The marshal finished, and a soldier stood ready to help him turn the ladder.

"Lord Jesus, receive my spirit!" William Leddra called and was hanged.

A fourth body swung, twitching, from the elm.

Richard was satisfied. The Quaker had invited his execution by ignoring the order of banishment. The law and the First Church must be upheld. He vowed that however many of the cursed sect sacrificed themselves in protest, the duty of the Great and General Court of Boston would remain clear. If nothing short of death would silence them, let the fanatics die. He thanked God the Quakers had not returned to the North Country since 1659. His town was pure, and Richard Walderne would do whatever circumstances demanded to keep it that way.

# Chapter 55

## LYDIA PERKINS WARDELL *CALLED*

May, 1663 Hampton, Newbury, and Ipswich, Massachusetts Bay Colony

Eli was pleased. The week after the missionaries left for Rhode Island, Lydia's apathy became a fever of organizational zeal. The change was marked, and in retrospect he realized it had been a warning sign, but he was preoccupied with selling thirty acres of tillage and meadow to Edward Gove among other affairs he must settle before they left Hampton. He was relieved that her energy had returned. The young husband had no idea that the source of Lydia's fervor was a divine call. She did not tell him of her bold plan, because she knew he would try to stop her.

The young couple spoke often of Rhode Island. It was the only colony that practiced religious toleration, and a strong community of Friends was established there. The men who had been banished from Winthrop's Boston in 1637 were now the leaders of the colony they had founded.

The coin from Gove's purchase provided means to move, and the Wardells determined to leave in early June by wagon. In the meantime, they struggled on the edge of penury. Lydia's family and the Hampton Friends helped, bringing gifts of food and paying generously for things she was leaving behind. Isaac Perkins offered to handle the sale of the house and remaining land for his son-in-law, if no buyer came forward by the time they left, but for the first time in their young lives, Lydia would not be planting a kitchen garden, and Eli would not be tilling the fields.

With only a month until their removal, Lydia's sister Rebecca was often with her, packing up the household, as well as helping with the persistent daily chores. The sisters had ever been close, for they contended with five elder brothers growing up. On the first laundry day after the missionaries had left, Rebecca came to help. They were behind the house, laying out bed linens to dry on the hydrangea bushes, and Lydia took the opportunity to confide in her sister, realizing she needed an ally to implement the plan to answer her call. Rebecca was skeptical and appalled that Lydia had told Eli nothing.

"I fear he would try to stop me," Lydia reasoned. "Or worse, insist on going with me. Then what should happen to Joseph?"

"Certes he would! To protect thee! No husband worth his salt would do otherwise, and I would rather take little Joe myself than have thee not tell thy husband," Rebecca retorted, arms akimbo.

Lydia turned away, and her eyes fell on their children. Theo was just five months older than Joseph. The two cousins were squatting over a fuzzy caterpillar on the back stoop, absorbed in its progress. Their brown-haired heads looked nearly identical, and a wave of love and doubt assailed her. She pushed the doubt aside.

"Eli is worth his weight in gold. He should not be kept in the dark!" Rebecca scolded. "Straighten that corner, Lyd. I cannot reach it," she added ever practical.

"And I cannot follow this call without thee," Lydia said, yanking the offending sheet. She lowered her voice and added, "Someone must help me, after I have said my piece."

Rebecca pursed her lips and did not answer, turning to the basket for more damp linen.

"Wouldst thou have me dragged off to gaol in such state?" Lydia pressed, laying a hand on her shoulder.

Rebecca straightened and threw her arms around her sister.

"They shall verily flog thee," she whispered her voice thick with impending tears. "I do not think I can stand to see thee so maltreated."

Lydia returned the embrace. "Then I beg thee be there for me, sister."

Rebecca tried to pull away, but Lydia grasped her shoulders and spoke intently.

"Becca, thou must believe me. I am called by God to do this. It came to me as we sang at Dover. I feel it in my bones, but I need thy help—not to accompany me, lest thou be punished too. Only be there for afterward. Say thou art curious to see the new church at Newbury, and John shall say yes. He denies thee nothing. Please, sister!"

Rebecca stared into her eyes. She sniffed and glanced over at the two children then back at Lydia.

"I shall help thee, Lyd," she said heavily, "but I fear I am helping thee to a flogging."

On the first Sabbath Day in May Lydia Perkins Wardell rose quietly and crept from her home in the predawn twilight. She left Eli and Joseph sleeping. She was impelled by a divine call so clear there could be no denial. The revelation had hit her as she sang with Mary Tomkins through her scourging at Dover. The woman exuded spiritual power, and Lydia had felt it, walking beside her, little Joe on her back. Although the call came in a moment, it took months to formulate her plan. She must testify against the corrupt clergy. Reyner's complaint caused her friends to suffer brutal punishment. Cotton had ruined Eli's prospects, forcing them to leave lifelong friends and family. The ministers were no longer men of God, but men of Greed. People were blind to their cruelty and lack of genuine spirituality. They must be publicly exposed with a statement so bold that all must heed her message. Throughout the winter she wrestled with doubt and was obsessed with planning the where and how. Mary Tomkins had renewed her courage and determination, by sacrificing herself to denounce Cotton's greed—just last Sabbath Day. Lydia would do her part today in Newbury.

All doubt was behind her, and the young woman strode purposefully down the road to Salisbury. It felt good to take action after months of fretting, though it was odd being unhampered by little Joseph. The warming air smelled of new life, and she settled into a brisk pace.

It was seven miles and a bit to Newbury, but Lydia reached the Salisbury dock in less than two hours. It was not yet eight of the clock, and the ferry waited at the landing. There would be time for a cup of tea and a bite at Coffin's publick house on the Newbury bank near her destination. She avoided the Emerys' place, as they knew her well and would ask too many questions. She knew no one else in the town and was glad. Her message would be more effective, if folk did not know her.

The sun was gaining strength by the time she boarded. A handful of people were making the crossing, and they glanced at her curiously. She was a woman alone, and that was unusual. She avoided eye contact, watching the Merrimack slide by and was relieved when no one spoke to her.

On the Newbury shore the other passengers dispersed, and Lydia entered the Coffins' ordinary alone. She went directly to the hearth and sat by the fire. She was not chilled, but the warmth was comfortingly familiar. One other person sat at a table in the corner—a gentleman, by his dress and bearing. A girl came from the kitchen with a steaming pitcher of tea and filled a mug for her. She offered to take Lydia's cloak, but the young Friend folded her arms and shook her head. The girl sniffed and turned away, stopping at the man's table en route to the kitchen.

"Would ye care for more tea, Mister Easton?" she asked.

Lydia pulled her gaze from the fire. Nicholas Easton was a friend of her husband's father. Eli had oft spoken of him, as he lived in the Rhode Island Colony. Easton and Thomas Wardell had been neighbors in Boston before being banished and following John Wheelwright north in 1637. Could this be the same man? He seemed too young, though older than Eli. When the girl moved on, he noticed Lydia looking at him and smiled.

"Good morrow, Friend," he said pleasantly. His address marked him a Quaker, encouraging her.

"Forgive me for staring," she apologized. "I overheard thy name and wondered if thou wert acquainted with my father-in-law, Thomas Wardell?"

"Why yes! He was a friend of my father's," Easton replied.

He rose and crossed to her table. Lydia straightened, clutching her cloak at the neck.

"Permit me to introduce myself. My name is John Easton. Nicholas is my father. May I join thee?" he asked.

"Please do," Lydia responded. "I am Lydia Wardell, wife to Eliakim."

He shook her free hand, smiling warmly, and sat down.

"I remember Eli but little, as he was ten years younger than I, but my father and Thomas Wardell were good friends and shared similar opinions on religion," he said. "I hope I do not appear old enough to be mistaken for my sire!" he added with mock horror.

Her response to this attempt at levity was weak, and Lydia's new acquaintance sobered, looking at her closely, "Is all well with thee, Friend Wardell?" he asked gently.

John was in Hampton representing his seventy-year-old father in the sale of his last piece of land in the North Country. The Eastons had lived in Hampton for several years before moving to Rhode Island in the '40s, driven by the Bay Colony's relentless pursuit of Anne Hutchinson's supporters. Lydia found a sympathetic ear with Nicholas' son. Once the girl had left the food on the table, she confided in the Rhode Island Friend.

"Thou art quite alone in this, I gather," John said quietly after a long pause.

"God is with me," she responded, staring at the steaming bowl of porridge in front of her. She had no appetite, but Lydia knew she must eat. They would not feed her in the gaol.

"Thy courage is admirable, but I fear for thee, Friend Wardell," he commented.

"Aside from our own tribulations, I have seen too many of those I love persecuted by these so-called ministers of God," Lydia answered. "Folk follow them blindly even though they are greedy and spiritually bereft. They serve themselves, not the people, and certes not God."

"Thy punishment will be severe," John cautioned.

"I answer a divine call. It cannot be ignored," she said, taking a small bite of porridge.

"How might I help thee?" he asked.

Lydia swallowed. "Wouldst thou accompany me to the church?" she asked shyly.

"'Twould be a privilege," her new friend answered.

When Lydia had finished eating, John Easton insisted upon paying her bill, and they walked to the Newbury Church together. She was glad of the distraction he provided, talking about Rhode Island along the way.

The last stragglers were on the steps, as they approached the building. Lydia planned to go in once the congregation was seated. The two Friends paused before the church.

"Shalt thou not reconsider this course, Friend Wardell?" John asked.

Lydia was shivering, and he knew she was not cold, for the day was mild, and she wore a heavy cloak. Still, she nodded definitively, gazing up at the closed doors. She looked small and vulnerable, and he wished he could help her more.

"When ye remove from this colony, Rhode Island shall welcome you," he said. "We are in Newport, and our community of Friends will embrace thy family. I beg thee to send word at thy leave-taking. My wife Meredith and I shall be privileged to entertain you and help you settle."

"I look forward to it, Friend Easton. Thou art exceeding kind. My thanks, for thy company and thy understanding," Lydia said.

They shook hands then she climbed the steps and disappeared into the church without looking back.

The vestibule was cold and dark after the bright sunshine. The new church had inner doors to the men's and women's sections, and they were closed. Reverend Timothy Parker was reading a psalm. His muted voice rose and fell in the way of preachers. Lydia closed her eyes briefly, praying for the faith to take this final step. She drew breath and pushed through the women's door.

It was new and opened silently. Parker's voice carried on, until Lydia reached up, pulling back the hood of her cloak. The movement caught his attention, and he looked up. Folk turned to see what had caught his attention. His voice faltered when cloaked figure remained standing in the aisle and did not immediately slink to a bench. Lydia saw Rebecca on the aisle to her right, next to her sister-in-law Elizabeth Hussey. The sight of her renewed Lydia's confidence, and she strode down the aisle, speaking clearly.

"Good people, harken to me for the ministers are false! God's Love dwells within your hearts not in their words!"

The Reverend Parker looked confused. "How now?" he exclaimed more surprised than angry. "Wh-what passes here?"

Lydia ignored him. "Our Heavenly Father bids me waken you to their perfidy!" She loosed the ties of her cloak and let it fall. There were audible reactions, as she wore only a loose woolen shift fastened at the neck with a drawstring.

"Good woman, cover yourself!" the minister exclaimed, putting a hand to his eyes.

"The ministers are not godly, they are greedy! They hunger for coin and power! Ye have no need of them, for God dwells in every breast!" Lydia grasped the ribbon at her neck.

The elders and deacons were rising from their seats before the pulpit.

"What say you? S-stop this!" Parker objected, as he realized he was under attack. He turned to descend from the pulpit. The murmurs grew to a buzz. She must act now or be thwarted. Lydia pulled the ribbon, and pushed the shift off her shoulders. It fell to the floor.

"Mark me, good people!" she asserted turning slowly with her arms outstretched. Everything froze. The air was thick with shock. This was the moment for her message.

"If my naked flesh offends you, how much more is God offended by the spiritual nakedness of your ministers!" she declared, pointing at Parker, who stood frozen.

Sound and movement erupted. Women screamed, infants wailed, and small children cried at the sudden noise and confusion. Mothers hid their children's faces and covered their own eyes to block the sight. Several recalcitrant boys were sitting at the feet of the deacons. They leapt to their feet, pointing with vociferous glee at the naked woman in the aisle. The deacon overseeing them stood with mouth agape, the switch in his hand forgotten. All the men were standing, craning their necks to see her. The congregation was in chaos.

Lydia Perkins Wardell stood before them all, arms extended. Her pale skin glowed like a beacon in the gloomy nave. She was the eye of the hurricane. Slowly she lowered her arms. Rebecca and Elizabeth hastened to cover her, lifting and re-tying her shift. Elizabeth secured the cloak around Lydia's shoulders, and Rebecca pushed a bundle of clothing into her arms. They returned to their bench quickly, barely noticed in the melee. The protest took two minutes, but the Sabbath Day Meeting in the Newbury

Church was a shambles. The miscreant was speedily apprehended and locked in the town's only cell. Constable Henry Jacques forbade anyone to see her.

"Such flagrant obscenity deserves no succor," he fumed, but he allowed Lydia to keep the clothes Rebecca had given her. She dressed quickly before he chained her in the cell.

The sisters communicated briefly through the back window of the gaol, although they could not see each other. Becca wept, but Lydia was calm. Events were now out of her hands. After months of wrestling with doubt and fear, of planning and guarding the secret from Eli, she was profoundly relieved.

Rebecca's husband John rode to the Wardells' farm to inform Eli. The young husband was appalled by the nature of his wife's protest and dismayed by her arrest, but her lack of trust hurt him most.

"I should have known something was amiss," he said grimly, when John had related the event. "She told me nothing. Ah, Lydia!"

They left little Joseph with his grandmother Perkins. Eli asked to borrow a mount, and Lydia's father, Isaac, insisted on accompanying his sons-in-law. The three men rode back to Newbury, arriving after noon.

Rebecca was waiting outside the gaol with John Emery, who had attended the morning service and was concerned for Lydia. It took some time to convince Henry Jacques to allow Eli and Isaac to see the prisoner, but eventually Lydia's father persuaded him.

The sight of his wife shackled hand and foot in the cell reduced Eli to tears. She tried to explain her call, but he was too upset to be comforted by her motivations. The more effective the protest, the harsher the punishment, and the authorities were outraged. They sent for the Hampton Magistrate, Thomas Wiggin, who insisted the prisoner be tried at the Ipswich Quarterly Court, her crime being too heinous for the lesser court at Newbury. Eli knew Lydia would be flogged, but how severely? He was frantic with worry. By contrast, Isaac Perkins was a pillar of strength. His own faith sustained his calm. He did not castigate his eldest daughter, but reached through the bars, embracing her awkwardly in her chains.

"There, Lyddie," he said, rubbing her back. "If thou wast answering a call from God, I understand. May He give thee strength to endure the test to come. Fear not for little Joseph. Thy mother and I shall care for him until thy return."

Lydia was grateful for his understanding and too giddy with relief to fear what might come. She had not wavered. She had answered her call. A ringing blow had been struck against the corrupt clergy in retaliation for all the injustices her family and dear friends had endured, and a strange euphoria was upon her. Now she need only endure the punishment. Certes, no scourging could dim the bright flame of faith burning in her heart. She would be strong, like Mary Tomkins.

Thomas Wiggin brought his own wagon to transport the prisoner to Ipswich the next Tuesday for her trial. The Hampton magistrate would preside at the court with the Ipswich magistrate, Samuel Symonds. The old captain rode on the seat beside Henry Jacques who drove for the ten-mile trip. Lydia was shackled in the back. The Wardells were charged for the constable's trouble, as well as a fee for the transportation. Eli did not have the coin and was too concerned for Lydia to muster a protest. Isaac quietly paid the inflated cost. John Emery rode behind the wagon with Eli and Isaac, as he was called to the same session for entertaining the Quaker missionaries earlier that spring.

Eli was grim on the road to Ipswich. It galled him to ride a borrowed mount, when he had owned one of the finest horses in the colony, but Socrates was now ridden by Seaborn Cotton. He stoked his anger for it dampened his fear. Eli had no doubt this day would end badly for his wife. It was a fine one too, unusually warm for early May, inspiring thoughts of planting, until he recalled that was denied him this season. Now, verily they must remove to Rhode Island. During the two-hour ride the young husband determined to quit Hampton as soon as possible.

The wagon pulled up before John Baker's tavern. The court convened in the common room, and it was busy with working men and boys taking noon refreshment. Curiosity was aroused by the sight of a comely young woman in chains. Several came out of the ordinary to ogle her, calling to their fellows to come and see. Eli, Isaac, and John glared at any who got too near, but they could not prevent them gawking. The Ipswich constable Edward Lumas helped Jacques escort the prisoner inside. The onlookers trailed after.

Symonds and Wiggin quickly determined that Lydia Perkins Wardell was guilty of speaking heresy and of lewd behavior in the Newbury House of Worship. She was sentenced to be publicly flogged on her bare back "to the satisfaction of the crowd" that was charged to witness her punishment. The "witnesses" celebrated with another round.

The quarterly court continued, hearing several other cases, John Emery's among them. When Constable Jacques accused him of entertaining Quakers, the indomitable innkeeper admitted it and told the court that if the Friends returned, he would "shake them by the hand and make them welcome again." He was severely fined, but John could afford it, and he was more concerned for Lydia's plight than his own. The inebriated state of the witnesses worried him. The few women present were leaving. He attempted to pay Lydia's fine as well, but the magistrates refused, saying her crime was too heinous. The miscreant must atone for her sin in blood lest God's wrath smite the community entire.

Once the court's business was done, it was time for Lydia's punishment. The common room emptied as the crowd moved outdoors. Nearly every man had a tankard in his fist, and for many, it was not the first that day. They spilled off the porch into the road and turned to watch, quaffing their ale and elbowing each other in anticipation. The magistrates stood on the porch.

Lumas pulled Lydia out as though leading a fractious mare, although she did not resist. Silence fell at the sight of her. She was a buxom lass, and the crowd was eager to see her stripped. Jacques removed the shackles. At a nod from Wiggin, Lumas cut her bodice and shift open at the back and yanked the material down to her hips. Her pale, full breasts were exposed, and the onlookers approved audibly. Eli gritted his teeth, and Isaac put a hand on his arm, as both comfort and restraint.

Lumas bound Lydia's wrists to a hook on the post designated for this purpose; however, she was shorter than the average male penitent and was forced to stand on tiptoe. The hook was positioned so that she faced the road, her breasts revealed to hungry eyes. There were catcalls, and a dark energy coursed through the men, as they pressed closer. This was a fine diversion from their labors. Their mood was celebratory, and bold voices called for the constable to pull the sinner's dress all the way down, followed by raucous laughter. Anticipation spiraled.

"Show us what they saw at Newbury!" and "Cheat us not by halves!" they urged.

There was a chorus of assent. Lumas looked to his superiors with raised eyebrows, but Wiggin frowned and shook his head, gesturing for the constable to get on with it. This was a legal procedure not a bawdy house. Some humiliation was in order but within legal limits.

Lumas set to his task with relish. Flogging was a regular thing in Ipswich, and he honed his technique at every opportunity. Few were as pleasing to the eye as this little maid, though. The crowd hushed as he shook out the nine-cord whip of knotted catgut. It was made to his specifications, and he kept it oiled and supple. He took his role as constable and disciplinarian seriously. Besides, he enjoyed the power.

The Ipswich constable began mildly enough, keeping to the middle of her back, but this sweet piece deserved special treatment. Verily, she had *asked* for it, appearing naked in in a House of God! Then there was the support—nay, the enthusiasm—of his audience. He must make a good show of it for their sake. She cried out immediately, and he exulted in it, though he kept his expression blank. No stalwart, this one, he thought with a licentious thrill.

The throng was soon calling out the number of each stroke with glee. The prisoner writhed prettily, but in vain, to escape the lash. Lumas found her movements seductive. Her breasts rubbed against the rough wood of the post, as she squirmed. Eyes glittered, relishing the sight.

As his arousal increased, the constable's strikes became more fervent. He was mastering her with every stroke. He lashed the sweet curve of her waist, letting the strands wrap around her delicate ribs and scour her midriff. The whip bit into the smooth skin of her back and licked the swell of buttocks showing above her dress. The knotted strands licked the sides of her breasts. She sobbed, she struggled, and she bled for him.

At twenty, he stopped, breathing heavily, and looked at the magistrates, who were watching dispassionately. They deemed the discipline correct, given her crime, and said nothing to stop it. Lydia hung from her wrists, no longer able to balance on her toes. Her sobs had stopped and her back was bright with blood; however, the mob objected to the pause. They took up a chant. "More! *More*! *MORE*!" At their urging Wiggin nodded for Lumas to continue. Her sentence depended on the satisfaction of the witnesses, and the crowd was clearly not satisfied.

Lumas wiped his sweaty hand on his pants and adjusted his grip on the handle. Then he resumed. He contemplated tumbling his sturdy goodwife later to relieve the ache in his groin. He would imagine this sweet piece under him, when he had his rime in ree.

Eli, Isaac, and John stood on the lowest step of the porch, facing the crowd. The innkeeper was outraged. How much harder must it be for Eli, powerless to protect his wife! And poor, sweet Lydia! The crowd's dark pleasure in her suffering struck him as obscene. The flogging was worse than any he had ever witnessed, for it was usually limited to ten stripes for women and fifteen for men. This young couple had suffered so much already at the hands of Seaborn Cotton. John looked at Isaac, but the man's face was a mask.

The onlookers resumed counting the stripes, goading Lumas on. A skinny fellow who smelled like a tanner stood closest to the steps, shouting with the rest.

"Twenty-two-oo! Twenty-three-ee!"

Eli snapped.

"'Tis enough!" he roared in anguished fury. Lumas ignored him.

"*Twenty-four-r-r! Twenty-five!*"

Eli rounded on the magistrates, and Isaac put a restraining hand on his shoulder.

"She has suffered *enough*," the young husband said to Wiggin. His voice shook.

"Hold," the magistrate said calmly, raising his hand.

Lumas paused, arming the sweat off his brow. The counting stopped raggedly, and a chorus of disappointment ensued. Wiggin regarded Lydia, hanging from her bonds, her lacerated back bled profusely. The strands of the whip pattered blood onto the boards.

"No!" the skinny fellow hollered, drunk on ale and the energy of the mob. "Not yet!" A chorus of agreement bolstered his courage further. "I allow…," he held up a finger and liquid spilled from the tankard in his other hand. "I allow 'tis proper treatment for a heretical who-ore!" he drew out the last word then chuckled, pleased with himself.

Isaac's firm grip kept Eli from assaulting the man, but it did not prevent him shouting into his pinched face, "She is no *WHORE*! She is my *WIFE*, and she is closer to God than thy sorry soul shall *ever* be, ye blackguard! Thou art a scurvy villain, leering and—"

John and Isaac tried to cut him off, but the damage was done.

"Slander!" the fellow cried, pointing at Eli. "He slanders me! In public! You all heard it!"

Wiggin and Symonds were satisfied with Lydia's punishment, and the flogging ceased, but the young husband was taken to task for public slander. Eli was fined five pounds or fifteen stripes to be administered at Hampton the next day. Constable Jacques took him into custody, shackling him in the wagon bed. Eli Wardell would not be able to comfort his wife that night. He would sleep in the Hampton gaol.

The day was cooling, as Isaac and John carried Lydia to the wagon. They had only her cloak to cover her nakedness and no means to treat her wounds. John thought it a blessing she was unconscious. Though shackled Eli held her tenderly across his lap in the bed of the wagon and gave what comfort he could, oblivious to the blood staining his own clothing.

Isaac asked the innkeeper's wife if he might purchase a blanket to cover his daughter, who shivered with the shock of her wounds. Mistress Baker fetched one for him readily. She refused his coin and looked shamefaced, as she gave it to him. It was unusually heavy, and when he unfolded it, a loaf and a quarter wheel of cheese fell onto the bed of the wagon. They were all hungry for there had been no opportunity to eat.

Isaac took a portion to Constable Jacques, as he climbed onto the seat. The man gave him a dubious look, suspicious of such generosity. Then he shrugged and took the food. Normal folk would have resented him after the day's events, but he reckoned the heretics were too daft to know their own enemies.

Isaac and John went ahead of the wagon, leading the horse Eli had ridden. Wiggin had consented to take Lydia to the Perkins' home in Hampton, and her father wished to alert his wife of their coming. Susannah had birthed ten healthy babies over twenty-two years and lost none to illness or injury. She had a fair knowledge of healing and would know how to treat her daughter's wounds. However, after the cruel debasement she had suffered at the whim of the rank crowd, Isaac was more worried about his daughter's spirit than her body.

The beat of the drum summoned the townsfolk to the whipping post in Hampton the next morning. Eli had spent a sleepless night in the gaol. Every time he closed his eyes he was tormented by images of Lydia's punishment. Had it not been for his father-in-law, Eli's assault on the inebriated tanner would have been more than verbal. The blatant injustices he had endured for almost three years were affecting him in ways he did not like. Violence had never been his way. He would be glad to quit the colony.

Henry Jacques led Eli out to the whipping post. The prisoner cut a daunting figure even in shackles. Lydia's blood marked his clothing, and his face was a mask of defiance. The drum had done its work, and the townsfolk were there to witness his punishment. Isaac Perkins and his brother Abraham stood with the Hampton Friends. Seaborn Cotton looked smug as Eli was stripped to the waist and tied to the whipping post.

"Fifteen stripes, Reverend?" Jacques inquired, shaking out the whip.

Cotton paused, relishing his power. "Fifteen will serve, Constable," he declared brightly. His eyes glittered. It had been a long battle with the Wardells, but he had triumphed in the end, and they had both been brought to heel by God's Will. Their punishments were a lesson to all dissenters, the consequences of spurning the authority of the First Church.

Jacques read the charge of public slander then laid on with the whip, drawing blood on the third strike. Eli did not cry out or writhe under the lash, as Cotton had hoped. The young man harbored such choler toward the minister, that although he gritted his teeth and his breath hissed audibly at each blow, his expression remained defiant.

When Jacques finished, Eli was released, wincing as his abraded wrists were unbound, and the blood rushed back into his fingers. He did not stagger or slump in pain, but walked unaided. Isaac and Abraham flanked him. As they came abreast of the minister, Eli stopped. Cotton took a step back, fearing the miscreant might strike him, but Eli only posed a question.

"Hath my pied heifer calved yet, Cotton?"

The reverend's face reddened. He laughed nervously and scanned the faces around him for support. They all stared back at him, awaiting his response. He could not deny he had the Wardells' heifer without lying outright. Seaborn Cotton sniffed, and turning on his heel, quit the scene.

# *Chapter 56*

## MARY AND ALICE *ESCAPE*

May, 1663 Salem, Massachusetts Bay Colony

On the second day out of Hampton, Walter put in at Salem Harbor. A front was building to the southwest, and he did not want to negotiate bad weather with his precious human cargo. He hoped to find Edward and George and wait it out in their company. The Salem men would have to come onboard, however, as it was dangerous for the missionaries on land. They were still within the jurisdiction of the Bay Colony.

They dropped anchor under massing clouds, and Walter sent Job in the dinghy to alert their friends and fetch some sustenance. The doctor roused Mary to dress her wounds, while Allie and Anne turned the feather tick and shook out her bedding. The bleeding had stopped but bandages were still necessary to prevent the salve rubbing off on her clothing. Mary was weak and lay down again, as soon as Walter finished. Her three companions huddled on the berth across from hers, talking quietly and waiting for Job's return.

Outside cooler air came with the front. Clouds obscured the sun, and the wind picked up, rocking the sloop at anchor despite the protection of the harbor. The craft was thirty-six feet long with three sails and a fully equipped cabin minus a galley, as Walter feared fire onboard and usually took refreshment onshore or ate cold food. There were four berths in the main cabin and two more in the bow. Walter called his craft the *Sister Sarah* for his adored sibling and only surviving family, Sarah Barefoote Wiggin, who had married Thomas Wiggin's son John two years earlier. Within two hours Job returned with the Salem men.

"Walter!" Edward called, as he hastened to climb aboard.

The hatch slid open, and the apothecary's head appeared from below. "We are here, Edward," he answered.

"Friend Clement says ye are come from Hampton with the English missionaries. What news? Are they in good health?" Edward's handsome features were creased with concern. He carried his hat and a satchel of food. The wind whipped the hair from his face.

"Apologies for the lack of warning. There is a storm building, and I judged it best we take shelter. Come below and see for yourself," Walter answered and disappeared.

Edward had not seen the missionaries since leaving them at Kittery Point in January. He greeted his three friends distractedly then went to Mary's berth. She sat up at the sound of his voice and managed a smile, but he was dismayed to find her worse off than he had left her. Her face was pale, and the skin beneath her eyes looked bruised. He sat beside her and gently took her hand. The gesture was more eloquent than words, and she leaned against his arm and closed her eyes, while Anne related the story of their protest at Hampton two days before.

Walter and Job wrestled the folding table from its recess in the floor between the berths, while George got out the ham, cheese, and bread they had brought. There was cider for the women and ale for the men. Walter produced a flask of brandy and added a medicinal shot to Mary's cider.

"The bleeding has stopped," he said to her, "and 'twill help you sleep, since I cannot brew a good tea here."

Outside rain began to fall, and the apothecary secured the hatch, then sat on Edward's other side. George had joined Anne and Allie on the berth opposite Mary's, and Job sat on the floor, already intent on his food. The soft pattering overhead rose to a drumming tattoo. The wind whined, and the sloop creaked and rocked as the storm descended upon them in earnest.

"We are en route to Rhode Island," Walter told the Salem men above the pounding rain. "The Scotts have offered our friends refuge at their home in Providence."

"'Tis another day up the river from Newport," Edward informed him. He had cut up some ham and cheese and was feeding Mary small morsels from the point of his knife, as any movement increased her pain. She was grateful for his consideration and realized it was evidence of his own past suffering under the lash. The fresh salve eased the heat of her wounds, and she knew in a matter of days the pain would give way to relentless itching. It was lessening already, and her appetite was returning. The food tasted wonderful and was all the more delicious because Edward's care was evident with each bite. Although he took up the task casually and talked with Walter throughout, being fed by him was strangely intimate. When she had had her fill, she relaxed against his solid warmth and drowsed, content and overwhelmingly relieved.

The men were discussing likely harbors on the way to Rhode Island, for it was evident that Walter was not familiar with the coast south of Boston. Edward cut some food for himself and gave his partner a significant look.

"George and I must go to Newport next week on business," he said.

"Mayhap we could arrange to leave sooner?" George hazarded in response.

Allie beamed at him.

"That would be marvelous!" Anne opined in her deep voice.

Mary straightened, as though coming out of a daze. Walter looked from George to Edward. The latter was nodding.

"Verily?" the doctor asked with undisguised hope, then shook his head. "Job and I shall work it out. I would not ask so much of you, my friends."

"We must go in any case, Walter. We have a shipment coming in—tools and seeds for planting season," Edward reasoned, "And besides that, I am familiar with the route."

Walter began a polite protest, but George overrode him saying, "We can be ready two days hence, I warrant."

The apothecary's relief was evident. The missionaries would be in good hands, and he could return to his neglected practice weeks sooner, but still Walter hesitated, making eye contact with each of the women.

"You do approve this plan?" he asked them.

The response was immediate and affirmative. Allie turned to the apothecary smiling, gratified that he considered their opinion for most men would not.

"Yes, Walter," she said fondly. "We can tend Mary's wounds. Only leave us some salve and bandages. I reckon thou hast done more than enough for us. Thou art a loyal friend, and we owe thee our lives many times over."

She leaned across the table and kissed his cheek. Walter blinked and nodded wordlessly. Parting would be hard, after all they had undergone together, but his friends would be in good hands with Edward and George. He could trust the two Salem Friends to transport the women safely to the refuge of the Scotts' home. Still, he felt torn between relief and regret for once they parted he doubted he would ever see them again.

They decided the *Sister Sarah* would remain at anchor until Edward and George were ready to depart. They could transfer the women to the *Sea Witch* in Walter's dinghy, and the missionaries need never set foot in Salem. Job and Walter would go ashore for supplies on the morrow, as soon as the weather cleared.

As they talked, Edward was aware of Mary's weight. He wanted to put his arm around her but feared putting pressure on her back. He turned his head slightly and saw she had fallen asleep. When he looked up, Walter was smiling at him.

"She has hardly slept for the pain," the apothecary said quietly. "Each time she is flogged, it takes longer to heal, and Cotton gave her fifteen stripes."

Edward's jaw clenched and his eyes closed briefly. "Then 'tis good she sleeps," he said.

"She has the best medicine in the entire world now," the apothecary added.

His friend looked at him quizzically.

"Your presence," Walter clarified. "Apparently it soothes her like nothing else."

Early on the morning of their third day at Salem, the missionaries prepared to change craft. Job held the dinghy steady, as the missionaries bade farewell to Walter.

"I fear my life shall be quite dull now," the apothecary said with a brave attempt at levity, but his eyes were sad.

Mary's condition had improved markedly. Her color had returned, and she was gaining strength. "Thou saved us, Walter. Without thy care and intervention we might have died long ago, our mission a failure." She kissed him on both cheeks. "God keep thee."

"Try to stay safe, Mary," he cautioned. "You cannot endure more flogging without permanent damage, I fear."

Anne looked up at him then threw her arms around his waist. Walter looked surprised, then smiled and embraced her.

"Thou art the best physician I have ever known. God bless thee, Walter," she said fervently.

Allie was the last to leave the *Sister Sarah*. The two friends faced each other, and Walter felt his eyes prickle. They stepped into an embrace and held each other for several moments before Allie could speak.

"Thou hast been a dear friend since the day we met," she whispered, tears slipping down her cheeks. "I shall think of thee every day and hold thee in my heart."

He nodded, too overcome for words.

On board the *Sea Witch*, the five Friends watched Walter and Job prepare to leave. The dinghy was secured at the stern, and the anchor was weighed. The limp mainsail rose, flapping, and the jib soon followed. The two men shortened the sails, catching some wind, and the sloop slowly moved off, making for open water. Walter looked back and waved from the cockpit, and his friends returned a final salute.

Mary was mending, and her pain lessened each day. Her range of movement improved, though she still tired quickly. The *Sea Witch* was familiar, and while not as swift as Walter's sloop, it was comfortable and felt like home. The weather cooled immediately after the storm but got warmer as they sailed south.

On board the five Friends enjoyed an informality that was not possible on land. The women dispensed with boots and stockings, and went barefoot. Long skirts were tucked into waistbands for ease of movement, exposing ankles and calves. Now free of bandages, Mary abandoned the long-sleeved, high-necked blouses and fitted jackets for her loose cotton shift and a skirt, unless she was on deck. Then she threw a shawl over her shoulders, knotting it at the neck. Allie and Anne followed suit. The men also shed their boots and coats and rolled up their shirtsleeves in the mild weather. They went hatless and did not shave. The wind worried everyone's hair constantly, and no one cared. The women bothered to brush and re-braid it once a day, as they prepared for sleep. Edward and George enjoyed this ritual, helping with stubborn snarls upon occasion. It was a quiet time of gentle intimacy, and the five Friends became closer for it.

There were four berths in the bow, forward of the area designated for cargo. On this trip the Salem men were transporting tools and sacks of seed for spring planting. Although the berths were wider than the ones on the *Sister Sarah* and could accommodate two comfortably, Edward elected to sleep on deck under the stars. In the event of rain Anne and Allie offered to share a berth, but after the storm in Salem, it did not rain.

Her limp did not keep Allie from scampering over the boat with the dexterity of an old sea hand. She was apt at raising or reefing the jib, and it became her job. The women kept things tidy, oiling the woodwork, polishing the brass fixtures, coiling rope, airing bedding, and preparing meals. They all sang together, delighting in the harmonies they created with George's tenor and Edward's base.

The first night, they put in at Scituate, but did not risk going ashore. The Plymouth Colony was nearly as strict as the Bay concerning Quakers, although they did not go so far as to execute them. The Friends shared silent worship and ate their evening meal on deck, watching the sun set. They talked of hardships endured and the fellowships that sustained them, for all but George had suffered imprisonment and flogging. After a lag in the conversation Edward spoke.

"Ye returned to Dover after we parted in January," he began, keeping his tone neutral.

Mary looked for reproach, but found none in his expression. She turned to Allie and her friend nodded. They had not talked of the second ordeal at Dover even between themselves. There would be no better time, or more sympathetic ears than here and now.

"Yes," she admitted candidly. "I did not credit thy warning, Edward, and I should have." Allie's eyebrows shot up, and she and Anne exchanged a glance. "We did not realize the constables would go beyond the rule of law," Mary finished.

"Walter told me he feared they meant to kill us from the first," Allie added.

"I have no doubt Richard Walderne approved both attempts," Edward agreed. He leaned back on the stern bench, crossing his arms. "I cannot fathom the man's vehemence against you," he added quietly.

"Being Quakers is enough, I warrant," George opined, "but ye are also women who preach. I doubt he approved that."

"I must tell you something," Mary said, straightening.

They all looked at her.

"Something passed between me and Richard Walderne the first time, during our flogging at Dover. I am at a loss to describe it." She paused, gathering her thoughts. "There was a moment when the Light made everything clear, and I *saw* him—the magistrate." She met their eyes, fearing disbelief, but no one laughed or looked at her askance. They regarded her gravely, waiting for her to go on. "I know not how, but his soul and his turmoil—his deepest self—was revealed to me. He is a man in torment, and I felt such sorrow for him…" She trailed off.

"Thou didst forgive him then?" Allie asked wonderingly.

Mary nodded. "I pitied him, and he remarked it. I think it frightened him."

Edward drew a hissing breath. "A frightened man is a dangerous enemy," he said softly.

"After that moment of insight he would not look at me, whereas before, his gaze was cruel and unrelenting. He stopped the cart soon after and left abruptly," Mary finished.

There was silence as they contemplated this wonder.

"You wounded his pride," Edward said. "Compassion and forgiveness are powerful weapons."

"'Twould explain why he wanted you dead," George added.

"At the time I did not understand how deeply it affected him," Mary went on. "Certes it did not occur to me that it would spur him to go outside the law in dealing with us."

"The second time we did not know the constables meant to kill us until the morning after our arrest. They said as much, before they took us from the root cellar," Allie said.

"I have never felt such fear," Mary confessed. "I could not even pray, although I tried. We faced death that day, and the men were laughing." She shivered, recalling Thomas Canney standing over her, rubbing his hands in gleeful anticipation.

"They laughed when I fell in the water, as well," Allie said. "I thought my time had come then."

"In the river? In that frigid water? For how long?" George asked, alarmed.

Allie shrugged and looked down. Mary's hand was clasped in her own, though she did not remember taking it. "I know not. It felt like hours, but I think verily 'twas moments. Long enough to lose this toe." She wiggled her foot.

George colored. "Forgive me, I did not realize how—"

"'Tis a small matter," she smiled, and they all chuckled at her pun.

"The storm stopped their murderous intent, but how did you escape them after?" Edward asked gently, when the humorous moment passed..

"Mistress Canney revived us and alerted Walter and Friend Roberts, God bless her," Mary answered fervently.

"She said the men planned to take us out after dark to perish in the storm in some uninhabited place," Allie added.

A muscle twitched in Edward's jaw. "Even after the storm? Then their guilt is certain."

"But God did not abandon you," Anne said solemnly. "The tempest was His instrument, and Jane Canney, Friend Roberts, and Walter were His angels."

As the *Sea Witch* plied her slow way south, Mary delighted in the camaraderie and gained strength with each passing day. She loved to sit on the stern bench and watch Edward maneuver current and wind. He radiated strength, and his impressive nautical skill soothed her. She never tired of looking at his handsome face. She liked his unshaven appearance and longed to touch the stubbly growth. She dangled her bare legs off the stern, watching the wake play out behind the solid, beamy *Sea Witch*. It was a world all their own, and she had never felt so content and free.

The third night out from Salem they rounded Cape Cod and anchored in a cove at its elbow. Edward called it Monomoit. An Englishman named William Nickerson had purchased four square miles of land from the Monomoyick *sôgmô Metaquason* seven years earlier, and the Salem merchants had become acquainted with him, when they brought supplies to the isolated settlement. Now Edward put in regularly on their many voyages around the cape. They enjoyed a fine hot meal ashore entertained by the Nickersons and returned to the *Sea Witch* sated and sleepy.

That night Mary startled from a dream no less terrifying for its lack of clarity. She was shaking, Richard Walderne's laconic sneer vivid in her mind's eye. She had been at his mercy, and he stood over her, rubbing his hands in gleeful anticipation. Fear hammered in her pulse and quickened her breath, fed by a confusing collage of images she was desperate to banish. Going back to sleep was impossible. She wrapped a blanket over her shift and crept up the ramp to the deck.

It was a calm, moonless night. The mass of stars overhead claimed her attention and calmed her racing heart. So *many*, glittering and pulsing in the black sky! She did not see Edward until he sat up and spoke her name.

"Mary? Is all well?" he asked, instantly alert. He was a dark silhouette against the starlight.

"An ill dream. Forgive me. I did not intend to disturb thee, Edward."

He shook his head then realized she might not see the gesture. "I was not sleeping," he answered and patted the bench. "Come, sit with me. The stars are wondrous bright."

She perched beside him, wrapped in her blanket, and they both gazed wordlessly at the sky for a time. She was grateful he did not ask her to recount the dream, but then Edward ever seemed to know when to speak and when not. It was one of the many things she treasured about him. Another two or three days, and the idyll they were sharing would end at Providence. She did not want it to. She sighed, and leaned against his arm.

Edward looked down then gently put his arm around her. He rested his hand on her hip, and it felt warm and solid. His embrace filled her with a sense of security as well as anticipation. When she did not object, he pulled her closer and put his mouth next to her ear.

"I have thought of thee each day since we parted," he whispered. His breath awoke a tingling energy in her spine, and she shivered. He mistook her reaction and went on quickly. "I expect nothing from thee. I understand thy calling, but I cannot leave thee again without declaring myself." He drew back to look in her eyes. He smoothed the hair from her forehead and cupped her cheek. "I love thee, Mary." She did not push him away, and he brushed the corner of her mouth with his lips, watching carefully for any sign that she wished him to stop.

Although the fearful images from her dream had dissipated, Mary's pulse was racing again. The wounds that had not throbbed for days were throbbing now, yet she felt no pain, only a yearning for Edward's touch. She knew she should protest, refuse him, stop this unseemly intimacy, but she realized she had been waiting—nay, *hoping*—for this. She wanted more. She met his eyes and reached up to stroke the new beard on his cheek, as she had imagined doing. Then Mary raised her chin. It was all the invitation Edward required. His hand cupped the back of her head, and he kissed her fully.

Mary closed her eyes and responded. His lips were warm and firm. Their teeth bumped then parted. Her face melted into his, as if the skin was gone and their blood mingled. They were falling, spiraling down together, joined by their mouths, their teeth, their tongues. The sensation eclipsed all thought or sense of self. Nothing had ever tasted so sweet or overwhelmed her so completely. A timeless interval passed before they broke apart.

Edward said nothing but reclined against a folded quilt, pulling Mary onto his lap with her back against his chest. Through her own blanket, she could feel his warmth along the length of her body—his torso and chest against her back, his legs and arms cradling her. Thus they lay together for the remainder of the night.

Overhead the stars danced.

END BOOK ONE of the VAGABOND TRILOGY

# GLOSSARY

Sources: ahdictionary.com, http://www.onelook.com, and colonialquills.blogspot.com

***Thou, Thee, Thy, Thine*** subjective and objective singular forms of you/your. Familiar forms used in Old English and some religious contexts. Friends used this "plain speech" because it was intrinsic to their belief that all people are equal before God.

***Ye*** subjective plural and the formal form of you as used in Old English and by Friends

***Apothecary*** physician, healer, pharmacist, doctor

***Anon*** soon

***Astonied*** stunned, amazed

***Betimes*** on occasion, once in a while

***Breeches, Britches*** pants

***Breeching*** rite of passage when boys graduate from nursery skirts to pants

***Certes*** certainly, sure

***Children of the Light*** another early title for the Society of Friends

***Combination*** a document of governance signed by the freemen of a town or settlement

***Convincement*** conversion to the Society of Friends

***Cooper*** barrel maker

***Cub*** prison cell

***Custom*** customers, business traffic

***Discomfitted, to discomfit*** uncomfortable in a situation, to cause discomfort

***Entertain, be entertained by*** to host or be hosted by (usually overnight)

***Factor*** one who acts for someone else, an agent

***Flakes*** a frame or platform for drying fish

***Forsooth*** indeed

***Gaol*** jail, prison

***Glazier*** one who repairs and makes glass windows and installs them

***Husbandman, Yeoman*** farmer, one who works the land

***La petite mort, the little death*** orgasm

***Mandamus*** a writ issued by a court or a monarch requiring a public official or entity to perform a duty associated with that office or entity.

***Name day*** birthday

***Naught*** nothing

***Nonce*** now

***Offscourings*** garbage, refuse

***Ordinary*** tavern, inn, public house dispensing alcohol, food, and sometimes lodging

***Pattens*** wooden overshoes with raised sole on an iron ring to avoid mud/snow

***Privily*** secretly, in private

***Publick house*** tavern, bar, ordinary

***Queue*** a long braid or hair gathered at the neck and secured in a ponytail

***To reef a sail*** to reduce the size of a sail by gathering in and securing part of it, as by lashing it to a yard.

***Religious Society of Friends*** the original and still formal title of the Quaker Faith

***Remark*** to notice, to see

***Rime in ree*** colloquial archaic expression for sexual intercourse

***Sôgmô*** a subordinate chief among the Algonquians of North America

***Sawyer*** one that is employed in sawing wood or operating the saw in a sawmill

***Small clothes*** (chiefly British) small items of clothing, underclothes or handkerchiefs

***Spatterdashes*** men's mud guards

***Stirrup stockings*** mud guards for women

***Trucking Station*** (archaic from the verb to truck) to exchange, barter; a place to trade goods or services without the exchange of money

***Verily*** truly, really

***Weirsman*** A person appointed to maintain weirs or low dams built across a river to raise the level of water upstream or regulate its flow; or to supervise the construction and maintenance of an enclosure of stakes set in a stream as a trap for fish

***Wheel lock pistol*** a kind of gun with a lock in which a steel wheel rubbed against a flint

# BIBLIOGRAPHY


Beals, Charles Edward, *Passaconaway in the White Mountains*, Boston: R. G. Badger, 1916.

Besse, Joseph, *A Collection of the Sufferings of the People Called Quakers*, London, 1753.

Bishop, George, *New England Judged by the Spirit of the Lord*, London: printed and sold by T. Sowle, 1703.

Bowden, James, *History of the Society of Friends in America*, London: Charles Gilpin, 1850.

Boyle, Frederick R., *Hatevil Nutter of Dover, New Hampshire,* Portsmouth, NH: Peter Randall, 2011.

Carroll, Kenneth Lape, *300 Years of Quakerism*, Maryland Historical Magazine, 1970.

Cutter, William Richard, *Memorial Encyclopedia of the State of Massachusetts, Volume 2*, New York: American Historical Society, 1918.

Currier, John James, *History of Newbury, Mass. 1635-1902*, Boston, Massachusetts: Damrell and Upham, 1902.

Dow, George Francis, *Everyday Life in the Massachusetts Bay Colony*, Boston, 1935.

Dow, Joseph, *Tuck Genealogy: Robert Tuck of Hampton, N. H. and his Descendants*, printed for private distribution, David Claff & Sons, 1877.

Earle, Alice Morse, *Customs and Fashions in Old New England*, New York: Charles Scribner, 1893.

Evans, Charles, *Friends in the Seventeenth Century*, ULAN Press, 2012 (original publication Philadelphia, For Sale at Friends' Bookstore, 1875).

Fiske, John, *The Dutch and Quaker Colonies in America*, Boston and New York: Houghton Mifflin & Co., 1903.

Frost, William J., *The Quaker Family in Colonial America*, New York, New York, St. Martin's Press, 1973.

Gordon, Charlotte, *Mistress Bradstreet*, New York and Boston, Little, Brown and Company, 2005.

Hallowell, Richard, *The Quaker Invasion of Massachusetts*, Boston: Houghton Mifflin, 1883.

Harrison, Samuel Alexander, "Wenlock Christison and the Early Friends of Talbot County, Maryland" in Maryland Historical Society Magazine, March 9, 1874.

Hubbard, Reverend William, *A General History of New England*, Cambridge, Massachusetts: Massachusetts Historical Society, 1815.

Hunt, Roger D., *The History of the Nutter Family*, self-published Tillamook, OR, 1998.

Hurd, Hamilton D., *History of Hillsborough County, New Hampshire*, Philadelphia: J. W. Lewis & Co., 1885.

Janney, Samuel M. (Samuel McPherson), *History of the Religious Society of Friends from its Rise to the Year 1828*, Philadelphia: T. Elwood Zell, 1867.

Jones, Rufus M. *The Quakers in the American Colonies*, London: MacMillan & Company, 1911.

Latimer, John, *The History of the Society of Merchant Venturers of the City of Bristol*, Bristol, England: J. W. Arrowsmith, 1903.

Lewis, Enoch, *Friends' Review: a Religious, Literary and Miscellaneous Journal*, Philadelphia: J. Tatum, edited by Samuel Rhoads, 1847.

Norton, Mary Beth, *Founding Mothers and Fathers: Gendered Power and the Forming of American Society*, New York: Knopf, 1996.

Palfrey, John Gorham, *A Compendius History of New England from the Discovery by Europeans to the First General Congress of the Anglo-American Colonies, Volume 2*, Boston: James R. Osgood, 1884.

Plimpton, Ruth Talbot, *Mary Dyer: Biography of a Rebel Quaker*, Wellesley, Mass: Branden Publishing Company, 1994.

Pope, Charles Henry, *The Pioneers of Maine and New Hampshire, 1623 - 1660*, Boston: Charles Pope, 1908.

Quint, Alonzo Hall, *Historical Memoranda of Persons and Places in Old Dover*, compiled by Reverend Alonzo Hall Quint and others and published in the Dover Enquirer from 1856 - 1888, edited by John Scales and printed at Dover, New Hampshire, 1900.

Rogers, Horatio, *Mary Dyer of Rhode Island: the Quaker martyr that was hanged on Boston Common, June 1, 1660*, Providence, RI: Preston and Rounds, 1896.

Rothbard, Murray, *Conceived in Liberty*, First Edition, 4 volumes, Arlington House Publishers, 1979.

Salter, Edward, *A History of Monmouth and Ocean Counties*, Bayonne, NJ: F. Gardner & Son Publishers, 1890.

Scales, John, *Colonial Era History of Dover, New Hampshire*, editor, John Scales, Westminster, Maryland: Heritage Books, 2008.

Ibid, *Piscataqua Pioneers, 1621 - 1775 Register of Member and Ancestors*, Dover, NH: Charles F. Whitehouse, 1919.

Sewel, William, *The History of the Rise, Increase and Progress of the Christian People Called Quakers*, Philadelphia: Samuel Keimer, 1728.

Sherwood, Mary B., *A Biography of William Brewster*, Falls Church, VA, Great Oak Press, 1982.

Stackpole, Everett Schermerhorn, *Old Kittery and Her Families*, Lewiston, Maine: Press of Lewiston Journal Company, 1903.

Ulrich, Laurel Thatcher, *Good Wives; Image and Reality in the Lives of Women 1650-1750*, New York, Vintage Books, 1991.

Wadleigh, George, *Notable Events in the History of Dover, New Hampshire, from the First Settlement in 1623 to 1865*, Tufts College Press, 1913.

Weeks, Stephen, *Southern Quakers and Slavery*, Baltimore, Maryland: Johns Hopkins Press, 1896.

Woodard, Colin, *American Nations: A History of the Eleven Rival Regional Cultures of North America*, New York, New York, Penguin Group, 2011.

## WEBSITES AND OTHER SOURCES

www.hallworthington.com, Worthington, Hall & Joan, "The Persecution of Quakers in America," online article.

http://dover1633.pbworks.com/FrontPage, Front Page Magazine, David Horowitz, Editor-in-Chief.

www.hampton.lib.nh.us, Lane Memorial Library, Hampton, NH

www.dover.lib.nh.us, Dover Public Library, Dover, NH

http://www.noblenet.org/salem/reference, Salem Public Library, Salem, MA

http://www.usgennet.org/usa/topic/newengland/savage/bk4/weymouth-wheeler.htm, *A Genealogical Dictionary of the First Settlers of New England before 1692, Volume 4, Weymouth - Wheeler*, Savage, James, Boston: Little Brown & Company, 1861.

http://freepages.genealogy.rootsweb.ancestry.com/

www.geni.com

www.shapleigh0tripod.com
Maintained by the Shapleigh Family Association
"The Shapleighs of England and America"

http://www.seacoastnh.com/history/colonial/massacre.html
New Hampshire Seacoast Association

https://minerdescent.com/
Maintained by Thomas Miner
"Miner Descent: tracing each branch back to their arrival in America"

http://www.nh.searchroots.com/strafford.html
---Early History of Dover, Strafford County, New Hampshire---
This Information (PDF FILE) is located on the web site: "History & Genealogy of New Hampshire" at SEARCHROOTS (address above)

http://www.genealogy.com/
*Genealogy*.com

http://marybarrettdyer.blogspot.com/2014/10/life-sketch-of-katherine-marbury-scott.html
© 2014 Christy K Robinson
"William and Mary Dyer"

# AUTHOR BIO

Olga R. Morrill studied theater arts and had a long and distinguished career as a librarian and storyteller. She facilitates the White Mountain Writers Group which published an anthology of their short stories and poetry called *The Literary Tourist.* She also wrote a weekly column for the *Conway Daily Sun*, "The Library Connection" for two decades.

Morrill lives with her husband, Stephen, in New Hampshire's White Mountains.

95920063R00252

Made in the USA
Columbia, SC
25 May 2018